George Gilbert Ramsay

Selections from Tibullus and Propertius

With an Introduction and Notes

George Gilbert Ramsay

Selections from Tibullus and Propertius
With an Introduction and Notes

ISBN/EAN: 9783337275709

Printed in Europe, USA, Canada, Australia, Japan

Cover: Foto ©Andreas Hilbeck / pixelio.de

More available books at **www.hansebooks.com**

Clarendon Press Series

SELECTIONS

FROM

TIBULLUS AND PROPERTIUS

WITH INTRODUCTION AND NOTES

BY

GEORGE GILBERT RAMSAY, M.A., LL.D., LITT.D.

PROFESSOR OF LATIN IN THE UNIVERSITY OF GLASGOW
AUTHOR OF 'LATIN PROSE COMPOSITION,' EDITOR OF 'LATIN VERSIONS'

SECOND EDITION, REVISED

Oxford
AT THE CLARENDON PRESS
1895

Oxford

PRINTED AT THE CLARENDON PRESS

BY HORACE HART, PRINTER TO THE UNIVERSITY

PREFACE.

THE following selection from Tibullus and Propertius has been prepared specially to meet the wants of the students of this University; but no apology need be offered for any attempt, however imperfect, to rescue from comparative neglect the best portions of two of the most fascinating and suggestive of Latin poets, and to supply such help for their interpretation as may bring them within the range of ordinary classical instruction, whether at Schools or Universities. It is scarcely creditable that in a country which avowedly places its higher instruction upon a classical basis, the works of two of the most characteristic poets of the best age of Latin poetry should be practically unknown to our schools, and ignored in University examinations. We may grant the transcendent merits, for educational purposes, of Virgil and of Horace; but it is impossible not to regret that the choice of Latin poets should run in so narrow a round, and that no place should be found for the graceful, refined Tibullus, or for that rare poetic genius whom Professor Postgate has justly styled ' the greatest elegiac poet of Rome.'

The works of both poets, no doubt, need to be read with discrimination, and lend themselves naturally to selection; but there are no poets who at once lose so little, and gain so much, by the process. There is no continuity of thought to be interrupted; the poems are unequal in quality; they are still more unequal in interest of subject; and there is an iteration of topic which becomes wearisome to the modern reader. It has been the fashion to assert that Cynthia was the maker of the muse of Propertius, and that when she failed him, his poetic gift departed from him. But some of his noblest poetry was written without reference to her; and I venture to think that if instead of leaving behind him sixty Cynthia elegies, and thirty-one elegies on other subjects, he had devoted but thirty-one elegies to Cynthia and given the sixty to other and nobler topics, his rank as a poet would have been higher than it is. And by discarding the less interesting of the Cynthia poems, and bringing into greater prominence the best of the remainder, we arrive practically at the same result.

The objects aimed at in the present selection have been these : (1) to include nothing that is not first-rate in quality, and up to the highest standard of its author's work ; (2) to include only poems of special interest, whether from the nature of their subject, or from their personal or historical references ; (3) to include nothing that can occasion any difficulty in teaching classes composed of the young of either sex. For educational purposes, the last condition is indispensable ; more especially in these days, when the classics are entering so largely into the higher education of women [1]. If the works of antiquity are to be used for their true educational purpose, to form the taste, and stimulate the imagination, of the young, it is essential that we should present them in their best and purest form, and draw an absolute line of demarcation between the deformities and the beauties of ancient life and literature. Not wholly uncalled-for is the Laureate's denunciation of those who

Feed the budding rose of boyhood with the drainage of your sewer ;
Pour the drain into the fountain, lest the stream should issue pure.

There are unhappily some modern editors who deem it due to the spirit of research to rake out and illustrate all the foul corners of antiquity: there are some who seem even to revel in the occupation [2]. Even from a merely literary point of view, it may be doubted whether we shall not more faithfully preserve the spirit of an ancient author by omitting that which is repugnant to modern notions, and which it is impossible for us to judge justly, because we can never perfectly understand the point of view from which it was written, never completely realise the surroundings to which it was addressed. That freedom of speech which ancient taste permitted was natural to a state of life and feeling which has now

---

[1] It is to be regretted that those responsible for setting the subjects for examinations in which women compete do not always sufficiently bear this condition in view.

[2] A recent German editor bitterly attacks the mediaeval critics for finding some ancient passages too strong for their stomach.

wholly passed away; and to reproduce, in the atmosphere of modern life, everything that an ancient writer held himself free to say, may be to suggest a wholly false and exaggerated view of his life and character [1]. Travellers tell us that when living amongst unclothed savages they are conscious of no sense of indelicacy: yet no sane man would maintain that by discarding clothes we could restore the simple morality of our first parents. And of all the purposes to which the study of antiquity can be put, none less deserves our sympathy than that which would use it to please the fancy of some prurient pedant, or to reward the patient but foul research of some senile commentator.

In compiling the explanatory notes, my object has been to make them sufficient and interesting in themselves, rather than to confine them within the meagre limits prescribed by the prudence of modern publishers, or the supposed requirements of schoolmasters and examiners. So many subjects are now pressed into the curriculum of our higher schools, that it is becoming impossible to give to any of them that time and amplification without which no genuine interest can be stimulated: and our best scholars vie with one another in producing editions of which the main excellence consists in packing into the closest space 'the irreducible minimum' of verbal and grammatical knowledge. But if only a minimum of information

[1] See the admirable remarks on this subject of the late H. A. J. Munro, Elucidations of Catullus, p. 75 sqq.

be provided, only a fraction of that minimum will be retained; and my experience is that the surest way to interest students in the classics, even in their grammatical difficulties, is to make them feel how rich and varied a field of human interest they present.

To make the notes as useful as possible to ordinary students, I have drawn illustrations, wherever possible, from the best-known authors, especially Horace and Virgil, rather than from obscurer sources; and I have given all the mythological and historical information necessary for the understanding of the text, even though it might be easily obtained from Classical Dictionaries. Not all students possess Classical Dictionaries: nor does their possession ensure that they will be consulted.

The critical notes make no pretension to completeness. They exhibit only the more important varieties of the best MSS., special prominence being given to those which bring out the comparative value of the different MSS., or which illustrate the kind of differences, whether as regards orthography or otherwise, which a student should learn to expect in comparing MSS. generally. In constituting the text of the selections from Propertius, I have aimed at carrying out the conclusions arrived at by M. Plessis in his most interesting work, 'Études Critiques sur Properce,' founding mainly on N, giving the most important readings of AFDV, and occasionally those of G, Hb and Per. I have occasionally followed N even in its varieties of orthography; not because such varieties can be regarded as representing the original text in the passages where they occur, but because it is well to familiarise students with the fact that in certain cases uniformity of spelling is not to be looked for, even in the best authorities. In two important passages, Prop. 3. 7. 22 and 3. 18. 21, I have ventured on conjectures of my own; in a good many more I have approved of readings which I have not ventured to introduce into the text.

I have followed Baehrens and Mr. Palmer in returning to the MS. division into four Books, an arrangement which has now met with the approval of Professor Postgate also. It is to be hoped that the confusion gratuitously introduced by Lachmann into Propertius references will now finally disappear. I have in my references throughout adopted the numbering of Mr. Palmer.

I have made a special feature of the English headings prefixed to each of the paragraphs into which I have divided the poems. A key to the general sense and structure of a poem is often of the greatest assistance to the young student, especially in an author like Propertius, whose train of thought it is often hard to catch. I have endeavoured to reproduce in the style of the headings the spirit of the original. I trust further that by exhibiting the connection of thought in the poems as they stand I have presented a strong argument against the many arbitrary transpositions suggested by Lachmann, Baehrens and other editors.

In the selections from Tibullus, I have had the advantage of being able to use an edition of extracts published by the late Professor William Ramsay. Some of the longer notes of that excellent scholar are too valuable to be lost, and I have quoted them in full within inverted commas.

In conclusion, I have to express my warm acknowledgments to Professor A. Palmer. Not only have I been largely guided by his admirable edition of the text, but he has rendered me substantial service by most kindly looking over my proofs, and by offering many valuable suggestions, which he has allowed me to incorporate in the notes. I owe much also to the edition of Dr. Postgate, whose selections coincide with those of this edition to the extent of some five hundred lines. His masterly Introduction is a most important addition to the fruits of British scholarship; and if I have ventured to differ from him occasionally in the notes, I have done so with much diffidence, and with a full sense of the authority with which he speaks. My best thanks are also are due to Professor E. L. Lushington for kindly furnishing me with the materials for the Egyptian note on Tibullus i. 7. 28; to Professor Veitch and the Rev. A. S. Aglen for suggesting to me some excellent illustrations; and to G. S. R. for the compilation of the Index.

University of Glasgow,
       Jan. 6, 1887.

My especial thanks are due to Mf. E. D. A. MORSHEAD, for his kindness in allowing me to print in this Edition (p. 369) his fine translation of the Cornelia poem, which appeared first in the *Journal of Education*, Sept. 1894.

Tibullus and Propertius, to face p. xiii.

PREFACE TO THE SECOND EDITION.

In this edition, the book has been revised throughout; some important corrections and additions have been made; and attention has been paid to various friendly criticisms. In particular, an Appendix has been added to the chapter on the MSS. of Propertius (Introd. pp. lix to lxv) for the purpose of indicating the results arrived at by Professor A. E. Housman and Dr. Postgate in their recent important contributions to Propertian criticism. All readings discussed by Prof. Housman in passages included in this selection are recorded in the critical notes.

G. G. RAMSAY.

The University, Glasgow,
May 1, 1895.

CONTENTS.

INTRODUCTION TO TIBULLUS.

Life of Tibullus.

THE following Biography is prefixed to the MSS. of Tibullus, and incorporated in the old Editions :—

'Albius Tibullus, eques Romanus, insignis forma cultuque corporis observabilis, ante alios Corvinum Messalam originem (*leg.* oratorem) dilexit, cuius et contubernalis Aquitanico bello militaribus donis donatus est. Hic multorum iudicio [et maxime Quinctiliani viri in studia [et] litterarum acerrimae licentiae] principem inter elegiographos obtinet locum. Epistolae quoque eius amatoriae, quanquam breves, omnino utiles sunt. Obiit adolescens [tempore Vergilii, ut indicat epigramma infra scriptum:

Te quoque Vergilio comitem, &c.']

Our sources of information for the life of the poet Tibullus are of the most scanty description. Of the little that we know by far the greater part is derived from the incidental notices of himself and his doings which are scattered here and there throughout his writings. The short Biography transcribed above adds but little to what he himself tells us, except the fact that he died young. In addition, we have an Epigram by a contemporary, Marsus Domitius, referred to in the same Biography ; two of the poems of Horace—Odes 1. 33 and Epistles 1. 4—are addressed to a poet Albius, whom the learned have unanimously identified with the poet Tibullus ; while there are frequent references to him in the works of Ovid. Amongst these is the exquisite elegy upon his death, Am. 3. 9.

The date of the poet's death is fixed by the Epigram of Domitius Marsus, mentioned above :

> *Te quoque Vergilio comitem non aequa, Tibulle,*
>   *Mors iuvenem campos misit ad Elysios,*
> *Ne foret, aut elegis molles qui fleret amores,*
>   *Aut caneret forti regia bella pede.*

'Thee too, in Virgil's company, Tibullus, unkindly Death despatched yet young to the Elysian fields, that there might be none either to sing the tearful elegies of love, or to tell in brave measure of the wars of kings.'

Now Virgil died at Brundusium on the 22nd Sept., B.C. 19, and the words of Domitius imply that Tibullus died at the same time, or at least shortly afterwards. We may therefore assume that his death took place at the end of B.C. 19, or the beginning of B.C. 18.

As to the date of his birth, however, there is more uncertainty. In the Third Book of the Elegies, there occurs the following passage, 5. 17, 18

> *Natalem nostri primum videre parentes*
>   *Quum cecidit fato consul uterque pari.*

'My parents saw my first birthday what time the two consuls fell by a common fate.'

If this couplet were genuine, it would fix the date of the poet's birth definitely to B.C. 43, when the consuls Hirtius and Pansa fell before the walls of Modena. But almost all scholars are now agreed in regarding the Third Book as not being the work of Tibullus ; and, even were it otherwise, this particular passage must be regarded as an interpolation for the following reasons :—

(1) The second of the two lines occurs *verbatim* in Ovid, Trist. 4. 10. 6, who tells us of his own birth :

> *Editus hic ego sum ; nec non, ut tempora noris,*
>   *Cum cecidit fato consul uterque pari.*

'Here was I born : and that thou may'st know the time, it was when, etc.'

Now the *Tristia* were written fully thirty years after the death of Tibullus, and it is extremely improbable that Ovid would have borrowed so remarkable a line without acknowledgment, or, if he did so, have failed to notice a coincidence so remarkable between his own life and that of Tibullus.

(2) But it is no less improbable that Tibullus was born so late as B. C. 43. In B. C. 31 we find him declining an invitation to follow his patron Messalla to the campaign which ended in the battle of Actium ; whilst in the year following he took part in his Aquitanian campaign. To suppose that he was only twelve and thirteen years old respectively on these two occasions is out of the question.

(3) Ovid himself, Trist. 4. 10. 51–54—a passage which we shall consider further in treating of the life of Propertius —states distinctly that disparity of age had prevented him from enjoying the friendship of Tibullus. This remark he further clenches in the next two lines: for arranging the four elegiac poets of his own age in chronological order, he puts Gallus first, Tibullus next, and then declares that Propertius was successor to Tibullus, while he himself was successor to Propertius. Now Gallus was born in B. C. 66, and Propertius somewhere between the years 50 and 47 B. C. (see Introduction to Propertius). It is therefore impossible that Tibullus can have been born so late as B. C. 43, and we must look for some date between B. C. 66 on the one hand, and B. C. 50, or at the latest B. C. 47, on the other.

What other clue have we to guide us to a more precise date ? We have seen that Domitius Marsus says he was a youth (*iuvenem*) at the time of his death in B. C. 19 or B. C. 18 : so too says the Biography, while the Life attributed to Hieronymus Alexandrinus, and which is, in fact, the same biography expanded, declares that he died *in flore iuventutis*. The term *iuvenis* was, however, used techni-

cally in a wide sense at Rome, as it included all citizens
liable to be called on for military service up to forty-six
years of age. Thus under the constitution of Servius
Tullius each Class was divided into an equal number of
Senior Centuries and Junior Centuries : all citizens up to
the age of forty-six were included in the latter. The
language of poetry, however, was not bound to conform
to such a use as this ; and we may fairly assume that
the fact of an early death would not have been insisted on
by Domitius had Tibullus been more than forty when he
died. Assuming this point therefore as an extreme limit,
we may assign B. C. 59 as the earliest possible date for the
poet's birth, whilst it is not possible for various reasons to
place it later than B.C. 54. The latter is the date assumed by
Lachmann, the former is that adopted by Dissen; and though
it is impossible to arrive at a certain conclusion on the subject, Dissen holds that the earlier date fits in best with the
poet's biography as a whole. It certainly suits well the
tone of Horace's Epistle, in which he treats Tibullus as
an equal to whose criticisms he attaches weight, while at
the same time he addresses him in that patronising but
kindly tone which he could only have employed to one
decidedly younger than himself. Horace was born in
B. C. 65.

The *praenomen* of our poet is unknown. He was a
Roman *eques*, and was probably born at Pedum, a Latin
town just at the foot of the Apennines, and a few miles
north of Praeneste, where his father possessed an ample
estate. He had been brought up, he tells us (I. 10. 16), on
this estate, and he had looked forward to inheriting a rich
patrimony ; but his fortunes came under a cloud, and he
lost either the whole or the greater portion of it. The
language which he uses upon the subject is not free from
ambiguity ; but it is certain that the losses which he sustained were connected with his landed estate, and that
they were only of a partial character. He still continued

to reside upon it : and though he speaks often of his poverty, it is always of a poverty which is not inconsistent with competency. Thus in 1. 1. 19–22 he compares his present with his former condition :

> *Vos quoque felicis quondam nunc pauperis agri*
> *Custodes, fertis munera vestra, Lares:*
> *Tunc vitula innumeros lustrabat caesa iuvencos,*
> *Nunc agna exigui est hostia parva soli.*

'Ye, too, my Lares, guardians of an estate once rich, now poor, receive your gifts; in those days would a calf be slaughtered to purify unnumbered steers, but now for my tiny farm there falls a little lamb.'

And when, at the end of the same poem, he resigns to the avaricious the hope of bringing back a fortune from the wars, he adds on his own account :

> *Ego composito securus acervo*
> *Despiciam dites despiciamque famem.*

'With pile stored up, I shall know no care : I shall envy not the rich, I shall fear not hunger.'

Thus his property is reduced, not lost altogether : and his tone throughout his poems is that of a man who possesses a modest competence, and whose aim in life it is to make the most of the simple pleasures which it could afford him. But the standard of wealth at Rome was high in the days of Tibullus ; and that he was still very comfortably off, in spite of his losses, is plain from the words of Horace, Ep. 1. 4. 7, who says to him

> *Di tibi divitias dederunt artemque fruendi ;*

'The gods have given thee wealth, with the knowledge how to enjoy it.'

While again in l. 10 he says that he has

> *Et mundus victus non deficiente crumena,*

'A tidy competence, and a purse that fails not.'

As to the actual cause of his losses, Tibullus preserves a discreet silence; but it is generally taken for granted that like Horace, Virgil, and Propertius, he was a victim of the confiscations perpetrated by Octavianus and Antony with the view of satisfying the demands of their disbanded soldiery. The confiscation from which Virgil and Horace suffered took place after the battle of Philippi in B. C. 42. There were other confiscations in B. C. 36, and again after Actium in B. C. 31.

The probability is that the confiscation took place on the first of these occasions, in B. C. 42 or 41. At that time Tibullus, according to Dissen's chronology, would have been 17 or 18 years of age, and therefore just liable for military service. To this date therefore he assigns the 10th Elegy of the First Book, which the poet wrote on the occasion of receiving his first summons to arms, and in which he expresses in passionate language his hatred of war and his longing for ease and peace. In this poem there is no mention of any loss of property; so Dissen conjectures that the confiscation took place after Tibullus had started for the wars, and that he did not return to his reduced estate till B. C. 32, when he would have completed his full period of ten years' service in the cavalry. According to this view, a period of ten years must be placed between the composition of the tenth and the first Elegies of the First Book, for in the latter poem, written in B. C. 31 (see Introduction), Tibullus tells us he has completed his term of service, and is determined to live the rest of his days in peace at home.

Dean Milman [1], however, has pointed out one serious difficulty in the way of this chronology. It is hard to believe that so finished a poem as I. 10 can have been written in boyhood: or that so long a period as ten years—ten years too of rough camp-life—can have elapsed

---

[1] Article 'Tibullus,' Smith's Classical Dictionary.

between the composition of elegies 10 and 1. The style certainly bears no trace of any such interval. We can hardly help suspecting that, with his strong dislike to arms, Tibullus may have found in the confusions of the time some means of evading or abridging his term of military service. It is hard also to understand how he could have spent ten of the best years of his life in active campaigning without leaving a single indication of the fact in his poems : more especially as he has left us an ample record of his subsequent achievements in the train of his patron Messalla.

Of that distinguished man—M. Valerius Messalla Corvinus—a short account is given in the note to Tib. 1. 1. 53. Not less distinguished in literature than in politics, he had originally been a warm supporter of the Republican cause, and only passed over to the side of Octavianus about the year 37 or 36 B. C. At what period his friendship for Tibullus began, we know not : but he was doubtless attracted to him through admiration for his poetry, and he became his firm friend and patron through life. In the commencement of the year B. C. 31 (see 1. 1.) we find him inviting Tibullus to form part of his suite in the campaign which culminated in the battle of Actium. In the autumn of the same year, Messalla was despatched by Octavianus to put down a rebellion amongst the Gauls of Aquitania : Tibullus accompanied him throughout the campaign, and in the seventh Elegy of the First Book has left a vivid account of the tribes and the places which he saw during its progress. Towards the end of B.C. 30, Messalla was invested by Augustus with a general commission to establish the affairs of the East (see Introd. to 1. 3) : Tibullus again accompanied him, but falling sick at Corcyra, was left behind, and was unable to rejoin his patron. It was during his illness on this occasion that he composed the despondent but beautiful poem 1. 3. From this time onwards the poet led a life of uneventful seclusion on the remains of his estate at Pedum, unconscious, it would seem, of the great revolution taking place around him, and without making any effort—beyond cultivating the friendship of Horace—to make his way into that brilliant literary circle which was repaying the patronage of the new government by conferring upon it an immortality not its own. The name of Augustus, so prominent, so worshipped, in the pages of Virgil, Horace and Propertius, never once occurs in those of Tibullus : amidst the baseness and the corruptions of the time, it is refreshing to find that there was at least one genius of the first rank who could practise the contentment which Horace preached, and live a life full of unaffected delight in simple rural pleasures, even when ungilded by the flattering consciousness of imperial patronage.

The works usually attributed to Tibullus consist of four Books of amatory Elegies. Of these the first two are invariably regarded as genuine, the third book is held by almost all scholars to be spurious, and to be the work of a hand very inferior to that of Tibullus. Mr. Cranston, however, in the Introduction to his excellent translation of our poet into verse (Blackwood, *Edinburgh*, 1872) has undertaken the vindication of this book on grounds that deserve consideration. Scholars will scarcely, however, be ready to accept his ingenious substitution of *decimum* for *primum* in 3. 5. 17, according to which the year B.C. 43 would mark his *tenth* birthday, not his first. The phrase *videre parentes* is not appropriate to any day except the actual day of his birth.

The Fourth Book opens with a dreary panegyric on Messalla in Hexameter verse, of very doubtful genuineness ; but the remainder of the elegies of that book, most of which relate to the love of a noble lady Sulpicia for Cerinthus—whether a real or imaginary personage is not known—have so much of the Tibullian charm about them that it is hard to believe they can be the work of an unknown poet. Some suppose them to have been written by Sulpicia herself, daughter or granddaughter of Cicero's contemporary, the famous jurist Servius Sulpicius, who was consul B.C. 51.

The first six elegies of the First Book are addressed to Delia—whose real name would seem to have been *Plancia, Plantia,* or *Plania* (Apuleius, Apol. 10)—for whom the poet had formed the most ardent and faithful attachment. Throughout the whole of this Book, the dream of his life is to retire with her to his country property, and to pass the rest of his days in the enjoyment of her love, and of the simple pleasures of country life. He nursed her tenderly during an illness which occurred after his return from Corcyra, but not long afterwards she threw him over, and united herself to another and richer lover. The Second Book is devoted mainly to another charmer of the name of Nemesis, of whom it is probable that Horace speaks under the name of Glycera, Od. 1. 33. Ovid, at any rate, in his beautiful elegy upon the poet's death, knows only of his having had two loves, Am. 3. 9. 31, 32

> *Sic Nemesis longum, sic Delia nomen habebunt,*
> *Altera cura recens, altera primus amor.*

'So will Nemesis, so will Delia, have an everlasting name : the last his first, the first his latter love.'

While in line 58 he tells us how both Delia and Nemesis were beside his sick bed, along with his mother and his sister, and that the latter claimed to have held his hand in death :

> *Me tenuit moriens deficiente manu.*

'He held me as he died with his failing hand.'

A charming picture of the character and person of Tibullus has been left to us by Horace in Epist. 1. 4.

1–9

Albi, nostrorum sermonum candide iudex,
Quid nunc te dicam facere in regione Pedana?
Scribere quod Cassi Parmensis opuscula vincat,
An tacitum silvas inter reptare salubres,
Curantem quidquid dignum sapiente bonoque est?
Non tu corpus eras sine pectore: di tibi formam,
Di tibi divitias dederunt artemque fruendi.
Quid voveat dulci nutricula maius alumno,
Qui sapere et fari possit quae sentiat, et cui
Gratia, fama, valetudo contingat abunde,
Et mundus victus, non deficiente crumena?

'What shall I say thou art doing, Albius, in thy region of Pedum, thou kindly critic of my satires? Art thou writing aught to outdo the trifles of Parmese Cassius, or art thou sauntering silent amongst the healthful woods, with thoughts bent on all that is worthy of one wise and good? No body without soul art thou: the gods have given to thee beauty, they have given thee wealth and the knowledge how to enjoy it. What more could fond nurse pray for the child she loves, than that he should have good sense, with power to express what he feels, good friends, a good name, abundance of good health, a trim but modest home, and a purse that is never empty?'

Ovid has frequent references to Tibullus, of whom he speaks in terms of the warmest admiration. Thus Am. I. 15. 27

Donec erunt ignes arcusque Cupidinis arma,
Discentur numeri, culte Tibulle, tui.

'So long as fire and bow shall be Cupid's weapons, so long thy numbers, polished Tibullus, shall be learnt.'

Quintilian, Inst. Or. 10. 1. 93, says, *Elegia quoque Graecos provocamus, cuius mihi tersus atque elegans maxime videtur auctor Tibullus: sunt qui Propertium malint: Ovidius utroque lascivior, sicut durior Gallus,*

i. e. he gives to Tibullus the palm for grace and polish, though some would assign it to Propertius : Ovid is more free, Gallus is deficient in tenderness. But the most beautiful tribute to his merit is the Elegy of Ovid, Am. 3. 9, of which mention has been already made. It is too long to transcribe as a whole, but here are the concluding lines :

Si tamen e nobis aliquid nisi nomen et umbra
Restat, in Elysia valle Tibullus erit.
Obvius huic venias, hedera iuvenilia cinctus
Tempora, cum Calvo, docte Catulle, tuo ;
Tu quoque, si falsum est temerati crimen amici,
Sanguinis atque animae prodige, Galle, tuae.
His comes umbra tua est. Si qua est modo corporis umbra,
Auxisti numeros, culte Tibulle, pios :
Ossa quieta, precor, tuta requiescite in urna,
Et sit humus cineri non onerosa tuo.

These lines have been thus gracefully rendered by Professor Nichol [1] :

Ah ! yet, if any part of us remains
But name and shadow, Albius is not dead ;
And thou, Catullus, in Elysian plains
With Calvus see the ivy crown his head.
Thou, Gallus, prodigal of life and blood,
If false the charge of amity betrayed,
And aught remains across the Stygian flood,
Shalt meet him yonder with thy happy shade.
Refined Tibullus! thou art joined to those
Living in calm communion with the blest ;
In peaceful urn thy quiet bones repose—
May earth lie lightly where thy ashes rest !

MSS. and Editions of Tibullus.

Up to a recent period, the best critical edition of Tibullus was that of Lachmann, published in 1829, pre-

---

[1] See the whole of Professor Nichol's translation, given in full in Mr. Cranston's Version.

ceded by a few years by that of Huschke, 1819. Lachmann relied mainly upon five MSS., none of them older than the fifteenth century. These MSS. were all, according to the fashion of the scholars of that time, much interpolated; the interpolations being due not only to the copying of readings from other MSS., but also, in many cases, to sheer invention. Lachmann was also acquainted with the readings noted by J. Scaliger from an old MS. of Extracts from Books I and II, possessed by Vincentius Bellovacensis, a writer of the thirteenth century; with the readings of the fragment of a MS. which Scaliger received from Cuiaccius; and with the readings of Franciscus Puccius, many of which were derived from a very old MS. But he was not able to exhibit the true connection between these MSS.; and the text has been put upon a new footing by the edition of Baehrens (1878), who claims to have discovered two MSS. of the first importance, and to have established the true relationship subsisting between the existing MSS. The following is the account he gives of the various MSS. First in importance is

A or Codex Ambrosianus discovered by Baehrens in the Ambrosian Library of Milan in 1876. It is on parchment, of quarto shape, contains only Tibullus in forty-eight leaves of twenty-two lines each, the last being blank. At the end, after the 'Vita Tibulli,' are the words, *Liber Colycii pyeri Cancellarii Florentini*, and, added in a different hand, *Liber Cosme Johannis de Medicis*. It is written in a beautiful hand, and has few mistakes. Its date is probably about 1374, as we know that *Colutius Salutatus* was hunting up copies of Propertius and Catullus about that time. It has been corrected here and there by a hand some fifty years later. Very like this MS., but inferior, is

V or Codex Vaticanus, on paper, folio size, containing Tibullus on leaves 1–37, and also Ovid's Remedia Amoris. It is probably of the end of the thirteenth or beginning of the fourteenth century. It has been corrected by various hands, but these corrections are all of little or no value.

These two MSS. resemble each other so closely, that it is evident they are derived from a common archetype. To this same family belong the various MSS. of the fifteenth century—including those relied upon by Lachmann—which departed more and more widely from the original, and suffered much from interpolations by Joannes Aurispa, Thomas Seneca, Jovianus Pontanus, and other scholars of that century.

But Baehrens believes that he has lighted upon a MS. which belongs to a different and older family than A.V. Lachmann set great store by certain readings noted in 1501 by Franciscus Puccius, who professed to have derived them from an old MS. This MS. Baehrens believes he has found in

G or **Codex Guelferbytanus**, a folio MS., now at Wolfenbüttel, on parchment, which contains the works of Tibullus on thirty-eight leaves, along with other matter. The writing is an imitation of the Langobardic character of the tenth or eleventh century, but Baehrens holds that it was written about 1425 A.D. It has been corrected by a later hand, not only on the margin, but between the lines, and even in the text itself. These corrections are sometimes taken from a MS. of the A.V. family, but are for the most part worthless. The text itself, from its similarity to the readings of Puccius, Baehrens holds to be the very MS. used by him : it seems to be derived from a different original from A.V., but to belong to the same family as the

Excerpta Parisina, a book of extracts from various ancient authors, compiled by some learned Frenchman between 1000 and 1100 A.D. This collection contained passages from Tibullus I and II : these were seen by Vincentius Bellovacensis, a writer of the thirteenth century, and other writers of that time : a copy came into the hands of Scaliger, and Meyncke has collected the passages from Tibullus which are to be found in two MSS. of the Florilegium now at Paris (Mus. Rhen., vol. 25, p. 369). Many of the readings are corrupt, and entirely bad, but those that are good seem to be derived from a different family from A. V., and to present great similarity to the readings of G. Wherever Par. has a good reading, G. agrees with it; where its reading is bad, it agrees rather with A. V. Hence Baehrens holds that A. and V. were derived from one common parent, while G. and Par. were derived from another and older parent, belonging possibly to the tenth or eleventh centuries. These two supposed MSS. however, though unequal in age, were themselves probably derived from a common archetype whose supposed readings, designated by the sign O., are to be ascertained from the consensus of the three MSS. A.V.G., supported by the readings of Par. where available.

But this is not all. There were at one time in existence two other MSS. of Tibullus, distinct both from each other and from O. Of one of these MSS. some fragments are preserved in the collection called

Excerpta Frisingensia, now at Munich, in a MS. of the eleventh century, and taken apparently from a MS. older and better than O [1]. Some excellent readings have been preserved in these extracts, especially that adopted in this edition in 1. 1. 25. The other MS. is preserved only in the

Fragment called F. This is the ancient fragment which Scaliger received from Jacobus Cuiaccius, on the readings of which Lachmann placed a high value. It began only from 3. 4. 65, and as the MS. itself has disappeared, only such of its readings were preserved as Scaliger thought fit to write out on to his own copy of the Plantinian edition of our poet (1560). That copy is now

---

[1] See Lachmann, pref. p. 8, and L. Mueller in Fleckeisen's Jahrbuch 1869, p. 63, as well as in his own edition.

in the library at Leyden, and has been examined by C. M. Francken and E. Hiller. These readings are marked by the sign *Plant.* in this edition. What is the relationship subsisting between O. F. and Fris. has not as yet been ascertained. O. itself was corrupt and interpolated, and it must have been experimented on by emendators at a very early age.

The text of the present edition has been largely founded upon that given in the excellent critical edition of E. Hiller (1885), compared throughout with that of Baehrens, and with occasional assistance from that of L. Mueller (1880). In every important or doubtful case, the authority is given in the critical notes.

The best general commentaries on Tibullus are contained in the edition of Heyne, fourth edition, 1817, and in that of Dissen, 1835. In the present edition considerable use has been made of an edition of Extracts from Tibullus published by the late Professor Ramsay in 1840, and now out of print: the notes transcribed from that edition are marked by inverted commas. For a complete list of editions and works on Tibullus see preface to E. Hiller's edition, 1885.

INTRODUCTION TO PROPERTIUS.

Life of Propertius.

OF the life and circumstances of Propertius we know little or nothing except what is recorded by himself, or can be gathered from a careful examination of his poems. Such an examination will tell us much of the poet's character, and enable us to construct for ourselves a tolerably complete picture of the man, of his temper and his tastes, of the strength and tenderness of his feelings, as well as of the characteristic features and limitations of his genius ; but it will furnish us with a very meagre account of the external incidents of his life. His poems are essentially poems of feeling, not of incident or description; and they revolve in a round so narrow, so intense, that beyond the special circumstances by which the feeling was called forth, they give little or no clue to the surroundings in which his life was passed. His love and his poetry were his all : and in leaving these behind him, he has left us the best record of his life.

His full name, so far as we know it, was Sextus Propertius. The praenomen does not occur in his writings, nor is it given in any MS.: but it is distinctly attributed to him by Donatus in his Life of Virgil. Many MSS. and, until recently, most editions, give him the additional name *Aurelius*, sometimes before, sometimes after, the *Propertius* : but apart from the improbability of a double gentile name being borne at so early a date as the time of Propertius, it is likely that a mistake has arisen from a confusion with the name of the poet Prudentius, whose full name was *Aurelius Prudentius Clemens*. Many MSS. add *Nauta* to the poet's name, as an agnomen: but this mistake has been shown to arise from a false reading *navita dives eras* instead of *non ita dives eras* in 2. 24. 38 [1].

As to the birthplace of our poet, a lively controversy has been waged. We know from himself that he was an Umbrian, but he does not fix the exact locality of his birth, and there are at least four towns whose claim to the honour have been supported with a good show of reason by different editors. These towns are *Asisium* (the modern Assisi, famed as the birthplace of St. Francis) ; *Mevania* (Bevagna) ; *Ameria* (Amelia) ; and *Hispellum* (Spello), to which may also be added *Perusia* (Perugia), though that town is not situated in Umbria at all. Almost all recent editors, however, are agreed in fixing upon *Asisium* : and yet, if the words of Propertius on which they rely be taken in their simple sense, nothing can be more clear than the fact that, while indicating each of the above-named places in connection with his birth, he does not state that he was born in any one of them. On the contrary, his references to the different cities show that his birthplace might be described in connection with them all ; and that he was in all probability born in some country house or village situated in the district which lay between them. The passages which bear on the subject are the following :—

1. The poem 1. 22 is written for the express purpose of answering the inquiries of his friend Tullus as to his home and family :

> *Qualis et unde genus, qui sint mihi, Tulle, Penates,*
> *Quaeris pro nostra semper amicitia.* ·

'Thou art ever asking, Tullus, as an old friend, what and whence my race, what my home.'

Propertius answers by referring him to the town of Perusia, and adds, ll. 9, 10

> *Proxima subposito contingens Umbria campo*
> *Me genuit, terris fertilis uberibus;*

---

[1] See M. Plessis, p. 172.

'In the plain below, where the rich fertile land of Umbria comes closest—there was I born;'

i. e. he was born in the rich plain of Umbria, at the point where it comes closest up to the walls of Perusia. It is impossible that in these words Umbria as a whole can be referred to: he clearly means to specify the particular part of Umbria with which he was connected.

2. In 4. 1. 61–66 he proclaims himself to be an Umbrian, and speaks in vague terms of his genius being connected with a city or cities set upon a height above the plain :

> *Ennius hirsuta cingat sua dicta corona:*
> *Mi folia ex hedera porrige, Bacche, tua,*
> *Ut nostris tumefacta superbiat Umbria libris,*
> *Umbria Romani patria Callimachi.*
> *Scandentes quisquis cernit de vallibus arces*
> *Ingenio muros aestimet ille meo.*

'Let Ennius crown his sayings with rugged wreath : but hand thou to me, Bacchus, a chaplet of thine own ivy, that Umbria be lifted up and boast her of my lays—Umbria the fatherland of the Callimachus of Rome. Whoever sees yon heights climbing out of the valley,—by my genius let him rate those walls.'

There is nothing in these words to show that Propertius had any particular town in view, or that he meant to speak of such town as his birthplace.

3. More definite information is afforded by 4. 1. 121–126

> *Umbria te notis antiqua Penatibus edit:*
> *(Mentior? an patriae tangitur ora tuae?)*
> *Qua nebulosa cavo rorat Mevania campo,*
> *Et lacus aestivis intepet Umber aquis,*
> *Scandentisque arcis consurgit vertice murus,*
> *Murus ab ingenio notior ille tuo.*

'Thy birthplace is ancient Umbria, in a home well-known: (Speak I false? or do I truly touch the region of thy fatherland?) where dank Mevania drips with its sunken plain; where reek, through summer days, the waters of the Umbrian mere; where rise the walls on the top of yon climbing height,—walls that have gathered name from genius of thine.' The MS. reading in l. 125 is *Asis* : but this is almost demonstrably wrong. There is no such name as *Asis*. Hertzberg in vain attempts to show that it was the name of the mountain *behind* Asisium, on the slopes of which also lay Hispellum. Hence Lachmann conjectures *Asisi* : but it has been shown that the first syllable of that word is long, not short. There is a Greek form of the name 'Aίσιον, used by Strabo; and Propertius might conceivably have used for his verse a form *Aisi*, genitive of *Aisium*. But the reading *Asis*, like *Asisi*, has evidently sprung from a desire to connect the poet with *Asisium*, and the position of that town, which is most remarkable, scarcely suits the words of the line. The modern town occupies the same site as the ancient town, and its peculiarity is that it is *not* on the top (*vertice*) of a hill, but actually forms a shelf on the side of a steep straight hill, which rises up no less steeply behind it. No room could be found even for the church of St. Francis, except by building out arcades as a foundation: so too with the great convent beside it. It would be quite impossible to describe the walls of the town as crowning a height [1]. Hertzberg suggests that *vertice* might be an ablative of the instrument, as though the wall was actually formed 'by the top of a hill;' but this is precisely what it was not. The words describe some town

---

[1] What is here said of Assisi is taken from personal observation. See Murray's Handbook, and the Quarterly Review, No. 208. Dante, Par. 11. 43, describes the site as hanging from the mountain side:

Fertile costa d' alto monte pende.

set on the top of a hill, doubtless the same town as that described in l. 65 in almost identical words :

> *Scandentes si quis cernet de vallibus arces;*

and *arcis*, not *Asis*, is the true reading. The town indicated is one of the towns in the valley of the Clitumnus, but it was not necessarily Asisium.

But even if *Asisi* were the true reading, the words of Propertius do not indicate more than that he was born in the neighbourhood of that town. It is clear that the poet here specifies a district, not a town. He again gives *Umbria* as his birthplace ; *patriae ora* has reference to what follows, and specifies the particular part of the province with which he was connected. This is then described as the part where the dank Mevania drips with moisture on a plain, where waters steam from the Umbrian lake in summer, and where the walls of a city rise up on a height. No known lake would satisfy the conditions of the *lacus Umber* : so the phrase is generally supposed to refer to a part of the river Clitumnus, which, according to the younger Pliny, 8. 8. 1-3, spreads out into a broad glassy pool not far below its source. The fact then that Propertius describes his Penates as being in a part of Umbria lying close under Perusia, where lay Mevania and the Umbrian lake, and the town set on a hill, is proof that he means to specify no particular town, but only to indicate a spot in the Clitumnus valley within reach of all the places he has named. The phrase *noti Penates* no doubt refers to the farm of which Propertius' father was deprived in the confiscations of B. C. 42, and implies that it was a property of some importance. It was in all probability situated nearer to *Asisium* than to the other towns named above, for the names *Propertius* and *Propertia* occur on several inscriptions found in or near that city. There is also evidence to show that he was claimed as a *municeps* of that town in the century after his death. For there exists at Assisi a stone with the following inscription :

C. PASSENNO

C. F. SERG

PAVLLO

ROPERTIO

BLAESO.

Now Pliny the younger, Epist. 6. 15. 1, speaks of a Passennus Paullus as a learned *eques* and a poet, adding, *Gentilicium hoc illi: est enim municeps Properti atque etiam inter maiores suos Propertium narrat.* There is no evidence that Propertius left any child behind him; the words of Pliny do not necessarily mean more than that Passennus counted Propertius as belonging to a previous generation of his family; and even if they do mean more, the claim of Passennus to be descended from Propertius as an ancestor is no more proof of the fact than the similar claim of the emperor Tacitus to be descended from the historian. Nevertheless, the statement of Pliny, taken along with the inscription, raises a strong probability that the Propertii were connected with Asisium, and that Asisium was the nearest important town to the property on which the poet was born.

The Propertii, it would appear, were a respectable family in comfortable circumstances, but neither patrician, noble, nor wealthy. Thus, in his childhood, Propertius wore the golden bulla that was the sign of *ingenuitas*, 4. 1. 131

> *Mox ubi bulla rudi dimissa est aurea collo,*
> *Matris et ante deos libera sumpta toga;*

'Soon, when I laid aside the golden boss from my neck, yet unfledged, and assumed the manly gown before my mother's gods,'

i.e. the Penates, so-called because his father was dead. Again, 2. 24. 36, he represents Cynthia as addressing him thus:

> *Certus eras, eheu! quamvis nec sanguine avito*
> *Nobilis, et quamvis non ita dives eras.*

'Faithful thou wert, ah me! though not sprung from noble ancestors, nor over rich withal.'

So again, 2. 34. 55

> *Aspice me, cui parva domi fortuna relicta est,*
> *Nullus et antiquo Marte triumphus avi.*

'See me, to whom but modest home and fortune have been left, and who have no ancestors that gained triumphs in ancient war.'

At an early age he lost his father, 4. 1. 127–130

> *Ossaque legisti non illa aetate legenda*
> *Patris, et in tenues cogeris ipse Lares :*
> *Nam tua cum multi versarent rura iuvenci,*
> *Abstulit excultas pertica tristis opes.*

'Thou didst gather thy father's bones at an age that was not meet, and wast thyself reduced to a slender home : full many a steer was wont to plough thy lands, but the accursed measuring-rod (i. e. of confiscation) took that well-tilled wealth away.'

The latter lines inform us that soon after his father's death his property was included, either in whole or in part—as the words *cui parva domi fortuna relicta est* seem to imply—among those confiscated by the triumvirs in B.C. 41. Dr. Postgate has pointed out that the horror with which the poet speaks of the siege of Perusia in B.C. 41 —in the course of which he lost one of his relatives—is to be explained by the fact that that event was associated with the lowest period of the family fortunes, and that Propertius himself, as a timid sensitive boy, may have witnessed some of the terrible scenes that attended it. His father dead, his property confiscated, he was brought up under the supervision of his mother, who in all proba- bility took him to Rome for his education, and expended upon him the same loving care that Horace informs us he experienced at the hands of his father. He received, at any rate, the best education which Rome could afford, and in due time, his mother being still alive, he assumed the *toga virilis.*

Like most well-educated young men of his time, he seems to have been intended for the bar; but we are not surprised that, with his temperament, like Ovid, he should have found the contentions of the forum intolerable, 4. 1. 133

> *Tum tibi pauca suo de carmine dictat Apollo,*
> *Et vetat insano verba tonare foro.*

'Then Apollo taught thee somewhat of his own gift of song, and forbad thee to thunder in the mad contests of the forum.'

The date of his birth can only be fixed approximately. Our only certain information on the subject is derived from Ovid, Trist. 4. 10. 41–54. In that passage Ovid gives a list of the poets whom he had known in his youth. Having first named Aemilius Macer of Verona, author of a poem on birds snakes and herbs, he proceeds:

> *Saepe suos solitus recitare Propertius ignes,*
> *Iure sodalicii qui mihi iunctus erat.*
> *Ponticus heroo, Bassus quoque clarus iambis,*
> *Dulcia convictus membra fuere mei.*
> *Detinuit nostras numerosus Horatius aures,*
> *Dum ferit Ausonia carmina culta lyra.*
> *Vergilium vidi tantum: nec amara Tibullo*
> *Tempus amicitiae fata dedere meae.*
> *Successor fuit hic tibi, Galle; Propertius illi;*
> *Quartus ab his serie temporis ipse fui.*

'Oft would Propertius recite to me his loves, close bound to me by bond of comradeship. Ponticus, famed in Epic verse, Bassus too in Iambic, were dearly-loved members of my band. Horace with his tuneful numbers held my ears fast-bound as he struck his polished lays from the lyre of Italy. Virgil I did but see: nor did the unkindly fates give Tibullus time to be my friend. He was thy successor, Gallus, and Propertius his: fourth from them was I in order of time.'

In the last four lines of the passage, it is evident that Ovid places the elegiac poets in a chronological order (*serie temporis*) in relation to each other. What he means to say is that Gallus was first in the series, then came Tibullus, then Propertius, whilst he himself closed the list as fourth in order from Gallus. A doubt has indeed been raised as to this interpretation in consequence of the two pronouns *hic* and *illi* being used in reference to the same person, viz. Tibullus: but there is no real difficulty in this, for as the subject of the sentence changes from Tibullus to Propertius, Tibullus is properly referred to as *hic* in the former clause, as *ille* in the latter. An exactly parallel instance occurs in Juv. 11. 23-5

> *Illum ego iure*
> *Despiciam qui scit quanto sublimior Atlas*
> *Omnibus in Libya sit montibus, hic tamen idem*
> *Ignoret quantum ferrata distet ab arca*
> *Sacculus,*

i.e. 'That man I should rightly despise who knows the height of Atlas, and who yet does not know,' etc. Here *illum* and *hic* refer to one and the same person, who is spoken of as *illum* when object, as *hic* when subject, to the verb. We thus establish the chronological sequence, (1) Gallus, (2) Tibullus, (3) Propertius, (4) Ovid. Now the poet C. Cornelius Gallus was born either in B.C. 69 or 66 and died B.C. 26; Tibullus was born possibly as early as B.C. 59, certainly not later than B.C. 54, and died probably B.C. 18; Ovid, lastly, was born B.C. 43, and died A.D. 18. We have thus to find a date for the birth of Propertius between the years B.C. 59 or 54 and B.C. 43. We have already seen that he was a boy in the years B.C. 42 and 41, old enough to be spoken of as the owner of property (4. 1. 129), and to be affected by the events of the Perusian war; but his education was not completed, and an interval must be left, corresponding to *mox* in 4. 3. 131, for his residence at Rome previous to his assumption of the manly gown in his sixteenth or seventeenth year. We may thus suppose that he was born not earlier than B.C. 50, nor later than B.C. 47, and that he assumed the manly gown between the years B.C. 34 and 30.

In the first flush of youth, Propertius came across his fate in the person of the famous Cynthia, at once his inspiration and his bane. The main work of his life was to record in passionate poetry the various phases of this attachment : and the ups and downs in his relations with her are the chief landmarks in his biography. Out of the · total number of ninety-one poems which he has left behind him, no less than sixty have relation to Cynthia : if we can arrange these in chronological order, we have practically the story of his life. The latest of the number are the two last elegies of Book III, in which, with a hardness and cruelty of tone almost amounting to brutality, he renounces his love for her, and finally bids her adieu. In the third line of poem 25, summing up the past, he says

Quinque tibi potui servire fideliter annos.

'For five years I was able to serve thee faithfully.'

The natural meaning of these words is that his whole attachment for Cynthia had lasted for five years : and though it is possible, as Dr. Postgate thinks, that a temporary reconciliation may have taken place after these words were written, it is certain that these two elegies are the last of which she was the theme. But before the final rupture, there was a previous period of estrangement which occurred in consequence of some quarrel between the lovers, the cause of which does not appear. Propertius puts it thus, 3. 16. 9

Peccaram semel, et totum sum pulsus in annum,

'Once had I sinned, and I was driven forth for an entire year.'

He had thus committed some fault, and she punished him by banishing him from her presence for a year. Now is this year to be counted amongst the five years

of 3. 25. 2? Are the words *potui servire fideliter* inconsistent with that hypothesis? The general opinion has
been that they *are* inconsistent with it; and this is the
view of Lachmann. He holds further that in 3. 15. 7, 8,
where the poet speaks of an attachment for Cynthia of
at least two years' standing, he must refer to a period
previous to the year of separation, so that the whole
period of the poet's connection with Cynthia must in
that case have extended over at least eight years. But
it is evident from the Cynthia elegies that there were
frequent quarrels and frequent reconciliations between the
lovers: their love was subject to all the vicissitudes of
caprice, disappointment, and satiety, which might be
expected to arise between two persons of ardent but
sensitive temperament, incapable of self-control, and
innocent of all restraint from moral or prudential con-
siderations. It were idle to look for five years of unbroken calm between such a pair; and a whole year of
interrupted relations might well be overlooked in a rapid
and indignant retrospect. Literal exactness is not to be
looked for in the protestations of a lover when at the
moment of a final rupture he recalls his devotion in the
past: and M. Plessis is doubtless right in holding that
when Propertius declares he had been for five years the
faithful slave of Cynthia, he meant to indicate the whole
duration of their attachment. It affords a strong cor-
roboration of this view, that the whole series of Cynthia
poems, so far as we can put an exact date upon them,
covers as nearly as possible a period of five years. None
of these elegies can be definitely ascribed to an earlier
date than B. C. 28: none can definitely be put later than
B. C. 23. There are many, no doubt, to which no date at
all can be assigned, and there are difficulties in the way
of any chronological scheme that can be constructed: but
the fact that some ten or twelve of the elegies, spread over
the three first books, can be dated, and that all fall within

the limits given above, affords a strong presumption which cannot be overthrown by problematical interpretations of particular poems or passages. The elegy 2. 10 which was probably written before the rupture, has been put as late as B.C. 22: but M. Plessis has shown that Hertzberg is probably correct in assigning it to B. C. 25[1].

The First Book was written during the earlier and happier period of the poet's attachment : many of the pieces included in it are in his lightest happiest vein, and its publication—which was perhaps delayed till B.C. 25[2]—at once established the reputation of its author. The book seems to have been known by the name of *Cynthia Monobiblos,* and is the book referred to by Martial, 14. 189

Cynthia, facundi carmen iuvenile Properti,
Accepit famam, nec minus ipsa dedit.

'Cynthia, the youthful poem of the eloquent Propertius, has conferred a name not less famous than she has received.'

It probably secured for Propertius admission to the circle of Maecenas, who soon began to suggest to him that he should employ his muse in the service of Augustus.

The Second Book was begun within a few months of the completion (not necessarily the publication) of the first; for in 2. 3. 3, after declaring his enslavement to Cynthia, he adds, addressing himself :

Vix unum potes infelix requiescere mensem,
Et turpis de te iam liber alter erit.

'Scarce, hapless one! canst thou rest one single month, and there will soon, to thy shame, be a second book about thee.'

The book opens with an elegy addressed to Maecenas; the poët is still in the full fervour of his love, and pleads

---

[1] Études critiques sur Properce, p. 222.
[2] See Postgate's Introduction.

the impossibility of tearing himself away from it as an excuse for declining the invitation of Maecenas to occupy himself with graver themes. As the book proceeds, the poet is still spell-bound by the fascinations of Cynthia, and there are some poems in the old exuberant key : but he speaks more frequently of her inconstancy and ingratitude ; complains of the hardness of her heart ; looks forward to a death brought about by her cruelty, and seems to struggle more resolutely against the slavery which enthralls him.

By degrees he turns his attention to other subjects ; declares he must now have done with love and sing of Caesar, and though he shows little alacrity to fulfil the promise, it is clear that Cynthia has a less exclusive hold on his regard than during the period covered by the first book. The poems are of various dates, and written in various moods: the twenty-eighth was written as early as B. C. 28 : the first and tenth were probably written in B.C. 25 or 24.

In the Third Book, only thirteen out of twenty-five poems refer to Cynthia. In it are included some of his noblest and most touching poems—amongst these the eighteenth, written on the occasion of the death of Marcellus in B.C. 23, and the exquisitely pathetic seventh, on the drowning of Paetus—which prove conclusively that Cynthia was by no means the only, or the noblest, inspirer of his muse. It concludes with the bitter and taunting poems in which he abjures his love for her, and finally casts her off.

The Fourth Book differs materially from all the rest. It contains but two poems referring to Cynthia. One of these belongs evidently to an early period ; the other— the seventh—was written after her death. The remainder are longer, and more formal in character than the elegies of the earlier books. Five of them are historical and antiquarian ; one is a poetical epistle from a

young wife to her absent husband; in another the
victory of Actium is celebrated, and the book closes
with the magnificent Elegy on the noble matron Cornelia. Two of the poems of this book, and two only,
can be dated. These are the sixth and eleventh, both of
which must be referred to the year B. C. 16. The former
was written to commemorate the celebration of the
ludi quinquennales; the latter, l. 66, alludes to the consulship of P. Cornelius Scipio, both of which events took
place in that year. Most editors are agreed in holding
that the whole book was published posthumously. Beyond the year B. C. 16, says Dr. Postgate, 'there is not
a shred for conjecture to lay hold of, and the obscurity
which wraps so much of the poetry of Propertius sinks,
like a pall, upon his life.'

It has generally been supposed that the antiquarian
poems of the Fourth Book—the first, second, fourth, ninth
and tenth—were written in the poet's first youth, and before
the Cynthia period of his life. But there is no proof for
this hypothesis; nor is it supported by any evidence to
be extracted from the poems themselves. Alike in subject and in treatment they display a calmness and a
continuity altogether foreign to the rapid fervour and
exuberant passionateness of the poet's earliest days;
they seem a very fulfilment of the poet's own promise
in 3. 5. 19 *sqq.*, that while devoted to Love and Bacchus
in his hot youth, he will turn, with advancing age, to graver
themes. Now had Propertius turned to antiquarian subjects in his youth, we may be certain that he would have
gone to the mythology of Greece for his subject. When he
began to write, he was saturated with the forms and the
spirit of Greek mythology; he had carried an imagination
and an enthusiasm into the study which burst through
all the artificial wrappings in which his Alexandrine
masters had embedded it; but there is nothing in his
earlier poems to show that he had expended any interest

or labour on the early legends of Rome or Italy. The question is not without interest : for by relegating to the poet's earlier days all the poems in Book IV which cannot be dated, it is possible to interpret literally the words of Propertius when he says 2. 1. 4

Ingenium nobis ipsa puella facit,

'my love herself is the maker of my Muse,' and to bestow on Cynthia the glory of having been the main, if not the only, inspirer of his genius. Dr. Postgate says, 'Without the stimulus of his love, and without the sympathy and encouragement of his beloved, his genius might never have broken the crust of lethargy which covered it . . . . With the extinction of his love decayed his poetic activity . . . . " His Muse," as Hertzberg says, " sank to silence with his love." ' There is no doubt that Cynthia's literary taste [1] did much to stimulate the poet's genius, and to throw his love for her into the imperishable form in which it has been embodied. No doubt also his rupture with her must have shaken his whole

---

[1] Cynthia's real name was Hostia, and her grandfather was probably the poet Hostius, who wrote a poem on the Illyrian war of B. C. 178, Festus s. v. *tesca*. Propertius says to her, 4. 20. 8

Splendidaque a docto fama refulget avo ;

he calls her *docta*, the characteristic epithet of poets in 1. 7. 11, 13. 11 and in a moment of anger declares, 2. 11. 5-6

Et tua transibit contemnens ossa viator,
   Nec dicet, Cinis hic docta puella fuit,

as though her title to 'learning' would naturally be acknowledged by everyone. In 2. 1. 27-32 he declares the causes of his love for her :

Quum tibi praesertim Phoebus sua carmina donet,
   Aoniamque libens Calliopea lyram ;
Unica nec desit iucundis gratia verbis,
   Omnia quaeque Venus quaeque Minerva probat.
His tu semper eris nostrae gratissima vitae,
   Taedia dum miserae sint tibi luxuriae.

See too the passage, 2. 3. 9-22.

nature, at once sensitive and passionate as it was : and the twenty-third and twenty-fourth poems of Book IV show how for a time at least it converted the tenderest of poets into the hardest. When there was no longer a Cynthia, there could no longer be Cynthia poems : but some of the finest, to a modern taste probably *the* finest, of the poems of Propertius are written on subjects in which Cynthia had no place ; and there is no need to exaggerate the influence which she exercised on his genius, and for that purpose to set aside the presumption afforded by the order of the poems as handed down to us that some of the noblest and most beautiful of his poems were composed after his love for Cynthia was a thing of the past. The fevered dissipation of his first youth no doubt left its effects behind, and the exuberance of his early muse departed from him ; but no dimness of poetic faculty, no seared heart, can be attributed to the poet who wrote the third and the eleventh poems of the Fourth Book ; and the latter, as we have seen, was written not earlier than B. C. 16.

Another argument, which is almost conclusive, can be drawn from the development in the structure of the elegiac couplet, and especially of the pentameter, which can be traced in the poems as they stand. In Books I and II Propertius constantly ends his pentameters with words of three, four, and five syllables : the number of such endings is far rarer in Book III, and ceases almost entirely in Book IV : in seven out of the eleven poems of that book not one of these endings occur. The following table will show at a glance how the facts stand :—

	Book I.	II.	III.	IV.
Trisyllabic endings	35	15	1	1
Quadrisyllabic endings	88	53	10	4
Quinquesyllabic endings	8	7	1	1

The above table speaks for itself. It shows that as the books proceed, Propertius eschews more and more all endings other than the dissyllabic, and that his verse was gradually conforming to the precise laws which became perfect and stereotyped in the verse of Ovid. It is evident that the whole of the poems of Book IV were written during the latest period of his art, and that it is impossible to refer any of them to the earlier period when he systematically revelled in the use of the longer endings. Some valuable observations on the metre of Propertius will be found in Dr. Postgate's Introd., p. cxxvi.

One more question has been started: was the rupture with Cynthia which took place in B. C. 23 absolutely final? We know that she did not long survive the rupture: was the old intimacy ever renewed before her death? One poem only, 4. 7, alludes to the death of Cynthia. This poem represents a dream in which the spirit of Cynthia appears to Propertius after death, rebukes him for forgetting their love so soon, and reproaches him with not having been present to conduct the ceremonies of her funeral. She then proceeds to give the poet various instructions. Dr. Postgate (Introduction, p. xxv) has made a most interesting analysis of this poem. He holds it to prove that the lovers had been once more reconciled, that she had died leaving to Propertius the disposal of her effects, that in the prostration of grief he had neglected all the 'death duties,' and that he wrote this poem as an expression of contrition. His interpretation is fair and ingenious; but it would unnecessarily lower Propertius in our estimation. If the quarrel was never made up, and she died while they were still estranged, it was quite natural that he should take no part in her obsequies, and the other arrangements connected with her death. But to suppose that they were friends at the time of her death, and that he proved utterly neglectful of the commonest offices of friendship to her remains, nay even outraged his former love by conduct showing blank indifference to her memory, is to suppose that he had lost

all sensibility, and that Propertius the man was something
wholly different from the Propertius disclosed to us in
his poems.   It is more pleasing to suppose that the
quarrel never was healed ; that Cynthia died in estrangement, and that Propertius in consequence took no part in
her funeral ; but that soon afterwards a feeling of remorse
and contrition came over him, to which he gave expression in a poem confessing his coldness, and acknowledging the claims which, after all, she still possessed upon
his regard.   But the poem is not the work of a heart-
broken man ; and its tone affords additional confirmation
of the view that Propertius' muse was not at once chilled
into silence by the death of Cynthia.

As might well be supposed, Propertius counted among
his friends all, or almost all, of the famous poets of his
time.   In 3. 26. 31 he pays a noble tribute to Virgil ;
Ovid, as we have seen, tells us that Propertius was his
intimate friend, and that he himself used often to hear
him recite his poems.   Ponticus, the epic poet, is addressed in 1.7, Bassus in 1. 4, and a tragic poet, Lynceus,
is mentioned in 2. 34.   But what of Horace, the period of
whose best lyrical activity so closely coincided with his
own ?   He is never named: yet the two must have met
on the common ground of literature, and in the house
of Maecenas.   They were men of very different temper:
the easy-going well-bred and self-controlled man of the
world may well have sneered at the morbidly sensitive
and capricious enthusiast whose key was often one
of exaggeration: and the ill-regulated impetuosity of the
Umbrian bard may have felt repelled by the serene and
critical self-confidence of the Epicurean, whose easy man-
ners might be mistaken by the vain self-conscious poet
for the airs of 'a superior person.'   Neither poet ever
names the other: and the careful analysis made by Dr.
Postgate of Hor. Ep. 2. 87 (Introd., p. xxxiii) leads strongly
to the conclusion that that passage is an elaborate attack

upon Propertius. Be that as it may, it is certain at
any rate that no intimacy can have existed between
the two poets. Tibullus also is never mentioned throughout the poems.

MSS. and Editions of Propertius.

The text of Propertius is notoriously in an unsatisfactory condition : amongst the texts of the great Roman
poets there is none which presents difficulties so great.
The comparative value of the existing MSS. of Propertius, and their mutual relation to each other, have not
even yet been settled beyond dispute. Of these the first
to be mentioned is

N or **Codex Neapolitanus.** The superiority of this
famous MS. had been established by Lachmann[1], and
accepted as an article of faith by succeeding editors,
including Professor A. Palmer, who published his admirable critical edition of the text in 1880 ; but it has
been called in question by L. Mueller, and more recently
by A. Baehrens, whose elaborate critical edition (1880)
is founded upon a theory which assigns to this MS. only
a subordinate position in the constitution of the text.
In 1884, however, there appeared a French work on
Propertius by M. Frédéric Plessis—a work which in
its grasp, lucidity, and critical acumen does honour to
French scholarship—which controverts the conclusions
of Baehrens, and, upon evidence which will probably
be accepted by future editors as conclusive, pronounces
the *Neapolitanus* to be beyond question the oldest, and,
in consequence, the most authoritative, of the MSS.
of our poet. In this he agrees with Professor Palmer,

---

[1] Who, however, places it only second in importance, after
the Groninganus.

who has himself carefully examined the MS. in question. This MS. is now in the ducal library at Wolfenbüttel: it is called *Neapolitanus* (or N. throughout this edition) because it was inspected at Naples by N. Heinsius; and from the fact that the name *Manetti* is written in faint letters on its last page, it seems to have once been the property of a scholar of that name who died at Naples in the year 1459. The MS. is on parchment, of large octavo size; it is composed of seventy-one leaves, and contains no writing but Propertius. At the beginning are the usual words *Incipit Propertius:* at the end *Explicit.* Books I and II are not separated: there is an interval between III and IV. There is no title, nor space left for a title, at the beginning of the different poems: but the initial word of each is marked by an illuminated letter. A good many of the leaves are damaged; one leaf, containing 4. 11. 17–76, has been lost altogether; and three different pens or hands can be recognised as having been employed in the transcription. The history of the MS. is not known. Lachmann, followed by Hertzberg, assigned it to the thirteenth century: L. Mueller puts it at the fourteenth, or more probably the fifteenth, while Baehrens declares it cannot be older than 1430. All agree that the writing presents certain characteristics of an earlier date than this; but Baehrens explains these away by supposing that the MS. was written in Italy, and that certain archaisms of writing lingered on in that country after they had been exploded elsewhere. M. Plessis has carefully examined the MS. anew; and backed by the authority of two French palaeographists—M. Léopold Delisle and M. Chatelain—he declares positively that it cannot be assigned to a later date than the beginning of the thirteenth century. This conclusion he founds upon six distinct peculiarities in the handwriting, the concurrence of which, he asserts, permits no doubt as to the date :—

1. The initial letters are frequently illuminated in green : green initial letters disappeared about A. D. 1220.

2. The writing of the diphthong *ae* by ę (with a cedilla) as *durę* for *durae* I. I. 10, *dominę* for *dominae* I. I. 21.

3. The placing of dots over double *i* (as in *Partheniis* I. I. 11) to distinguish them from the letter *u*, whereas the single *i* has no dot.

4. The use of the sign *&* in place of *et* at the end of a word, as in *oport&* 4. 2. 1, *val&* 4. 2. 7, etc.

5. The constant use of the straight letter ſ in preference to the curved form s.

6. The use of a *t* written so that the head never rises above the line, as thus, *t*[1].

A controversy of this kind can only be decided by experts in palaeography; but a careful study of the various readings given in this edition will, it is believed, bring out clearly the great superiority, on intrinsic grounds, of the readings of N. as compared with those of any other single MS.

In the rank next to N. come four MSS., as to the value of which again Baehrens holds views differing from those of other editors.

V. or Codex Ottoboniano-Vaticanus, No. 1514. This MS. is at Rome, in the Vatican Library. Attention was first called to it by Baehrens, who has collated it, and given to it, together with the three other MSS. to be named next, a rank superior even to that of N. It is written on parchment (M. Plessis says on vellum); it is

---

[1] These indications L. Mueller disposes of by supposing that a transcriber in the fifteenth century amused himself by imitating the writing of the thirteenth—an argument which might be pushed so as to destroy all evidence of antiquity derived from handwriting; M. Baehrens by the hypothesis that the form of character in S. Italy was two centuries (!) behind that of N. Europe. See M. Plessis, p. 12 *sqq.*

in large octavo form; it contains eighty-three leaves, and contains Propertius only. A series of corrections and erasures have been made in it by a later hand; these occur not only in the margin and between the lines, but actually in the text itself. The readings of this hand are indicated by the sign V^2. M. Baehrens assigns the MS. definitely to the end of the fourteenth century, the corrections to the fifteenth century. M. Plessis, on the other hand, has had the MS. examined by competent experts, who place it as late as the year 1450. The first letter of the poems, as well as the first letters of the third and fourth books, is illuminated. Almost all the elegies have a coloured title at their head.

D. or **Codex Daventriensis,** so called because it is now at *Deventer* in the Netherlands, numbered 1792. It is oblong in shape, is on parchment, occupies sixty-eight pages, and contains Propertius only. The first leaf, containing up to I. 2. 14, is lost. It is written in a beautiful hand : there are no corrections in the text, but there are a number of various readings by a contemporaneous hand in the margin. Baehrens declares it to be 'unus ex optimis codicibus Propertianis,' and dates it from 1410–1420. M. Plessis is inclined to assign to it the same date as to V., i. e. about 1450.

F. or **Codex Laurentianus,** so called because now in the Laurentian Library at Florence. It is in quarto, written on parchment, contains seventy-three leaves, and has at the end the words *Liber Colucii pyerii,* and then, added in another hand, *Liber Cosme Johannis de Medicis.* There are many corrections, taken from various sources, by a somewhat later hand, some in the margin, some between the lines : the readings of this hand are indicated in the notes by the sign F^2. Baehrens assigns this MS. to the very beginning of the fifteenth century.

A. or **Codex Vossianus,** now at Leyden, is in large octavo, on parchment; it has sixteen leaves, and extends only as far as 2. 1. 63. Its style of writing and abbreviations prove it to belong to the fourteenth century: there are no intervals between the poems, but the initial letters are distinguished, and there are titles on the margin. Baehrens gives 1360 as its date.

G. or Codex Groninganus, so called because now at Groningen, is of a small octavo size, and contains forty-six leaves. It was written by an Italian in the fifteenth century, and Professor Palmer, who has examined it, agrees with Baehrens in pronouncing it of no value. It has an importance however in the history of the text from the fact that Lachmann considered it the best of all the MSS. of our poet, assigning to N. only the place next below it. Worthy of mention also is

Per. or Codex Perusinus, which is in fact none other than the *Codex Cuicianus* of Scaliger, and which was re-discovered by Professor Palmer in 1874 in the library of Mr. H. Alan. It was written at Perugia in 1467 by the poet Pacificus Maximus, whence Mr. Palmer has given it the name of *Perusinus*. He has given a collation of it at the end of his edition, and attaches some value to its readings. One reading at least has been restored from it in this edition. Lastly may be mentioned the

Codex Hamburgensis, now at Hamburg, a small quarto, written in Italy at some period of the fifteenth century. It contains Catullus, Tibullus, and Propertius. It has been much corrected, but Hertzberg attaches considerable weight to it, and M. Plessis considers it scarcely inferior to the MSS. of Baehrens. It follows mainly the authority of F., and agrees generally with N. A. and F., though it sometimes agrees with D. and V. It may be considered as one of the best of the fifteenth century MSS.; Baehrens, while valuing it because transcribed from F. — though not till after F. had suffered corruption — does not distinguish it from the rest of the interpolated family which he designates by the sign ς (=Z in this edition).

With regard to the relationship of the four MSS., A. F. V. and D., Baehrens has propounded a theory of his own, the grounds for which, such as they are, he has explained in his *Prolegomena.* He believes that the original MS. of Propertius, which was discovered some time in the fourteenth century and is now lost, was twice copied about the middle of that century: one of these copies, he holds, is represented by the MSS. A. and F., of which the latter is inferior to and later than the former. The other copy is preserved to us in V. and D. Thus A. and F. constitute one family of copies, D. and V. constitute another family; and the corrections of the second hand in V. and F. (called in this edition V^2. and F^2.) are due to the scholars of the fifteenth century, who corrected mistakes in some cases by transferring readings from the one family to the other, in others by sheer invention. He thus holds that a judicious comparison of the readings of these two families (excluding the corrections in V. and F.) will enable us to reconstruct in great measure the original archetype from which the first two copies were derived. To this supposed archetype he gives the sign of O., a mode of designation which has been adopted for convenience sake in this edition, although, as will be seen, with a somewhat different meaning.

We have now to ask, what weight is to be attached to this ingenious theory? A careful examination of the recorded readings will show that Baehrens is right in classing A. F. as one family, and D. V. as another: but what of O. and N.? It is obvious that his view of O. must depend upon his being able to show that N. is a more recent, and a less trustworthy, MS. than the four upon which he chiefly relies: whereas Mr. Ellis, Mr. Palmer, M. Plessis—and to a considerable .extent F. Léo[1]—agree in holding it to

---

[1] Rheinisches Museum, vol. xxxv, 1880, p. 431.

be the oldest and most authoritative of all. Baehrens dates it about 1430: he regards it therefore as a MS. of the interpolated type, belonging to the same family as A. F., but taking some of its readings for D. V., and disfigured in some places by Italian conjectures, in others by reproducing the corrections of F². and V². But M. Plessis, as we have seen, upsets Baehrens' dates on palaeographic grounds: he makes N. some 200 years older, V. some 50 years younger, than does Baehrens: while he regards A. D. F. as being all about the same age, viz. of the end of the fourteenth century. Further, both Mr. Ellis[1] and M. Plessis have pointed out various passages in which A.F.D.V. are all corrupt, while N. alone has preserved the true reading: while both F. Léo and M. Plessis point out that wherever F². and V². agree with N., the reading is correct. In addition, N. is distinctly superior in orthography; it does not give the false name of *Aurelius* or *Nauta* to the poet; and Mr. Ellis[1] has ingeniously shown that even in passages where it blunders, it blunders because the copyist preferred faithfully to copy the MS. before him, rather than introduce obvious corrections. Finally, M. Plessis' view as to the date of N. is confirmed by Mr. E. Maunde Thompson, of the British Museum, an authority of the highest mark[2].

From these arguments the conclusion remains that N. is the best existing MS., being the oldest representative of the family A. F.; that D.V. form another family, equal to A. F. but inferior to N.; that the corrections of F². and V². have been largely taken from N. or from some equally good MS.; while G. and H. G. have mixed in an uncertain degree the readings of the two families. A careful examination of the readings given in the critical notes

---

[1] American Journal of Philology, vol. i. no. 4.
[2] See Mr. R. Ellis' review of M. Plessis' book in the Amer. Journal of Phil. 1886.

will confirm these conclusions, and show that while paramount importance is to be attached to N., the readings of F². and V². are extremely valuable, while the agreement of the three, as M. Plessis says, amounts to a certainty. The important reading *natat*, 3. 7. 22, comes from F².

In this edition the sign O. is used, as by Baehrens, but in a slightly different sense. Baehrens uses it to denote the supposed archetype, the readings of which are to be gathered from a consensus either of all the MSS. or of what he regards as the good MSS., viz. A. D. F. V. in opposition to N. F². V². In this edition O. is used to denote the consensus of these same MSS. (or, what is the same thing, the archetype of those four MSS.), but to the exclusion of N., the readings of which are stated separately. Baehrens' O. includes N., except·when the contrary is stated ; and as he does not attach much importance to N., he has been less particular in recording its readings.

The *Editio Princeps* of Propertius appeared at Venice in 1472, and from that day to this new editions have been poured forth in a continuous stream. The most important are those of Muretus (1558), of Scaliger (1577), who confused the text by endless and arbitrary transpositions, of Dousa (1588), of Passerat (1608), containing a perfect storehouse of illustrations, of G. Barth (1777), of Burmann (1780), and the somewhat lumbersome edition of Kinnoel (1805). The first great step to the purification of the text was made by Lachmann in his first edition of 1816 : he was the first to distinguish the comparative value of the leading MSS., in the main correctly : but he has been the author of infinite confusion by re-arranging many of the poems, and by introducing on arbitrary grounds the division into five books against the authority of the MSS. In 1829 he published a second edition, in which, without explanation, he gave up almost all the conjectures of his first edition. The references to Lach-

mann in the notes of this edition are to the readings of the edition of 1816. In 1835 appeared the very
useful French edition published by Lemaire; and from
1843 to 1845 appeared the great edition of Hertzberg,
both critical and explanatory. It is the great standard
edition, full of matter of every description, but unequal
and ill-arranged, and, like so many learned German works,
frequently deficient in taste and judgment. Of Baehrens'
work we have already spoken. His critical apparatus is
the most complete that has yet been published; but his
text is injured by his predisposition to depreciate N., and
disfigured by many wild and tasteless conjectures. Many
of these, doubtless, will be abandoned in his next edition,
and it may be thought that too many of them have been
noticed in this edition. But his authority is great, his
edition is quoted as a standard edition, and it is well
to show in particular instances what are the taste and
judgment of the critic who makes such large demands
upon our confidence. The edition of L. Mueller in the
Teubner series is less adventuresome, and follows mainly
in the lines of Lachmann. In England we have the very
full and serviceable commentary of Paley, published
in 1853 and 1872; and in 1880 Professor Palmer published his admirable critical edition of the text, which
has brought out in a striking way the true value of N.
by exhibiting in italics every word, even every letter, in
which the reading adopted departs from that MS. The
notes are in the best spirit of modern critical scholarship:
their only fault is that they are too few. Different altogether in scope and aim is the delightful selection of
Professor Postgate (1881), which includes about one-fourth
of the works of our poet, selected on a principle different
from that followed in this edition. The explanatory notes
are of first-rate quality; but the chief value and originality
of the book lies in the Introduction, which contains the
most complete and thoughtful study that has yet appeared

of the style, the language, the grammar, the temperament and literary position of our poet. Nor can we omit to mention the very useful school selections of Schultze (Second Edition, Berlin, 1882), and the scholarlike notes of Mr. Pinder contained in his 'Selections from the less-known Latin Poets,' Clarendon Press, 1869. Propertius has been well translated into English Verse by Dr. Cranstoun (1875) and by Mr. C. R. Moore (1870).

Jan. 6, 1887.

APPENDIX TO THE SECOND EDITION.

SINCE the above was written, a new advance has been made in the criticism of Propertius by the appearance of three masterly articles by Professor A. E. Housman in the Journal of Philology, Nos. 41, 42, and 43 (Vols. xxi and xxii). Amid the masses of dull ill-digested learning which are too often put forth under the name of textual criticism, it is refreshing to find a critic who puts life and reality into the discussion of various readings, and applying to his facts sound sense and vigorous logic, shows exactly what conclusions may, or may not, be fairly drawn from them. To see what interest and vitality may be imparted to such a subject, by the mode of treatment, the student must refer to the articles themselves : it is enough here to put before him the conclusions at which Prof. Housman has arrived, and to indicate the kind of reasoning by which he has reached them. His results do not radically alter the view taken above of the general relative value of

the MSS. of Propertius ; but they put the whole criticism
of our author upon a firmer basis by showing exactly, from
internal evidence, what contribution each of the principal
MSS. has made towards the constitution of the true Propertian text, and by brushing aside exclusive theories
unduly favouring one MS. at the expense of the rest.

His conclusions are as follows. There are seven independent authorities, every one of which must be employed
if we would reconstruct the Propertian archetype. These
are (as given above) N. A. F. D. V. F^1., and V^2. No
other existing MS. has any independent value. A. F. D.
and V. are all the offspring of a lost original O., A. and F.
representing one family of descendants, D. and V. another.
N. is an independent MS. of great value, containing certain
elements not derived from O., but derived from a MS.
parallel to O., which he calls Z. This Z. must have been
of at least equal authority with O., both of them being
descended (through whatever number of links) from the
original archetype, to which may be assigned the name
of ω. But while N. has elements which are independent
of the four MSS. A. F. and D. V., nevertheless it has also
many elements which are common to them: and the
facts seem to show that though the transcriber of N. did
not have access to any one of those four MSS., he
nevertheless derived some readings from a MS. (not
known) belonging to the same family as A. F. and also
some readings (fewer in number) from a MS. belonging
to the family D. V. Thus N. is derived from three
different sources:

(1) From a MS. allied to A. F.;

(2) From a MS. allied to D. V.;

(3) From a MS. Z., wholly independent of both the
above families, and also independent of their common
progenitor O.

Thus N., valuable as it is, is valuable rather as an
edition, drawing from different good sources, than as

being itself a MS. of incontestable integrity, claiming superiority as the single and best transmitter of the original text.

F^2. and V^2. had also access to Z. ; hence their frequent similarity to N.

The following propositions give the principal steps in the argument by which the above conclusions are arrived at. Each proposition is founded upon a critical examination of the variants given by the different MSS. in disputed passages. Those who wish to master all the evidence adduced, must refer to the articles themselves; the references given below are solely to passages contained in the present selection. The student can thus look up each passage for himself, examine the various readings given in the notes, and pass his own judgment upon them.

(1) The following (amongst many other) passages show that N. has an element superior to O. (O. standing for the four MSS. A. F. D. and V. when in agreement with one another), viz. 1. 18. 16; 3. 5. 6; 3. 7. 49; 4. 3. 55.

(2) The following show a slight corruption in N., a more advanced corruption in O.: 2. 13. 49; 3. 4. 4; 3. 22. 3.

(3) In the following N. is absolutely right, or nearly so while O. is wrong : 1. 18. 19; 2. 28. 9; 3. 1. 5; 3. 1. 27; 3. 4. 19; 3. 5. 34; 3. 11. 14; 3. 22. 27; 4. 3. 51; 4. 3. 59; 4. 4. 30; 4. 6. 79.

(4) In various cases N. exhibits a superior spelling to O. *The inference from the above is that N. contains a genuine element which was not contained in O.*

(5) But, on the other hand, there are passages in which O. has preserved readings superior to those of N. See 2. 2. 1; 3. 1. 23; 3. 2. 3; 3. 7. 46; 3. 18. 24; 3. 11. 25; 3. 22. 14.

(6) In some cases the spelling of O. is superior to that of N.

(7) In some passages N. and O. have both gone wrong,

and seem equidistant from the truth (as in 4. 3. 11); in others, both have good readings, between which it is impossible to decide. See 1. 8. 45; 2. 13. 58; 3. 7. 25; 4. 4. 57.

The inference from the above is that O. *contains a genuine element not contained in* N., *and hence that neither can be derived from the other.* Their common source must be superior to both.

If, again, we examine the two families A. F. and D. V. respectively as representatives of O., we find that

(8) A. F. is sometimes better than D. V.: see 1. 8. 26; 1. 19. 13; 2. 3. 23, 24; 2. 10. 11; 2. 28. 47; 2. 31. 10; 3. 11. 44; 4. 6. 25.

(9) In other passages, D. V. is better than A. F.: 1. 8. 7; 1. 8. 19; 1. 8. 27; 2. 10. 22; 2. 11. 2; 2. 28. 29; 3. 2. 4; 3. 5. 24; 3. 11. 51; 4. 6. 75.

(10) In some passages where A. F. and D. V. differ, they are equidistant from the true reading (as in 3. 2. 22; 4. 11. 60); in others they have different, but equally good readings: 1. 8. 15; 4. 3. 8; 4. 11. 26.

(11) The spelling is sometimes better in A. F., sometimes in D. V.

It thus appears that we must use both the families, A. F. and D. V., *if we would get at the true reading of* O.

(12) If again we take these four MSS. singly (A. F. D. and V.), we find that each of them in turn is the sole preserver of a true reading in one or more passages: hence *all four deserve attention as representatives of* O. A. has alone preserved the true spelling of *solacia* in 1. 5. 27; F. has a striking superiority over both D. V. and N. in 2. 1. 32 (*atratus*), and in 2. 1. 49. D. alone preserves the true reading in seven passages; V. alone in 3. 1. 26 (*isse*) and in perhaps two or three others.

(13) Next comes the question, what is the relation of N. to O.? When the two families differ, N. more often sides with A. F., but sometimes also with D. V.: and it

generally shows the best reading. But N. did not know
O. directly : it seems to have derived its knowledge of O.
mainly from a MS. of the A. F. family (it will be noted
that A. only extends down to 2. 1. 63) but also in part
from one of the D. V. family.

Thus N. so far as it represents O. is to be regarded as
founded mainly on A. F., but adopting many true and
easy readings from D. V.

(14) Lastly, what of F². and V².? In many places
where N. is better than O., that same better reading is
found in F². or V².; in some passages, these alone
preserve the true reading (see 2. 2. 4 ; 2. 12. 28 ; 4. 4. 64).
But many of N.'s readings, when they differ from O., are
not in V². or F².: and these give many readings not in N.
It is clear, therefore, that they are not copied from one
another, but that where both have common elements
they were taken from some common source.

Prof. Housman thus sums up his conclusions :

'It has been demonstrated, against Baehrens, that N.
contains a genuine element which A. F. D. V. do not
contain, and it has been demonstrated, against Solbisky,
Plessis, and Weber, that this genuine element in N. is not
derived from the archetype of A. F. D. V., but from an
independent source whence F². and V². have also derived
a genuine element not possessed by A. F. D. V. It
has been further shown that N. contains a second element
drawn from a MS. of the family A. F., and a third and
smaller element from a MS. of the family D. V. It has
been demonstrated, against Mr. Leo, that A. F. D. V.
contain a genuine element which N. does not contain,
and it has been demonstrated, against Mr. Solbisky, that
the two families A. F. and D. V. deserve equal credence
as witnesses to their archetype O. It has been shown
also that each of the four codices A. F. D. V. preserves
fragments of truth peculiar to itself.

'Hence follows as a necessary consequence, that the

e

seven authorities N. A. F. D. V. F². V². are independent witnesses and must all be employed if we would reconstruct the Propertian archetype.

' Finally it has been shown that the residue of the MSS. exhibit no element of genuine tradition not possessed by one or other of these, whence it follows that they are derived from these, and are therefore to be cast aside.'

More recently still, an important contribution to Propertian criticism has been made by Dr. Postgate in the Transactions of the Cambridge Philosophical Society for 1894. In that paper he publishes, *inter alia*, a collation, with a facsimile, of a MS. now in the Holkham Library, to which he assigns the name of L. This MS., written in 1481, is closely related to F., and appears to be derived, in the main, from the same source as F.; it is therefore of value as affording evidence of the readings of the A. F. family from 2. 1. 63, the point at which A. fails us. But whilst L. is thus probably derived from the exemplar of F., it contains other elements also, which seem to be derived from the D. V. family, not from N.: and Dr. Postgate concludes that before L. was copied from the exemplar of F., that exemplar had been corrected from a MS. belonging to the family D. V.

Dr. Postgate accepts, in the main, the conclusions of Mr. Housman, though he considers that he is disposed to attach too much weight to the testimony of single manuscripts, and that he scarcely does justice to N., either as regards its date or its authority. He holds the view given above as to the early date of N., whereas Mr. Housman is prepared to acquiesce in the later date suggested by Mueller and Baehrens; and he defends the primacy of N. with no uncertain sound :

'At the end of his paper Mr. Housman puts the question, "Which is the best MS. of Propertius?" and returns himself the answer, "There is no best MS. of Propertius." This denial of supremacy is of course aimed at the "worshipped Neapolitanus," as it is elsewhere invidiously denominated. If it means that there is no codex of Própertius . as eminent as the Parisinus of Demosthenes or the Vaticanus of Valerius Flaccus, no one will dispute it. But if it means that N. is not *primus*, or rather *facile princeps*, *inter pares*, the judgment will not, I imagine, receive the assent of the critics of the future, who will, unless I am much mistaken, pronounce on the contrary that the Neapolitanus *is* the best MS. of Propertius—best as being the oldest of our witnesses, best again as the one that presents the greatest amount of truth with the smallest amount of falsehood.'

THE UNIVERSITY, GLASGOW,
  May 13, 1895.

SIGNS USED TO DESIGNATE THE MSS.

1. TIBULLUS.

A = Codex Ambrosianus.
V = Codex Vaticanus.
G = Codex Guelferbytanus.
G² = the second hand of the same MS.
O = the consensus of AVG.
Par. = Excerpta Parisina.
Fris. = Excerpta Frisingensia.
Plant. = the readings of the Fragment (F) preserved by Scaliger in
    his Plantinian Edition.
Z = the readings of the more modern and interpolated MSS.

2. PROPERTIUS.

N = Codex Neapolitanus.
A = Codex Vossianus.
F = Codex Laurentianus.
D = Codex Daventriensis.
V = Codex Ottoboniano-Vaticanus.
F² V² = the second hands of F and V.
G = Codex Groninganus.
Hb = Codex Hamburgensis.
Per = Codex Perusinus.
O = the O of Baehrens, except that it does not include N, the readings
    of which are given separately.   Baehrens thus defines his use of
    the sign O:
        'O = archetypus saeculo XIV repertus ex consensu sive om-
    nium codicum sive bonorum A. D. V. m. 1 V. m. 1 (oppositis
    N. F. m. 2 V. m. 2) restitutus.'
Z = the readings of the Italian Scholars in MSS. of the interpolated
    class.

The abbreviation *Hous.* refers to the articles by Professor A. E.
Housman in the Journal of Philology, Vols. xxi and xxii.

NOTE.—The readings attributed to Lachmann in the notes are
taken from his first edition of 1816.   These were practically all given
up in the second edition of 1829.   In the following cases the readings
attributed to Lachmann are only suggested in his notes, but not
inserted in his text, viz. *unde* for *omne* 1. 14. 5; *dignus amor* for
digna soror 2. 2. 6; *Ipsa ... sorte* for *Illa ... fata* 2. 28. 26; *Ei
scelus !* for *Et satis* 4. 4. 17 ; and *meis* for *malis* in 4. 11. 70.

TIBULLUS, I. 1.

1—6. Let others seek for wealth through war and peril; be mine a life of poverty and peace at home.

DIVITIAS alius fulvo sibi congerat auro
  Et teneat culti iugera multa soli,
Quem labor assiduus vicino terreat hoste,
  Martia cui somnos classica pulsa fugent :
Me mea paupertas vitae trąducat inerti,   5
  Dum meus assiduo luceat igne focus.

7—24. Here will I plant the vine and apple, and look for in-crease in my fruits, giving service due to every rustic god: nor shall ye, Lares, be forgotten out of my humble store.

Ipse seram teneras maturo tempore vites
  Rusticus et facili grandia poma manu :
Nec Spes destituat, sed frugum semper acervos
  Praebeat et pleno pinguia musta lacu.   10
Nam veneror, seu stipes habet desertus in agris
  Seu vetus in trivio florida serta lapis :
Et quodcumque mihi pomum novus educat annus,
  Libatum agricolae ponitur ante deo.

The parts of this poem have been variously transposed by different editors. Baehrens arranges it thus: vv. 1–6, 25–36, 7–24, 37–78. L. Mueller (Teubner edition), following Haase, thus: 1–6, 25–34, 7–12, 15–18, 13, 14, 19–24, 35–78.
2. *multa* G Par. Fris. Diomedes. *magna* AVG². 5. *vite* (= *vitae*) AV *vita* G Par. Fris. 7. *feram* Par. 12. *florida* O *florea* Z. 13. *donum* conj. L. Mueller. 14. *agricolae* ... *deum* O *agricolae* ... *deo* Muretus *agricolam-deum* Pucci.

Flava Ceres, tibi sit nostro de rure corona   15
    Spicea, quae templi pendeat ante fores:
Pomosisque ruber custos ponatur in hortis
    Terreat ut saeva falce Priapus aves.
Vos quoque, felicis quondam, nunc pauperis agri
    Custodes, fertis munera vestra, Lares.   20
Tunc vitula innumeros lustrabat caesa iuvencos:
    Nunc agna exigui est hostia parva soli.
Agna cadet vobis, quam circum rustica pubes
    Clamet 'io messes et bona vina date.'

25—36. *So may I live content by stream and shade, thinking no shame to tend my flock, and honouring Pales for their good.*

Iam modo iam possim contentus vivere parvo,   25
    Nec semper longae deditus esse viae,
Sed Canis aestivos ortus vitare sub umbra
    Arboris ad rivos praetereuntis aquae.
Nec tamen interdum pudeat tenuisse bidentem
    Aut stimulo tardos increpuisse boves;   30
Non agnamve sinu pigeat fetumve capellae
    Desertum oblita matre referre domum.
At vos exiguo pecori, furesque lupique,   .
    Parcite: de magno est praeda petenda grege.

---

15. *sit* O *fit* conj. Lambinus.   17. *ponatur* O *donatur* Lambinus, Baehrens.   19. *felicis* G V *felices* A.   23. *cadet* O. Bae. conj. *cadit*.   24. *Clamat* V *Clamet* G.   25. *Iam modo iam possim* Fris. *Iam modo non possum* O *Quippe ego iam possum* Par. *Iam mihi iam possim* Mueller *Iam modo iam possum* Guy *Iam modo si possum* Lach. Dissen conj. *Iam modico possum contentus vivere in agro.*   28. *rivos* O *rivum* Burmann *rivom* Bae.   29. *bidentem* G Par. *bidentes* V *ludentes* A.   32. *donum* V.   34. *est* O om. by Fris.

Hic ego pastoremque meum lustrare quot annis   35
   Et placidam soleo spargere lacte Palem.

37—48. *Spurn not my humble gifts, ye Gods, for I seek not
wealth ; enough for me to lie in ease, and hear the wild
wind and rain without.*

Adsitis, divi, nec vos e paupere mensa
   Dona nec e puris spernite fictilibus.
Fictilia antiquus primum sibi fecit agrestis
   Pocula, de facili composuitque luto.   40
Non ego divitias patrum fructusque requiro,
   Quos tulit antiquo condita messis avo:
Parva seges satis est, satis est requiescere lecto,
   Si licet, et solito membra levare toro.
Quam iuvat immites ventos audire cubantem,   45
   Et dominam tenero detinuisse sinu !
Aut, gelidas hibernus aquas cum fuderit auster,
   Securum somnos imbre iuvante sequi !

49—58. *Seek thou, Messalla, for the spoils of war: I court no
glory, if only Delia be mine.*

Hoc mihi contingat: sit dives iure, furorem
   Qui maris et tristes ferre potest pluvias.   50
O quantum est auri pereat potiusque smaragdi,
   Quam fleat ob nostras ulla puella vias.
Te bellare decet terra, Messalla, marique,
   Ut domus hostiles praeferat exuvias:

---

37. *Vos quoque adeste dei* Par.   *neu* O   *nec* Par. Z.   41. *fructusque* AV   *fructusve* G Par.   43. *satis est uno* Par.   44.
Scilicet O Par.   46. *detinuisse* Z   *continuisse* O   *tum tenuisse*
Bae.   48. *imbre* G Par.   *igne* AV.   49. *sit* G Par.   *si*
AV   *iure* O   *rure* Par.   50. *et celi nubila ferre potest* Par.
51. *pereat potiusque* O   *pereat pereantque* Bae.   54. *hostiles* G
exiles AV (V² *ostiles*).

B 2

Me retinent vinctum formosae vincla puellae,   55
Et sedeo duras ianitor ante fores.

57—74. *When Death comes, Delia, thou wilt duly weep for me: let us love meanwhile, till sluggish Age steals on.*

Non ego laudari curo, mea Delia: tecum
Dum modo sim, quaeso segnis inersque vocer.
Te spectem, suprema mihi cum venerit hora,
Te teneam moriens deficiente manu.   60
Flebis et arsuro positum me, Delia, lecto,
Tristibus et lacrimis oscula mixta dabis.
Flebis: non tua sunt duro praecordia ferro
Vincta, nec in tenero stat tibi corde silex.
Illo non iuvenis poterit de funere quisquam   65
Lumina, non virgo, sicca referre domum.
Tu Manes ne laede meos, sed parce solutis
Crinibus et teneris, Delia, parce genis.
Interea, dum fata sinunt, iungamus amores:
Iam veniet tenebris Mors adoperta caput: 70
Iam subrepet iners aetas, nec amare decebit,
Dicere nec cano blanditias capiti.
Nunc levis est tractanda Venus, dum frangere postes
Non pudet, et rixas inseruisse iuvat.

75—78. *No wars but these be mine, and to despise wealth and penury alike!*

Hic ego dux milesque bonus: vos, signa tubaeque,
Ite procul, cupidis vulnera ferte viris.   76

59, 60. *Te . . . Te* Z   *Et . . . Et* O   cf. Ovid Am. 3. 9. 58.
63. *duro* G   *dura* V corr. V².   **64.** *Vincta* G Fris.   *iuncta* AV.
67. *Tu* O   *tum* Haupt. Bae.   **72.** *capiti* Z   *capite* O Par. Bae.
Hiller.   **74.** *conseruisse* Z   *inseruisse* O.

Ferte et opes: ego composito securus acervo
Despiciam dites despiciamque famem.

I. 3.

1—10. While thou speedest on, Messalla, here must I stay, alone and ill. O spare me, Death! I have no mother here, no sister, to honour me if I die: no Delia.

Ibitis Aegaoas sine me, Messalla, per undas;
   O utinam memores ipse cohorsque mei!
Me tenet ignotis aegrum Phaeacia terris:
   Abstineas avidas Mors modo nigra manus.
Abstineas, Mors atra, precor: non hic mihi mater,   5
   Quae legat in maestos ossa perusta sinus;
Non soror, Assyrios cineri quae dedat odores,
   Et fleat effusis ante sepulcra comis;
Delia non usquam; quae me cum mitteret urbe,
   Dicitur ante omnes consuluisse deos.   10

11—22. When Delia sought the omens, all seemed fair for my departure: yet how she wept, how loth I was to go! Ah! let no man ever more go forth against the behests of Love.

Illa sacras pueri sortes ter sustulit: illi
   Rettulit e triviis omina certa puer.

---

78. *Dites despiciam* **AV.**
I. 3. 4. *mors modo nigra* **O**   *mors precor atra* **G²Z.**   **12.**
triviis **O** *trinis* Muretus, Bae.

Cuncta dabant reditus: tamen est deterrita
   nusquam,
   Quin fleret nostras respiceretque vias.
Ipse ego solator, cum iam mandata dedissem,   15
   Quaerebam tardas anxius usque moras.
Aut ego sum causatus aves aut omina dira,
   Saturni aut sacram me tenuisse diem.
O quotiens ingressus iter mihi tristia dixi
   Offensum in porta signa dedisse pedem!   20
Audeat invito ne quis discedere Amore,   .
   Aut sciat egressum se prohibente deo.

23—34. *What now avail me, Delia, thy prayers to Isis? Oh
help me, Goddess! grant to Delia that she may duly pay
her vows to thee, while I do honour to my own Penates.*

Quid tua nunc Isis mihi, Delia, quid mihi prosunt
   Illa tua totiens aera repulsa manu?
Nunc, dea, nunc succurre mihi (nam posse mederi
   Picta docet templis multa tabella tuis),   28
Ut mea votivas persolvens Delia voces
   Ante sacras lino tecta forẹs sedeat;   30
Bisque die resoluta comas tibi dicere laudes
   Insignis turba debeat in Pharia.
At mihi contingat patrios celebrare penates
   Reddereque antiquo menstrua tura Lari.

---

13. *nusquam* G V *nũquam* A *nostras* G² *haud deterrita frustra est* Z.   14. *Quin* Aldine ed. 1502   *Cum* O   *despueretque*
Haupt *respiceretque* O *respueretque* Z.   17. *aut* Z *dant* O
omina A G *omnia* V *omine diro* Bae.   18. *Saturni sacram* O
Saturni aut sacram G²Z *Saturnive* Broukh, Mueller, Hiller.
21. *nequis* Z *neuquis* O.   25. *dum* G *deum* A   29. *Ut* A V
et G *voces* O *noctes* Scaliger, Bae.   34. *thura* O.

35—50. *How well it was when Saturn ruled on earth: when men knew nor ships nor voyages, nor sword nor battle; when was no evil for man nor beast; no barred door, no stone-marked boundary; when oaks dropped honey, and flocks brought full udders home untended.*

Quam bene Saturno vivebant rege, prius quam   35
    Tellus in longas est patefacta vias !
Nondum caeruleas pinus contempserat undas,
    Effusum ventis praebueratque sinum ;
Nec vagus ignotis repetens compendia terris
    Presserat externa navita merce ratem.   40
Illo non validus subiit iuga tempore taurus,
    Non domito frenos ore momordit equus ;
Non domus ulla fores habuit, non fixus in agris,
    Qui regeret certis finibus arva, lapis.
Ipsae mella dabant quercus, ultroque ferebant   45
    Obvia securis ubera lactis oves.
Non acies, non ira fuit, non bella, nec ensem
    Immiti saevus duxerat arte faber.
Nunc Iove sub domino caedes et vulnera semper,
    Nunc mare, nunc leti mille repente viae.   50

51—56. *O spare me, Father Jove! for I am pure; but if my days are run, may a stone be set to tell how Tibullus died, how soon, how sadly.*

Parce, pater, timidum non me periuria terrent,
    Non dicta in sanctos impia verba deos.

---

37. *contempserat* O   *conscenderat* G² Bae.   **47.** *facinus* Bae. *rabies* Burmann.   **50.** *repente* GV² *reperte* AV¹ *multa reperta via* Z Heyne.

Quod si fatales iam nunc explevimus annos,
    Fac lapis inscriptis stet super ossa notis:
'Hic iacet immiti consumptus morte Tibullus,   55
    Messallam terra dum sequiturque mari.'

57—66. *Then will Venus lead me to Elysium, to the land of dance and song, where casia and rose grow unbidden, where bands of youths and maidens ever sport with Love.*

Sed me, quod facilis tenero sum semper Amori,
    Ipsa Venus campos ducet in Elysios.
Hic choreae cantusque vigent, passimque vagantes
    Dulce sonant tenui gutture carmen aves;   60
Fert casiam non culta seges, totosque per agros
    Floret odoratis terra benigna rosis;
Ac iuvenum series teneris immixta puellis
    Ludit, et assidue praelia miscet Amor.
Illic est, cuicumque rapax mors venit amanti,   65
    Et gerit insigni myrtea serta coma.

67—82. *But in the dark profound lies the accursed Tartarus, where rages Tisiphon, and Cerberus ever guards; where are Ixion and Tityos, Tantalus and the daughters of Danaus.*

At scelerata iacet sedes in nocte profunda
    Abdita, quam circum flumina nigra sonant;
Tisiphoneque impexa feros pro crinibus angues
    Saevit, et huc illuc impia turba fugit: 70
Tunc niger in porta serpentum Cerberus ore
    Stridet et aeratas excubat ante fores.

---

54. *inscriptis* O   *inscriptus* or *his scriptus* Z Heyne.   63. *Ac*
AG   *at* V   *hac* or *hic* Z.   69. *impexa* O Par.   *implexa*
Frut. Bae.   71. Palmer suggests *per centum Cerberus ora.*

Illic Iunonem temptare Ixionis ausi
  Versantur celeri noxia membra rota :
Porrectusque novem Tityos per iugera terrae   75
  Assiduas atro viscere pascit aves.
Tantalus est illic, et circum stagna : sed acrem
  Iam iam poturi deserit unda sitim ;
Et Danai proles, Veneris quod numina laesit,
  In cava Lethaeas dolia portat aquas.   80
Illic sit, quicumque meos violavit amores,
  Optavit lentas et mihi militias.

83—92. *But do thou be true, my Delia ; and may the day come when thou mayest fly to meet me when I come back to thee, unannounced, as if sent to thee from the heavens.*

At tu casta precor maneas, sanctique pudoris
  Assideat custos sedula semper anus.
Haec tibi fabellas referat, positaque lucerna   85
  Deducat plena stamina longa colu :
Ac circa gravibus pensis affixa puella
  Paulatim somno fessa remittat opus.
Tunc veniam subito, nec quisquam nuntiet
       ante,
  Sed videar caelo missus adesse tibi.   90
Tunc mihi, qualis eris, longos turbata capillos,
  Obvia nudato, Delia, curre pede.
Hoc precor, hunc illum nobis Aurora nitentem
  Luciferum roseis candida portet equis.

---

73. *temptare* **A**   *tentare* **GV.**   79. *quod* **AV**   *quae* **G.**
83. *casta precor coniunx maneas* Par.   86. *colo* **O** Par. *colu*
Fris. Bae. Hil. Muel.   87. *Ac* **O**   *At* Par. Bae.

I. 7.

1—8. *The Fates sang true, Messalla, at thy birth, that the Atax should tremble before thee, and that thou shouldest bear along captive kings in triumph.*

Hunc cecinere diem Parcae fatalia nentes
  Stamina, non ulli dissoluenda deo:
Hunc fore, Aquitanas posset qui fundere gentes,
  Quem tremeret forti milite victus Atax.
Evenere: novos pubes Romana triumphos   5
  Vidit et evinctos brachia capta duces:
At te victrices lauros, Messalla, gerentem
  Portabat niveis currus eburnus equis.

9—12. *I saw thy glory gained: witness too was the Ocean and the Pyrenees, the Arar and the Rhone, the Loire and the Garonne.*

Non sine me est tibi partus honos: Tarbella
    Pyrene
  Testis, et Oceani litora Santonici;   10
Testis Arar Rhodanusque celer magnusque
    Garunna,
  Carnutis et flavi caerula lympha Liger.

I. 7. **3.** *frangere* G *fundere* AV.   **4.** *Atur* Scaliger.   **6.**
evinctos G *victos* A (*in* added by hand 2) *evictos* V.   **7.** *lauros* G
lauros AV.   **8.** *niveis* Z   *nitidis* O.   **9.** *me est tibi* O
marte ibi Bae.   *Tarbella* Scaliger   *tua bella* O.   **11.** *Atur*
Duranusque Scaliger   *garunna* Z   *garumna* O   *geronna* Fris.
12. *Carnutis* Fris. *Carnuti* Z   *Carnoti* O   *caerula* A Fris.
Garrula Gruppe.

13—22. *Or shall I tell of thee, Cydnus, with thy silent stream, or thee, mighty Taurus? of Syria or of Tyre, or of the wealth-bringing waters of the Nile?*

An te, Cydne, canam, tacitis qui leniter undis
    Caeruleus placidis per vada serpis aquis;
Quantus et aetherio contingens vertice nubes   15
    Frigidus intonsos Taurus alat Cilicas?
Quid referam, ut volitet crebras intacta per urbes
    Alba Palaestino sancta columba Syro;
Utque maris vastum prospectet turribus aequor
    Prima ratem ventis credere docta Tyros;   20
Qualis et, arentes cum findit Sirius agros,
    Fertilis aestiva Nilus abundet aqua?

23—28. *O where hast thou hid thy head, Father Nile? 'Tis because of thee that thy land thirsts not for rain: thee the youth worship, with Osiris and with Apis.*

Nile pater, quanam possim te dicere causa
    Aut quibus in terris occuluisse caput?
Te propter nullos tellus tua postulat imbres,   25
    Arida nec Pluvio supplicat herba Iovi.
Te canit atque suum pubes miratur Osirim
    Barbara, Memphiten plangere docta bovem.

29—42. *For 'twas Osiris that first tilled the ground, and planted fruit and vine tree: 'twas Osiris first taught the joyous juice to flow that prompts to dance and song, that gladdens the weary husbandman, and loosens the captive's chain.*

Primus aratra manu sollerti fecit Osiris,
    Et teneram ferro sollicitavit humum;   30

---

13. *An* Z *At* O *tactis qui leniter ulvis* Lach. **14.** *Caerulea ad placidas . . . aquas* Bae. **15.** *aerio* Z *aetherias* Bae. **18.** *arat* O. **20.** *dicta* G². **23.** *possum* G *possim* AV.

Primus inexpertae commisit semina terrae
    Pomaque non notis legit ab arboribus.
Hic docuit teneram palis adiungere vitem,
    Hic viridem dura caedere falce comam;
Illi iucundos primum matura sapores   35
    Expressa incultis uva dedit pedibus;
Ille liquor docuit voces inflectere cantu,
    Movit et ad certos nescia membra modos.
Bacchus et agricolae magno confecta labore
    Pectora tristitiae dissoluenda dedit: 40
Bacchus et afflictis requiem mortalibus affert,
    Crura licet dura compede pulsa sonent.

43—48. *Not care and grief are thine, Osiris, but chaunt and
dance and love, but flowers and flowing robes, soft flute
and sacred chest.*

Non tibi sunt tristes curae nec luctus, Osiri,
    Sed chorus et cantus et levis aptus amor;
Sed varii flores et frons redimita corymbis,   45
    Fusa sed ad teneros lutea palla pedes;
Et Tyriae vestes et dulcis tibia cantu,
    Et levis occultis conscia cista sacris.

49—54. *Hither then to honour the Genius of the day with
sport and dance, with perfume and with chaplet! so will
I pay thee thy due.*

Huc ades et Genium ludo centumque choreis
    Concelebra et multo tempora funde mero: 50

---

35. *iocundos* Fris.   42. *compede* G   *cuspide* AVZ.   47.
et O   *set* Bae.   *dulcis* AV *dulci* G.   49. I have ventured on
genium ludo centumque   *centum ludos geniumque* O   *centum
ludis* Z   *genium ludo* Heyne.

Illius et nitido stillent unguenta capillo,
    Et capite et collo mollia serta gerat.
Sic venias hodierne: tibi dem turis honores,
    Liba et Mopsopio dulcia melle feram.

55—64. *Long live thy race, Messalla: long may men tell of thy*
work, as they pass along the Latin way; and oft may
this day, ever brighter and more bright, return.

At tibi succrescat proles, quae facta parentis   55
    Augeat et circa stet veneranda senem.
Nec taceat monumenta viae, quem Tuscula
        tellus
Candidaque antiquo detinet Alba Lare.
Namque opibus congesta tuis hic glarea dura
    Sternitur, hic apta iungitur arte silex.   60
Te canit agricola, e magna cum venerit urbe
    Serus, inoffensum rettuleritque pedem.
At tu, Natalis, multos celebrande per annos,
    Candidior semper candidiorque veni.

I. 10.

1—10. *Who was it that first forged the sword, and brought*
battle and slaughter upon earth? There were no wars
on earth, no towers or ramparts, till men lusted after
gold: O had those days been mine!

Quis fuit, horrendos primus qui protulit enses?
    Quam ferus et vere ferreus ille fuit!

---

51. *et* O *e* Z.   **54.** *Liba* AV *Libem* G *Libaque* Z *melle* GZ
mella AV.   **56.** *veneranda* O *venerata* Z *venerande* Muel.
57. *nec* GV *ne* A *quem* Z *que* A *quae* GV   **58.** *Candidaque*
AV *Candida quae* G *Candida quem* Broukh, Bae.   **61.** *e* Z,
om. by O.

Tum caedes hominum generi, tum praelia nata,
    Tum brevior dirae mortis aperta via est.
An nihil ille miser meruit, nos ad mala nostra   5
    Vertimus, in saevas quod dedit ille feras?
Divitis hoc vitium est auri, nec bella fuerunt,
    Faginus astabat cum scyphus ante dapes.
Non arces, non vallus erat, somnumque petebat
    Securus varias dux gregis inter oves.   10
Tunc mihi vita foret, vulgi nec tristia nossem
    Arma, nec audissem corde micante tubam.

13—28. *But now I am dragged off to war: keep me safe, ye
Lares of my fathers: ye have ever been duly honoured, and
ye shall be honoured ever.*

Nunc ad bella trahor, et iam quis forsitan hostis
    Haesura in nostro tela gerit latere.
Sed patrii servate Lares: aluistis et idem,   15
    Cursarem vestros cum tener ante pedes.
Neu pudeat prisco vos esse e stipite factos:
    Sic veteris sedes incoluistis avi.
Tunc melius tenuere fidem, cum paupere cultu
    Stabat in exigua ligneus aede deus.   20
Hic placatus erat, seu quis libaverat uvam,
    Seu dederat sanctae spicea serta comae :
Atque aliquis voti compos liba ipse ferebat
    Postque comes purum filia parva favum.
At nobis aerata, Lares, depellite tela,   25
    Hostiaque e plena rustica porcus hara.

I. 10. 5. *An* **AV** *at* **G** *forsan et ille nihil meruit* Par.   8.
aptabat Par. For *dapes* Par has *merum.*   10. *saturas* Heins.
vacuas Broukh *sparsas* **Z.**   11. *vulgi* **O** *dulcis* Heins. **Z.**   12.
tremente **V.**   18. *veteris* **Z** *veteres* **O.**   23. *ipse* **Z** *ipsa* **O.**   26.
Hostiaque e **O** *Hostia de* **G²** *Hostia erit* **Z** *mystica* **G** *rustica* **AVG².**

Hanc pura cum veste sequar myrtoque canistra
Vincta geram, myrto vinctus et ipse caput.

29—34. *Not for me to boast of arms and victories: what madness is it to quicken the stealthy foot of Death!*

Sic placeam vobis: alius sit fortis in armis,
    Sternat et adversos Marte favente duces,   30
Ut mihi potanti possit sua dicere facta
    Miles, et in mensa pingere castra mero.
Quis furor est atram bellis arcessere mortem?
    Imminet et tacito clam venit illa pede.

35—42. *For below there is no corn, no wine, no calm old age, with family and flocks around, but only Styx, and Cerberus, and pallid grief-worn shades.*

Non seges est infra, non vinea culta, sed audax   35
    Cerberus et Stygiae navita turpis aquae:
Illic perscissisque genis ustoque capillo
    Errat ad obscuros pallida turba lacus.
Quam potius laudandus hic est, quem prole parata
    Occupat in parva pigra senecta casa!   40
Ipse suas sectatur oves, at filius agnos,
    Et calidam fesso comparat uxor aquam.

43—68. *Then be it mine to live till age; to see arms lie rusted, and ploughshares busy; and to behold field, and vine, and countryman made glad by the fair face of Peace.*

Sic ego sim, liceatque caput candescere canis,
    Temporis et prisci facta referre senem.

---

30. *adversos* **G V**²   *adverso* **A V.**   33. *arcessere* **G** Par. **V**²
accersere **A V.**   36. *turpis* **Z** *puppis* **O** Par.   37. *perscissis*
Par. *percussis* **O** *perculsis* **Z** *exesis* Heins.   39. ·*Quam* **G** Par.
Quin **A V**   41. *at* **A** Par. *ac* **Z** *ut* **V** *aut* **G.**

—

    Interea Pax arva colat: Pax candida primum   45
      Duxit araturos sub iuga panda boves ;
    Pax aluit vites et sucos condidit uvae,
      Funderet ut nato testa paterna merum ;
    Pace bidens vomerque nitent, at tristia duri
      Militis in tenebris occupat arma situs ;   50
    Rusticus e lucoque vehit, male sobrius ipse,
      Uxorem plaustro progeniemque domum.
    At nobis, Pax alma, veni spicamque teneto,   67
      Perfluat et pomis candidus ante sinus.

---

46. *panda* G Par. *curva* **AV**.   49. *bidens* G Par. **V²** *nitens* **AV** *vomerque vigent* G *vomerque nitet sed* Par. *vomer viderit* **AV** *nitent* conj. by Guy.   51. *ipse* Z *ipso* O.   68. *Perfluat* Z *Prefluat* **AV** *Profluat* G *Perpluat* Heins.

TIBULLUS, II. 1.

1—12. *Silence, all, while we purify our fields and flocks!
Hither come, we pray, Bacchus and Ceres ; now rest man
and beast ; crowned be every head, and pure be every hand.*

QUISQUIS adest, faveat: fruges lustramus et agros,
    Ritus ut a prisco traditus exstat avo.
Bacche, veni, dulcisque tuis e cornibus uva
    Pendeat, et spicis tempora cinge, Ceres.
Luce sacra requiescat humus, requiescat arator,   5
    Et grave suspenso vomere cesset opus.
Solvite vincla iugis: nunc ad praesepia debent
    Plena coronato stare boves capite.
Omnia sint operata deo: non audeat ulla
    Lanificam pensis imposuisse manum.   10
Casta placent superis: pura cum veste venite   13
    Et manibus puris sumite fontis aquam.

15—24. *O gods of our fathers ! as ye see the holy lamb pass on
to the altar, drive ill away! Bring fatness to field and
fold, bring store and joy into our homes.*

Cernite, fulgentes ut eat sacer agnus ad aras   15
    Vinctaque post olea candida turba comas.
Di patrii, purgamus agros, purgamus agrestes:
    Vos mala de nostris pellite limitibus.

II. 1. 1. *faveat* Scal.   *valeat* O   *ades faveas* Dousa, Heyne.
8. *vertice stare boves* Par.   9. *sint* G V²   *sunt* A V¹ Par.   13.
mente Par.   15. *ignis* G.   17. *Di* G   *Dii* A V.   18. *tol-
lite* G.

C

Neu seges eludat messem fallacibus herbis,
  Neu timeat celeres tardior agna lupos.   20
Tunc nitidus plenis confisus rusticus agris
  Ingeret ardenti grandia ligna foco,
Turbaque vernarum, saturi bona signa coloni,
  Ludet et ex virgis exstruet ante casas.

25—32. *See ye, the signs are good ? Forth then with the Chian
and Falernian ! let all be merry, and drink with every
cup to our Messalla.*

Eventura precor: viden ut felicibus extis   25
  Significet placidos nuntia fibra deos?
Nunc mihi fumosos veteris proferte Falernos
  Consulis, et Chio solvite vincla cado.
Vina diem celebrent: non festa luce madere
  Est rubor, errantes et male ferre pedes.   30
Sed 'bene Messallam' sua quisque ad pocula dicat,
  Nomen et absentis singula verba sonent.

33—50. *Come hither, thou conqueror of Aquitania, and help me
while I sing of the country, and the country's gods : how
they have gifted us with corn, and house, and wine, with
fruit and garden, with harvest, wine, and honey.*

Gentis Aquitanae celeber Messalla triumphis
  Et magna intonsis gloria victor avis,
Huc ades aspiraque mihi, dum carmine nostro 35
  Redditur agricolis gratia caelitibus.
Rura cano rurisque deos. His vita magistris
  Desuevit querna pellere glande famem :
Illi compositis primum docuere tigillis

---

22. *Ingeret* A *Ingerat* GV.   24. *arte* G²Z.   29. *celebrent*
AVG¹ *celebrant* G Par.   34. *avis* Z Scal.   *ades* O.   38.
glande GV² *grande* AV¹.

Exiguam viridi fronde operire domum :   40
Illi etiam tauros primi docuisse feruntur
   Servitium, et plaustro supposuisse rotam.
Tum victus abiere feri, tum consita pomus,
   Tum bibit irriguas fertilis hortus aquas,
Aurea tum pressos pedibus dedit uva liquores,   45
   Mixtaque securo est sobria lympha mero.
Rura ferunt messes, calidi cum sideris aestu
   Deponit flavas annua terra comas.
Rure levis verno flores apis ingerit alveo,
   Compleat ut dulci sedula melle favos.   50

51—58. *Thus blessed, the husbandman first beat foot to song, first tuned the pipe, and in honour of thee, Bacchus, essayed the rustic dance.*

Agricola assiduo primum satiatus aratro
   Cantavit certo rustica verba pede,
Et satur arenti primum est modulatus avena
   Carmen, ut ornatos diceret ante deos ;
Agricola et minio suffusus, Bacche, rubenti   55
   Primus inexperta duxit ab arte choros.
Huic datus a pleno, memorabile munus, ovili
   Dux pecoris curtas auxerat hircus opes.

59—66. *Here gather we flowers for our Lares ; here grows the bright wool for maiden's task, with distaff or with loom.*

Rure puer verno primum de flore coronam
   Fecit, et antiquis imposuit laribus.   60

---

41. *primi* O Par. *primum* Z.   45. *Aurea* G Par. *Antea* AV.
49. *ingerit* G Par. *ingerat* AV.   50. *ut* G Par. *et* AV¹.
54. *diceret* GV² *duceret* AV¹.   58. Probably corrupt. *hauxerat* A *hauserat* GV *duxerat* G² *hirtas duxerat hircus oves* Heyne *curtas auxerat hircus opes* Waardenburg, Muel. Hil.

Rure etiam teneris curam exhibitura puellis
  Molle gerit tergo lucida vellus ovis.
Hinc et femineus labor est, hinc pensa colusque,
  Fusus et apposito pollice versat opus:
Atque aliqua assidue textrix operata Minervae   65
  Cantat, et applauso tela sonat latere.

67—86. *Here Love was born: here first he held the bow, here
first pierced young and old. Come thou too to our feast, but
come unarmed: so shall all breathe their vows to thee.*

Ipse interque greges interque armenta Cupido
  Natus et indomitas dicitur inter equas.
Illic inducto primum se exercuit arcu:
  Ei mihi, quam doctas nunc habet ille manus!   70
Nec pecudes, velut ante, petit: fixisse puellas
  Gestit, et audaces perdomuisse viros.
Hic iuveni detraxit opes, hic dicere iussit
  Limen ad iratae verba pudenda senem:
Hoc duce custodes furtim transgressa iacentes   75
  Ad iuvenem tenebris sola puella venit,
Et pedibus praetemptat iter suspensa timore,
  Explorat caecas cui manus ante vias.
A miseri, quos hic graviter deus urget! at ille
  Felix, cui placidus leniter adflat Amor.   80
Sancte, veni dapibus festis, sed pone sagittas
  Et procul ardentes hinc precor abde faces.

---

65. *assidue...Minervam* O *assiduae...Minervae* Z   *textrix* O
textis Z. **66.** *applauso* Z *appulso* O. **67.** *Ipse interque greges*
G *Ipse quoque inter agros* A   *Ipse quoque inter greges* V¹   *Ipse
agros interque greges* V²   *quoque inter apros* Klotz.   **70.** *Hei*
GV.   **72.** *atroces* conj. Bae.   **73.** *opes* G²Z *opus* O.   **78.**
cui O   *dum* conj. Heyne.

Vos celebrem cantate deum pecorique vocate
   Voce : palam pecori, clam sibi quisque vocet.
Aut etiam sibi quisque palam : nam turba iocosa   85
   Obstrepit, et Phrygio tibia curva sono.

87—90. *Then sport your fill: Night comes with her starry train : soon Sleep and Dreams will follow.*

Ludite : iam Nox iungit equos, currumque sequuntur
   Matris lascivo sidera fulva choro,
Postque venit tacitus furvis circumdatus alis
   Somnus, et incerto somnia nigra pede.   90

II. 5.

1—10. *Hither, Phoebus, with thy lyre! thou hast a new priest to-day. Hither, radiant God, with laurel on thy brow, and in thy festal robe !*

Phoebe, fave : novus ingreditur tua templa
   sacerdos :
   Huc age cum cithara carminibusque veni.
Nunc te vocales impellere pollice chordas,
   Nunc precor ad laudes flectere verba meas.
Ipse triumphali devinctus tempora lauro,   5
   Dum cumulant aras, ad tua sacra veni.
Sed nitidus pulcherque veni : nunc indue vestem
   Sepositam, longas nunc bene pecte comas,
Qualem te memorant Saturno rege fugato
   Victori laudes concinuisse Iovi.   10

---

88. *choro* G·V¹   *thoro* A·N¹.   89. *furvis* G   *fulvis* A·V Par. *fuscis* Z Heyne.   90. *nigra* O Par.   *vana* Z   *pigra* Heyne.   II. 5. 3. *me* Bae.   4. *meas* O   *tuas* Z   *mea* Lach.   *tua* Wisser.   7. *Sed* O   *Et* Bae.   9. *Qualem* O   *Quali* Bae.

11—18. *All prophecy is thine, through bird, through entrails, and through lot: grant thou to Messalinus to touch the sacred Sibyl's leaves, and truly to unfold her song.*

Tu procul eventura vides, tibi deditus augur
  Scit bene quid fati provida cantet avis;
Tuque regis sortes, per te praesentit aruspex,
  Lubrica signavit cum deus exta notis.
Te duce Romanos numquam frustrata Sibylla, 15
  Abdita quae senis fata canit pedibus.
Phoebe, sacras Messalinum sine tangere chartas
  Vatis, et ipse precor quid canat illa doce.

19—38. *She it was that gave lots to Aeneas when he yet turned his eyes to Ilium, and Romulus had built no wall; when herds strayed over the Palatium, and the shepherd hung his rude gift to Pan or Pales under the tree; when maidens ferried over the Velabrum to meet their lovers.*

Haec dedit Aeneae sortes, postquam ille parentem
  Dicitur et raptos sustinuisse lares: 20
Nec fore credebat Romam, cum maestus ab alto
  Ilion ardentes respiceretque deos.
Romulus aeternae nondum formaverat urbis
  Moenia, consorti non habitanda Remo,
Sed tunc pascebant herbosa Palatia vaccae, 25
  Et stabant humiles in Iovis arce casae.
Lacte madens illic suberat Pan ilicis umbrae,
  Et facta agresti lignea falce Pales;

---

11. *debitus* O *deditus* Z.   17. *chartas* GV² *cartas* AV¹.   18. *quid* Z *quos* O *quod* Z *canit* G *canat* AV.   19. Bae. thinks 19-22 spurious. Bubendey Quaest. p. 28 thinks the same of 21-38. 20. *raptos* Z *captos* O.   22. Bae. suspects *domos* is the true reading for *deos*.   23. *formaverat* O *firmaverat* Z.

Pendebatque vagi pastoris in arbore votum,
　　Garrula silvestri fistula sacra deo,　　　　30
Fistula, cui semper decrescit arundinis ordo:
　　Nam calamus cera iungitur usque minor.
At qua Velabri regio patet, ire solebat
　　Exiguus pulsa per vada linter aqua.
Illa saepe gregis diti placitura magistro　　　35
　　Ad iuvenem festa est vecta puella die,
Cum qua fecundi redierunt munera ruris,
　　Caseus et niveae candidus agnus ovis.

39—54. *She sang to him of Laurentum and the Numicius ; how the camp of the Rutulian would burn, how Lavinium and Alba Longa grow ; how Ilia would be loved by Mars.*

'Impiger Aenea, volitantis frater Amoris,
　　Troica qui profugis sacra vehis ratibus,　　40
Iam tibi Laurentes assignat Iuppiter agros,
　　Iam vocat errantes hospita terra Lares.
Illic sanctus eris, cum te veneranda Numici
　　Unda deum caelo miserit Indigetem.
Ecce super fessas volitat Victoria puppes,　　45
　　Tandem ad Troianos diva superba venit.
Ecce mihi lucent Rutulis incendia castris :
　　Iam tibi praedico, barbare Turne, necem.
Ante oculos Laurens castrum, murusque Lavini est,
　　Albaque ab Ascanio condita longa duce.　　50

---

32. *nam* **AV** *et* **G** Bae. *dum* Heyne.　34. *pulla* **O**　*pulsa* **Z.**
35. *illaque* **AV**　*diti* **Z**　*ditis* **A.**　　38. After l. 38 a new elegy
commences in **O.** Perhaps a couplet has dropped out.　43. *venerande* Mueller.　49. *castrum* **Z**　*castris* **O.**

Te quoque iam video, Marti placitura sacerdos
  Ilia, Vestales deseruisse focos,
Concubitusque tuos furtim, vittasque iacentes,
  Et cupidi ad ripas arma relicta dei.

55—64. ' *Feed on, ye bulls,' she said, ' while ye may; here Rome
  shall stand, and rule from East to West: once more shall
  Troy be great, and glory in your wanderings.*'

Carpite nunc, tauri, de septem montibus herbas, 55
  Dum licet: hic magnae iam locus urbis erit.
Roma, tuum nomen terris fatale regendis,
  Qua sua de caelo prospicit arva Ceres,
Quaque patent ortus et qua fluitantibus undis
  Solis anhelantes abluit amnis equos.   60
Troia quidem tunc se mirabitur, et sibi dicet
  Vos bene tam longa consuluisse via.
Vera cano: sic usque sacras innoxia laurus
  Vescar, et aeternum sit mihi virginitas.'

65—80. *So sang she, and called on thee, Phoebus: blot out, we
  pray thee, all omens dire of comet or of stone-shower, of
  embattled sky or speaking grove, of failing sun or cloud-
  wrapped year, of voiced ox or weeping God.*

Haec cecinit vates et te sibi, Phoebe, vocavit, 65
  Iactavit fusas et caput ante comas.
Quidquid Amalthea, quidquid Marpesia dixit
  Herophile, Phyto Graiaque quod monuit,

---

53. *vittasque* Z   *victasque* O.   62. *longa . . . via* Z Scal.
longam . . . viam O.   63. *lauros* G.   64. *Vescar* ZV² *Noscar*
A   *Noscat* GV¹.   65-80 Bae. holds to be spurious, interpolated
in consequence of there having been a gap after l. 64.   67. *Quid
quod* A.   68. *Eryphile* G   *Heriphile* AV.   *Phoeto Graia*

Quasque Aniena sacras Tiburs per flumina sortes
    Portarit sicco pertuleritque sinu: 70
Hae fore dixerunt belli mala signa cometen,
    Multus ut in terras deplueretque lapis:
Atque tubas atque arma ferunt strepitantia caelo
    Audita, et lucos praecinuisse fugam:
Ipsum etiam Solem defectum lumine vidit   75
    Iungere pallentes nubilus annus equos,
Et simulacra deum lacrimas fudisse tepentes
    Fataque vocales praemonuisse boves.
Haec fuerant olim: sed tu iam mitis, Apollo,
    Prodigia indomitis merge sub aequoribus.   80

81—94. *Now let the laurel crackle, let field and cask be full: the glad shepherd shall leap over the straw, young and old shall make merry together.*

Et succensa sacris crepitet bene laurea flammis,
    Omine quo felix et sacer annus erit.
Laurus ubi bona signa dedit, gaudete coloni:
    Distendet spicis horrea plena Ceres,
Oblitus et musto feriet pede rusticus uvas,   85
    Dolia dum magni deficiantque lacus.
Ac madidus Baccho sua festa Palilia pastor
    Concinet: a stabulis tunc procul este lupi.

Lach.   *Phoebo grata* O   *Phyto grata* Huschke   *que quod monuit* Z   *quod admonuit* O.   Rossbach puts a comma after *dixit*, and reads *Phoebo grata*.   69. *Quasque* Z   *Quodque* AV   *Aniena* Z   *Albana* O   *Albuna* Scal.   *Tiburs* Z   *Tiberis* O.   70. *pertuleritque* Z   *perlueritque* O.   71. *Hec* AV   *Hae* Z.   Notice *haec* in ll. 65, 79.   72. *ut* G²Z   *et* O   *deplueretque* Z   *deplueritque* AG   *depuleritque* V.   81. *Et* GV²   *Ut* AV¹.   83. The words *gaudete coloni* may be taken parenthetically.   87. *Ac* O   *At* Z Lach.

Ille levis stipulae sollemnes potus acervos
 Accendet, flammas transilietque sacras.   90
Et fetus matrona dabit, natusque parenti
 Oscula comprensis auribus eripiet,
Nec taedebit avum parvo advigilare nepoti,
 Balbaque cum puero dicere verba senem.

95—104. *The youth shall build leafy bowers, and hold banquet on the sod: if cups bring angry words to any, he will wish them unsaid when sober.*

Tunc operata deo pubes discumbet in herba, 95
 Arboris antiquae qua levis umbra cadit,
Aut e veste sua tendent umbracula sertis
 Vincta, coronatus stabit et ante calix.
At sibi quisque dapes et festas exstruet alte
 Caespitibus mensas caespitibusque torum. 100
Ingeret hic potus iuvenis maledicta puellae,
 Postmodo quae votis irrita facta velit:
Nam ferus ille suae plorabit sobrius idem,
 Et se iurabit mente fuisse mala.

105—112. *But perish thou, Love, with thy evil ways! what mischief hast thou wrought! most of all to me, who lie love-sick for my Nemesis, and love so to lie.*

Pace tua pereant arcus pereantque sagittae, 105
 Phoebe, modo in terris erret inermis Amor.
Ars bona: sed postquam sumpsit sibi tela Cupido,
 Heu heu quam multis ars dedit ista malum!

---

92. *comprensis* G Z *compressis* A V. 95. *operata* G *operta* A.
98. *ante* Z *ipse* O. 99. *extruet* G² *extruat* O. 100. *thorum*
A V. 103. *Nam* A V *Iam* G Bae.

Et mihi praecipue. Iaceo cum saucius annum,
    Et faveo morbo, cum iuvat ipse dolor,   110
Usque cano Nemesim, sine qua versus mihi nullus
    Verba potest iustos aut reperire pedes.

113—122. *But spare, maiden, spare the holy bard, that he may sing of Messalinus, and swell the glory of his triumph. O Phoebus, hear my prayer!*

At tu, nam divum servat tutela poetas,
    Praemoneo, vati parce, puella, sacro,
Ut Messalinum celebrem, cum praemia belli   115
    Ante suos currus oppida victa feret,
Ipse gerens lauros: lauro devinctus agresti
    Miles 'io' magna voce 'triumphe' canet.
Tunc Messalla meus pia det spectacula turbae,
    Et plaudat curru praetereunte pater.   120
Annue: sic tibi sint intonsi, Phoebe, capilli,
    Sic tua perpetuo sit tibi casta soror.

II. 6.

1—10. *Macer is going off to war: will Love go with him? or brand him a traitor to his cause? Then I too will go to the camp with him: farewell to my maiden and my Love!*

Castra Macer sequitur: tenero quid fiet Amori?
    Sit comes et collo fortiter arma gerat?
Et seu longa virum terrae via seu vaga ducent

---

109. *iaceo* **Z** *taceo* **A**.   110. *cum* **O** *tam* **Z** *quod, nam, quin* have been suggested. Older edd. place a comma after *praecipue*.   112. *reperire* **A** *reperisse* **GV**.   116. *feret* **G** *ferent* **AV**.   117. *lauros* **G**.
II. 6. 3. *terre* **AV**[1] *terret* **GV**[2].

Aequora, cum telis ad latus ire volet?
Ure, puer, quaeso, tua qui ferus otia liquit, 5
    Atque iterum erronem sub tua signa voca.
Quod si militibus parces, erit hic quoque miles,
    Ipse levem galea qui sibi portet aquam.
Castra peto, valeatque Venus valeantque puellae:
    Et mihi sunt vires, et mihi facta tuba est. 10

11—18. *How brave my words! but how feeble is my foot!
Ah, cruel Love, would that thy shafts were broken, and
thy torch put out!*

Magna loquor, sed magnifice mihi magna locuto
    Excutiunt clausae fortia verba fores.
Iuravi quotiens rediturum ad limina numquam!
    Cum bene iuravi, pes tamen ipse redit.
Acer Amor, fractas utinam tua tela sagittas, 15
    Si licet, extinctas aspiciamque faces!
Tu miserum torques, tu me mihi dira precari
    Cogis, et insana mente nefanda loqui.

19—28. *I should have perished, but Hope bids me live: Hope,
that brings solace to the husbandman, to the fowler, to the
slave, still promises to me my Nemesis.*

Iam mala finissem leto, sed credula vitam
    Spes fovet, et fore cras semper ait melius. 20
Spes alit agricolas, Spes sulcis credit aratis
    Semina, quae magno fenore reddat ager:

---

8. *levem* **AV** *levi* **G** Bae. *portet* **AG** *portat* **VG³**. **16.**
Si licet **Z** *Scilicet* **O**. **20.** So **O** *et melius cras fore semper
ait* Par.

Haec laqueo volucres, haec captat arundine
   pisces,
   Cum tenues hamos abdidit ante cibus:
Spes etiam valida solatur compede vinctum: 25
   Crura sonant ferro, sed canit inter opus.
Spes facilem Nemesim spondet mihi, sed negat illa︵
   Ei mihi, ne vincas, dura puella, deam.

29—42. *Ah spare me, Nemesis! By thy dear sister • dead, whose grave I tend, who pleads my cause, and who standing over thee, all blood-stained as she fell, will break thy sleep: be hard to me no more. Enough: not mine to bring tear into thine eye.*

Parce, per immatura tuae precor ossa sororis:
   Sic bene sub tenera parva quiescat humo.   30
Illa mihi sancta est, illius dona sepulcro
   Et madefacta meis serta feram lacrimis,
Illius ad tumulum fugiam, supplexque sedebo,
   Et mea cum muto fata querar cinere.
Non feret usque suum te propter flere clientem: 35
   Illius ut verbis, sis mihi lenta veto,
Ne tibi neglecti mittant mala somnia Manes,
   Maestaque sopitae stet soror ante torum.
Qualis ab excelsa praeceps delapsa fenestra
   Venit ad infernos sanguinolenta lacus.   40
Desino, ne dominae luctus renoventur acerbi:
   Non ego sum tanti, ploret ut illa semel.

23, 24. Heyne and Fischer (Quaest. Prop.) think these lines spurious.   28. *Hei* O.   32. *feram* GV² *ferant* AV¹.
38. *thorum* AV.

TIBULLUS, III. 3.

1—10. What boots it, Neaera, that I have filled heaven with my prayers? not for marble house or rich estate, but to share all joys with thee, and live happy in thy love till death.

QUID prodest caelum votis implesse, Neaera,
 Blandaque cum multa tura dedisse prece,
Non ut marmorei prodirem e limine tecti,
 Insignis clara conspicuusque domo,
Aut ut multa mei renovarent iugera tauri,   5
 Et magnas messes terra benigna daret,
Sed tecum ut longae sociarem gaudia vitae
 Inque tuo caderet nostra senecta sinu,
Tum cum permenso defunctus tempore lucis
 Nudus Lethaea cogerer ire rate?   10

11—24. What to me were gold or pearl or marble, what grove or gilded roof? With thee, Neaera, poverty were sweet: no kingly wealth can please without thee.

Nam grave quid prodest pondus mihi divitis
   auri,
 Arvaque si findant pinguia mille boves?
Quidve domus prodest Phrygiis innixa columnis,
 Taenare sive tuis, sive Caryste tuis,
Et nemora in domibus sacros imitantia lucos,   15
 Aurataeque trabes marmoreumque solum?

III. 3. **2.** *Multaque cum blanda* Bergk.   **7.** *sociarē* G   *sociarent* AV.   **9.** *permenso* O   *praemensae* ZH   *permensae* Huschke.   **11.** *quid prodesse potest pondus grave* Par.

Quidve in Erythraeo legitur quae litore concha
 Tinctaque Sidonio murice lana iuvat,
Et quae praeterea populus miratur? in illis
 Invidia est: falso plurima vulgus amat. 20
Non opibus mentes hominum curaeque levantur:
 Nam Fortuna sua tempora lege regit.
Sit mihi paupertas tecum iucunda, Neaera:
 At sine te regum munera nulla volo.

25—38. *O thrice bright and happy the day that should give me
back my wife, in my poor but peaceful home! But if the
Fates say nay, then may Orcus call me to his dark and
dismal streams.*

O niveam, quae te poterit mihi reddere, lucem! 25
 O mihi felicem terque quaterque diem!
At si, pro dulci reditu quaecumque voventur,
 Audiat aversa non meus aure deus,
Non me regna iuvant nec Lydius aurifer amnis
 Nec quas terrarum sustinet orbis opes. 30
Haec alii cupiant, liceat mihi paupere cultu
 Securo cara coniuge posse frui.
Adsis et timidis faveas, Saturnia, votis,
 Et faveas concha, Cypria, vecta tua.
Aut si fata negant reditum tristesque sorores, 35
 Stamina quae ducunt quaeque futura neunt,
Me vocet in vastos amnes nigramque paludem.
 Dives in ignava luridus Orcus aqua.

---

20. *Invidia est* G Par. *Invida quae* **AV**. **22.** *regit* G Par.
gerit **AV** Fris. **28.** *adversa* O *aversa* **V²Z**. **29.** *Non* G Par.
Nec **AV** *iuvant* **AV** Par. *iuvent* G. **32.** *Securo vitae munere*
Par. **33.** *Assis* O. **36.** *canunt* Heyne *regunt* Dis. **38.**
Dives in O *Ditis et* **Z** Bae. *Ditis ab* Mueller.

III. 5.

1—6. *While ye, my friends, are at the waters of Etruria, I am ill and like to die.*

> Vos tenet, Etruscis manat quae fontibus unda,
>> Unda sub aestivum non adeunda canem,
> Nunc autem sacris Baiarum proxima lymphis,
>> Cum se purpureo vere remittit humus:
> At mihi Persephone nigram denuntiat horam: 5
>> Immerito iuveni parce nocere, dea.

7—20. *Yet have I done no ill, no crime or sacrilege: I have lodged no evil thought, spoken no evil word: why should I be cut off so young?*

> Non ego temptavi nulli temeranda virorum
>> Audax laudandae sacra docere deae;
> Nec mea mortiferis infecit pocula sucis,
>> Dextera nec cuiquam trita venena dedit;   10
> Nec nos sacrilegos templis admovimus ignes,
>> Nec cor sollicitant facta nefanda meum;
> Nec nos insanae meditantes iurgia mentis
>> Impia in adversos solvimus ora deos;
> Et nondum cani nigros laesere capillos,   15
>> Nec venit tardo curva senecta pede.

III. 5. 1. *Vos* G² *Nos* AG.   3. *proxima* Sciopp. *maxima* O
Plant.   7. *virorum* Z *deorum* O Plant.   10. *trita* F *certa*
O Plant. *tetra* G².   11. *sacrilegos* G Plant. *sacrilegis* AV
sacrilegi Z *admovimus ignes* G² Plant *amovimus egros* A
egros GV.   12. *facta* O Par. Plaut. *furta* Bae.   13. *meditantes*
G Plant. *meditantis* AV.

[Natalem primo nostrum videre parentes,
    Cum cecidit fato consul uterque pari.]
Quid fraudare iuvat vitem crescentibus uvis,
    Et modo nata mala vellere poma manu?   20

21–34. *Oh! spare me, gods of the world below: grant to me to reach old age. Live happily, my friends, and forget not to do sacrifice for me.*

Parcite, pallentes undas quicumque tenetis,
    Duraque sortiti tertia regna dei.
Elysios olim liceat cognoscere campos,
    Lethaeamque ratem Cimmeriosque lacus,
Cum mea rugosa pallebunt ora senecta,   25
    Et referam pueris tempora prisca senex.
Atque utinam vano nequiquam terrear aestu!
    Languent ter quinos sed mea membra dies.
At vobis Tuscae celebrantur numina lymphae,
    Et facilis lenta pellitur unda manu.   30
Vivite felices, memores et vivite nostri,
    Sive erimus, seu nos fata fuisse velint.
Interea nigras pecudes promittite Diti,
    Et nivei lactis pocula mixta mero.

---

21. *undas* O Plant. *umbras* Z.   29. *At vobis* GV² *Atque nobis* AV¹.   31. 'Perhaps *sed* (*set*).' Palmer.   32. *volent* Z.

PROPERTIUS, I. 8.

1—8. What? art thou indeed ready to give thine heart to another? and to brave for his sake the perils of the deep, and the frosts of Dalmatia?

' TUNE igitur demens, nec te mea cura moratur?
    An tibi sum gelida vilior Illyria,
Et tibi iam tanti, quicumque est, iste videtur,
    Ut sine me vento quolibet ire velis?
Tune audire potes vesani murmura ponti?   5
    Fortis et in dura nave iacere potes?
Tu pedibus teneris positas fulcire pruinas,
    Tu potes insolitas, Cynthia, ferre nives?

9—16. Long last the wintry storms! May no ill breeze arise to waft thee from these shores!

O utinam hibernae duplicentur tempora brumae,
    Et sit iners tardis navita Vergiliis!   10
Nec tibi Tyrrhena solvatur funis arena,
    Neve inimica meas elevet aura preces!
Atque ego non videam tales subsidere ventos,
    Cum tibi provectas auferet unda rates,

---

6. *mane* **AF**.   7. *fulcire* **NO** Per. Hertz.   *sulcare* old edd., Palmer, who however suggests *nunc ire pruinas* : cf. 2. 30. 19. Other conj. are *calcare, super ire, superare pruinas* **DV**   *ruinas* **NAF**. 11. *harena* **N** *ab ora* conj. Burmann.   13. So **NO** *Aut* **Z** Huschke *non* **NO**   *iam* Bae. **F** has *subdire* : Graevius conj. *tali sub sidere*.

Et me defixum vacua patiatur in ora   15
  Crudelem infesta saepe vocare manu!

17—26. *Yet may Galatea prosper thy voyage; where'er thou
mayest be, my heart is thine, and I shall ever hold thee mine.*

Sed quocumque modo de me, periura, mereris,
  Sit Galatea tuae non aliena viae;
Utere felici praevecta Ceraunia remo;
  Accipiat placidis Oricos aequoribus.   20
Nam me non ullae poterunt corrumpere taedae,
  Quin ego, vita, tuo limine verba querar;
Nec me deficiet nautas rogitare citatos
  'Dicite, quo portu clausa puella mea est?'
Et dicam: 'licet Atraciis considat in oris,   25
  Et licet Hylaeis, illa futura mea est.'

27—32. *Joy! Joy! I have conquered! She hears my prayer
and consents to stay!*

Hic erit! hic iurata manet! rumpantur iniqui!
  Vicimus! assiduas non tulit illa preces!

---

15. *patiatur* NO *patietur* old edd. Hertz. Bae. Palmer *patiaris*
Beroaldus *patienter* Lach. *in hora* AF *arena* DV.   17. *quodcunque*
NA.   19. *Ut te* NAF Hertz. *Utere* D and prob. V too, Bae. Palmer
Vites felici praevecta Lach. *Ut te felici post lecta* Mueller *provecta*
DV *praevectam felice* Guy, H. A. J. Munro.   21. *de te* NO Per. Bae.
taedae Z old edd.   22. *Quin ego vita* NF²V *Quin ego tuta* AFD
Quin ego fida Lach. *Quin arguta* conj. Bae. The MSS. have *verba*.
Palmer and Mueller adopt the conj. *vera*, for which P. quotes 3. 6.
35 and Cat. 66. 18.   22. *lumine* O Per.   23. *deficiat* AF.
25. The reading in this couplet is very uncertain. N Per. Lach.
have *licet atraciis*, A *licet a traciis*, D *a thraciis licet haec*. Hertz.
and others *Autaricis*, Mueller *Autariis*, Palmer *Artaciis*, comparing Apoll. Rhod. Arg. 1. 954 κρήνη ὑπ' 'Αρτακίη and Arg. Orph.
496.   26. *Hyleis* AF *Hylleis* Muretus *hileis* N *ellaeis* DV
Eleis Z Hertz. Palmer now prefers *Hylaeis*: see notes.   27. *erit*
DV Hertz. *erat* NAF Palmer, who translates 'She was here *all the
while*, and here she remains.' But that sense spoils the passage.

Falsa licet cupidus deponat gaudia livor :
  Destitit ire novas Cynthia nostra vias.   30
Illi carus ego et per me carissima Roma
  Dicitur, et sine me dulcia regna negat.

39—46. *It is not gold nor pearls that have won for me her love ;*
it is my gift of song.

Hanc ego non auro, non Indis flectere conchis,
  Sed potui blandi carminis obsequio.   40
Sunt igitur Musae, neque amanti tardus Apollo,
  Quis ego fretus amo : Cynthia rara mea est.
Nunc mihi summa licet contingere sidera plantis :
  Sive dies seu nox venerit, illa mea est.
Nec mihi rivalis certos subducet amores :   45
  Ista meam norit gloria canitiem.

I. 14.

1—8. *Though all luxury be thine, Tullus, as thou gazest on*
wood and river, no wealth may equal the riches of my love.

Tu licet abiectus Tiberina molliter unda
  Lesbia Mentoreo vina bibas opere,
Et modo tam celeres mireris currere lintres,
  Et modo tam tardas funibus ire rates,
Et nemus omne satas intendat vertice silvas,   5
  Urgetur quantis Caucasus arboribus :
Non tamen ista meo valeant contendere amori :
  Nescit Amor magnis cedere divitiis.

---

42. amo NO Bae. conj. *ovo*.   45. *certos* NF²V *summos* AF
somnus D   *subducet* F² *subducit* N.
4. *iam* AF *finibus* AF.   5. *omne* NO *unde* Lach.   6.
quantus DV.

9—16. *When she is by, all gold, all gems, are mine: no wealth is wealth without her.*

Nam sive optatam mecum trahit illa quietem,
  Seu facili totum ducit amore diem,   10
Tum mihi Pactoli veniunt sub tecta liquores,
  Et legitur rubris gemma sub aequoribus:
Tum mihi cessuros spondent mea gaudia reges;
  Quae maneant, dum me fata perire volent.
Nam quis divitiis adverso gaudet Amore?   15
  Nulla mihi tristi praemia sint Venere!

17—24. *Love tames the stout heart, Love climbs upon the purple couch: if Love smile true on me, I can despise Alcinous.*

Illa potest magnas heroum infringere vires,
  Illa etiam duris mentibus esse dolor:
Illa neque Arabium metuit transcendere limen,
  Nec timet ostrino, Tulle, subire toro,   20
Et miserum toto iuvenem versare cubili:
  Quid relevant variis serica textilibus?
Quae mihi dum placata aderit, non ulla verebor
  Regna vel Alcinoi munera despicere.   •

I. 17.

1—8. *Ah! truly I deserved to die deserted on this lonely shore, amid the chiding of the wind, since I could leave my Cynthia.*

Et merito, quoniam potui fugisse puellam,
  Nunc ego desertas alloquor alcyonas!

---

11. *veniant* **AF**[1].   13. *sua gaudia* Burmann.   19. *arabtum*
F (**A**?) *atratum* Graevius *auratum* or *aeratum* Heinsius   *limen*
om. by **AF**[1].   20. *thoro* **NAF**.   22. *relevant* **NF**[J] *relevent*
O.   24. *vel* **NO**   *nec* **Z**.

Nec mihi Cassiope solito visura carinam est,
Omniaque ingrato litore vota cadunt.
Quin etiam absenti prosunt tibi, Cynthia, venti : 5
Aspice, quam saevas increpat aura minas !
Nullane placatae veniet Fortuna procellae ?
Haeccine parva meum funus harena teget ?

9—14. *Yet spare me now, Cynthia: see not my sad fate un-
moved.*

Tu tamen in melius saevas converte querelas :
Sat tibi sit poenae nox et iniqua vada.   10
An poteris siccis mea fata reponere ocellis,
Ossaque nulla tuo nostra tenere sinu ?
Ah pereat, quicumque rates et vela paravit
Primus et invito gurgite fecit iter !

15—18. *Were it not better to have borne with that hard heart,
than to be thus, in strange lands, alone ?*

Nonne fuit levius dominae pervincere mores   15
(Quamvis dura, tamen rara puella fuit),
Quam sic ignotis circumdata litora silvis
Cernere, et optatos quaerere Tyndaridas ?

19—24. *Had I died there, she had honoured my remains, and
prayed over my grave.*

Illic si qua meum sepelissent fata dolorem,
Ultimus et posito staret amore lapis,   20

---

3. *casiope solito* **NO** *solitam* Passerat *Cassiopes statio* Lach.
salvam L. Mueller *Casiopest olim* Bae. *est* is om. by **NO** Hertz.
Palmer reads *carinamst.*   4. *Omnia que* **AD** *Omniaque* **N**
Hertz. etc. *Omine et* Paley.   6. *increpat* **NAFV¹** *increpet*
DV.   8. *harena* **NDV** Per. (as elsewhere) *querelas* **NO.**   11.
reponere **NO** Palmer *opponere* **Z** Hertz. Mueller *exponere*
Graevius.   13. *Ha* **AF** *et bella* **F**.   15. *levius* **NO** *melius* **GZ.**

Illa meo caros donasset funere crines,
  Molliter et tenera poneret ossa rosa:
Illa meum extremo clamasset pulvere nomen,
  Ut mihi non ullo pondere terra foret.

25—28. *Help, ye sea daughters of Doris! if ye too know Love,*
make kind to me your shores.

At vos aequoreae formosa Doride natae,   25
  Candida felici solvite vela choro:
Si quando vestras labens Amor attigit undas,
  Mansuetis socio parcite litoribus.

I. 18.

1—4. *In this silent forest, to these lonely rocks, I may pour*
forth my pain.

Haec certe deserta loca et taciturna querenti,
  Et vacuum Zephyri possidet aura nemus.
Hic licet occultos proferre inpune dolores,
  Si modo sola queant saxa tenere fidem.

5—10. *Whence came thy pride, Cynthia? where began my*
fault?

Unde tuos primum repetam, mea Cynthia, fastus? 5
  Quod mihi das flendi, Cynthia, principium?
Qui modo felices inter numerabar amantes,
  Nunc in amore tuo cogor habere notam.

---

26. *choro* **NAF** *noto* **DV.** **28.** *choribus* **F** *pectoribus* Hous.
3. *impune* **AD** *inpune* **N** and the rest. **7.** *numerabar inter* **AF.**

Quid tantum merui? quae te mihi carmina
    mutant?
An nova tristitiae causa puella tuae?   10

11—16. *None other have I loved: and for all thy cruelty, never would I give pain to thee.*

Sic mihi te referas levis, ut non altera nostro
    Limine formosos intulit ulla pedes.
Quamvis multa tibi dolor hic meus aspera debet,
    Non ita saeva tamen venerit ira mea,
Ut tibi sim merito semper furor, et tua flendo 15
    Lumina deiectis turpia sint lacrimis.

17—22. *Bear witness of my love, ye trees, that tell of Cynthia's name.*

An quia parva damus mutato signa colore,
    Et non ulla meo clamat in ore fides?
Vos eritis testes, si quos habet arbor amores,
    Fagus et Arcadio pinus amica deo.   20
Ah quotiens teneras resonant mea verba sub
    umbras,
    Scribitur et vestris Cynthia corticibus!

---

9. *carmina* NO Per.   *crimina* Z Lipsius, Hertz. Paley, Bae. Mueller. 12. *illa* N. 16. *deiectis* Z *delectis* NV² *dilectis* O. 17. *parva* O *rara* Burmann *dura* Bae.   *colore* NO *calore* V² Lach. 19. *arbor* NV² *ardor* O. 20. *amica* NAF Hertz. etc. *amata* DV Bae.   21. *Ha* AF *Ah* the rest   *teneras* O *vestras* l. 21 and *teneris* l. 22 Schrader, Palm. *tenera has* Bae. 22. *vestris* N edd. *nostris* AFV².

23—32. *All wrong, all cruelty I have borne: yet here on cold rocks, in rough paths, I sing, and shall ever sing, of Cynthia.*

An tua quod peperit nobis iniuria curas,
    Quae solum tacitis cognita sunt foribus
Omnia consuevi timidus perferre superbae   25
    Iussa, neque arguto fata dolore queri.
Pro quo divini fontes et frigida rupes
    Et datur inculto tramite dura quies;
Et quodcumque meae possunt narrare querelae,
    Cogor ad argutas dicere solus aves.   30
Sed qualiscumque es, resonent mihi 'Cynthia'
    silvae,
    Nec deserta tuo nomine saxa vacent.

I. 19.

1—10. *I fear not death, Cynthia: I fear only to be forgotten by thee when dead.*

Non ego nunc tristes vereor, mea Cynthia, Manes,
    Nec moror extremo debita fata rogo:
Sed ne forte tuo careat mihi funus amore,
    Hic timor est ipsis durior exequiis.
Non adeo leviter nostris puer haesit ocellis,   5
    Ut meus oblito pulvis amore vacet.
Illic Phylacides iucundae coniugis heros

---

23. *An tua quod* NO Hertz. etc.   *Ah tua quot* Z Bae.   *En tua quot* Mueller.   24. *foribus* NO edd. *foliis* conj. Bae.   26. *fassa* F¹ *facta* N Hertz. etc. *fata* Z Palm.   27. *divini fontes* O *dumosi montes* Heinsius, Bae. *Clusini* R. Ellis. Post. (in Corp.) reads *Pro quo mi nudi montes.*   29. *querellae* DV¹ *querelae* the rest.   30. *ut argutae* conj. Bae.   31. *resonant* A.F¹¹ Per. (and *vacant*).

1. *non tristos* N.   4. *obsequiis* F¹.   5. *nostris* V² *noster* NO. 7. *iocundae* or *iocunde* NO *iucundae* Lach. Hertz. Palm. *iocundae* Bae. Paley.

Non potuit caecis inmemor esse locis,
Sed cupidus falsis attingere gaudia palmis
Thessalis antiquam venerat umbra domum.   10

11—24. *Death shall not cool my love for thee: ah! let no rival bid thee dry thy tears for me.*

Illic quidquid ero, semper tua dicar imago:
Traicit et fati litora magnus amor.
Illic formosae veniant chorus heroinae,
Quas dedit Argivis Dardana praeda viris;
Quarum nulla tua fuerit mihi, Cynthia, forma   15
Gratior, et Tellus hoc ita iusta sinat.
Quamvis te longae remorentur fata senectae,
Cara tamen lacrimis ossa futura meis.
Quae tu viva mea possis sentire favilla!
Tum mihi non ullo mors sit amara loco.   20
Quam vereor ne te contempto, Cynthia, busto,
Abstrahat heu! nostro pulvere iniquus Amor,
Cogat et invitam lacrimas siccare cadentes!
Flectitur assiduis certa puella minis.

25—26. *Meanwhile, let us love while life shall last.*

Quare, dum licet, inter nos laetemur amantes: 25
Non satis est ullo tempore longus amor.

---

8. *inmemor* N   *immemor* ADV.   10. *Thessalis* DV Ital.
Thessalus NAG   *venerat* NA   *verberat* DV.   11. *quicquid* N.
12. *Traicit* NHb.   13. *veniat* DV.   15. *Quarum* NO Hertz.
Harum Bae. Palm. Heinsius.   17. *longe te* NA.   18. *tuis* Scaliger.
19. *tu viva mea possis* NO edd.   *cum mixta mea possim* conj. Bae. (!)
22. *Abstraat* N   *Abstrat* AF   * l* (for *heu*) N   *a* Z   *e* O Per.

I. 22.

1—10. *What my birth, thou askest, Tullus, and my birth-place? Knowest thou Perusia? Close under Perusia, in Umbria, I was born.*

Qualis et unde genus, qui sint mihi, Tulle, Penates,
  Quaeris pro nostra semper amicitia.
Si Perusina tibi patriae sunt nota sepulcra,
  Italiae duris funera temporibus,
Cum Romana suos egit discordia cives,   5
  Sed mihi praecipue, pulvis Etrusca, dolor :—
Tu proiecta mei perpessa es membra propinqui,
  ʻTu nullo miseri contegis ossa solo :—
Proxima supposito contingens Umbria campo
  Me genuit, terris fertilis uberibus.   10

---

3. For *patriae* Bae. suggests *patrum*.   For *sepulcra* Scaliger conj. *sepultae*.   6. *Sed* (*set*) Palm.   *Sit* **N O** Per. Hertz.   *Sis* Scal.   *Sic* **Hb Z** Lach. Mueller   *praecipue* **NV¹**.   9. *subposito* **NA** *supposito* the rest.

PROPERTIUS, II. 1.

1—16. *Thou askest, Mæcenas, why love is ever the burden of my song? My muse comes all from Cynthia: whatever she wears, or does, or says, is to me a fount of song.*

QUAERITIS, unde mihi totiens scribantur amores,
 Unde meus veniat mollis in ora liber.
Non haec Calliope, non haec mihi cantat Apollo:
 Ingenium nobis ipsa puella facit.
Sive illam Cois fulgentem incedere coccis,   5
 Hoc totum e Coa veste volumen erit:
Seu vidi ad frontem sparsos errare capillos,
 Gaudet laudatis ire superba comis:
Sive lyrae carmen digitis percussit eburnis,
 Miramur, facilis ut premat arte manus: 10
Seu cum poscentes somnum declinat ocellos,
 Invenio causas mille poeta novas:
Seu quidquid fecit sive est quodcumque locuta, 15
 Maxima de nihilo nascitur historia.

17—26. *Had mine been the gift to sing of heroes and their deeds, I should have sung first of Cæsar's glories, then of thine.*

Quod mihi si tantum, Maecenas, fata dedissent,
 Ut possem heroas ducere in arma manus,

---

2. *moris* N   *ora* O   *ore* N.   **5–10.** Lach. and Bae. invert the order of these lines. Lach. (followed by Mueller) places them thus: 9, 10–7, 8–5, 6.   Baehrens thus: 7, 8–5, 6–9, 10.   **5.** *chois* NO *coccis* Lach. Hertz. Bae. Mueller   *cogis* NAF   *togis* DV   *vidi* Z Palm.   *novi* Huschke.   **6.** *Hoc* NO   *Hac* Bae.   *Hoc totum in Coa* conj. Lach.   **10.** *facilis* N   *faciles* DV   **11.** *cum* O   *iam* Bae. **15.** N has *quicquid*: and so elsewhere.

Non ego Titanas canerem, non Ossan Olympo
    Impositam, ut caeli Pelion esset iter,   20
Non veteres Thebas, nec Pergama nomen
    Homeri,
    Xerxis et imperio bina coisse vada,
Regnave prima Remi, aut animos Carthaginis
    altae,
    Cimbrorumque minas et benefacta Mari :
Bellaque resque tui memorarem Caesaris, et tu   25
    Caesare sub magno cura secunda fores.

27–36. *Wherever Cæsar fought, wherever Cæsar triumphed, the Muse links thy name with his—true loyal heart, in camp or council!*

Nam quotiens Mutinam aut civilia busta Philippos
    Aut canerem Siculae classica bella fugae,
Eversosque focos antiquae gentis Etruscae,
    Et Ptolemaeei litora capta Phari,   30
Aut canerem Aegyptum et Nilum, cum atratus
    in urbem
    Septem captivis debilis ibat aquis,
Aut regum auratis circumdata colla catenis,
    Actiaque in Sacra currere rostra Via :
Te mea Musa illis semper contexeret armis,   35
    Et sumpta et posita pace fidele caput.

---

20. *Impositam* **NAF** Per. *Impositum* **DV** Hertz. 21. *pergam* **N**. 22. *Xerxive inperio* Lach. 30. *Et* **NO** *aut* Schrader, Bae. *ptolomenei* **N** *Ptolemaeei* Hertz. Palm. Mueller *ptholomeae* **D** *Ptolomaei* Bae. 31. *Et* Schrader, Bae. Palm. *Aut* **NO** Hertz. *cyptum* **NA** *Cyprum* Per. **DV** Hertz. *Aegyptum* edd. *Coptum* Bae. *atratus* Bae. Palm. *attractus* **NA** *tractus* **DV** Per. Hertz. *atractatus* **F** *urbem* **N** Per. Hertz. *urbe* Palm. 35. *contexerit* **NO**.

37—42. *Callimachus could not sing of Jove's battles, nor can I of Cæsar's.*

Theseus infernis, superis testatur Achilles,
 Hic Ixioniden, ille Menoetiaden,
Sed neque Phlegraeos Iovis Enceladique tumultus
 Intonet angusto pectore Callimachus, 40
Nec mea conveniunt duro praecordia versu
 Caesaris in Phrygios condere nomen avos.

51—70. *No spells can win me from my love: I die of an ill that no medicine may heal, no charm drive away.*

Seu mihi sunt tangenda novercae pocula 51
  Phaedrae,
 Pocula privigno non nocitura suo,
Seu mihi Circaeo pereundum est gramine, sive
 Colchis Iolciacis urat aena focis,
Una meos quoniam praedata est femina sensus, 55
 Ex hac ducentur funera nostra domo.
Omnes humanos sanat medicina dolores :
 Solus amor morbi non amat artificem.
Tarda Philoctetae sanavit crura Machaon,
 Phoenicis Chiron lumina Phillyrides ; 60
Et deus extinctum Cressis Epidaurius herbis
 Restituit patriis Androgeona focis ;
Mysus et Haemonii iuvenis qua cuspide vulnus

---

37. *infernis* O *ut larvis* conj. Bae. **41.** *praeveniunt* **AF**.
51. *sunt* **NAF** Hertz. Bae. *sint* **DV** Paley. **54.** *cholcis* **NDV**
colchiacis (or *cholchiacis*) O Hertz. : *Iolciacis* Scaliger, Bae. Palm.
ahena **DV**. **58.** *habet* Schrader, Bae. who thinks *amat* has crept
in from *non amat artificem* I. 2. 8. **61.** *craesis* **N** *cresis* O.
63. *Missus* **N** *Misus* **VF** *emonia* **A** *aemonia* **D** *Haemonii*
conj. Heinsius, Palm. Muel.

Senserat, hac ipsa cuspide sensit opem.
Hoc si quis vitium poterit mihi demere, solus   65
 Tantalea poterit tradere poma manu:
Dolia virgineis idem ille repleverit urnis,
 Ne tenera assidua colla graventur aqua:
Idem Caucasia solvet de rupe Promethei
 Brachia, et a medio pectore pellet avem.   70

71—78. *Only do thou, Mæcenas, thou glory of my life, my death,*
stay thy car beside my grave and say: ''Twas a maiden's
hard heart that slew him.'

Quandocumque igitur vitam mea fata reposcent,
 Et breve in exiguo marmore nomen ero,
Maecenas, nostrae spes invidiosa iuventae,
 Et vitae et morti gloria iusta meae,
Si te forte meo ducet via proxima busto,   75
 Esseda caelatis siste Britanna iugis,
Taliaque illacrimans mutae iace verba favillae:
 'Huic misero fatum dura puella fuit.'

II. 2.

5—8. *How fair her hair, her hands, her form! how stately*
her gait!

Fulva coma est, longaeque manus, et maxima toto   5
 Corpore, et incedit vel Iove digna soror,
Aut cum Dulichias Pallas spatiatur ad aras,
 Gorgonis anguiferae pectus operta comis.

---

66. *Tantelea* **N**   *Tantalea* **O** Per. Hertz.   *Tantaleae* Beroaldus,
Bae. Palm.   With *Tantalea, carpere* or *radere* have been conj.
67. *urnis* **O**   *umbris* conj. Bae.   71. *me* conj. Heinsius.   73.
spes **NO**   *pars* **GZ** Hertz. Paley.   75. *ducit* **DV**.
  6. *Corporeque incedit* **F**   *ceu Iove digna viro* Heinsius   *vel Iove*
dignus amor Lach.   7. *Aut cum* **O** Hertz.   *Ut cum* **Z** Bae.   *Dul-*
chias **V**[1]   *Munychias* **Z** Mueller.

II. 3.

1—8. *Alas, that I so late boasted I could love no more! my boast is vain.*

Qui nullam tibi dicebas iam posse nocere,
    Haesisti: cecidit spiritus ille tuus.
Vix unum potes, infelix, requiescere mensem,
    Et turpis de te iam liber alter erit.
Quaerebam, sicca si posset piscis harena   5
    Nec solitus ponto vivere torvus aper,
Aut ego si possem studiis vigilare severis:
    Differtur, numquam tollitur ullus amor.

9—26. *'Tis not her face only that enslaves me: her gifts of dance, of voice, of song, were granted to her at birth by the Gods.*

Nec me tam facies, quamvis sit candida, cepit—
    Lilia non domina sint magis alba mea: 10
Ut Maeotica nix minio si certet Hibero,
    Utque rosae puro lacte natant folia;—
Nec de more comae per levia colla fluentes,
    Non oculi, geminae, sidera nostra, faces;
Nec si qua Arabio lucet bombyce puella—   15
    Non sum de nihilo blandus amator ego,—
Quantum quod posito formose saltat Iaccho,
    Egit ut euantes dux Ariadna choros,
Et quantum, Aeolio cum temptat carmina plectro,
    Par Aganippeae ludere docta lyrae,   20
Et sua cum antiquae committit scripta Corinnae,
    Carmina quae quaevis non putat aequa suis.

---

1. *nullam* Heinsius, edd. *nullum* NO. 10. *sint* NF Hertz. Palm. *sunt* DV Per. Bae. 11. *Ut* NDV Hertz. *Et* F Bae. *certet* O *certat* Z Bae. 15. *si qua Arabio* O Hertz. Palm. *sic quom Arabio* conj. Bae. 17. *quod* O *quom* Lach. Bae. 18. *euhantes* NV² *euantes* DV *eufaues* F *coros* F. 19. *tentat* DV. 22. *quae quivis* NO Per.

Num tibi nascenti primis, mea vita, diebus
Candidus argutum sternuit omen Amor?
Haec tibi contulerunt caelestia munera divi, 25
Haec tibi ne matrem forte dedisse putes.

II. 10.

1–10. *'Tis time now my Muse were taking a wider and a
graver theme; I have sung my love: I must now sing
Cæsar, and Cæsar's deeds in arms.*

Sed tempus lustrare aliis Helicona choreis,
Et campum Haemonio iam dare tempus equo.
Iam libet et fortes memorare ad praelia turmas,
Et Romana mei dicere castra ducis.
Quod si deficiant vires, audacia certe 5
Laus erit: in magnis et voluisse sat est.
Aetas prima canat Veneres, extrema tumultus:
Bella canam, quando scripta puella mea est.
Nunc volo subducto gravior procedere vultu,
Nunc aliam citharam me mea Musa docet. 10

11–18. *Rise, then, my soul! and tell how East and West are
trembling before his touch.*

Surge, anima, ex humili; iam, carmina, sumite vires;
Pierides, magni nunc erit oris opus.

---

quae qüaevis conj. Palm. *quae quivis putet* Post. **G** has *Carmina quae lyrnes*: whence *Carminaque Erinnes* Volscus, Hertz.
Mueller. **23.** *Num* **F** Hertz. Bae. *Nunc* **DV** *Non* **N** Mueller
Nascenti et primis Lach. **24.** *Candidus* Macrobius, Bae. Mueller,
Palm. edd. *Ardidus* **NF** Hertz. *Aridus* **DV** *Arridus* Per.
augustae Macrobius. **25.** *tibi* om. by **N** *Haec haec* Palm.
contulerint **NF** Per. *contulerunt* **Z** *cum tulerint* **D.**
 1. *coreis* **F.** **2.** *hemonio* **NFG** *emonio* **DV** *Aonio* Heinsius, Bae. *Emathio* Muel. *Maeonio* has been conj. **10.** *Nunc*
NV Hertz. etc. *Nanque* **D** *Näque* **F** *Iamque* Bae. **11.** *carmina* **F** Lach. Palm. Bae. *carmine* **NDV** Hertz. Some punctuate
ex humili iam carmine; sumite vires, Pierides.

E

Iam negat Euphrates equitem post terga tueri
  Parthorum, et Crassos se tenuisse dolet:
India quin, Auguste, tuo dat colla triumpho,   15
  Et domus intactae te tremit Arabiae:
Et si qua extremis tellus se subtrahit oris,
  Sentiat illa tuas post modo capta manus.

19—26. *This be my task: and if my humble Muse may not deck Cæsar's brows, it may cast a chaplet before his feet.*

Haec ego castra sequar: vates tua castra canendo
  Magnus ero: servent hunc mihi fata diem!   20
Ut caput in magnis ubi non est tangere signis,
  Ponitur hic imos ante corona pedes,
Sic nos nunc, inopes laudis conscendere carmen,
  Pauperibus sacris vilia tura damus.
Nondum etiam Ascraeos norunt mea carmina
      fontes,   25
  Sed modo Permessi flumine lavit Amor.

II. 11.

1—6. *Let others sing of thee, Cynthia, or die unknown: so when thou shalt have lost all thy charms in death, no traveller shall stop to say 'Here lies a learned maid!'*

Scribant de te alii vel sis ignota licebit;
  Laudet, qui sterili semina ponit humo:

---

15. *quis* NO *quin* Z.   17. *horis* N.   22. *hic* DV *hac* NF.
23. *carmen* NO Hertz. etc.   *culmen* Z Heinsius, Bae.   *currum*
Markland.   24. *thura* O.   25. *etiam* NO *etenim* Bae. Mueller.
  II. 11. F joins this fragment to the previous poem: the other
MSS. give it as a separate poem.
  1. *vel* NDV   *ne* F Bae. Hous.   2. *Laudet* DV *Ludet* NFV².

Omnia, crede mihi, secum uno munera lecto
　　Auferet extremi funeris atra dies:
Et tua transibit contemnens ossa viator,　　　5
　　Nec dicet: ' Cinis hic docta puella fuit.'

II. 12.

1—8. *How wondrous clever was the painter who first drew*
Love as a giddy Boy, and endowed with wings !

Quicumque ille fuit, puerum qui pinxit Amorem,
　　Nonne putes miras hunc habuisse manus ?
Is primum vidit sine sensu vivere amantes,
　　Et levibus curis magna perire bona.
Idem non frustra ventosas addidit alas,　　　5
　　Fecit et humano corde volare deum;
Scilicet alterna quoniam iactamur in unda,
　　Nostraque non ullis permanet aura locis.

9—16. *Rightly too is he armed with a bow and with quiver:*
how swift and sure he strikes ! In my breast his shafts are
fast: he has lost his wings, and drains my life-blood dry.

Et merito hamatis manus est armata sagittis,
　　Et pharetra ex humero Gnosia utroque iacet; 10
Ante ferit quoniam, tuti quam cernimus hostem,
　　Nec quisquam ex illo vulnere sanus abit.

---

3. *secum* **Z** Hertz. etc. *tecum* **NO** Per. Bae.　　6. *cuius* **F.**
1. *primus* **F.**　　3. *Is* **NDV**　*Hic* **F.**　　6. *humana sorte* Heinsius　*immani corde* Burmann.　Bae. suggests *humano calce.*　　8.
Bae. conj. *umbra* for *aura.*　　10. *uterque* **N.**　　12. *abit* **NV**
erit **DF** Bae.

In me tela manent, manet et puerilis imago:
   Sed certe pennas perdidit ille suas,
Evolat heu! nostro quoniam de pectore nusquam, 15
   Assiduusque meo sanguine bella gerit.

17—24. *Oh! turn thy shafts elsewhere and slay me not: else who will sing the head, the hands, the eyes, the gait of Cynthia?*

Quid tibi iucundum est siccis habitare medullis?
   Si pudor est, alio traice tela tua.
Intactos isto satius temptare veneno:
   Non ego, sed tenuis vapulat umbra mea.   20
Quam si perdideris, quis erit qui talia cantet?
   (Haec mea Musa levis gloria magna tua est),
Qui caput et digitos et lumina nigra puellae
   Et canat ut soleant molliter ire pedes?

II. 13.

17—26. *When I die, Cynthia, let there be no pomp and parade at my funeral; no images, no trumpets, no perfumes, no splendidly adorned bier: enough if my poems be my procession.*

Quandocumque igitur nostros mors claudet ocellos,
   Accipe quae serves funeris acta mei.
Nec mea tunc longa spatietur imagine pompa,
   Nec tuba sit fati vana querella mei,   20

---

15. *l* (for *heu*) **N** *e* **O** *a!* Bae.   **18.** *Si puer est alio* **NO** *pudor* **V²** Bae. conj. *I, puer, en alio* *tela tua* or *bella tua* **Z** *puella tuo* **NO** *loco* **N²** *tela puer* **V²** Si puer est alio traijce *puella loco* Per.   **19.** *temptare* **N** *tentare* **DV**.   **24.** *canit* **V¹**.
   19. *Nec* **NO** *Ne* Burmann. Bae.   **20.** *querela* **NO**.

Nec mihi tunc fulcro sternatur lectus eburno,
  Nec sit in Attalico mors mea nixa toro;
Desit odoriferis ordo mihi lancibus; adsint
  Plebei parvae funeris exequiae.
Sat mea sat magna est si tres sint pompa libelli, 25
  Quos ego Persephonae maxima dona feram.

27—38. *But let thy loving care be there to give me one last kiss, to place a laurel-branch over my tomb, and to write on it the undying epitaph ' He lived a faithful lover.'*

Tu vero nudum pectus lacerata sequeris,
  Nec fueris nomen lassa vocare meum,
Osculaque in gelidis pones suprema labellis,
  Cum dabitur Syrio munere plenus onyx. 30
Deinde, ubi subpositus cinerem me fecerit ardor,
  Accipiat manes parvula testa meos,
Et sit in exiguo laurus superaddita busto,
  Quae tegat extincti funeris umbra locum.
Et duo sint versus : 'Qui nunc iacet horrida
    pulvis,   35
  Unius hic quondam servus amoris erat.'
Nec minus haec nostri notescet fama sepulcri,
  Quam fuerant Phthii busta cruenta viri.

39—42. *Long mayest thou live: but slight not thou my ashes— they will know the slight—and when thou diest, come to me.*

Tu quoque si quando venies ad fata, memento,
  Hoc iter ad lapides cana veni memores. 40

---

23. *at sint* conj. Heinsius. 24. *obsequiae* NF. 25. *mea sat* Z *mea sit* NO *mea sic* conj. Bae. *magna si* O *magna est si* Z. 27. *Tum* DV. 31. *subpositus* N *suppositus* O. 34. Bae. conj. *funebris.* 36. *Unus* N. 40. *Hoc iter* O *Hoc itere* Scaliger *Huc ferri ac lapides cana subire meos* Heinsius *Huc cura ad lapides, cara, vehi memores* Bae.

Interea cave sis nos aspernata sepultos:
Non nihil ad verum conscia terra sapit.

43—50. *Ah! why did I live beyond the cradle? Why live to tremble for death, or, like Nestor, to deem it late in coming?*

Atque utinam primis animam me ponere cunis
    Iussisset quaevis de tribus una soror!
Nam quo tam dubiae servetur spiritus horae?   45
    Nestoris est visus post tria saecla cinis.
Cui si tam longae minuisset fata senectae
    Gallicus Iliacis miles in aggeribus,
Non ille Antilochi vidisset corpus humari,
    Diceret aut: 'O mors, cur mihi sera venis?' 50

51—58. *Yet wilt thou weep for me, as Venus wept Adonis; and though all in vain, thou wilt call on my spirit for an answer.*

Tu tamen amisso non numquam flebis amico:
    Fas est praeteritos semper amare viros.
Testis, qui niveum quondam percussit Adonem
    Venantem Idalio vertice durus aper.
Illis formosum iacuisse paludibus, illuc   55
    Diceris effusa tu, Venus, isse coma.

---

45. *serventur* **F** *servatur* Ital.   **46.** *visus* **NF** *iussus* **DV** Bae. suggests *ustus* or *tostus*.   **47.** *Quis tam longaevae* **NO** *Cui tam longaevae* Hertz. Bae. conj. *Quoi stamen longae renuisset.* Another conj. is *Cui si tam longae. minuisset* **NF**ᵗ**V**² *meminisset* **DV** *iuravisset* **F** *meruisset* Per.   **48.** *Gallicus* **O** Per. Hertz. *Callidus, Bellicus* (adopted by Palm.), *Saucius, Troicus, Ilius, Caerulus* have all been conj.   **49.** *ille* is om. in **N.**   **50.** *aut* the MSS.: Bae. conj. *unde.*   **53.** *qui* **NO** *cui* Huschke, Hertz. *quoi* Bae.   *Adonem* **NO** *Adonim* **Z.**   **55.** *illic* **Z** Bae. *lavisse* **Z** Scaliger (from Per.) Palm. who states H. A. J. Munro approved *iacuisse* **NO** Hertz.   **56.** *esse* **F.**

Sed frustra mutos revocabis, Cynthia, manes:
Nam mea qui poterunt ossa minuta loqui?

II. 28.

1—8. *O! spare my fair one, Jupiter, struck down by the raging Dog-star, or perchance, it may be, for vows forsworn.*

Iuppiter, affectae tandem miserere puellae:
Tam formosa tuum mortua crimen erit.
Venit enim tempus, quo torridus aestuat aer,
Incipit et sicco fervere terra Cane.
Sed non tam ardoris culpa est neque crimina
caeli,   5
Quam totiens sanctos non habuisse deos.
Hoc perdit miseras, hoc perdidit ante puellas:
Quidquid iurarunt, ventus et unda rapit.

9—14. *Hast thou boasted thyself to Venus? hast thou scoffed at Juno or at Pallas? Ill words have aye been fair maiden's bane.*

Num sibi collatam doluit Venus? illa pcraeque
Prae se formosis invidiosa dea est.   10
An contempta tibi Iunonis templa Pelasgae,
Palladis aut oculos ausa negare bonos?
Semper, formosae, non nostis parcere verbis:
Hoc tibi lingua nocens, hoc tibi forma dedit.

---

58. *qui* N Palm. *quid* all other MSS. and edd.
8. *iurarem* N *iuratur* Per. 9. *Num* DF *Non* N *Nun*
others *illa* NO *ipsa* Z *peraeque* or *peraequae* N Hb. *parem-*
que FG *peraegre* Per. *ipsa paremque* Paley, Bae. Muel. *illa?*
peraeque old edd. and Palm. who quotes Cic. Att. 2. 19 *tam perae-*
que omnibus ordinibus offensa. See notes. 11. *At contenta* V².
12. *Pallidis* N.

15—24. *Yet will better days come to thee: as to Io and to Ino,*
to Andromeda and to Callisto.

> Sed tibi vexatae per multa pericula vitae   15
>   Extremo veniet mollior hora die.
> Io versa caput primos mugiverat annos:
>   Nunc dea, quae Nili flumina vacca bibit.
> Ino etiam prima terris aetate vagata est:
>   Hanc miser inplorat navita Leucothoen.   20
> Andromede monstris fuerat devota marinis:
>   Haec eadem Persei nobilis uxor erat.
> Callisto Arcadios erraverat ursa per agros:
>   Haec nocturna suo sidere vela regit.

25—34. *Bear thyself humbly, Cynthia, for even Doom may be*
turned; and if thou diest, thou shalt be first among all
maids of story.

> Quod si forte tibi properarint fata quietem,   25
>   Illa sepulturae fata beata tuae.
> Narrabis Semelae, quo sit formosa periclo:
>   Credet et illa, suo docta puella malo:
> Et tibi Maeonias omnis heroidas inter
>   Primus erit nulla non tribuente locus.   30
> Nunc, utcumque potes, fato gere saucia morem:
>   Et deus et durus vertitur ipse dies.
> Hoc tibi vel poterit coniunx ignoscere Iuno:
>   Frangitur et Iuno, si qua puella perit.

---

15. *vexata . . . vita* Z.   16. *veniet* V² *venit* NO *veniat* Z.
18. *vacha* F.   20. *inplorat* N *implorat* DV.   21. *devota*
NF²V² edd. *monstrata* O *sacrata* conj. Bae.   24. *sidera* F.
26. *Illa* NO *Ipsa* Z *Igne* conj. Bae. *fata* NO *facta* Z Bae. *Ipsa,*
sepulturae sorte beata tuae. Narrabis Lach.   29. *inter heroidas*
omnis NF *omnis herodias* (sic) *inter* DV; see Ov. Trist. 1. 6. 33.
G has *interque*: so Paley.   33. *poterit* N *poterat* O.

35—40. *Alas! every magic spell has failed: one dark boat is to carry off my love.*

Deficiunt magico torti sub carmine rhombi,   35
  Et iacet extincto laurus adusta foco,
Et iam Luna negat totiens descendere caelo,
  Nigraque funestum concinit omen avis.
Una ratis fati nostros portabit amores
  Caerula ad infernos velificata lacus.   40

41—46. *O spare us, Jupiter, and let us both pay glad vows to thee!*

Si non unius, quaeso, miserere duorum.
  Vivam, si vivet: si cadet illa, cadam.
Pro quibus optatis sacro me carmine damno:
  Scribam ego: 'per magnum salva puella
    Iovem,'
Ante tuosque pedes illa ipsa operata sedebit,   45
  Narrabitque sedens longa pericla sua.

47—56. *Long be this mercy thine, Pluto, and thine, Persephone! ye have so many fair ones in your realm: the fair of Troy and of Achaia, and, save this one only, all the fair of Rome.*

Haec tua, Persephone, maneat clementia, nec tu,
  Persephonae coniunx, saevior esse velis.

---

35. In **N** a new poem commences here. Bae. ends the poem at l. 46 and holds that ll. 1 and 2 belong to ll. 33–46, and that the passage so adjusted should precede ll. 3–32. **35.** *sub imagine* **F.** **36.** *iacet* **O** *tacet* Bae. **38.** *concinit* **V²** edd. *condidit* **NO**: Bae. cps. Ov. Am. 3. 12. 2. **40.** *lacus* **NO** *locos* conj. Bae. **43.** For *carmine* of the MSS. Palmer conj. *crimine*, as it would be absurd to call the words *per magnum . . . . Iovem* a votive poem. He supposes *sacro crimine damnatus* could be equivalent to *voti reus.* **44.** *est* is inserted after *magnum* in **O**, om. by **NZ.** **45.** *operta* **NO** *adoperta* **V²** *operata* Heinsius (to which *opata* of Hb. seems to point). ll. 47–62 are joined to the preceding poem in **NO**, Lach. Bae. Palm. Mueller snppose them to form a separate poem. **47.** *maneat* **NF** *moveat* **DV.**

Sunt apud infernos tot milia formosarum:
  Pulchra sit in superis, si licet, una locis.   50
Vobiscum est Iope, vobiscum candida Tyro,
  Vobiscum Europe, nec proba Pasiphae;
Et quot Troia tulit vetus et quot Achaia formas,
  Et Thebe et Priami diruta regna senis,
Et quaecumque erat in numero Romana puella, 55
  Occidit: has omnis ignis avarus habet.

57—60. *Further or nearer, Death comes to all: pay thou thy
vows, my dear one, to Diana!*

Nec forma aeternum aut cuiquam est fortuna
      perennis:
  Longius aut propius mors sua quemque manet.
Tu quoniam es, mea lux, magno dimissa periclo,
  Munera Dianae debita redde choros.   60

II. 31.

1—16. *Thou askest why I come so late? I have seen Cæsar's
glorious temple to Phœbus dedicated this day, with its statues
and marble columns, its sun-chariot and ivory gates, and
the Pythian God himself in minstrel's robe.*

Quaeris, cur veniam tibi tardior? aurea Phoebi
  Porticus a magno Caesare aperta fuit.

---

49. *aput* V¹ Bae. *millia* V².   **50.** *si licet* NV *scilicet* DV²F².
53. *Troia* NO   *Eoa* Hertz.   *Creta* Bae.; *Phthia, Iona, Sparta,
Thraca,* have been conjectured.   **54.** *phebi* N   *ph(o)ebi* O
Phoebei et muri Hertz. *Thebae* Scaliger. Palmer has *Thebe* and cps.
Ov. Am. 3. 12. 15.   **56.** *omnis* N   *omnes* DV.   Bae. says *ignis*
is indefensible: why? and suggests *Ditis* or *Orcus.*   **57.** *perennis*
DV *peremnis* F *perhennis* N.   **59.** *dimissa* Z *demissa* NO.

Tanta erat in speciem Poenis digesta columnis,
    Inter quas Danai femina turba senis.
Hic equidem Phoebo visus mihi pulchrior ipso   5
    Marmoreus tacita carmen hiare lyra,
Atque aram circum steterant armenta Myronis
    Quattuor artificis, vivida signa, boves.
Tum medium claro surgebat marmore templum,
    Et patria Phoebo carius Ortygia,   10
In quo Solis erat supra fastigia currus,
    Et valvae, Libyci nobile dentis opus,
Altera deiectos Parnasi vertice Gallos,
    Altera maerebat funera Tantalidos.
Deinde inter matrem deus ipse interque sororem 15
    Pythius in longa carmina veste sonat.

---

3. *Tanta* **NO** *Tota* Per. **Z** Hertz. edd. *Quanta* Bae.   **5.** Hertz.
and others place ll. 5–8 after l. 16. *equidem.* So the MSS. Palm.
conj. *Phoebus Phoebo.* See notes.   7. *steterant* **NDV** *steterunt* **F**
Bae. *steterantque* **F²**.   8. *Quatuor* **O** *artificis* **O** *artifices* edd.
10. *carius* **NFV²** edd. *clarior* **DV**.   11. *Et quo* **NO** *In quo* or
Auro **Z** *aurea* Per. *aequos* Bae. which he explains 'i.e. itidem
marmoreus.' *Et duo . . . erant* Hertz. See Ov. Pont. 4. 6. 48.
16. *Pithius* **N**.

PROPERTIUS, III. 1.

1—6. *Shades of Callimachus and Philetas! 'Tis I first that bring your rites to Italy: tell me, whence came your wondrous art?*

CALLIMACHI Manes et Coi sacra Philetae,
    In vestrum, quaeso, me sinite ire nemus.
Primus ego ingredior puro de fonte sacerdos
    Itala per Graios orgia ferre choros.
Dicite, quo pariter carmen tenuastis in antro?   5
    Quove pede ingressi? quamve bibistis aquam?

7—14. *Farewell to arms! My Muse has triumphed with the fine and finished songs of love: all poets swell my train.*

Ah valeat, Phoebum quicumque moratur in armis!
    Exactus tenui pumice versus eat;
Quo me Fama levat terra sublimis, et a me
    Nata coronatis Musa triumphat equis,   10
Et mecum in curru parvi vectantur Amores,
    Scriptorumque meas turba secuta rotas.
Quid frustra missis in me certatis habenis?
    Non datur ad Musas currere lata via.

---

1. *coi* NV² *choi* O   For *sacra* Bae. conj. *fata* (= umbra).   4. *coros* F.   5. *tenuastis* NF² *tenuistis* O.   7. *Ha* F. 10. *nota* Z.   11. *currum* N.   13. *missis* MSS. *inmissis* Auratus *admissis* Palm.

15—20. *Others will sing of Rome and her greatness: be mine the poet's tender chaplet, not the stern crown of War.*

> Multi, Roma, tuas laudes annalibus addent,   15
>   Qui finem imperii Bactra futura canent:
> Sed, quod pace legas, opus hoc de monte Sororum
>   Detulit intacta pagina nostra via. .
> Mollia, Pegasides, date vestro serta poetae:
>   Non faciet capiti dura corona meo.   20

21—24. *Envy may carp at me now: but my fame will grow all the greater after death.*

> At mihi quod vivo detraxerit invida turba,
>   Post obitum duplici fenore reddet Honos.
> Omnia post obitum fingit maiora vetustas:
>   Maius ab exequiis nomen in ora venit.

25—32. *Who would know of Troy and all her woes if she had had no singer?*

> Nam quis equo pulsas abiegno nosceret arces,   25
>   Fluminaque Haemonio cominus isse viro,
> Idaeum Simoenta Iovis cunabula parvi
>   Hectora per campos ter maculasse rotas?

---

16. *canant* Z.   **17.** *de fonte* Z.   **19.** *nostro* F   *vestro date* V² Hertz.   **21.** *detraxit* F   *detraxerat* V².   **22.** *duplicei* N   *reddet* F²V²   *reddit* NO   *Ut mihi . . . reddat* Markland   *honos* Z   *onus* NO.   **23.** *Omnia* NO   *Fame . . . vetustae* N.   **24.** *hora* F.   **25.** *ab regno* V   *artes* NO.   **26.** *isse viro* V   *esse viro* ND   *ille raro* F.   **27.** *Idaeum Simoenta* N   *iovis cunabula parvi* O   N has *iovis* with the rest of the line omitted Bae. follows the conj. of G. Wolff, *Iovis cum prole Scamandro* Palm. conj. *Idaeos montes Iovis incunabula parvi*, remarking that *Simoenta* has been introduced because of *flumina* in l. 26, and quoting Virg. Aen. 3. 105, Cic. Att. 2. 41. See notes.   **28.** For *per* Fruter conj. *ter*: so Lach.

Deiphobumque Helenumque et Pulydamantas in
armis?
Qualemcumque Parin vix sua nosset humus. 30
Exiguo sermone fores nunc Ilion, et tu
Troia bis Oetaei numine capta dei.

33—40. *And as Homer's fame grew ever greater as time went
on, so too shall mine.*

Nec non ille tui casus memorator Homerus
Posteritate suum crescere sensit opus ;
Meque inter seros laudabit Roma nepotes :   35
Illum post cineres auguror ipse diem.
Ne mea contempto lapis indicet ossa sepulcro
Provisum est Lycio vota probante deo ;
Carminis interea nostri redeamus in orbem,
Gaudeat ut solito tacta puella sono.   40

III. 2.

1—8. *If Orpheus, Amphion, and Polyphemus wrought marvels
with their song, is it strange that maidens should be moved
by words of mine?*

Orphea delinisse feras et concita dicunt
Flumina Threicia sustinuisse lyra :
Saxa Cithaeronis Thebas agitata per artem
Sponte sua in muri membra coisse ferunt :

---

29. So Hertz. Paley, Palm. *poliledamantes in armis* N *puli leda-
mantes* F *Polydamanta sub armis* Z *Polydamanta et in armis*
Bae. Mueller. **30.** *pari* N *parim* O *noscet* DV. **33.** *memo-
ratur* N. **35.** *Me quoque per seros* conj. Bae. **36.** *auguror ipse
deae* N. **37.** *lapsis* N. **39.** The MSS. begin the 2nd Poem
here. See notes. **40.** *ut* V²Z Hertz. Palm. *insolito* N *in
solito* DHG Hertz. Bae.

1. *delinisse* conj. Ayrmann *detinuisse* NV² Hertz. *detenuisse*
FV¹ Per. (and l. 2) *te tenuisse* D *delenisse* Bae. Mueller. **2.** *sustinuisse* NF edd. *detinuisse* DV. **4.** *in muri* DV *innumeri* N.

Quin etiam, Polypheme, fera Galatea sub Aetna 5
    Ad tua rorantes carmina flexit equos :
Miremur, nobis et Baccho et Apolline dextro,
    Turba puellarum si mea verba colit ?

9—16. *Though no gorgeous house, no fruitful lands are mine, yet is the Muse my comrade and my friend.*

Quod non Taenariis domus est mihi fulta columnis,
    Nec camera auratas inter eburna trabes,   10
Nec mea Phaeacas aequant pomaria silvas,
    Non operosa rigat Marcius antra liquor :
At musae comites, et carmina cara legenti,
    Nec defessa choris Calliopea meis.
Fortunata, meo si qua est celebrata libello !   15
    Carmina erunt formae tot monumenta tuae.

17—24. *Happy she whose fame I sing! more stable than Pyramid, or monument of Mausolus, my name will know no death.*

Nam neque pyramidum sumptus ad sidera ducti,
    Nec Iovis Elei caelum imitata domus,
Nec Mausolei dives fortuna sepulcri
    Mortis ab extrema condicione vacant.   20
Aut illis flamma aut imber subducet honores,
    Annorum aut ictu pondere victa ruent.
At non ingenio quaesitum nomen ab aevo
    Excidet : ingenio stat sine morte decus.

---

5. *fera* MSS. edd.   11. *pheacias* **ND**   *feacias* **F.**   12. *ante* **N.**   13. *comitis* **NDV** *comiti* **F** *comites* **FV²**.   14. *Nec* conj. Bae. Palm. *Et* O Hertz., omitted by **N.**   21. *subducit* **N** *subducet* Hertz. edd.   22. *ictu* **NF** *ictus* **DV** *ipso* Bae. *pondere* **NDV** *pondera* **F** Palm., following Burmann, reads *Annorum aut ictu, pondere victa, ruent.*

III. 3.

1—12. Methought I lay on Helicon, and sang of Alba and the Horatii, of Æmilius and Fabius, of Cannæ's fatal field, of the Capitol saved from the Gallic host.

Visus eram molli recubans Heliconis in umbra,
 Bellerophontei qua fluit humor equi,
Reges, Alba, tuos et regum facta tuorum,
 Tantum operis, nervis hiscere posse meis;
Parvaque tam magnis admoram fontibus ora,   5
 Unde pater sitiens Ennius ante bibit,
Et cecini Curios fratres et Horatia pila,
 Regiaque Aemilia vecta tropaea rate,
Victricesque moras Fabii pugnamque sinistram
 Cannensem et versos ad pia vota deos,   10
Hannibalemque Lares Romana sede fugantes,
 Anseris et tutum voce fuisse Iovem:

13—24. But Apollo chid me and said: ' Not thine to sing of heroes in heroic strain, but only soft lays of love: leave not the course prescribed for thee.'

Cum me Castalia speculans ex arbore Phoebus
 Sic ait, aurata nixus ad antra lyra: .
'Quid tibi cum tali, demens, est flumine? quis te 15
 Carminis heroi tangere iussit opus?
Non hic ulla tibi speranda est fama, Properti:
 Mollia sunt parvis prata terenda rotis,
Ut tuus in scamno iactetur saepe libellus,
 Quem legat expectans sola puella virum.   20

---

5. Mueller conj. *Pronaque   tam* O   *iam* Heinsius, Bae.   6.
sciens N   *ibit* N.   7. *cecinit* MSS. Hertz. Bae.   *cecini* old edd.
11. *lares* F   *lacies* N.

Cur tua praescriptos evecta est pagina gyros?
    Non est ingenii cymba gravanda tui.
Alter remus aquas, alter tibi radat arenas:
    Tutus eris: medio maxima turba mari est.'

25—36. *With that he led me to a green mossy cave, where were
the Muses and all signs of their art: each busied with her
proper task.*

Dixerat, et plectro sedem mihi monstrat eburno,   25
    Quo nova muscoso semita facta solo est.
Hic erat adfixis viridis spelunca lapillis,
    Pendebantque cavis tympana pumicibus.
Ergo Musarum et Sileni patris imago
    Fictilis, et calami, Pan Tegeaee, tui;   30
Et Veneris dominae volucres, mea turba, columbae
    Tingunt Gorgoneo punica rostra lacu,
Diversaeque novem sortitae iura puellae
    Exercent teneras in sua dona manus.
Haec hederas legit in thyrsos, haec carmina nervis 35
    Aptat, at illa manu texit utraque rosam.

37—50. *Then spake Calliope: 'Not thine to sing of steed or
trump of war, of German or of Gallic rout, but of lovers,
revels, and serenades.'*

E quarum numero me contigit una dearum;
    Ut reor a facie, Calliopea fuit:

---

21. *perscripto* N   *praescriptos evecta gyros* Scal. etc.   *sevecta* N
Per. Hertz. Bae.   Palm. now gives up the *devecta* of his edd. 1880.
23. *harenas* N.   **26.** *Quo* N   *Qua* Per. Hertz. Bae. etc.   **29.**
Ergo O   *Plectraque* or *Orgia* Heinsius   *Organa* Bae. *musarum* O
Bae. conj. *Nysaei (Nusaei)*   Unger conj. *mystarum.*   **32.**
pumica N   *rostra* F²V   *nostra* NDF.   **33.** *Divorsaeque* DV
Diverseque NF Bae.   *Diversaeque* edd.   *iura* Scaliger Palm. *rura*
the MSS and edd.   **35.** *ederas* V.   **36.** *apta* N *et* F; the rest *at.*

' Contentus niveis semper vectabere cycnis,
　　Nec te fortis equi ducet ad arma sonus.　　40
Nil tibi sit rauco praeconia classica cornu
　　Flare, nec Aonium tinguere Marte nemus ;
Aut quibus in campis Mariano praelia signo
　　Stent, et Teutonicas Roma refringat opes,
Barbarus aut Suevo perfusus sanguine Rhenus　45
　　Saucia maerenti corpora vectet aqua.
Quippe coronatos alienum ad limen amantes
　　Nocturnaeque canes ebria signa fugae,
Ut per te clausas sciat excantare puellas,
　　Qui volet austeros arte ferire viros.'　　50

51–52. *And with that she touched my lips with water from Philetas' spring.*

Talia Calliope, lymphisque a fonte petitis
　　Ora Philetaea nostra rigavit aqua.

III. 4.

1–6. *Cæsar is going forth to the East : the Tigris and Euphrates are to pass under his sway.*

Arma Deus Caesar dites meditatur ad Indos,
　　Et freta gemmiferi findere classe maris.
Magna, viri, merces ; parat ultima terra triumphos ;
　　Tigris et Euphrates sub tua iura fluent.

---

41. *praeconia* N　*praeconica* O　Bae. suggests *praeconis.*　42.
Flere the MSS. Palm. cps. 1. 9. 10, remarking that Prop. uses *flere*
of singing a doleful song, as *lacrimae* in 1. 3. 46, 1. 6. 24, 4. 1. 120
Flare Fruter, Hertz. Pal.　Cp. Mart. 11. 3. 8　*tinguere* N　*tingere*
DF　*cingere* V.　45. *scevo* N　*saevo* DV　*Suevo* edd.
1. Palm. suggests *meus* for *Deus.*　4. *nova* conj. Bae.　Ilous.
conj. *Thybris, ...fluet :* see J. of Phil. xxi. p. 119.

Sera, sed Ausoniis veniet provincia virgis.:   5
  Adsuescent Latio Partha tropaea Iovi.

7—10. *Forth with you, men, ships, and steeds! Avenge the Crassi, write a new page of History for Rome!*

Ite agite, expertae bello date lintea prorae,
  Et solitum armigeri ducite munus equi.
Omina fausta cano: Crassos clademque piate:
  Ite et Romanae consulite historiae.   10

11—22. *And may I live to see the day of Cæsar's Triumph, and swell the plaudits on the Sacred Way!*

Mars pater et sacrae fatalia lumina Vestae,
  Ante meos obitus sit, precor, illa dies,
Qua videam spoliis oneratos Caesaris axes,
  Ad vulgi plausus saepe resistere equos;
Inque sinu carae nixus spectare puellae   15
  Incipiam, et titulis oppida capta legam,
Tela fugacis equi, et braccati militis arcus,
  Et subter captos arma sedere duces.
Ipsa tuam serva prolem, Venus: hoc sit in aevum,
  Cernis ab Aenea quod superesse caput.   20
Praeda sit haec illis, quorum meruere labores:
  Mi sat erit Sacra plaudere posse Via.

---

5. *Sera sed* NO   *Seres et* conj. Gulielmius, Bae.   *venient* Heinsius, Bae.   6. *Adsuescent* N edd.   *Assuescent* O   *Adcrescent* Bae. *parta* N Per.   8. *equi* NO   Bae. conj. *equos* and writes *Armigeri*. 11. Some MSS. have *numina*.   13. *onerato axe* Muretus   *oneratos axes* MSS. Hertz. Bae.   15. Bae. thinks *nixus* corrupt, as *spectare* needs an object, and suggests *exuvias*. He is quite wrong. *Spectare* is regularly used without object, as Ov. A. A. 5. 99; Quint. 6. 3; Plaut. Poen. Prol. 32.   *Vinctos, nexos* have been conj.   22. *Me* NO Per. edd.   *Mi* Z Palm.   *Sacra* NV   *media* DF.

F 2

III. 5.

1—6. *My God is Love, a God of Peace : I care not for gold,*
nor gems, nor acres wide.

Pacis Amor deus est, pacem veneramur amantes :
    Stant mihi cum domina praelia dura mea.
Nec tamen inviso pectus mihi carpitur auro,
    Nec bibit e gemma divite nostra sitis ;
Nec mihi mille iugis Campania pinguis aratur,   5
    Nec miser aera paro clade, Corinthe, tua.

7—12. *Ill-starred Prometheus ! how little deftly didst thou mix*
thy clay ! how crooked, how unstable, how prone to war, didst
thou make the souls of men !

O prima infelix fingenti terra Prometheo !
    Ille parum caute pectoris egit opus.
Corpora disponens mentem non vidit in arte :
    Recta animi primum debuit esse via.   10
Nunc maris in tantum vento iactamur, et hostem
    Quaerimus, atque armis nectimus arma nova.

13—18. *Yet shall we carry nought to Acheron : rich and poor,*
captive and captor, will be mingled in the shades together.

Haud ullas portabis opes Acherontis ad undas,
    Nudus at inferna, stulte, vehere rate.

---

2. *Stant* the MSS. Hertz. Muller   *Sat* from Livineius, Bae.
3. *tamen* NO   *tantum* Lach.   *tale* Bae. (scil. ' ut bella cupiam ').
4. *gemina* N.   6. *miser* O   *mixta* Bae. *aere* N   *ire* O.   7.
frangenti N.   8. *caute* NO   *cauti* Z Hertz. Palcy, Mueller.
13. *Haut* N   *Haud* O.   14. *ad infernas . . . rates* NO   *ab*
inferna rate Per. Z   *at inferna rate* Schraeder, Hertz. Bae.   *ad*
infernos conj. Palm. who also suggests *in inferna rate.*

Victor cum victis pariter miscebitur umbris :   15
  Consule cum Mario, capte Iugurtha, sedes.
Lydus Dulichio non distat Croesus ab Iro ;
  Optima mors, acta quae venit apta die.

19—22. *Be it mine, while youth shall last, to court the Muses
and the wine-cup;*

Me iuvat in prima coluisse Helicona iuventa,
  Musarumque choris inplicuisse manus :   20
Me iuvat et multo mentem vincire Lyaeo,
  Et caput in verna semper habere rosa.

23—46. *In age, to search out Nature, and to scan the ways of
Moon and Storm, of Earthquake, Star, and Sea: what
comes after Death, or whether there be an After.*

Atque ubi iam Venerem gravis interceperit aetas,
  Sparserit et nigras alba senecta comas,
Tum mihi naturae libeat perdiscere mores :   25
  Quis deus hanc mundi temperet arte domum ;
Qua venit exoriens, qua deficit, unde coactis
  Cornibus in plenum menstrua luna redit ;
Unde salo superant venti, quid flamine captet
  Eurus, et in nubes unde perennis aqua ;   30
Sit ventura dies, mundi quae subruat arces ;
  Purpureus pluvias cur bibit arcus aquas ;

---

15. *miscebimur* Z   Palm. suggests *Victor cum victis pariter
miscebimur umbrae* Lach. reads *Indis* for *umbris.*   18. *parca* NO
(*parta* F¹) Hertz. Palm.   *tarda* Guy *propera* Heinsius *carpta* Bae.
Parcae conj. Lach. I read *acta*, believing the *acta* of N has got out
of place.   *apta* O Bae.   *acta* N Muel. Palm.   See note on
whole line.   20. *coris* F.   21. *iuvat* DV *iuvet* NF *vincire* O
fulcire Bae.   24. *Sparserit et integras* N *Sparserit et nigras* Z
Sparserit integras DV Per.   *Sparsit et integras* F.   30. *perennis*
DV Hertz. etc.   *perhennis* N *perhemnis* F *peremnis* Per. Bae.
Palm. conj. *perennet.*   31. *arces* NV² Palm. etc.   *arcem* O Bae.

Aut cur Perrhaebi tremuere cacumina Pindi,
    Solis et atratis luxerit orbis . equis ;
Cur serus versare boves et plaustra Bootes,   35
    Pleiadum spisso cur coit igne chorus ;
Curve suos fines altum non exeat aequor,
    Plenus et in partes quattuor annus eat ;
Sub terris sint iura deum et tormenta nocentum,
    Tisiphones atro si furit angue caput ;   40
Aut Alcmaeoniae furiae aut ieiunia Phinei,
    Num rota, num scopuli, num sitis inter aquas ;
Num tribus infernum custodit faucibus antrum
    Cerberus, et Tityo iugera pauca novem ;
An ficta in miseras descendit fabula gentes,   45
    Et timor haud ultra quam rogus esse potest.

47—48. *But do ye, that love arms, bring back the standards of Crassus !*

Exitus hic vitae superet mihi : vos, quibus arma
    Grata magis, Crassi signa referte domum.

III. 7.

1—4. *Ah ! Gold, what havoc dost thou work in the heart and life of man !*

Ergo sollicitae tu causa, pecunia, vitae es !
    Per te immaturum mortis adimus iter.

---

34. *atratis* N edd.   *attractis* O   *actractis* Per.   *auratis* F².
35. *seros* N   Palm. approves *segnis* of Per. comparing Iuv. 5. 23.
36. *choit* F   *imbre* Heinsius.   39. *gigantum* FV Per.   N has a blank : Palm. adopts Haupt's conj. *nocentum*.   42, 43. N has *Non* for *Num*.   44. *pauca* NO   Bae. conj. *operta*   Palm. now prefers *pressa*, see n.   46. *haut* N   *aut* O.   47. *superest* O.
III. 7. The parts of this poem have been variously transposed. See Bae. Palm. thinks with him that ll. 21, 22 should be placed after 38. R. Ellis is doubtless right in holding 23, 24 to be spurious. 1. *es* DVF² edd. : omitted by NF.

Tu vitiis hominum crudelia pabula praebes :
Semina curarum de capite orta tuo.

5—12. '*Tis thou hast whelmed Pætus in the deep! Far off he lies, so young, where no mother can tend his remains, with the wide Carpathian for a tomb!*

Tu Paetum ad Pharios tendentem lintea portus　5
　　Obruis insano terque quaterque mari.
Nam dum te sequitur, primo miser excidit aevo,
　　Et nova longinquis piscibus esca natat ;
Et mater non iusta piae dare debita terrae,
　　Nec pote cognatos inter humare rogos,　　　10
Sed tua nunc volucres astant super ossa marinae,
　　Nunc tibi pro tumulo Carpathium omne mare est.

13—18. *What spoils hadst thou here to gain, cruel Aquilo? O Neptune, why wreck the innocent? These waters have no Gods to hear thee, Pætus.*

Infelix Aquilo, raptae timor Orithyiae,
　　Quae spolia ex illo tanta fuere tibi?
Aut quidnam fracta gaudes, Neptune, carina?　15
　　Portabat sanctos alveus ille viros.
Paete, quid aetatem numeras? quid cara natanti
　　Mater in ore tibi est? non habet unda deos.

19—24. *In the dark storm the cable parted and thou wast lost: even so was lost Argynnus, dear to Agamemnon.*

Nam tibi nocturnis ad saxa ligata procellis
　　Omnia detrito vincula fune cadunt.　　　20

---

5. *petum* **FN** *poetum* **VD**, throughout.　　11. *astant* **N**.
18. *tibi in ore est* **N**　*non pavet unda deos* Burmann.

Sunt Agamemnonias testantia litora curas,
    Qua natat Argynnus poena minantis aquae.
[Hoc iuvene amisso classem non solvit Atrides,
    Pro qua mactata est Iphigenia mora.]

25—28. *O Waves, give up his body! be his sepulchre a warning to the brave!*

Reddite corpus humo, posita est in gurgite vita: 25
    Paetum sponte tua, vilis arena, tegas;
Et quotiens Paeti transibit nauta sepulcrum,
    Dicat: ' Et audaci tu timor esse potes.'

29—36. *Out upon you. ye that build ships! ye do but open up new paths of death, and labour for the winds!*

Ite, rates curvas et leti texite causas:
    Ista per humanas mors venit acta manus.   30
Terra parum fuerat: fatis adiecimus undas:
    Fortunae miseras auximus arte vias.
Ancora te teneat, quem non tenuere Penates?
    Quid meritum dicas, cui sua terra parum est?
Ventorum est, quodcumque paras: haud ulla carina   35
    Consenuit, fallit portus et ipse fidem.

---

22. *Qua* N   *Quae* V Per. Hertz. Palm.   *notat* NO   *natat* F[2]
nota Z   *Agynni* N   *argynni* V[2]   *arginni* F   *argivum* DV
argynnus conj. Waardenb. (see Bae.)   *poena minantis aquae* NO
natantis aquae V[2] Per.   *poena minacis aquae* Lach[1].   *Athamantiadae*
Hertz. Muel.   *poenam inhiantis aquae* Bae.   *poena Mimantis aquae*
(or *aquas*) R. Ellis. I have ventured on the reading of the text.
See explanatory note.   23. *Hoc* NVF[2]   *Nec* O   *Hic* Lach.   25.
posita est N   *positaque* O Hertz.   *positumque in gurgitis ora* Bae.
positumque in gurgite, venti Lach[1].   26. Most MSS. have *harena*.
29. *Ire* N   *curvas* Passerat.   *curvae* NO   *curvae leti contexite* Per.
curvate W.T. Lendrum   *terite* N.   35. *haud* O   *haut* N.

37—42. *The sea is but nature's snare for greed : witness Ulysses
and the Argive host.*

Natura insidians pontum substravit avaris :
    Ut tibi succedat vix semel esse potest.
Saxa triumphales fregere Capharea puppes,
    Naufraga cum vasto Graecia tracta salo est : 40
Paullatim socium iacturam flevit Ulixes,
    In mare cui solum non valuere doli.

43—50. *Had Pætus heeded me, he had been living now ; poor,
but honoured, in his own home, with no storm to vex him,
and all comfort round him.*

Quod si contentus patrios bove verteret agros,
    Verbaque duxisset pondus habere mea,
Viveret ante suos dulcis conviva Penates,   45
    Pauper, at in terra, nil ubi flare potest.
Non tulit hic Paetus stridorem audire procellae,
    Et duro teneras laedere fune manus,
Sed Thyio thalamo aut Oricia terebintho
    Effultum pluma versicolore caput.   50

51—54. *But now he lies engulfed in water, a mangled corpse.*

Huic fluctus vivo radicitus abstulit ungues,
    Et miser invisam traxit hiatus aquam ;

---

37. *insidians* N Palm. Bae. etc. *insidias* Z Hertz.   41. *Paula-
tim* O *Palantum* Heinsius, Bae.   42. *soli* NO *soliti* Lipsius,
Hertz. *solum* Z.   43. *O si* Lach. *contentos* DF *patrio* the
MSS. *patrios* Heinsius.   46. *ubi* N *nisi* O *flare* Heinsius (?)
flere NO Per. See Palmer's n. *nil nisi fleret opes* Bae. *flere sat est*
Post.   47. *hic* Z *hoc* F *hunc* DV *haec* N.   49. *chio* the
MSS. *thyio* Hertz.   50. Most MSS. have *Et fultum ; Effultum*
Hertz. Palm. suggests *Est fultum.*   51. Perhaps *vivos* should be
read.   52. *miser* NO *invisam* NF²V² *invitam* Per. *miseri* Palm.

Hunc parvo ferri vidit nox improba ligno :
Paetus ut occideret, tot coiere mala.

55—66. *With his last breath he prayed: ' O ye Gods of the
Ægean, why do ye snatch from me my young life so rudely ?
O waft my body to my native shore, and to my mother's
care !'*

Flens tamen extremis dedit haec mandata que-
      rellis,   55
  Cum moribunda niger clauderet ora liquor :
' Di maris Aegaei quos sunt penes aequora, Venti,
  Et quaecumque meum degravat unda caput,
Quo rapitis miseros primae lanuginis annos ?
  Attulimus longas in freta vestra manus.   60
Ah miser alcyonum scopulis adfligar acutis :
  In me caeruleo fuscina sumpta deo est.
At saltem Italiae regionibus evehat aestus :
  Hoc de me sat erit si modo matris erit.'
Subtrahit haec fantem torta vertigine fluctus : 65
  Ultima quae Paeto voxque diesque fuit.

67—72. *O hundred daughters of Nereus ! O Thetis with thy
mother's heart ! why did ye not put out a hand to save ?
Never shalt thou see sail of mine, cruel Aquilo !*

O centum aequoreae Nereo genitore puellae,
  Et tu materno tacta dolore Thetis,
Vos decuit lasso subponere brachia mento : .
  Non poterat vestras ille gravare manus.   70

---

55. *querelis* O.   **57.** *Di* N *Dii* O.   **60.** *longas* the MSS.
castas, puras, lotas, sanctas have been conj. But Palm. remarks that
length is characteristic of a youth's hands. **63.** *advehat* Per. **66.**
voxque N *noxque* O Per. **68.** *tacta* V[2] *tracta* O *fracta* Heinsius.

At tu, saeve Aquilo, numquam mea vela videbis:
Ante fores dominae condar oportet iners.

III. 11.

1—8. *What marvel that a woman sways my life? Hear thou from me, who know, of woman's power.*

Quid mirare, meam si versat femina vitam,
    Et trahit addictum sub sua iura virum,
Criminaque ignavi capitis mihi turpia fingis,
    Quod nequeam fracto rumpere vincla iugo?
Venturam melius praesagit navita mortem,   5
    Vulneribus didicit miles habere metum.
Ista ego praeterita iactavi verba iuventa:
    Tu nunc exemplo disce timere meo.

9—28. *Who knows not of the marvels wrought by Medea? of the valour and loveliness of Penthesilea? how Omphale tamed the tamer? how Semiramis built Babylon, took Bactra, and turned the Euphrates? how Jupiter himself has fallen before woman?*

Colchis flagrantis adamantina sub iuga tauros
    Egit, et armigera praelia sevit humo,   10
Custodisque feros clausit serpentis hiatus,
    Iret ut Aesonias aurea lana domos.
Ausa ferox ab equo quondam obpugnare sagittis
    Maeotis Danaum Penthesilea rates;

---

5. *Venturam* the MSS. Palm. adopts the conj. *Iactura   mortem*
NO *noctem* **F** etc. Lach. Hertz. *molem* R. Ellis.   9. *flagrantis*
(acc.) so **N**. The Ald. and some MSS. have *flagranteis*.   10.
saevit **D**.   13. *obpugnare* **N** *oppugnare* **O** Per.   14. *Meotis*
NF² Hertz. *iniectis* **O** Per. Bae.

Aurea cui postquam nudavit cassida frontem,   15
   Vicit victorem candida forma virum.
Omphale in tantum formae processit honorem,
   Lydia Gygaeo tincta puella lacu,
Ut, qui pacato statuisset in orbe columnas,
   Tam dura traheret mollia pensa manu.   20
Persarum statuit Babylona Semiramis urbem,
   Ut solidum cocto tolleret aggere opus,
Et duo in adversum missi per moenia currus
   Ne possent tacto stringere ab axe latus;
Duxit et Euphratem medium, qua condidit arces,   25
   Iussit et imperio surgere Bactra caput.
Nam quid ego heroas, quid raptem in crimine
      divos?
   Iuppiter infamat seque suamque domum.

29—38. *And what of her, our shame, that late asked for our
City and our Senate as a lover's present, and from the shore
where Pompey fell, stamped eternal infamy on Rome?*

Quid, modo quae nostris opprobria vexerit armis,
   Et famulos inter femina trita suos?   30
Coniugii obscaeni pretium Romana poposcit
   Moenia, et addictos in sua regna patres.

---

15. *cui* NF²V² *qui* O *quoi* Bae.   17. *Omphale* NV Per.
Hertz *Omphaliae* D   Palm. conj. *Iardanis* (Omphale was dau.
of Iardanus) believing *Omphale* to be a gloss, and cps. Ov. Her.
9. 103, pointing out that Prop. was fond of female patronymics,
as *Iasis, Tyndaris, Tantalis, Minois, Inachis,* etc. He further
remarks that such an *hiatus* as Ŏmphălē in is unexampled in
Prop. and that the scribe of N probably pronounced *Omphāle* : q. v.
see notes.   23. *dño* (= *domino*) N   *missi* N Hertz.   *misit* Z
immissi Dousa   Palm adopts Tyrrell's attractive conj. *mitti.*   24.
Nec NF Palm.   *Ne* the rest.   25. *qua* NF² *quam* O Bae.
arcis Bae.   27. *crimine* NO *crimina* V² Bae.   29. *obprobria* N
vexerit N   *vexerat* Z Hertz. Bae.   31. *coniugis* NO Hertz.
coniugii Passerat, Bae. Palm. etc.

· Noxia Alexandria, dolis aptissima tellus,
　Et totiens nostro, Memphi, cruenta malo,
Tres ubi Pompeio detraxit arena triumphos!　　35
　Tollet nulla dies hanc tibi, Roma, notam.
Issent Phlegraeo melius tibi funera campo,
　Vel tua si socero colla daturus eras.

39—46. *For she, forsooth, she—the foul Queen of Egypt—would fain have set up Anubis against Juppiter, have silenced the Roman trumpet with the rattle, have paraded her luxury, and dealt forth her laws, among the arms of Marius!*

Scilicet incesti meretrix regina Canopi,
　Una Philippeo sanguine adusta nota,　　40
Ausa Iovi nostro latrantem opponere Anubim,
　Et Tiberim Nili cogere ferre minas,
Romanamque tubam crepitanti pellere sistro,
　Baridos et contis rostra Liburna sequi,
Foedaque Tarpeio conopia tendere saxo,　　45
　Iura dare et statuas inter et arma Mari!

47—58. *Why was Tarquin driven forth, if a woman was to rule? Give Augustus all thy thanks, Rome, that she that had scared our city was hunted to the Nile, enchained, and done to death.*

Quid nunc Tarquinii fractas iuvat esse secures,
　Nomine quem simili vita superba notat,
Si mulier patienda fuit? Cape, Roma, triumphum,
　Et longum Augusto salva precare diem.　　50

---

35. *arena* **FV²**　*harena* **N** (as generally).　　**45.** *canopeia* **NO** *canopia* **V²**.　　**46.** *dare* **N** Per.　*dare et* **Z** Hertz. etc.　*dare;* Palm. with interrogation at end of line.　　**48.** *quae* **N**.

Fugisti tamen in timidi vaga flumina Nili :
    Accepere tuae Romula vincla manus.
Brachia spectavit sacris admorsa colubris,
    Et trahere occultum membra soporis iter.
'Non hoc, Roma, fui tanto tibi cive verenda,' 55
    Dixit, ' et assiduo lingua sepulta mero.'
Septem urbs alta iugis, toto quae praesidet orbi,
    Femineas timuit territa Marte minas.

59—66. *What now of the Scipios, of Camillus? of Pompey?*
what of our victories over Syphax, Hannibal, and Pyrrhus?
what of Curtius, of Cocles, or of Corvus ?

Nunc ubi Scipiadae classes ? ubi signa Camilli ?
    Aut modo Pompeia, Bosphore, capta manu ? 60
Hannibalis spolia et victi monimenta Syphacis,
    Et Pyrrhi ad nostros gloria fracta pedes ?
Curtius expletis statuit monimenta lacunis,
    At Decius misso praelia rupit equo ;
Coclitis abscissos testatur semita pontes, 65
    Est cui cognomen corvus habere dedit.

67—72. *With Cæsar safe, Rome has none to fear, nay, scarce*
Jove himself: Apollo will tell of Actium, and thou, sailor,
of the peaceful seas.

Haec di condiderunt, haec di quoque moenia servant :
    Vix timeat, salvo Caesare, Roma Iovem.

---

51. *vaga* DV   *vada* NF.   **53.** *spectavit* Per. *spectavi* other
MSS. and edd.   **55.** *fuit* NO *fui* Z.   **56.** *Dixit et* O *Et
ducis* D Heinsius.   **57.** *toto* N Per. Hertz. etc.   **58.** Omitted
by **N**. In Per. *Marte* is om.: Palm. suspects that the word was
wanting in the archetype, and suggests *turpe*.   **59, 60.** This
couplet is placed in the MSS. after l. 68. Pass. pointed out that its
proper place is after l. 58. So Palm. The lines have been variously
placed.   **62.** *monimenta* so N, as elsewhere.   **63.** *Curius* NV.
64. *At Decius misso* N Hertz. *Admisso Decius* Scal. Palm.   **66.**
Est Broukh, edd. *Et* NO Per.   **67.** *dii . . . dii* NO, as elsewhere.
condiderant O.

Leucadius versas acies memorabit Apollo;
  Tantum operis belli sustulit una dies.   70
At tu, sive petes portus seu, navita, linques,
  Caesaris in toto sis memor Ionio.

III. 18.

1—10. *Near dark Avernus and the warm pools of Baiæ, where Misenus lies and where clanged the cymbals of Hercules— in that ill spot he lay low his head.*

Clausus ab umbroso qua alludit pontus Averno
  Fumida Baiarum stagna tepentis aquae,
Qua iacet et Troiae tubicen Misenus arena,
  Et sonat Herculeo structa labore via,
Hic, ubi, mortales dextra cum quaereret urbes,   5
  Cymbala Thebano concrepuere deo:
At nunc, invisae magno cum crimine Baiae,
  Quis deus in vestra constitit hostis aqua?
His pressus Stygias vultum demisit in undas,
  Errat et in vestro spiritus ille lacu.   10

11—16. *What availed his race, his worth, his father's name, his mother's help? Just twenty years his life had run.*

Quid genus aut virtus aut optima profuit illi
  Mater, et amplexum Caesaris esse focos?
Aut modo tam pleno fluitantia vela theatro,
  Et per maternas omnia gesta manus?
Occidit, et misero steterat vigesimus annus: 15
  Tot bona tam parvo clausit in orbe dies.

---

1. *ludit* NO Per.   *alludit* Lambinus, edd.   *tundit* Bae.   2.
Fumida Scaliger, edd.   *Humida* O.   5. *mortales* N   *mortalis* O
dextra DV   *dexter* NF.   8. *nostra* F.   10. *nostro* F.   15.
ut Heinsius for *et*.   16. *quam parvo* Heinsius.

17—24. *Go to! dream thou of triumphs, pile up thy gauds!*
that ill path must be trod, that fatal ferry must be passed,
by first and last alike.

I nunc, tolle animos, et tecum finge triumphos,
　　Stantiaque in plausum tota theatra iuvent;
Attalicas supera vestes, atque omnia magnis
　　Gemmea sint ludis: ignibus ista dabis.　　　　20
Hoc manet, hoc omnes, huc primus et ultimus
　　ordo:
　　Est mala, sed cunctis ista terenda via est;
Exoranda canis tria sunt latrantia colla,
　　Scandenda est torvi publica cymba senis.

25—30. *Not arms can guard from death, not fair face or strong*
arm, not all the gold of Pactolus.

Ille licet ferro cautus se condat et aere:　　　　25
　　Mors tamen inclusum protrahit inde caput.
Nirea non facies, non vis exemit Achillem,
　　Croesum aut Pactoli quas parit humor opes.
Hic olim ignaros luctus populavit Achivos,
　　Atridae magno cum stetit alter amor.　　　　30

31—34. *Grant only, ferryman, that by the same road over which*
Claudius and Cæsar passed, his spirit may pass to the stars.

At tibi, nauta pias hominum qui traicit umbras,
　　Huc animae portet corpus inane tuae,

---

18. *teatra* F. 19. *supra* N. 20. *sint* NV² *sunt* O. 21. *Sed*
tamen hoc omnes huc NO *hoc omnes hic primus* Per. *hoc omnes hoc*
Lach. Bae. (i. e. 'facimus' or 'erunt') *huc omnes huc* Hertz. edd.
Palm. makes the excellent suggestion *Sed manet hoc.* I adopt *manet,*
and read *Hoc* for *Sed*, see notes. 22. *tenenda* F¹. 24. *troci* N
torti O. 29, 30 Bae. thinks out of place, and suspects they should
be placed after l. 8. He places a lacuna after them, as well as after
l. 31. 30. *altus* Lach. 31. *At tu* Burmann *traicis* NO Per.
Hertz. Bae. etc. *traicit* Palmer, who attributes the mistake to the
transcriber's not seeing that *tibi* and *nauta* refer to different persons
(Marcellus and Charon). 32. *Huc* N Hertz. etc. *Hoc* Lach.

Qua Siculae victor telluris Claudius et qua
  Caesar ab humana cessit in astra via.

III. 22.

1—4. *How is it, Tullus, that thou hast so long been charmed*
by Cyzicus and the Propontis?

Frigida tam multos placuit tibi Cyzicus annos,
  Tulle, Propontiaca qua fluit Isthmos aqua,
Dindymus et sacra fabricata e vite Cybelle,
  Raptorisque tulit qua via Ditis equos?

5—18. *If thou carest more for travel than for thy friends,*
know thou that all the sights and marvels of all lands, from
West to East, are outdone by those of thine own Italy.

Si te forte iuvant Helles Athamantidos urbes,   5
  Nec desiderio, Tulle, movere meo,
Tu licet aspicias caelum omne Atlanta gerentem,
  Sectaque Persea Phorcidos ora manu,
Geryonis stabula, et luctantum in pulvere signa
  Herculis Antaeique, Hesperidumque choros: 10
Tuque tuo Colchum propellas remige Phasim,
  Peliacaeque trabis totum iter ipse legas,
Qua rudis Argoa natat inter saxa columba
  In faciem prorae pinus adacta novae:

Mueller *hac* Guy, Palm.   *portent* N Hertz. etc.   *portet* Palmer
tuae N Hertz.   *suae* Lach. Palmer, etc.
    1. *annus* O.   2. *qua* DV   *quae* NF.   3. *Dindymus*
NO edd. *Dindymis* Palm.   *sacra fabricata iuventa* O (*inventa*
N) *Cybelle* DV Bae. *Cybille* F   *Cibile* N   *sacrae fabricata iuvenca Cybebae* Vossius   *e vite* Haupt. Bae   *Dindyma sacra Rheae,*
et fabricata iuvenca Cybelae Hertz.   5. *Si* O   *Sic* Bae.   *iuvat* NF.
6. *Nec* Z   *Et* O.   9. *Geryonis* DV   *Girionis* N   *Geryonae*
edd.   13. *argoa* NF²V²   *argea* O Hons.

G

Et si qua Ortygiae visenda est ora Caystri,   15
   Et quae septenas temperat unda vias,
Omnia Romanae cedent miracula terrae:
   Natura hic posuit, quidquid ubique fuit.

19—38. *A truly famous land! a land ever victorious, ever merciful; full of fair lakes and streams; where no savage or loathsome beasts, no hideous crimes, no cruel wrongs are known.*

Armis apta magis tellus quam commoda noxae,
   Famam, Roma, tuae non pudet historiae: 20
Nam quantum ferro tantum pietate potentes
   Stamus: victrices temperat ira manus.
Hic Anio Tiburne fluis, Clitumnus ab Umbro
   Tramite, et aeternum Marcius humor opus,
Albanus lacus et socii Nemorensis ab unda,   25
   Potaque Pollucis lympha salubris equo.
At non squamoso labuntur ventre cerastae,
   Itala portentis nec fluit unda novis,
Non hic Andromedae resonant pro matre catenae,
   Nec tremis Ausonias, Phoebe fugate, dapes,   30
Nec cuiquam absentes arserunt in caput ignes
   Exitium nato matre movente suo,

---

15. Corrupt. N and Per. have *Et si qua origae.* Lach. and Hertz. give *Et si qua Ortygiae.* Scaliger conj. *Et si quadrigae.* Bae. has *Aut si quadriga et. Si quave olorigeri* is in the marg. of the Aldine Ven. 1700. *Et qua Gygaei* others. Palmer conj. *Et si quoi rigui.* **18.** *fuit* NO *nitet* Heinsius *viget* Bae. **22.** *ira* NO *illa* Z Bae. **23.** *Tirburne flues* N *fluis* Z. **25.** *Albanus locus et* N *abunda* N. Hertz. and Palm. read *Albanusque lacus* and *et unda.* **26.** *nympha* O *lympha* Z. **27.** *nunc* N *labuntur* N *lambuntur* O. **28.** *fuit una* N *furit* or *fluit* Z *unda* or *ora* Z.

Penthea non saevae venantur in arbore Bacchae,
  Nec solvit Danaas subdita cerva rates,
Cornua nec valuit curvare in pellice Iuno,   35
  Aut faciem turpi dedecorare bove,
Arboreasve cruces Sinis, et non hospita Grais
  Saxa, et curvatas in sua fata trabes.

33—42. *Here, Tullus, is thy true abode: here seek a life of honour and a home.*

Haec tibi, Tulle, parens, haec est pulcherrima
    sedes,
  Hic tibi pro digna gente petendus honos,   40
Hic tibi ad eloquium cives, hic ampla nepotum
  Spes et venturae coniugis aptus amor.

---

35. *pelice* **N** *pellice* **O**.   36. *Aut* **O** *Ac* Bae.   37. *senis*
ON[1] *cinis* **N**[2]   *Grais* so **NO** Per.   41. For *cives* **Z** have *cursus*
via fert Heinsius *vires* Burmann.   *nepotum* **NO** *penatum* Bae.

1—6. This message Arethusa sends to her own Lycotas: if aught be wanting to it, it has been blotted by her tears.

Haec Arethusa suo mittit mandata Lycotae,
    Cum totiens absis si potes esse meus.
Si qua tamen tibi lecturo pars oblita deerit,
    Haec erit e lacrimis facta litura meis:
Ac si qua incerto fallet te littera tractu,   5
    Signa meae dextrae iam morientis erunt.

7—10. All nations have seen thee: the Bactrian and Sarmatian, the Briton and the Indian.

Te modo viderunt iteratos Bactra per ortus,
    Te modo munito Neuricus hostis equo,
Hibernique Getae, pictoque Britannia curru,
    Ustus et Eoa decolor Indus aqua.   10

11—14. Is this thy plighted troth? Surely I wedded under some evil omen, and with no God to bless.

Haecne marita fides, et sic pactae mihi noctes,
    Cum rudis urgenti brachia victa dedi?
Quae mihi deductae fax omen praetulit, illa
    Traxit ab everso lumina nigra rogo.

---

1. *Haec* om. by **NF**   *Aretusa* **DV** Per.   *Haretusa* **F**   *Harethusa* **N**.   5. *Aut* (or *Et?*) **N**   *Ac* **D**   *Et* **F** Per.   8. *munitus hericus* **N**   *hernicus* **D**   *Neuricus* Iacob.; others *Sericus, Noricus,* etc.   10. *Ustus* **O**   *Postus* Bae.   *discolor* **NO** Per.   *decolor* Passerat, Bae. Palmer.   Munro reads *Eoae decolor . . aquae.* See notes.   11. *et parce avia* **N**   *et pacate mihi* **F**   *hae sunt pactae mihi* **DV**   *sic pactae mihi* Paley   *pactae iam mihi* Per. Palmer. See Hous., J. of Phil. xxi. p. 148.

15–22. *Thou art now four years away: perish he that first fashioned trees into palisades, and forged the trump of war!*

Et Stygio sum sparsa lacu, nec recta capillis   15
    Vitta data est, nupsi non comitante deo.
Omnibus heu portis pendent mea noxia vota:
    Texitur haec castris quarta lacerna tuis.
Occidat, inmerita qui carpsit ab arbore vallum,
    Et struxit querulas rauca per ossa tubas,   20
Dignior obliquo funem qui torqueat Ocno,
    Aeternusque tuam pascat, aselle, famem.

23–28. *Art thou worn and wasted? I pray it may be for love of me!*

Dic mihi, num teneros urit lorica lacertos?
    Num gravis imbelles atterit hasta manus?
Diceris et macie vultum tenuasse: sed opto,   27
    E desiderio sit color iste meo.

29–42. *When night comes, I kiss thy arms, I toss restless on my bed: I ply my winter task, or learn where flows the Araxes, what parts are scorched with heat or numb with cold, what wind will waft thee back to Italy.*

At mihi cum noctes induxit Vesper amaras,
    Si qua relicta iacent, osculor arma tua.   30
Tum queror in toto non sidere pallia lecto,
    Lucis et auctores non dare carmen aves.
Noctibus hibernis castrensia pensa laboro
    Et Tyria in radios vellera secta suos.

---

16. *Vitta* **N**   *Vita* **O.**   23. *dum* **NO**   *num* **V.**   34.
gladios **NO** Per.   *radios* **Z.**

Et disco, qua parte fluat vincendus Araxes,   35
　　Quot sine aqua Parthus milia currat equus.
Cogor et e tabula pictos ediscere mundos,
　　Qualis et haec docti sit positura dei,
Quae tellus sit lenta gelu, quae putris ab aestu,
　　Ventus in Italiam qui bene vela ferat.   40
Assidet una soror, curis et pallida nutrix
　　Peierat hiberni temporis esse moras.

43—50. *O that I could bear arms like Hippolyte, and follow thee over Scythia's snows! no love can match the love of a true wedded wife.*

Felix Hippolyte! nuda tulit arma papilla,
　　Et texit galea barbara molle caput.
Romanis utinam patuissent castra puellis!   45
　　Essem militiae sarcina fida tuae,
Nec me tardarent Scythiae iuga, cum Pater altas
　　Africus in glaciem frigore nectit aquas.
Omnis amor magnus, sed aperto in coniuge maior:
　　Hanc Venus, ut vivat, ventilat ipsa facem.   50

51—52. *What help are my purples or my gems? All is dumb and dead. I scarce pray to the Lares: I have but my Glaucis' voice to comfort me. If the owl cry, if the lamp sputter, I sacrifice for thy return.*

Nam mihi quo Poenis si purpura fulgeat ostris,
　　Crystallusque meas ornet aquosa manus?

---

36. *Quod* N　*equs* N.　**37.** *Cogor* NO　*Conor* Broukh. Hertz.
48. *Africus* O　*Affricus* N Per.　*Aprico* Hertz.　*Aeris* (Bae.)
Aeolus, Arctoo (Lach.), *Tetricus, Aetheris* (Mueller), *Arcticus* (R.
Ellis), have been proposed.　**51.** *te* N　*tibi* O　*si* Heinsius.　*nova*
(or *ter*) Palm.　*Nam mihi quo? Poenis tibi* Lach. Bae. Muell.
52. *meas* N　*tuas* O Bae.　Hous. conj. *nunc* for *si* in 51, with *meas*
in 52.　See J. of Phil. xxi. p. 129.

Omnia surda tacent, rarisque adsueta kalendis
Vix aperit clausos una puella Lares.
Glaucidos et catulae vox est mihi grata que-
rentis :   55
Illa tui partem vindicat una toro.
Flore sacella tego, verbenis compita velo,
Et crepat ad veteres herba Sabina focos.
Sive in finitimo gemuit stans noctua tigno,
Seu voluit tangi parca lucerna mero,   60
Illa dies hornis caedem denuntiat agnis,
Succinctique calent ad nova lucra popae.

63—72. *Ah, think not of glory but return! Come back to me
victorious and true: and let thine arms, hung up at the
city gate, tell of a wife's gladness for the safety of her lord.*

Ne, precor, ascensis tanti sit gloria Bactris,
Raptave odorato carbasa lina duci,
Plumbea cum tortae sparguntur pondera fundae, 65
Subdolus et versis increpat arcus equis.
Sed, tua sic domitis Parthae telluris alumnis
Pura triumphantis hasta sequatur equos,
Incorrupta mei conserva foedera lecti :
-Hac ego te sola lege redisse velim.   70
Armaque cum tulero portae votiva Capenae,
Subscribam : ' Salvo grata puella viro.'

---

54. *laros* N.   **59.** *finitimo* NF²V² *furtivo* O.   **61.** *ornis*
NF.   **62.** *Succincteque* NO.   **64.** *carbasa lina* the MSS.
Palmer holds *lina* to be a gloss, and that Prop. wrote *picta*.   **68.**
triumphantis (acc.) so N and other MSS.

IV. 4.

1—2. *I will tell the tale of Tarpeia and the Tarpeian rock.*

Tarpeium nemus et Tarpeiae turpe sepulcrum
Fabor et antiqui limina capta Iovis.

3—18. *Hard by a fountain, dark with cave and wood, King Tatius lay encamped ; here drank the horses, here Tarpeia filled her pitcher for Vesta's service.*

Lucus erat felix hederoso consitus antro,
    Multaque nativis obstrepit arbor aquis :
Silvani ramosa domus, quo dulcis ab aestu   5
    Fistula poturas ire iubebat oves.
Hunc Tatius fontem vallo praecingit acerno,
    Fidaque suggesta castra coronat humo.
Quid tum Roma fuit, tubicen vicina Curetis
    Cum quateret lento murmure saxa Iovis ?   10
Atque ubi nunc terris dicuntur iura subactis,
    Stabant Romano pila Sabina foro.
Murus erant montes : ubi nunc est curia saepta,
    Bellicus ex illo fonte bibebat equus.
Hinc Tarpeia deae fontem libavit : at illi   15
    Urgebat medium fictilis urna caput.
Et satis una malae potuit mors esse puellae,
    Quae voluit flammas fallere, Vesta, tuas ?

---

1. *tarpelae* N.   3–14. Bae. transposes these lines thus ; 7–10 ; 13, 14 ; 11, 12 ; 3–6.   3. *conditus* NO *consitus* Z *concavus* Bae. 7. *fontem* O   *montem* Heinsius, Bae.   9. *Curitis* (= *Quiritis*) Bae.   10. *saxa* NF²V³ *facta* O.   12. *foro* F²V *foco* NO.   15. *Hinc* O *hic* Z Bae. *tarpela* N.   17. *una* the MSS.   *urna* Lach¹. Hertz.   Lach¹. reads *Ei, scelus! urna.*

19—28. *She saw King Tatius, she loved: now for this cause, now for that, she was ever descending to the fount.*

Vidit arenosis Tatium proludere campis,
    Pictaque per flavas frena levare iubas.   20
Obstupuit regis facie et regalibus armis,
    Interque oblitas excidit urna manus.
Saepe illa immeritae causata est omina lunae,
    Et sibi tinguendas dixit in amne comas;
Saepe tulit blandis argentea lilia Nymphis,   25
    Romula ne faciem laederet hasta Tati.
Dumque subit primo Capitolia nubila fumo,
    Rettulit hirsutis brachia secta rubis;

29—46. *Then prayed she with tears that she might become a captive in the Sabine court, deserting her father, her country, and the goddess whom she served.*

Et sua Tarpeia residens ita flevit ab arce
    Vulnera, vicino non patienda Iovi: 30
' Ignes castrorum, et Tatiae praetoria turmae,
    Et formosa oculis arma Sabina meis,
O utinam ad vestros sedeam captiva Penates,
    Dum captiva mei conspicer ora Tati.
Romani montes et montibus addita Roma   35
    Et valeat probro Vesta pudenda meo.
Ille equus, ille meos in castra reponet amores,
    Cui Tatius dextras collocat ipse iubas.

---

20. *frena* the happy conj. of Palm. see notes.   *arma* NO *aera*. Heinsius, Bae., others *ora*.   23. *omina* NV² *omnia* O.   24. *tinguendas* N *tingendas* the rest, Bae. etc.   28. *bracchia* O *brachia* N. 30. *non patienda* NV² Hertz. etc. *compatienda* O Per. *comperienda* Bae.   34. *arma* V² Hertz. etc. *esse* NO *ora* Gronov., which may be right as *er* precedes.   37. *reponet* NO *reportet* Hertz. Bae.

Quid mirum in patrios Scyllam saevisse capillos,
   Candidaque in saevos inguina versa canes? 40
Prodita quid mirum fraterni cornua monstri,
   Cum patuit lecto stamine torta via?
Quantum ego sum Ausoniis crimen factura puellis,
   Improba virgineo lecta ministra foco!
Pallados extinctos si quis mirabitur ignes,   45
   Ignoscat: lacrimis spargitur ara meis.

47—66. ' *To-morrow there will be a feast,*' *she said;* '*follow thou the silent slippery path: then take me to wife, with Rome betrayed for my dowry: so shall the Sabine maidens be avenged.*'

Cras, ut rumor ait, tota cessabitur urbe:
   Tu cape spinosi rorida terga iugi.
Lubrica tota via est et perfida: quippe tacentes
   Fallaci celat limite semper aquas.   50
O utinam magicae nossem cantamina Musae!
   Hanc quoque formoso lingua tulisset opem.
Te toga picta decet, non quem sine matris honore
   Nutrit inhumanae dura papilla lupae.
Sic, hospes, pariamne tua regina sub aula?   55
   Dos tibi non humilis prodita Roma venit.

---

40. *foedos* Heinsius, Bae.   47. *pugnabitur* NO Per. Hertz. etc. *cessabitur* is the excellent conj. of Palmer, who points out that the phrase *tota in urbe pugnari* is absurd in itself, and that the day following was to be a feast-day. On the other hand *ut rumor ait* scarcely applies to a festival fixed for the morrow; and l. 81 presents the idea of taking advantage of the holiday as a new one. Palm. now prefers *potabitur*, C. R. ii. p. 39.   50. Palm. proposes *caespes* for *semper*. 51. *magine* N   *magicae* edd.   *magnae* (vocative) Palm.   52. *Haec* NO *Hanc* Bae. Others *Hac* (i. e. via), *nunc, sic.*   55. *Sic hospes* NO   *Sim compar* Bae.   *Dic hospes; spatiorne tuam . . . aulam* Heinsius *pariamne* N *patiare* DV *patriaeve* Hertz.

Si minus, at raptae ne sint impune Sabinae,
　Me rape, et alterna lege repende vices.
Commissas acies ego possum solvere nupta;
　Vos medium palla foedus inite mea.　　　60
Adde, Hymenaee, modos: tubicen, fera murmura
　conde:
Credite, vestra meus molliet arma torus.
Et iam quarta canit venturam bucina lucem,
　Ipsaque in Oceanum sidera lapsa cadunt;
Experiar somnum, de te mihi somnia quaeram: 65
　Fac venias oculis umbra benigna meis.'

67—82. *Unrestful that night she slept: on the morrow, the feast
of Pales, she sped forth in frenzy, and made the traitorous
pact.*

Dixit, et incerto permisit brachia somno,
　Nescia se furiis accubuisse novis.
Nam Vesta, Iliacae felix tutela favillae,
　Culpam alit, et plures condit in ossa faces.　70
Illa ruit, qualis celerem prope Thermodonta
　Strymonis abscisso fertur aperta sinu.
Urbi festus erat—dixere Parilia patres—
　Hic primus coepit moenibus esse dies—
Annua pastorum convivia, lusus in urbe,　　75
　Cum pagana madent fercula divitiis,

---

57. *ne* NV² Hertz. etc. *non* O Bae.　　59, 60. *solvere nupta;
Vos* so Madvig, Palm. instead of *solvere: nuptae, Vos* with the MSS.
and most edd.　60. *medium* NO *media* Bae.　62. *thorus* NF.
63. *E?* NO *En* Bae. *bucina* N *buccina* O.　64. *oceanum* NO.
68. *nefariis* NO Per. *se furiis* Pass. Livin. *vae furiis* Iacobus
Hertz. etc.: but Mueller remarks that *vae* is not used by Prop.
72. *fertur* NO *pectus* Hertz. Bae. Hous.　73. *parilia* NF
palilia Per. etc.　74. *coepi* N.　76. *divitiis* NO edd. *delitiis*
V· *deliciis* Bae.

Cumque super raros faeni flammantis acervos
   Traicit inmundos ebria turba pedes.
Romulus excubias decrevit in otia solvi,
   Atque intermissa castra silere tuba.   80
Hoc Tarpeia suum tempus rata convenit hostem ;
   Pacta ligat, pactis ipsa futura comes.

83—88. *The gate was betrayed: the Sabine host poured in :
' Now take me for thy wife,' she said.*   ·

Mons erat ascensu dubius, festoque remissus :
   Nec mora, vocales occupat ense canes.
Omnia praebebant somnos : sed Iuppiter unus 85
   Decrevit poenis invigilare tuis.
Prodiderat portaeque fidem patriamque iacentem,
   Nubendique petit, quem velit, ipsa diem.

89—94. *' Have then thy wish,' said the King, ' but take also
the dowry that is thy due !'   And with that she fell, borne
down by the Sabine shields.*

At Tatius—neque enim sceleri dedit hostis hono-
      rem—
   'Nube,' ait, 'et regni scande cubile mei.'   90
Dixit, et ingestis comitum superobruit armis.
   Haec, virgo, officiis dos erat apta tuis.
A duce Tarpeio mons est cognomen adeptus :
   O vigil, iniustae praemia sortis habes.

---

78. The MSS. have *inmundas dapes.*   **83.** *remissis* O and Bae.
who supposes a lacuna between *festo* and *remissis*   *remissos* G.
85. *praebebant* NO   *carpebant* Bae. *praebebant somni* Lach. *Iupiter* N.   **88.** *ipsa* NO Hertz. Paley *ipse* V² Bae. Mueller.   **93.**
Tarpeio NO Per. Hertz. Paley, etc. *Abs te Tarpeius* Bae. *Tarpeius* or *Tarpeium* Palmer *Tarpeia* Mueller.   **94.** Guy conj. *virgo.*

IV. 6.

1—10. Prepare for the poet's sacrifice! Make ready the victim and the incense, the wreath, the altar and the sacred song! Away with every ill word and deed!

Sacra facit vates: sint ora faventia sacris,
    Et cadat ante meos icta iuvenca focos.
Cera Philetaeis certet Romana corymbis,
    Et Cyrenaeas urna ministret aquas.
Costum molle date et blandi mihi· turis honores, 5
    Terque focum circa laneus orbis eat.
Spargite me lymphis, carmenque recentibus aris
    Tibia Mygdoniis libet eburna cadis.
Ite procul fraudes, alio sint aere noxae:
    Pura novum vati laurea mollit iter.   10

11—14. Of Apollo's temple, and in Cæsar's praise, I sing.

Musa, Palatini referemus Apollinis aedem:
    Res est, Calliope, digna favore tuo.
Caesaris in nomen ducuntur carmina: Caesar
    Dum canitur, quaeso, Iuppiter ipse vaces.

15—18. There is a port sacred to Phæbus in the Ionian Sea that tells of Cæsar.

Est Phoebi fugiens Athamana ad litora portus, 15
    Qua sintis Ioniae murmura condit aquae,

---

1. *sunt* V².   2. *Et cadet* O   *En cadet* Bae.   *Et cadat* N Hertz. etc.   3. *Cera* NO Hertz. etc.   *Serta* Scaliger, Bae. *Ara* Haupt. *philippeis* NO   *Philetaeis* Beroaldus.   5. *thuris* DV.   8. *modis* Per.   11. In most MSS. a new poem begins here.   14. *iupiter* NF.

Actia Iuleae pelagus monimenta carinae,
Nautarum votis non operosa via.

19—24. *Here clashed the world in arms ; on this side the foul Queen of Egypt, on that Augustus with his country's gods.*

Huc mundi coiere manus: stetit aequore moles
Pinea: nec remis aequa favebat avis.   20
Altera classis erat Teucro damnata Quirino,
Pilaque feminea turpiter acta manu:
Hinc Augusta ratis plenis Iovis omine velis,
Signaque iam patriae vincere docta suae.

25—36. *As the moon-shaped line passed on, Apollo, with his torch of flame, alighted on Augustus' ship: not arrayed as a minstrel he, but as when he scourged the Greek host, or slew the Python.*

Tandem acies geminos Nereus lunarat in arcus,   25
Armorum et radiis picta tremebat aqua,
Cum Phoebus linquens stantem se vindice Delon
—Nam tulit iratos mobilis una Notos—
Astitit Augusti puppim super, et nova flamma
Luxit in obliquam ter sinuata facem.   30
Non ille attulerat crines in colla solutos,
Aut testudineae carmen inerme lyrae,
Sed quali aspexit Pelopeum Agamemnona vultu,
Egessitque avidis Dorica castra rogis,

Aut qualis flexos solvit Pythona per orbes   35
   Serpentem, inbelles quem timuere ferae.

37—54. *'O saviour of the world!' he said; 'conquer thou by
sea as thou hast conquered by land: free thy country from
fear, the sea from shame! Let no terrors fright thee: no
cause is strong that is not just: forward, and Phœbus shall
be thine aid!'*

Mox ait: 'O longa mundi servator ab Alba,
   Auguste, Hectoreis cognite maior avis,
Vince mari! iam terra tua est: tibi militat arcus,
   Et favet ex humeris hoc onus omne meis.   40
Solve metu patriam, quae nunc te vindice freta
   Inposuit prorae publica vota tuae.
Quam nisi defendes, murorum Romulus augur
   Ire Palatinas non bene vidit aves.
Et nimium remis audent: proh turpe Latinos   45
   Principe te fluctus regia vela pati.
Nec te, quod classis centenis remiget alis,
   Terreat: invito labitur illa mari.
Quodque vehunt prorae Centauros saxa minantis,
   Tigna cava et pictos experiere metus.   50
Frangit et attollit vires in milite causa;
   Quae nisi iusta subest, excutit arma pudor.

---

36. *inbelles* **N** *imbelles* **DV** *quom tacuere lyrae* L. Mueller *lyrae*
NDVF Hertz. etc.: apparently from l. 32 : Post. defends it. Bae. has
deae: Palmer *viri* (comparing Ov. Met. 1. 438 sqq.) or *ferae* which I
have adopted.   **42.** *Inposuit* **N** *Imposuit* **O.**   **45.** *Et ni-*
mium **NFV²** *Et nunc, en, remis audent prope* Bae. *prope* **NO**
Per. *proh turpe* **Z** *Latinis* **NO** *Latinos* Markland, Bae. Post.   **49.**
Centaurica the MSS. *Centauros* Guy. *minantis* **NF** *minantes* **V.**

Tempus adest, committe rates : ego temporis auctor
   Ducam laurigera Iulia rostra manu.'

55—58. *So saying, he sped his shafts ; forth leapt the spear of*
Cæsar, and the Eastern Queen lay conquered, her sceptre
shattered on the waters.

Dixerat, et pharetrae pondus consumit in arcus : 55
   ·Proxima post arcus Caesaris hasta fuit.
Vincit Roma fide Phoebi : dat femina poenas :
   Sceptra per Ionias fracta vehuntur aquas.

59—68. *The great Julius rejoiced from heaven : the gods of the*
sea rejoiced as she fled to die in her own time—'twas better
so—and Phœbus wins the praise.

At pater Idalio miratur Caesar ab astro :
   'Sum deus : et nostri sanguinis ista fides.'   60
Prosequitur cantu Triton, omnesque marinae
   Plauserunt circa libera signa deae.
Illa petit Nilum cymba male nixa fugaci,
   Hoc unum, iusso non moritura die.
Di melius : quantus mulier foret una triumphus, 65
   Ductus erat per quas ante Iugurtha vias !
Actius hinc traxit Phoebus monimenta, quod eius
   Una decem vicit missa sagitta rates.

69—74. *Enough now of war ! Apollo calls to song and feast, to*
the wine-cup and the rose !

Bella satis cecini : citharam iam poscit Apollo,
   Victor et ad placidos exuit arma choros.   70

---

54. *uilia* N (acc. to Bae.).   **56.** *furit* Heinsius.   **59.** *Italio*
N.   **60.** *Sum deus* NO   *Tu meus* Bae.   *Tum deus* Lach.   *est*
NFV   *et* DV² Per.   *en* Markland, Hertz.   **63.** *Illa* NFV²
Ille O.   For *nixa* Paley reads *nacta*.   **67.** *monimenta* N.   **68.**
sagita N.   **69.** *cytharam* N.

Candida nunc molli subeant convivia luco,
  Blanditiaeque fluant per mea colla rosae,
Vinaque fundantur praelis elisa Falernis,
  Terque lavet nostras spica Cilissa comas.

75—86. *Let Bacchus aid our muse, and tell of German, of Ethiopian, and of Parthian, or if there be aught for Cæsar's sons to conquer: so shall day break in upon our feast.*

Ingenium potis irritet Musa poetis: 75
  Bacche, soles Phoebo fertilis esse tuo.
Ille paludosos memoret servire Sicambros,
  Cepheam hic Meroen fuscaque regna canat,
Hic referat sero confessum foedere Parthum:
  Reddat signa Remi: mox dabit ipse sua.   80
Sive aliquid pharetris Augustus parcet Eois,
  Differat in pueros ista tropaea suos.
Gaude, Crasse, nigras si quid sapis inter arenas:
  Ire per Euphraten ad tua busta licet.
Sic noctem patera, sic ducam carmine, donec   85
  Iniciat radios in mea vina dies.

IV. 11.

1—14. *Weep not for me, Paulus: the black gate opens not for prayer or tears: when once the trump has sounded, nor husband nor ancestors nor sons can move the heart of Fate.*

Desine, Paule, meum lacrimis urgere sepulcrum:
  Panditur ad nullas ianua nigra preces.

---

72. *Blanditiaeque* NO Per.   *Blanditaeque* Scaliger   *Blandae utrimque* Lach¹.   **74.** *Terque* V   *Perque* NO.   **75.** *potis* DV   *positis* NF Per.   **81.** *aliquis* NO   *aliquid* Z   *almus* Bae.   **82.** *trophea* O.   **83.** *arenas* NFV²   *harenas* N.   **85.** *carmina* N.
  1. NO Per. have *Paule*, and so throughout   *sepulchrum* N.

Cum semel infernas intrarunt funera leges,
  Non exorato stant adamante viae.
Te licet orantem fuscae deus audiat aulae,   5
  Nempe tuas lacrimas litora surda bibent.
·Vota movent superos: ubi portitor aera recepit,
  Obserat herbosos lurida porta rogos.
Sic maestae cecinere tubae, cum subdita nostrum
  Detraheret lecto fax inimica caput.   10
Quid mihi coniugium Pauli, quid currus avorum
  Profuit, aut famae pignora tanta meae?
Num minus immites habuit Cornelia Parcas?
  En sum, quod digitis quinque legatur, onus!

15—26. *I die young but guiltless: deal gently with me, Pluto.
Come forth to judge, ye judges of the realms below: let the
Furies be at your seat, let Sisyphus and Ixion, let Tantalus
and Cerberus listen as I plead.*

Damnatae noctes, et vos vada lenta paludes,   15
  Et quaecumque meos implicat unda pedes,
Immatura licet, tamen huc non noxia veni:
  Det Pater hic umbrae mollia iura meae.
Aut, si quis posita iudex sedet Aeacus urna,
  In mea sortita vindicet ossa pila;   20

---

8. *herbosos* **NF** Hertz. Paley   *umbrosos* **DV** Palmer, Bae. Mueller
rogos **NO**   *locos* Bae. after Markland, who reads *umbrosos lurida
Parca locos*. Palmer suggests *Obserat umbrosas lurida porta fores*.
But why should the *fores* be called *umbrosae?*   Heinsius conj.
domos.   **9.** *Sic* **NO**   *Ut* Bae. with comma after *caput* l. 10.
13. *Num* **F** Hertz. etc.   *Non* **ND**   *habuit* **NO** edd.   *habui*
old edd. Bae.   **14.** *En* **Z** Hertz. etc.   *Et* **NO** Per.   *legatur* **NO**
levatur **Z** Hertz. Bae. etc.   **17.** The leaf of **N** containing ll. 17–76
has been lost.   **18.** *Det Pater* **O** edd. *Deprecor* Bae.   *huic* **Z**
hinc old edd.   **19.** *Aut* **O**   *At* Bae.   **20.** *In* **O**   *Is* Heinsius
vindicet **F**   *iudicet* **DV**   *indicet* Per.

Assideant fratres, iuxta et Minoida sellam
  Eumenidum intento turba severa foro.
Sisyphe, mole vaces, taceant Ixionis orbes,
  Fallax Tantaleus corripiare liquor,
Cerberus et nullas hodie petat improbus umbras, 25
  Et iaceat tacita laxa catena sera.

27—32. *Of my father's ancestors let Africa and Numantia tell:
nor less noble my mother's house of Libo.*

Ipsa loquor pro me: si fallo, poena sororum
  Infelix humeros urgeat urna meos.
Si cui fama fuit per avita tropaea decori,
  Nostra Numantinos regna loquuntur avos.   30
Altera maternos exaequat turba Libones,
  Et domus est titulis utraque fulta suis.

33—44. *In wedlock I have known but thee, Paulus: I call all
my sires to witness that I have brought no shame upon their
house, no stain upon the name of wife.*

Mox, ubi iam facibus cessit praetexta maritis,
  Vinxit et acceptas altera vitta comas,

---

21. *Assideant fratres* the MSS. Palm. reads *Assideant, fratrem
iuxta Minoia sella, et* O Hertz. Paley have no *et* after *iuxta*
minoia O *minoida* Z   *sellam* Z *sella* DF *sella et* Hamb. Per.
24. *Tantaleus* Z Bae. *Tantaleo* O with which Aurntus (followed
by Palmer and Mueller) reads *corripere ore* Hertz. has *Tantaleo
corripiare liquor*.   26. *laxa* DV Bae. *lapsa* F Hertz. Palmer,
etc.   27. *loquor* O *loquar* Z Hertz. Bae. etc. *fallo* Z *fallor* O.
29. *trophea decori* Z   *decora trophei* O.   30. The MSS. have
Et or *Aera* which Palmer defends, reading *una* 'one set of brasses.'
Scaliger conj. *Afra* Bae. has *nostra*, which he considers is required by *Si cui   regna* O edd. *signa* Bae. Palm. suggests as possible *Aera . . . nostra* ('family coins').   31. So the MSS. The
line is probably corrupt. Most edd. follow the MSS. Palmer has
*materni exaequatur   hisce aequat, materni hos exaequant, materno
se exaequat*, etc. have been proposed.   32. *Et* O *En* Bae.

Iungor, Paulle, tuo sic discessura cubili :   35
  In lapide hoc uni nupta fuisse legar.
Testor maiorum cineres tibi, Roma, colendos,
  Sub quorum titulis, Africa, tonsa iaces,
Et Persen proavi simulantem pectus Achilli,
  Quique tuas proavo fregit Achille domos,   40
Me neque censurae legem mollisse, nec ulla
  Labe mea vestros erubuisse focos.
Non fuit exuviis tantis Cornelia damnum,
  Quin et erat magnae pars imitanda domus.

45—54. *As my blood is pure, so my life has been pure also : not purer were the Vestals Claudia and Aemilia.*

Nec mea mutata est aetas, sine crimine tota est :   45
  Viximus insignes inter utramque facem.
Mi natura dedit leges a sanguine ductas,
  Ne possem melior iudicis esse metu.
Quaelibet austeras de me ferat urna tabellas :
  Turpior assessu non erit ulla meo,   50
Vel tu, quae tardam movisti fune Cybellen,
  Claudia, turritae rara ministra deae,
Vel cui, commissos cum Vesta reposceret ignes,
  Exhibuit vivos carbasus alba focos.

---

36. *Ut* Graevius, Bae.   *hoc* O Bae.   *huic* Marcilius, Palmer.
37. *colendos* O Per. Bae.   *verendos* Z Hertz. Palmer.   38. *tunsa* O
Bae. *tanta* Per. *tonsa* other MSS.   39. *simulantem* Z edd. *stimulantem* O   *Achilli* O Bae.   *Achillis* V² Hertz. etc.   40. For
tuas Post. conj. *tumens*   Per. has *tuas* corr. to *tuus*   *proavus* V².
44. *et erat* O   *erat et* Z   *et eram* Ital.   48. *Ne possem* Z   *Ne
possis* O.   49. *Quamlibet* Livineius   *una* Wyngaarden.   50.
assessu Z   *assensu* DV   *asensu* F   *ascensu* V².   51. *Cybellen* DV
Cibelem F   *Cybelen* Hertz. *Cybehen* Palmer.   53. *cui commissos* Z Hertz. etc.   *cuius rasos* O   *cui sacra suos* Bae.

55—60. *To thee, dear mother, I have brought no grief but by my death: Cæsar himself bewails my lot.*

Nec te, dulce caput, mater Scribonia, laesi :   55
    In me mutatum quid nisi fata velis ?
Maternis laudor lacrimis urbisque querellis,
    Defensa et gemitu Caesaris ossa mea.
Ille sua nata dignam vixisse sororem
    Increpat, et lacrimas vidimus ire Deo.   60

61—72. *I have gained honour from my sons; twice has my brother borne consul's office; my daughter is worthy of her race; I have a fair name, a woman's highest glory.*

Et tamen emerui generosos vestis honores,
    Nec mea de sterili facta rapina domo.
Tu, Lepide, et tu, Paule, meum post fata
      levamen,
    Condita sunt vestro lumina nostra sinu.
Vidimus et fratrem sellam geminasse curulem,   65
    Consule quo facto tempore rapta soror.
Filia, tu specimen censurae nata paternae,
    Fac teneas unum nos imitata virum,
Et serie fulcite genus: mihi cymba volenti
    Solvitur aucturis tot mea fata meis.   70
Haec est feminei merces extrema triumphi,
    Laudat ubi emeritum libera fama rogum.

---

63. *Te . . . te* O   *Tu . . . tu* Z.   65. *sella in gemuisse curuli* Bae.   66. *Consul quo factus tempore* Lach. Bae. has *falso* for *facto* H. A. J. Munro conj. *festo* or *fati*.   70. *aucturis* Z edd. *uncturis* DV   *nupturis* F For *fata* Post. conj. *facta*   *meis* Lach. Palm. Bae.   *malis* O Hertz.

73—78. *And now I commend to thee our sons: play thou a mother's part to them, and add my kisses to thine own.*

Nunc tibi commendo communia pignora natos:
  Haec cura et cineri spirat inusta meo.
Fungere maternis vicibus, pater: illa meorum   75
  Omnis erit collo turba ferenda tuo.
Oscula cum dederis tua flentibus, adice matris:
  Tota domus coepit nunc onus esse tuum.

79—84. *Let them see no tears upon thy cheek; enough that thou grieve for me by night, and speak to mine image as though it would answer thee again.*

Et si quid doliturus eris, sine testibus illis:
  Cum venient, siccis oscula falle genis.   80
Sat tibi sint noctes, quas de me, Paule, fatiges,
  Somniaque in faciem credita saepe meam;
Atque ubi secreto nostra ad simulacra loqueris,
  Ut responsurae singula verba iace.

85—90. *If the couch be strewn for another wife, my sons, bear with her; subdue her love by gentleness: nor praise your mother over much.*

Seu tamen adversum mutarit ianua lectum,   85
  Sederit et nostro cauta noverca toro,
Coniugium, pueri, laudate et ferte paternum:
  Capta dabit vestris moribus illa manus.
Nec matrem laudate nimis: conlata priori
  Vertet in offensas libera verba suas.   90

---

76. *ferenda* O *fovenda* Mueller, Bae.   77. *matris* Z *mater* O.
79. *quid* NV² edd. *quis* O *eris* Z edd. *erit* NO.   81. *sint* N
sunt O.   84. *iace* Z *tace* NO.   86. *thoro* FN.   87. *placati
ferte* Mueller.   89. *conlata* N *collata* O.

91—98. *If he be content with memory of me, feel for his coming age : add my years to yours : 'tis well I leave you all behind me.*

Seu memor ille mea contentus manserit umbra,
  Et tanti cineres duxerit esse meos,
Discite venturam iam nunc sentire senectam,
  Caelibis ad curas nec vacet ulla via.
Quod mihi detractum est, vestros accedat ad annos: 95
  Prole mea Paullum sic iuvet esse senem.
Et bene habet : numquam mater lugubria sumpsi :
  Venit in exequias tota caterva meas.

99—102. *My cause is said.   Do ye witness for me as ye weep, and help my course to heaven.*

Causa perorata est.   Flentes me surgite testes,
  Dum pretium vitae grata rependit humus.   100
Moribus et caelum patuit: sim digna merendo,
  Cuius honoratis ossa vehantur equis.

---

94. *valet ulla vias* N.   97. *lubrica sumptum* O   *lubrica* Z edd. *lubrigia sumptum* NV². 99. For *me* Palmer suggests *ne.* 102. *vehantur* NV² *vehuntur* O   *aquis* NFV² Palmer (who compares 3. 18. 31, 32) *equis* DV Per. Hertz   *avis* Heinsius, Bae. Hous., who quotes Cons. ad Liviam 329

  *Ille pio si non temere haec creduntur in aevo
  Inter honoratos excipietur avos.*

NOTES ON TIBULLUS.

WEARY of war and danger, the poet declares he has no care for wealth: he will give up a soldier's life with all its hopes and honours, and retiring to his humble country estate, will live a life of peace and simple ease, cultivating his fields and tending his flocks, and happy till death with the love of Delia.

The introduction of Messalla's name, l. 53, implies that Tibullus had received an invitation from his patron to accompany him on some military expedition, from joining in which, as part of the great man's suite, substantial profit might be looked for. There was no surer way for a young man to push his fortunes, and to lay the foundation of a good balance at his banker's, than to attach himself to the *cohors* or suite of a provincial governor: and we know with what furious invective Catullus assails the provincial governor whose meanness (or sense of justice?) permitted his suite to return home empty-handed (Cat. 28). What then is the occasion to which the invitation of Messalla refers? It could not have been Messalla's command in Aquitania, nor his subsequent mission to the East, for Tibullus accompanied him on both occasions (see Tib. I. 3 and 7), and we know of no foreign service of Messalla's after the latter event. We must look therefore to some earlier employment; and as we know that Messalla took an important part in the Actian campaign, and commanded a division of the fleet in the battle itself, we may with all probability infer that this poem was composed in the spring of B.C. 31, on the occasion of the poet's being invited to take a part in that memorable campaign. It will be noted that the allusions in the piece itself are more applicable to a campaign in which active fighting was expected, than to an ordinary provincial command. Assuming this view to be correct, it is interesting to compare this poem with the 1st Epode of Horace, composed under precisely similar circumstances, and on the same occasion. Like Tibullus, Horace disclaims all desire to make money out of his

attachment to his patron (ll. 25–34); but whereas Tibullus refuses
an invitation to accompany Messalla, Horace volunteers unsolicited,
and apparently against remonstrance, to follow Maecenas through
every danger to the extremities of the earth. As a matter of fact,
Horace enjoyed at home the peace and comfort for which Tibullus
sighed: but whether his abstention was due to accident or policy,
his Muse has not betrayed him.

At the time supposed, if Tibullus was born in B.C. 59, he would
have arrived at the age of 28. · His term of ten years' service as
an *eques* would have expired; and the contemplative indolent poet
was little disposed to embark again on the troubled waters from
which he had just emerged.

1. The conditions of modern warfare make it hard for us to
realise that over the greater part of human history, whether
ancient or modern, the chief attraction in the military profession
has been the hope of enrichment. The profession of arms, now
emphatically the 'poor man's' profession, has been mainly filled
by men anxious to make their fortunes, whether on a big or little
scale. The Celtic races have never known but two motives to
war—plunder and revenge. The Scottish Celt was able to live
up to his principles till put down by the strong arm of England
in the middle of last century. At Rome, until the Emperors introduced a stable and tolerably just government throughout the
provinces, Roman soldiers, whether generals or legionaries, came
home gorged with plunder. When legitimate plunder failed, as
during the Civil Wars, honest citizens had to be despoiled of their
lands to satisfy the demands of the soldiery; and the triumvirs
swelled their legions by promising grants of lands to their ad-
herents, just as Cromwell did to the army which he took over to
Ireland in 1649.

Divitias, as defined by **auro**, refers to the former mode of pay-
ment: **iugera multa soli** to the latter. When Horace hears that
his friend Iccius is going to join the expedition of Aelius Gallus
against Arabia, he takes it as a matter of course that thirst for gold
is his motive, Od. 1. 29. 1

> *Icci beatis nunc Arabum incides*
> *Gazis ?*

Similarly, Propertius prophesies great wealth to those who join
Augustus' expedition to the East, 3. 4. 3 *Magna, viri, merces*
and (like Tibullus) excuses himself from joining it because he has
no thirst either for gold or gems or land, 3. 5. 3–8

Nec tamen inviso pectus mihi carpitur auro,
   Nec bibit e gemma divite nostra sitis ;
Nec mihi mille iugis Campania pinguis aratur,
   Nec miser aera paro clade, Corinthe, tua.

sibi congerat, 'pile up for himself.' **Divitias** includes all forms
of wealth, **fulvo auro** is one of the means by which it may be accu-
mulated. The two main forms are distinguished, Hor. Sat. 2. 1. 13
   Dives agris, dives positis in fenore nummis.
   2. teneat, ' have and hold.' The word avoids all awkward questions as to how possession is to be obtained.
   culti, 'land fully tilled,' and therefore necessarily gained by
expropriation.
   multa, A. has *magna*: a similar mistake occurs Ov. Am. 3. 15. 12
where P. (Palatinus primus) reads *campi iugera parva* for *pauca*.
But Hor. Sat. 1. 6. 4 has *magnis legionibus;* so Sallust, Cat. 53.
Iugera magna might therefore ▬ ' whole acres.' The Roman
iugerum contained two *actus quadrati,* and the *actus quadratus* was
a square whose side was one hundred Roman feet. Hence a
iugerum ▬ a rectangular plot of ground 240 feet by 120. The
English acre represents a square whose sides are nearly 209 feet, and
contains 43,560 square feet. By reducing Roman feet to English
(the Roman foot equals about 11·64 inches imperial measure), it
will be found that the Roman *iugerum* contained 27,097 square
feet, and so was less than two-thirds of the English acre.
   The line is obviously imitated by Ov. Fast. 3. 192
      Iugeraque inculti pauca tenere soli.
   3. labor assiduus, here used of the hardships and dangers
of a soldier's life. So Caesar B. G. 7. 41 of an attack on his camp
nostros assiduo labore defatigarent. Hor. Epod. 1. 15 alluding (as
here Tibull.) to the Actian campaign
   - *Roges tuum laborem quid iuvem meo?*
So Soph. Phil. 864
      πόνος δ μὴ φοβῶν κράτιστος.
   Quem . . . terreat, the subj. because no individual is pointed
at in *alius* l. 1. *Quem* has thus a consecutive force, ▬' one of such
a kind as.'
   4. Classica. The history of the word *classicum* is remarkable.
It is here used to denote ' a trumpet,' as in Virg. Geo. 2. 539
      Necdum etiam audierant inflari classica.
Its proper meaning is ' a military signal,' a signal given to the
'Classes' into which the Roman people were divided for military
purposes by the constitution of Servius Tullius. The word *classis*

is connected with *calo* (καλέω), whence come *calendae, concilium, clamo*, etc. Thus *classis* meant the people, or a division of the people, called together especially for war purposes. Hence it originally meant 'an army:' a use which evidently puzzled Livy, for he tells us 4. 34. 6 *Classi quoque ad Fidenas pugnatum cum Veientibus quidam in annales retulere, rem aeque difficilem atque incredibilem.* The word is used in the same sense by Virg. Aen. 7. 716

> *Hortinae classes populique Latini.*

When Servius divided the people into divisions according to their wealth, each of the five divisions into which the wealthier citizens (i. e. those possessing as much as 12,500 asses) were divided was called a '*classis*'; while those who belonged to the first, i. e. wealthiest, class, were emphatically called *classici*. From this meaning sprang the phrases 'classical authors' and 'the classics,' as we learn from a passage in Gell. 19. 8. 15 *classicus assiduusque aliquis scriptor, non proletarius*, the term *proletarius* denoting those who were too poor to be enrolled: 'the masses' as distinguished from 'the classes.' Subsequently *classis* came to be used exclusively for 'a fleet,' and *classici* are 'marines.'

pulsa, here used improperly of a wind-instrument. Thus in Arist. Av. 682 κρέκειν αὐλόν, and Claud. de Cons. Theod. 313

> *Cui tibia flatu,*
> *Cui plectro pulsanda chelys.*

5. mea paupertas. *Paupertas* is evidently here used in a relative sense, for Hor. Ep. 1. 4. 7 addresses the poet

> *Di tibi divitias dederunt artemque fruendi.*

The word *mea* of itself qualifies the *paupertas*: 'such poverty as is mine;' a poverty which, as he goes on to explain, enabled him to live in idleness. From the allusions in ll. 19, 20 it would appear that Tibullus' property was not so valuable as it had been. It is generally assumed that it must have been in part confiscated during the confiscations of B. C. 42. But confiscations were seldom if ever partial: and Tibullus' own words point rather to his property having fallen in value than to its loss. More probably, therefore, he was only a sufferer from 'the agricultural depression' which followed the civil wars.

traducat, in allusion to his past military service.

vitae. *Ad vitam* would be a more usual construction, but *transduco*, like *obduco*, is essentially a trajective verb, and is followed by the dat. after the analogy of *dare, tradere*, etc. Hence Hor. Od. 1. 24. 18

Nigro compulerit Mercurius gregi,

quoted by the commentators, is scarcely in point.

6. dum . . . luceat, i. e. ' provided only.' An ' ever-blazing hearth ' is a sign of comfort : enumerated by Mart. 10. 474 among the constituents of a happy life,

Non ingratus ager, focus perennis.

See too Cat. 23. 2. Statius had this passage in view Silv. 1. 2. 255

Divesque foco lucente Tibullus.

7. Ipse, emphatic, ' with my own hands,' unlike the owners of the vast estates called *latifundia,* which were cultivated by hordes of slaves.

8. facili, ' ready,' ' skilful,' ' able to turn to anything,' in strict accordance with its derivation from *facio.* The same root appears in *facetus* which in early Latin bears the meaning of ' smart,' ' handy,' ' graceful,' without any reference to the humorous.

poma, here for *pomos,* apple-trees : **grandia** in contrast to *teneras vites.*

9. Spes is here personified as a goddess. Altars were erected to *Spes* in gardens, etc., as the giver of increase. Cp. Tib. 2. 6. 21

Spes alit agricolas, Spes sulcis credit aratis
Semina, quae magno fenore reddat ager.

frugum includes cereals as well as fruits.

10. musta lacu. *Mustum* (properly an adjective meaning ' young' or 'new '), sc. *vinum,* was the name given to the sweet juice of the grape, when first extracted from it, first by treading, afterwards by pressing. The *lacus* was a kind of cistern into which the juice flowed from the press, and in which it was left to ferment. Cp. Ov. Fast. 4. 887

Qui petis auxilium, non grandia divide mecum
- Praemia, de lacubus proxima musta tuis.

The alliteration in this line, as below l. 34, is obviously intentional.

11. nam, used elliptically. 'And I have good ground for hope, for I am careful to worship the gods.' Rude images of rustic deities were set up in fields and at crossways. They consisted of rough blocks of stone or trunks of trees, sometimes carved into the similitude of a head. Silvanus, Priapus, and Terminus were frequently represented in this way : thus Ov. Fast. 2. 639

Termine, sive lapis, sive es defossus in agro
Stipes ab antiquis, sic quoque numen habes,

and Lactantius De Falsa Rel. 1. 20 *Quid, qui lapidem colunt informem atque rudem, cui nomen est Terminus?* The god Ter-

minus was worshipped by the proprietors on each side of the march-
stone : Ov. l. c.

> *Te duo diversa domini pro parte coronant,*
>   *Binaque serta tibi, binaque liba ferunt.*

desertus, i. e. standing by itself in a field, as opposed to *in
trivio,* l. 12.

14. libatum. The verb *libo* (λείβω) properly means 'to pour,'
and is specially used of libations poured upon the ground or upon an
altar to a god.   Hence it means generally 'to offer in sacrifice,' as
exta canum Ov. Fast. 1. 389, *munera* ib. 647, and figuratively,
Prop. 4. 6. 7

>   *Spargite me lymphis, carmenque recentibus aris*
>   *Tibia Mygdoniis libet eburna cadis.*

agricolae . . . deo should be read. No special god is intended.
The singular is used collectively = 'the gods of agriculture:' cp. 2. 1. 36

>   *Redditur agricolis gratia caelitibus.*

Many MSS. have *deum,* obviously because *ante* was supposed to be
the preposition.   In Prop. 4. 2. 45 Vertumnus says

>   *Nec flos ullus hiat pratis, quin ille decenter*
>   *Inpositus fronti langueat ante meae.*

Ante no doubt means 'before I take any for myself.'   There is a
similar confusion caused by *ante* the adv. preceding an acc. in 1. 2. 10.

15. Corona spicea, 'a wreath of corn-ears,' the natural offering to Ceres : so Hor. Car. Sec. 29

>   *Fertilis frugum pecorisque tellus*
>   *Spicea donet Cererem corona.*

Compare the Scottish custom of hanging up in the kitchen of a farm-
house 'the maiden,' or last-cut handful of the harvest, decked with
blue ribbons.

17. ruber, i. e. painted with vermilion.   So Ov. Fast. 1. 415
describes Priapus

>   *At ruber, hortorum decus et tutela, Priapus.*

Plin. 33. 36. 1 informs us that it had been the custom to paint the face
of Jupiter's image on feast days with vermilion, and that the censors
let out the job on contract.   He adds that the bodies of triumphing
generals, of whom he cites Camillus, were similarly treated. Similarly
Pan is represented in Virgil E. 10. 27 as

>   *Sanguineis ebuli baccis minioque rubentem,*

and in Tib. 2. 1. 55 the countryman in worshipping Bacchus paints
himself with the same substance,

>   *Agricola et minio suffusus, Bacche, rubenti.*

See Plut. Qu. Rom. 98.

18. Priapus, the God of Gardens, was unknown alike to Italian and to early Greek mythology. The main seat of his worship was Lampsacus, on the Hellespont, where he was worshipped as the son of Dionysus and Aphrodite. He was regarded as the protector of flocks and of the vine, but especially of bees and all garden produce, which he protected from thieves and birds, being thus the ancestor of the modern scare-crow or 'tatie-bogle.' His statue was to be found in all gardens, with a falx or gardener's knife in his hand, and a cudgel; he bore a horn of plenty in his arms, and other emblems of fruitfulness. Virg. Geo. 4. 109

Et custos furum atque avium cum falce saligna
Hellespontiaci servet tutela Priapi.

Martial 8. 40 treats him with scant respect : the poet threatens he will cut him up for firewood if he does not protect his wood properly from thieves. See also Hor. Sat. 1. 8. 3–8.

19, 20. These lines refer to the loss of property which the poet had sustained from whatever cause. See Introd.

20. fertis, i. e. 'receive.' So Hor. Od. 4. 3. 5

neque tu pessima munerum

Ferres,
and Ov. Am. 3. 6. 66

Munera promissis uberiora feres.

Lares. The *Lares* here meant are the *Lares Rurales*, who presided over the fields and guarded the interests of the husbandman.

'The word *Lar* is of Tuscan origin, and was used in that language as a title of honour, equivalent, apparently, to chief or prince. Thus we read of Lar or Lars Porsenna, king of Clusium, Lar Tolumnius, king of the Veiientes, etc.

'Among the Romans, the deities denominated Lares were certain spirits of dead men who were supposed to watch over and protect the living. They were very numerous, and were ranked in classes according to the departments over which they presided. Thus there were *Lares Privati* and *Lares Publici*, the former being the objects of family worship, while the latter were worshipped by the whole community.

'The *Lares Privati*, or *Domestici*, or *Familiares*, were tutelary spirits worshipped by all residing under the same roof. The spot peculiarly sacred to them was the *focus* or hearth situated in the *Atrium*, where stood the altar for domestic sacrifice. Near to this there was usually a niche, containing little images of these gods, called *lararium*, or *aedicula*. The offerings to the Lares consisted chiefly of flowers, frankincense, and wine, which were presented from time to time, and regularly on the Kalends of each month. A portion of the viands consumed at each meal was also placed before them in little dishes, and victims were occasionally sacrificed. Marked reverence was paid to the Lares at the most important periods of life; to them the youth dedicated his *bulla* when he assumed the manly gown; to them the bride presented a piece of money when betrothed, according to the form termed *coemptio;* to them she made a solemn offering on the day after her nuptials, before entering on the discharge of her matron duties; to them a grateful salutation was addressed by the master of the mansion when he returned in safety from a foreign land; and to them the soldier dedicated his arms when the toils and dangers of war were over. Thus in the Aulularia of Plautus, the Prologue is spoken by a Lar Familiaris, to whose guardianship the father of the actual proprietor of the house had committed a treasure buried beneath the hearth. The spirit, after complaining of the neglect of the son, continues thus,

> *Huic filia una est : ea mihi quotidie*
> *Aut ture, aut vino, aut aliqui semper supplicat:*
> *Dat mihi coronas.*

Cato, when describing the duties of a Villica, R. R. 43 *Focum purum circumversum quotidie, priusquam cubitum eat, habeat. Kalendis, Idibus, Nonis, festus dies cum erit, coronam in focum indat. Per eosdem dies Lari familiari pro copia supplicet.*

'In the above passages a single Lar only is supposed to belong to the dwelling; the plural, however, is quite common, as in Juv. S. 9. 137

> *O parvi nostrique Lares, quos ture minuto,*
> *Aut farre, et tenui soleo exorare corona.*

Also Hor. C. 3. 23. 2

> *Nascente luna, rustica Phidyle,*
> *Si ture placaris et horna*
> *Fruge Lares avidaque porca.*

Cp. also Tibull. 1. 3. 33; 1. 10. 15-27; 2. 1. 59; Cato R. R. 2; Ov. Trist. 4. 8. 21;. Pers. S. 5. 30

> *Cum primum pavido custos mihi purpura cessit,*
> *Bullaque succinctis Laribus donata pependit;*

and Prop. 4. 1. 131

> *Mox, ubi bulla rudi dimissa est aurea collo,*
> *Matris et ante deos libera sumpta toga.*

Consult also Macrob. S. 1. 15; Nonius, p. 531.

'Of the *Lares Publici* the most important were the *Lares Rurales,* guardians of flocks and herds and fruits, propitiated by sacrifices of calves and lambs; the *Lares Compitales*, worshipped at the spot where two or more roads crossed each other; the *Lares Viales*, probably the same with the preceding, so called because their images were erected in streets and highways: invoked by travellers when setting forth on a journey (see Plaut. Merc. 5. 2. 23); the *Lares Vicorum*, or guardians of the streets; the *Lares Praestites*, protectors of the city; the *Lares Permarini*,, worshipped by mariners (a temple was dedicated to them in the Campus Martius, B.C. 179); and the *Lares Grundules*, who stood under the *grundae* or projecting eaves of houses.

'It is obvious from what has been said that the Roman Lares bear a marked resemblance to the saints of the Roman Catholic Church. Like them, the saints are believed to be the spirits of dead men, to whose protection cities, streets, roads, ships, families, and private individuals are commended; statues or pictures of saints are to be found in streets, crossways, bridges, ships, dwelling-houses, and all places of public and private resort; these are honoured with garlands and offerings of every description, while lamps fed with perfumed oil burn before their shrines. The *Lares* must be distinguished from the *Penates*. The word *Penates* is apparently a local adjective like *nostras, cuias, Casinas, Arpinas*, etc., connected with *penitus, penetro, penetralia*, etc., so that the term properly denotes the deities worshipped in the *penus*[1] or innermost part of the house. But we have already seen that the *focus* or hearth situated in the *Atrium* was considered the central point of the dwelling, and was invested with peculiar sanctity. Hence *Penates* is in fact a generic term, and, in its strict sense, comprehends *all the gods worshipped at the hearth*, and will thus include the *Lares*, who are continually mentioned in conjunction with the *Penates*, and frequently in such terms as to imply that they were the same. But it is quite certain that other gods, besides the Lares, were worshipped at the hearth, especially *Vesta*, who was herself the Goddess of the Hearth, and to these the term *Penates* is often applied, so as to distinguish them from the *Lares*. This is evident from a single passage in Plautus, Merc. 5. 1. 5

Di Penates meum parentum, familiaeque Lar pater,
Vobis mando meum parentum rem bene ut tutemini.
Ego mihi alios Deos Penates persequar, alium Larem.

It would be vain to enquire who the Penates were, since they might

---

[1] 'Nam et ipsum *penetral, penus* dicitur, et hodie quoque *penus Vestae claudi* vel *aperiri* dicitur.' Serv. on Virg. Aen. 3. 12.

be different for every family, and the statements of ancient authors upon this point are very contradictory. Varro, however, distinctly asserts that the number and names of Penates were indeterminate.

' As there were Public as well as Domestic Lares, so there were Public Penates who exercised a general influence over the destinies of the whole Roman people. Thus Tacitus tells us, Ann. 15. 41, that *delubrum Vestae cum Penatibus Populi Romani* was consumed along with other very ancient temples in the great fire during the reign of Nero. Apparently the temple of Vesta, being the common hearth or central point of the city, was the proper abode of the Public Penates. Dionysius also, R. A. 1. 68, describes a temple in the Velia (that part of the Forum immediately under the Palatine) in which were "images of the Trojan Penates, two young men in a sitting posture, with spears in their hands, a work of ancient art;" and adds that he had seen many other effigies of these gods in ancient shrines, always represented as two young men in martial equipment. These we should naturally suppose to be the Trojan or Phrygian Penates mentioned so often in the Aeneid, supposed to have been rescued from the flames of Troy by Aeneas, and transported by him to Italy.'

21-24. The principal rural festivals at which the fields, flocks, and countrymen were purified were the *Ambarvalia* (see below Tib. 2. 1), the *Palilia* (Ov. Fast. 4. 721 sqq.), and the *Feriae Sementivae* (Ov. Fast. 1. 6󠀠8).

21. Tunc, i. e. in better times.

22. exigui seems to imply that the property had been reduced in size.

25. A. reads *Iam modo non possum*, which can only mean ' I am now only not able,' i. e. ' I am all but able,' as Virg. Aen. 9. 141
> *penitus modo non genus omne perosos,*

'in all but utter hatred of the whole of womankind.' But to say 'I am *all but* ready to be content with little' is at once weak and inconsistent with the lines which follow, which imply a definite assertion, or hope, of contentment. The reading of the text is from M.: see critical note. *Possim* is supported by *pudeat*, l. 29.

vivere parvo. Cp. Hor. Od. 2. 16. 13
> *Vivitur parvo bene cui paternum*
> *Splendet in mensa tenui salinum.*

26. longae . . . viae, of military marches. So Hor. Od. 2. 6. 7
> *Sit modus lasso maris et viarum*
> *Militiaeque.*

These lines imply that Tibullus had only just given up the pro-

‚fession of arms, and did not feel sure how he would enjoy his modest retirement.

deditus implies not so much ‘devoted to’ as simply ‘engaged in.’   Cp. Ov. Met. 13. 920, where Glaucus says,

> *Ante tamen mortalis eram: sed scilicet altis*
> *Deditus aequoribus, iam tum exercebar in illis.*

So Lucr. 4. 996.

27. Canis aestivos ortus. ‘Two constellations were known to the Greek astronomers by the name of the Dog, and were distinguished as the greater and the lesser.

‘The greater, or *Canis*, rose, according to Columella, on the 26th of July, and the bright star in its mouth was called *Canis*, or *Canicula*, or *Sirius*,—the terms *Canis* and *Canicula* being used to denote sometimes the whole constellation, and sometimes the principal star.

‘The lesser, or *Procyon* (προκύων), that is, in Latin, *Antecanis*,

> *Antecanis, Graio Procyon qui nomine fertur*[1],

rose, as its title imports, before the great Dog, according to Columella, on the Ides of July.   Although *Canicula* is usually employed with reference to the greater Dog, yet, from its being a diminutive of *Canis*, it is occasionally applied to the lesser, and we may observe generally that the two groups are frequently confounded by ancient writers, and the fables proper to the one transferred to the other. See Ovid, Fast. 4. 939 and n.

‘Since their rising served to mark the period of greatest heat, they are commonly spoken of by the poets in connection with this circumstance. Cp. Tibull. 1. 7. 21; 2. 1. 47; 3. 5. 1, and Hor. C. 3. 29. 17

> *Iam clarus occultum Andromedae pater*
> *Ostendit ignem : iam Procyon furit*
> *Et stella vesani Leonis*
> *Sole dies referente siccos*[2],

and C. 3. 13. 9, addressed to the Bandusian fount,

> *Te flagrantis atrox hora Caniculae = Nescit tangere . . .*

and C. 1. 17. 17

> *Hic in reducta valle Caniculae = Vitabis aestus . . .*

to which add Ov. A. A. 2. 231 ; ˙Pers. S. 3. 5, etc.   In like manner Virg. G. 4. 425

---

[1] Arat. ap. Cic. N. D. 2. 44.   Many edd. have *Ante Canem*, connected in construction with the line preceding it.

[2] According to Columella the Sun enters Leo on 20th July; the bright star in the heart of the Lion rises on the 29th July; Cepheus rises in the evening on the 9th July.

> *Iam rapidus torrens sitientes Sirius Indos*
> *Ardebat,*

and Virg. Aen. 3. 141

> *tum steriles exurere Sirius agros,*
> *Arebant herbae, et victum seges aegra negabat.*

Our own familiar expression of " The Dog-days " is, of course,
derived from the same source.'

28. Cp. Hor. who as a poet describes himself, Od. 1. 1. 21, as

> *nunc viridi membra sub arbuto*
> *Stratus, nunc ad aquae lene caput sacrae.*

29. tenuisse bidentem, 'to hold the hoe or mattock.' The
bidens was a hoe with two strong teeth of iron (δίκελλα): referred to
by the poets as the typical instrument of agricultural industry. So
Lucr. 5. 209 speaks of the human race as *Vitai causa valido consueta*
bidenti = Ingemere.

Tenuisse and *increpuisse* l. 30, beside *referre* l. 32, show that
little or no distinction can be drawn in such cases between the use
of the pres. and perf. infin.

30. The **stimulus** was a goad, i. e. a long stick with a sharp
spike at the end of it. Such an instrument is constantly in use in
South Italy at the present day.

34. est is placed by some MSS. at the end of the line. But
Dissen shows that the proper position for *est* is after *magno* as being
the emphatic word. Cp. above l. 22 and 1. 5. 68

> *Ianua, sed plena est percutienda manu.*

35. Hic, on my farm. The allusion is to the *Palilia*, the feast
of *Pales*, god of flocks and shepherds, held on the 21st of April.
The day was supposed to mark the birthday of Rome: and is at
this day celebrated at Rome in honour of that event. For the
Palilia or *Parilia* cp. Ov. Fast. 4. 72ỷ. Part of the ceremony of
purification consisted in leaping over heaps of burning straw. See
Tib. 2. 5. 87.

36. spargere lacte. It would seem that the statue of the god
was actually sprinkled with milk: Tib. 2. 5. 27

> *Lacte madens illic suberat Pan ilicis umbrae,*
> *Et facta agresti lignea falce Pales.*

38. fictilibus. Vessels of common pottery were long used in
public rites, in retention of the simplicity of early times. In private
rites silver, and even gold, vessels came to be used: cp. Pers. 2. 57

> *Aurum vasa Numae Saturniaque impulit aera,*

while Juv. 11. 116 laments the good old days when Rome worshipped

> *Fictilis et nullo violatus Iuppiter auro.*

40. facili. We have seen this word above, l. 8, used in an active sense, 'that can make easily.' Here it is used passively, 'that can be easily made or moulded,' 'ductile.' So Ov. Met. 15. 169

Utque novis facilis signatur cera figuris.

41. requiro approaches very nearly in meaning to *desidero* 'to miss,' 'to feel regret for the loss of something once enjoyed;' and is sometimes coupled with it, as in Cic. Verr. 2. 5. 67 *cives Romani vestram severitatem desiderant, vestrum auxilium requirunt.* Here *desiderant* is 'feel the loss of;' *requirunt,* 'demand to have restored to them.'

42. condita, of the harvest gathered in and safely 'stored' in the garner.

43. lecto ... toro. 'Differunt enim *lectum* et *torus* ut λέχos et εὐνή,' D. *Lectus* is the bed as a whole: connected with *lex, lĕgo,* our 'lay,' etc. *Torus* connected with στορέννυμι, *sterno, stramen, toral,* etc., refers to the cushions or bedding: hence such phrases as *praebuit herba torum,* etc. Ov. Her. 5. 14.

44. levare, 'to make light;' hence 'to remove a weight,' 'to refresh.'

46. tenero, 'loving.'

detinuisse, for the tense see above on l. 30 and below ll. 73, 74.

48. imbre iuvante. 'Compare the quotation from Sophocles in Cic. Epp. ad Att. 4. 7, " Cupio, ut ait tuus amicus Sophocles,

κἂν ὑπὸ στέγῃ
πυκνᾶς ἀκούειν ψεκάδος εὐδούσῃ φρένι." '

50. Note the trisyllabic ending of the pentameter, much rarer in Tibullus than in Catullus, though more frequent than in Ovid.

51. The allusion to precious stones has been held to indicate that the proposed campaign was to be in the East. Propertius in the same way expects rich booty of jewels from Augustus' projected campaign against the Parthians, 3. 4. 2 ; 3. 5. 4, etc.

smaragdi. 'It appears extremely probable that the ancients gave the name *smaragdus* not merely to the precious gem which we call an emerald, but extended the term to fluor spar, green vitrified lava (green Icelandic agate), green jasper, and green glass. There is a curious passage in Pliny, H. N. 37. 5, where he tells us that Nero used to view the combats of gladiators "in an emerald," which is generally understood to mean a smooth polished mirror made of some of the above substances ; although, from the peculiar phraseology employed, others maintain that the emperor was near-sighted, and used a concave eyeglass formed out of the gem. See Beckmann, History of Inventions, vol. 3. p. 176.'

With regard to the quantity of a short vowel before *smaragdus* see Ramsay's Latin Prosody, p. 261. 2.

'Observe the position of **que**, which is irregular, since it ought to be attached to the latter of the two words which it connects. A prose writer would have said, *O quantum est auri smaragdique ;* but the poets not unfrequently indulge in this license, e. g. Tib. 1. 3. 56

> *Messallam terra dum sequiturque mari.*

Similar to these are Hor. C. 2. 19. 27

> *Sed idem ▬ Pacis eras mediusque belli,*

and Hor. Sat. 1. 4. 17

> *Di bene fecerunt, inopis me quodque pusilli*
> *Finxerunt animi, raro et perpauca loquentis.'*

The 'misplacing' of *que* or *ve* in such passages is a marked feature of Horace's style. The word to which the particle is attached is always emphatic, and its meaning usually is common to both clauses. See Wickham on Od. 1. 30. 7.

52. vias, of military marches, cp. l. 26.

53. Messalla. 'Appian, De Bello Civili 4. 38, gives a summary of the history of M. Valerius Messalla Corvinus, which is useful for the student of Tibullus. According to this and other authorities, Messalla, while yet a very young man, was proscribed by the triumvirs, and fled to Brutus and Cassius. His name was almost immediately struck out of the fatal list, but he remained true to the cause of the republic until after the battle of Philippi, when, the soldiers who escaped having chosen him for their general, he persuaded them to yield to fortune and surrender. For a considerable period, Messalla remained in close alliance with Antony, but, disgusted by the conduct of Cleopatra, he passed over to Octavianus, who received him with the greatest distinction, and admitted him at once to full confidence. He fought well for Augustus in Sicily B. C. 36, against the Salassi B. C. 34, and at Actium B. C. 31, where he commanded the centre of the fleet, holding the office of consul in the place of Antonius. At the end of the same year he proceeded to Aquitania as pro-consul, was despatched thence to the East and did not return to Rome till his triumph in B. C. 27. He was the first person named to hold the important office of Praefectus Urbi, a charge which, however, he soon resigned. He was born about B. C. 60, and died before A. D. 3.

'Messalla enjoyed also the highest reputation in literature, and his compositions are warmly praised by Seneca, Quinctilian, and the two Plinys. He was the author of a History of the Civil Wars, and of a treatise *De Romanis Familiis;* but his fame rested chiefly on his oratorical efforts, which were characterised by great purity of style and neatness of expression, and by a lofty and generous tone, though considered deficient in strength. None of his works have been preserved, with the exception of a few insignificant fragments.'

54. Referring to the custom of hanging up upon the door-posts spoils won from the enemy. So Prop. 3. 9. 26

Atque onerare tuam fixa per arma domum.

See Virg. Aen. 7. 183.

56. Roman slaves who acted as janitors were not unfrequently chained, like dogs, to their posts. So Ov. Am. 1. 6. 1

Ianitor, indignum! dura religate catena.

57. laus is especially used of military renown: Prop. 1. 6. 29

Non ego sum laudi, non natus idoneus armis.

60. Imitated by Ovid in his Elegy on Tibullus, Am. 3. 9. 58

Me tenuit moriens deficiente manu.

63, 64. ferro Vincta. This phrase does not mean merely a heart ' enclosed in ' or ' encased by ' iron (Pind.), but rather a heart 'tight bound (or hard), as being made of iron.'

67. manes ne laede. *Flere et crines solutos habere consentaneum, si vero etiam abscinderet crines Delia et genas laceraret, aegre ferrent hoc Manes poetae, quibus etiam in Orco cura formosae puellae.* D. *Immodico luctu carorum Manes offendi aut putabant, aut poetae saltem eleganter pronuntiant.* H. 'We find the same idea in Prop. 4. 11. 1

Desine, Paulle, meum lacrimis urgere sepulcrum.'

69. iungere in this sense is properly used with an acc. of the persons joined together, as Ov. Met. 4. 156

Ut quos serus amor, quos hora novissima iunxit;

cp. the word *coniux,* one joined to another. But it is also used, as here, with a quasi-cognate acc. of the union formed, in such phrases as *iungere pacem, foedera, amicitiam,* or as here *amorem;* cp. Cat. 64. 372

Quare agite, optatos animis coniungite amores.

72. If **capiti** be read, it should probably be taken as an old form of the abl. as in Cat. 66. 124. *Capite* is supported by Plaut. Merc. 2. 2. 34

Tun' capite cano amas?

On the other hand, the dat. with an infin. after it is not unexampled with *decet:* e. g. Liv. 34. 58. 8 *Sicut aut sola aut prima certe pensari decet principi orbis terrarum populo.* So Dig. 32. 1. 23.

Tib. I. 2. 91 further suggests that the *blanditiae* might be repeated by the old lover to himself:

Et sibi blanditias tremula componere voce.

73, 74. Of the drunken revels and brawls of lovers.

inserere used by Liv. 35. 17 with *expostulationes*, by Tac. Hist. I. 23 with *querelas.* The phrase is analogous to *iungere amores* above l. 69.

75. The poets often speak of Love in terms analogous to those of War. Pindar well quotes Ov. Am. I. 9 where an elaborate comparison is drawn between the Lover and the Soldier. See esp. l. 19

Ille graves urbes, hic durae limen amicae
Obsidet ; hic portas frangit, at ille fores.

I. 3.

THIS poem was written at Corcyra. Messalla was despatched direct from Aquitania on his mission to the East. Finding this enterprise more to his mind than the prospect of joining in the campaign against Antony in B. C. 31, Tibullus had attached himself to his patron. He fell ill, however, on the journey, was compelled to remain behind at Corcyra, and returned to Rome on his recovery. The sad thoughts of a sick bed and the disappointed hopes of the adventurer are curiously mingled, in a tone half serious, half playful, with the expectation of a poetic Elysium if he die, and the picture of a happy and unexpected return home to Delia if he survive.

1. Ibitis . . . Messalla. The poet first addresses the whole *cohors comitum,* then specially their chief.

2. cohors, it must be noted, is the technical term for the personal retinue of a commander ; not merely his military or official staff, but all the friends who accompanied him. So Horace writing to a friend on the staff of Tiberius in the East, Ep. I. 8. 14

Ut placeat iuveni, percontare, utque cohorti ;
and Cat. 28. 1

Pisonis comites, cohors inanis.

3. Corcyra was fixed upon by the later Greeks as the abode of Alcinous and the Phaeacians, upon equally good authority as that which selected the isles between Capri and Surrento as the haunt of the Sirens, Formiae as the abode of the Laestrygones, and the bold headland near Terracina as the dwelling of the enchantress Circe. Cp. Ov. Am. 3. 9. 47, where Ovid alludes to this illness of Tibullus.

ignotis terris, foreign lands, as distinguished from *nota sedes*.

5-8. The following passage from Tib. 3. 2. 9–26 contains minute information on the ceremonies connected with preserving the ashes of the dead:

> *Ergo cum tenuem fuero mutatus in umbram,*
> *Candidaque ossa super nigra favilla teget,*
> *Ante meum veniat longos incompta capillos*
> *Et fleat ante meum maesta Neaera rogum.*
> *Sed veniat carae matris comitata dolore:*
> *Maereat haec genero, maereat illa viro.*
> *Praefatae ante meos Manes animamque precatae*
> *Perfusaeque pias ante liquore manus,*
> *Pars quae sola mei superabit corporis, ossa*
> *Incinctae nigra candida veste legant;*
> *Et primum annoso spargant collecta Lyaeo,*
> *Mox etiam niveo fundere lacte parent,*
> *Post haec carbaseis humorem tollere velis*
> *Atque in marmorea ponere sicca domo.*
> *Illuc, quas mittit dives Panchaia merces*
> *Eoique Arabes, pinguis et Assyria,*
> *Et nostri memores lacrimae fundantur eodem:*
> *Sic ego componi versus in ossa velim.*

See also the interesting and detailed instructions given by Propertius with regard to his own funeral rites 2. 13. 17 (extracted below).

7. Assyrios here, as elsewhere, for 'Syrian' and so 'Oriental,' as Eastern wares were shipped to Rome through Syrian ports. See note on Prop. 2. 13. 30, Cat. 66. 12. Thus *Syra merx* is used of the spices of India and Arabia, as well as of the gems, silks, cottons, etc. of central Asia. Thus Virg. describes Tyrian purple as *Assyrium venenum*, the incense of Arabia as *Assyrium amomum*, and Ovid Indian ivory as *Assyrium ebur*.

9. cum mitteret, i. e. 'at the moment of saying farewell.' Pind. compares Cat. 66. 29 *maesta virum mittens*.

11, 12. 'Among the superstitious Romans fortune-tellers drove a brisk trade, and frequented the Forum, the Circus Maximus, and other places of public resort. Ennius, in a fragment preserved by Cicero, De Divin. 1, exclaims,

> *Non habeo denique nauci Marsum augurem,*
> *Non vicanos haruspices, non de Circo astrologos,*

i. e. "soothsayers that stroll about the streets, and astrologers that haunt the Circus." Horace, Sat. 1. 6. 113, says that when taking an evening walk,

> *Fallacem circum vespertinumque pererro*
> *Saepe forum, adsisto divinis ;*

and there is a very interesting passage in Juvenal, Sat. 6. 542, regarding foreign impostors, Jews, Armenians, Syrians, and Chaldaeans, who passed from house to house vending their prophecies. It would appear from the lines before us, that boys were wont to sit in the streets for the purpose of affording the passers by an opportunity of trying the divination by *sortes*. These *sortes* were slips of parchment or pieces of wood, upon which certain words or sentences were inscribed. They were mixed together in a box or urn, one was drawn or shaken out, at random, and a conclusion formed from the expressions which it contained, as applied to the particular circumstances of the person who made the experiment [1]. The *sortes* of the temple of Fortune at Praeneste were among the most celebrated in Italy. Cicero has a dissertation upon the subject in general, and upon these in particular in his treatise De Div. 2. 41.

'Some understand that the *puer*, l. 11, was employed only to draw out the lots, because Cicero says of those at Praeneste, *Fortunae monitu, pueri manu, miscentur atque ducuntur;* but the words *illa sustulit* seem to preclude that interpretation here. Again, a question has been raised with regard to the second clause, *illi Rettulit e triviis omina certa puer,* whether these words are merely a continuation and explanation of those which precede, or whether they relate to another species of divination, and point out that, in addition to drawing the *sortes,* Delia sent a boy to a place where three ways met, in order that he might watch for an omen and announce to her what he had seen. This last interpretation seems somewhat forced, but has been adopted by Dissen. Finally, we may notice the ingenious conjecture of Muretus, which has been adopted by several editors, who would substitute *trinis* for *triviis*, making the prediction depend upon the result obtained by drawing the lots three times, *three* being a mystical number.'

13. dabant, here used for 'offered,' 'promised.' This meaning is perhaps to be derived from the imperf. tense: 'were for giving.'

14. nostras ... vias, for the plural used of a voyage cp. Prop. 1. 8. 30

> *Destitit ire novas Cynthia nostra vias.*

---

[1] Tacitus, Germ. 10, gives an account of a species of divination, practised among the Germans, resembling this.

respiceret. *Respicere*, lit. ' to look back,' is constantly used of that repeated, respectful, or loving looking, to which we give the name of 'regard.' Here it means 'to regard with fear and anxiety,' and though the use of *vias* as an object is remarkable, there is no reason to adopt the inferior MS. reading *respueret*, or Haupt's conj. *despueret*, in reference to the well-known ancient superstition (still shared apparently by so many of our countrymen) that spitting brings good luck.

15. cum iam mandata dedissem, 'after my last parting instructions.'

17. causatus aves, 'alleged the omens in excuse.' In the next line the construction is changed to an infin.

> *Causatus sum me tenuisse.*

So Hor. after *cantare* Od. 2. 9. 19

> *Cantemus Augusti tropaea*
> *Caesaris, et rigidum Niphaten,*
> *Medumque flumen gentibus additum*
> *Victis minores volvere vertices.*

18. Saturni . . . diem. 'The Jewish Sabbath, the seventh day, seems to have been always called *Saturni dies* (whence our *Saturday*), from the time when the division of time into weeks of seven days became known to the nations of the west. We find many passages in the writers of the Augustan age, and their immediate successors, which prove that, scorned as the Jews were who had migrated to Rome, some of their peculiar tenets were well known and respected, by the vulgar at least. Thus Ov. A. A. 1. 415

> *Quaque die redeunt rebus minus apta gerendis*
> *Culta Palaestino septima sacra Syro;*

and again R. A. 220

> *Nec pluvias vites, nec te peregrina morentur*
> *Sabbata, nec damnis Allia nota suis;*

and Horace, alluding, it would seem, to the Sabbath of the passover, Sat. 1. 9. 69

> *Hodie tricesima Sabbata, vin' tu*
> *Curtis Iudaeis oppedere?*

and Pers. 5. 184

> *Labra moves tacitus recutitaque Sabbata palles;*

to which add Juv. Sat. 14. 105.' It is to be noted that the lax principles of Tibullus and Ovid enabled them to adopt a tone of respect towards the Jewish and other foreign observances very different from the tone of hate and scorn in which Juvenal speaks of them. Tacitus, Hist. 5. 4, when giving an account of the Sabbath and the Sabbatical year, and of the different opinions entertained with regard to the origin of these observances continues : *Alii honorem eum Saturno haberi, seu principia religionis tradentibus Idaeis, quos eum Saturno pulsos et conditores gentis accepimus, seu quod e septem sideribus, quis mortales reguntur, altissimo orbe et praecipua potentia stella Saturni feratur: ac pleraque caelestium vim suam et cursum septimos per numeros commeare.*

'The passage before us is remarkable as being the first in which we find mention made of a day of the week named after a planet, and it is by no means certain that the planetary names for the other six were at this time known to the Romans. Josephus, born A. D 37, asserts, Ap. 39, that there was no Greek city whatsoever, and no foreign nation, to which the use of the week of seven days had not penetrated ; but Dion Cassius, who flourished A. D. 200, tells us, 37. 17. 18, that the practice of referring the days of the week to the seven stars, called planets, arose among the Egyptians, but had not come into general use until a short time before the period when he wrote. It was introduced into the Roman Calendar by Constantine.' See dissertation on the names of the week and days of the week in the Philolog. Museum, vol. i. p. 1.

tenuisse, 'observed.' Or *me* may be the object : 'detained me.' Cf. Prop. 2. 10. 14 and *n.*

20. Stumbling on the threshold was considered the most unpropitious of all omens to a person setting out from home, or embarking on any enterprise. To avoid the possibility of such a mischance, a bride was always lifted over the threshold of her future home. Cp. Ov. Met. 10. 452

> *Ter pedis offensi signo est revocata.*

23. Like so many women at the time, Delia was a worshipper of the Egyptian goddess Isis. Her worship was introduced by Sulla, and she had a temple in the Campus Martius.

24. aera refers to the *sistrum*, or rattle, made of bronze, frequently represented on ancient monuments. It was shaped like a racquet, and the jingling was produced by transverse rods which fitted loosely into the frame. See Rich. The rattling of these instruments by the worshippers, together with the white linen vestments of the priests, were the two prominent features of the worship of Isis. Cp. Ov. Am. 3. 9. 33; A. A. 1. 1. 77; E. P. 1. 1. 51

> *Vidi ego linigerae numen violasse fatentem*
> *Isidis, Isiacos ante sedere focos.*

28. Picta tabella, referring to the votive pictures and models which were hung up at the shrine of the goddess, just such as can be seen nowadays in the chapels of saints in Catholic countries.

30. lino tecta. See above. These garments of linen excited wonder at Rome, where woollen clothes chiefly were worn. The introduction of lighter fabrics from the east is considered to have contributed to the greater unhealthiness of Rome in later times. Warm clothing is essential as a preservative against the malaria which infests so large a portion of Italy.

31. Bisque die. At sunrise and sunset.

32. Pharia, i. e. Egyptian, from the isle of Pharos, opposite the harbour of Alexandria. Cf. Lucan, ix. 1.

33. celebrare, properly used of a concourse of people for a feast or other event at some particular spot, or on some particular day: hence used of individuals ‘ to celebrate,’ or, as here, ‘ to worship.’ It was customary for a traveller, on his return home, to pay solemn salutations to his Lares and Penates: hence l. 33 is equivalent to a prayer that he may return to his own home safe and sound. Cp. Ter. Phorm. 2. 1. 81, where Demipho says, on his return from foreign parts,

> *At ego Deos Penates hinc salutatum domum*
> *Devortar.*

34. menstrua tura. In allusion to the offerings, chiefly of frankincense, flowers, and wine, which were made to the Lares on the kalends, i. e. the 1st of every month, at the new moon. Cp. Hor. Od. 3. 23. 2

> *Nascente Luna, rustica Phidyle,*
> *Si ture placaris et horna*
> *Fruge Lares avidaque porca.*

35. Saturno rege, i. e. in the golden age: cp. 2. 5. 9 and note.

36. We speak in the same way of a new country being ‘ opened up.’ **in longas vias,** so as to make journeys to them possible, acc. of result. For *vias* see 1. 1. 26.

37. contempserat, i. e. had got over its primitive and natural fear of the unruly element: had not yet learnt to be indifferent to. Cp. Juv. 10. 123.

Note the poetical variety caused by placing **que** after the second, instead of after the first, word in the sentence. See below l. 56 and Prop. 2. 20. 12

> *Ferratam Danaes transiliamque domum.*

39. compendia here stands for ‘ gain.’ *Compendium* is properly a gain effected by saving, being the opposite of *dispendium*, ‘ a paying or weighing out.’ The phrase *facere compendium* or *com-*

pendii is frequently used by the early dramatists, generally in a colloquial sense, for 'to save,' 'cut short;' thus Plaut. Capt. 5. 2. 12

> *Satis facundus : sed iam fieri dictis compendium volo.*

40. presserat, i. e. 'had laden.'   Cp. Virg. Geo. 1. 303

> *Ceu pressae quum iam portum tetigere carinae.*

44. regere fines, 'to rule,' or 'define the marches' between
properties : a technical phrase of Roman law, often found in Cicero.
The heading of one section of the Justinian code is '*Finium regun-
dorum.*'   Ovid gives an account of the god Terminus, Fast. 2. 639
sqq. : see especially l. 659

> *Tu populos urbesque et regna ingentia finis :*
> *Omnis erit sine te litigiosus ager.*

Cf. also Virg. Aen. 12. 897, where Turnus sees

> *Saxum antiquum, ingens, campo quod forte iacebat,*
> *Limes agro positus, litem ut discerneret agris.*

45. The idea was that honey dropped spontaneously from the
leaves of the oak : as in Virg. E. 4. 30

> *Et durae quercus sudabunt roscida mella.*

48. duxerat used here of the art of the forger : 'had hammered
out.'   So the Greek ἐλαύνειν.   Cp. Aen. 7. 633

> *alii thoracas aenos,*
> *Aut leves ocreas lento ducunt argento.*

The word is used also of the sculptor working in bronze : Hor. Epp.
2. 1. 240

> *aut alius Lysippo duceret aera*
> *Fortis Alexandri vultum simulantia.*

49. Nunc.   Tibullus takes cognisance here of two ages only,
the gold and the iron.   See on 2. 5. 9.

50. mare.   With special reference to ll. 37, 38.

repente is used here almost with the force of an adjective ;
perhaps to contrast with *semper* in l. 49.   So *super* in Virg. Aen. 3.
487

> *O mihi sola mei super Astyanactis imago.*

51. timidum refers to the same cause of fear as **terrent,** the
two words merely intensifying the meaning.   The sense is 'I have
committed no perjuries, I have uttered no impious words, to give me
reason to fear the wrath of the gods.'   So Prop. 2. 28. 6 declares the
true cause of Cynthia's illness to be *totiens sanctos non habuisse deos.*
Pater of course is Jupiter.   This gives a more natural sense than to
take it 'I *am* afraid, but it is not my sins which terrify me.'

53. fatales, 'the term of years assigned to me by destiny.'

54. fac ... stet, *ut* omitted, as frequently.

55. immiti, because premature. *Acerbus* is the word usually employed of an early death, as Virg. Aen. 6. 429, where *funere mersit acerbo* is used of those dying in infancy.

57–82. ' It is interesting to examine into the ideas entertained by the earlier Greeks of the lower world and a future state, as expressed by Homer, and to mark the modifications introduced by Virgil into his narrative.

' According to Homeric Geography, the earth was a flat circular plain or disc, completely encompassed and bounded by the great stream of Ocean. The abode of departed spirits, the kingdom of Hades, was called *Erebus*, and lay under the world inhabited by men ; the entrance was placed on the western bank of the Ocean stream, at a spot where the rivers Pyriphlegethon and Cocytus, the latter of which is a branch of Styx, unite at a rock and pour their waters into (the marsh of?) Acheron, Od. 10. 513. The natural objects in this nether-world are shadowy representations of those in the world above. There is a sky, and clouds, and storms, meadows, hills, trees, and fruits. The only thing wanting is a Sun. The bright light of day never penetrates into those dismal regions, which are overspread by a gloomy twilight. As upon earth, good and bad men are mingled together without distinction ; the former enjoy no reward, the latter suffer no punishment. A few only who have broken their oaths, Il. 3. 276, or openly outraged the majesty of heaven, are tortured as the enemies of the gods. Such are Tityus, Tantalus, and Sisyphus. The ghosts of the dead wear the same external aspect as at the moment when they departed from life, follow the same pursuits, and cherish the same feelings and passions. Thus Odysseus recognises, at once, all his former friends, as they throng the edge of the pit, eager to drink the blood of the victims which he had slain. He beholds Minos grasping a sceptre, laying down laws, and deciding the controversies of the dead, and Orion, club in hand, pursuing and slaying the beasts of chase, while Ajax, still cherishing vindictive wrath, turns away and refuses to hold communion with his former foe.

' On the whole, the inmates of Erebus are discontented and unhappy, comparing their actual nothingness with their former vigour and power. Achilles, in reply to the compliments of Odysseus, exclaims,

> *Extol not death to me, illustrious chief,*
> *For rather would I toil on earth for hire,*
> *The bonded servant of some needy swain,*
> *Than rule supreme o'er all the shadowy hosts.*

' *Tartarus* is perfectly distinct from *Erebus ;* it is a dark abyss as far below earth as earth is below heaven, Il. 8. 17 ; a brazen anvil, says Hesiod, Theog. 720, dropped from heaven, would fall for nine days and nine nights, and on the tenth day would reach the earth ; a brazen anvil dropped from earth would fall for nine days and nine nights, and on the tenth day would reach Tartarus.   In this gloomy dungeon, closed in with gates of iron, Il. 8. 15, sit Kronus and Iapetus, Il. 8. 479, on whom the sun never shines, and the breeze never blows, and who, along with the other Titans, rebels against Zeus, are guarded by Cottus and Gyges, and high-souled Briareus, Il. 14. 274, 279, Hes. Theog. 720.

'*Elysium*, again, is a happy plain on the western confines of the earth, cooled by Ocean breezes, where certain favoured men live a life of bliss.   The description in Homer Od. 4. 562 forms part of the prophecy delivered by Proteus to Menelaus, and is well known on account of its exquisite beauty.

'Let us now briefly compare these statements with the picture drawn by Virgil, who, although following in the steps of the great master, has embellished his descriptions with many particulars derived, in part, perhaps, from his own imagination, but chiefly from the later Greek poets and philosophers.

1. 'The rivers Acheron, Styx, Cocytus, Phlegethon, are all *in* the nether world. It is not easy to seize the conception formed by Virgil of their position and connection, but it is clear that they formed a boundary, and that it is necessary that one of them should be crossed by the spirits of the dead before they can gain access to their destined abode.

2. 'They are transported across by the grim ferryman Charon, a personage unknown to Homer, and those only are allowed to pass who have received the rites of sepulture. Those whose bodies remain unburied are compelled to wander disconsolate for the term of a hundred years, a condition unknown to Homer. On the farther side of the stream is the cave of Cerberus (Homer speaks of the dog of Hades, and he is named by Hesiod), and beyond is a region tenanted by those who have died a violent death before the hour appointed by fate.

3. ' *Tartarus*, at the entrance of which sits the fury Tisiphone, is a deep gulph which opens out of the realms of Pluto, and is the general place of punishment for the Titans, the Hundred-handed, Tantalus, Sisyphus, the Danaids, and all impious men.

4. '*Elysium* is *in* the lower world, and is the blissful abode of all the virtuous.

5. 'Minos and Rhadamanthus act as judges, and decide the lot of the spirits whether for weal or woe.

6. 'The Pythagorean doctrine of the transmigration of souls is introduced. The inhabitants of Elysium, after a certain period, drink of the river *Lethe*, which induces perfect oblivion of the past, and then ascend to upper air to animate new bodies.

'See Voss, "Homer's Unterwelt," to be found in his "Kritische Blätter," vol. 2. Consult also Heyne on Virg. Aen. 6.'

57. facilis, 'obedient,' 'compliant,' 'kindly.' Cp. Ov. Her. 16. 282
> *Sic habeas faciles in tua vota deos,*
'that lend themselves kindly to.'

61. casiam. 'This is a perfume or spice, the same as that spoken of by Virgil, Geo. 2. 466
> *Nec casia liquidi corrumpitur usus olivi.*
It is the *Casia* of Pliny (H. N. 16. 32), the κασία of the Greeks, which Theophrastus describes as coming from Arabia, and which must, from his words, have resembled our cinnamon. It was, in all probability, the bark of the *Laurus Cassia* (Linn.) the substance well known in commerce as *Cassia Lignea*. We must carefully distinguish this from a sweet smelling herb growing commonly in Italy, and frequently spoken of by Virgil, e. g. E. 2. 49
> *Tum casia, atque aliis intexens suavibus herbis,*
and Geo. 2. 213
> *Vix humiles apibus casias roremque ministrat,*
and again, Geo. 4. 30, 184, 304 ; Ciris, 370.

'This last is believed to be the same with the κνέωρον or θυμελαία of the Greeks, and the *Daphne Gnidium* of Linnaeus (see "Flore de Virgile par A. L. Feé.")'

non culta seges. Note that *seges* signifies (1) a growing crop, (2) as here, the land on which a crop grows. The former meaning appears in Virg. Geo. 1. 77
> *Urit enim lini campum seges, urit avenae,*
the second in Geo. 1. 47
> *Illa seges demum votis respondet avari*
> *Agricolae, bis quae solem, bis frigora sensit.*

63. series, from *sero*, 'to bind' or 'twine,' is applied to any number of objects linked together: thus here of a band of·youths and maidens dancing hand in hand.

64. praelia, not, as H. supposes, of the quarrels of lovers, but after the fashion of the Elegiac poets, who love to compare the feats

K

of love with feats of war. The meaning is the same as in 1. 10. 53

  Sed Veneris tum bella calent.

Our word ' engagement ' has a similar twofold application, and in all tongues the language of Love has borrowed such terms as ' conquest,' ' captivating,' ' killing,' ' chains,' etc., from the operations of the sterner art.

  66. Note the change of construction : *qui* has to be supplied before **gerit.**

  insigni, because wreathed with a chaplet ; **myrtea,** because the myrtle was sacred to Venus. Cp. Virg. Aen. 6. 442

   Hic, quos durus amor crudeli tabe peredit,
   Secreti celant calles, et myrtea circum
   Silva tegit.

  67. scelerata. It may be doubted whether this word here means ' hateful,' ' accursed,' or is used as = *sceleratorum,* i. e. the abode of the guilty. Similarly Ov. Met. 4. 455 of the infernal regions

   sedes scelerata vocatur,

and Virg. Aen. 6. 563

   Nulli fas casto sceleratum insistere limen.

The former interpretation is rendered probable by *impia Tartara* Virg. Aen. 6. 543, and *lugentes campi* ib. 441.

  69. Tisiphone. Cp. Virgil's description, Aen. 6. 570

   Continuo sontes ultrix accincta flagello
   Tisiphone quatit insultans, torvosque sinistra
   Intentans angues vocat agmina saeva sororum.

  ' The 'Ερινύες of the Greeks, who are the same with the *Furiae* of the Latins, appear as independent goddesses in Homer and Hesiod. According to the latter, they sprang from the blood drops which fell from the wound inflicted by Kronus (Saturn) on his father Uranus (Coelus), Theog. 183. Their number was first defined to be three by Euripides, Orest. 408, 1650, and the names *Alecto, Megaera, Tisiphone,* are not found until we come down to the authors of the Alexandrian school. In the popular creed they were viewed as ever wakeful, ever active avenging spirits, who inflicted punishment upon impious criminals, by awakening remorse and expelling them from society in this life, and by torturing them in the nether-world. They were worshipped by the Greeks under the propitiatory titles of Εὐμένιδες (benevolent), and Σεμναὶ θεαί (Venerable Goddesses), of which the former appellation is said to have originated at Sicyon, the latter at Athens, although both were familiar to the tragedians. See " Muller's Dissertations on the Eumenides of Aeschylus." '

pro crinibus. The snakes are here represented as actually forming her hair: elsewhere they are twined into it. Note that *pro crinibus* must be taken exclusively along with *feros angues*: 'the wild snakes which are to her in place of hair.'

71. serpentum . . . ore stridet, 'hisses through his serpent throat.' Cerberus had three mouths, but Hor. in the same way uses the singular *ore trilingui* Od. 2. 19. 31. Virgil places the snakes on his neck, Aen. 6. 419; Horace on his head, Od. 3. 11. 17.

niger. In the metaphorical sense of the word *ater* is more common: as Hor. Od. 2. 13. 34 of Cerberus

> *Demittit atras bellua centiceps*
> *Aures.*

73. Ixionis. ' " Legends preserved by the clans of northern Greece, and stamped, as it seems to me, with evident marks of high antiquity, represent Ixion, the Phlegyan chieftain, as the first example of an expiation from blood-guiltiness, but withal repaid by ingratitude. Ixion, in slaying the father of his bride, is the first among men who has shed kindred blood (Pind. Pyth. 2. 32). Then wild frenzy seizes him; he wanders like Cain; none either of gods or men will give him expiation (Pherecyd. frag. 69), until Jupiter himself at last takes compassion upon him and cleanses him. But, unmindful of the sacred obligation which binds the expiated to the expiator, he stretches forth his audacious arms even to Juno." (Mueller.) Deceived by the goddess, who substituted a cloud moulded into her own shape, he became the father of Centaurus, from whom sprung the monster race half man, half horse. Zeus, to punish his insolent ingratitude, launched his bolt and hurled him down to Erebus, where, bound to an ever-revolving wheel, he atones for his offence by eternal torments.'

75. Tityos. 'The giant Tityos is in Homer a son of Earth, but according to Apollodorus, of Zeus and Elara, daughter of Orchomenus. He insulted Leto, who summoned to her assistance her children, Apollo and Artemis, by whose shafts the monster was slain. He endures eternal torture in the realms of Hades, where vultures prey upon his liver, Hom. Od. 11. 575, Apollod. 1. 4. 1. His crime and punishment are described in the Odyssey, and Virg. Aen. 6. 595 has closely imitated the passage in six magnificent lines:

> *Nec non et Tityon Terrae omniparentis alumnum,*
> *Cernere erat: per tota novem cui iugera corpus*
> *Porrigitur; rostroque immanis voltur adunco*
> *Immortale iecur tondens, fecundaque poenis*
> *Viscera, rimaturque epulis, habitatque sub alto*
> *Pectore; nec fibris requies datur ulla renatis.*

'Lucretius, 2. 997, considers the fable of Tityos as an allegorical representation of the tortures caused by the various passions and desires which gnaw the heart of man.'

77. 'Tantalus was king of Lydia, son of Jupiter and the nymph Pluto, and father by Dione, or, as others say, Euryanassa, one of the Atlantides, of Pelops and Niobe. The cause, as well as the form of his punishment, in the infernal regions, are differently narrated by different writers. Ulysses, in the Odyssey, 11. 581, thus depicts his fate,—

> And Tantalus I saw in grievous plight,
> All in a lake he stood, it reached his chin;
> Thirsty he stood, but might not quench that thirst;
> Oft as the old man stooped, eager to drink,
> So oft the water shrunk and disappeared,
> While round his feet dark earth was seen—the might
> Of some divinity dried up the flood.
> From tall green trees rich fruits depending swung,
> Pomegranates, pears, and apples shining bright,
> The luscious fig, the olive in its pride,
> But when the old man raised his oustretched hand
> To satisfy his hunger, straight the breeze
> Whirled them aloft to the dark clouds of heaven.

The account of Homer is followed by Propertius, 2. 1. 66; Horace, Sat. 1. 1. 68; Ovid, A. A. 2. 605; Seneca, Herc. Fur. 752, and others. On the other hand, Pindar, Olymp. 1, says that an enormous stone was hung over his head by Zeus, and that he is tormented by the endless dread of danger, because he stole away nectar and ambrosia from the table of the gods, and conveyed it to his earthly peers. Euripides[1], who to a certain extent adopts the same version of the tale, represents him as swinging aloft midway between heaven and earth, while the rock suspended from golden chains whirls above his head,

> For that, so runs the tale, a mortal man
> By gods admitted to communion high,
> He failed to curb his tongue—disease most foul.

Compare, among the Latins, Lucretius 3. 993

> Nec miser impendens magnum timet aere saxum
> Tantalus, ut fama est, magna formidine torpens.'

stagna, the nominative case.

---

[1] Orest. 4 and 980. For further particulars see Eustathius and the Scholia upon Homer, and the Scholia upon Pindar and Euripides.

79. Danai proles. 'According to Apollodorus, 2. 1, 4, 5, Epaphus, son of Zeus and Io, became king of Egypt, and wedded Memphis, daughter of Nilus, by whom he had a daughter, Libya. Líbya bore to Poseidon twin sons, Agenor and Belus; Agenor passed over to Phoenicia, where he reigned and became the patriarch of a mighty tribe, while Belus remained in Egypt and married Anchinoe, daughter of Nilus, who gave birth to twin sons, Aegyptus and Danaus. Belus established Aegyptus in Arabia, and Danaus in Libya; the former, by many wives, was the father of fifty sons, the latter of a like number of daughters. Discord having arisen between the brothers, Danaus, fearing the sons of Aegyptus, by the advice of Pallas, constructed a ship and fled to Argos, where Gelanor, the reigning monarch, surrendered to him the sovereignty[1]. The sons of Aegyptus followed their uncle, entreated him to forego his anger, and to bestow on them his daughters in marriage. Danaus distrusted their professions and still harboured resentment, but consented to their proposal. On the day of the nuptials, after the marriage feast, he distributed daggers to the damsels, who murdered their husbands while asleep, all save Hypermnestra, who spared Lynceus. The rest were purified from their blood-guiltiness by Hermes and Athene at the bidding of Zeus. Danaus, in his wrath, cast Hypermnestra[2] into prison, but afterwards forgave her, and bestowed her upon Lynceus. The rest of his daughters he offered as prizes in a gymnastic contest, and awarded them to the victors. Apollodorus says nothing of any punishment inflicted on the Danaids, but other writers feigned that they were sentenced in the realms of Hades to draw water in a vessel full of holes. Lucretius treats this as an allegory representing discontent, 3. 1021

Hoc, ut opinor, id est aevo florente puellas
Quod memorant laticem pertusum congerere in vas,
Quod tamen expleri nulla ratione potestur.'

numina. Note that the plural *numina* is here spoken of in relation to a single deity. This is common in the poets: as in Virg. Aen. 7. 297, where Juno exclaims indignantly

At, credo, mea numina tandem
Fessa iacent.

See too 3. 543 and Geo. 1. 30. The same use explains the difficult

---

[1] The circumstances are detailed by Pausan. 2. 19.
[2] Told somewhat differently by Pausan. 2. 19.

expression Aen. 1. 8, also in reference to Juno; *quo numine laeso,* 'at what point, in what respect, was her divinity outraged that.'

82. lentas ... militias, i. e. wished that my campaign might be spun out so as to keep me away from Delia.

84. anus. From 1. 6. 57 it would seem that the *duenna* who is to keep guard over Delia, tell her stories, and set her a-spinning, was her mother: otherwise the unceremonious way in which she is spoken of might lead us to surmise that she was the counterpart of the modern nurse, developed into a lady companion.

85. posita. *Ponere* is specially used of setting down things on a table: of a lamp or candle, therefore, it is equivalent to our phrase 'to bring in' lights: of a dish put down at a meal, it means 'to serve up.' Thus Pers. 1. 53 *Calidum scis ponere sumen,* 'you know how to serve up a sow's paunch piping hot.'

86. Deducat, 'to draw out,' the regular word used of spinning, and so often used metaphorically of the drawing out or spinning of verses. See Prop. 1. 16. 41. We learn from various passages, e. g. Ov. Met. 4. 32-45, that the correct way of spending the evening for the female part of an ancient household was to be busy with spinning or weaving, while one of the party would tell stories. Cp. the well known story of Lucretia, Liv. 1. 58, Ov. Fast. 2. 741 sqq.

Lumen ad exiguum famulae data pensa trahebant.

87. circa is peculiar, used of a single *puella.* Yet we speak of one person being always 'about' another, meaning 'in their company.' *Puella* can scarcely stand for 'a group of maidens.'

91. qualis eris, 'just as you are,' without making any change on my account. *Ut eras* is frequently used in the same way; Ov. Met. 4. 473

Tisiphone canos, ut erat, turbata capillos.

92. nudato, i. e. 'without taking time to put on your shoes.'

93. hunc illum. This phrase well illustrates the meaning of these two pronouns. *Illum* is 'that distant, much-hoped for, glorious day, when I shall return to you;' *hunc* (which contains the predicate of the sentence) means 'just such a day as I have now described.' The meaning then is 'may that glorious day when it comes be like this,' 'such be that day.'

I. 7.

THIS poem is a birthday panegyric in celebration of the triumph of his patron Messalla, and of the various great services by which that triumph was earned. The triumph took place on the 24th Sept. B. C. 27, and it would seem that Messalla's birthday must have fallen a few days after that event, so that the poet is able dexterously to weave together the two causes of congratulation. An outline of Messalla's career has been given already in the note to 1. 1. 53. The poet begins by celebrating his patron's victories in Aquitania, and enumerates the various tribes which he subdued. He then passes on to describe his mission to the East, to which he appears to have been appointed at the close of B. C. 30. During the course of that year Augustus had received the submission of Syria from Antony's legate Didius; the Antonian troops in Egypt had surrendered, Antony and Cleopatra had committed suicide, and from the 1st of August Egypt had formally been made into a Roman province. Augustus prepared once more to winter at Samos rather than return to Rome, not only because Samos was a central spot from which he could keep an eye upon the course of affairs in the East, but also because he wished to allow matters to ripen in the City, and to make the need of his presence there the more keenly felt. With this view he had to keep his own hands free : so he summoned over Messalla from Aquitania, and entrusted him apparently with a general mission to make a progress in the East, to settle the provinces, and to see that the dispositions made by himself were carried into effect. In the course of this mission he passed through Syria, Cilicia and Egypt. Augustus himself returned to Italy in B. C. 29; Messalla did not return to Rome till B. C. 27 when he celebrated his triumph for his Aquitanian successes. Tibullus accompanied Messalla upon this mission as far as Corcyra, where he was taken ill, as we saw in Elegy 3, and was obliged to stay behind.

It will be noted that Tibullus in this poem gives especial prominence to Egypt, its gods and its fertility, and connects the acquisition of that country with the inauguration of a new era of peace and plenty. Egypt had by this time become the main granary of Rome ; its safe keeping became a matter of special concern to the emperor ; and its inclusion within the strong grasp of the Roman system was justly regarded as a pledge not less of economic prosperity than of political security.

1. nentes, 'while spinning.' The ancient idea was that the Fates, as they span the thread of each man's destiny at his birth, chaunted at the same time a song in which the main events of his life were foretold. Sometimes the prediction was made at the marriage of the parents, as in the famous case of the marriage of Peleus and Thetis, Catull. 64, where the fortunes of Achilles are told to the recurring refrain,

Currite ducentes subtemina, currite fusi.

In Tib. 4. 5. 3 the prophecy is made at the birth,

Te nascente, novum Parcae cecinere puellis
Servitium et dederunt regna superba tibi.

Ovid imitates this passage in Trist. 5. 3. 25.

2. dissoluenda. The *u* is here vocalised as in Cat. 66. 38

Pristina vota novo munere dissŏlŭō.

So in l. 74 *ēvŏlŭăm* and Hor. Epod. 13. 2 *nunc mare, nunc sĭlŭāe.*

3. Hunc perhaps implies that the victory was gained on Messalla's birthday. This supposition removes the harshness of identifying the day and the man.

Aquitanas. The limits of Aquitania are thus defined by Caesar, B. G. 1. 1 *Aquitania a Garumna flumine ad Pyrenaeos montes et eam partem Oceani quae est ad Hispaniam pertinet, spectat inter occasum solis et septemtriones.*

4. quem tremeret, 'at thought of whom the vanquished Atax should tremble.' *Atax* is a river in Gallia *Narbonensis*, now the *Aude*, which flows from the Pyrenees into the Mediterranean; as it nowhere passes through Aquitania, Scaliger ingeniously conjectured *Atur*, for the usual form *Aturus*, the modern *Adour*, which flows into the Bay of Biscay through the centre of that province. But the *Atax* may well have been the scene of some preliminary victory, as its valley affords the natural access to Aquitania.

5. Evenere, i. e. the facts foretold by the Fates at their spinning.

pubes Romana, i. e. 'the manhood of Rome,' 'the Roman people:' so *Dardana pubes* for the Trojans, Virg. Aen. 7. 219.

6. No distinction of meaning can be established between **evinctos** and *vinctos*, as though the former were a stronger word. It is used of gentle bindings, as by garlands or fillets, Virg. Aen. 5. 494, Ov. Am. 3. 6. 57. Captives were usually represented with their arms bound behind their backs, but this meaning is not expressed by *evinctos.*

7, 8. In allusion to Messalla's triumph. The imperf. *portabat* is used for graphic effect.

9. We thus see that Tibullus accompanied Messalla in the campaign. The *Tarbelli* are named by Plin. N. H. 4. 19 amongst the Aquitanian tribes. Their country, id. 30, 2, was celebrated for its hot and cold springs. They lived on the *Aturus*, and are mentioned by Lucan and other authors as living on that stream, 1. 419

> nunc rura Nemosi
> *Qui tenet, et ripas Aturi, qua litore curvo*
> *Molliter admissum claudit Tarbellicus aequor,*
> *Signa movet, gaudetque amoto Santonus hoste.*

Ausonius speaks of *Tarbellicus Aturus*, and the tribe has given its name to the modern *Tarbes*.

10. The *Santones* dwelt to the N. of the Garonne, giving their name to the modern province *Santoigne*.

11. Arar. The Arar is the modern *Saone*, a river which flows into the Rhone with a course due Southwards at Lyons, and has its origin on the S. slopes of the Vosges mountains, not far from the sources of the Meuse and the Moselle, which, rising on the Northern side of the same chain, flow Northwards towards the Rhine and the Atlantic. Geographically speaking, the valley of the Saone is, in fact, the continuation, or rather the commencement, of the great Rhone valley, so that the Rhone ought rather to be considered the tributary of the Saone, than the Saone the tributary of the Rhone. But with rivers, as with nations, might often triumphs over right: and the superior volume of the Rhone, fed by the snows of Switzerland, has enabled it to usurp the title which belonged by right to the placid Gallic stream. Caesar thus describes the Saone: *Flumen est Arar, quod per fines Aeduorum et Sequanorum in Rhodanum fluit incredibili lenitate, ita ut oculis, in utram partem fluat, iudicari non possit* B. G. 1. 12.

12. Carnutis. So M.: but A. has *Carnoti*. Caesar calls the people Carnutes: but as the Greek form is Καρνοῦτοι, the Latin form should be *Carnūtes*, not as here *Carnŭtis*. This people in Caesar's time occupied the country to the W. of the upper Seine, upon both banks of the Loire. They give their name to the province called *Chartrain*, and to the modern town of *Chartres* (Autricum). It is to be noted that in this and other cases, the name of modern French towns is derived not from the Roman name of the ancient city on the same site, but from that of the Gallic tribe which occupied the surrounding country. Thus *Paris* derives its name from the *Parisii*, not from *Lutetia*; *Bourges* from the *Bituriges*, not from *Avaricum*; *Tours*, not from *Augustodunum*, but from the

Turones. Similarly *Trèves* takes its name from the *Treviri;* *Amiens* from the *Ambiani,* *Rheims* from the *Remi, Soissons* from the *Suessiones, Angers* from the *Andecavi, Nantes* from the *Nam-netes,* etc.

flavi, because the Celts of Gaul appeared light-haired to the inhabitants of Italy.

Liger, the Loire. It will be noted that Tibullus takes a wide sweep through the names of Gaul, and by no means confines himself to Aquitania. The epithet *caerula* must either refer to the estuary of the Loire, with its sea water, or else be an unmeaning general epithet applicable to streams in general; for no epithet could be less applicable to the Loire itself. As a rule, the Roman poets had a true eye for streams and rivers, and generally describe them by characteristic terms. Their descriptions of mountain or forest scenery, on the other hand, are in the last degree conventional and vague.

13. The poet now passes on to describe Messalla's exploits in the East, and begins by addressing the Cydnus (the *Tersoos*), the one famous river of Cilicia, which rises in Mount Taurus and passes by the walls of Tarsus, birth-place of the apostle Paul.

14. This line is generally thought corrupt from the redundancy of **placidis aquis.** It is impossible, as some propose, to take these words as datives for *ad aquas,* 'creepest on to the calm waters of the lake' (Pind.), in allusion to the swamp called the ῥῆγμα, into which Strabo says the Cydnus emptied itself. The words **per vada,** however, do seem to refer to such shallows: if so, *tacitis undis* will describe the general character of the river, *placidis aquis* the broad smooth surface of the swamp or lake into which it passed.

- 15. quantus et, 'I will tell too how great.'

16. arat, the MS. reading, is obviously corrupt, and all editors now agree in substituting **alat.** This makes good sense; for Strabo tells us that Mount Taurus was cultivated to the very summit. The construction of the passage requires the subjunctive mood, and even if it were not so, the idea that *Taurus arat Cilices* can be equivalent to *Cilices arant Taurum,* gravely put forward by Scaliger, is as absurd as to say that 'the cat killed the mouse' is equivalent to 'the mouse killed the cat.' Scarcely less absurd· is H.'s interpretation 'Mount Taurus cuts through or traverses the land of the Cilicians.' Mount Taurus does nothing of the kind, nor can the Latin be made to say so.

18. sancta, not 'hallowed by' (Pind.) as if *Palaestino Syro* were an ablative, but 'sacred to, holy in the eyes of, the Syrian of Palestine.'

Palaestino is an adj., 'the Palestine Syrian.' Note that the term *Syria* was used in a loose sense by the Romans, being applied to the whole country bordering the Levant from Cilicia to Egypt, and stretching inward to the Euphrates and Arabia. Thus all Phoenicia and Palestine were included within its limits.

Pigeons were sacred to the Syrian Goddess *Astarte* or *Ashtaroth*, identified by the Greeks with Aphrodite.

20. Tyros, which became the chief city of Phoenicia after the decay of Sidon, is here put for the Phoenicians as a whole. As is well known, they invented navigation, and for many centuries monopolised the commerce not of the Mediterranean only, but of the world.

credere docta. This Graecism—an infin. depending directly upon an adjective or participle—is common in all the Augustan poets, but especially in Horace. Cp. Od. 4. 13. 7 *doctae psallere Chiae;* and Ib. 1. 1. 18 *indocilis pauperiem pati.* See below l. 28.

21-26. We may here transcribe a passage from Heeren on the ancient Egyptians: ' The cause of the yearly inundations of the Nile was an object of much research even in ancient times. Herodotus formed many conjectures respecting it, and decided for the most reasonable of them (Herod. 2. 20, etc.). Agatharchides, however, seems to have been the first to discover the truth (Agatharchid. ap. Diodor. 1. p. 50). The constant rains, to which the districts of Upper Ethiopia are subject during the wet season, from May to September, swell all the rivers in those regions, the whole of which pour their floods into the Nile, which consequently becomes the reservoir of this prodigious accumulation of water. In the middle of June, about the time of the summer solstice, the Nile begins to rise in Egypt. It continues to increase till the end of July, though still confined within its channel; but in the first half of August it overflows its banks, inundates the neighbouring territory[1], and its waters continue, without intermission, to extend themselves till September. About this time, the torrents of rain in Ethiopia having ceased, the Nile begins gradually to fall, but so slowly, that the greater part of the territory of Egypt remains covered with its waters till the commencement of October; and it is not till towards the end of this month that they completely return into their bed. The period of the inundation, therefore, continues from the middle of August to the end of October; and during this time all the fertile valley of Egypt

---

[1] It is usual to cut through dams and open canals on the 9th of August.

has the appearance of one vast lake, in which its cities jut up like so many islands. Ancient writers, indeed, are wont to compare it to the Aegean sea, where the Cyclades and Sporades offer a similar appearance, on a larger scale.'—Again, the same writer—' Although Lower Egypt is not altogether without rain, yet this so rarely falls, as we retire from the sea, that, under the constantly serene sky of Thebes, the whole period of man's life may pass away without the earth being refreshed from above with more than a moist dew. The irrigation and fertility of the soil, therefore, entirely depend upon the river, without which Egypt would have shared the fate of the rest of Africa, and have been partly a sandy waste, and partly a stony desert.'

The mystery of the sources of the Nile—the mighty beneficent river which unfailingly carries down its life-giving waters through hundreds of miles of rainless country from the great unknown continent within—a mystery which has only been solved in our own day by our great countryman Livingstone—exercised the imagination of the ancients fully as much as it has done that of moderns. Thus Horace, Od. 4. 14. 45

Te fontium qui celat origines
Nilus,

and Ov. Am. 3. 6. 39

Ille fluens dives septena per ostia Nilus
Qui patriam tantae tam bene celat aquae.

Claudian, Nilus 13, has the fine phrase, *Fertur sine teste creatus.*

27. Osirim. 'Everything connected with Egyptian mythology is involved in the deepest obscurity, which has arisen, in a great measure, from the doctrine sedulously inculcated by the priesthood, that the religion of Greece had flowed from Egypt as from a fountain head, and that the prototypes of all the Grecian divinities were to be found on the banks of the Nile. Herodotus seems to have entertained no doubts of the general truth of this assertion, supported as it was by a mass of bold and ingenious fabrications. But, as an acquaintance with the subject became more accurate and extensive, subsequent writers found that many of the powers and attributes of the Egyptian gods would, by no means, apply to the members of the Grecian Pantheon, with whom they had been identified by the father of history; and although they seem never to have had any difficulty in acknowledging the general principle, yet they differed widely from him and from each other, in applying it. Hence the statements of these authors, when taken collectively, present a tissue of confusion and contradiction, which, in many cases, becomes inextricable, from the practice of employing the Greek denominations at once, without noticing the native names. Thus Greek writers, when discussing Egyptian mythology, speak of the rites of Apollo, Pan, Artemis, Hermes, Hephaestus, Latona[1] and others, just as familiarly as if they were describing the ceremonies of Athens or Argos; while, in many instances, we have no means of ascertaining, beyond some vague and fortuitous resemblance, the nature of the personages to whom they refer.

'There seems, however, to be no doubt that *Osiris,* and his consort *Isis,* were two principal objects of popular adoration among the Egyptians, and that their worship was not confined to any particular district, as was the case with many of their deities, but prevailed over the whole land. As to the nature of this pair, we find, as might be expected from the remarks made above, various and conflicting accounts: By some, Osiris was considered to be the Sun (Plutarch. Isid. et Osirid.; Diog. Laert. in prooemio; Macrob. Sat. 1. 21); by others, to be a personification of the river Nile (Eusebius—Selden, de Dis Syriis 1. 4; see Prichard's Egyptian Mythology, p. 76); but, according to the idea generally entertained by the Greeks, he was the same with their Dionysus or Bacchus, the Liber Pater of the Latins, and as such he is represented by Tibullus in the lines before us

'*Isis* again was by many regarded as the Moon (Plutarch de Isid. et Osirid.; Diodor. 1. 11); by others, as Pallas Athene (Plutarch as before); but generally by the Greeks as the same with their Demeter, or Mother Earth, the Ceres of the Latins. This is expressly asserted by Herodotus, 2. 156, and corroborated by Diodorus, 1. 13. She is, however, often confounded with Argive Io, e. g. Ov. Met. 1. 588, 724.

28. Memphiten ... bovem. 'He means the sacred, oracular bull, *Apis,* which was kept at Memphis, the capital of Lower Egypt, in a magnificent temple, to which were attached spacious pleasure grounds, where he might take healthful exercise (Aelian. de Animal. 2. 10). This animal was believed to be an incarnation of Osiris (Strabo 17; Diodor. 1), and was recognised by a number of peculiar marks described by Pliny, H. N. 8. 46, and Aelian, De Animal. 2.

---

[1] Latona is mentioned as an Egyptian Goddess by Herodotus and many others, but we should have been entirely ignorant of her native appellation had it not been for a passage in a late grammarian, Stephanus Byzantinus, from which we learn that it was *Bouto.*

10.   He was said to live for twenty-five years, at the end of which period he was supposed to drown himself by leaping into the Nile,

Quos dignetur agros, aut quo se gurgite Nili
Mergat adoratus trepidis pastoribus Apis

Stat. Sylv. 3. 2. 115.   He was then interred with great pomp, and the priests wandered about for some days, shrieking, beating their breasts, and exhibiting every outward form of grief, until a new Apis was found, when the discovery was celebrated by a joyful festival, termed the Theophania, or Manifestation of the god.   This lasted for five days.   All the ceremonies, together with an account of the nurture of the young Apis, are detailed by Aelian.   See Prichard's Egyptian Mythology, p. 305; Jablonski, Pantheon Aegypt. 4. 2, etc.

'There were other sacred bulls besides Apis.   Such was *Mnevis*, worshipped at On or Heliopolis; *Pacis*, at Hermonthis; and one of vast size, with his hair reversed, called *Onuphis*.   See Prichard, as above.

'We may conclude this notice by quoting the words of Pliny, H. N. 8. 46 *Bos in Aegypto etiam numinis vice colitur, Apim vocant. Insigne ei, in dextro latere candicans macula, cornibus Lunae crescere incipientis: nodus sub lingua, quem cantharum appellant. Non est fas eum certos vitae excedere annos, mersumque in sacerdotum fonte enecant, quaesituri luctu alium, quem substituant, et donec invenerint, maerent, derasis capitibus: nec tamen umquam diu quaeritur. Inventus deducitur Memphim a sacerdotibus.*   He then goes on to give an account of his oracular powers, and of his having been consulted by Germanicus Caesar.'

According to the view of Brugsch (Religion u. Mythologie der alten Aegypter, 1884) and that of many recent Egyptologers, the fundamental conception of the Egyptian religion was that there was one universal divine essence, which expanded itself into various distinct deities, such as *Ra, Amen, Ptah, Osiris;* while by a reverse process, each of these derived deities might also assume the form and the attributes of the one supreme originating power.   Thus *Nun* is distinctively the primal water element, from which all things were formed by the one soul of the whole, which is at once identical with, and yet distinct from it; and *Ra* is the principal title for the Sun, who is one main symbol of the divine permeating force.   Yet in localities specially sacred to *Amen*, he may be invoked, not only under his own name, but also as *Amen-Nun*, or as *Amen-Ra*.   *Ra* is especially the rising Sun, as *Tum* or *Atum* is the setting Sun: and as the Sun sets and rises again, so Osiris is held to live again after his murder by Typhon (Set). This myth probably typifies the struggle of darkness with light, and also of good with evil. In the same manner, the departed human soul was held to follow the Sun in his course through the nether world and to rise again. One special function of Osiris is that of Judge of the Dead : a function apparently assigned to no other deity. He frequently appears in this capacity in representations of Hades ; he is swathed as a mummy, and beside him is his minister *Anubis*, with the face of a dog or jackal, who assists in laying out the dead, etc.

Isis again affords an instance of the self-dividing process of the one original power in the matter of sex, as into active and passive. Just as several male gods may be fused into one, so Isis becomes Athor, Neith, Bast, etc. And the male power himself, becoming ἀρσενό-θηλυς, is styled both 'father of fathers,' and also 'mother of mothers,' the stronger sex absorbing the properties of both. Osiris, too, as primal spirit, being identified with primal matter, becomes the water which is the womb of the world, and hence passes on to be the Nile or even the Ocean. It is obvious that this quasi-Hegelian process may account to some extent for the different accounts given by Greek authors of Osiris and other Egyptian deities.

The river Nile was worshipped both in his own right, and also as representing Osiris. Hymns addressed to the Nile have been found: and Brugsch gives an inscription from a sarcophagus, on which the four gods, representing the four elements, who bestowed favours on the departed, are thus enumerated :

Ra, he gives thee light.
S'u, he gives thee sweet breath of air.
Qeb (or Seb, the Earth), he gives thee all growing fruits.
Osiris, he gives thee the Nile, thou livest again.

The two aspects of the Nile—the earthly and the heavenly—give a further illustration of the transforming tendency of Egyptian mythology. For as the earthly Nile is often named *Nun* or *Oceanus*, in one inscription he is styled 'Ocean-Nile (Nun-Hāpi), Father of Deities.' So too the heavenly stream assumes sometimes the name Hāp or Hāpi, which was the Egyptian title for the earthly river [1].

plangere ... bovem. '*Plangere* signifies—(1) Generally, 'to beat,' 'to strike.' (2) Specially, 'to beat the breast,' etc., in token of grief, and is construed either (1) with the accusative of the object

---

[1] For the substance of the above note I am indebted to my friend the late Professor Lushington.

struck, or (2) of the object of sorrow, or (3) absolutely, without a regimen, thus,

(1) *Plangebant alii proceris tympana palmis*

Catull. 64. 262.

Adspicit Alphenor, laniataque pectora plangens

Ov. Met. 6. 248.

(2) *Nec dubium de morte ratae, Cadmeida palmis*
Deplanxere domum, scissae cum veste capillos

Ov. Met. 4. 544.

(3)   *planxere sorores*
Naides, et sectos fratri posuere capillos.

Planxere et Dryades: plangentibus adsonat Echo

Ov. Met. 3. 505.

30. teneram, because the earth was yet young: cp. Virg. Geo. 2. 343

Nec res hunc tenerae possent perferre laborem.

inexpertae, l. 31, has the same reference.

sollicitavit. In the same sense Virg. Geo. 2. 418

Sollicitanda tamen tellus, pulvisque movendus.

33. palis, 'stakes' or 'props.' The vines of ancient (as of modern) Italy were trained along espaliers, most usually formed of growing elm trees. Hence continual reference in the poets to the 'widowed' or 'unwedded' vine when separated from its supporting elm.

34. See Virgil's directions for pruning the vine, Geo. 2. 362-370. **dura,** in antithesis to *tenera* l. 33.

36. incultis, . . . **pedibus,** i. e. 'to feet untrained to such work,' in the same sense as *nescia* l. 38.

37. voces inflectere cantu. *Inflectere* is 'to bend,' and *inflectere vocem* expresses the simple idea that the voice, when it changes its note, is as it were bent out of the straight line. Lucr. 5. 1406 varies the expression,

Ducere multimodis voces et flectere cantus.

Here the song itself is said to be bent, just as we say 'to turn a song.' The same idea survives in the term 'inflections' applied to the changes in a form by declension, etc.

40. tristitiae dissolvenda, 'to be freed of his gloom.' Here *solvere*, following the analogy of words of emptying, etc., is used with the genitive. Cp. Hor. Od. 3. 17. 12 *cum famulis operum solutis,* 'loosened in respect of,' i. e. 'loosened from, their work.'

42. Referring to the chains in which slaves were frequently forced to work.

44. aptus, 'fitted,' 'suitable.'

45, 46. For the repetition of *sed* Pind. compares Virg. Geo. 2. 467.

46. corymbis. *Corymbus* is a branch of ivy with the berries hanging from it. The ivy was sacred to Bacchus, and his locks were crowned with it.   Hence Ov. Fast. 1. 393

> *Festa corymbiferi celebrabat Graecia Bacchi.*

palla is the long woman's robe of saffron colour (*lutea*, κρο-κωτός) worn by Bacchus.   A purple or scarlet cloak (*Tyriae vestes*) was apparently thrown over the *palla*.

48. cista (Scottice ' kist ') was the box or case in which the sacred utensils and emblems were kept which formed the principal part of the mysteries in which the god Bacchus was worshipped. The articles were kept covered up with ivy leaves: hence Hor. Od. 1. 18. 11

> *Non ego te, candide Bassareu,*
> *Invitum quatiam, nec variis obsita frondibus*
> *Sub divum rapiam.*

See too Catull. 64. 259

> *Pars obscura cavis celebrabant orgia cistis.*

49. genium. 'The word *Genius* is derived from *geno* or *gigno*, signifying to *create* or *beget*, and the name was applied to a spiritual being who presided over the birth of man, attended upon and watched over him during life, and perished at his death.   Each individual had a separate genius who regulated his lot, and was represented as white or black, according to his fortunes.

'Horace, Ep. 2. 2. 187, in answer to the question—why are the natural dispositions and characters of those around us frequently so much opposed to each other?—replies,

> *Scit Genius, natale comes qui temperat astrum,*
> *Naturae deus humanae, mortalis in unum*
> *Quodque caput, vultu mutabilis, albus et ater;*

and Censorinus, De Die Natali 3 *Genius est deus, cuius in tutela, ut quisque natus est, vivit.   Hic, sive quod ut genamur curat, sive quod una genitur nobiscum, sive etiam quod nos genitos suscipit ac tuetur, certe e genendo Genius appellatur.   Eundem esse Genium et Larem, multi veteres memoriae prodiderunt.   Hunc in nos maximam, immo omnem habere potestatem, creditum est.   Nonnulli binos genios in iis dumtaxat domibus, quae essent maritae, colendos putaverunt. Euclides autem Socraticus duplicem omnibus omnino nobis Genium dicit appositum. . . .   Genio igitur potissimum per omnem aetatem quotannis sacrificamus. . . . Genius autem ita nobis assiduus obser-*

L

*vator appositus est, ut ne puncto quidem temporis longius abscedat,
sed ab utero matris exceptos ad extremium vitae diem comitetur.*

'The Genius of women was called a *Iuno.* Thus Pliny, H. N. 2. 7
*Quamobrem maior caelitum populus etiam quam hominum intelligi
potest, cum singuli quoque ex semetipsis totidem Deos faciant, Iunones
Geniosque adoptando sibi.* So Tibull. 4. 6. 1

> *Natalis Iuno, sanctos cape turis honores.*

Women accordingly swore by their Juno. Tibull. 3. 6. 47

> *Etsi perque suos fallax iurarit ocellos,*
>   *Iunonemque suam, perque suam Venerem.*

So also Petronius Arbiter 25 and Senec. Ep. 110.

'Such being the Genius, it will be easily understood why the
Natalis Dies, or birthday, was particularly set apart for his worship.
The nature of the sacrifices offered is fully illustrated by the lines
now under consideration, and by the following passages. Tibullus,
2. 2, celebrates the birthday of his friend Cerinthus:

> *Dicamus bona verba: venit Natalis ad aras:*
>   *Quisquis ades, lingua, vir mulierque, fave.*
> *Urantur pia tura focis, urantur odores,*
>   *Quos tener e terra divite mittit Arabs.*
> *Ipse suos Genius adsit visurus honores,*
>   *Cui decorent sanctas florea serta comas.*
> *Illius puro destillent tempora nardo,*
>   *Atque satur libo sit madeatque mero,*
> *Annuat et, Cerinthe, tibi quodcumque rogabis:*
>   *En age, quid cessas? annuit ille, roga.*

And 21

> *Hac veniat Natalis avi prolemque ministret,*
>   *Ludat et ante tuos turba novella pedes.*

See also 4. 5. 19. To which add Hor. Ep. 1. 1. 143, describing the
rural festivals of the olden time,

> *Tellurem porco, Silvanum lacte piabant,*
>   *Floribus et vino Genium memorem brevis aevi.*

'Varro, quoted by Censorinus 2, says that bloody offerings were
never presented to the Genius on a birthday feast, because men
thought that it was unbecoming to take away life on the day when
they themselves received it. This did not apply, it would seem, to
the feast in honour of another; for we find in Horace, when he is
making preparations to celebrate the birthday of Maecenas, Od. 4. 11. 6

> *Ridet argento domus, ara castis*
>   *Vincta verbenis avet immolato*
>   *Spargier agno.*

'The Genius was naturally believed to exercise an especial superintendence over wedlock; the marriage bed was under his protection,
and was called *genialis torus*[1], and the expression *genialis praeda*
is appropriately applied by Ovid A. A. 1. 125 to the Sabine women,
whom the Romans had forcibly seized for their brides. Observe
also that *genialis* is used generally as an epithet for anything which
conduces to festivity, mirth, or pleasure. *Genialis dies* is a day of
joviality, *Genialis hiems* points out winter as the season of convi-
viality, expressions arising from the comfortable doctrine held by the
ancients, that in taking care of themselves, and looking after their
own enjoyments, they were performing an acceptable service to their
Genius. Those who practised abstinence were said *defraudare
Genium suum*, Terent. Phorm. 1. 1. 9 *belligerare cum Genio*[2];
while the precept of Persius, S. 5. 151 *indulge Genio*, is an exhor-
tation to eat, drink, and be merry. In like manner, as there were
public *Lares* and *Penates*, the whole Roman people, taken collectively,
was supposed to have a Genius. When we read in Livy 21. 62 that
the Genius was propitiated by the sacrifice of five full-grown victims,
we must understand the historian to mean the Public Genius, to whom
we find votive tablets inscribed with the words GENIO. P. R. We
find similar tablets to the Genius of an Army, of a Century, of a
Colony; nay more, places also had their Genius[3], and Prudentius,
C. Symm. 2. 369, 444, twits his opponent with the fact, that walls,
gates, baths, stables, all had their Genii, so that scarce a corner of
the city could be found without a god of its own. The Genius of a
place was represented by a snake, Servius, Virg. Aen. 5. 85; and
hence to paint a snake upon the walls of any place of public resort
was the method adopted to point out that it was sacred, and not to
be defiled, Pers. S. 1. 113.

'Somewhat more mystical is the statement of Aufustius, an unknown writer quoted by Festus[4], that the Genius is the son of the
gods, and the creator of men (*deorum filius et parens hominum*), the
instrument, as it were, employed by the gods in the formation of men.

---

[1] Thus in Juv. Sat. 6. 22 *sacri genium contemnere fulcri* means
'to violate the marriage bed.'
[2] Plaut. Truc. 1. 2. 81. Compare also Plaut. Pers. 1. 3. 28 and 2.
3. 11; Stich. 4. 2. 42; Hor. Od. 3. 17.
[3] Servius on Virg. G. 1. 302 'Genium autem dicebant antiqui na-
turalem deum uniuscuiusque *loci vel rei vel hominis*.' In Aen. 7.
136 Aeneas invokes *Geniumque loci*.
[4] In voce *Genius*. See Müller, Die Etrusker, 3. 4, 5.

This seems to be connected with the ancient doctrine, Macrob. Sat. 1. 10, that the souls of men proceeded from Jupiter, and after death were restored to him again.   We can thus understand how a Genius might be attributed to the gods themselves—the Genii being, according to this view, agents who executed their will ; and, in fact, we read of *Genius Iovialis*[1], *Genius Infernus* (Fabrett. Inscrip. 2. 71), *Genius Plutonis* (Gruter. Inscrip. 1073. 8), *Genius Priapi* (Petron. Arb. 21), *Genius Famae* (Mart. 7. 11), and the like.   It is possible, however, that these are mere circumlocutions, indicating the divinities themselves.'

49. The MS. reading *centum ludos geniumque* is insupportable, as involving a harsh zeugma.   'Celebrate a hundred games and (honour) the Genius with a dance.' *Genium ludo geniumque choreis*, adopted by Hiller, is no better.   The probability is that the two words *genium* and *centum*, being so extremely like one another, got accidentally interchanged, and that the true reading is that of the text, *genium ludo centumque choreis.*   The change from *ludo* to *ludos* would naturally follow from the misplacement of *centum*, and the sense requires *centum* to go with the second substantive, not the first, and thus create a climax.   *Chorea* is usually found in the plural, so that *centum* is quite a permissible exaggeration, and harmonises with *multo* in the next line.   See Prop. 1. 3. 5 ; 3. 10. 23 ; Hor. Od. 2. 19. 25 ; Ov. Met. 8. 746.

tempora. The brow of the Genius was to be moistened with wine, just as his hair was to run down with unguents.   As above explained, the Genius was in all respects the representative and counterpart of the man himself.

51. Illius, sc. Genii : see 2. 2. 5 seqq. quoted above. The image of the Genius, in the form of a youth, stood in the *atrium ;* on festal days it was adorned with wreaths and unguents ; viands and wine were placed before it.

53. hodierne, for *hodie.*   Or it may be the vocative by a confusion of construction, as in Pers. S. 3. 28

Stemmate quod Tusco ramum millesime ducis.

honores here means ' a complimentary offering,' ' an offering paid as an honour.'   The word *honor* is generally used not with a mere abstract meaning, but with the additional sense of some external or material result.   Thus *honor, honores,* are the characteristic words to use for any of the great offices of the state.   See Juv. Sat. 1. 117

Sed quum summus honor finito computet anno,

---

[1] Caesius quoted by Arnob. adv. Gent. 3. 40. Varro quoted by Augustin. de Civ. Dei, 7. 2. 13.

where *summus honor* stands for 'our highest magistrates.' In Virg. Aen. 5. 308 it means 'a present;' so in 5. 534. For the present passage cp. Virg. Aen. 4. 207 and 1. 736

> *in mensam laticum libavit honorem.*

54. Liba. The *libum* was a cake much used in sacrifices; it was made of cheese, wheaten flour, and an egg. Cato, R. R. 75, gives a minute receipt for making it. When there was any feast in a house there was a large baking of *liba:* in Juv. 3. 187, when a favourite in a great house dedicates his beard or his hair,

> *Plena domus libis venalibus;*

i. e. 'the house is full of *liba:* but we, the poor clients, are made *to pay for them*,' because they had to fee the menial who distributed them.

Mopsopio. *Mopsopus* was a mythical king of Attica: hence *Mopsopii muri* Ov. Met. 6. 423, and *Mopsopius iuvenis* id. 5. 661 for 'Attic.'

56. veneranda. It may be doubted whether *veneranda* is not here used in an active sense 'venerating' or 'meet to venerate,' in accordance with the original meaning of the participle in -*dus*. Thus we have the gerundives of deponent verbs, as in Hor. Od. 4. 4. 68

> *Praelia coniugibus loquenda,*

'for wives to tell of.' So *Viribus utendum est* Luc. 1. 347, 'there is a using, or a need for using, of strength.'

57. monumenta viae, in reference to the repairing or re-making of the *Via Latina* by Messalla. Amongst the various public works carried out by Augustus, not the least important was the restoration or improvement of the great military roads, which had fallen into disrepair during the civil wars. Undertaking himself the reconstruction of the great North road—the *Via Flaminia*—as far as the Adriatic at Ariminum, he committed the rest to the generals to whom he accorded triumphs, who were to defray the expense out of their spoils, Suet. Oct. 30. Messalla, being amongst the number, had to repair the *Via Latina*, one of the two main roads to the South. Starting from the Porta Capena, like the *Via Appia*, it diverged from it almost immediately to the left or North, and making straight for the northern shoulder of the Alban group, passed close to Tusculum, leaving the Alban mount upon the right, and came down upon the upper waters of the Trerus near Anagnia. Thence descending the Trerus and the Liris, it ultimately joined the *Via Appia* at Beneventum. To this road probably Mart. alludes 8. 3. 5

> *Et quum rupta situ Messallae saxa iacebunt.*

59, 60. The Romans were great as engineers; and none of their engineering works are more impressive or durable than their great military roads. So solidly were they built that the phrase used for making a road is *munire viam* : and the architect Vitruvius, who lived under Caesar and Augustus, has left an exact account of the mode of their construction. First the earth was levelled and rammed down till it was solid; then came a layer of rough stones for a foundation, with or without cement; above this a second layer of rubble, mixed with lime, and rammed down to a thickness of nine inches. On the top of all was a layer of hard pavement stones, generally irregular in shape, laid carefully in a bed of cement. These giant roads extended up to the extreme limits of the empire; many portions of them exist still—notably of the *Via Appia*—almost as firm as when they were first laid down. The superintendence and repairs of the roads were offices of high distinction; Augustus himself had charge of a district. The *glarea* of l. 59 refers to the layers of rubble; the *silex* of l. 60 to the flat stones, usually of basaltic lava, or other hard rock, which formed the surface. The words *apta iungitur arte* show how nicely the stones were fitted.

64. *Candor* and *candidus* imply a bright glistening whiteness, as contrasted with the dead dull white denoted by *albus*. Hence they are the natural words to use of the bright sunlight, of the brightness of joy and happiness, of the shining radiance of a god, of the bright beauty of a young face, or the unclouded transparent openness of a clear soul.

I. 10.

THIS piece is probably the earliest of Tibullus' poems, and resembles much the first of the first book in tone and subject. Our poet was a lover of peace; and this poem was apparently written on the occasion of his being called out as a youngster to serve his time as an *eques* in the cavalry. He is to be torn, against his will, from the peaceful pursuits and secure joy of his ancestral acres; but in what cause, or in what quarter, he was to serve, we have no hint to tell. If he were born, as supposed, in the year B. C. 59, his obligation to military service would naturally have commenced in B. C. 42, when he was seventeen years of age; if so, he may have been called upon to form part of the forces that were being raised in that year in preparation for the campaign of Philippi. It is interesting to think that Tibullus may have formed part of the pursuing host before which Horace ran, having 'ingloriously thrown his shield away;' but had he taken part in so memorable a campaign, his writings would surely have borne some trace of it. The circumstance too that he was shorn of part of his ancestral property is an indication that he was not considered to be an adherent of the triumvirs; unless indeed we regard the fact that he was allowed to keep a portion of it as a mark of especial favour, whilst opponents like Horace, or neutrals like Virgil, lost their all. It is to be noted that in this poem Delia has not yet appeared upon the scene; the poet looks forward in hope to the simple pleasures of the country, and the sweets of domestic life; but there is no parting to look back to, as in I. 3, no loved one to whose arms he hopes to return.

1. protulit, i.e. 'brought forward,' 'brought to light,' 'invented;' cp. Prop. 2. 6. 31 and Hor. A. P. 130, of the coining of new terms,

> *Quam si proferres ignota indictaque primus.*

2. ferus et ferreus occur together Cic. ad Q. F. 1. 3.

4. mortis via. Cp. *animi via* Prop. 3. 5. 10, and notes on *mortis adimus iter* 3. 7. 2, and *fortunae vias* ib. 32.

5. An has better MS. authority than *at*, and gives a better sense. After calling the inventor of arms *vere ferreus*, it is somewhat abrupt to say, 'But he, poor wretch, did no harm: ours is the blame.' With *an* the transition is softened: 'Or is it rather true to say that ours is the blame, not his?'

5, 6. Note the distinction between *ad* and *in* when followed by accusatives. *Ad* is vague, of general direction, without purpose; *in* is followed by the immediate, seen, object of a hostile attack.

7. He returns to the theme of I. 1, that lust for gold is the cause of war.

8. astabat, i.e. 'stood ready for use,' 'was set upon the table.' Cups made of beechwood are part of the regular furniture of primitive country life. In Ov. Met. 8. 669 they go along with vessels of delf: see Virg. E. 1. 36. When the rustic Hyrieus entertained Jupiter and Mercury unawares, Ov. Fast. 5. 522

> *Terra rubens crater, pocula fagus erant.*

10. varias, 'parti-coloured:' used by Virgil of lynxes, Geo. 3. 264, by Hor. of veined marbles, Ep. 1. 10. 22, by Claudian of tigers. The meaning is that in primitive times no pains were taken to secure even whiteness and fineness in the fleece—sheep might be spotted. Varro, R. R. 2. 2, pays attention to this subject, and directs that for breeding purposes rams with black or spotted tongues should be rejected, as the fleeces of their offspring will be spotted also. See Virg. Geo. 3. 387 and Columella 7. 3.

dux gregis, i. e. the shepherd, who as in Biblical times, and to this day in the East, walked before his flock.

11. foret, for the more strictly correct *fuisset*, is used for pictorial effect, as though to hide, as it were, the impossibility that the wish could ever be gratified. Or by making *tum* the predicate rather than *vita foret*, the tense is still more natural : ' O that I were living then, in those happy days!' Very similar is Ov. Her. 10. 133, where imperf. and plup. are joined together in a single wish :

> *Di facerent ut me summa de puppe videres !*
> *Movisset vultus maesta figura tuos.*

Lit. ' Oh, that the gods were granting me to see thee from the ship! My sad form would have moved thee.'

vulgi. Dissen supposes the weapons of the mob—clubs, knives, staves, etc.—to be contrasted with the *tuba* of regular warfare. This is far-fetched : the contrast is rather between acquaintance with arms in general, and his own present circumstance, when he must himself obey the trumpet-call.

Vulgus is used of the ordinary passion for arms, from which Tibullus separates himself, just as Horace separates himself for other reasons from the unholy crowd, 3. 1. 2

> *Odi profanum vulgus et arceo.*

12. micante, i. e. ' quivering,' 'fluttering.' *Mico* properly means ' to move rapidly backwards and forwards,' ' to vibrate :' applied by Virgil to the ears of a well-bred horse, Geo. 3. 84, and the darting of a serpent's tongue, ib. 439. It is frequently applied to mental agitation.

13. trahōr before a vowel, being in arsis. Tibullus evidently was a most unwilling conscript, and reminds us of the hero in R. Buchanan's ' Shadow of the Sword.'

quis seems here to be used for *aliquis ;* but no other instance of this use is quoted except in relative sentences. *Quis* is constantly used for *aliquis* after *si, nisi, num, ne, cum ;* in Liv. 6. 40 it is used without any such conjunction in a mere relative sentence, *quae ab nostrum quo dicentur,* ' the things which shall be said by any *one of us.*'

15. The images of the *Lares,* as we have seen, stood at or near the hearth of the *atrium,* enclosed in a kind of niche or chapel called *lararium.* **idem** is the contracted form of the nom. plur.

16. tener, i. e. in childhood ; as above 1. 7. 30 *teneram humum,* ' the earth in her young days.'

Cursarem. So 2. 2. 22 addressing the *Genius Natalis*,

> *Ludat et ante tuos turba novella pedes.*

18. veteris seems here used almost as = *senis*. There is perhaps the additional implication that he is speaking of a time long gone by.

19. melius tenuere fidem, i. e. the men of those days were simpler and more true.

cultu refers to ornaments.

20. aede exigua, i. e. the *Lararium*.

21. Note the difference between *uva*, 'a bunch of grapes;' *racemus*, 'a bough with leaves and clusters;' *acinus*, 'a single berry.' Juvenal fitly compares a hive of bees swarming to a *uva*, 13. 68

> *Examenque apium longa consederit uva*
> *Culmine delubri.*

In the present passage *uva* is used for 'wine.'

23. voti compos. *Votum* is properly 'a vow:' i. e. a prayer accompanied by a promise that if the thing prayed for be granted, some offering or service shall be given in return for it. Being thus a promise accompanied by a condition, the word is used sometimes specially of the promise, sometimes specially of the condition. Thus *voti compos* means 'having gained or become possessed of the thing prayed for;' *voti reus*, *voti damnatus*, mean 'having become bound to fulfil the promise,' i. e. in consequence of having obtained the prayer. In both cases the same fact is stated, only from a different point of view.

24. So Ov. Fast. 2. 651

> *Inde ubi ter fruges medios immisit in ignes,*
> *Porrigit incisos filia parva favos.*

26. hostiaque is joined in the prayer with *Lares*, as being able to secure his safety.

rustica is read by good MSS. and is a safer reading than *mystica*. On the other hand, it was less likely to be changed to *mystica* than *vice versa:* and *mystica* derives confirmation from χοιρία μυστηρικά, χοίρους μυστηρικάς Arist. Ach. 747, 764, in connection with the worship of Ceres. So Virg. has *mystica vannus Iacchi*, and Tib. 3. 6. 1 *mystica vitis*, in connection with the worship of Bacchus. *Rustica* can only mean 'as a humble country offering.' Horace mentions both *porcae* and *myrtle* as offered to the Lares, Od. 3. 23. 4 and 16.

27. canistra, 'baskets,' in which the offerings of incense, cakes, *far*, etc., were held. See the description 2. 1. 11–14.

32. Cp. Ov. Her. 1. 31

> *Atque aliquis posita monstrat fera praelia mensa,*
>   *Pingit et exiguo Pergama tota mero:*
> *Hac ibat Simois, hic est Sigeia tellus,*
>   *Hic steterat Priami regia celsa senis;*
> *Illic Aeacides, illic tendebat Ulixes,*
>   *Hic lacer admissos terruit Hector equos.*

So also Voltaire,

> *Et le vieux nouvelliste, une canne à la main,*
>   *Trace au Palais Royal Ypre, Farne et Denain,*

where the tracing is done with a stick on the gravel.

33. Quis furor . . . ? A common formula = 'what madness to . . . !'

34. tacito clam. Each word adds to the strength of the other.

35-38. 'This picture corresponds closely with the account of the Infernal Regions, to be found in Homer, who represents the realms of Hades as a gloomy and desolate region, where the spirits of the departed, although not suffering actual pain, are strangers to enjoyment. See Tib. 1. 3. 56.'

36. Stygiae navita turpis aquae. *Turpis* here means 'ugly,' 'rough and unkempt.' So Virg. uses the word of a horse's head, 'ugly,' 'clumsy,' Geo. 3. 52; of the scab, ib. 441; of the loss of looks in old age, ib. 96; of limbs fouled with mud, Aen. 5. 358. The best MSS. read *puppis:* but the words would be readily interchanged, and *puppis* was evidently introduced to suit *navita* by a scribe who could not understand *turpis.* Charon is described by Virgil as *horribili squalore* Aen. 6. 299; by Propertius as a *torvus senex* 3. 18. 24; by Juvenal as a *porthmeus teter* 3. 265.

37. The reading of A. is **percussisque**, which makes no good sense. The words *usto capillo* show that some word is needed describing the condition of the cheeks after death, whilst still visible on the flaming pyre. Strangely enough, the popular ancient belief was that the shades bore in the infernal regions the same appearance as at the moment of death, or even when half consumed by the flames. In Virg. Aen. 495 Deiphobus appears with his body all mangled: and Prop. 4. 7. 7-10 draws his vision of the deceased Cynthia thus,

> *Eosdem habuit secum, quibus est elata, capillos,*
>   *Eosdem oculos: lateri vestis adusta fuit;*
> *Et solitum digito beryllon adederat ignis,*
>   *Summaque Lethaeus triverat ora liquor.*

Percussis can only refer to striking the cheeks, *perscissis* to tearing them in grief: neither is appropriate as applied to the shades of themselves. *Exesis*, the conjecture of Heinsius, makes the best sense, but involves a great change in the text.

40. Occupat, 'comes upon him,' 'overtakes him,' with the implication 'before he is aware of it.'

42. Cp. Hor. Epod. 2. 42.

46. araturos, to be taken closely with *duxit.*

48. testa paterna. 'The amphora stored up, or laid in, by his father.' Cp. Ov. A. A. 2. 695

> *Qui properant, nova musta bibant ; mihi fundat avitum*
> *Consulibus priscis condita testa merum.*

The *amphora* was the earthenware vessel in which wine was kept stored up for use, after all the processes of making had been gone through. Though holding over five and a half quarts, it was thus the counterpart of the modern bottle ; it was long in shape, had two handles at the neck, and ended in a point at the bottom which was stuck into the ground, whilst the head leant against the wall, or against other amphorae. Great numbers of amphorae have been found in this position, just as they were left by their owners.

50. situs (from *sino*) properly means 'a lying,' 'a situation :' it is hence used of every kind of filth, such as dust, rust, mould, weeds, etc., which gather upon things which are left untouched. Thus Prop. 4. 5. 72

> *inmundo pallida mitra situ.*

51. E luco. Another touch to describe the happy times of peace. The father with his wife and family have been to a festival in some sacred grove close by: so Hor. Od. 1. 4. 11 of spring,

> *Nunc et in umbrosis Fauno decet immolare lucis ;*

and Virg. Aen. 11. 739

> *Hic amor, hoc studium ; dum sacra secundus haruspex*
> *Nuntiet, ac lucos vocet hostia pinguis in altos.*

From such a feast it would appear that the father might be expected to come home in the same condition as too many a modern farmer from fair or market : so Hor. A. P. 223

> *Illecebris erat et grata novitate morandus*
> *Spectator, functusque sacris et potus et exlex ;*

and Tib. 2. 1. 29

> *non festa luce madere*
> *Est rubor, errantes et male ferre pedes.*

ipse. Only the father got drunk. Some editors suppose *ipse* to mean 'with his own hands' as having no slave. But if he were himself *male sobrius*, it is to be hoped that his wife, or some other member of the family, held the reins.

    male sobrius, i. e. 'by no means sober,' 'very drunk.' The use of the adverb *male* is apt to embarrass the young scholar, when he finds that it apparently bears two opposite meanings. Thus *male sanus*, Cic. Att. 9. 15, is equivalent to 'not at all sane' or 'insane;' whereas *non dubito quin me male oderit*, Cic. Att. 14. 1. 2, means 'he hates me very much;' *male metuo*, Ter. Hec. 3. 2. 2, 'I am very much afraid;' *male laxus calceus*, Hor. Sat. 1. 3. 21, 'a very loose shoe.' The explanation is that *male*, like our 'badly,' naturally varies in meaning according to the meaning of the word to which it is joined. 'To be badly wounded' is to be very much wounded, because wounding is an undesirable, evil thing. But 'to fit badly' is to fit not at all, because fitting is the thing desired, and to add 'badly' implies that the object is imperfectly attained or not attained at all. So with *male*: *male sanus*, 'badly sane,' i. e. 'not sane;' cp. singers *male rauci* Hor. Sat. 1. 4. 66, 'very hoarse,' because hoarseness is a bad thing. To do a *bad* thing *badly* is to do it *very badly*; to do a *good* thing *badly* is to do it imperfectly, or not at all. Cp. our 'ill;' 'I can ill brook,' i. e. 'scarcely.'

    68. Perfluat, 'overflow.' The idea is taken from representations of *Pax* on coins and elsewhere: she holds an ear or ears of corn in her hand, her lap runs over with apples and other fruit.

    candidus, 'snow-white.' See note on 1. 7. 64.

II. 1.

    'THE subject of this Elegy is the *Ambarvalia* or *Sacrum Ambarvale*, a festival celebrated in spring time by the rustic population of Latium, for the purification of themselves, their flocks, and fields. As the name imports, the victims were led round the limits of each farm or district, and the holy influence of the sacrifice was supposed to extend to everything included within this circle. Such is the solemnity described by Virgil, when he enjoins the husbandman to pay due honour to the gods, Geo. 1. 338

    In primis venerare deos, atque annua magnae
    Sacra refer Cereri laetis operatus in herbis,
    Extremae sub casum hiemis, iam vere sereno.
    Tunc pingues agni et tunc mollissima vina;
    Tunc somni dulces, densaeque in montibus umbrae.
    Cuncta tibi Cererem pubes agrestis adoret.

Cui tu lacte favos et miti dilue Baccho,
Terque novas circum felix eat hostia fruges,
Omnis quam chorus et socii comitentur ovantes,
Et Cererem clamore vocent in tecta ; neque ante
Falcem maturis quisquam supponat aristis,
Quam Cereri, torta redimitus tempora quercu,
Det motus incompositos et carmina dicat.

Cato (R. R. 141) gives, at length, the form of prayer most fitting for such occasions.

' Besides the *Ambarvalia,* celebrated by private individuals or small communities, there was a public festival, whose name and object were the same, in which the sacred rites were performed by a college of priests, denominated the *Fratres Arvales.* These, according to tradition, were first instituted by Romulus, and, originally, it was their duty to march in solemn procession round the boundaries of the state, accompanied by the victims—a boar, a ram, and a bull—constituting the sacrifice called *Suovetaurilia,* singing hymns as they paced along. When, in later times, from the extension of territory, this became impossible, the sacrifices were still offered at certain spots which marked the original limits of the Roman domain[1].'

The only clue as to the date is given in l. 33, in which Messalla's Aquitanian triumph is alluded to. The poem must therefore have been composed after that event, not earlier than the spring of B. C. 26. The interest of the piece is great, as it is not a mere theoretical description, but an account of the ceremony which he was himself about to celebrate on his own farm, as an act of regular worship.

The shortness of the Second Book of Tibullus' Elegies has been explained by the supposition that the poems contained in it were collected and published after his death. Ovid, however, must have known of the book before he wrote the elegy on the death of Tibullus, and some time before he wrote A. A. 3. 535

Nos facimus placitae late praeconia formae :
Nomen habet Nemesis, Cynthia nomen habet.

1. A. and most MSS. have *valeat :* but *faveat* is a certain correction. Tibullus uses the regular formula with which a sacrifice or any holy rite was opened, as *linguisque animisque favete* Ov. Met. 15. 677. Ill-omened words must be avoided on such occasions ; and as the only mode of securing that no ill-omened words should be pronounced was that no words should be uttered at all, the phrase *favete linguis* is equivalent to ' keep silence.'

---

[1] See Strabo, 14. § 34 (p. 645), and Ov. Fast. 2. 639 sqq.

2. prisco avo, because supposed to have been instituted by Romulus.

Though the *Ambarvalia* were mainly in honour of the gods connected with the fertility of the soil, other gods besides were worshipped. In the remarkable *Carmen Fratrum Arvalium,* one of the very earliest specimens of Latin extant, the god addressed throughout is Mars. The worship of Ceres (i.e. the Greek Demeter) was not introduced at Rome till B. C. 494, when a temple was erected to her along with her children *Liber* and *Libera,* close to the Circus Maximus. The temple was restored by Tiberius, Tac. Ann. 2. 49. *Liber* and *Libera,* who were no doubt native Italian deities, were afterwards identified with Bacchus and Proserpina. Cic. pro Balbo 24 dwells at length on the circumstance that the worship of Ceres was introduced from Greece.

Bacchus was represented on coins with horns, as a symbol of strength and plenty. The same idea seems to have given rise to the *cornucopia,* the horn of the goat Amalthea.

5, 6. Cp. the description of the *Sementiva,* a festival celebrated at the close of the seed-time, in Ov. Fast. 1. 657 sq. especially l. 667

> *Villice, da requiem terrae, semente peracta:*
> *Da requiem terram qui coluere, viris;*

and l. 663

> *State coronati plenum ad praesaepe iuvenci:*
> *'Cum tepido vestrum vere redibit opus.*

6. suspenso vomere. 'Ancient ploughs were so light that they were easily carried, and hung up when not wanted: so Ov. Fast. 1. 665

> *Rusticus emeritum palo suspendat aratrum.'* Pinder.

7. iugis. The abl., not the dat., as Pind. says: Virg. Aen. 1. 562

> *Solvite corde metum.*

9. operata. *Operari* is simply 'to be busy,' 'to work,' and in this sense is followed either by the dat. or by the abl. with *in,* as (1) *eo tempore quo corpus operatum rei publicae esset,* 'busied for the republic,' Liv. 4. 60. 2, and (2) Hor. Ep. 1. 2. 29

> *In cute curanda plus aequo operata iuventus.*

But the word is frequently restricted to attendance upon sacred duties, especially sacrifice, as Hor. Od. 3. 14. 5

> *Unico gaudens mulier marito*
> *Prodeat iustis operata divis;*

or without any case, as Prop. 2. 33. 2

> *Cynthia iam noctes est operata decem.*

The neuter seems to have the same sense as in the Psalm: 'Let everything that hath breath praise the Lord.'

non for *ne* in prohibitive sentences has a gentle dissuasive meaning, amounting rather to a recommendation than an order: Hor. Sat. 2. 5. 91

> *Difficilem et morosum offendet garrulus ultro*
> *Non, etiam sileas:*

'you should not keep silence.' Pers. 1. 5

> *non, si quid turbida Roma*
> *Elevet, accedas.*

Other instances are Hor. Ep. 1. 18. 72, A. P. 460. In these passages the prohibitive meaning shades nearly off into the conditional: 'you would not keep silence,' i. e. if you followed my advice.

15. eat. The lamb was sacrificed after having been led thrice round the farm: Festus says, *Ambarvalis hostia est quae rei divinae causa circum arva ducitur ab iis qui pro frugibus faciunt.* So Virg. Geo. 1. 345

> *Terque novas circum felix eat hostia fruges.*

19. neu seges eludat messem. The harvest or crop itself is said to be mocked with vain hopes, in place of the husbandman. Hor. 3. 16. 30 expresses exactly the same idea by *et segetis certa fides meae*, as though the crop had given a promise which it loyally redeemed. Cp. Virg. Geo. 1. 225. The *herbae* are the green blades which never come to maturity. Ov. Her. 17. 263 puts the idea into a proverb,

> *Sed nimium properas et adhuc tua messis in herba est.*

21. nitidus, 'spruce:' Hor. Epp. 1. 4. 15.

23. The master, having feasted royally, is in a good temper, feeds his slaves from his table, and looks kindly on their sports. Cp. Hor. Od. 3. 17. 16, Epp. 2. 1. 142, and especially Sat. 2. 6. 67–9

> *O noctes cenaeque deum! quibus ipse meique*
> *Ante Larem proprium vescor, vernasque procaces*
> *Pasco libatis dapibus.*

24. The allusion seems to be to extempore arbours (*pergula, trichila*) put up by the slaves near the altar, in which to drink and be merry. See Tib. 2. 5. 97, and Ov. Fast. 3. 527

> *Sub Iove pars durat: pauci tentoria ponunt:*
> *Sunt quibus e ramis frondea facta casa est;*
> *Pars sibi pro rigidis calamos statuere columnis,*
> *Desuper extentas imposuere togas.*

25. Eventura, i. e. 'prayers that will be fulfilled.'

26. nuntia fibra. *Fibra*, according to Varro and Festus, means 'an extremity,' being the fem. of the adj. *fiber :* in divination it denoted the thread-like extremities of the liver, which were of great importance in that science. Thus Tib. 1. 8. 3

Nec mihi sunt sortes, nec conscia fibra deorum.
Cic. Tusc. 3. 6 has *omnes radicum fibras evellere.*

27. fumosos, because wine was kept in an upper room (*Fumarium*) where the wood smoke of the chimney might play about it : just as many appreciate the 'peat reek' of Highland whisky.

27, 28. Falernos . . . Chio. 'The Italian wines most esteemed by the Romans, were all produced in the favoured district of the "happy Campania" or on its confines. The *Massicum* and *"immortale Falernum,"* Mart. Ep. 9. 95, grew upon the sunny slopes to the south of Sinuessa (*Rocca di Monte Dragone*). The *Caecubum* and *Calenum,* so often and so earnestly eulogised by Horace, came, the former from the marshes around Fundi, the latter from Cales (*Calvi*); the heights of Setia (*Sezza*) yielded the *Setinum*, prized above all others by Augustus and his court, Plin. H. N. 14. 6, while the volcanic ridges of Mons Gaurus (*Monte Barbaro*), between Puteoli (*Pozzuoli*) and Cumae, supplied the scarcely less celebrated *Gauranum.* From the bay of Sinuessa, says Pliny H. N. 3. 5, *incipiunt vitiferi colles, et temulentia nobilis succo per omnis terras inclyto, atque, ut veteres dixere, summum Liberi patris cum Cerere certamen. Hinc Setini et Caecubi obtenduntur agri : his iunguntur Falerni, Caleni : dein consurgunt Massici, Gaurani, Surrentinique montes.*

'Among the various delicious sweet wines of the Greek islands, those of Lesbos and Chios seem to have been most relished. Of the latter, immense quantities must have been imported, if we can believe the accounts given by Pliny, H. N. 14. 14, of the number of casks bequeathed by Hortensius to his heir, and of the largesses of Lucullus upon his return from Asia.'

29. madere, 'to be soaked in wine,' 'to be drunk :' Plaut. Most. 1. 4. 7

Ecquid videor tibi ma—ma—madere ?
So *uvidi* Hor. Od. 4. 5. 38 and Tib. 2. 5. 89.

30. male ferre, 'to be scarce able to direct :' see note on 1. 10. 67.

31. Bene Messallam. A shortened form of toast, for *precor bene valere* or *valiturum* : cp. Plaut. Stich. 5. 4. 26

Tibi propino decem : affunde tibi tute inde si sapis :
Bene vos! bene nos! bene te! bene me! bene nostrum
etiam Stephanium !
The dative may also be used.

34. intonsis. Varro, R. R. 2. 11. 10, says shaving was introduced into Rome from Sicily B.C. 300; while Pliny, H. N. 7. 59,
attributes the 'daily shave' to Scipio Africanus. Thus *intonsus,
barbatus, incomptus* are standing epithets of 'the ancients:' of a
bold and truthful witness Juv. 16. 31 says,

> *Et credam dignum barba dignumque capillis*
> *Majorum.*

38. Cp. Virg. Geo. 1. 8

> *Liber et alma Ceres, vestro si munere tellus*
> *Chaoniam pingui glandem mutavit arista.*

44. irriguas, in a transitive sense, 'watering,' as in Virg.
Geo. 4. 32

> *Irriguumque bibant violaria fontem;*

in a passive sense 'well-watered' in Hor. Sat. 2. 4. 16

> *Irriguo nihil est elutius horto;*

figuratively id. 2. 1. 9

> *Irriguumque mero sub noctem corpus habento.*

46. securus = *sine cura,* 'without care or anxiety;' here 'that
knows no care,' or possibly 'care-dispelling.'

48. Deponit, 'surrenders.' Cp. Prop. 2. 19. 12 *vitem docta
ponere falce comas.* **comas,** of the harvest. **annua,** 'year by year.'

49. verno goes here with *alveo,* as with *flore* in l. 59, not with
rure in either line.

51. satiatus, 'having had enough of.'

55. suffusus is here equivalent to *inductus.* The word is
usually applied to a flush or a paleness *under* the skin, as Ov. Am. 3.
3. 5, Fast. 1. 215; here to something laid over it. Lucr. 6. 479 says
of the clouds,

> *Suffunduntque sua caelum caligine;*

but that rather suggests the idea that the clouds form a lining to the
sky as looked at from outside its sphere. For the use of red paint,
not only for painting the faces of the gods, but also those of the
worshippers, see above on I. 1. 17.

56. ab is not redundant. It denotes the beginning 'from which.'

55, 56. For these early rustic performances see Hor. Ep. 2. 1.
139–155 and Virg. Geo. 2. 385–396.

58. This line is corrupt, but *parcas* or *curtas* seems a certain
correction. The best MS. reading is

> *Dux pecoris hircus auxerat hircus oves,*

which is unmeaning, besides the metrical difficulties involved. The
meaning seems to be that the *agricola* was enriched by receiving
a *hircus* as a prize.

M

61. exhibitura, 'will occasion,' 'cause;' so *molestiam alicui exhibere* Cic. Att. 2. 1. 2.

64. 'Catullus 64. 312 gives us a most vivid description of the primitive method of spinning, with the distaff (*colus*) and spindle (*fusus*) which was common in this country until within a few years, and is still universally employed by the peasantry of southern Italy and of Greece:'

> *Laeva colum molli lana retinebat amictum;*
> *Dextera tum leviter deducens fila supinis*
> *Formabat digitis; tum prono in pollice torquens*
> *Libratum tereti versabat turbine fusum:*
> *Atque ita decerpens aequabat semper opus dens,*   .
> *Laneaque aridulis haerebant morsa labellis,*
> *Quae prius in levi fuerant exstantia filo.*
> *Ante pedes autem candentis mollia lanae*
> *Vellera virgati custodibant calathisci.*

Here the left hand holds the distaff with the mass of wool at the top; the fingers of the right, palm uppermost, draw down and gradually shape the fibres which are to form the thread, while the thumb turned downwards keeps the spindle twirling, assisted by a weight at the bottom; as the thread is formed, the spinner watches that it shall come out evenly, biting off any lump or irregularity with her teeth, as neither of her hands is free. In front are baskets full of the cleaned and carded fleeces wherewith to replenish the distaff. In the present passage **apposito pollice** refers to the thumb of the right hand keeping the thread down so as to give it the proper degree of tension, and at the same time regulating the motion of the spindle.   .

65. Minervae, dat. after *operata;* see note on l. 9. Minerva is the patroness of spinning: cp. Hor. Od. 3. 12. 5 *Operosaeque Minervae studium.* The whole operations connected with spinning are to be seen sculptured on the fragment of the Temple called ' Pallas Minerva' in the forum of Augustus at Rome, now forming the front of a bakery.

66. applauso tela sonat latere. The web (*tela*), fitted in the framework of the loom, rattles as it moves from side to side when the threads of the woof (*subtemen*) are driven home by the lay (*pecten*). This is the operation described by Virg. Geo. 1. 15 where the wife

> *Arguto tenuis percurrit pectine telas,*

while the peculiar ' rattle' mentioned is familiar to every one who has passed through a village where hand-looms are still in use. See the careful description of weaving in Ov. Met. 6. 54

> *Haud mora, consistunt diversis partibus ambae,*
> *Et gracili geminas intendunt stamine telas.*
> *Tela iugo vincta est; stamen secernit arundo;*
> *Inseritur medium radiis subtemen acutis,*
> *Quod digiti expediunt, atque inter stamina ductum*
> *Percusso feriunt insecti pectine dentes.*

73. detraxit, iussit. Perfects of Habit; what has happened once may be expected to happen again, so that the tense expressing a single occasion may stand for a repeated act. A good instance is Virg. Geo. 4. 214

> *rege incolumi mens omnibus una est:*
> *Amisso rupere fidem, constructaque mella*
> *Diripuere ipsae.*

Cp. Geo. 1. 49.

75–79. A charmingly natural picture of a maiden stealthily getting up in the dead of night, slipping past the slaves who guard the door, and feeling her way in the dark, by foot and hand, that she may meet her lover.

77. Pedibus suspensa, 'on tip-toe.'

78. Cp. Ov. Met. 10. 455

> *Nutricisque manum laeva tenet: altera motu*
> *Caecum iter explorat.*

cui manus, 'while her hand.' The force of *cui* here is not so much that of *simul,* or *atque etiam,* or *dum,* as Pinder says, but rather is pictorial, as though a picture or a statue were being described: the foot feeling its way, the expression of fear, the exploring hand, form evidently one representation; the two lines give not a narrative, but an attitude. So 2. 3. 43, quoted by Pinder, describes a *character,* not a course of conduct: while Virg. Aen. 4. 138 is exactly parallel to the passage before us:

> *Cui pharetra ex auro, crines nodantur in aurum,*
> *Aurea purpuream subnectit fibula vestem.*

In all these cases we may translate by 'while,' using the word however not in its temporal, but in its adversative, sense.

81. veni dapibus, not so much *to,* as *for,* the feast.

83. deum, i. e. Cupid.

pecori, a similar dative to *dapibus* above; but the conjunction of *pecori vocate voce,* 'call upon him for the flock with the voice,' is somewhat harsh.

86. Obstrepit, 'makes a din *against,*' i. e. so that your prayer will not be heard. In allusion to the Phrygian, or somewhat orgiastic, mode of music of which the *tibia* was the appropriate instrument, connected especially with the worship of the Phrygian Cybele. The *tibia*, flute or flageolet, had various shapes: the Phrygian flute was a straight tube of wood, at the end of which was fastened a curved metallic end (κώδων) like the end of a French horn. Hence the epithet *curva:* so Virg. Aen. 11. 737, Cat. 63. 22, and *adunco tibia cornu* Ov. Met. 3. 531. There were often, however, two branches proceeding from the same stem; hence Virg. Aen. 9. 618

> *biforem dat tibia cantum.*

For the various kinds of *tibiae* see Rich.

88. fulva. This use of the word throws light upon the colour of Cynthia's hair, Prop. 2. 2. 5, where see note. Not 'brown,' but 'golden,' 'shining,' is the idea of the word. The stars are Daughters of the Night, and sport joyously in her train: imitated by Ov. Met. 3. 683. Theocr. 2. fin. calls the stars

> ἀστέρες εὐκήλοιο κατ' ἄντυγα Νυκτὸς ὀπαδοί.

See Eur. Ion 1150.

89. furvis. The *fulvis* of some MSS. has evidently dropped down from *fulva* in l. 88.

90. nigra, not *atra,* because dreams may be pleasing, and only the darkness of night is indicated. Ov. Fast. 4. 662 also has *somnia nigra.*

incerto pede, of the unstable, indistinct, character of dreams.

II. 5.

M. VALERIUS MESSALLA had two sons, M. Valerius Messallinus, who was consul along with Cn. Cornelius Lentulus, B.C. 3; and Lucius, who was consul along with Cn. Cornelius Cinna Magnus, A.D. 5. The latter was adopted into the Aurelian gens, and was known as L. Aurelius Cotta Volusus, or sometimes as Maximus Cotta. The former took the name of Messallinus after the death of his brother. He was the friend of Ovid, to whom the poet addresses two of the epistles written in exile, F. ex P. 3. 2 and 5.

Tacitus, Ann. 3. 34, mentions Marcus in honourable terms: *Valerius Messallinus cui parens Messalla, ineratque imago paternae facundiae.* 'The present Elegy was composed, probably about B.C. 16, to celebrate the admission of Marcus, the elder, into the college of the quindecimviri, the fifteen priests to whom was committed the custody of the Sibylline Books. These prophecies occupied a conspicuous place in the history of the internal affairs of Rome, and formed, for a long period, a political engine of great power. They were originally deposited in a stone chest, under ground, in the temple of Jupiter Capitolinus, and were committed to the charge of inspectors or commissioners chosen from among the patricians, whose duty it was to consult them when authorised by the Senate. The number of commissioners was originally two, who were styled *duumviri sacrorum* or *duumviri libris adeundis*. In the year B. C. 368, a bill was brought in by the tribunes to increase the number of commissioners from two to ten, with the condition that one-half of these should be plebeians. After great opposition, the bill was carried the following year, and continued in force until the dictatorship of Sulla, by whom the number was further augmented to fifteen.

'The books remained in safety until the year B. C. 83. when they were destroyed in the conflagration which consumed the temple of Jupiter Capitolinus. The Senate, upon the restoration of the shrine, nominated three ambassadors, who were enjoined to visit the cities of Italy and Greece, and especially to pass over to Erythrae in Asia, for the purpose of collecting any Sibylline oracles which might be preserved either in sanctuaries or by private individuals. In this manner about a thousand lines were procured and brought to Rome[1]. When Augustus entered upon the duties of the high priesthood, he commanded that all books of prophecies, resting upon no sufficient authority, of which upwards of a thousand were in circulation, should be brought together and burned[2]. He then directed his attention to the Sibylline verses preserved by the State, and took great pains to separate the genuine from such as were deemed spurious. The former were transcribed by the pontifices, and deposited in two gilded cases in the Temple of Palatine Apollo (Ammianus 23). A fire, in the time of Julian the Apostate, nearly destroyed this second edition of the Sibylline verses, and all writings of this description which remained were finally swept away by an edict of the emperor Honorius. The compilation now extant under the name of "Sibyllina Oracula" is well known to be a forgery.'

As the Sibylline books were now kept in the Temple of the Palatine Apollo, the ceremony of inauguration was held in the same

---

[1] Fenestella quoted by Lactant. 1. 6 and Dionys. as above.
[2] Tacit. Ann. 6. 12; Suet. Octav. 31; Dion. 54. 17. Tiberius made a similar clearance, see Dion. 57. 18.

place. The dedication of that temple is described by Prop. 2. 31 ;
see Hor. Od. 1. 31.

3. impellere chordas, i. e. ' of *my* lyre.'

4. meas. Lachmann's conjecture *mea* should be adopted, i. e.
' bend my words to praise.' Hiller adopts the conjecture *novas.*

5. triumphali, in allusion probably to the triumph of the
father.

6. cumulant. So Virg. Aen. 11. 49 *Cumulatque altaria donis.*

7. nitidus pulcherque. Characteristic epithets of Apollo :
' the radiant, handsome god.'

8. Sepositam, ' laid aside ' for great days: in Scottish phrase,
' put past.' The god was to deck himself out for the great day ' in
his braws.' So Ovid in exile, on his birthday,

> *Quaeque semel toto vestis mihi sumitur anno*
> *Sumatur fatis discolor alba meis*

Trist. 5. 5. 7.

9, 10. These lines represent Apollo as the singer of Zeus'
great triumph in his contest with the Giants. Seneca in the same
way speaks of Apollo as singing dignified strains at the previous
victory over the Titans, Agam. 331. Horace, following the more
usual account, makes Apollo take a leading part in the conflict
along with Pallas, Vulcan, and Juno, in the fine passage Od. 3. 4.
53-64, his warlike character being especially insisted on in the line

> *Numquam humeris positurus arcum.*

Of all the curious identifications invented by the Romans in their
anxiety to connect Italian mythology with that of Greece, none is
more strange than their belief that their own Saturnus was the
same as the Greek Kronos. According to Greek mythology, Kronos
was youngest and chief of the Titans: who, having deposed and
mutilated their father Uranus, were themselves vanquished in turn
by his sons the Kronidae, headed by Zeus. Zeus and his brothers
and sisters became thus the ruling powers, and maintained their
position against three successive assaults: (1) from the Giants ; (2)
from the monster Typhon or Typhoeus ; and (3) from the Aloidae,
Otus and Ephialtes. Horace only connects Apollo with these
later struggles ; Tibullus, in the lines before us, as also Seneca, makes
him take part in the original victory over Kronos and the Titans. But
these great dynastic struggles are altogether foreign to the character
of *Saturnus.* Saturnus was an Italian god of agriculture and plenty :
his name being obviously connected with *sat, satur,* etc., from the
root *sa* (Germ. *säen*), whence *sero* and our ' sow.' The native story
made him a king of Italy, who reached its shores in the reign of

Janus, introduced agriculture, wealth (his wife was called *Ops*), and the civilised arts of life, and settled on the banks of the Tiber on the height originally called *Saturnia*, subsequently known as the *Capitolium*. This account is given in detail by Virgil, Aen. 8. 314 sqq. and 355, where Saturnus is represented as coming direct from Olympus after his defeat by Jupiter. The one intelligible connection between the two is that Hesiod, Op. 111, tells us that the golden age on earth was while Kronos ruled in heaven: an idea which exactly fitted in with the Italian idea of Saturnus, a god of peace and plenty, in whose days war and greed and wrong were alike unknown.

11–16. In these lines the four principal methods of divination are enumerated: (1) From the flight of birds (*augurium*); (2) by lots (*per sortes*), see note on Tib. 1. 3. 11; (3) by the entrails of victims (*haruspicina*); (4) by consulting the Sibylline books.

11. eventura vides. So Apollo says of himself, 3. 4. 47

> *At mihi fatorum leges, aevique futuri*
> *Eventura pater posse videre dedit,*

which expresses the sense of the well-known line, Aesch. Eum. 19

> Διὸς προφήτης ἐστὶ Λοξίας πατρός.

12. fati goes with *quid*, rather than with *provida*.

13. Tiberius, with his strong and hard common sense, wished to do away with the oracles near the city: *sed maiestate Praenestinarum sortium territus destitit* Suet. 63.

14. Lubrica, both literally, of the entrails themselves, and also figuratively, of the difficulty of their interpretation.

notis. *Nota* here = Gk. σημεῖον.

16. Thus the Sibylline answers were expressed in Dactylic Hexameters. They were in Greek.

19. The commentators have no reason for imagining a response given to Aeneas before starting on his wanderings by the Sibyl of Erythrae. Obviously Tibullus alludes to the visit to the Cumaean Sibyl as told by Virgil.

21–38 form a long parenthesis on the topic which the Roman poets dwelt on with peculiar complacency, viz. the appearance presented by the site of the future Rome in the time of Aeneas.

23. formaverat. Probably *firmaverat* (i.e. with a rampart), found in some MSS., should be read. Cp. Prop. 3. 9. 50.

25. pascebant. Virg. also uses the active form of the verb in an intransitive sense: Geo. 1. 143

> *Saltibus in vacuis pascunt.*

27. Lacte madens, i. e. from the offering of the worshippers: cp. on 1. 1. 36.

29. votum, 'the offering.'

30. silvestri deo, i. e. Silvanus.

31. 'A Pandean pipe, made of several stalks of the reed or cane, of unequal length and bore, fastened together and cemented with wax: hence called *arundo cerata* Ov. Met. 11. 154; Suet. Jul. 32.' Rich. See Virg. E. 2. 35

> *Est mihi disparibus septem compacta cicutis*
> *Fistula.*

33. The *Velabrum* was the level ground or 'haugh' between the Capitol, Palatine, and Aventine, extending from the river to the Forum. It was a swamp, until drained by the Cloaca Maxima, and was constantly flooded by the Tiber. Cp. Prop. 4. 9. 5

> *Qua Velabra suo stagnabant flumine, quaque*
> *Nauta per urbanas velificabat aquas.*

It was in such a flood that the cradle with the twins was floated to the foot of the Palatine. Cp. Ov. Fast. 6. 405 sqq.

35-38. The rustic maiden ferries across the lake on a holiday to visit her sweetheart, owner of a rich flock, and returns home with a gift of a lamb and a cheese. The *magistro* is, of course, the same person as the *iuvenem*.

35. placitura, 'to meet,' 'for the sake of.'

39. The proper subject of the poem is here resumed. The prophecy of the Sibyl to Aeneas begins with the words '*Impiger Aenea.*'

frater Amoris, because Cupid or Amor, like Aeneas, was the son of Venus This relationship to the volatile Amor of the staid, pious Aeneas is very rarely touched on by the poets. It is to be noted all through the history of Aeneas, especially as told in the Aeneid, that Venus herself always appears in a higher character, and discards the lighter elements of her nature, in relation to her exemplary son. The story of Rome required that Venus should be represented as a noble, dignified matron, worthy of her place as the progenitrix of the Roman race. To effect this result, the ennobling features of the maternal relationship are worked out in a way which is very true to nature.

41. Laurentes agros. The *Laurens ager*, or territory of Laurentum, was that on which Aeneas first landed when he disembarked on the south bank of the Tiber. It is to be noted how carefully the Aeneas legend has invented stepping-stones to connect Rome naturally with Troy and Aeneas. The native Roman tradition pointed to Alba Longa as the cradle of the race: thus the Trojans had to be brought to Alba. But how was Alba to be reached by a small colony arriving by sea? They sail up the Tiber, land near its mouth, on the territory of Latinus, king of Laurentum. Their first encampment is called *Laurentia castra* Aen. 10. 635. The war over, Aeneas marries Lavinia, and founds a new settlement, which he calls after his wife Lavinium, well on the way to Alba. Thirty years later his son Ascanius moves the remaining step, and transfers the government to Alba. The motive of the whole story is plain. The *laurus* still grows in profusion on the low sandy tract where Aeneas landed.

43, 44. Cp. Liv. 1. 2 *Secundum inde praelium Latinis, Aeneae etiam ultimum operum mortalium fuit. Situs est, quemcunque eum dici ius fasque est, super Numicium flumen; Iovem Indigetem appellant.* See Ov. Met. 14. 598. Topographers generally identify a small stream called the *Rio Torto* with the *Numicius*; and *Pratica*, which lies close to it, with *Lavinium.*

44. caelo miserit. Note the construction. It is not so much that *caelo* stands for *ad caelum*, as that *miserit* has a trajective force: 'handed over to,' 'transferred.' In the case of *caelum*, the idea of motion towards, as if it were a terrestrial journey, is put out of sight. Thus *Italiae miserit* would be impossible.

47. mihi lucent. A good example of the *Dat. Ethicus.* 'I see the camp blazing.' Here the camp of Turnus is burnt: an incident not given by Virgil.

49. Ante oculos, i. e. in prophecy: she sees the whole future course of Roman history.

51. placitura. Cp. above, 3. 35. Here, of course, no intention is signified: 'destined to find favour in the eyes of.'

52. deseruisse. The effect of the perfect here (with the present-perfect sense) is to add vividness, as if the scene were being enacted before her eyes: 'thou hast left the Vestal hearth.'

53. furtim, going closely with *concubitus*, has the force of an adjective. The explanation is not so much that the phrase is a Graecism, = τὰς λάθρα συνουσίας, as Orelli puts it—a mode of expression contrary to the genius of Latin, which has no article— but rather it is an elliptical phrase, the adverb being taken with a participle suggested naturally by the context. Thus *iterum consul* stands for *iterum consul creatus; populum late regem* Virg. Aen. 1. 21 suggests *late regnantem; omnes circa populi* Liv. is short for *circa habitantes.*

iacentes, as if she could no longer wear the maiden's fillet.

57. fatale has by no means the same meaning as our word 'fatal.' It denotes simply what is ordained by, or done in accordance with the will of, the fates, i.e. 'fated.' It thus carries with it necessarily a serious and solemn, but not necessarily a disastrous, meaning. Thus Cic. Div. 2. 7. 9 *Omnia quae fiunt quaeque futura sunt ex omni aeternitate definita dicis esse fataliter.* So *fataliter mori* Eutr. 1. 11 is 'to die a natural death,' i.e. one that comes in the regular course of fate.

terris regendis is the dative denoting the end or sphere with respect to which the decree of destiny applies.

58–60. i.e. over the whole habitable globe, from east to west. Lines 59 and 60 are an expression and definition of *qua prospicit arva.*

59. Quaque ... et. 'Both where ... and.'

ortus, not in connection with *solis* in l. 60, but used absolutely. 'The rising' = 'the East.'

patent, used not with reference to the wide realms of the East, but to the opening day. Cp. the fine lines of Virg. Geo. 1. 250

Nosque ubi primus equis Oriens afflavit anhelis,
Illic sera rubens accendit lumina Vesper.

60. amnis, for the Ocean: Homer's ποταμοῖο ῥέεθρα ὠκεανοῦ Il. 14. 245, and παρὰ ῥόον ὠκεανοῖο 16. 151. Cp. Tib. 3. 4. 18

Iam nox aetherium nigris emensa quadrigis
Mundum caeruleo laverat amne rotas.

In Il. 21. 195 Achilles says no river can contend with Zeus, not even Ocean:

οὐδὲ βαθυρρείταο μέγα σθένος Ὠκεανοῖο,
ἐξ οὗπερ πάντες ποταμοὶ καὶ πᾶσα θάλασσα,
καὶ πᾶσαι κρῆναι καὶ φρείατα μακρὰ νάουσι.

61. se mirabitur. Cp. the slang phrase of a conceited person : 'fancies himself.' Troy will plume herself upon the greatness of her offspring Rome.

62. tam longa via, 'that you have done well in taking so long a voyage.'

63. The use of *sic*, like our word *so*, is frequent in vows or adjurations, and always bears the same meaning, viz. 'on this condition.' The clause with *sic* has its verb in the subjunctive, or rather optative, mood ; and it is always attached to another clause in which either (*a*) a statement, or (*b*) a prayer, is made. The 'condition' to which *sic* refers is either (*a*) that the statement made is true ; or (*b*) that the prayer preferred be granted. The passage before us is an example of (*a*). *Vera cano,* 'what I sing is true.' *Sic,* 'On this condition, and on this condition only (viz. that I sing the truth), may I continue to feed on the sacred laurel unharmed, and preserve my maiden purity.' In other words, she is willing to risk her future position as priestess on the truth of her statements. Precisely similar is our own form of oath, 'So help me God;' before which comes the promise, ' I speak, or will speak, the truth.' In other words, 'I am willing to rest all my hopes of help from God upon the truth of my statements.' Sometimes, instead of a declaratory indicative, as here *vera cano*, we have *ut* before the indicative, as *ut vera cano*. The meaning would still be the same : ' as I tell,' ' as surely as I tell,' ' in proportion as I tell, the truth, *so*, on that condition, may such and such a thing happen to me.' An excellent instance of this is Catull. 45. 13-16

> *Sic, inquit, mea vita, Septimille,*
> *Huic uni domino usque serviamus,*
> *Ut multo mihi maior acriorque*
> *Ignis mollibus ardet in medullis,*

i. e. ' *So*, on this condition, may we ever be slaves to the God of Love *as it is true that* a fiercer flame burns in my heart than in thine.' She risks the hope of their future happiness on the truth of her protestation. Cp. Ov. Met. 8. 867.

In case (*b*), where a prayer is preferred, the main clause has an imperative instead of an indicative, with or without *ut :* thus Virg. E. 10. 1 sqq.

> *Extremum hunc, Arethusa, mihi concede laborem :*
> *Sic tibi, quum fluctus praeterlabere Sicanos,*
> *Doris amara suam non intermisceat undam,*

i. e. ' *If* thou grantest my prayer, I will pray in turn for thee that,' etc. Exactly similar are Virg. E. 9. 30 sqq. ; Ov. Her. 4. 168 ; ib. 3. 135 ; Hor. Od. 1. 3. 1, 7 ; ib. 1. 28. 23, 27, and below l. 121. In all cases alike *sic* goes with an optative verb. We may thus typify in a simple form the three possible constructions :

> (1) *Vera dico : sic felix sim ;*
> (2) *Ut vera dico, sic felix sim ;*

i. e. ' may my future happiness depend upon the truth of what I say.'

> (3) *Dic mihi vera : sic felix sis ;*

i. e. ' Tell me the truth, and may your future happiness depend upon your telling it.'

63, 64. laurus Vescar. 'The Pythia, before she ascended the tripod, bathed in the water of Castalia, crowned herself with laurel, and chewed its leaves to increase the inspiration. This is what Lycophron terms Δαφνηφάγων ἐκ λαιμῶν ὄπα, "a voice proceeding from a laurel-eating throat," and so also Lucian, in the Bis Accusat. ἡ πρόμαντις πιοῦσα τοῦ ἱεροῦ νάμιτος καὶ μασαμένη τῆς δάφνης, etc.'

63. innoxia, 'in a passive sense, "suffering no harm," "un-harmed." So Lucan 9. 891

> *Gens unica terras*
> *Incolit a saevo serpentum innoxia morsu.*

We find it also in the active sense of "doing no harm," in Plaut. Capt. 3. 5. 7

> *Decet innocentem servum atque innoxium*
> *Confidentem esse, suum apud herum potissimum.*

In like manner *innocuus* signifies either "harmless," or, "unhurt."

> 1. *Innocuum rigido perforat ense latus*

Ov. Trist. 3. 9. 26.

> 2. *Donec rostra tenent siccum, et sedere carinae*
> *Omnes innocuae*

Virg. Aen. 10. 301.'

64. Vescar is here followed by the accusative. Lucretius, and still more frequently Plautus, use verbs like *potior, fruor, fungor, utor* with the accusative. This phenomenon has not as yet been satisfactorily explained. The ablative after these verbs is required by their original, not their acquired meaning. Thus *vescor* means, 'I feed on,' *utor*, 'I employ myself by,' etc. We should naturally expect that the ablative would be *more* rigorously insisted on in the infancy of the language, when the original meaning of the words still survived, than when by frequent use they had acquired a conventional mean-ing. It would seem that in grammar, as in prosody, the knowledge of Greek brought with it an artificial tendency towards purism which forced the literary language into a conventional correctness, from which it again burst itself free upon the decay of letters. It certainly is remarkable that what are called the corruptions of a debased age should appear in some instances in the earliest records of the language.

66. Her hair, after the manner of inspired priestesses—and modern poets—was tossed back in disorder from her forehead.

67-70. 'These lines present many difficulties, and the text has been moulded into various forms by different editors. The general meaning of the passage is clear enough. The prophecy of the Sibyl, who foretold to Aeneas the high fortunes of his posterity, being concluded, the poet continues, "Other Sibyls, it is true, pre-dicted the appearance of many prodigies ominous of woe, and these portents have already been made manifest, but may Apollo ward off all calamities in time coming." Some of these prophetesses of evil are specified in the lines before us, in which Tibullus seems to have taken at random names commonly current, without investigating very closely their origin or their relations to each other.

'*Amalthea* is in Varro[1] the *Sibylla Cumana*, who, he says, by others is called Herophile or Demophile. Again Herophile, in Pausanias, is the *Sibylla Erythraea*, but he quotes certain verses, said to be composed by herself, in which she declares that she was a native of Marpessus[2], a city of which, Pausanias adds, traces still remained in his time upon Phrygian Ida. A Marpessus, however, in this situation is mentioned by no other ancient authority[3], while Stephanus Byzantinus[4], Suidas and others place a *Mermessus* on this very spot. Hence Salmasius would change Μάρπησσος, in Pausanias, into Μέρμησσος, and read *Mermessia* in Tibullus, instead of *Marpessia*. But whether we adopt *Marpessia* or *Mermessia*, it must be taken as an epithet of Herophile, and the punctuation of Huschke,

> *Quidquid Amalthea, quidquid Mermessia dixit,*
> *Herophile Phoebo grataque quod monuit,*

by which *Mermessia* is made to indicate a personage distinct from Herophile, can scarcely be received. On the other hand, if we place the comma after Herophile, as in our text, the words *Phoebo grataque quod monuit* stand isolated without any noun to which *grata* can be referred. Hence critics have supposed that *Phoebo* has been substituted by some ignorant transcriber for the name of a Sibyl, and Vossius would substitute *Demo*, who, according to Hyperochus, was the *Cumana*, while Lachmann conjectures *Phaeto Graiaque*; Φύτω (*Phyto* Huschke), in Suidas, being the Samian Sibyl.' Hiller reads *Phyto Graia quod admonuit*. In Cat. 66. 58 the MSS. read *Gratia*, where Lachmann has restored *Graia*.

'The next couplet, if we follow the best MSS., and read *Albana . . . Tiberis* is absolutely unintelligible. The description, given by Varro, of the tenth Sibyl seems to afford the clue required to guide us. *Decimam Tiburtem, nomine Albuneam ; quae Tiburi colitur, ut Dea, iuxta ripas amnis Anienis ; cuius in gurgite simulacrum eius*

---

[1] Serv. Aen. 6. 72 says it is not clearly known which of the Sibyls composed the Roman oracles, yet it is certain that they were brought to Tarquin by a woman named Amalthea.

[2] Salmasius, however, has a very happy conjecture, according to which the Sibyl will declare that she herself was of Erythrae, and the Nymph, her mother, of Mermessus.

[3] Except Varro ap. Lactant., and the reading is disputed.

[4] Μερμησσός, πόλις Τρωική, ἀφ' ἧς ἡ 'Ερυθραία Σίβυλλα. The MSS. have also Μύρμισσος, and Suidas Μάρμισσος.

inventum esse dicitur, tenens in manu librum.   Cuius sacra (some
MSS. *sortes*) *senatus in Capitolium transtulerit.*   From this, Scaliger, with much plausibility, conjectured *Albuna,* instead of *Albana,*
although *Aniana* (i e. *Aniena*) *Tiburs,* which appears in some
Italian MSS., is,. perhaps, to be preferred.'

71–78. This passage describes the portents which took place
before Caesar's assassination, and bears a marked likeness to the
similar passages Hor. Od. 1. 2. 1–20, and Virg. Geo. 1. 466–492.
In ll. 466–8 the darkening of the sun after the eclipse of B. C. 44 is
referred to :

> *Ille etiam exstincto miseratus Caesare Romam,*
> *Quum caput obscura nitidum ferrugine texit,*
> *Impiaque aeternam timuerunt saecula noctem.*

This phenomenon is specially mentioned by Plin. H. N. 2. 30, and
Plutarch.

72. deplueret, the proper tense after *dixerunt fore ut.*   Note
this extreme case of the misplacement of *que.*   It comes after the
fifth word in the sentence.

74. Audita, i. e. *audita esse*

lucos; cp. Virg. Geo. 1. 476

> *Vox quoque per lucos vulgo exaudita silentes*
> *Ingens.*

75. defectum lumine, for the more usual *deficientem ;* lit.
'worn out,' 'enfeebled in its light,' as Ov. Fast. 3. 674.   So exactly
Luc. x. 280 *Defectusque epulis et pastus caede duorum.*

76. pallentes . . . equos.   Plut. says of the sun throughout
that year ὠχρὸς μὲν ὁ κύκλος καὶ μαρμαρυγὰς οὐκ ἔχων.   Prop. 3.
5. 34 *solis atratis equis* is not in point, as that passage points to
mourning, this to the sun's having lost his wonted fires.

79. fuerant.   The tense puts all this catalogue of ill portent
far back into the past and gone.

Horace in like manner, Od. 1. 2. 29, turns first to Apollo to
cleanse the people from the guilt of which the portents were a sign.

80. indomitis, implying that the waters have power to wash
off every pollution, however great.   Monstrous births, etc., were
thrown into the sea.

81. At sacrifices, and especially in magical incantations, laurel
leaves were thrown into the fire, and omens were drawn from their
modes of crackling.   Prop. 2. 28. 35

> *deficiunt magico sub carmine rhombi,*
> *Et tacet extincto laurus adusta foco.*

And the witch in Virg. E. 8. 83 says

Daphnis me malus urit, ego hanc in Daphnide laurum.

Cp. Theocr. 2. 24. Compare our own divination by burning chest-nuts, etc., on the night of Halloween.

83. ubi, not exactly = *postquam*, 'as soon as' (Pind.); but rather a general statement 'in cases where,' and so = 'whenever.'

85. Oblitus musto, a universal incident of wine-pressing ; but the words also suggest a general idea of abundance.

86. As already stated on 1. 1. 10, the *lacus* was the large cistern into which the *mustum*—the new-pressed grape-juice—was received from the press; the *dolia* were the large vats in which the fermentation was completed. Cato's direction R. R. 113 is as follows, *De lacu quamprimum vinum in dolia indito, post dies xl diffundito in amphoras.*

deficiantque. Here again *que* is misplaced. It will be observed that when this particular place in the Pentameter—the commencement of the second Penthemimer—is occupied by a verb, it seems specially privileged to carry with it a postponed *que*. See again l. 90 *transilietque.*

87. The *Palilia*, or *Parilia*, as we have seen, was the feast of Pales—who, according to Tibullus, Virgil, and Ovid, was a goddess, but a god according to Varro—which was held on the 21st of April, the supposed birthday of Rome. Ovid gives a detailed account of the various purifications gone through, and prayers offered upon this day, Fast. 4. 721 sqq. The characteristic ceremony of the day was leaping across heaps of blazing hay and straw, *his Palilibus se expiari credentes* Varro ap. Schol. Pers. 1. 72.

sua, because the *Palilia* was essentially the shepherd's feast.

90. For the leaping over the straw bonfires see Prop. 4. 4. 73 and notes. Both poets make it an essential part of the ceremony that the leaper should be *madidus* and *potus.*

91. fetus dabit, 'will bear offspring,' being blest with fertility.

92. The ancients were curious in kisses. The Greeks had a special name for the kiss indicated in the text, calling it χύτρα, or the Pitcher-kiss, because the kisser held the kissee by the ears as one would hold a pitcher (such as the *amphora*) by its two handles. The Latin name was *Osculum Florentinum*. Whole books have been written containing enumerations and descriptions of the various modes in which kisses can be given and received.

93. Grandpapa was to stay at home and 'keep' or 'mind' the baby.

l. 93 implies that the child was put to sleep; but in l. 94 he wakes up, and has to be amused with baby-language.

95. operata deo. See above on 2. 1. 9.

discumbet. Properly used of a number of people sitting down to a meal, each taking his proper place. But it is also used of a single person, Juv. 5. 12

Primo fige loco quod tu discumbere iussus,

i. e. 'when invited to dinner.'

96. levis umbra. Surely the epithet *levis* needs no explanation. Pinder after D. laboriously explains it as either 'the glancing, wavy shade,' or 'airy,' 'not close and oppressive from the boughs being low.' How *levis* could bear either meaning is not stated.

97. Cp. above 2. 1. 24.

98. stabit, i. e. on the table. For *coronatus* cp. Virg. Aen. 1. 724

Crateras magnos statuunt et vina coronant.

So Geo. 2. 528. Wreaths of flowers were twined round the goblets, as well as round the heads of the drinkers.

101. Ingeret, a word specially used of opprobrious language.

102. Postmodo, 'after a while.'

103. suae apparently must go with *ferus:* 'he that was late so cruel to his love.'

105. Pace tua, called in the P. S. Lat. Primer an 'Ablative of Condition.' It is, in reality, an ablative of attendant circumstance, closely allied to the ablative absolute. 'There being peace, i. e. no objection, on thy part.'

108. dedit ... malum, 'wrought mischief to,' 'injured.' Cp. the old repartee of the Metelli to the poet Naevius :

Dabunt malum Metelli Naevio poetae.

110. faveo morbo, 'foster or encourage my distemper,' make no effort to throw it off. Note *cum iaceo, cum iuvat,* as in Plautus, where we should expect the subjunctive. Or the indic. may denote duration of time, as in *multi sunt anni cum in aere meo est,* Cic. Fam. 15. 14.

111. mihi nullus. A very unusual ending for a hexameter.

Nemesis. The second flame of our poet : Ov. Am. 3. 9. 31

Sic Nemesis longum, sic Delia nomen habebunt,
Altera cura recens, altera primus amor.

116. Referring to the representations or models of captured towns carried along as part of a triumphal procession, Hor. Ep. 2. 1. 193

Captivum portatur ebur, captiva Corinthus ;

also Prop. 3. 4. 16 and note.

119. pia, here used of the father's affection for the son.

121. Annue : sic ... sint. Cp. note on l. 63.

II. 6.

THE poet Aemilius Macer had gone forth to the wars; taking courage from his example, and distracted by the cruelties and caprice of his beloved Nemesis, Tibullus determines to buckle on his armour and to cure himself of his love by absence. But alas! the very thought of leaving Nemesis behind unmans him; once more he turns and implores her to take pity on him. Hope will not desert him: he implores her by the memory of her sister, who had died by a tragic and untimely death, to heal his wounds and restore him to her favour.

1. Macer. We have to distinguish between two contemporaneous poets of the same name.

(1) Aemilius Macer of Verona, who according to the Eusebian chronicle died in Asia B.C. 16. He was apparently a friend of Virgil, for Serv. ap. E. 5 says that by Mopsus *intelligitur Aemilius Macer Veronensis poeta, amicus Vergili*. He wrote a poem on birds, snakes, and plants, as appears from Ov. Trist. 4. 10. 43

> *Saepe suos volucres legit mihi grandior aevo*
> *Quaeque necet serpens, quae iuvet herba, Macer.*

Manilius alludes to this poem Astr. 2. 43 in similar terms. Quintilian contrasts him with Lucretius, whom he terms *difficilis*, while Macer is *humilis*, both being *elegantes in sua materia*.

(2) The Macer addressed by Ovid in Am. 2. 18 and in E. P. 2. 10. 13, and therefore alive in B.C. 12. Ovid speaks of him as an old companion, and thus describes his poetry:

> *Tu canis aeterno quidquid restabat Homero,*
> *Ne careant summa Troica bella manu.*

In E. P. 4. 16. 6 he calls him *Iliacus Macer*, which implies that there were two of the name, and that one of them was known as a compiler of Homeric poems. See Wernsdorff on the Homeristae Latini in his *Poetae Latini Minores*.

quid fiet Amori. 'What will become of Love?' *Fiet* in this sense is constructed both with (*a*) the dative, and (*b*) the ablative: the former being the dative of the thing or person affected, 'what will happen to;' the latter being the ablative of the instrument, 'what will be done by or with.' Thus for (*a*) see Liv. 45. 39 *Quid deinde tam opimae praedae, tam opulentae victoriae spoliis fiet?* So Ov. A. A. 1. 536; for (*b*) Cic. Epp. Att. 6. 1 *Quid illo fiet quem reliquero? quid me autem si non tam cito decedo?*

3. vaga, 'unstable,' 'uncertain.' So Tib. 2. 3. 39

> *Praeda vago iussit geminare pericula ponto.*

N

4. ad latus, i. e. 'at the side of Macer.' *Claudere latus* is a regular word for walking side by side with a person, especially on the left side. Cp. Hor. Sat. 2. 5. 18

> *Utne tegam spurco Damae latus?*

5. Ure here = 'torture,' from the practice of branding slaves, especially runaways. So Tib. I. 9. 21

> *Ure meum potius flamma caput, et pete ferro*
> *Corpus, et intorto verbere terga seca.*

6. erronem, a wandering or loitering slave. Hence here of a truant soldier.

7. hic quoque, i. e. himself. *Hic* is the pronoun of the first person, as *iste* is of the second and *ille* of the third.

8. Ipse, i. e. as a common soldier or *gregarius,* who had to perform all duties for himself. The helmet was the soldier's natural drinking-cup: Prop. 3. 12. 9

> *Tu tamen iniecta tectus, vesane, lacerna,*
> *Potabis galea fessus Araxis aquam.*

levem apparently is intended to suggest the simpleness of his fare, and the humble scale on which his comforts are supplied.

10. mihi facta tuba est seems to mean 'the trump has sounded for me,' 'I obey the trumpet-call.'

11. Magna loquor, 'big words!' So in Greek μέγα εἰπεῖν, μεγάλη γλῶσσα, etc., and Hor. of Apollo 4. 6. I *magnae vindicem linguae.* We have the converse Ov. Met. 6. 151

> *Cedere caelitibus verbisque minoribus uti.*

12. Excutiunt. Pinder scarcely gives the force when he translates 'dash to the ground,' or 'empty of their force.' *Excutio* is 'to shake out,' and is properly applied to clothes or materials of any kind when shaken out to see what they contain. Thus of a suspected person it is 'to search,' as Plin. H. N. 7. 36, of a girl visiting her mother in prison, *a ianitore semper excussa ne quid inferret cibi.* Of mental sifting and examination, Pers. 1. 49

> *nam belle hoc excute totum:*
> *Quid non intus habet?*

'Shake out the meaning of these "Bravos:" what will you not find contained in them?' Of offering the inmost heart to be read, Pers. 5. 20

> *tibi ...*
> *Excutienda damus praecordia,*

'I present my heart to be shaken out by,' i.e. 'laid bare to, to you.' So here 'the sight of the closed door shakes all my brave words out of me.' Cp. Cic. pro Sull. 8.

16. aspiciamque. See note on 2. 5. 86.

18. nefanda loqui, 'to talk blasphemy.'

22. fenore reddat. The field is said to give back what is put into it *fenore*, just as a borrower is said *pecuniam accipere fenore*, i.e. ' at 'interest,' ' on terms of interest,' an ordinary modal ablative. *Cum fenore* is also used, as in the parallel passage Ov. R. A. 173

> *Obrue versata Cerealia semina terra*
> *Quae tibi cum multo fenore reddat ager.*

26. The change of subject in **canit** is harsh. It has to be supplied from *vinctum*.

Ovid imitates this passage, E. P. 1. 6. 31, of Hope,

> *Haec facit ut vivat vinctus quoque compede fossor:*
> *Liberaque a ferro crura futura putet.*

29. immatura ossa, as Pinder remarks, is an expression after the manner of Propertius: but Propertius would have introduced it less harshly.

parce ... Sic ... quiescat. See note on 1. 5. 63.

30. tenera, probably 'which lightly presses on.' Cp. Pers. 1. 37

> *Non levior cippus nunc inprimit ossa?*

and the common formula on tombs S. T. T. L. i.e. *sit tibi terra levis.*

31. mihi, ' in my eyes.'

34. cum cinere querar, i.e. 'complain *to*,' after the analogy of *pugnare cum*, 'to quarrel *with* a person,' or of any act which requires more than one person for the doing of it.

35. clientem. As though he had formally ranged himself as her client, and therefore was entitled to her aid.

36. lenta, i.e. ' slow in hearing my prayer,' and so ' obdurate.'

41. Desinŏ, read by all the best MSS. One of the very few cases in the Augustan poets where final *o* in a verb is short, with the exception of *scio, nescio, puto, volo*. See Ramsay's Latin Prosody on *o* final. Probably *desine* should be read.

III. 3.

As to the genuineness of the 3rd Book of Tibullus, see the Introduction. It presents obvious differences of style, if compared with Books 1 and 2.

The writer is separated from Neaera, and laments that neither vows nor offerings have effected their re-union. He has sought not wealth nor splendour, only to have her love, and to live till old age

in her company. Poverty with her were happiness: without her not
kingdoms, not all the riches of Pactolus, can bring content. In conclusion, he prays that if the Fates have indeed ordained that their
separation is to be eternal, he may speedily pass down to the gloomy
realms of Orcus.

1. caelum votis implesse. So Virg. Aen. 9. 24

> *oneravitque aethera donis.*

2. Blanda, i. e. 'propitiating,' 'likely to win favour.' In Plaut.
Cas. 2. 3. 55 *Experiemur nostrum uter sit blandior,* 'which of us
two is the more persuasive.' So Prop. 4. 6. 5 *blandi turis honores,*
and Hor. Od. 3. 23. 17

> *Non sumptuosa blandior hostia.*

5. renovarent, 'plough up anew.' So *novalis* or *novale,*
'fallow land,' Virg. Geo. 1. 71, or 'land ploughed for the first time,'
Plin. H. N. 7. 5. 3.

7. sociarem, 'share.'

8. caderet, 'fail,' almost = *occideret.*

13. Phrygiis. The Phrygian marble was one of those most
highly prized at Rome, when all the quarries of Europe were opened
up to fulfil Augustus' famous boast 'that he had found Rome
made of brick, and left her made of marble.' This marble is of a
white colour, seamed with wavy streaks of purple, and came from a
village near Synnada, in Phrygia Magna, whence it is often called
lapis Synnachius. It is called *Pavonazetto* by antiquaries, and is
found in considerable fragments in Rome. Statius, Silv. 1. 5. 36, thus
describes it along with Numidian marble:

> *Sola nitet flavis Nomadum decisa metallis*
> *Purpura, sola cavo Phrygiae quam Synnados antro*
> *Ipse cruentavit maculis liventibus Atys.*

14. Taenare. Black marble was obtained from the promontory
of *Taenarum* in Laconia (C. Matapan) and is now known as *nero
antico.* There was another Lacedaemonian marble, green in colour
(*serpentino*), from Mount Taygetus.

Caryste. Carystus was in Euboea. The marble obtained
there was white and green, and in consequence of its being streaked
like the outer coat of an onion, is called *cippolino.* References to
these marbles are perpetual in the Latin poets. Martial enumerates
the three above-mentioned, with the Numidian, or common yellow
marble (*giallo antico*), 9. 76. 6

> *Idem beatus lautus extruit thermas*
> *De marmore omni, quod Carystos invenit,*

Quod Phrygia Synnas, Afra quod Nomas mittit,
Et quod virenti fonte lavit Eurotas.

15. The wealthy Romans had gardens and shrubberies behind
their houses, surrounded and enclosed by peristyles or colonnades,
where they might sit, walk, or even drive, protected from rain in
winter, or from noontide heat in summer. The remains of Hadrian's
villa near Tivoli show to what an incredible extent private luxury in
such matters could be carried. See the description of it in Murray's
Handbook for Rome. Even in Horace's time, Ep. 1. 10. 22

Nempe inter varias nutritur silva columnas.

Cp. Od. 3. 10. 5 and Seneca, Controv. 5. 5 *Intra aedificia vestra*
undas et nemora comprehenditis.

sacros imitantia lucos, i.e. so large, so retired.

16. trabes, the main beams between which were the panels
which formed the fretted ceiling (*lacunar*). Cp. Hor. Od. 2. 18. 1–4
and Prop. 3. 2. 9

Quod non Taenariis domus est mihi fulta columnis,
Nec camera auratas inter eburna trabes.

17. Erythraeo littore. The Persian Gulf: *E. lapilli* are
pearls.

19. in illis Invidia est. Huschke well quotes Plin. Pan. 88. 5
An satius fuit felicem vocare? quod non moribus, sed fortunae datum
est: satius magnum? cui plus invidiae quam pulchritudinis inest.
So Prop. 2. 25. 34

Invidiam quod habet non solet esse diu.

21. mentes hominum curaeque levantur. A zeugma: the
mind is lightened, or eased, of its load; the burden of care is made
lighter. A still stronger instance occurs 1. 4. 65

Quem referent Musae, vivet, dum robora tellus,
Dum caelum stellas, dum vehet amnis aquas.

So Virg. Aen. 2. 320

Sacra manu, victosque deos, parvumque nepotem
Ipse trahit,

where *trahit* is only applicable to *nepotem*. A still stronger instance,
almost amounting to a pun, occurs Ov. Met. 2. 505

– Arcuit omnipotens; pariterque ipsosque nefasque
Sustulit,

i. e. 'both raised them to the skies, and prevented the unholy deed.'

28. non goes closely with *meus,* 'by no means favourable,'
'hostile,' 'angry.' So Hor. Epod. 9. 30 of Antony after Actium,

Ventis iturus non suis,

while in Virg. Geo. 4. 22 the bees go forth *vere suo*, 'in the spring that is all their own.' Cp. Ov. Her. 12. 84

>   *Sed mihi tam faciles unde meosque deos?*

The Pactolus and the Tagus are coupled together by the ancients on account of their golden sands. The Pactolus (now Bagouly) rose in Mount Tmolus—celebrated for saffron—flowed under Sardis, and joined the Hermus. See Virg. Aen. 10. 141 and Juv. 14. 298.

33. Juno, daughter of Saturn, is invoked as the patroness of wedded life.

35. tristes, 'inexorable.'

III. 5.

THE poet is lying alone in Rome, worn with fever, and expecting death: he pours out his lamentations to his friends who are visiting the hot springs of Etruria. Protesting the innocence of his life, he implores the gods not to let him die in youth, but to prolong his days to a good old age, and begs his friends to offer sacrifices for his recovery.

1, 2. 'Etruria was celebrated in ancient, as it is in modern times, for its hot springs. Among the most famous of these were the *Aquae Caeretanae*, now the *Bagni di Sasso*, in the neighbourhood of the important city of Agylla or Caere; the *Aquae Pisanae*, now the *Bagni di Pisa*, within a few miles of Pisae, the still celebrated *Pisa*; the *Aquae Tauri*, now *Bagni di Ferrata*, near Centumcellae, or Traiani Portus (*Civita Vecchia*), etc. The poet gives no hint of the particular spot he alludes to, but many of these places are situated near the sea, and the proverbial insalubrity of this low-lying coast of Tuscany (*the Maremma*) in hot weather, will sufficiently explain the meaning of the second line.' Strabo 5. p. 227 speaks of the fame of the Etruscan waters, and says they were as much frequented as the more famous waters of Baiae. This confirms the reading *proxima.*

3. proxima, the conj. adopted by Hiller for the *maxima* of the MSS., gives a good sense: 'the Etruscan springs, which near the dog-days are not to be approached, but at the present season rank next to the sacred waters of Baiae.' For this use of *proxima* implying a comparison in point of merit cp. Ov. Met. 12. 398

>   *Pectoraque artificum laudatis proxima signis,*

'not inferior to.' No satisfactory explanation of *maxima* has been suggested. Scaliger supposes *Baiae* to stand for hot springs in general, like the word 'Spa :' 'greatest amongst hot springs, on account of its holy waters.' But no proof of such a use has been adduced, to say nothing of the intolerable ambiguity which it would introduce here. Others wrest *maxima* into the sense of *maior*, meaning 'superior.' This is no less inadmissible. It has been noted that *autem* is not elsewhere used by Tibullus. The words *maximus* and *proximus* are not unfrequently interchanged in MSS.

4. se remittit, 'unbends from,' 'is released,' i. e. from the cold of winter. Ov. Fast. 4. 126

> *Vere nitent terrae, vere remissus ager.*

The winter is regarded as presenting an interruption to the normal state of the earth.

purpureo vere, 'under the influence of spring.'

5. nigram contrasted, as D. points out, with *purpureo* l. 4. For *nigra hora* cp. *niger dies* Prop. 2. 24. 34.

denuntiat. This verb is often used in the sense of threatening: *inimicitias, caedem, vim denuntiare*, etc. occur in Cicero.

8. laudandae deae. The Bona Dea, to whose rites no male might be admitted. Tib. 1. 6. 22

> *Sacra bonae maribus non adeunda Deae.* ˙

It is well known what serious consequences, political and personal, were entailed by the violation of these rites by Clodius in Caesar's house B.C. 62.

9. infecit pocula, 'drugged a bowl.'

10. trita, 'pounded.' A. has *certa*. *Trita venena* occurs also Prop. 2. 17. 14.

11. sacrilegos is not quite so well supported as *sacrilegi*, but it gives a better sense. And if *sacrilegi* would readily be changed to *sacrilegos* to agree with *ignes* (Pinder), *sacrilegos* might still more readily be changed to *sacrilegi* to agree with *nos*.

13. iurgia mentis. Lachmann illustrates by this phrase the *iurgia saevitiae* of Prop. 1. 3. 18. 'Brooding over the resentments of a frenzied mind' Pinder.

18. This line occurs in Ovid's autobiography, Trist. 4. 10. 6, and it is extremely unlikely that Tibullus would have borrowed so marked a line literally, and without acknowledgment. Further, it is certain that he was born at least eleven years, probably sixteen years, before the event indicated, which took place B. C. 43. See Introduction. Either, therefore, these lines are interpolated, or else the author was not the poet Tibullus. As a matter of fact, the lines are quite out of place where they stand.

19, 20. Ovid closely imitates these lines, Am. 2. 14. 23–4

Quid plenam fraudas vitem crescentibus uvis,
Pomaque crudeli vellis acerba manu.

22. Dura ... tertia regna. The inelegance of the double epithet is relieved by the circumstance that *tertia regna* go together as one idea. The three kingdoms of course are those of Zeus in the heavens, of Poseidon over the water, and of Pluto over the shades.

sortiti for *sortiti estis.*

23. olim, 'on some far distant day.'

24. The Cimmerians were known to Homer as living in the far West, on the borders of the Ocean, near the entrance to Hades. Their land is shrouded in mists and clouds, and the sun never shines on them, Od. 11. 14 sqq. In Herodotus, the Cimmerians possessed the country round the Palus Maeotis. They were expelled by the Scythians and made an irruption into Asia. They gave their name to the Cimmerian Bosphorus.

30. The water is **facilis** because it yields to the hand; the hand is **lenta,** 'pliant,' ' flexible,' because it knows how to overcome the resistance of the water.

33. Black steers were sacrificed to the gods below; white to the gods above.

Interea, i. e. until my fate is decided, one way or the other.

NOTES ON PROPERTIUS.

I. 8.

THIS poem is addressed to Cynthia, and consists of two parts. In the first part—ll. 1–26—the poet writes in an agony of terror that she has transferred her affections to a rival who was at that time praetor designate, and in the belief that she had actually made up her mind to leave Rome and sail with him to the province of Illyricum and Dalmatia, of which he had been appointed governor. If the project was indeed entertained, Cynthia was diverted from it by the indignant and heart-broken remonstrances of Propertius, and he writes the second part in a tone of enraptured triumph, assured that he has won the love of Cynthia, and attributing the hold he has acquired over her to his gift of poesy. We hear again of this same praetor on his return from Illyria in 3. 7. 1, when he is still an object of suspicion ; in l. 8 Propertius gives vent to his feelings by calling him *stolidum pecus*, 'a dull sheep.'

1. igitur, with a question, expresses surprise and indignation, marking an abrupt conclusion to a lost train of argument. So Hor. Sat. 2. 5. 101

> *Ergo nunc Dama sodalis*
> *Nusquam est ?*

and id. Od. 1. 24. 5. Cp. the Greek ἄρα. 'What then, art thou mad ?'

cura, as elsewhere, is used especially of the pangs of love. So Hor. A. P. 85

> *Et iuvenum curas et libera vina referre.*

Sometimes, like *amor*, and ' love ' in English, it is used for the loved object, as Virg. E. 10. 22 *tua cura Lycoris.*

2. tibi, ' in thy eyes,' the Dativus Ethicus, or Dative of Reference. Cp. Pers. 6. 62 *Sum tibi Mercurius.*

Illyria. The Province of Illyricum (or Illyria) and Dalmatia included the whole Eastern sea-board of the Adriatic from the peninsula of Histria as far south as the Acroceraunian promontory, where Macedonia began, and comprised the modern territories of Croatia, Dalmatia, Bosnia, Herzegovina, Montenegro, and Albania.

gelida, because all mountainous countries alike, and all countries

to the north of Rome, were regarded by the Romans as cold and
inhospitable.

3, 4. tanti . . . ut . . . velis. 'Of so great value that (for his
sake) thou art willing.' Cp. Juv. 3. 54

tanti tibi non sit opaci
Omnis arena Tagi, quodque in mare volvitur aurum,
Ut somno careas, ponendaque praemia sumas.

i. e. 'be of such value in your eyes that (for its sake) you will do
without sleep,' etc.

iste, with a notion of contempt : ' that fellow, whoever he may
be.' *Iste* implies properly pointing at a person who is present, and
hence suggests familiarity and contempt.   In a court of justice, the
accused person is always *iste* to the prosecutor, *hic* to his own advo-
cate.   Cp. 2. 9. 1.

4. vento quolibet may be taken together, 'taking advantage of
any wind, no matter what,' i. e. ready to sail in any weather, or at
any season of the year.   But it is better to take *quolibet* as the adverb,
'ready to sail in any direction,' ' to start for any country.'   *Vento* is
Abl. of the means or instrument of transit, as in Virg. Aen. 2. 180
Vento petiere Mycenas.   So we say 'to go by road' or ' by rail.'

5, 6. potes . . . potes.   Emphatic : ' Canst thou bring thyself
to?' ' hast thou the hardihood to?'

vesani, of the wild, wintry sea.   So Hor. Od. 3. 4. 30 *insanientem
Bosporum*, and id. 3. 7. 6 *Post insana Caprae sidera*, and Epp. 1. 11. 10
Neptunum procul e terra spectare furentem.

6. dura nave.   So in Pers. 5. 145 *Luxuria* is represented as
dissuading the indolent youth from going to sea :

Tun' mare transilias ? tibi, torta cannabe fulto,
Cena sit in transtro?

7. positas, 'deposited,' and so = 'lying.'   Hor. Sat. 2. 3. 142
Pauper Opimius argenti positi intus et auri.

Postgate well compares Od. 3. 10. 7
Positas ut glaciet nives
Puro numine Iuppiter.

fulcire.   Postgate (App. B.) has clearly proved that we have here
an example of the proper meaning of the word *fulcio*, which is ' to
press.'   From this is derived the secondary meaning ' to prop,' ' support,' 'strengthen.'   The word comes from the same root as *farcio*,
meaning ' to press,' ' to pack,' and so ' to stuff.'   The sense ' to
press ' is clearly made out from the present passage, from Celsus 7. 19
linamenta super non fulcienda sed leviter tantum ponenda sunt,

and from the MS. reading of Lucr. 2. 98, where the crushing together and rebounding of the primordial atoms is described :

> *Partim intervallis magnis confulta resultant.*

Less certain instances occur in Virg. E. 6. 53, Pers. 1. 78.

8. insolitas, in passive sense 'unaccustomed,' 'unknown to
thee.' Sometimes it is used actively in the sense of 'contrary to one's
habit,' as of the seals rushing up rivers, Virg. Geo. 4. 543 *insolitae
fugiunt in flumina phocae.*

For ll. 5–8 we may compare

> *Yet take good heed, for ever I dread*
> *That ye could not sustain*
> *The thorny ways, the deep valleys,*
> *The snow, the frost, the rain,*
> *The cold, the heat.*   The Nut-brown Maid, Anon. 1521.

9. hibernae, 'stormy.'

tempora, i. e. 'the length' of the stormy season.

10. iners (*in* and *ars*), 'sluggish,' 'inactive,' as of the winter
itself, Hor. Od. 4. 7. 12 *et mox Bruma recurrit iners ;* i. e. 'in
which no work is done.'

tardis Vergiliis, Abl. of Cause, 'in consequence of the late
rising of the Vergiliae.' The morning rising of the Vergiliae, or, to
use their Greek name, the Pleiades, was held in a rough way to mark
the commencement of spring, and of the sailing season. As to the
precise date indicated, there is great confusion in the writings of the
Roman poets, arising mainly from two causes : (1) they did not distinguish between the *true* morning rising of a star (i. e. when it rises
at the same moment with the sun) from its *apparent* rising (i. e. when
it rises long enough before the sun to be visible before daylight) ; and
(2) they occasionally (Ovid especially) copied dates from Greek
astronomical writers without correcting their calculations for the date
or for the latitude of Rome. In the year 44 B.C. at Rome the true
morning rising of the Pleiades was on April 16 ; the apparent or
heliac rising was on May 28. According to the division of the seasons
in Caesar's Calendar, the beginning of summer was marked by the
morning rising of the Pleiades, but whether the true or heliac rising
was meant is not stated. See W. Ramsay's Appendix on the Roman
Calendar, Selections from Ovid, p. 358 sqq.

11. Tyrrhena . . . arena. These words form a kind of rhyme
called leonine : cp. 1. 17. 5

> *Quin etiam absenti prosunt tibi Cynthia venti,*

and 2. 8. 16

> *In nostrum iacies verba superba caput.*

For a similar jingle, either intentional or not avoided, cp. 2. 26. 27 (26ᵇ. 5)

> *Multum in amore fides, multum constantia prodest,*
> *Qui dare multa potest multa et amare potest.*

Tyrrhena, i. e. the shore of the *Mare Tyrrhenum* on the West coast of Italy.

solvatur funis, the 'loosening of the cable' was equivalent to our 'setting sail.'

12. elevet, 'carry off,' 'waft away,' as fruitless: lit. 'make light,' so that an air could blow them away. The sense 'to disparage' as in Pers. 1. 6

> *non, si quid turbida Roma*
> *Elevet, accedas*

comes from 'making light' in a scale, and so 'depreciating.'

11-20. Propertius first prays that his prayer may be heard, and that Cynthia may not be able to sail ; then, imagining her ship started, he hopes that the winds which have not deterred her may still rage around her, while he, stupefied with grief, rates her for her cruelty from the shore. Then repenting of his cruel words, he hopes that after all she may have a prosperous passage. Postgate follows those editors who invert the order of the two distichs ll. 13–16, partly to give *tales* a better meaning, partly to assist a supposed symmetrical division of the poem into passages of 4, 4, 6, 6, 6 lines respectively, each giving a complete thought. But the change is unnecessary, for (1) **tales** has a good sense as given above, referring to the fierce and stormy winds which he has hoped may prevent her from sailing altogether. These winds he hopes, in his anger, may still continue after she has set sail, and that she may have the further agony of seeing and hearing him upbraiding her from the shore. (2) **Atque ego** will thus have its natural sense, instead of 'And yet' as required by Postgate's order. (3) Symmetrical divisions should be regarded with much suspicion. They may be multiplied indefinitely to suit the caprice of editors, and once the principle of transposition is admitted it cannot be kept within reasonable limits. An examination of the transpositions suggested in Propertius by recent editors, with the reasons for them, will convince a sober critic that his safest course is to take and explain the order as he finds it in the best MSS., rather than to expend ingenuity in showing how our poet might have been more symmetrical or logical in his arrangement. The English headings given in this edition will, it is hoped, serve to bring out that the order of the MSS. is in almost every case natural and intelligible ; and in this case there are no corresponding divisions in the second part of the Ode.

14. provectas, 'advanced on their way,' 'having set sail,' used proleptically, so that *auferet provectas* = 'bear thy ship away.' The word is usually employed of 'getting under weigh,' as in Virg. Aen. 3. 72 *Provehimur portu*, but may be used of any amount of progress achieved, however small, as in Aen. 2. 24

　　　Huc se provecti deserto in litore condunt,

where it means 'having launched and sailed a certain distance.' In prose it is often used with *longius*, in the sense of 'carried far,' or 'too far.'

　　rates. The Plur. seems used poetically, and is not inappropriate to the original meaning of the word which Festus, p. 273 (Müller), gives thus : *Rates vocantur tigna inter se colligata quae per aquam aguntur, quo vocabulo interdum etiam naves ipsae significantur.* Varro, de L. L. c. 2, suggests a reason for the use of the Plural : *Ratis dicta navis longa propter remos quod hi cum per aquas sublati sunt dextra et sinistra duas partes* (Scaliger's corr. for *rates*), *efficere videntur.* So Plin. 3. 5. 9, § 13 of the Tiber, *trabibus potius quam ratibus meabilis*, which shows that the Plural might be used of a single structure. The word *ratis* seems to have been used by the early writers (Attius and Ennius) for 'an oar :' this may have been its original meaning, and would suit well its connection with the root *ar* or *ra*, whence come *aro, ars, arma, remus, rota*, etc. That *rates* here means Cynthia's vessel only seems more poetical and natural than to suppose with Postgate that Prop. was thinking of a crowd of vessels storm-stayed by the same storm, and all setting sail together. The interpretation above adopted, by which Cynthia is supposed to sail in spite of high winds, is inconsistent with that view.

　　15. The construction is *patiatur me defixum vocare (se) crudelem* : 'may she endure (to see) me stupefied with grief (and to hear me) oft call her cruel with outstretched hand.' Prof. Palmer would take *patiatur* as referring to *aura*. **vacua** is added to intensify the sense of the lover's loneliness and desertion, as in 1. 18. 2. The same word in a different connection may be used to give a sense of complete repose, or of a mind untroubled by thought or care. Cp. 3. 17. 11

　　　Semper enim vacuos nox sobria torquet amantes.

　　defixum, 'deadened,' 'stupefied,' is the natural meaning ; but this, as Postgate points out, is inconsistent with *infesta vocare manu* in the next line. Why should not *defixum* have a still simpler meaning, 'rooted to the ground ?' The picture would then be of the poet standing in one spot, helpless to follow, but crying out upon her cruelty with voice and hand.

patiatur is peculiar, as instead of being used prolately with an infinitive, it has an accusative with the infinitive after it. This construction is not uncommon with verbs of wishing, etc., in Plautus.

16. infesta manu. Clearly used of the threatening or upbraiding hand. Postgate's suggestion that the words may mean 'with hand hostile to myself' of beating the breast, etc., though possible, does not seem in harmony with the passage, and destroys the contrast of *crudelem infesta.*

vocare manu may be either, as Postgate suggests, a compression of two things or two stages, 'speaking by hand and voice,' into one, after the manner of Propertius (see his Introduction), or it may be a somewhat harsh zeugma (if it may be so called), implying that his hand was now his only instrument of speech.

The maledictions are scarce uttered, when the poet repents of having uttered them : he recants, and prays that after all she may have a prosperous voyage.

17. quocunque modo, equivalent to *utcunque*: the phrase would be more naturally connected with a transitive verb.

18. Galatea, a sea-nymph, taken as representative of the powers of the deep. In Aen. 9. 102 Jupiter promises Cybele that such of Aeneas' ships as reach Italy in safety shall be changed into sea-goddesses,

> *qualis Nereia Doto*
> *Et Galatea secant spumantem pectore pontum.*

It is possibly from a recollection of this passage that Horace gives the name of Galatea to a maiden whom he would dissuade from crossing the *ater sinus Hadriae* in time of storm, Od. 3. 27

non aliena viae, imitated by Ovid, Am. 2. 11. 34. **aliena**, 'hostile,' 'unfriendly,' as frequently in Cic., with or without *animus* or *animo*: Tac. Hist. 2. 74 *Muciani animus nec Vespasiano alienus.*

19. praevecta, as the reading stands in the MSS. (*ut te . . . praevecta*) must be the vocative for the accusative, just as it stands for the nom. in the well-known passages in Pers. 1. 123 and 3. 29

> *Stemmate quod Tusco ramum milesime ducis.*

In both passages the use of the Vocative is harsher than it is here, as it stands as the predicate of the sentence. Postgate is inclined to adopt *utere* with Baehrens, pointing out that the imperative is often used in inscriptions, in short prayers, and that the omission of *te*, involved by that reading, is quite Propertian (see Introduction). Harsh as is the transition thus involved from the 3rd person in *sit* to the 2nd in *utere*, and then back to the 3rd in *accipiat*, this reading is the best yet proposed.

praevecta, used of riding or gliding past, as in Tac. Ann. 2. 6 of the Rhone, *servat nomen qua Germaniam praevehitur*. H. A. J. Munro (Journal of Phil. 6. p. 49), besides objecting to the asyndeton of the MS. reading, and to the omission of *te* l. 20, holds that it is impossible to use the past part. *praevecta* in the sense of the present part., showing that Lachmann's instances of *praetervehor* are all in the present tense, and comparing Livy's *praetervehens equo* with Cicero's use of *praetervecta* in the pass. (pro Cael. 51). He therefore repeats the conj. *Ut te praevectam felice Ceraunia remo*, pointing out that *felice* occurs in Cicero, and *infelice* in Catullus. But *praevecta*, as practically equivalent to a pres. part., may be illustrated by *provectas* l. 14; and if we read *utere*, the objection to *praevecta* is practically removed. The rowing would not be pronounced *felix* until the dangers were passed.

Ceraunia, referring to the precipitous cliff and acute promontory called *Acroceraunia*, which forms the termination of the Ceraunian Mountains. This promontory was just to the north of *Oricum* (or *Oricos*), and was the main terror of the passage from Italy to Greece. Bold indeed must have been the man, says Hor. Od. 1. 3. 19, who first dared to face the sea :

> *Qui vidit mare turgidum et*
> *Infames scopulos Acroceraunia.*

20. Oricos or **Oricum**, a town on the confines of Illyria and Epirus, at which passengers bound for Rome would wait for favourable weather. Thus Asteria's lover Gyges is detained at Oricum, Hor. Od. 3. 7. 5

> *Ille Notis actus ad Oricum*
> *Post insana Caprae sidera.*

Oricum and Dyrrhachium (further north on the same coast) were the Calais and Boulogne, as Brundusium was the Dover or Folkestone, of the Roman world.

21. Non ullae taedae. The torch was so essential a part of the marriage procession, as it was also of the funeral procession, that the word *taeda* by itself may stand for either ceremony. Thus in Prop. 4. 11. 46 the shade of Cornelia describes her whole wedded life by the words

> *Viximus insignes inter utramque facem,*

and Ov. Her. 21. 172

> *Et face pro thalami fax mihi mortis erit.*

Here *taeda* stands for 'marriage,' as in Virg. Aen. 4. 18, where Dido says,

Si non pertaesum thalami taedaeque fuisset.

Nam. Postgate seems to miss the force of this word: 'the argument is, "to pass on to me, I shall always be true to you."' Surely *nam* gives the reason for the sudden change of tone introduced by *sed* in l. 17, 'Nay, after all, I must pray for thy happy voyage : *for* I can never give up my love for thee, and wherever thou goest, thou shalt yet be mine.'

21. corrumpere. It should be noticed that this word does not exactly correspond to our word 'to corrupt.' It means 'to break through,' 'to break utterly,' 'to destroy,' and so to render a thing useless for its proper object. To a people who worshipped strength above all things, a word signifying loss of strength came naturally to have a moral meaning ; but the ideas associated with it were rather those of loss of fibre, weakness, and luxury, which the Roman moralists especially connected with loss of manly virtue, than what we denote by moral corruption. Thus Sallust, Jug. 39. 5 *milites . . . licentia atque lascivia corruperat;* Tac. Hist. 3. 49 *disciplinam corrumpere;* Virg. Geo. 2. 466

Nec casia liquidi corrumpitur usus olivi,

i.e. 'deteriorated,' 'spoiled,' and Hor. Sat. 1. 5. 95 of a road,

utpote longum
Carpentes iter et factum corruptius imbri,

i. e. 'broken up.' In the passage before us the word may mean that no second love, no marriage, shall 'break down' or 'weaken' the love he bears to Cynthia.

22. Quin is only used, as Postgate points out, after negative or quasi-negative sentences (such as questions), and introduces the thing which one is *not* prevented from doing. Its meaning is equivalent to 'so as not :' as here, 'No marriage shall change me *so that* I shall *not* complain.' Its most usual use is after verbs of doubting : *non dubium est quin eam viderim* means literally, 'No doubt exists so that I did not see her' = 'No doubt exists which interferes with, or prevents, my having seen her,' i. e. 'There is no doubt but that I saw her,' or 'as to my having seen her.' *Quominus* has precisely the same sense after verbs of preventing or hindering.

verba querar. As Postgate points out, there is no need to alter this reading. *Verba* is the cognate accusative after *querar*, which is used in the sense of 'to pour forth by way of complaint.' Thus *Verba queri* is 'to pour forth complaining words' or 'words of

complaint.' Parallel to *queri*, 'to utter complainingly,' is Virgil's
use of *rumpere* with *vocem*, etc., as in Aen. 11. 377

rumpitque has imo pectore voces,

which means 'To send forth in a breaking or broken manner,' ' To
utter burstingly.' So Aen. 4. 553

Tantos illa suo rumpebat pectore questus.

For *verba querar* Postgate compares Ov. Met. 9. 304 *verba queror*,
and points out that Propertius frequently uses *verba* where one
would expect the particular kind of words—whether of joy, sorrow,
or otherwise—to be indicated. Most editors have adopted Passerat's
conjecture *vera*, which Palmer supports by 3. 6. 35

Quae tibi si veris animis est questa puella.

But in that passage the whole point turns upon the truth of the
complaint made; here there is no question of true or false, only of
his persistence in his love. Catull. 66. 18 also quoted is quite
beside the mark. 'I shall pour forth my woe in words upon thy
threshold' is surely more forcible than 'I shall utter well-founded
complaints.'

The **limen** of the loved one's door was the natural confidant of
all a Roman lover's woes and disappointments, and the recipient of
his most earnest protestations. In 1. 16 a whole poem is devoted
to retailing the varied experiences of a *limen*, which betrays the
confessions of a rejected but still hopeful lover. Strange that the
one merit of such a confidant—that it could keep a secret—should
be so wantonly sacrificed. Cp. Catull. 67.

23. deficiet, used impersonally, or rather perhaps, by a curious
inversion, with the infinitive *rogitare* as a subject. 'The continual
questioning of sailors shall never fail me.' An accusative of the person
after *deficere* is common, as Hor. Sat. 2. 1. 13 *Cupidum, pater
optime, vires Deficiunt.*

citatos. He will send for, summon, all sailors who arrive in
port, to question them about Cynthia. The interpretation 'moving
quickly' is very weak. As Paley points out, *citare* is a regular word
to use of summoning witnesses.

24. clausa, safe somewhere in harbour, as though she were
only detained by stress of weather from returning to him, like Gyges
in Hor. Od. 3. 7. 5-8, and were watching for the first opportunity to
cross.

Dicite . . . est. The direct question indicates the urgency and
rapidity of his questions.

25, 26. 'I shall ever hold her to be true;' *dicam*, not merely
because, as Postgate observes, Propertius frequently puts something as

said where another writer would say that it *is*, but because he wishes
to express a conviction to which he is determined to give utterance,
and which is rapturously justified in the lines which follow.

25. licet ... licet. On this pleonastic repetition see Postgate's Introduction.

Atraciis is read by the best MSS. Atrax is a town in Thessaly.
There is also a river *Atrax* in Aetolia. Pucci conjectured *Autaricis*,
which would refer to an Illyrian tribe mentioned by Strabo under the
name of Αὐταριᾶται. Palmer writes *Artaciis*, resting on Apoll. Rhod.
Arg. I. 954, where a harbour is spoken of

Κρήνῃ ὑπ' 'Αρτακίῃ.

considat, of a lasting settlement. Dido asks Aeneas, Aen. I. 572

Vultis et his mecum pariter considere regnis?

26. Most editions have **Eleis**. The MSS. have **hileis**, for
which **Hylleis**, referring to an Illyrian tribe Ὕλλειοι or Ὑλληεῖς,
seems, as Postgate says, a very probable correction. Yet *Eleis*
would do well enough, and seems confirmed by l. 36. Professor
Palmer now prefers *Hylaeis*, the reading of the text, which is near N.:
'Though my lady moors her bark in the furthest regions of the
earth, she will be true to me.' Hylaea was a region of Scythia,
mentioned in connection with Cyzicus, near which was Artace, by
Herodotus. See Hermathena, 1883.

27. erit, 'will remain.' **iurata,** 'on oath.' She remains, and
remains for certain, as she has sworn it. Palmer prefers **erat**: 'She
was here *all the while*, and here she remains.' As she never actually
set sail at all, this must refer to the time when he imagined that she
had done so.

rumpantur iniqui. 'Let my enemies burst through envy.'
Rumpor, a natural phrase, used of envy as here by Virg. E.
7. 26

invidia rumpantur ut ilia Codro;

of anger, by Hor. Sat. I. 3. 136 *miserque Rumperis et latras.* Postgate well compares the Fable of the Frog: Hor. Sat. I. 3. 319

non si te ruperis, inquit,
Par eris.

28. Vicimus. 'I have gained the day,' 'I have carried my
point:' as we might say 'Victory!'

non tulit. 'Has not been able to endure,' 'to stand out
against.'

29. licet ... deponat, simply 'may now lay aside,' 'give
up.'

falsa, of a joy without foundation, and therefore doomed to disappointment. The same idea is expressed elsewhere by *vana gaudia*, an empty joy founded on no reality.

livor, blackness, is taken as the personification of Envy: as Ov. R. A. 387 *Rumpere livor edax.*

cupidus, 'full of eagerness,' i. e. to do its proper work. Translate, 'the envy of their hearts.'

30. Destitit, 'has ceased,' 'has given up the idea of going.' Constructed with the infinitive as in Hor. Epod. 11. 5

> *Hic tertius December, ex quo destiti*
> *Inachia furere.*

novas vias, 'new, strange courses.' Used literally of her journey, with a suggestion of the metaphorical meaning as well.

31. Illi, to be joined with *carus*. 'She tells me I am dear to her.' **per me**, 'for my sake.'

32. dulcia negat, 'declares they have no charms for her.' Or *negat* may stand for *abnegat*, as in Suet. Aug. 40. Postgate well remarks upon the skill shown in this couplet.

39. concha, 'a pearl-oyster,' and hence 'a pearl,' as Tib. 2. 4. 30; Ov. Met. 10. 260; Am. 2. 11. 13.

39, 40. The sense of these lines is given in a less serious spirit by a modern writer:

> *I did not buy her (out upon it!*
> *I had no gold to buy :*
> *The duns are at me for the bonnet*
> *I sent her—just to try—)*
> *What won her was the seely sonnet*
> *That praised her to the sky!*

40. blandi, 'caressing,' 'loving.' *Blandus* is the characteristic epithet assigned to Propertius by Ovid, Trist. 5. 1. 17.

obsequio, 'by the loving homage of my song.'

41. Sunt, emphatic. 'Do really exist,' 'are no fiction.' **tardus**, 'slow to help.'

42. rara, 'such as is rarely found:' similar in sense to, but not quite so strong as, *unica*. Cp. 1. 17. 16

> *Quamvis dura tamen rara puella fuit,*

and Stat. Silv. 5. 1. 11 *coniux rarissima. Rarus* is properly used of a substance which has intervals between its parts : hence applied to nets (Virgil), air (Lucretius), a sieve (Ovid), friable soil (Virgil), etc. It is then used of the parts so separated, and thus means 'far apart,' 'rare.'

43. A hyperbolical way of speaking, as when Horace says that if Maecenas ranks him among lyric bards

> *Sublimi feriam sidera vertice.*

Postgate declares this to be not to the point, maintaining that Propertius means ' I shall walk a god among the gods.' The reference to the gods is scarcely in place, and destroys the simple realism of the idea. The plain meaning is, ' I shall tread on the very stars as I walk along' in triumph and exultation. Cat. 66. 69 *me nocte premunt vestigia divom* is hardly in point. Berenice's hair, changed into a star, says quite simply 'the gods plant their steps on me,' ' I form the road over which they walk.'

licet. Postgate well points out in this and other passages, how fond Propertius is of softening his meaning, so that he prefers to say that he *may*, or that he *will*, or that he *desires*, or that he *intends*, to do a thing, rather than that he actually does it. This tendency he connects with irresolution and weakness of will, as characteristic of the poet. See his Introduction.

45. certus, 'true,' 'faithful:' so Enn. in Cic. Lael. 17. 64
Amicus certus in re incerta cernitur,
the happily selected motto of one of our principal Insurance Societies.

subducet. Most MSS. *subducit*, which is perhaps better, expressing both the certainty and the endurance of his love.

amores, either the affection of Cynthia for him, or perhaps Cynthia herself, the loved object, which no rival can now filch from him. So Cic. Div. 1. 36 *amores et deliciae tuae.*

I. 14.

This charming little poem is addressed to the poet's friend Tullus, a young man of wealth and good family, to whom also are addressed several of his most intimate pieces. Happy in the consciousness of Cynthia's love, he tells his friend that he has no envy of his beautiful villa on the Tiber, with its costly furniture and lovely view, for he possesses in his love a joy and a wealth that far transcend all the joys and wealth of kings. From the Sixth Elegy of the First Book it appears that Tullus was the nephew of a man of distinction, L. Vocatius Tullus, who was consul in the year B.C. 33, along with Octavian himself. This uncle, probably in the year 27 B.C., was setting out as proconsul to the senatorial province of Asia, and taking with him his nephew Tullus as his legatus. On that occasion Tullus offered to find a place for the poet on his uncle's staff: but Propertius declared (1. 6) that he could not tear himself away from Cynthia. After his uncle's term of office was over, Tullus remained some time in the East for travel and enjoyment: and in

3. 22 the poet writes to him upbraiding him with his long absence, as showing indifference to his friends and the beauties of his own country. The First Elegy of the First Book, in which Propertius declares his absolute devotion to Cynthia, is also addressed to Tullus: and it is highly probable that it was through Tullus that the poet first obtained an introduction to Maecenas.

1. Tu, in antithesis to *meo amori* in l. 7.

abiectus. This word usually carries with it the idea of despondency or meanness, as in its English equivalent ; but here it is to be taken simply in the sense of 'stretched at ease,' 'lying prostrate,' in connection with the local ablative **Tiberina unda.** Cp. Ov. Her. 7. 1 of the swan who sings upon the Maeander, *udis abiectus in herbis.* The word carries with it the notion of that complete ease and abandon which was the ideal of the Epicurean poet : Hor. Od. I. 1. 21

> *nunc viridi membra sub arbuto*
> *Stratus, nunc ad aquae lene caput sacrae.*

For the ablative *unda* cp. the common reading in 2. 13. 55 *Illis formosum iacuisse paludibus.* See also 4. 3. 10 and note.

2. Lesbia. The wine of Lesbos was sweet and light : Hor. Od. 1. 17. 21 describes it as *innocens*, and Athenaeus 1. 22 calls it οἰνάριον, a phrase exactly equivalent to the French term *petit vin* for a light, weak wine, of no particular pretensions.

Mentoreo. Mentor was the most celebrated chaser of silver among the Greeks, especially famous for his cups. He lived shortly before 356 B.C., as we are told that many of his cups were destroyed in the burning of the temple of Ephesus in that year. Enormous prices were paid for his works : Juvenal 8. 104 describes the wealthy days of the East by asserting

> *rarae sine Mentore mensae ;*

and Martial 4. 39. 5 thus addresses a wealthy connoisseur :

> *Solus Mentoreos habes labores.*

Propertius characterises Mentor's work by the complicated character of his subjects, 3. 9. 13

> *Argumenta magis sunt Mentoris addita formae.*

3, 4. Tullus lies lazily stretched upon the river bank, watching the barges gliding down the current or being towed against it.

5. intendat vertice silvas. This phrase has been strangely misunderstood. Paley translates, ' Though all the woodland around you should wave with trees,' without explaining how the meaning is to be extracted from the words. *Intendere* can only mean ' to

stretch:' and the idea here is analogous to that of stretching or
pitching tents on a plain (*tabernacula carbaseis intenta velis* Cic.
Verr. 2. 5. 12. § 30), or of stretching or spreading sails upon a mast.
Nemus is the woodland, situated on a hill overlooking the Tiber,
on the slope of which—probably the Janiculum or the Vatican—
Tullus' villa was built.   The wooded hill is thus said 'to stretch out
the planted trees on its top:' and l. 6 makes it clear that Propertius
is dwelling on the size of the trees, not, as Burmann and others suppose, on the extent of the wood.   Nor can *intendat* mean 'to
thicken,' = *arboribus denset*, as Schultze supposes.   The only other
possible interpretation is 'how the wood stretches out, i. e. rears
high, the trees at their top' or 'with their top:' but this is weak
and tautological.

    7. **contendere**, 'to vie with,' here used with the dative as in
1. 7. 3

        Atque, ita sim felix, primo contendis Homero.

    The more usual construction is with *cum* followed by the person,
and the ablative of the subject of rivalry as in 2. 24. 7 (Vulg. 28)

        Contendat mecum ingenio, contendat et arte.

    7, 8. With these lines, and ll. 11, 12, compare—

        No pearls, no gold, no stones, no corn, no spice,
        No cloth, no wine, of Love can pay the price.   Anon.

    9, 10. trahit . . . ducit. The verbs *trahere* and *ducere* both
carry with them the notion of *length:* here of the long hours or
live-long day spent in the dalliance of love.   Cp. *ducere somnos*
Virg. Aen. 4. 560.   Kinnoel compares Sen. Herc. 645 *Vigilesque
trahit purpura noctes.*

    The metaphors are strangely abrupt: 'Then do the waters of
Pactolus pour under my roof, then do I gather gems under the Red
Sea.'   The Red Sea of the ancients was the whole Indian ocean, and
they had a fancy that its bed was rich with gems.   Thus of the pearl
or 'shell of Venus,' Prop. 3. 13. 6

        Et venit e rubro concha Erycina salo.

So Martial 5. 37. 34 has *lapilli Erythraei*.   See note on Tibull. 2.
2. 15, 16, and Curtius 8. 9. 19 *gemmas margaritasque mare litoribus
infundit.*

    11, 12. Compare the following lines from the *Chloris* of William
Smith (1596):

        Some make their love a goldsmith's shop to be,
        Where orient pearls and precious stones abound;
        In my conceit these far do disagree,
        The perfect praise of beauty forth to sound:

> *O Chloris, thou dost imitate thyself,*
> *Self-imitating passeth precious stones;*
> *For all the Eastern-Indian golden pelf,*
> *Thy red and white with truest fair atones.*

How far removed is the elaborate 'conceit' of the modern poet from the simplicity and directness of Propertius!

13. 'Assure me that kings will yield to me,' i. e. in point of happiness.

13, 14. There is much in this poem, as well as in poems 8, 17, and 18, which remind us of passages in Shakespeare's Sonnets. Cp. Sonnets 25 and 29, which ends with the lines

> *For thy sweet love remembered such wealth brings,*
> *That then I scorn to change my state with kings.*

Cp. lines 23, 24. But every comparison only brings out more clearly the essential differences between the ancient and modern conceptions of love. How unintelligible to Propertius would have been the spirit of Scott's well-known lines, though they reproduce the main idea of ll. 17–24:

> *In peace love tunes the shepherd's reed,*
> *In war he mounts the warrior's steed,*
> *In halls, in gay attire is seen,*
> *In hamlets, dances on the green.*
> *Love rules the court, the camp, the grove,*
> *For love is Heaven, and Heaven is love.*

15. adverso ... Amore. 'If Love be unpropitious.' Hertzberg quotes Mimnermus:

> Τίς δὲ βίος, τί δὲ τερπνόν, ἄτερ χρυσῆς 'Αφροδίτης;
> τεθναίην ὅτε μοι μηκέτι ταῦτα μέλοι.

16. sint, conditional. 'No wealth would be wealth to me.'

tristi, of a maiden who will not smile on her lover: so Prop. 1. 6. 10, and Tib. 4. 4. 17

> *lacrimis erit aptius uti*
> *Si quando fuerit tristior illa tibi.*

17–22. 'Not strength or sternness, not wealth or luxury, can keep Love away.'

18. dolor. The nominative, as elsewhere in Propertius, is here put for the more usual dative of predication. See 1. 18. 15 and the passages referred to in the Index.

19. Arabium limen, i. e. a threshold paved with *onyx*, or Oriental alabaster, which was brought from Arabia (Plin. N. H. 36. 12) and was much used for cups, pillars, and other ornamental work at Rome.

20. ostrino, 'purple.' An adjective derived from *ostrum* (ὄστρεον), lit. 'the blood of the purple-snail,' used several times by Propertius.

22. relevant, lit. 'lift up,' 'lighten,' used in the sense of our 'alleviate.' For the sense cp. Tib. 1. 2. 77–80.

23. verebor, used in a somewhat peculiar sense, 'shall have no scruples about,' 'shall not hesitate to.' For the Infinitive after *vereor* cp. Hor. Sat. 2. 3. 40

Insanos qui inter vereare insanus haberi.

I. 17.

This poem, together with the one which follows it, is among the most charming and touching of all the love-poems of Propertius. They are poems which none other of the amatory poets of Rome could have written, and which alone would be enough to give a distinguishing mark to his genius. They are essentially modern in their character. There is no tinge of coarseness or artificiality, no trace of the laboured and pedantic conceits of the Alexandrine school in the love which they breathe. The pain and the love which the poet pours forth are essentially romantic rather than classical in their character; and as pure and true to nature as the winds, the waves, and the rocks which he addresses. The cast of the pieces is entirely modern: it may be doubted whether there are any poems in antiquity which come so near to the spirit of the Nature school of English poetry. Driven to despair by Cynthia's hardness, he embarks upon a voyage, he buries himself in some lonely spot in the hope of driving her image from his mind; but the first breath of a storm, the soughing of the trees, and the songs of birds, only add fuel to his passion: he curses the folly which has induced him to tear himself away from her, and every sight and sound only makes him feel the more that in leaving her he has left the whole world behind him. He speaks to the winds with the passion of a Lear, to the trees and the birds and the streams with the tenderness of a Rosalind; he calls on the beeches and the pines to bear witness to his love; he carves Cynthia's name upon their trunks, he shouts it aloud to the rocks; he colours all nature with the intensity of his own feelings, and looks for her help and sympathy in every phase of his passion. There is throughout that refined appreciation of the beauties of nature, and that sense of their mysterious correspondence with the various moods of man's mind, which we are accustomed to regard as characteristic of our own modern poets.

1. There is nothing to show whether the voyage of this piece was real or imaginary. In 1. 15 the poet speaks as if he were about to undertake a voyage in consequence of the treatment he had received from Cynthia.

Et marks an abrupt beginning. The poet plunges *in medias res :* he starts in the middle of a gust of feeling, leaving what has preceded to be understood. Cp. Ov. Am. 3. 12. 9

> *Et merito, quid enim formae praeconia feci?*

potui, 'could bring myself to,' 'had the heart to,' like the Greek ἔτλην.

2. **Alcyonas.** Alcyone, daughter of Aeolus, and her husband Ceÿx were for their presumption changed into sea-birds. The ancient fable was that the halcyon made her nest upon the waters, and that during that time calm prevailed. Hence our 'halcyon days;' here Propertius calls on the halcyons in hopes that they will allay the storm. See Ov. Met. 11. 742-749, and Servius on Virg. Geo. 1. 399. So Theocr. 7. 57

> Ἀλκυόνες στορεσεῦντι τὰ κύματα.

3. **Cassiope,** wife of Cepheus and mother of Andromeda, was changed into a constellation, whose appearance through the storm would be a sign of brightening weather. Some suppose the allusion to be to the town *Cassiope* or *Cassope* on the shores of Epirus, mentioned by Strabo 7. 7 as a point made for in the voyage to Greece. The remains of the town between Nicopolis and Pandosia are at some distance from the sea, in the hills : it was thus rather a point to be sighted than a harbour to be made for. This would perhaps give a better meaning both to *visura* and to *solito*.

solito is peculiar: it must be used adverbially, =*ex solito ;* perhaps such forms as *gratuito, incerto,* etc. may be regarded as analogies. Hertzberg makes the prosy conjecture *solidam,* understanding Cassiope of the town. Paley makes the conjecture *omine et* for *omnia* l. 4 ; but we are not aware of any omen specially connected with the constellation, and *omnia* seems needed for emphasis.

6. **increpat.** The indicative gives greater emphasis, the indirect question being ignored. See note on 1. 8. 24.

8. **funus,** as elsewhere in Propertius, is used for 'a dead body.' So Virg. Aen. 9. 489 and 6. 510

> *Omnia Deiphobo solvisti et funeris umbris.*

11. **reponere** is the reading of N., and, if correct, must mean 'to represent,' 'to portray in imagination,' or, as Lemaire puts it, 'remettre sous les yeux.' *Ponere* is used of any portrayal or description of a thing, whether in words, painting, or otherwise ; and the *re*

will denote the calling up of the occurrence by the mind's eye. *Opponere* would mean 'to place before the eye,' 'imagine.'

12. ossa nulla, emphatic : 'no bones of mine:'. 'to be utterly without remains of mine to hold.' Paley well recalls the striking picture given by Tac. Ann. 2. 75 of Agrippina embarking from Asia for Rome, and carrying the urn with her husband's ashes clasped upon her bosom. Cp. Tib. 1. 3. 5.

13. paravit, 'equipped.'

15. Pinder suggests that Propertius may have had the similar passage of Virgil in his eye, E. 2. 14.

17. The scene is now shifted; the poet is no longer out at sea hoping to sight the land; he is sailing along unknown wooded shores.

18. Tyndaridas, the well-known meteoric phenomenon called 'St. Elmo's fire,' which was a sign of fine weather and was attributed by the ancients to Castor and Pollux. See Hor. Od. 1. 3. 1. So in the Battle of Lake Regillus :

> *If once the great twin Brethren*
> *Sit shining on the sails.*

See also Hayes' account of Sir Humphry's voyage (quoted by Froude, Short Studies, vol. i. p. 486) : *We had also upon our mainyard an apparition of a little fier by night, which seamen do call Castor and Pollux.*

19. Illic, i.e. 'Had I remained and died at Rome.' *Sepelissent, donasset, clamesset* refer to acts over once for all ; *staret*, to the abiding monument ; while *poneret*, l. 22, represents the act of placing the ashes amongst roses in the urn as actually proceeding.

20. posito ... amore combine in one expression the ideas of the remains laid in the grave, and the love laid down and done with, as we might speak of 'a buried love.'

23. extremo pulvere, 'the dust which is my end.' See n. 1. 19. 2.

24. =the usual formula S. T. T. L., i.e. *sit tibi terra levis.*

25. Doridae natae, i.e. the Nereids.

26. felici ... choro, 'appearing as a glad band ;' lit. 'by your glad band.' Strictly, the nominative should have been used, as the *natae* are to form the *chorus*.

solvite vela, i. e. 'enable us to unreef our sails.'

28. socio, i. e. 'your partner in love.'

Mansuetis litoribus, 'by making calm your shores.'

I. 18.

1. taciturna, to be taken closely with *querenti* : 'that will keep my complaints to themselves.' So *tenere fidem* l. 4.

1–4. Cp. Tennyson, Oenone:
Hear me, O Earth, hear me, O hills, O caves,
That house the cold crown'd snake! O mountain brooks,
Hear me, for I will speak, and build up all
My sorrow with my song.

5. Unde repetam, i.e. 'To what point am I to go back to find.'

8. habere notam, an image taken from the *nota* or mark of infamy attached by the censors on their roll to the name of any citizen whom they wished to stigmatise as having been guilty of some disgraceful act. So Cleopatra is described 3. 11. 40 as
Una Philippeo sanguine adusta nota.

9. carmina. So the MSS. If correct, the meaning must be 'spells.' But Lipsius' emendation *crimina* is to be preferred. The two words are often confused.

11. Sic ... ut. See note on Tib. 2. 5. 63.

levis, emphatic: 'capricious that thou art,' nominative case. Palmer puts a comma before *levis* as well as after it.

13. multa ... aspera. So *multa dura* 1. 15. 1.

14. venerit, nearly equivalent to the future, though there is probably also an optative sense: 'may I never become so enraged,' 'may it never be said that I have become.'

15. furor; cp. *dolor* 1. 14. 18.

17. colore, unquestionably the best reading, rather than *calore* adopted by Baehrens and Mueller. See 1. 6. 6
Mutatoque graves saepe colore preces.
'Do you doubt my love,' asks the poet, 'because I do not change colour, with the bashfulness of a young lover, at every instant?' *Calore* would mean practically the same thing, but less directly. A lover might well be said to grow hot and cold with hope and fear alternately, but the point of the line is in *signa damus*. Do you doubt my love, he asks, because you do not see the outward signs of feeling on my cheek? So *clamat in ore* in l. 18.

18. fides, the sincerity or loyalty of the lover, which does not proclaim itself in his face.

20. The nymph Pitys (Πίτυς) was loved by Pan; she was changed into a fir-tree, which tree became sacred to Pan in consequence. See Virg. E. 7. 24.

It is possible that here and elsewhere the beech-tree is mentioned specially in connection with love, because its bark admits of being carved with letters more readily than that of any other tree. See l. 22 and Ov. Her. 5. 21

Incisae servant a te mea nomina fagi,
Et legor Oenone, falce notata, tua.

21—22. The quotation at once suggests itself from 'As you like it,' Act 3 :

O Rosalind! these trees shall be my books,
And in their barks my thoughts I'll character.

Again, the Faery Queene, 4. 7. 46 :

And eke by that he saw on every tree
How he the name of one engraven had
Which likely was his liefest love to be.

Compare too, for *mea verba* l. 21, as well as for ll. 31, 32, Drayton's Quest of Cynthia :

Forth roved I by the sliding rills
To find where Cynthia sat,
Whose name so often from the hills
The echoes wondered at.

. . . . . .

When on upon my wayless walk
As my desires me draw,
I like a madman fell to talk
With everything I saw.

So too Sir Robert Aytoun :

O happy happy tree
Unto whose tender rynd
The trophies of our love shall live
Eternally enshryn'd ;
Which shall have force to make
Thy memory remain,
Sequester'd from the bastard host
Of trees which are profane !

And again :

Bear me record that while I passed by,
I did my duteous homage to your dame ;
How thrice I sigh'd, thrice on her name did cry,
Thrice kissed the ground for honour of the same,
Then left these lines to tell her, on a tree,
That she made them to live and me to die !

23. An, etc. 'Or can it be because.' The line recalls the well-known maxim of the cynic, that men hate those whom they have injured.

24. The MSS. have *foribus,* a reading which seems almost unworthy of the tone of this beautiful poem. The reference would be to the commonplace subject of the excluded lover, pouring out his sorrows to the door which shuts him out.   See the whole poem, I. 16.   Baehrens' conjecture *foliis* is tempting.   It is in harmony with the piece, containing a pathetic assurance on the part of the poet, in the very moment that recalls to him his wrongs, that he has breathed them to none but the silent leaves.

quae is a general neuter, referring to *curas*: 'matters which are known only,' etc.

25. Note the contrast of *timidus* and *superbae*.

26. arguto ... dolore, a grief that vents itself in words.

27. The address to the Fountains and their Naiads, implied in the usual punctuation, is somewhat abrupt, and it seems better to leave the question open whether *fontes* is the nominative or the vocative.   The only reason for supposing it to be the latter is contained in the epithet *divini*, which is inconsistent with *frigida*, *inculto*, *dura*, all pointing to the hardships of the poet's present surroundings.   But this is outweighed by the ambiguity and harshness of taking the words out of their natural sequence: *divini fontes et frigida rupes et ... dura quies*.   The conjecture *dumosi montes* is quite unnecessary.   Mr. R. Ellis, Journal of Phil. vol. xv. p. 12, has made the ingenious conjecture *Clusini fontes*.   *Divini* is out of place; and he suggests a coincidence with the passage in Horace, Epp. I. 15. 5, where Horace complains that Baiae and its hot springs were being deserted for the cold founts of Clusium.   Propertius, sick with love or ill, may have retired for change of air to *Clusium*, and poured forth this eighteenth elegy in some unfrequented spot in the neighbourhood.

28. tramite.   Sellar (Elegiac Poets, p. 273 *n.*) would translate 'hill-side.'   He compares 3. 13. 44, where *trames* apparently is a translation of ὅρος in a poem by Leonidas of Tarentum.

31. Cynthia, i.e. ' the name "Cynthia"': object to *vacent*.

I. 19.

A beautiful and touching elegy, written apparently in anticipation of an early death, and, with the exception of the relief afforded by the two concluding lines, in a tone of deep despondency.   The poet is filled with terror at the thought that Cynthia may forget him when dead, while he vows that his own love will endure beyond the grave.   Let them enjoy their love, at least, while they live.

1. Vereor, seldom if ever used with exactly the same sense as *timeo* or *metuo*.   Cicero carefully distinguishes the words, Sen.

11. 37 *Metuebant eum servi, verebantur liberi*, and Phil. 12. 12. 29
*Quid? Veteranos non veremur? nam timeri se ne ipsi quidem
volunt.* The same contrast is brought out in Ad Quint. 1. 1, and
Liv. 39. 37. 17.

2. moror. Just as Virgil's *nec dona moror*, Aen. 5. 400,
means 'I do not stop the gifts,' 'I let them go past me,' and so 'I
do not care for them;' so here *moror fata* means, 'I would do
nothing to avert,' and so 'am indifferent to.'

extremo, an ornamental, intensifying epithet. It is not used to
part off one kind of *rogus* from another—as in such common phrases
as *extremo tempore*, etc.—but to indicate a quality which is universal: 'the pile which is life's end.' The word is used in exactly
the same way in 1. 17. 23

    Illa meum extremo clamasset pulvere nomen,
and in 3. 2. 18 (20)

    Mortis ab extrema conditione vacant.

debita fata rogo. Nothing can be more crude and unpoetical
than to say, with Kinnoel and Pinder, that *fata* 'stands for "a
dead body";' or, with Paley, that it is a periphrasis for *fatum
rogi*, whatever that might mean. Surely neither poetry nor sense
requires anything to 'stand for' so fine a phrase as 'Nor would
I stay the fate that is my funeral pyre's due.'

3. ne goes with *Hic timor est*, the emphatic *Hic* being explanatory of the sentence *ne careat:* 'But I *have* a fear—a fear
more stern than death itself—that thy love may be absent from my
burial.'

5. Puer is of course Cupid. It is possible, as Hertzberg
suggests, that there may have been running through the poet's mind
a conceit which he illustrates from two passages from the Greek
Anthology, according to which the eyes of Aphrodite are represented as anointed with bird-lime to enable her to catch her
prey. This is bad enough; but when Paley translates this into
'The lover goes about with his eyes smeared to catch Cupid as he
flies, and so is unable to shake him off again,' the idea becomes
intolerable. The eyes are the seat of Love; it is through the eyes
that Love is caught up and answered. Olivia in Twelfth Night says,

    Methinks I feel this youth's perfections,
    With an invisible and subtle stealth,
    To creep in at mine eyes.

It was by the eyes that Cynthia first captured Propertius, 1. 1. 1

    Cynthia prima suis miserum me cepit ocellis.

The figure therefore of Cupid having settled on the poet's eyes, and

clung to them so firmly that it was inconceivable that he should
leave him when dead, and allow his remains to be neglected by her
whom he had loved, is a perfectly natural and beautiful idea. The
idea of the Anthology is quite different. There Venus, or the
ministers of Venus, anoint their eyes with bird-lime that they may
catch the lover; here Love has fastened himself so firmly on to the
lover's eyes, that he cannot be forgotten by love, even after death.
The old song says

> *Love in her eyes sits playing;*

Shakespeare thinks it necessary to controvert the common opinion,
when he says,

> *Love looks not with the eyes but with the mind.*

6. oblito, generally taken in a passive sense, as in Virg. E. 9.
53 *Nunc oblita mihi tot carmina.* So also Val. Flac. 2. 38. 8.
But is this necessary? Could it not be taken in a quasi-proleptic
sense, to mean 'Love has not clung so lightly to my eyes that my
ashes can be left untended by a forgetting love.' L. 3 shows that
the *amore* is not his love for her, but hers for him; it is her forgetfulness of him which he dreads. Thus *oblito amore vacet* means
'shall lie unhonoured by a love—a love that has forgotten me.'
In other words, there is a double predication combined in one expression. He might either have said 'that my ashes should be
unhonoured by Love,' or that 'Love should be forgetful of my
ashes.' Here both phrases are welded into one. Moore brings out
this meaning:

> *Too well I've loved, too blindly, that my bier*
> *Should be unhonoured by a single tear.*

Pinder's explanation 'Not even in death will thy love be forgotten by me' misses the point. Is it possible that *vacet* may be
used absolutely, 'lack the honour due to it,' as uncultivated lands
are said *vacare*? *Oblito amore* would then be the ablative absolute,
'thy love forgetting,' 'through the forgetfulness of thy love.' Cp.
4. 11. 94

> *Caelibis ad curas nec vacet ulla via.*

7. Phylacides. Protesilaus is meant, whose father Iphiclus
was son of Phylacus. The love of Protesilaus for Laodamia is
well-known from Ov. Her. 13. He obtained leave from the gods
to return to see her for a single day.

Illic, of the regions below, suggested by the word *pulvis* in
l. 6.

8. caecis in locis. These words take up and expand the *Illic*
of l. 7 by a kind of apposition, and contrast finely with *immemor*.

'Not there—even in that land of darkness—could Protesilaus,' etc.

9. cupidus goes with Phylacides, l. 7, and *Thessalis umbra* is the predicate: 'He came in the character of a shade.'

falsis goes primarily with *palmis*. Just as *gaudia* were called *falsa* in 1. 8. 29 because there was no solid ground for their existence, so here the hands are *falsae* because unsubstantial. But a reference to that line will show that the idea of *falsis* is intended to be thrown over *gaudia* as well as *palmis*:

> *Falsa licet cupidus deponat gaudia livor.*

The recurrence of the three words *falsa, cupidus, gaudia* can scarcely be accidental.

11. imago. Pinder suggests an allusion to the 'image' of Protesilaus, which Laodamia made and worshipped after his second death.

tua dicar imago. It is hard to determine whether the predicate of the sentence be *tua imago* or *tua* only. In the latter case, *imago* will mean only a shade: 'Shade though I be,' or 'In my phantom form I shall still be called *thine*.' In the former case, *imago* must have some further meaning, 'I shall be called *thy* semblance or representative.' 'I shall be held to present thy form,' i. e. not merely that he would be known as a shade to be still devoted to her, but that he was so identified with her, their personalities were so joined together, that his shade would be said to be not his only but hers also.

dicar. In accordance with his usual tendency, Propertius prefers to say 'I shall be *called* thine,' than simply 'I shall *be* thine.'

12. Traicit, in its intransitive sense, 'passes the bounds of Fate,' i. e. of Death. *Traicere* is also used transitively when it may be constructed with two Accusatives, one of the object crossed, the other of the thing sent across it. Thus Caesar B. G. 1. 83 *Caesar Germanos flumen traicit*, 'sends the Germans across the river.'

fati litora. Cp. *una ratis fati* 2. 28. 39.

magnus amor. The epithet is either specific, 'A *potent* love' or general, 'The mighty power of Love.'

With this magnificent line—read in connection with ll. 18–20— cp. Byron, who thus speaks of a love severed by death:

> *Yet did I love thee to the last*
> *As fervently as thou,*
> *Who didst not change through all the past,*
> *And can'st not alter now.*

> *The Love where Death has set his seal*
> *Nor age can chill nor rival steal,*
>   *Nor falsehood disavow:*
> *And—what were worst—thou can'st not see*
> *Or wrong or change or fault in me.*

Propertius, on the contrary, held that love *was* continued after death (l. 12); that the shade of the dead one would still feel for the living (l. 18), and resent any want of affection (2. 13. 41–42).

13. chorus, in apposition to *heroinae:* 'let them come in a body.' Hous. thinks the Latin requires *formosus.*

14. The fate of which Hector emphatically warns Andromache in the Iliad when he goes out to battle. The most famous of the class were Cassandra, Andromache, Helen.

15. If **Quarum** be retained, it must be equivalent to *Sed earum.* Heinsius, followed by Palmer, reads *Harum.*

fuerit, fut. perf., implying that his judgment will be final and abiding.

16. ita probably goes with *sinat:* 'May Earth grant this to be so.' As this is somewhat tautological, some would take *ita* with *iusta:* 'May Earth, just only on the condition that she does so, grant,' i.e. in no other way than by granting his prayer can she deserve the name of Just. This use of *ita* is analogous to that where it is followed by *ut* with the indicative. The full phrase would be *Tellus ita iusta est ut sinit:* 'May Earth grant my prayer; she is only just in proportion as she does so.' See note on Tib. 2. 1. 63.

17. fata senectae, i.e. 'fate consisting of old age.'

18. ossa, 'thy bones.' *Sunt* is omitted. The line is a harsh way of saying that whenever her death comes, he, though a shade, will moisten her remains with his tears.

19. Quae refers to the general idea of the preceding line, his love for her when dead.

mea favilla, a very peculiar ablative: 'on the occasion of my death.' So exactly *morte mea* 3. 6. 24.

20. non ullo loco, i.e. 'come when or where it may.'

21. contempto, of indifference or neglect. *Bustum,* connected with *uro, buro,* is properly the place where the body was burned. As the spot was frequently marked by a monument, and as the most usual form of monument was a sarcophagus with half-length sculptures of the deceased and his family upon the top, the word thus came to bear the meaning of a half-figure or 'bust.'

22. heu. So H., no doubt correctly, for the MS. *e* or *è,* apparently a common abbreviation.

P

iniquus, of a rival in love. So above, 8. 27, *rumpantur iniqui.*
It is hard to see how Pinder gets the meaning 'a passion alien to me.'

24. certa, i. e. even a faithful maiden.

minis, the threats of interested friends. Paley quotes Ov. Fast.
2. 806

> *Nec prece, nec pretio, nec movet ille minis.*

25. Quare. Prosaic as the word seems, Propertius is fond of
introducing a final couplet with it: so 1. 5. 31 and 9. 33. The
word has reference not to the lines immediately preceding, but to
the general sense of the whole piece. 'With the grave and all its
doubts thus before us, let us love while we may.' The absence of
caesura in this line makes it very inharmonious.

26. ullo tempore can only mean 'in any time, however long :'
'No time is long enough for love.' This indefinite use of *ullus*, to
signify time of boundless duration, is peculiar. The idea is, 'You could
name no time—i.e. no period of time—which would be long for love.'

25, 26. This last couplet recalls the exquisite lines of Catullus:

> *Vivamus, mea Lesbia, atque amemus:*
>
> .   .   .   .
>
> *Soles occidere et redire possunt:*
> *Nobis, quum semel occidit brevis lux,*
> *Nox est perpetua una dormienda.*

I. 22.

Propertius closes this first Book of his Elegies after the manner of
Roman poets (see esp. Hor. Epp. 1.20) with an autobiographical reference to himself. It is addressed to Tullus—the same Tullus, presumably,
to whom the 1st, 6th, and 14th Elegies of this book are addressed—in
answer to his queries as to the poet's birth. He was born, he says, in
Umbria, where that province comes closest to the walls of Perusia.

1. Qualis, as well as *unde*, is to be taken with *genus.* 'What
and whence my family, you ask.' The double interrogation is frequent
in Greek, commonly without a copula, as ποῦ πόθεν γεγώς ; etc.

qualis genus can scarcely mean, as Postgate puts it, 'of what
kind of family,' but rather 'of what kind in point of family,' i. e. 'of
what family.'

Penates, the proper Latin equivalent for 'Home.' It is
doubtful whether the word *domus* ever bears this meaning.

2. pro nostra amicitia, a common phrase. In this and
similar phrases *pro* indicates that there is a proportion, a correspondence, a natural connection, between the thing said or done and
the noun governed by the preposition. You ask me 'as a friend ;'

'as befits our friendship;' 'as is natural for you, being my friend, to do.' So the common phrase *pro virili parte* means 'as befits a man;' 'as a man should do;' 'to the utmost of his ability.'

semper should be taken with *quaeris*. Postgate's references (especially Virg. Aen. 1. 198) scarcely justify the extreme harshness of taking the word with *amicitia* as if it were an adjective.

3. He marks his birthplace by its neighbourhood to *Perusia*, a town which had gained evil notoriety by the terrible scenes attending its siege and capture by the army of Octavianus in B.C. 41. The consul, L. Antonius (brother of the Triumvir), had declared against him, and finding himself unable to keep the field, shut himself up in that strongly posted town.

The Perusian War is always spoken of with horror by the Augustan poets. Its outbreak gave rise to a feeling of despair: it seemed as if there was to be no end of civic discord. It was this war which prompted Horace's most despondent utterances, Epod. 7 and 16. Interesting memorials of the siege and sufferings attendant upon it are preserved in the Museo Kircheriano at Rome, in the shape of leaden and other bullets hurled from slings between the combatants, some of them inscribed with insulting messages. The mere name of the place calls up to Propertius' mind the notions of Death and Discord.

'The Perusian tombs of our country' may mean either (1) 'That Perusia in which our countrymen found their tomb,' i. e. 'The tombs of our countrymen at Perusia,' or (2) 'That Perusia in which our country (i. e. our country's hopes) found a grave.' In the former case the expression is analogous to such phrases as *Tyrrhenusque tubae clangor*, etc., so common in Lucretius. Line 4 seems to suggest the latter interpretation, and is well illustrated by Cat. 68. 89

> *Troia (nefas!) commune sepulcrum*
> *Europae Asiaeque,*

and cp. 2. 1. 27

> *civilia busta Philippos.*

4. Italiae, doubtless to be constructed both with *funera* and *temporibus*. Translate: 'In that dire hour of Italy;' 'In Italy's hardest, darkest hour.' *Funera* is in apposition to *sepulcra*.

3, 4. These lines exhibit strongly a characteristic of Propertian, and indeed of all ancient, poetry. They are deeply pathetic; yet there is not one word which of itself suggests feeling. The simple external reality is put before us in all its hardness and coldness, without one softening touch; but so truly is the description drawn, that if we only fairly realise it, the appropriate feeling rises of itself, and as if created by our own minds, affects them with double force. How different from the gush of much modern so-called poetry or oratory, where words of passionate feeling are thrown away before an attempt has been made to depict the things, to summon up the ideas, which would justify them ! The lines before us form a composition of the deepest tragedy : ' Perusia—our country's grave—the hard death-time of Italy.' Every touch is instinct with feeling, yet not one word expresses it. It is hard to refrain from translating *dura* by 'sad :' yet that would be perhaps to modernise the passage.

5. discordia, personified. ' The demon of civic strife.'

egit Postgate translates 'hounded on,' quoting Ov. Met. 14. 750

> *quam iam deus ultor agebat,*

and Hor. Epod. 7. 17.

But surely this idea is quite foreign to the word. 'To hound on' is to set dogs on to attack some one. There is no one here to be attacked. The notion of *agere* is simply 'to drive,' best illustrated by the common phrase for plundering, 'agere et ferre,' *agere* referring to cattle, *ferre* (or *rapere*) to portable property. The picture is that of a Fury or other evil power driving on remorselessly jaded and worn-out herds, and allowing them no rest. We say 'to drive distracted' in much the same sense. ·Cp. the fate of Io, οἰστροπλήξ. Postgate also quotes Luc. 6. 777

> *Effera Romanos agitat Discordia Manes ;*

but the sense of 'hounding on' would require some object of attack or purpose to be named, as in the fine but quite different passage, Virg. Aen. 8. 678, where Augustus before Actium is gathering all Italy to war :

> *Hinc Augustus agens Italos in praelia Caesar*
> *Cum patribus populoque, Penatibus et magnis Dis.*

Here the meaning is not ' hounding on,' but ' gathering in.'

6. sed. So Palmer, I have no doubt correctly. There is an anacoluthon here. *Tibi,* l. 3, refers to *Tullus,* and the whole passage 2–10 amounts to this: 'If thou knowest Perusia, then know that I was born just outside her walls.' But the mention of Perusia turns the poet into a digression in which he apostrophises the soil of the Perusian plain, on which his relative was cast out unburied: ' Yet mine chief should be the grief.' The reading *sit* arose from the connection not being understood.

pulvis, feminine, as in Ennius and several times in Propertius, who however has it masculine also.

7. perpessus es, ' couldst endure to see.' Or rather perhaps, 'the casting forth of my friend's body was a thing thou didst endure,' i.e. as an indignity. This seems better than to suppose *esse* omitted.

8. solo. The expression is peculiar: the *pulvis* is represented as not covering the body with the *solum*, though both *pulvis* and *solum* refer to the same thing.

9. contingens adds nothing to the sense of *proxima*, except to define it more closely. 'Next to the plain below, and coming right up to it.'

10. terris, 'soil.' In French the plural *terres* is used for a country estate.

II. 1.

It would appear from this poem that Maecenas had been exerting his influence with his *protégé*, Propertius, to induce him to employ his muse in the service of Augustus and his government. It has been frequently pointed out with what consummate political tact Maecenas turned to account his own undoubted literary tastes in the interests of his patron, with a view to reconciling the Roman world to the government of its new master. The marvellous originality of this idea, as well as its singular and immense success, has perhaps been less generally acknowledged. Having ascended to power by a short and unscrupulous career of violence—a career unrelieved by a tinge of unselfish patriotism, and darkened by cold-blooded crime—Augustus succeeded, not merely in arresting for a time that disintegration of the empire which Horace thought imminent when he wrote the Sixteenth Epode; not merely in securing for himself a period of un-resisted authority: besides all this he succeeded in imposing himself upon the imagination of his countrymen—not for his lifetime merely, but for succeeding generations—as a beneficent and all-wise ruler, as the healer of his country's sores, as the long-expected deliverer who was to restore the peace and prosperity of the Golden Age, as the legitimate and divinely-appointed successor of Aeneas, of Romulus, and of every true Roman worthy; as not only entrusted with a divine mission, but as being himself worthy to become a god, and to trans-mit a claim to divinity not only to every one of his own descend-ants, but to an infinite series of successors. So magnificent a political success has never before or since been achieved in this world: never before or since have not only the physical forces of a great country, but its whole mind and imagination, been carried into so complete and abiding a captivity. The secret of this great achievement lies in the fact that under the inspiration, and through the help, of a minister marvellously fitted to play such a part, Augustus succeeded

in laying hold of the whole intellect of a people which had just risen
to its full intellectual strength, and in attaching to himself and his
government, as enthusiastic champions, the master-minds in whom
that intellectual strength was embodied. Napoleon III tried in vain
to attach to himself the intellect of France, and he fell : Augustus
succeeded. And if we reflect how weary of the display of brute
force, how polished, how receptive of ideas, how sensitive to artistic
form, was the Rome of the Augustan age, we can without difficulty
understand how irresistible was the force exerted upon the imagination
of the time by a cause which was accepted as a fundamental article of
faith by its noblest spirits, which was proclaimed as a gospel, and
ardently advocated on every ground—personal, political, literary, religious—by the whole power of a literary cluster of which Virgil, Horace,
Livy, Ovid, Propertius, and Tibullus were, after all, only the brightest
stars. All this advocacy was obtained silently, and mainly through
the instrumentality of Maecenas. With Propertius, as with Horace,
Maecenas used all his influence, under cover of a regard for his
literary reputation, to induce him to turn his muse to higher themes,
to urge her to soar a higher flight ; Propertius, like Horace, under
cover of a refusal, adds a new point to the praises which he professes
himself inadequate to render. His whole inspiration, he declares,
comes from Cynthia ; he is unworthy of a loftier theme ; had the
power been his, he would have chosen to sing of the exploits of
Caesar and Maecenas before all other topics: but he must needs
refrain, like Horace, Od. 1. 6. 9,

> *Dum pudor*
> *Imbellisque lyrae Musa potens vetat*
> *Laudes egregii Caesaris et tuas* •
> *Culpa deterere ingeni.*

1. amores, poems on Love. Writers of Love poetry are constantly apologising for not turning to graver themes. Cp. Spenser,
Faerie Queene, Bk. 4, Introduction :

> *The rugged forehead that with grave foresight*
> *Welds kingdomes causes and affairs of state,*
> *My looser rimes, I wote, doth sharply wite*
> *For praising Love, as I have done of late,*
> *And magnifying lovers' dear debate.*

2. veniat mollis, lit. ' comes soft (i.e. amorous) in the mouth,'
mollis being the real predicate. *In ora* may refer to the mouth of
some one reading out the poems, or to the poet's own mouth ;
probably the latter. The poet is supposed to recite as he composes.

3. Calliope, the Epic muse.

5. The construction of *sive*, repeated in each couplet down to l. 16, is peculiar. The usual construction of *sive—sive*, as of our disjunctives 'whether—or,' is that each has a verb to itself in protasis, while the apodosis consists of one single verb, which is applicable to both or more alternatives. Thus Plaut. Trin. 1. 2. 146

> *seu recte seu perverse facta sunt,*
> *Egomet fecisse confiteor.*

'Whether it was well or badly done, I confess that I did it.' In the passage before us, each fresh alternative introduced by *sive* has an apodosis of its own, so that the sense is not represented by 'whether —or—or,' but by 'If—or if—if again,' etc. See Ovid. Am. 2. 7. 9

> *Sive bonus color est, in te quoque frigidus esse,*
> *Seu malus, alterius dicor amore mori.*

In l. 15 again *seu* and *sive* are thrown in almost as surplusage, adding nothing to the sense, which is completely expressed by the summing-up words *quidquid fecit, quodcumque est locuta*. It is impossible to translate *seu* and *sive* in that line, unless we allow *quidquid, quodcumque* to lose their relative force ('whatsoever') and simply stand for 'anything at all.' A somewhat similar use of *seu* occurs 4. 2. 11, where it joins together two principal verbs, without any subordinate verb:

> *Seu, quia vertentis fructum praecepimus anni,*
> *Vertumni rursus creditur esse sacrum.*

Here *seu* simply means 'or else.' An exactly similar example occurs 4. 10. 47.

incedere, of the stately, majestic walk of a tall person, or a goddess, as Virg. Aen. 1. 405, of Venus, *Et vera incessu patuit dea*, and of Cynthia herself, 2. 2. 6

> *incedit vel Iove digna soror.*

coccis, a conjecture of Lachmann, can scarcely be right, for though Cynthia was doubtless fond of gay colours (see 2. 29. 26) a finite verb is needed to go with *sive*, and it seems harsh to understand *vidi* from l. 7. Some propose *vidi*, which would give a clumsy repetition. Possibly *cogis*, read by some MSS., may be right: but the passage seems to require a verb in the first person. Lachmann alters the order of the third, fourth, and fifth couplet, putting them in this order: five, four, three. In this way the reference to the lyre comes immediately after that to *Apollo* and her *ingenium* in the second couplet, and *vidi* can be supplied readily in l. 5 if preceded by ll. 7, 8.

6. Coa veste. Silk was manufactured in Cos from an early time, and its introduction into Rome was denounced as a sign of corrupt luxury, Hor. Sat. 1. 2. 101

> *Cois te paene videre est*
> *Ut nudam.*

6 Coa veste . . . erit, 'will be wholly made up of.'

7. It would seem from this line that the Roman ladies had adopted 'the bang' of modern fashion.

8. laudatis, the emphatic word.

9. lyrae carmen would seem to be used not of the voice only, but of the melody of the instrument, as in 4. 6. 32

> *Aut testudineae carmen inerme lyrae.*

So too 2. 3. 19

> *Et quantum, Aeolio cum temptat carmina plectro.*

carmen percussit, 'struck out the tune' by striking the chords. So κρέκειν μέλος Theocr. Epig. 5. 2. 5 and Ovid Trist. 4. 10. 50 *ferire carmina lyra*. The line last quoted seems to show that striking by the *plectrum* is referred to, and not by the fingers: *digitis eburnis* will in that case be used metaphorically to indicate the material of which the plectrum was made.

10. facilis, 'skilful,' 'handy.' This is analogous to the use of *facetus* in Plautus, which, coming from *facio*, means regularly 'clever,' 'handy,' 'dexterous,' scarcely ever 'witty' or 'facetious.'

premat manus, of pressing the fingers against the strings, with or without the plectrum. Our word is 'touches.'

11. One MS. gives *somnus*, a tempting reading. *Somnum* of course goes with *poscentes*.

12. Notice the artistic position of **poeta**: 'a thousand new reasons for my poetry.'

15. Explained above on l. 5.

5-16. For this whole passage we may compare

> *There is an epic in her eyes,*
> *A drama in her wavy tresses,*
> *An idyll in her low replies ;—*
> *Even the rustle of her dresses*
> *As, light of foot, she trips along,*
> *Is matter for a lover's song.*   Anon.

17. Quod . . . si. Very rarely separated as here by an intervening word.

tantum, expanded by *ut* in l. 18: 'so much as this that,' etc.

18. heroas ducere manus. The poet, by a common figure, is said himself to do the things which he describes. Cp. Thuc. 1. 5 καὶ οἱ παλαιοὶ τῶν ποιητῶν, τὰς πύστεις τῶν καταπλεόντων πανταχοῦ ὁμοίως ἐρωτῶντες εἰ λῃσταί εἰσιν.

19, 20. The allusion is to the attempt made by Otus and

Ephialtes, sons of Aloeus (hence called the *Aloidae*), to scale the
heavens by piling the three mountains here mentioned upon each
other. Propertius avoids the error of Virgil, according to which
Olympus, the biggest of the three mountains, is placed upon the
top: Geo. 1. 281

> *Ter sunt conati imponere Pelio Ossam,*
> *Scilicet, atque Ossae frondosum involvere Olympum.*

See Ramsay's Extracts from Ovid, p. 246. Here Olympus is placed
at the bottom, and Pelion on top of Ossa.

20. ut, connected with *impositam*, as though that word had
ita before it: 'Ossa so placed on Olympus that Pelion was the way
to heaven,' i. e. was placed on the top. Some MSS. read *impositum*,
but *Ossa* is feminine in Ov. Am. 2. 1. 14.

22. The reference apparently is to the cutting through of the
isthmus of Mount Athos, by which 'two seas' could be said to have
'come together.' Juvenal sceptically alludes to this undoubted
achievement, Sat. 10. 174

> *Creditur olim*
> *Velificatus Athos, et quidquid Graecia mendax*
> *Audet in historia.*

The gigantic work—of which traces still exist—employed a vast
multitude of men, and took three years to execute. But it is not
impossible that the words may refer to the bridging of the Hellespont,
which made the two continents one, and therefore appealed more
to the imagination than the much greater, though useless, work of
cutting through the isthmus of Mount Athos. *Vadum* is used strictly
of shallow water, the water close to the shore. Thus, with reference
to a swimmer's danger, we have the proverb, *Omnis res est iam in
vado*, 'All is now safe.' *Bina coisse vada* might therefore refer to
the shore-waters of the two continents joined together by the bridge.

·**24.** The allusion of course is to the magnificent victory of
Marius over the Cimbri at Campi Raudii, near Vercellae, in his fifth
consulship, B.C. 101.

benefacta, 'the splendid exploits,' should perhaps be written in
two words, as in the line quoted by Cic. 2. 18. 62 from Ennius:

> *Bene facta male locata male facta arbitror.*

25. res, in contrast to *bella*, would seem to denote the political
achievements of Augustus.

26. cura, 'the object of my attention,' 'of my song.' *Cura*
is often used specially of love, as Prop. 1. 15. 31 *tua sub nostro ...
pectore cura*, and so of a loved object, as in Virg. E. 10. 22 *tua cura
Lycoris.*

27. Mutinam, referring to the outbreak of civil war after Caesar's murder. The consuls Hirtius and Pansa, at the head of the senatorial forces, were both killed in the moment of victory before Mutina in B. C. 43 : Ovid marks his birth by that event, Trist. 4. 10. 6

> *Cum cecidit fato consul uterque pari.*

civilia busta Philippos. A very harsh apposition, like *patriae sepulcra, Italiae funera* in 1. 22. 3, 4.

28. classica, 'naval.' In allusion to the final campaign carried out with great vigour against Sextus Pompey in Sicily, B. C. 36. For *classica* see note on Tib. 1. 1. 4.

29. Alluding to the siege of Perusia : see 1. 21. 2, and note on 1. 22. 3.

30. Ptolemaeei. This seems the proper form of the adjective. The Latin form of the name is *Ptolemaeus*, corresponding to the Greek Πτολεμαῖος ; from this the Greek adjective would be Πτολεμαίειος, which would naturally become *Ptolemaeeus* in Latin. The MSS. and edd. vary much, as might be expected.

Pharos is usually feminine, but occurs masculine in Suet. Claud. 20. It is properly the name of the island still called Faro, opposite the mouth of the harbour of Alexandria, on which Ptolemy Philadelphus (reigned B. C. 285–247) built his famous lighthouse. Caesar speaks of it with admiration B. C. 3. 112. Hence the word came to signify ' a lighthouse ' in general, in which sense it is preserved in the French *phare*. The event alluded to is the capture of Alexandria by Octavianus in B. C. 30, which was the immediate consequence of the battle of Actium. From this final victory dates the true commencement of the reign of Octavianus as the undisputed ruler of the Roman empire. Horace celebrates the event—or rather the death of Cleopatra which immediately succeeded it—in an ode of triumphant exultation, 1. 37, and fifteen years afterwards he emphatically dates the Empire of Augustus from that day : Od. 4. 14. 34

> *nam tibi, quo die*
> *Portus Alexandrea supplex*
>   *Et vacuam patefecit aulam,*
> *Fortuna lustro prospera tertio*
> *Belli secundos reddidit exitus,*
>   *Laudemque et optatum peractis*
>   *Imperiis decus arrogavit.*

31. Aegyptum, so the old edd. Hertzberg follows G. and Per. in reading *Cyprum*, which certainly is close to the *Cyptum* of N. Cyprus, after having long been attached to Egypt, had become an independent kingdom ; it was annexed to Rome by the shameful Bill of

Clodius, B.C. 58; Antony presented it to the children of Cleopatra; and after the battle of Actium it became an imperatorial province. Its fate therefore might well be mentioned separately from that of Egypt.

cum atratus. N. has *cum attractus,* others *contractus* or *contactus,* from which Palmer and Baehrens have both independently conjectured *atratus.* With that reading the idea will be that the Nile was in mourning when representations of himself and his seven mouths were borne along in the triumph of Octavianus. Prop. 3. 5. 34 affords an excellent illustration, both as to sense and reading. The Sun's horses in eclipse are represented as being in mourning:

> *Solis et atratis luxerit orbis equis;*

and there, as here, *atratis* has been changed, in Gron. to *attractis,* in Per. to *actractis.* With *atratus* Palmer reads *urbe.* That pictures of rivers were carried along in triumphs is well known: thus Pers. 6. 47

> *ingentesque locat Caesonia Rhenos.*

So Ovid, Art. 1. 223, where the Tigris and Euphrates are pointed out as part of a triumphal show. More to the point is Virg. Aen. 8. 711, where the Nile himself is represented on the shield of Aeneas as grieving at the defeat of Cleopatra, and in immediate connection with Caesar's triple triumph:

> *Contra autem magno maerentem corpore Nilum,*
> *Pandentemque sinus, et tota veste vocantem*
> *Caeruleum in gremium latebrosaque flumina victos.*

If we read *tractus in urbem* the idea will be that of the Nile brought in triumph from Egypt to Rome, which is merged l. 32 in the more natural idea of the great seven-mouthed river flowing weak through sorrow.

32. Mark the stately but subdued cadence of this line, so fitting to the sense. The very division into seven seems to proclaim the loss of power and glory to the river, as though a victim to the maxim *Divide et impera.* The idea of 'the Nile enchained and dragged to Rome as a captive *with its seven mouths*' scarcely deserves the epithet 'happy' given to it by Paley.

33. As a Roman could never be supposed to conquer, or obtain a triumph over, Romans, the triumph was ostensibly held over the native princes who had befriended Antony, such as Philadelphus, king of Paphlagonia, Amyntas of Pisidia, Deiotarus of Galatia. In the same way Caesar in B.C. 46 did not triumph over Pompey, Scipio, or Cato, but over Pharnaces and Juba.

These lines are an exact counterpart to Hor. Od. 4. 3. 6, where it is said of the poet

> *neque res bellica Deliis*
> *Ornatum foliis ducem,*
> *Quod regum tumidas contuderit minas,*
> *Ostendet Capitolio;*

and again Epod. 7. 7

> *Intactus aut Britannus ut descenderet*
> *Sacra catenatus via.*

The Triumphal Procession entered the city from the Campus Martius, where it was marshalled by the *Porta Triumphalis* (close to the river, used only on such occasions), made the entire circuit, or more strictly a three-quarter circuit, of the Palatine, passing through the Circus in its course. On reaching the summit of the Velia—where now stands the Arch of Titus—it descended into the Forum by the *Via Sacra*, having now the Capitol full in front.

34. currere, joined with *Cyprum, Nilum, colla*, as an object to *canerem* in l. 31. Somewhat similar is Virg. Aen. 8. 656, of the goose,

> *Gallos in limine adesse canebat.*

It would hence appear that the prows of the ships conquered at Actium were carried in the triumphal procession.

35. The art of the poet is here compared to that of weaving, as it so often is to that of spinning. In the latter case the idea seems to be simply that of drawing out verses like a thread or 'line,' as in Hor. Epp. 2. 1. 225 *tenui deducta poemata filo*, and Prop. 1. 16. 41

> *At tibi saepe novo deduxi carmina versu.*

In the former case the idea is that of composition as a whole, as Sen. Epp. 114. 18 *contexere librum*. Quint. 9. 4. 19 distinguishes an *oratio vincta atque contexta* from one *soluta*, i.e. 'compact,' 'well put together.' Cp. our word 'context.' Here the idea is that the name of Maecenas would necessarily be woven into—bound up with —any account of Caesar's exploits.

36. There is nothing in the words *sumpta et posita pace* to suggest the idea that Maecenas actually took part in any of Augustus' campaigns. There is every reason to believe he did not: though Hor. Epod. 1. 1. 8 shows that Maecenas had contemplated taking part in that of Actium.

fidele caput. There is tenderness, as well as praise, in these words. It is instructive to note the difference between the Latin and English uses of the words 'head' and 'heart.' The ancients believed the heart to be the seat of intelligence: hence Pers. 6. 10 *Cor jubet hoc Enni*, in imitation of Lucilius' *Egregie cordatus homo*, who meant that Ennius was a man of genius, i.e. 'had a good head.' *Caput*, on the other hand, denoted primarily the physical life: to expose the *caput* to peril was to expose the life, or as we should

say 'the body,' as distinguished from the mind or soul.   From thus
meaning 'the physical life' or 'body,' the word came to be used
specially as a term of endearment, as what is primarily loved, or
at least caressed, is the body, not the mind.   Thus in Plautus we
have such phrases as *caput carum, festivum, lepidissimum, ridiculum,*
and in Virg. Aen. 4. 354

Me puer Ascanius capitisque iniuria cari.

It thus comes about that while we may sometimes, as above, have
to translate *cor* by 'head,' so we may sometimes render *caput* by
'heart,' as in the passage before us.   *Carum caput* is just 'dear
heart;' cp. the Greek φίλον ἦτορ.   Other special meanings of *caput,*
such as *capitis poena,* 'capital punishment,' *caput,* 'the sum of a
Roman citizen's rights,' etc., are derived from the sense of 'life.'

37, 38. These lines have been generally misunderstood, and
in consequence the connection of ideas has been made to appear
more abrupt than it really is.   Two cases of famous friendships are
appealed to—that of Theseus and Pirithous, and that of Achilles
and Patroclus.   Theseus, king of Athens, proved his friendship for
Pirithous, son of Ixion (hence *Ixionides*), by assisting him in his
mad endeavour to carry off Proserpine from the lower world.
Achilles showed his affection for Patroclus, son of Menoetius (hence
Menoetiades), by the fury with which he avenged his death, and by
giving up for that purpose his anger against the Greeks.   According to the common interpretation, these cases are referred to simply
as instances of great friendships, with which Propertius wished to
compare the friendship of Augustus and Maecenas.   Thus the two
lines serve to illustrate only l. 34, and the meaning is, 'Theseus
in the world below,' lit. 'to those below,' 'Achilles in the world
above, call Pirithous and Patroclus as witnesses to their friendship.'
But this rendering breaks the coherence of the passage, and dis-
connects entirely l. 36 from ll. 37–40, which contain its main idea.
Testatur may mean not only 'calls to witness,' 'summons as
witnesses,' but also 'bears witness to,' 'attests,' as in 3. 7. 21

Sunt Agamemnonias testantia littora curas.

Propertius has just said, ' I would sing the deeds of Augustus and
thine, Maecenas, his faithful friend, had I the power.'   He goes on,
'Theseus to the world below, Achilles to the world above, bear
testimony to their friends Pirithous and Patroclus ; but Callimachus
had not the power to thunder forth the battles of Zeus, nor have I
the power to tell in heroic verse the glories of Augustus.'   Thus the
connection of ideas is complete.   No doubt in naming these heroic
friendships the poet intended *also* to imply that the friendship of
Augustus and Maecenas was as notable as theirs; but his main

point was that these heroes had each a friend who could worthily celebrate their praises, but that he had not the power to celebrate the glories of Augustus.

39. Phlegraeos. The *Phlegraei campi* (τὰ φλεγραῖα πεδία) was the name given to the volcanic region which extends along the coast of Campania to the north of Naples (now called *Solfatara*), and which was the supposed scene of the victory over the Titans and their punishment by Zeus.   Cp. 3. 9. 48.

40. Intonet, with potential force, implying not merely that Callimachus did not sing the battles of Zeus, but that he felt himself incompetent to do so.

angusto pectore gives the reason for his incompetence. F. has *augusto*, a not impossible reading : ' with all that great heart of his, he yet,' etc.

41. conveniunt, personally, by a rare use, instead of the usual impersonal *convenit*.   Such phrases however as *res convenit*, even *condiciones (pacis) convenerunt* (Nepos), are found.   Here the sense is 'nor is my genius fitted.'

duro . . . versu, of epic hexameter verse, in distinction to the soft and tender strains of elegiac poetry.   Cp. the Epigram of Domitius Marsus upon Tibullus :

> *Te quoque Vergilio comitem non aequa, Tibulle,*
> *Mors iuvenem campos misit ad Elysios,*
> *Ne foret, aut elegis molles qui fleret amores,*
> *Aut caneret forti regia bella pede.*

Cp. too 2. 34. 44

> *Inque tuos ignes, dure poeta, veni,*

where the contrast is between amatory poetry (*ignes*) and Lynceus' efforts in tragedy (*dure poeta*).

Mollis is the regular word used by Propertius to describe his own poetry ; in 3. 3. 18 he speaks of his own *mollia prata* in contrast to heroic verse ; cp. l. 2 above.

42. condere is used in a somewhat grandiloquent sense for ' to compose,' with such words as *carmen, poema,* etc.   Ovid, in a passage similar to this, Trist. 2. 336, has

> *Divitis ingenii est immania Caesaris acta*
> *Condere.*

Here there seems to be an additional idea taken from other meanings of *condo*, such as 'to store up,' 'to lay by,' of treasure, etc., so as to give a sense at once of value, of permanence, and of remoteness ; he is unfit to go back, as it were, to the remotest times, and assign Caesar a lasting place among his Phrygian ancestors.

51. Prop. here assumes that Phaedra in vain attempted to secure the love of her stepson Hippolytus by a love-potion.

53. gramine, of the magic herbs used by Circe.

54. Iolciacis. Iolcus, a town in Thessaly, on the Pagasaean gulf, was the birthplace of Jason. Here Medea by her incantations restored his aged father Aeson to youth.

urat, i. e. 'set a boiling.' Propertius is not thinking of the rejuvenescence of Aeson, as some editors suppose, he simply quotes Medea as a sorceress, and as compassing the death of Pelias. What he means is that whatever magical arts may be tried upon him, he will remain true to Cynthia, and die in no arms but hers.

57. A new idea here comes in. Love is a disease which alone of all diseases knows no curing.

58. non amat, ' will have nothing to say to,' ' knows not.'

morbi artificem, i. e. a treater—not a manufacturer—of disease. For the whole expression cp. I. 2. 8

> *Nudus Amor formae non amat artificem.*

59. Machaon, son of Aesculapius, cured Philoctetes of his wound.

Chiron, the gifted and artistic centaur, skilled in medicine, son of Cronos and Philyra, cured Phoenix, son of Amyntor, of his blindness. See Ov. A. A. 1. 337.

61. deus Epidaurius, i. e. Aesculapius, who was specially worshipped, and according to some accounts born, at Epidaurus. He restored to life Androgeos, son of Minos king of Crete, who had been wounded by the Athenian youth in jealousy of his success at their games.

63. Mysus iuvenis, i. e. Telephus, king of Mysia. He was wounded by Achilles in endeavouring to prevent his landing on the coast of Mysia, and was afterwards cured by the rust of the spear which had wounded him, Plin. H. N. 25. 5.

65. vitium is properly 'a defect' or 'flaw;' such as a crack in a jar, Pers. 3. 21

> *Sonat vitium percussa, maligne*
> *Respondet viridi concocta fidelia limo.*

'The jar, made of green ill-baked clay, betrays the flaw by its unsound ring when struck.' Ovid calls the hole in the wall through which Pyramus and Thisbe conversed a *vitium*, Met. 4. 67. Any defect in taking the auspices was called a *vitium* : hence the phrases *magistratus vitio creati, tabernaculum vitio captum. Mendum* or *menda* was a lesser defect, Ov. A. A. 2. 361

> *Rara tamen mendo facies caret.*

Here, the *vitium* or 'weakness' referred to is of course Propertius' love for Cynthia. In the preceding lines he has declared that all maladies can be cured except love.

66. Tantalea manu. I have retained, though not without hesitation, the reading of the MSS., on the principle that a MS. reading should not be rejected if a satisfactory sense can be extracted from it. *Tantalea manu*, if correct, would mean 'with the hand of Tantalus,' or 'with the hand of a Tantalus;' and though the dative would be more natural after *tradere*, it is perfectly good sense to speak of 'offering, or passing on, apples with the hand of a Tantalus.' In the Odys. 11. 581, where the position of Tantalus is described, emphasis is laid on the fact that he cannot reach the fruit, etc., *with his hand* (see the passage quoted on Tib. 1. 3. 77); and to invert the phrase by using *tradere* instead of some word meaning to reach or obtain, is quite in the style of Propertius. The point was that Tantalus could not handle, though he could see, the apples: so Propertius can feel, but cannot remove, his own weakness. 'To hand apples *to* Tantalus' is a different idea, and imports another person into the scene. At the same time, *Tantaleae* is a very tempting correction. Propertius nowhere uses the dative in *-ui* : in 1. 11. 12 he has the contracted form

Alternae facilis cedere lympha manu,

and again, 2. 19. 19, *reddere pinu Cornua.* The same form occurs Tac. Ann. 3. 30, 33, 6. 23. Horace has the similar form *fide* for *fidei* Od. 3. 7. 4, and Virg. Geo. 1. 208 has *die* for *diei*. The correction to *Tantalea* is just the correction which an ignorant scribe would make. A similar doubt as between the dative and the ablative occurs in 4. 6. 22, where Palmer adopts the reading

Pilaque femineae turpiter apta manu.

Just as in this passage, N. reads the ablative *feminea manu*, though *apta* (as here *tradere*) suggests the dative, and the dative, on the whole, is best suited to the sense of the passage. See notes.

67. virgineis, referring to the 49 Danaids, who, for murdering their husbands on their bridal night, were condemned to pour water everlastingly into a bottomless cask.

idem. Note the Latin idiom by which, when two predicates are referred to a common subject, the English *also* is represented not by *etiam*, but by *idem*, agreeing with the subject. Cp. Hor. Od. 2. 19. 28

idem
Pacis eras mediusque belli.

Prometheus was punished for his defiance of Zeus by being chained

to a rock on Mount Caucasus, where his liver was incessantly
fed upon by an eagle.

repleverit. The sense points to the successful performance of
the hopeless task, and therefore the future perfect is the appropriate
tense to use, while the simple future is used in ll. 65, 66, 69 and 70.

71. reposcent. The prefix *re* is used here, as in many other
words, not to denote restitution, but that the thing is suitable,
natural, or due. *Poscent* would be a demand which might have no
justification ; *reposcent* implies a natural, proper, inevitable demand.
' When they shall come to ask,' ' When in the due course of things
they shall ask,' etc. Cp. Juv. 3. 202, of the roof,

> *molles ubi reddunt ova columbae,*

because pigeons may be expected to lay their eggs on the roof.
Again, a field is said *reddere fructum*, not because it gives back the
seed put into it, or makes a return, but because ' it duly yields.'

72. breve in exiguo. Note the emphasising of the sense by
the juxtaposition of two words of similar meaning. Cp. Hor. Od.
1. 3. 10 and Wickham's note.

73. A difficult line. The text gives *spes*, the reading of N ;
but I believe that *pars*, the reading of G, should be adopted.
Whether we read *spes* or *pars*, the meaning of *invidiosa* will be
the same, ' full of the envy of others,' ' the object of envy,' i. e. the
word is used objectively, not, as more usual, subjectively, in the sense
of ' full of envy towards others.' If we read *spes*, then *nostrae* must
refer to Propertius himself, who in the phrase *nostrae s. i. iuventae*
styles Maecenas the hope of his youthful fortunes, adding that his
expectations from Maecenas have made him the object of envy.
Literally the words will mean, ' Thou envy-attracting hope of my
youth.' The phrase is strained and ungainly in itself; but the idea
also is out of place. The poet has declared that his wound cannot
be healed, and, anticipating an early death, calls on Maecenas, his
chief boast and pride, in life and death alike, to linger one moment
at his tomb, and let fall the words, ' Died of unrequited love.'
The idea of hope is foreign to the passage. The poet's race is run ;
he only begs that the one great pride of his life—his connection with
Maecenas—a connection which has brought envy on him in the
past—may not desert him in death, and that Maecenas may stop to
say one word of sympathy over his grave. Hertzberg and Paley,
reading *pars*, take *nostrae iuventae* to signify ' our Roman youth,'
quoting the well-known phrase *princeps iuventutis*, applied to the
young Caesars, and Horace's *Maecenas equitum decus*. Hertzberg
also laboriously shows that Maecenas might come under the Roman

Q

military definition of youth, which included all up to forty-six years
of age under the name *Iuniores*.   But the whole passage is personal
and passionate in feeling ; the poet never travels from himself ; and
to give a whole line to a description of Maecenas' position breaks
the current of the thought.   Propertius simply adjures Maecenas, as
part and parcel of his life, as his boast and glory in life and death
alike, to pay him this last tribute. For *pars iuventae* cp. Virg. Geo.
2. 40, also addressed to Maecenas,

> *O decus, o famae merito pars maxima nostrae,*

and 1. 21. 4

> *Pars ego sum vestrae proxima militiae.*

75. meo ... busto.   The dative, apparently after *proxima*,
but perhaps to be taken along with *ducet* as well, just as *iace* in
l. 77 goes with *favillae*.

76. Esseda, properly a Celtic war-chariot, from which apparently the pattern of a Roman travelling coach was taken.

Britannus. The gentile name is here used instead of the adjective *Britannicus*. So Horace has *Flumen Rhenum*, *Metaurum
Flumen*, etc., and Propertius *Liburna* 3. 11. 44 ; *Inda* 3. 13. 5.

78. fatum . . . fuit. Cp. our colloquial phrase 'was the
death of him.' *Fato* would be the more usual construction.

II. 2. 5–8.

This passage gives a description of Cynthia's personal appearance.

5. Fulva, connected with *fulgeo*, *fulmen*, *fulgur*, and so probably with *flagro*, *flamen*, *flavus*, denotes a gleaming, golden brightness, not equivalent to the 'light flaxen hair so common in those
of Saxon descent' (Paley), but probably corresponding rather to
the shade of golden brown to which we give the name of 'auburn.'
Thus the term is applied to lions, Lucr. 5. 902, to wolves, Virg.
Aen. 1. 275, to gold, id. 7. 279 and elsewhere, to the eagle, id. 12.
247.   The Greek equivalent is ξανθή.

6. maxima toto corpore gives the notion of proportion as well
as height : she was tall, and on a large scale throughout. This
prepares us for the stately, graceful walk implied in *incedit*, and
the comparison which follows with the matronly Juno and the
martial Pallas, the two most majestic of the goddesses of Olympus.
The remains of ancient Greek statuary show us that the ancients had
no admiration for tight-drawn waists and spindle ankles, nor for the
smallness and fineness which go to making up our idea of 'pretty.'
They loved to see in a woman, as in a man, fully-developed limbs,
giving a sense of power as well as freedom ; and the ancient female

dress was calculated more to set off the beauty of the figure as a whole, than to call special attention to the face. Our word 'figure' is often so narrowed as to refer to the waist only; but no ancient statue has a slender waist, and the ankles of all the most celebrated statues of Venus—as e.g. the Venus de Medici and the Venus of the Capitol—have that robust healthy thickness about them which a horse-fancier would describe by the word 'gummy.'

longae manus. A well-developed tapering hand, fitted to do well its work in life; here again the ancients had no idea that a woman's hand was beautiful in proportion to its approximating to the hand of a doll. Cp. 3. 7. 60

· *Attulimus longas in freta vestra manus.*

In Catull. 44. 2 long hands are specially mentioned as an essential to beauty.

incedit, used especially of the majestic walk of Juno, Virg. Aen. 1. 46, in a passage probably imitated here by Propertius:

Ast ego quae Divum incedo regina Iovisque
Et soror et coniux.

Iove digna soror, lit. 'worthy of Jove as his sister,' i.e. worthy to be Jove's sister.

7. Aut cum Pallas spatiatur is wrongly explained by Hertzberg as a kind of *anacoluthon.* The peculiarity of the construction is that *Pallas* is placed by attraction inside the clause dependent on *cum* instead of outside it. The meaning is ' she moves a very Juno or a Pallas.' ' she moves as a sister worthy of Jove, or as Pallas *when* she walks before the altars.' The change suggested to *ut cum* is no improvement; *aut ut* would make the sense clear were it not too violent a change. The difficulty is that the particle of comparison is omitted: Propertius does not say 'She moves *as* Juno or Pallas,' but actually identifying Cynthia with the goddess to whom she is compared: 'She walks a sister worthy of Juno or Pallas when,' etc.

7. Dulichias. Dulichium was one of the group of islands called Echinades, off the coast of Acarnania. Homer, Il. 2. 625, speaks of 'Dulichinm and the sacred islands Echinae, which lie beyond the sea, opposite to Elis.' Strabo identifies *Dulichium* with one of the islands called Dolicha (Δολίχα) in his day. The island formed part of the kingdom of Ulysses, and was therefore probably the seat of the worship of his special patroness Pallas.

8. It is evident that at Dulichium the goddess was worshipped in her martial character, and represented in complete warlike array, with the *aegis* on her breast.

II. 3.

The poet enlarges on the charms of Cynthia, which justify the absorbing character of his passion.

1. nocere, of the harm, damage, or 'wounding' caused by love.

2 spiritus, i. e. the poet's boasting that he had cast himself clear of his love, and was a free man once more. For *spiritus,* 'breath,' in the sense of pride and boasting, cp. Hor. Sat. 2. 3. 311

> *Corpore maiorem rides Turbonis in armis*
> *Spiritum et incessum.*

The similar use in the Scottish dialect of the word 'wind' is well illustrated in the Litany ascribed to the ancestor of the present Mr. Maxtone-Graham of Cultoquhey. Laird of a small property, surrounded by four great families, he daily prayed at 'the wishing well' of the domain :

> *From the craft of the Campbells,*
> *From the pride of the Graemes,*
> *From the ire of the Drummonds,*
> *From the wind of the Morays,*
> > *Good Lord, deliver us.*

4. liber alter. These words are generally referred to the publication of the First book of the Elegies, as though within one month the poet began the writing of the Second (see Introd.). But the reference might be merely to a temporary abjurement of Cynthia—perhaps the same as that referred to in 2. 2. 1 *Liber eram,* etc.—and the *liber* might only be a *maxima historia,* or one of the *longas Iliadas* which the beauty of Cynthia was perpetually forcing from him, 2. 1. 16, 14.

5. quaerebam—si, 'I was casting about to see if,' 'I was trying to discover whether ;' and then follow two impossibilities to show the futility of the attempt to give up his love.

6. Neo solitus is here equivalent to *vel si non solitus* or *insolitus,* as is evident from a comparison of *si posset* l. 5 with *si possem* l. 7. The use of *nec* as equivalent to *et non* is frequent in cases where the negative qualifies the whole sentence which follows. But here Propertius uses *nec* in such a way that its negative only qualifies the single word *solitus.* So in 2. 28. 52

> *Vobiscum Europe nec proba Pasiphae,*

nec proba is equivalent to *et non proba* or *et improba.* Similarly

2. 25. 33 *nec umquam vorans Charybdis* is equivalent to *et Charybdis quae numquam vorat.*

7. studiis vigilare. *Vigilare*, with the dative, is uncommon. *Invigilare* is more usual in this sense.

11. minium, cinnabar, or ore of mercury, of which there are mines in Spain. Paley refers to the μίλτος of Homer as showing that red-lead was used very early as a paint. For *minium* see Virg. E. 10. 27.

12. Cp. Virg. Aen. 12. 68

Indum sanguineo veluti violaverit ostro
Si quis ebur, aut mixta rubent ubi lilia multa
Alba rosa: tales virgo dabat ore colores.

With ll. 9–12 we may also compare

There is a garden in her face
Where roses and white lilies grow;

and the following lines recall many of the ideas in the passage ll. 9–20 :

It is not beauty I demand,
A crystal brow, the moon's despair,
Nor the snow's daughter, a white hand,
Nor mermaid's yellow pride of hair:
Tell me not of your starry eyes,
Your lips that seem on roses fed,
Your breasts where Cupid tumbling lies,
Nor sleeps for kissing of his bed.

15. si qua may be for *si aliqua*, as though he were not thinking of Cynthia only : 'I am not the man to be captivated *by every maiden who*,' etc. But as the whole point of the passage is that it gives a description of Cynthia's charms, it seems more in place to suppose that *qua* stands for the ablative, as in the line Virg. Aen. 6. 883

O miserande puer, si qua fata aspera rumpas,

'If in any way, at any time, she dress herself up in silk,' etc.

16. de nihilo, i. e. having no ground to proceed from, without sure reason.

17. posito . . . Iaccho, 'when the wine has been put upon the table,' i. e. after supper. This use of 'ponere,' to place upon the table, and so 'to serve up,' is frequent in later Latin. So Pers. 1. 53

Calidum scis ponere sumen.

So H. quotes Copa 37

Pone merum et talos : pereat qui crastina curet.

The interpretation 'laid aside' is out of place.

20. Par may be either the nominative agreeing with the

subject, or the accusative after *ludere*. For *ludere docta*, the favourite Graecism of Horace, cp. Od. 4. 13. 7

Doctae psallere Chiae

and *passim*.

19. Et ... cum. Instead of repeating *quod* after *quantum*, he uses a new expression, in agreement with the general sense of the passage : ' as that (I love her) when,' etc.

21. cum is probably the preposition, and the construction is

Committit scripta sua cum (scriptis) Corinnae.

Exactly parallel is 2. 8. 23

Et sua cum miserae permiscuit ossa puellae,

where *miserae puellae* is the reading of N. (Tyrrell, Hermathena, vol. 2, corr. *misera puella*).

The only objection to this natural construction is that Propertius usually uses the Greek form of genitive and accusative in Greek names of the first declension, such as *Antigones, Persephones, Helenen,* etc. But there are exceptions, as *Helenae* 3. 8. 32, *Hermionae* 1. 4. 6, *Antiopae* 1. 4. 5, *Ariadna* sup. 18, and probably *Achilli* 4. 11. 39, which are enough to break the rule (see Hertz. Qu. P. 164).

If *Corinnae* be the dative, *cum* must be the conjunction, and the name must go directly with *committit*, as in Juvenal 6. 378, the poetess being identified with her poems, so that *Corinnae* will be equivalent to *scriptis Corinnes*. *Committere*, ' to join,' or ' match,' is used with an accusative, either of the engagement, as in the phrase *committere praelium*, ' to join battle,' or of the combatants engaged. So Juvenal 1. 162

licet Aeneam Rutulumque ferocem
    Committas,

and 6. 436, where the literary pretensions of the ' blue stocking ' are well hit off, *Committit vates et comparat.* Cp. Mart. 7. 24. 1.

22. quae quaevis. So Palmer, interpreting the words of Corinna's pride in her own poems : ' who deems no poems, whatever they be, equal to her own.' But *carmina* refers more naturally to *scripta*, Cynthia's own verses : and the emphasis requires that the couplet should close with a strong statement of Cynthia's excellence, not of Corinna's. N. has *quae quivis.* Gron. has *quae lyrnes*, from which Beroaldus conj. *Carminaque Erinnes*, which is plausible. *Corinna* was a poetess of Tanagra in Boeotia, who flourished in the fifth century, B.C. *Erinna* was a Lesbian poetess, cotemporary with Sappho. *Quae quivis* might possibly mean ' poems which any author, however famous, cannot deem equal to his own,' i.e. only equal : he must deem them superior. R. Ellis,

Phil. Journal, xv. p. 13, quotes in illustration of this line Lucian de Mercede Conductis 38 ἐν γάρ τι καὶ τοῦτο τῶν ἄλλων καλλωπισμάτων αὐτοῖς δοκεῖ ἢν λέγηται ὡς πεπαιδευμέναί τε εἰσὶ καὶ φιλόσοφοι καὶ ποιοῦσιν ᾄσματα οὐ πολὺ τῆς Σαπφοῦς ἀποδέοντα.

23. Num. The **Non** of N. has been unnecessarily changed to *Num* by the editors. If *num* be read, it must be interpreted as said playfully or ironically, so as to be equivalent in meaning to *non* or *nonne*, just as we might say ' *Is* it true then?' where the implication is, ' Is it not true?'

Candidus, a certain correction for *ardidus*. *Candidus* implies beauty as a whole: *candida Dido* Virg. Aen. 5. 571. So of Maia, id. 8. 138, and of Apollo, Hor. Od. 1. 2. 31

Nube candentes humeros amictus,

where however the idea is rather of the radiant glory of a god.

Sneezing was a favourable omen, especially for lovers. Cp. Catullus 43. 9, where in the loves of Acmen and Septimius

Amor sinistra ut ante
Dextra sternuit approbationem.

Burm. quotes Theocr. 7. 96 Σιμιχίδᾳ μὲν ἔρωτες ἐπέπταρον: cp. Aristoph. Av. 720.

II. 10.

Lachmann and other editors, followed by Paley, believe that this Elegy marks the commencement of a new book. The poem reads like a pröoemium, containing a formal announcement that the poet has determined to give up the writing of love verses, and to betake himself henceforth to singing of wars and warlike deeds, or, in other words, to add one more to the panegyrists of Augustus. In his own simple words, l. 6

Bella canam quando scripta puella mea est.

Unfortunately the promise is not fulfilled; for, as Postgate observes, there is but one poem in the book (2. 31 according to the usual numbering, on the dedication of the Temple of Apollo), which specially relates to Augustus, and that poem was obviously written, as it purports to be, with quite a different motive. Lachmann's theory quite breaks down; it is not supported by any evidence to show that a common purpose can be traced running through any one of the books of our poet; it is opposed by the authority of the MSS., and it assigns to the second book a bulk so small—nine poems in all —as to be out of all proportion with the length of the remaining books. The best recent editors of Propertius—Palmer, Postgate, and

Baehrens—have rejected Lachmann's arrangement, and all that survives of his arbitrary changes is the double numbering which causes
such confusion in the references to our poet.   The date of the poem
before us is fixed to the year B. C. 24 by the references to the expedition of Aelius Gallus.

1. **Sed** denotes a sudden break in the author's purpose, and a
turning in a new direction.

lustrare here is 'to career over,' as in Hor. Od. 3. 25. 11 *Pede
barbaro Lustratam Rhodopen.*   Virgil also associates the word with
choral dancing, Aen. 10. 224

> *Agnoscunt longe regem lustrantque choreis.*

2. 'To give field to his horse' is a natural expression for giving
free scope to his song, i. e. no longer to be confined to one kind of
poetry.

Haemonia is a poetical name for Thessaly, and Thessaly
was famed from the earliest times both for horses and riders.   The
metaphor here is not drawn expressly from chariot-racing, as in
Virg. Geo. 2. 542 ult. and Juv. 1. 19.   Cicero ad Q. fratrem 2. 15
imitates Pindar's phrase, Pyth. 10. 65, of 'a four-in-hand of poetry,'
where, talking of his own poems, he says *cursu corrigam tarditatem,
tum equis, tum vero (quoniam scribis poema ab eo nostrum probari)
quadrigis poeticis.*   Hertz. quotes Stat. Silv. 4. 7

> *Iamdiu lato spatiata campo*
> *Fortis heroos Erato labores*
> *Differ, atque ingens opus in minores*
> *Contrahe gyros.*

3. **fortes ad praelia.**   So. Tib. 1. 9. 46

> *Nam poteram ad laqueos fortior esse tuos.*

4. **mei ducis,** i. e. Augustus.

5. Notice the subjunctive *deficiant* in the protasis followed by
the indicative *erit* in the apodosis.

6. **Laus,** in the nominative, for the more usual construction
laudi.

et voluisse, 'the mere will.'

7. **tumultus** is properly distinguished from *bellum* as denoting
a rising in Italy, and especially an outbreak in Cisalpine Gaul.   Thus
Cic. Phil. 8. 1. 2 *Itaque maiores nostri tumultum Italicum, quod
erat domesticus; tumultum Gallicum, quod erat Italiae finitimus,
praeterea nullum nominabant.   Gravius autem tumultum esse quam
bellum hinc intellegi licet, quod bello vacationes valent, tumultu non
valent.*

8. quando for *quandoquidem.* So Juv. 5. 93

> *Quando omne peractum est*
> *Iam mare.*

9. subducto seems to refer, as Postgate explains, to the 'draw-ing up' of the face or eyebrows as a mark of austerity. Thus Gell. 19. 7. 16 *Vituperones suos subducti supercilii carptores appellavit.* The other meaning of *subductus,* 'withdrawn,' 'retired,' is not appropriate.

10. aliam, 'another and a new lyre,' i.e. a more dignified strain.

11. As the reading stands, *anima, carmina, Pierides,* are all vocatives: *ex humili* goes closely with *surge,* and is exactly parallel to Hor. Od. 3. 30. 12

> *Dicar . . . ex humili potens*
> *Princeps Aeolium carmen ad Italos*
> *Deduxisse modos,*

where the meaning is 'rising to lordly greatness out of a humble lot.' Paley retains *carmine,* the reading of N., and follows those editors who punctuate thus:

> *Surge, anima, ex humili iam carmine sumite vires.*

But though his poetry might rise *ex humili,* it could scarcely be said to gather strength *ex humili ;* and the position of *iam* points clearly to its being taken with *sumite* rather than with *surge.*

12. magni oris opus, 'a grandiloquent, big-mouthed, work.' The genitive is descriptive: the phrase, *magnum os,* which occurs also Virg. Geo. 3. 294, is analogous to *os rotundum* Hor. A. P. 323, *os magna sonaturum* Sat. 1. 4. 44, and conveys the idea of spouting and declamation. Hence it is used here and elsewhere to denote the more high-flown language of Epic poetry.

13. The one terrible and as yet unavenged defeat which the Roman arms had sustained at the hand of a foreign foe was the fatal field of Carrhae, B.C. 53, when Crassus and his son were slain and the whole Roman army destroyed or captured by the Parthians. Hence the Parthian name became a name of terror and shame to the Romans. Caesar was about to set out on a Parthian campaign when he was assassinated ; and it was the great ambition of Augustus' life to wipe out the disgrace of Carrhae. This he effected by diplomacy and a display of force in B.C. 20, when, taking advantage of the internal dissensions of the Parthians, he obtained the restoration of the standards lost with Crassus at Carrhae, received the homage of the king Phraates, and placed Tigranes upon the throne of Armenia. This event was regarded as the crowning triumph of Augustus' foreign policy ; and it was deemed so essential to his position as sole ruler of Rome that he should obtain a great success over the Parthians, that it is not only perpetually celebrated in terms of triumph by the court poets after it was obtained, but it is frequently referred to in anticipation. Thus the mere mention of a Parthian victory is by no means sufficient in itself to prove that the passage in which it occurs was written after B.C. 20. The famous lines in Virg. Geo. 3. 30 sqq., in which the Armenian and Parthian successes of Augustus seem to be alluded to, were in all probability written in a tone of prophecy; for Virgil died in B.C. 19, and the Georgics were written at least ten years before the events supposed to be referred to occurred. The same explanation is to be given with regard to Hor. Od. 2. 9. 18-20, where Parthian successes are spoken of in an Ode which from other causes can scarcely be dated later than B.C. 23.

In the magnificent statue of Augustus, which now adorns the Braccio Nuovo in the Vatican, and which was dug up in the Villa Livia at the Sacra Rubra (now *Prima Porta*) in 1863, the cuirass is beautifully sculptured with figures indicating the leading events of his life. The principal place in the centre is occupied by a representation of the Parthian envoys handing over the standards to Tiberius.

13. equitem post terga tueri. In allusion to the mode of fighting peculiar to the Parthians, which struck terror into the Roman imagination. Their chief arm was a light cavalry, who were armed with bows and shot from horseback, advancing or retreating with great rapidity, and so peculiarly adapted to a desert country where the great heat, the want of water and supplies, the long distances and the burning sand, rendered the Roman system of fighting practically impossible. Thus Virg. Geo. 3. 31

Fidentemque fuga Parthum, versisque sagittis.

Cp. Hor. Od. 2. 13. 17 ; in Sat. 2. 1. 15, in a passage exactly parallel to this, he declares it is not every poet that can sing of wars,

Aut labentis equo describat vulnera Parthi.

Cp. Persius 5. 4

Vulnera seu Parthi ducentis ab inguine ferrum.

So again, Prop. 3. 9. 54 describes the Parthian flying shots as

Parthorum astutae tela remissa fugae.

R. Ellis, Phil. Journ. xv. p. 14, objects to the usual rendering of this passage, as not giving the natural meaning of the words. He thinks that the expression is obviously taken from an army or commander *retreating before a victorious foe*, and looking back continually to see whether he is pursuing. But the Euphrates is here represented as a Parthian river, not as a Roman river (*Crassos se tenuisse dolet*), and there would be no point in saying that the Parthian river was no longer running away from a victorious foe. The point is that the Euphrates repents of having kept the Crassi, and declares that his horsemen no longer cast that terrible glance behind them.

14. tenuisse, 'that it kept them,' i. e. instead of sending them back unhurt.

15. The word **India** is probably here used in poetic exaggeration. The only known relation between Augustus and India is that an Indian embassy is mentioned amongst others as having reached him in B. C. 20 when in the East. Postgate supposes the reference to be to a previous embassy of which Dion Cassius speaks in vague terms, 54. 9. The poet speaks grandly, as though the whole East were submitting to Augustus; the only foundation in fact for such a boast being that Augustus was meditating an expedition against Arabia, and had begun to intrigue in Parthian affairs. Arabia was probably looked upon vaguely as being on the road to India; hence Horace couples the two together, Od. 3. 24. 1

> *Intactis opulentior*
> *Thesauris Arabum et divitis Indiae.*

16. intactae, 'unrifled.'

Arabiae. The allusion is to the disastrous expedition against Arabia, conducted by Aelius Gallus in B.C. 24. Horace alludes to this expedition, Od. 1. 29. 1

> *Icci, beatis nunc Arabum invides*
> *Gazis.*

As the commentators point out, the words *te tremit* point to a time previous to the disaster.

Arabia has here the first syllable long, for sake of the metre, as in 1. 14. 19. Poets allow themselves great license in the case of proper names. Thus we have *Ítălŭs* and *Ītālŭs, Sĭcānŭs, Sĭcănŭs* and *Sĭcănĭs, Cȳthēră* and *Cȳthĕrăă*, and we need not feel squeamish about admitting *Āpŭlŭs* side by side with *Āpŭlǽ* in the much-tortured passage Hor. Od. 3. 4. 9, 10

> *Me fabulosae Vulture in Appulo*
> *Altricis extra limen Apuliae,*

where none of the proposed emendations deserve adoption.

17, 18. These lines complete the circle of prophetic boastfulness. The reference in l. 17 is of course to Britain. So Horace in Od. 1. 21. 13, an Ode which was probably written in B. C. 28, prophesies victories to Augustus over East and West alike :

Hic bellum lacrimosum, hic miseram famem
Pestemque a populo et principe Caesare in
  Persas atque Britannos
    Vestra motus aget prece.

17. si qua for *si aliqua*, 'if there be any that' would be quite indefinite, but that the indicative *subtrahit* shows that a particular country is meant. So Virg. Aen. 7. 225.

se subtrahit. Our proud insular isolation has perhaps never been more simply and finely expressed.

19. Haec castra sequar, i.e. 'this is the cause to which I shall attach myself as a poet,' referring to *bella canam* l. 8. He will follow the conquering course in spirit. There is no idea of his actually accompanying the expedition as an official poet, counterpart of the modern War Correspondent, as Paley seems to suggest. Ovid has an exact parallel, Am. 2. 18. 11, 12: his love is ever enticing him from singing deeds of war:

Frangor, et ingenium sumptis revocatur ab armis,
  Resque domi gestas et mea bella cano.

20. hunc. This use of *hunc* Postgate well illustrates from Tib. 1. 3. 93, Ov. Pont. 1. 4. 57. Propertius uses *ille* in exactly the same connection, 3. 1. 36

Illum post cineres auguror ipse diem.

21. in magnis signis, lit. 'in the case of tall statues,' or as we should say 'of a tall statue.' For this use of *in*, used to localise or specify, cp. Hor. Epod. 11. 4

Amore, qui me praeter omnes expetit
  Mollibus in pueris aut in puellis urere.

22. hic, further defined by *ante pedes*: 'just here, before my feet,' as though he were pointing to the very spot. So 1. 19. 7, quoted by Postgate, where *illic* is explained by *caecis locis*.

23. inopes conscendere. Another instance of Horace's favourite Graecism. *Conscendere carmen laudis*, 'To climb up to the height of a song of praise' is an intelligible and graphic expression, expressing both the difficulty of the task in itself, and the grandeur of the merit that calls for such an effort. It is scarcely necessary to assume that *laudis* means 'thy merit' in particular; or that there is a frigid reference to the stock phrase of climbing the hill of the Muses.

24. The figure is slightly changed here; instead of crowning a statue in honour of a victory, the poet represents himself as offering a humble offering at the festival of a god. The idea of *vilia tura* is exactly illustrated by Horace in his beautiful address

to the rustic Phidyle, who can afford no costly offering, Od. 3.
23. 17

> *Immunis aram si tetigit manus,*
> *Non sumptuosa blandior hostia*
> *Mollivit aversos Penates*
> *Farre pio et saliente mica.*

In **sacris** the idea is no doubt that so carefully worked out by
Horace, Od. 3. 1. 1–4. There the poet represents himself as the
priest of the Muses; at the Muses' feast, and in their name, he gives
forth his holy song ; as at a solemn sacrifice, no words of evil omen
are to be heard; and he sings to none but to the pure ears of boys
and maidens. Akin to this is the idea in 3. 1. 3 *puro de fonte
sacerdos*, where the water is from the Muses' spring, to be used in
purifying the worshippers. See too 4. 6. 1–10 and note.

25. Ascra was a village in Boeotia, near Mount Helicon, famed
as the birthplace of Hesiod. Close past it flowed the small stream
Permessus, which has its source in the celebrated inspiring spring of
Aganippe. The sense thus is, 'I have not yet climbed up to the
source of the Muses' stream, and quaffed at the fountain-head ; I
have been but dipped by Love in its lower reaches.'

II. 11.

This short Elegy is evidently the expression of a moment of
pique ; its bitterness of tone is not to be mistaken for indifference.

1. For the reading *ne* for *vel* see Hous., J. of Phil. xxi. p. 186.

2. sterili semina ponit humo, i. e. ' is engaged in a thankless
task.' Cp. Juv. 7. 49 *tenuesque in pulvere sulcos Ducimus, et litus
sterili versamus aratro.*

3. munera, ' thy gifts and graces' whether natural or super-
added. For the latter sense cp. 1. 2. 4, where *peregrina munera*, in
the shape of silks and scents, are contrasted with *naturae decus* ; for
the former cp. *iocosi munera Liberi* Hor. Od. 4. 15. 26.

uno lecto is of course the couch of the funeral-bier; *uno*
conveys the notion of ' last and fatal :' that couch which is strewn
once and for all for each of us.

4. extremi, thus used constantly in reference to death : ' that
closes all things.'

5. transibit ... viator. It must be remembered that the tombs
of the Romans were for the most part placed along the sides of the
great high roads leading out of the city, and not huddled together in

modern fashion in cemeteries. Hence the frequent invocations to travellers to stop their chariots (2. 1. 75) or their horses to pay a tribute of respect to the dead—invocations often senselessly repeated on modern tombstones. No man could approach the Eternal City but through this City of the Dead: and it must have afforded a strange sensation to the traveller visiting Rome for the first time to have to pass for miles and miles, before the city itself was in view, between two lines of the ancient dead, each tomb telling in simple words the story of the occupants, and, as a rule, surmounted with their images.

II. 12.

This charming little poem describes a picture of the God of Love, and explains the meaning of the symbols under which the god was represented. The subject was a common one for decorative and other purposes; and as it was essential for an ancient artist to adhere rigidly not only to the general type and character, but also to all the details and accessories, of the representation of any recognised mythical personage, we know that we have here an exact description of a picture perpetually before every Roman's eyes, and to be found painted on the walls or elsewhere in almost every Roman house.

1. Quicunque ille fuit, of a definite, though unknown, person: hence the indicative mood.

puerum, predicatively, 'as a boy.'

2. miras manus, 'wondrous clever hands.' The phrase should properly apply only to the execution of the picture; it is here used of the conception. What he praises is the *idea* of representing Love as a boy. The phrase *miras manus* is exactly analogous to that of 'having good hands,' commonly applied to a rider or driver who knows how to handle a horse's mouth. Analogous is the phrase 'a good touch,' applied to manual performance on musical instruments.

3. Is, referring to the same person as *ille*, line 1.

sine sensu, as nearly as possible equivalent to 'without sense.' The word *sensus* here has no technical meaning: it does not mean, as often elsewhere, either 'sensation' or 'sensibility,' which it would be absurd to deny to lovers, or 'perception' as Postgate says ('to lie in *insensibility*, without *perceiving* obvious facts'); it means just that amount of intelligence and understanding, whether we call it reflection or judgment or purpose, which distinguishes the ordinary man in the conduct of his affairs, and which enable us to call him a 'man of sense.' The distinction between *sensus* and *mens*, appropriate elsewhere, is here out of place; more parallel are such phrases as *latet in animo ac sensu meo* Cic. de Leg. 2. 1, or *ut id maxime excellat quod longissime sit ab imperitorum intelligentia sensuque disiunctum* de Orat 1. 3, and especially the phrase *communis sensus*, on which so much has been written : see Lucr. 1. 422

> *Corpus enim per se communis dedicat esse*
> *Sensus.*

Cp. Mayor on Juv. 8. 73, where *communis sensus* is said to be wanting to the man who is inordinately puffed up by his pedigree, just as Hor. S. 1. 3. 66 says the same of the man who senselessly interrupts another who wishes to read or to be quiet. Deficient in 'tact' we should say: i. e. in that amount of sense and intelligence and judgment which we expect to find in our fellow-creatures. 'Without sense' or 'thought' will suit the present passage : ἀφρόντιστος, as Postgate points out, is similarly used of Love by Theocritus 10. 19.

4. levibus curis, an ablative of cause, to be taken with *perire,* which is equivalent to the unused passive of the verb *perdere.*

curis, as frequently in love poems, is equivalent to 'love' or 'the loved object.' For the former sense cp. Ov. Rem. Am. 311

> *Haeserat in quadam nuper mea cura puella;*

for the latter, Prop. 2. 34. 9

> *Lynceu, tune meam potuisti, perfide, curam*
> *Tangere?*

Cp. the Greek ἐμὸν μέλημα.

bona, all solid advantages: not wealth only.

ventosas. So Virg. Aen. 12. 848: 'light and airy.'

6. Fecit, the regular word for artistic representation: as in Ovid. Met. 6. 109

> *Fecit olorinis Ledam recubare sub alis,*

or to representation by words, as in Cic. N. D. 1. 12. 31 *Xenophon facit Socratem disputantem.*

The latter part of the line is difficult. Paley, following Hertz., translates 'to flit in the human heart.' 'To flutter within the human heart' would well express the uncertainty of lovers. Postgate also makes *corde* the ablative of place, and supposes that in the picture Love was represented as 'flying from heart to heart.' This sense, however, is scarcely to be got out of the words *humano corde :* and so Postgate suggests that Propertius, though he has failed to express himself clearly, meant to convey the idea found in Moschus 2. 17

καὶ πτερόεις ὡς ὄρνις ἐφίπταται ἄλλον ἐπ' ἄλλῳ
ἀνέρας ἠδὲ γυναῖκας, ἐπὶ σπλάγχνοις δὲ κάθηται.

But here two ideas are conveyed : (1) the god flits from one person to another, (2) he sits *upon* the σπλάγχνα.   But can the words *humano corde volare* mean either the one or the other ? and what is the meaning of love sitting upon the σπλάγχνα ?   It may either be that he takes his station on the heart, as his natural seat and abode ; or that he perches there as a bird of prey, to feed on the vitals of the man, as the eagle on the liver of Prometheus.   Postgate quotes line 15 in favour of his view ; but the very next lines seem to show the true meaning of ἐπὶ σπλάγχνοις κάθηται :

Evolat heu ! nostro quoniam de pectore nusquam,
Assiduusque meo sanguine bella gerit,

i e. the god never leaves his breast but carries on the war with, or at the cost of, his (i.e. the poet's) blood.   The Abl. is one of Attend. Circums.   In lines 5 and 6 there is nothing about war, blood, or preying : they simply say that the artist properly represented Love as furnished with wings, and ' made him *humano corde* fly as a god.' Can these words not mean ' possessed of the *cor* (i. e. the heart, the feelings, and so almost the personality), of a man, but flying with wings as a god ? '   *Humano corde* would thus be an ablative of quality.   *Cor* is used, and especially *corculum*, to denote a person ; and the position of the words suggests an antithesis between *humano* and *deum*.   In such a connection it is not unnatural to say that Love is represented as having a human heart, i.e. as a man, and at the same time flying as only a god can fly.   If *humano corde* be an ablative of place, the only way of extracting Postgate's meaning would be to translate ' flies *from* the human heart,' i.e. from one to another.   Baehrens reads *humano calce*.   He probably means the allusion to be to the *talaria*, or small wings attached to the heel, which we see in representations of Cupid and Mercury.

7. The idea of flying in air suggests that of floating on rising and falling waves, at the caprice of every wind.

8. nostra, like *suus*, applied to a wind, naturally suggests the idea of 'favourable.'   But in itself, as here, 'our wind' simply means 'the wind which bears us,' any further meaning depending on the context.

non ullis locis, exactly parallel to *nusquam* line 15.

10. pharetra Gnosia, i. e. Cretan, from Gnosus or Gnosos (Κνωσός), now Cnosson, the abode of Minos and the ancient capital

of Crete.   The Roman poets loved to particularise a general term
by some local or specific epithet, not merely to give a flavour of
learning (whence 'doctus' is the characteristic epithet of a poet),
but also because they understood that representative art attains its
object best when it calls up concrete individual images.   The object
of poetry is to rouse feeling ; and feeling gathers round the particular,
not the general.   On this principle Horace's sailor is *Poenus* Od. 2.
13. 15 ; wine is Falernian, Massic, Chian, Lesbian, etc.; merchan-
dise is Syrian (1. 31. 12) or Thynian (3. 7. 3), Cyprian or Tyrian
(3. 29. 60); a sea is the Myrtoan (1. 1. 14) or the Tyrrhenian (1. 11.
5) or the Cretan (1. 26. 2) or the Caspian (2. 9. 2), etc.   Such instances could be multiplied indefinitely from Horace and Virgil alone.

utroque.   Thus the quiver hung from both shoulders.   Paley
supposes that two positions of the quiver are referred to : one at the
back, when it was not in use, and hung from both shoulders; the
other when drawn to one side for the purpose of taking out an
arrow.   *Utroque* shows that here the former position is indicated :
thus *quoniam*, line 11, means 'Love holds the barbed arrow
ready in his hand because (*quoniam*) he aims instantaneously
and does not wait to draw the arrow from the quiver.'   In other
words, 'Love shoots so rapidly that he keeps his quiver where it is
not ready for use!'   The reference of *quoniam* to *manus armata*
is far-fetched : the word merely explains why he is portrayed as an
equipped archer.

11. tuti, i. e. in our supposed safety.   The word is used ironically ; for *tutus* implies emphatically protection from actual danger.
Securus, 'without care,' implies only an unconsciousness of the existence of danger, and *incolumis*, 'unharmed,' that as yet no injury has
been sustained.

12. ex, 'out of,' 'immediately after,' and so 'in consequence
of,' as here.

13. In me, cp. sup. 10. 6.   But the words may mean simply,
'his darts remain fast in me.'

puerilis imago corresponds to *humano corde* l. 6.   'He
remains fast, in his boyish image ; but his wings (cp. *volare*) are
gone.'

15. heu, as not unfrequently, is represented only by *ĕ* in N.

nusquam, 'does not fly out anywhither,' i. e. at all.   As Postgate remarks, Latin has no one word for 'no whither.'   *Non aliquo*
or *non alio* would be the nearest equivalents : cp. *alio* l. 18.

Hertz. well illustrates ll. 14–15 from the *Anthology*.   A lover
complains that Love has emptied on him all his quiver :

R

μὴ πτερύγων τρομέοι τις ἐπήλυσιν· ἐξότε γάρ μοι
λάξ ἐπιβὰς στέρνοις πικρὸν ἔπηξε πόδα,
ἀστεμφής, ἀδόνητος ἐνέζεται, οὐδὲ μετέστι,
εἰς ἐμὲ συζυγίην κειράμενος πτερύγων.

Here Love tramples on the lover's breast, and, having lost his wings, cannot fly away.

16. See note on l. 6.

17. siccis medullis. Love has drained him of his life-blood, either by the wounds of his arrows, or actually by drinking it. Thus Theocr. Id. 2. 55 represents Love as fastening like a leech on to the lover's flesh and drinking his blood dry.

18. 'Carry thy darts elsewhither.' Hous. defends *tela, puer* (V²).

19. veneno, a new metaphor : but perhaps the idea may be that of a poisoned arrow, to which the word *vapulat*, l. 20, is more appropriate.

20. tenuis umbra mea, probably in allusion to the poet's slender make, inf. 2. 22. 21
   Sed tibi si exiles videor tenuatus in artus ;
and 1. 5. 21
   Nec iam pallorem totiens mirabere nostrum,
   Aut cur sim toto corpore nullus ego.

21. talia, 'such verses as mine.'

23, 24. The authority of N. for *qui* in l. 23, and *canat* in l. 24, is conclusive. L. 22 must be taken parenthetically. *Quae canit* may make, as Pinder says, a smoother ending, but *qui canat* is more forcible; it implies not merely that he sings his mistress's charms, but that it would be an unbearable loss to Love that they should remain unsung.

II. 13.

THE following elegy has an exordium of sixteen lines prefixed to it in the MSS., which Lachmann and other editors believe, without sufficient reason, to have formed a separate poem. Those lines repeat the oft-told, well-worn theme that love for Cynthia is the inspirer of the poet's muse ; and though lighter in tone than the succeeding verses, which deal with the poet's death and funeral, the contrast is scarcely stronger than is to be found in other passages. His love for Cynthia is the one portal through which Propertius approaches every subject ; and we have seen elsewhere (especially 2. 1. 71-78) in how morbid (or shall we say puerile?) a fashion he drags in the idea of his death whenever his love has met a check. Our own Laureate has coupled ' Love and Death :' Propertius constantly couples the two ideas, but in a spirit very different from that which prompted the words,   •

> *I know not which is sweeter, no not I.*

17. igitur; cp. *igitur* in the exactly parallel passage, 2. 1. 71

> *Quandocumque igitur vitam mea fata reposcent.*

In both passages a contemplation of his death is made to follow, as by a natural consequence, upon an emphatic protestation of his love.

18. acta, 'the arrangements' or 'dispositions' for his funeral. They are called *acta*, because made, decided upon, during his life. Postgate well compares the phrase *acta Caesaris*, which occurs so often in Cic. Phil. 2, of the various dispositions for the future conduct of affairs made (or at least pretended by Antony to have been made) by Caesar before his death.

19. He desires no long array of ancestral images to follow him to the grave—for the very good reason that he had no claim to such a distinction. All *nobiles*, i. e. descendants of men who had held curule office, were allowed to have waxen images or busts of their distinguished ancestors ranged round the *atrium* of the house. This right was called *ius imaginum*. The relationship between the originals of the busts was indicated by garlands or strings, *stemmata*, the prototype of the modern pedigree or genealogical table. Hence the well-known *Stemmata quid faciunt?* of Juv. 8. 1. At a funeral, these busts, which seem to have been hollow, were put on by persons who represented the dead worthies, and who, wearing the dress and insignia which the dead would have worn, walked before the bier in long procession to the place of burning or interment, so that the deceased seemed actually to be escorted to the grave by the whole series of his ancestors. In the case of the older families, these processions must have been extraordinarily imposing. In recording the death of Tiberius' son Drusus, Tacitus himself was moved at the thought of what must have been one of the most grotesque and yet impressive sights ever witnessed. There passed forth, says the historian, 'in long array all the fathers of the Julian house—Aeneas, all the Alban kings, then the Sabine nobility with Attus Clausus, and all the rest of the Claudii,' Ann. 4. 9. See Juv. 8. 2 sqq.; Ov. Fast. 1. 591; Hor. Epod. 8. 12.

imagine, in the singular, as though it were a collective noun.

20. tuba. At the head of the funeral procession marched musicians, flute-players, hornblowers, and trumpeters; hence *tuba* sometimes stands for death, as in Pers. 3. 103

> *Hinc tuba, candelae.*

fati is an objective genitive after *querela*.

21. fulcro eburno, ablative of quality or description; the *lectus* is the funeral bier, often richly ornamented, on which the body was carried to burial.

Attalico, either ' sumptuous,' from the wealth of the kings of Pergamus, as in Hor. Od. 1. 1 *Attalicis condicionibus ;* or, as Postgate suggests, ' embroidered with gold,' an art which Plin. N. H. 8. 48 attributes to the last Attalus. Cp. *Attalicas vestes* 3. 18. 19. In 2. 32. 12 the handsome hangings in the *Porticus Pompeia* are called *aulaea Attalica.*

22. mors mea, i. e. 'my body when dead,' 'my dead body.' Exactly similar are the expressions *nostrae vitae,* 1. 2. 31, 'to me so long as I live ;' *mea poena* 2. 20. 31, 'my shade while undergoing punishment ;' *meum funus* 1. 17. 8, 'my dead body.' Cp. Virg. Aen. 9. 491

> *Et funus lacerum tellus habet ?*

23. lancibus. Descriptive Abl. 'Let there be no train of incense-bearing chargers.' Cf. Virg. Aen. 3. 618 *domus sanie dapibus-que cruentis.* Post. compares II. 32. 13, *creber platanis surgentibus ordo.* Perfumes were thrown on the body when first laid out, Pers. 3. 103 ; they were carried in chargers along with the procession, as here ; they were thrown on to the body when placed on the *rogus ;* they were finally mingled with the ashes before they were deposited in the urn. The senses of smell and hearing must thus have been fully occupied at a Roman funeral. When Juvenal wishes to describe an over-scented fop he makes him reek *quantum vix redolent duo funera* Sat. 4. 109 ; and when Horace describes an overpowering din, he says

> *Cornua quod vincatque tubas,*

i. e. those of a funeral, Sat. 1. 6. 44. A funeral conducted without pomp was called *tacitum funus,* 'a quiet funeral :' a phrase which strikes strangely on our ears. Cp. Ov. Tr. 1. 3. 22.

25. This line has not unnaturally been interpreted to prove that Propertius when he wrote this Elegy must have published at least two complete books, and have been engaged upon a third. But we have already seen that the arguments for supposing that the first ten Elegies of Book II. formed a completed book are of little weight ; and the whole treatment of the subject of death in this elegy is so imaginative and unreal—not real enough to be called morbid—that it is unnecessary to suppose a reference here to any actual number of completed or even contemplated books. Three books form a modest complete number ; less than three would be meagre, either for a poet or a procession ; three was the number of books which Horace first published as a completed edition of his

Odes.　And whatever inference could be drawn from this passage is more than overborne by 2. 24. 1, 2

> *Tu loqueris cum sis iam noto fabula libro.*

26. feram, probably the subjunctive, ' for me to present.'

27. pectus lacerata, with middle sense. The futures *sequeris, pones*, imply a softened, courteous imperative, a hope or recommendation, rather than a command, as in Hor. A. P. 385

> *Tu nihil invita dices faciesque Minerva.*

Hence the usage is mainly confined to epistles and similar friendly communications.

28. fueris, probably the future perfect, as *nec* precedes.　Yet Prop. uses *nec* for *neu*, as in 2. 28. 47.

lassa vocare.　Postgate seems somewhat to over-refine here when he says that the infinitive denotes ' the cause of the weariness, not the result arrested by it.'　Like other infinitives dependent on an adjective, it is used vaguely to denote the sphere within which the adjective applies : *lassa vocare* is ' wearied in calling,' just as *doctae psallere Chiae* (Hor.) is ' learned in playing,' and *celerem sequi Aiacem* (id.) is ' swift in following.'

30. Syrio.　The Roman poets call all wares which came from the far East *Syrian*, because they were shipped at a Syrian port —chiefly Antioch.

onyx, in reference to the costly perfumes poured on to the pyre, or mingled with the ashes in the urn.　*Onyx* or *Onychites* or *Lapis Alabastrites* was a kind of gypsum or spar, so called from its colour resembling the white of the human nail.　This material was much used to make vessels for holding perfumes, as it was supposed to possess the property of preserving their fragrance.　Such flasks were usually made with a narrow neck—such as we see in museums —from which the liquor was allowed to escape drop by drop. Hence the extravagance of the woman in St. Mark 14. 3, who, ' having an alabaster box of ointment of spikenard very precious,' instead of letting it out by drops, ' brake the box and poured it on his head.'

31. ardor, for ' flame.'

32. manes, here equivalent to *cineres*, from the idea of the spirit hovering about them.　Cp. Virg. Aen. 4. 34 and 427.

testa, an urn of common pottery.

33. laurus, the bay or laurel of Apollo ; hence used to denote poetic fame.

busto.　See note on 1. 19. 21, where the origin of our word ' bust' is explained.　The effigies of the dead and their families which were commonly placed on the lid of a Roman sarcophagus, may sometimes have been likenesses of the deceased; but it is evident from modern excavations that they were kept ready-made by the stone-cutters, and executed after conventional patterns. It seems a novel and interesting idea that a man might 'choose' his father or mother—though not till after their decease.

34. funeris, his remains, now reduced to ashes; cp. sup. on l. 22.

umbra, of the shade of the laurel bough, in predicative apposition to *quae:* translate, 'to cover with its shade the spot where lie my lifeless remains.'

35. horrida, of the revolting, loathsome ashes, so out of keeping with the idea of joyous love.

37. notescet fama. The expression is redundant; it was not the *fama* of his sepulchre, but the sepulchre itself, which would become known. Postgate has some interesting observations (Introd. p. lxvii) on Propertius' tendency to what he terms 'disjunctiveness,' or 'polarisation' of an idea, by which he charges his meaning doubly, serving up one idea in two forms, and treating each form as a new idea. A good example is 3. 1. 17

> *Sed, quod pace legas, opus hoc de monte sororum*
> *Detulit intacta pagina nostra via.*

Here the *opus* and the *pagina* are one and the same thing; yet the latter is said to bring down the former from the mount of the Muses.

38. Phthii viri, i. e. Achilles.

cruenta, because Polyxena, daughter of Priam, was sacrificed by Neoptolemus, his son, upon his tomb.

39. si quando, denoting an indefinite, though certain, time: 'when the day comes, whenever that may be.'

venies ad fata, a euphemism for death: later Latin was fond of such softened modes of expressing death. See especially in Tacitus, where such phrases as *decessit, excessit, exiit,* etc., are constant. Cp. our own phrase 'he is gone,' or 'he's away.'

40. lapides, his monument.

cana, he trusts she may not die till of ripe age.

For **memores** cp. Hor. Od. 3. 11. 51

> *nostri memorem sepulcro*
> *Scalpe querelam,*

and 4. 14. 4

> *Per titulos memoresque fastos.*

It is far-fetched to suppose that *memores* anticipates the idea of the next couplet, that his ashes will have some consciousness of her: especially as *interea,* l. 41, marks a new transition.

42. ad verum sapit, 'has some sense towards, in the direction of, truth.'

conscia, is simply 'conscious,' 'sentient:' here the spirit is not only conscious, but *ad verum sapit*, i. e. can form true ideas.

43. primis cunis, 'the cradle that ushers in life;' exactly like *extremus* in 3. 2. 22

> *Mortis ab extrema condicione vacant.*

ponere, 'to lay down,' 'give up.'

45. quo, 'for what purpose?' constructed both with the nom. and acc.

47. The MSS. have *Quis tam longaevae*, which is clearly corrupt. Hertz. has *Cui si longaevae:* the correction *Cui si tam longae* seems best. *Cui si* written in one word would become *quis*, and then *longae* would be lengthened into *longaevae* for the metre.

48. The first word is quite uncertain: the two first letters were probably lost in the archetype, as Palmer suggests. **Gallicus** is a very unnatural word to use of a Phrygian in reference to the Homeric period: *Ilius* (Lachmann) would give a harsh jingle: and *bellicus* (Palmer) is tame. Postgate justly thinks that a proper name is required; and would defend *Gallicus* as referring to Hector, the Γάλλος being a river in Phrygia (Herodian 1. 11. 2), with which Hector *may* have been connected in some legend. If Memnon be referred to, who killed Antilochus while defending his father, he thinks the passage corrupt.

49. See Juv.'s imitation, S. 10. 246–255. Hous. approves Müller's *aut* for *ille*: see J. of Phil. xxi. p. 114.

51. flebis, a gentle request, as above, ll. 27, 29.

53. qui, the MS. reading, has been needlessly altered to *cui*. Palmer well quotes Ov. Her. 20. 103: the word *testis* does not imply that 'a boar was a witness to a moral truth' (Paley), any more than Hor. Od. 3. 4. 69

> *Testis mearum centimanus Gyas*
> *Sententiarum*

implies that the giant Gyas gave evidence in support of Horace's opinions. *Testis* simply means 'affords proof or evidence of.'

55. Illis, with reference to *Idalio vertice*.

By an awkward construction, *diceris* must be supplied to go with *lavisse* from *diceris isse* l. 56.

iacuisse: so NO. Palmer adopts *lavisse*, the reading of Per. which was adopted by Scaliger. He informs me that H. A. J. Munro approved of it. To make Adonis *lie* in marshes seems absurd, and

iacuisse is just the correction which a scribe might make who supposed *paludibus* to refer to the boar.

57. revocabis, partly in the sense of 'recalling,' as in 2. 27. 15,
partly in that of 'calling on him in the hope of a reply,' as l. 58
suggests.

58. qui. Palmer appears to be the first who has supported
here the reading of N., which has been changed without reason to
quid by the editors. *Qui* gives a much richer, more pathetic meaning.

II. 28.

THIS again is one of the most touching and natural of the Cynthia
poems. It is written in genuine anxiety, on the occasion of some
serious illness of Cynthia's. With earnest prayers for her recovery
the poet mingles admonitions, half serious, half playful, that the illness has been brought on as a punishment for some fault of her own,
either for neglect of some god, or for lover's vows forsworn. In the
contemplation of the possibility of her death, while paying a very
touching tribute to her charms, the poet exhibits that matter-of-fact
coolness which is a constant characteristic of the ancients in treating
of death and its surroundings, and which conveys a feeling of insensibility, almost of hardness, to the modern reader. If the ancients
had less of the hope, they had also less of the sense of awe and
mystery, which we feel in the contemplation of death.

The poem is divided into three parts: and some editors, amongst
them Palmer, consider that they form three distinct poems. In the
first part, ll. 1-34, the poet expresses his fears as to her illness, suggests its cause, and both warns and comforts her by mythological examples. In the second part, ll. 35-46, he fears the worst, and makes
an impassioned appeal for her recovery. In the third, ll. 47-62, he
thanks Persephone for having spared for a while longer her intended
victim, and bids her pay the vows due for her recovery. Baehrens,
as will be seen from the critical notes, unnecessarily turns the poem
upside down. The same illness is alluded to in 2. 9. 25

Haec mihi vota tuam propter suscepta salutem,

but there is little to suggest the dates at which the two poems were
written. See, however, Hertz., Quaest. p. 224.

1. affectae, i. e. *morbo.*

2. tuum crimen, i.e. 'the death of so lovely a maiden will be
laid as a charge at thy door,' *tuum* being here used objectively. So
Ov. Am. 2. 11. 35, to the Nereids,

Vestrum crimen erit talis iactura puellae.

3. The illness occurred at the most unhealthy period of the year; the time when attention to business, according to Hor. Ep. 1. 7. 9

> *Adducit febres et testamenta resignat.*

4. **fervēre.** Archaic for *fervēre:* so Virg. Aen. 8. 677.

8. **ventus et unda rapit**, an image for forgotten words or vows, frequent in the ancient poets.   So Cat. 70. 3

> *Dicit: sed mulier cupido quod dicit amanti*
> *In vento et rapida scribere opertet aqua.*

See Ov. Am. 1. 8. 106; 2. 16. 45.

9. **illa**, read by NO, is probably right: cf. *Juppiter ille =* ' yonder,' ' in the heavens.'   See Hous., J. of Phil. xxi. p. 131.

peraeque.   So N., followed by Palm. and Post.   Most editors adopt the reading of Gron. *paremque*, which must be translated ' compared, ay and placed on a level with, herself.' Palmer follows N. in reading *illa peraeque*, and places the mark of interrogation after *Venus;* and he justifies *peraeque invidiosa* by Cic. Att. 2. 19 *tam peraeque omnibus ordinibus offensa.*   But the addition of *omnibus* makes an important difference, ' to all orders equally.' Cicero would not have written *peraeque ordinibus offensa.* If the reading of the text be correct, *formosis* must be taken as equivalent to *formosis omnibus.*

10. **Prae se**, with *formosis:* ' those whose beauty outshines her own.'

11. **Pelasgae**, emphatic epithet = ' Greek,' or rather ' Argive,' as Juno is essentially the friend of the Greek or Argive cause, the enemy of the Trojan.   So in Virg. Aen. 547 Aeneas propitiates her anger:

> *Iunoni Argivae iussos adolemus honores.*

12. **bonos**, ' beautiful.'   So Ov. Met. 8. 678 *super omnia vultus Accessere boni*, just as we speak of ' good looks,' ' good-looking,' ' a good head,' etc.   To the Greeks and Italians, accustomed to dark eyes, it was apparently a moot point whether the gray or blue eye of γλαυκῶπις Ἀθήνη could be considered a beauty; and indeed the epithet γλαυκῶπις refers rather to the fierceness than to the colour of her eye.   The ancients associated fierceness with light eyes as we do with dark : thus Tac. Germ. 4 describes the fair-haired Germans as having *truces et caerulei oculi, rutilae comae.*

11, 12. **tibi ... ausa.**   The construction abruptly changes : *tibi* in l. 11 leads up to *tu* to be supplied before *ausa.*   So in 1. 6. 21, 22 *tibi* has to be supplied from *tua:*

> *Nam tua non aetas umquam cessavit amori,*
> *Semper et armatae cura fuit patriae.*

13. semper ... non nostis, 'Ye have never known.' Cp. 1. 16. 7

> *Et mihi non desunt turpes pendere corollae*
> *Semper.*

14. lingua nocens, 'an ill tongue.' The poet means that she was punished by the Gods for talking proudly.

16. mollior hora, 'a happier time.' So in 1. 7. 4 *mollia* means ' favourable : '

> *Sint modo fata tuis mollia carminibus.*

Cp. Ov. Trist. 4. 8. 32.

17. Io, daughter of Inachus, king of Argos (whence she is called *Inachis* 1. 3. 20), loved by Zeus and turned into a cow by the jealousy of Here, after many wanderings found peace on the banks of the Nile, where she became associated or identified with the goddess Isis. Ovid describes her metamorphosis from a cow into a goddess, Met. 1. 728–750, till at last l. 743

> *De bove nil superest, formae nisi candor, in illa ;*

and l. 747

> *Nunc dea linigera colitur celeberrima turba.*

19. Ino, daughter of Cadmus, was married as a second wife to Athamas, and became mother of Learchus and Melicertes. The jealousy of the first wife Nephele wrought ruin in the house: Athamas, in madness, slew Learchus. Ino flung herself with Melicertes into the sea. She was then admitted amongst the sea-gods under the name *Leucothea,* and subsequently, by some strange confusion, was identified with the Latin goddess Matuta. See Ov. Fast. 6. 545 ; Cic. Tusc. 1. 12. 28.

21. Andromede, daughter of Cepheus and Cassiopeia, saved from the sea-monster by Perseus, became his wife : she was afterwards placed among the stars. See Ov. Met. 4. 662 foll.

23. Callisto, an Arcadian huntress and follower of Artemis, was loved by Zeus and metamorphosed into a she-bear. Slain in the chase by Artemis, she was transformed by Zeus into the famous constellation of Arctos or Septemtrio, which we still know by the name of the Great Bear.

26. This line is very harsh, and has been variously emended. See critical notes. As it stands in the text, *fata* in l. 25 must be the fates, *fata* l. 25 Cynthia's lot or portion after death. *Illa* must refer to the description of her future condition given in ll. 27-30, and is used instead of *haec* in order to express the distance and grandeur of the scene. 'In these grand respects will the lot of thy burial be happy.'

27. Semele, daughter of Cadmus, being loved of Zeus, requested that he would visit her in all his splendour: he appeared as the god of thunder, and she was consumed.

There is no need to change **sit** into *sis*, for which, as Hertz. points out, *fueris* would be required. **formosa** stands for the class of the beautiful: 'at what peril a fair maiden lives,' 'what are the perils of the fair.'

periclo is an ablative of attendant circumstance, analogous or equivalent to the ablative of price.

29. Maeonias, 'Lydian :' either for 'Eastern' in general, or specially 'Homeric,' as not unfrequently in Ovid. Thus we have *Maeonium carmen* E. P. 3. 3. 31, *Maeoniae chartae* id. 4. 12. 27, etc.

The young student will observe that **omnis** here is the accusative plural, which was frequently written with *is* for *es* in the case of *i* nouns. So in l. 56.

32. durus dies, i. e. 'the day of death,' called *niger ille dies* 2. 24. 34.

33. Schultze supposes this line to be addressed to Jupiter, the *deus* of l. 32. 'Spare Cynthia, Jupiter : Juno herself will permit this, without feeling a wife's jealousy.' But this is far-fetched, and the address to Jupiter is out of place. Cynthia is addressed throughout; 'even fate may relent: even Juno with all her jealousy as a wife will forgive thee in this,' lit. 'will pardon this to thee,' i. e. will permit her to live, instead of unrelentingly pursuing her, as in the cases given above. The poet throughout assumes that it is the fatal gift of beauty that is the cause of Cynthia's illness.

coniunx may carry with it the additional idea that Juno is the goddess of marriage and married women, and that her compassion might specially be appealed to on a wife's behalf.

34. frangitur, i. e. *animo* : 'is touched,' 'grieved.' Cp. our 'heart-broken.'

35. At this point a new poem commences in N., whilst Jacob and Lachmann make a third separate poem of ll. 47–62. But in reality these points only mark subdivisions in the sense of an essentially connected whole. See the argument as given in the English headings. The first part, ll. 1–34, is addressed to Cynthia : he declares the cause of her malady, comforts her by mythological examples, and bids her, even yet, have hope. In the second part, ll. 35–46, his panic becomes acute : he has all but lost hope, magic rites have failed, he makes one last despairing appeal for her recovery. The concluding portion is a paean of joy over her safety : she has been spared by Persephone, who indeed, he thinks, might well spare her for a while longer, and she is bidden to pay the vows offered during her illness.

The *rhombus* or *turbo*, a four-sided wheel or reel, was a favourite implement of ancient sorceresses, and was used mainly in love incantations. To this the *licia*, or threads, were attached, and as the reel revolved the witch was supposed to control the fate of her victim. See Ov. Fast. 2. 573 (Ramsay's n.). In Cynthia's case it had been used as a healing spell, or to forecast the result of her illness. Cp. 3. 6. 25

> *Non me moribus illa, sed herbis improba vicit:*
> *Staminea rhombi ducitur ille rota.*

For a new explanation see Dict. Ant. (new ed.).

36. Omens were taken from the burning of laurel leaves in the fire : it was a favourable sign if they burnt brightly and crackled on the hearth. See Tibull. 2. 5. 79, and note, and Ov. Fast. 4. 742. So too with sacrifices, it was an unfavourable sign if the flesh was not well consumed, Soph. Antig. 1006

> ἐκ δὲ θυμάτων
> Ἥφαιστος οὐκ ἔλαμπεν, ἀλλ' ἐπὶ σποδῷ
> μυδῶσα κηκὶς μηρίων ἐτήκετο
> κάτυφε κἀνέπτυε.

37. For the power of witches to call down the moon from the sky see 1. 1. 19

> *At vos deductae quibus est fallacia Lunae,*

and Virg. E. 8. 69, Hor. Epod. 5. 45, Ov. Met. 12. 263.

38. nigra avis, apparently the owl, whose cry was ill omened (*nigra*): Arethusa deems it so 4. 3. 59, and Virgil, Aen. 4. 462, speaks of *ferali carmine bubo*. Paley suggests that ' the black bird ' is the raven, but quotes no parallel.

39. ratis fati, a very modern expression, ' the bark of fate ; ' the genitive being used loosely to indicate any kind of connection. So *lumina fastus* 1. 1. 3, *mortis lacrimae* 4. 7. 69, *tela fugae* 3. 9. 54.

40. velificata, 'making sail.' Used passively by Juv. 10. 174 *velificatus Athos*, ' sailed through.'

41. miserere. We may assume from l. 44 that Jupiter is the deity here addressed : it is implied in the earlier part of the poem that Jupiter is the natural friend, as the jealous Juno is the natural enemy, of fair maidens.

43. ' I mulct myself in a poem,' i. e. undertake to write one.

Professor Palmer reads *crimine*; and there certainly is a difficulty in *carmine*. Many passages might be quoted where an *offering* is mentioned in such cases as this, and the *carmen* is the dedicatory

verse or verses; but where is the offering here? After *puella* in
l. 44, *dedicavit hoc munus* is clearly understood : where and what is
the *munus?* Arethusa, in 4. 3. 71, dedicates her husband's arms
and writes the *carmen* under them :

> *Armaque cum tulero portae votiva Capenae,*
> *Subscribam ' salvo grata puella viro.'*

It is probable, therefore, that some sacred gift is referred to in l. 43,
for which Propertius was to write an inscription.   The words *per
magnum salva puella Iovem* seem too insignificant for an offering by
themselves. ' Operosum sane carmen !' is Palmer's note : but it is not
clear what he means when he adds ' *sacro crimine damnatus* idem
significat atque illud " voti reus."' What is the force of *crimine?*
A gift or vow of some sort is no doubt implied, for which Propertius was to write an inscription : the gift might be trivial, but to
Propertius the important thing was that he was to write the verses,
and so he mentions them only, saying nothing about the offering.
For *damno* with an ablative in the sense of 'mulct' cp. Plaut.
Pers. 69 *Sed legirupam qui damnet det in publicum Dimidium*,
where *qui* is the ablative.

45. operata, the correction of Heinsius. If *adoperta* were
read, the reference would be to the fact that in prayer or thanksgiving
to a god the head was veiled, while the right hand was raised to
the lips—hence *adoro*, ' to worship.'

46. In the critical note N should be added to O as joining ll.
47–62 to the preceding part of this poem.

49,50. I. e. ' You have so many fair ones with you in the shades,
you may surely spare this one.'

51. Iope is the reading of the best MSS. Others read *Io*, *Iole*,
Antiope. Iope, usually known by the longer form of the name as
Cassiopeia, was daughter of Aeolus, wife of Cepheus, and mother of
Andromeda. According to one version of the legend, Cassiopeia
roused the anger of the Nereids by boasting of her own beauty as
surpassing theirs.

Tyro, loved by the river-god Enipeus, to whom she bore Pelias
and Neleus.

52. Europe, the famous daughter of Phoenix (or Agenor), from
whom the continent derives its name. She was carried off by Zeus in
the form of a bull from Phoenicia to Crete, where she gave birth to
Minos: see Hor. Od. 3. 27.

nec proba Pasiphae, 'the infamous Pasiphae,' wife of Minos.
For the remarkable expression *nec proba* standing for *et improba* cp.
nec umquam vorans Charybdis 2. 26. 53, 54 = *numquam vorans.*

53. There is, perhaps, no sufficient objection to the MS. reading in this line, though the repetition of *Priami regna* in the next line, and the coupling of *Phoebi* and *Priami*, are suspicious. Hertzberg, founding on the *Hioa* or *Hiona* of Scaliger's MS., reads *Eoa*, supposing that it may be used as a feminine substantive for 'the region of the East.' But see critical notes.

55. in numero, as we say 'was accounted of:' placed in the number of those worthy of being mentioned. Cp. Cic. de Orat. 3. 56 *sine hac* (actione) *summus orator esse in nullo numero potest.* But *numerus* may be used for the mere multitude, those not worthy of being taken into consideration : as Hor. Epp. 1. 2. 27

> *Nos numerus sumus et fruges consumere nati.*

The Greek ἀριθμός is similarly used in both senses: cp. Plut. 2. 682 F οὐδεὶς ἀριθμοῦ ἐστί τινος (= *nullo est in numero*), with Eur. Her. 997

> εἰδὼς μὲν οὐκ ἀριθμόν, ἀλλ' ἐτητύμως
> ἀνδρ' ὄντα τὸν σὸν παῖδα.

58. Cp. Hor. Od. 2. 3. 25, Ov. Met. 10. 33.

59. The MSS. have *demissa*: the confusion between *de* and *di* is continual.

II. 31.

THIS poem gives an account of the famous temple of Apollo on the Palatine, built by Augustus to celebrate his Sicilian victory over Sextus Pompeius, and to fulfil a vow made in the Actian campaign. It was begun B.C. 36, and dedicated on the 24th of October, B.C. 28. Propertius had made an appointment to visit Cynthia: he arrived late, and he offers as his excuse that he has been present at the dedication of the temple. In honour of the same event Horace wrote Od. 1. 31. The temple, with the colonnades round it, was attached to Caesar's palace. Its distinguishing feature was that it contained the famous Palatine library, adorned with the busts of poets, so frequently mentioned by the Roman poets. The first librarian was C. Julius Hyginus. Cp. Hor. Epp. 1. 3. 17

> *Scripta Palatinus quaecunque recepit Apollo,*

and 2. 1. 216 *munus Apolline dignum :* see Suet. Aug. 29.

1. veniam. The poet presents the poem as his excuse on arrival.

aurea, probably a general epithet denoting splendour. No doubt there was much gilding about the woodwork of the temple. Cp. the famous so-called 'Golden House' of Nero.

2. aperta, here used in its proper but rare sense as a participle.

The portico or colonnade ran all round the building, like an out-side cloister. The library was placed in one part of this cloister; in another part meetings of the Senate, etc., were held.

3. in speciem, 'dazzlingly,' 'so as to make a show.'

Poenis, here for 'African,' referring to the well-known marble *giallo antico*, so called from its yellow colour, with occasional red veins running through it. Roman shops are full of little saucers, etc., made out of the fragments of this marble.

digesta refers to the regular intervals at which the columns were placed. *Digerere* is the word used for planting trees in rows, as in Virg. Geo. 2. 267. So of asparagus beds, Cato, R. R. 161. 3, and of evenly arranged curls, Mart. 3. 63. 3.

4. femina for *feminea*, like *Romula* for *Romulea, flumen Rhenum*, etc. See note on 3. 2. 11, 3. 3. 7.

5. equidem, with the third person, undoubtedly presents a difficulty, and Palmer's conjecture *Phoebus Phoebo* deserves attention. Ussing however, on Plaut. Amph. 757, quotes various passages to controvert Bentley's dictum that *equidem* is never used with the second or third person or with the plural number before the time of Nero. Persius and Lucan certainly so use it; Pers. 1. 110

> *Per me equidem sint omnia protinus alba,*

and in the present passage, though the verb is in the third person, there is a reference to the first person in *visus mihi,* which might justify the use of *equidem.*

5, 6. Between the columns on one side were placed statues of the fifty daughters of Danaus; opposite to them on the other side were the sons of Aegyptus, their unhappy bridegrooms. See Ov. Trist. 3. 1. 61

> *Signa peregrinis ubi stant alterna columnis*
> *Belides, et stricto barbarus ense pater.*

Hertz., Postgate, Bae., etc., place ll. 5–8 at the end of the piece, to make the description follow the order from the outside to the interior. But in an extempore piece like this it is vain to look for an exact order, and there is a special awkwardness in placing *tacita lyra* l. 6 in immediate juxtaposition to *carmina sonat* l. 16. The order rather is that the poet first mentions the colonnades, then the statues, then the temple itself. In the last couplet he reverts, as the crowning and central point of interest, to the statue of the god himself, arrayed as a *citharoedus,* placed between those of Latona and Diana. Ll. 7, 8 give a very feeble ending to the poem. But, besides this, it is possible that two distinct statues of the god may be referred to. Pliny speaks of a colossal statue of the Tuscan Apollo, in bronze, placed inside the library, and there may have been one in marble in the exterior colonnade. If so, *tacita lyra*, and *in longa carmina veste sonat*, may be characteristic descriptions of the two statues : in the one the lyre was only held in the hand, in the other the god was represented as playing upon it. *Hic equidem* defines the position of the statue first named, as being in the outer colonnade, near the Danaids.

7. steterant. For the tense cp. 1. 12. 11

Non sum ego qui fueram ; mutat via longa puellas ;

and 3. 11. 67

Haec di condiderant, haec di quoque moenia servant.

Myron, the famous Boeotian statuary, born about B.C. 480. He especially excelled in depicting animals.

9. Tum, i. e. in his progress through the building.

claro. The marble used was the white marble of Luna (*Carrara*) still used by statuaries.

The tenses *surgebat, erat*, l. 11, and *steterant*, l. 7, all represent the temple as its contents presented themselves to Propertius at the dedication.

11. The MSS. have **In quo**, but N. omits the **In**. *In quo* does not stand very well for 'upon which' after *templum ;* Hertzberg (followed by Postgate) reads *Et duo*, explaining that there were two chariots, one on each side of the *fastigium*.

12. The folding doors were of ivory; on one panel was carved a group of Gauls being hurled down from the rock at Delphi by the god, on the other the slaying of Niobe's children. This refers to the attack of the Gauls on Delphi in the irruption of B.C. 279.

14. funera, 'the tragic calamity;' or possibly 'the dead children.'

Tantalidos. Niobe was daughter of Tantalus.

15. The repetition of **inter**, as Postgate points out, gives importance to the two goddesses as making us think separately of each. See note on 3. 18. 21 and Hor. Sat. 1. 7. 11, 12.

16. in longa veste, i. e. the long-trailing robe (*palla*) of the citharoedus. Cp. Virg. Aen. 6. 645. A copy of the *Apollo citharoedus* is in the Vatican at Rome.

III. 1.

IN this Elegy Propertius asserts his claims as a poet, acknowledges his masters and his models, proclaims his originality, and
declares that after death his fame will rise triumphant out of all
the attacks of his detractors. It is interesting to compare it with
Hor. Od. 4. 3, which is one of Horace's most artistic Odes, and is
devoted to the same subject. Many of the same ideas run through
both pieces, though the manner of working them in, and the
tone and temper of the two poems, are very different. There is in
the Horatian poem a sense of power, a calm dignity and self-
restraint, a simplicity and faithfulness to fact, an absence of self even
when speaking of self, a true conception of what makes the poet
and what the poet is, lastly a tender music running through the
whole piece, which stamp it as the work of true poetic genius.
We have in the Horatian Ode, as in the Propertian, the idea of the
triumph of the chariot-race, of the influences which mould the
poetic faculty, of the detracting work of envy, of the certainty of
Rome's approving verdict; but Horace has the consummate art to
put every idea in its right place, and give it its importance with
reference to the whole; he speaks with the simplicity and modesty
of true greatness, and proves his right to fame by the very manner
of his renouncing it. Propertius is somewhat fussy in his self-
assertion; he pushes his rivals rudely by; he does not observe a
due order in his ideas, but proclaims his triumph first, records the
grounds for it afterwards, and acknowledges lastly that, after all, it
has not been yet awarded to him : he acquaints us with the source
of his inspiration before he has made us feel that he is inspired,
whereas Horace first makes us *feel* that he is a poet, and not till
then does he tell us that all his merit is the Muse's gift. Lastly, while
Propertius has to glorify his models if he would exalt the copyist,
and looks to such frigid sources of inspiration as Muses' grottoes
and Muses' inspiring founts, Horace appeals to Nature as the true
fashioner of poets in those noble and tuneful words which Words-
worth might fain have written :

> *Sed quae Tibur aquae fertile praefluunt,*
> *Et spissae nemorum comae,*
> *Fingent Aeolio carmine nobilem.*

1–4. Addressing the shades of Callimachus and Philetas, the
poet prays for admission to their sacred grove : then assuming that
his prayer is granted, he claims to be the first inspired bard who
has wedded the rites of Italy to the song of Greece. **Callimachus**

S

and **Philetas** were the two great masters of the Alexandrine
Elegiac School, a school whose characteristic feature was a mixture
of poetry with erudition. Philetas of Cos was the younger of the
two ; he lived under the first Ptolemy, by whom he was appointed
to be tutor to his son Philadelphus, and died probably between 290
and 270 B.C.   Callimachus, a member of the noble family of the
Battiadae of Cyrene, was patronised by Philadelphus and was chief
librarian of the famous Alexandrine library (of which the main part
was burnt during the blockade of Julius Caesar) from circ. 260 to
240 B.C.   Besides being a poet, Callimachus was one of the most
famous grammarians and critics of the Alexandrine school, and his
poems were a marvel of laboured and affected learning.   Fragments
of his hymns and epigrams remain ; but he was especially deemed the
prince of elegiac poetry, and in this branch the best idea of his tortuous
and erudite style is to be obtained from Catullus' adaptation of his
Coma Berenices.   Philetas was deemed second to Callimachus : less
oppressed with learning, he had probably more genuine poetic
feeling. His main works were elegies in praise of his mistress
Bittis or Battis. Propertius speaks of both with the utmost reverence as his masters.   Besides the passage before us, see 3. 9. 43

> *Inter Callimachi sat erit placuisse libellos,*
> *Et cecinisse modis, Coe poeta, tuis.*

In 2. 34. 31–2, whatever reading be adopted, the two poets seem
placed on a par ; but in 3. 3. 51–2 he derives his inspiration from
Philetas alone,

> *Talia Calliope, lymphisque a fonte petitis*
> *Ora Philetaea nostra rigavit aquà.*

l. sacra. As Postgate observes, the word *sacra* may be used
in the widest possible sense, of any 'sacred things' ; whether sacred
rites, or sacred reliques, or even possibly the disembodied spirits of
the departed.   The idea is the same which we have had above,
2. 10. 24.

> *Pauperibus sacris vilia tura damus,*

where see note. The poets are priests of the Muses ; to be admitted to their holy grove, to take part in their holy rites, is to be
admitted a brother of the guild. Callimachus and Philetas being
dead, Propertius addresses their Manes ; and using that 'disjunctiveness' of expression which has been illustrated on 2. 13. 37 (see
Postgate's introduction), he speaks of the *Manes* of Callimachus and
the *sacra* of Philetas as if he meant two distinct things.   What he
means is simply 'O Shades of Callimachus and Philetas, admit me to
your holy grove, and let me too have a share in your holy rites.'

3. ingredior has immediate reference to *ire* l. 2: in l. 4 he changes the idea, and uses the word in the metaphorical sense of 'beginning' or 'undertaking.' Thus instances of the infinitive after *ire*, *pergere*, etc., are not quite in point.

puro de fonte, partly from the idea of priests sprinkling themselves and the worshippers with pure water: partly from that of drinking in inspiration from springs sacred to the Muses. Cp. 3. 3. 51 quoted above.

4. orgia, 'secret rites,' like μυστήρια, especially of the rites of Bacchus. Thus the idea is that the sacred rites and emblems of Italian worship are to be carried on and worshipped under the forms of Greek choric dance and song. In other words, the boast is the same as that more simply expressed by Hor. Od. 3. 30. 13 under a different metaphor,

> *Dicar* . . . . . .
> *Princeps Aeolium carmen ad Italos*
> *Deduxisse modos.*

To take *per* with *Itala orgia*, even if admissible, would be to remove a slight harshness of meaning by a greater harshness of language.

5. pariter, 'side by side;' implying not only that the two poets are equal, but equal in the same style of poetry.

tenuastis, referring to the fineness and finish of their verses. The idea is taken from spinning, to which the drawing out of verses (like our 'spinning a yarn') is so often compared. Cp. Hor. Ep. 2. 1. 225, imitated by Columella 10. 40

> *Pierides tenui deducite carmine Musae.*

So Virg. E. 6. 5

> *deductum dicere carmen.*

antro. Caves and grottoes were specially regarded as haunts of the Muses: artificial grottoes were frequently manufactured in the grounds of Roman villas, and called *musea*. In 3. 2. 14 such grottoes are called *operosa antra* : see too 3. 3. 27.

6. quove pede has no reference to the superstition that it was more lucky to enter a place with the right foot (cp. Juv. Sat. 10. 5

> *Quid tam dextro pede concipis?*

where see Mayor), for (1) *utro* would be required with that sense ; (2) it seems absurd to pronounce these poets unrivalled, and in the same breath to ask whether they had begun their career auspiciously or not; (3) the sense of the whole passage requires a question as to the cause and secret of their success. Postgate is doubtless right in supposing that *pede* conveys a double meaning : (1) the natural one of 'gait,' and so 'march,' 'progress,' 'success;'

(2) a reference to metrical feet. He well quotes a similar confusion or union of ideas from Ov. Am. 3. 1. 8

> *Venit odoratos Elegeia nexa capillos,*
> *Et puto pes illi longior alter erat.*

The ancients were constantly led into false reasonings from not distinguishing between the literal and metaphorical uses of words.

quamve bibistis aquam? continues the same sense, 'From what spring did you gain your inspiration?' The allusion, as in 2. 10. 25, is to the inspiring properties of Hippocrene and other springs.

7. valeat, as we might say 'Good-bye to,' 'Farewell to,' 'Away with.' Cp. Plaut. Amph. 3. 2. 46 and Cic. N. D. 1. 44. 124 *Si talis est deus ut nulla hominum caritate teneatur, valeat,* i. e. 'let me have nothing to say to him.' So Hor. Ep. 2. 1. 180.

Phoebum moratur. Cp. the legal phrase *nihil morari aliquem* = 'to dismiss.'

in armis, i. e. occupies his poetic genius with singing feats of arms.

8. A powerfully concentrated line, in which every word tells. **Exactus** implies finish ; **tenui,** subtlety, fineness, point ; **pumice,** polished smoothness ; **eat,** the stately gliding march or flow of the line, as in Johnson's *With fatal sweetness elocution flows.* To say that *tenui,* 'fine,' stands for 'refining,' is unnecessary ; nothing is commoner, both in ancient and modern poetry, than to court variety by using an adjective with some noun to which it does not strictly apply, leaving the mind insensibly to alter the relation between the words. When Hor. Ep. 1. 19. 18 says *exsangue cuminum,* we translate 'the bloodless cumin,' and need no commentator to tell us that it is the cheek, not the plant, to which the epithet applies. So with *pallidam Pirenen* Pers. Prol. 4, *timor albus* id. 3. 115 ; to translate 'pallor-causing' is to destroy the poetry. Cp. *divitis Nili* Juv. 13. 27. In the present passage, *tenui* could not mean 'refining,' because pumice-stone makes things smooth, not fine ; and it is clear that the epithet derives its point from *versus,* not from *pumice.* Pumice-stone no doubt was used to smoothe the edges of a parchment-roll when finished and rolled up ; but there is no allusion here to a finished book, only to the smooth finish of a line.

eat, used specially of 'flowing,' as in Virg. Aen. 8. 726

> *Euphrates ibat iam mollior undis,*

and so of the flow of verses, Hor. S. 1. 10. 58 *versiculos . . . euntes mollius,* quoted by Post.

9–14. These lines show a rapid development of changing metaphor. In 9 the poet's verse is a flying car, in which Fame carries him aloft; in 10 the car becomes a triumphal chariot, in which his muse, i. e. himself, is borne away, his Loves, like children, by his side (11), and a crowd of poets following at the wheels (12). In 13 he is in a chariot-race, on a course too narrow (14) for his rivals to have any hope of passing him.

9. a me Nata, 'sprung from myself,' 'child of my brain' (Postgate), like the *carmina non prius audita* of Hor. Od. 3. 1. 2.

10. coronatis, the horses of a triumphing general were wreathed with garlands ; and

11. his young sons rode with him in the car: those who had attained to manhood rode on horseback. Tacitus tells us that when Germanicus triumphed he had five children in the car along with him.

12. The crowd of imitator poets follow after the car, as soldiers after their general. **secuta** cannot exactly go with *vectantur*, as they were on foot. Either the general sense of ' marching,' ' advancing,' is to be extracted from *vectantur*, or else *secuta* stands for *secuta fuerit* or *sit = sequatur*.

13. missis, for the more usual *immissis*, of the reins shaken loose upon the horses' necks to urge them on. Thus *immissis habenis* Virg. Aen. 5. 662 ; *immissis frenis* id. 11. 889: the horses themselves are *immissi* Cic. Fam. 10. 30. 3, etc.

in me goes both with *missis* and *certatis*, of the goal or object aimed at. Keats likens a poet to a charioteer in his ' Sleep and Poetry:'

> *For lo! I see afar*
> *O'ersailing the blue cragginess, a car*
> *And steeds with streamy manes—the charioteer*
> *Looks out upon the winds with glorious fear:*
> . . . . *Most awfully intent*
> *The driver of those steeds is forward bent.*

14. currere lata, a rather harsh Greecism: 'broad in the running.' Cp. note on 2. 13. 28. The peculiarity here is that the noun agreeing with the adjective could not be (as usual) the subject of the verb. It is the same kind of harshness to say *via currit* as *pagina detulit opus* below, l. 18. *Currere* might possibly also be taken with *datur ;* or with the whole sentence, instead of with *lata* only. There is no broad-running road, no ' royal road,' to the Muses. Pinder says that two constructions are mixed up here, *non datur ad musas lata via*, and *non datur currere lata via* (ablative). What does this mean? Is it not like saying that ' *lata* should be in the ablative, only it wouldn't scan?'

16. Here again we have the usual prophecy that Augustus will extend the Roman empire to the eastern confines of Parthia. See above, and Virg. Aen. 8. 688, where Bactra (as elsewhere Britain) is called *ultima*.

17, 18. See note on 2. 13. 37. *Pagina detulit opus* is somewhat like *cantarunt scripta Catulli* 2. 34. 87.

Sororum, of the Muses, as in 2. 30. 27.

18. intacta via. Cp. Hor. Od. 3. 2. 22

Virtus . . . negata tentat iter via,

while in Sat. 1. 10. 66 he speaks of Lucilius as

Graecis intacti carminis auctor.

All the poets of the Augustan age are equally emphatic in proclaiming their own originality: so Virg. G. 3. 293 and Hor. Epp. 1. 19. 21

Libera per vacuum posui vestigia princeps,

Non aliena meo pressi pede,

though confessing, in the same breath, that it was only an originality of imitation.

19. Mollia refers to amatory poetry in opposition to the *dura* of Epic. Cat. 16. 4 couples *molliculi* with *parum pudici* of his own verses. So in 4. 1. 61 Ennius has a *hirsuta corona*, he himself asks for one *ex hedera*. See note on 2. 1. 41.

Pegasides, i.e. the Muses. The Greeks knew nothing of Pegasus as the horse of the Muses, beyond the fact that by a kick of his hoof he called up the inspiring fount of Hippocrene. The Roman poets abound in allusions to the poetic character of Pegasus, and go so far as to attribute to the spring of Pirene, near Corinth, where Pegasus was caught by Bellerophon, the same inspiring properties which were possessed by Hippocrene. Thus Persius couples both the *fons caballinus* (Hippocrene) and *pallida Pirene* with the Muses, Prol. 1. 4.

20. faciet used absolutely, without a case. Cp. the phrase *facere*, 'to sacrifice,' where *sacra* must be supplied, Virg. E. 3. 77

Cum faciam vitula pro frugibus, ipse venito.

So *facere ad*, like Mr. Matthew Arnold's phrase, 'to make for righteousness.' Cp. 'the things which make for peace,' Rom. 14. 19. The verb is thus reduced to the mere expression of action, as in the auxiliary use of our *do, does*. We may almost translate here with Postgate 'will do for.'

21. At implies a transition to a new theme, the disparagement of his verses by detractors. Like Horace, Propertius suffered from, and complained of, the unworthy jealousy of rivals: Horace could speak of it with the toleration and temper of a man of the world, and boasts at last that he has lived it down, Od. 4. 3. 16

Et iam dente minus mordeor invido.

21, 22. Cp. Keats:

> *Happy he who trusts*
> *To dear Futurity his darling fame;*

and again

> *These are the pleasures of the bard,*
> *But richer far Posterity's award.*

23, 24. The idea is similar to, but not quite the same as, that of Hor. Od. 3. 24. 31, 32

> *Virtutem incolumen odimus*
> *Sublatam ex oculis quaerimus invidi:*

the contrast here is merely as to the extent of a man's fame.

22. Honos. This passage, with its imitation by Ov. Am. 1. 15. 40, is enough to disprove the dictum that *Honor*, especially in the singular, means necessarily some concrete thing and especially 'a public office.' It is here personified as a quality and is equivalent to *gloria*. See note on Tib. 1. 7. 53.

23. Omnia . . . fingit maiora, 'fashions everything on a larger scale.' *Fingere* refers essentially to the plastic arts and processes, and is applied to the moulding of any ductile substance. It does not therefore mean here simply 'makes greater,' 'magnifies' (Postgate), but it refers to making up, as it were, and fashioning the materials of the past on a new and larger scale. *Fingent nobilem* Hor. Od. 4. 3. 12 is 'will shape into nobility.'

vetustas is the abstract quality implied by *vetus*, which properly means 'old' in the sense of 'having lasted for a long time.' Thus it is applied by Horace to old trees, old wine, old friends, old stories, old poems. *Vetustas* therefore is simply 'length of time,' 'age,' which is here said, in its simplest meaning, to magnify the past. Thus Postgate's explanation is unnecessarily elaborate: 'a prospective-retrospective use, an age to come when the present shall be a distant past.' Pinder is right in translating 'The oldness of things makes them seem greater.' Cp. *vetustate dilapsum* in the Inscription quoted on 3. 2. 12.

24. ab, 'after.' The phrase is imitated, as Postgate points out, by Ov. P. 4. 16. 3.

25. Nam, proceeding to give instances.

pulsas is not very appropriate to **arces**, but this kind of confusion is precisely in the manner of Propertius. The explanation of Paley and Postgate, that when he said *equo pulsas* he had a battering-ram in mind, seems harsh and unpoetical. For the following passage cp. Joanna Baillie:

O who shall lightly say that fame
Is nothing but an empty name,
When but for that our mighty dead,
   All ages past, a blank would be,
Sunk in oblivion's murky bed
   A desert bare, a shipless sea.

26. Haemonio viro, i. e. Achilles, from *Haemonia,* the old name of Thessaly.

27. Postgate adopts G. Wolff's conjecture *Iovis cum prole Scamandro* on the ground that *flumina* shows that *two* rivers must be intended, and that Propertius is referring to Hom. Il. 21. 2, where the Scamander summons the Simois to help him against Achilles. But this change, as Palmer says, is *rescribere non emendare Propertium.* Reading the whole passage 25-30 through, it will be seen that each line contains a single and separate idea, so that Postgate's argument that *flumina,* l. 26, ' shows *two* rivers must be mentioned ' falls to the ground. . Rather the mention of Achilles' river-fight—mainly with the Scamander—calls up the Simois as being famous on another ground. Palmer ingeniously conjectures

Idaeos montes (or *Idaeo sub monte*) *Iovis incunabula parvi,*

quoting Virg. Aen. 3. 105, to show that Crete was looked upon as the ' cradle ' of Jove,

   Mons Idaeus ubi et gentis cunabula nostrae,

and Cic. Att. 2. 41 to illustrate the connection of *montes* with *incunabula: Ad montes patrios et ad incunabula nostra.* R. Ellis, Journal of Phil. 15. p. 18, supports the MS. reading. He well quotes Manilius 2. 25 *Iovis et cunabula magni,* and Ovid's *Iovis incunabula Creten,* and points out that Pacatus Paneg. Theodos. 4 has the very expression of Propertius, *terra Cretensis parvi Iovis gloriata cunabulis.* The confusion between the Trojan and Cretan Ida, and between other similar names in Crete and the Troad, is frequent and well known. See Herz.'s note. But see also Hous., J. of Phil. xxi. p. 126.

28. per campos. Postgate adopts the conjecture *ter* for *per,* regarding it as a certain correction. So Palmer. But it is unnecessary, and does not improve the sense. To say that Hector ' thrice through or across the plain stained the chariot-wheels of Achilles ' is an intelligible mode of saying that three turns or courses were made through the plain, i. e. that he was thrice dragged round the city. But to say that he ' thrice stained the plain, thrice the wheels ' is less obvious in meaning.

29. The termination of this line is unsatisfactory. Polydamas is quoted by Cic., Pers., etc., as the Mrs. Grundy of the time, from his croaking advice to the Trojans to retire behind their walls. But Sil. Ital. 12. 212

> *Polydamanteis iuvenis Pedianus in armis*

shows that there was some story, hitherto unexplained, about the arms of Polydamas which might explain *Polydamantis in armis.* Simpler is *Polydamanta sub armis*, Polydamas being mentioned merely as a Trojan warrior. That *Polydamantis in armis* refers to Paris in l. 30 is unlikely: see n. to l. 27. Palm. now conj. *Polydamanta sine annis*, 'had it not been for their antiquity'; Class. Rev. ii. 39.

30. Paris is reserved for the last, to complete the climax. Paris himself, the *fons et origo* of the whole Trojan disaster, would be unknown to the soil of his own country, were it not for the poets.

Qualemcunque, used absolutely, not relatively: 'of whatever kind he was.' Cp. Quint. 11. 1. 14 *Hoc qualecunque discrimen raro admodum eveniet.*

31. Exiguo sermone. An extension, not uncommon, of the ablative of quality to an absolutely external circumstance. Applied to an individual it would be natural enough, meaning 'with small powers of talk,' just as *exiguo corpore* would mean 'with a small body' (Nep. Ages. 8). The peculiarity here is that the *sermo* is not that of Ilion, but of people *about* Ilion: in other words, Ilion is the *object*, not the *subject*, of the talk.

32. No satisfactory distinction has been established between Ilion (or Ilium) and Troia. In Virg. Aen. 3. 3 both words are used to denote the town exclusively:

> *ceciditque superbum*
> *Ilium, et omnis humo fumat Neptunia Troia.*

Oetaei dei, i.e. Hercules, so called because he erected his funeral pyre on the top of Mount Oeta. Troy was twice taken by Hercules: once by himself, because Laomedon defrauded him of his promised reward for saving his daughter Hesione from the sea-monster; a second time because it was by his arrows, bequeathed to Philoctetes, that Paris was wounded, and the Greeks thus enabled to take the city.

34. Posteritate, simply 'in the after-time.' Surely not, as Postgate suggests, an ablative of the means, 'through posthumous lapse of time.' *Posterus* is not equivalent to 'posthumous:' *postumus* itself does not necessarily, only by implication, mean 'after death;' and *posteritas* means simply 'subsequent-ness.' Cp. Hor. Od. 3. 30. 7

> *usque ego postera*
> *Crescam laude recens,*

where note *crescam* in the same sense as *crescere* here. So Virg. E. 7. 25.

35. It is an over-refinement to say that *Roma* and *seros nepotes* are identical. Rome is the abiding personality of the city which lives through all generations of her sons; she may perfectly well therefore be said 'to praise Propertius amongst her distant grandchildren.'

36. **Illum,** prophetic of the far-off day when his reputation will grow to its full height.

37, 38. His true fame will only be recognised *inter seros nepotes*: but he has secured at least that there shall be no dishonour done to his remains upon his death. The allusion may be either to the directions he has given to Cynthia, above, 1. 19 and 2. 13. 41, 42; or, as some hold *Lycio deo* to indicate, to the admission of his works into the Palatine Library, founded by Augustus, B. C. 28. See 2. 31 and introduction.

39, 40. Most of the MSS. commence a new Elegy with this couplet: Hertz. and other editors place it at the end of El. 1. The two poems seem in any case to be connected together. In the first, Propertius asserts his position as a poet in somewhat high-flown language, and compares himself to Homer. In the second, he descends from this lofty pedestal, and declares that his true function is to sing the praises of maidens. The two lines before us mark the transition; and they seem less abrupt at the end of the First Elegy than at the beginning of the Second. If we so place them, they serve to soften down the high pretensions just made, as though the poet felt he had pitched them in too high a key, and to give a natural unpretending close to the poem. Exactly similar is the light playful ending with which Horace loves to close his more high-strung Odes.

39. in orbem. The usual round or routine of subject which he had struck out for himself. Cp. Ov. Rem. Am. 398

> *gyro curre, poeta, tuo.*

40. N. gives **insolito;** but l. 39 makes that reading impossible.

III. 2.

1. detinuisse. Palmer, following Paley, adopts Ayrmann's conj. *delinisse*. But I feel sure that N.'s reading *detinuisse* is right. The correspondence between *detinuisse* and *sustinuisse* seems intentional. *Detinuisse* is applied to the animals, who were chained to the spot, and kept from going on their ways: *sustinuisse* implies effort and resistance, of the rivers whose onward course was stopped.   So Ov. Fast. 5. 662 applies *sustinere* to water, *cursum sustinuistis aquae*, while Mart. 14. 166 uses *detinere* of the wild beasts :

> *Qui duxit silvas detinuitque feras.*

Similar is the use of *tenere* in 2. 10. 14 where the Euphrates *Crassos se tenuisse dolet.*   *Detineo* is specially used of a subject which occupies the attention : Ov. Trist. 2. 520

> *Saepe oculos memini detinuere meos,*

and Trist. 5. 7. 39

> *Detineo studiis animum falloque labores.*

3. Referring to Amphion : cp. Hor. Od. 3. 11. 2

> *Movit Amphion lapides canendo.*

agitata, simply 'moved.'   **Thebas,** accusative of motion to-wards.   For *Thebas* prob. *Phoebeam* should be read (see Hous.).

5. fera.   Palmer conjectures *freto* without sufficient reason.

8. colit, the indicative mood, because the poet states it as a fact.

9. Quod is here equivalent to 'whereas,' 'although.'   It is properly an accusative of respect 'with regard to the fact that.'

9–11.   This passage gives unmistakeable evidence of a careful study of Horace.   Every one of the ideas in it is to be traced in Horace, though with a different application.   L. 9 corresponds to Od. 3. 1. 45

> *Cur invidendis postibus et novo*
> *Sublime ritu moliar atrium?*

l. 10 to 2. 18. 1–5

> *Non ebur neque aureum*
>   *Mea renidet in domo lacunar ;*
> *Non trabes Hymettiae*
>   *Premunt columnas ultima recisas*
> *Africa :*

and for the meaning of the whole cp. Epod. 1. 25–30.

L. 11 recalls Od. 3. 16. 41

> *Quam si Mygdoniis regnum Alyattei*
> *Campis continuem.*

See too id. 33–36.   For ll. 13, 14, cp. Od. 3. 4. 25

> *Vestris amicum fontibus et choris.*

On the parallel to ll. 17–22, see note on l. 17 : and the concluding lines 23, 24 are a paraphrase on 4. 8. 28, 29

> *Dignum laude virum Musa vetat mori :*
> *Caelo Musa beat.*

11. Phaeacas, acc. plural, from *Phaeacus.*   *Phaeax* is 'a

Phaeacian,' used as a synonym for 'fat and comfortable,' Hor. Ep.
1. 13. 24, and as an adjective by Juv. 15. 23 *Phaeax populus.*

mea, emphatic.

aequant, here intransitive, 'rises to the level of,' 'is equal
to.' The proper meaning is transitive, 'to make equal,' i. e. 'to make
one thing equal to another.' In Virg. Geo. 1. 113

Cum primum sulcos aequant sata,

the meaning is ambiguous : the word may either mean 'make the
furrows equal,' i. e. to each other, by obliterating all signs of the ridges;
or else ' rise to the level of, become equal to, the furrows.'

12. For **operosa antra** see 3. 1. 5 and note. The water for the
grotto was to come from the famous *Aqua Marcia,* the first of the
great Roman aqueducts which was conducted for a considerable
distance on arches. It was built by Q. Marcius Rex, B.C. 145, bringing its water from Sublaqueum (the modern *Subiaco*), a distance of
over sixty Roman miles. Of this distance more than seven miles was
above ground : and the remains of these arches, together with those
of the more magnificent Aqua Claudia (built by the emperor
Claudius), form to this day one of the most impressive features of the
Roman Campagna. In an archway in the ancient walls, close to the
modern Porta S. Lorenzo, are still to be seen high in air the *specus*
or channels by which three of the principal sources of water-supply
reached the city, the *Marcia,* the *Tepula,* and the *Julia.* The lowest
of the three is the Marcia : and it bears the following inscription,
recording its restoration by Vespasian : *Imp. Titus Caesar Divi F.
Vespasianus Aug. Pont. Max. tribuniciae potest. IX Imp. XV Cens.
Cos. VII Design. VIII rivum aquae Marciae vetustate dilapsum
refecit et aquam quae in usu esse desierat reduxit.* Propertius again
speaks of this aqueduct 3. 22. 24

Aeternum Marcius humor opus

The distribution of the water through the city was effected by leaden
pipes (see Hor. Ep. 1. 10. 20) : and Propertius in the present passage
refers to the possibility of 'laying on' the Marcian water by such a
pipe to an artificial Muses' grotto. But though the Romans used
pipes to distribute water downwards from the higher points of the
aqueducts, and apparently knew that water, confined in pipes, rises
to its own level, they preferred the aqueduct as the easiest method.
Nor did they know how to make pipes strong enough to bear the
strain. The *Anio Novus* travelled over fourteen miles of arches,
some of them 109 feet in height !

13. cara. Lachmann quite unnecessarily adopts the variant
grata.

14. Calliope or **Calliopea** (so Virg. E. 4. 57) was specially the Muse of Epic poetry; but the Roman poets paid little regard to the provinces of the Muses, and appealed to them indifferently.   Horace addresses in turn Calliope, Clio, Euterpe, Polyhymnia, and Melpomene, as the sources of his inspiration.   Mr. Verrall's ingenious attempt to show that the poet varied his muse with his mood will scarcely bear examination (Studies in Horace).

choris.   The dance and the song were so inseparably bound together that the former is used as synonymous with the latter.   So in 3. 1. 4: and Horace, when addressing the Muses, speaks of himself, Od. 3. 4. 25, as

> *Vestris amicum fontibus et choris.*

15. si qua est. The *si qua* gives a general meaning to the phrase: the indicative *es* makes it apply to Cynthia alone.

16. Cp. Shakespeare, Sonnet 81

> *Your monument shall be my gentle verse.*

17. The following lines have an echo of Hor. Od. 3. 30. 1–5 running through them: here again we may note the statelier march, the more natural order, the more self-restrained power, of the Venusian poet:

> *Exegi monumentum aere perennius,*
> *Regalique situ pyramidum altius,*
> *Quod non imber edax, non Aquilo impotens*
> *Possit diruere, aut innumerabilis*
> *Annorum series, et fuga temporum.*

Pyramidum sumptus, i. e. *Pyramides sumptuosae*, as Pinder points out, comparing Horace's *Pyramidum situs.*   *Situs* is the finer idea, so suggestive of immovability and permanence.

ducti, in reference to the height of the Pyramids.   *Duco* is used specially of all things or operations which imply length: hence *ducere murum*, 'to build a wall;' *ducere pocula*, 'take a long draught,' ' a pull;' *ducere bellum*, ' to prolong;' *ducere versus*, ' to write verses,' etc.

18. Of the handsomely fretted or spangled ceiling.   But the words might refer to the vaulted ceiling, or to the mere height of the building, as in Hor. Od. 3. 29. 10

> *Molem propinquam nubibus arduis.*

19. Mausolus was a king of Caria, who died B. C. 353, to whom his wife *Artemisia* erected the magnificent and marvellous monument which has given its name to all similar erections.

dives fortuna sepulcri, ' a poetical periphrasis for the tomb itself, like the *sumptus Pyramidum* just before,' Pinder.

20. Mortis extrema conditione. See note above on 1. 19. 2.

21. subducet, scarcely an appropriate word with *flamma* and *imber,* as it properly implies a silent stealthy withdrawing. Possibly, like Horace's *edax,* it may apply to the gradual corrosion and decay of damp.

22. Pondere victa, 'crushed by their overweight.' Hous. reads *ictus pondera*: 'the strokes of years will overcome the massy piles and cast them down.'

23. quaesitum again suggests the *superbiam Quaesitam meritis* of Hor. Od. 3. 30. 15.

ab aevo, 'at the hands of time' or 'in consequence of.' Or the *ab* might be instrumental, stronger than *aevo* alone. Pinder translates 'shall fall away from time' or 'life.' But *aevum* does not signify 'life' as distinguished from 'death,' but only 'a life-time.' Possibly the meaning may be 'shall be wrested from time.'

With these last lines cp. Shelley, Adonais:

> *And he is gathered to the kings of thought*
> *Who waged contention with their time's decay,*
> *And of the past are all that cannot pass away.*

III. 3.

ONCE more Propertius returns to the theme that Apollo and the Muses have forbidden him to sing in heroic verse the glories of Roman history, and warned him to confine himself to elegiac verse. So exactly Hor. Od. 4. 15. 1

> *Phoebus volentem praelia me loqui*
> *Victas et urbes increpuit lyra,*
> 　*Ne parva Tyrrhenum per aequor*
> 　　*Vela darem.*

So completely had the examples of Homer and Ennius placed Epic poetry upon a level above all other, that those who laboured in any other field felt that they could not make good their claim to be poets at all without apology. But it is to be marked, that while there is a truer note of manly modesty in Horace's estimate of his own powers and his aims, so, in the very act of self-depreciation, he has thrown an undying historical halo round the very men and acts whose praises he announces himself unwilling to sing. The hum of the toilsome bee of Mount Matinus has sounded not less bravely, has ministered to Fame no less notably, than the note of the Dircaean swan.

The piece is in the form of a dream or allegory in which Apollo warns the poet away from severer studies, and Calliope promises him inspiration in Elegiac poetry.

1. Visus eram goes with *recubans* and *hiscere posse*, ' Me-thought I lay, and dreamed I could,' etc.

molli, with reference partly to the easy lounging of the poet's life, as Hor. has it Od. 1. 1. 21

> *nunc viridi membra sub arbuto*
> *Stratus, nunc ad aquae lene caput sacrae,*

(cp. the phrase *vita umbratilis*, etc.), partly to the character of ama-tory poetry.   See above note on 3. 1. 19.

2. Bellerophontei. See note on 3. 1. 19. Cp. *caballinus fons*, ' the hack's spring,' Pers. Prol. 1.

4. Tantum operis.   A common phrase = *Tantum opus*. The words are in apposition to the whole sentence.   So Virg. Aen. 6. 223

> *pars ingenti subiere feretro,*
> *Triste ministerium, et subiectam more parentum*
> *Aversi tenuere facem ;*

ib. 10. 311

> *primus turmas invasit agrestes*
> *Aeneas, omen pugnae.*

The construction is commoner in Greek than in Latin.

nervis hiscere posse, ' that I had strength to gasp forth.' *Ner-vus* means ' a muscle,' and is the regular term for denoting physical strength.   Hence *nervosus* is ' muscular,' ' powerful :' *Quis Aristotele nervosior ?* Cic. Brut. 31. 121, and so our phrase ' nervous energy.'

hiscere, ' to lisp,' or ' gasp,' because of the greatness of the task. *Hisco* implies generally that utterance is choked by fear, nervousness, sense of guilt, etc.

5. Parva ora, of small unworthy lips, with reference to *fontibus* ; not surely parallel to *os magnum* 2. 10. 12 (where see note) or *os rotundum* Hor. A. P. 323. · In a passage imitated from this Pers. Prol. 1 uses *labra prolui*, ' soused my lips.'

6. pater, a term of respect to Ennius, as the father of Roman song.   So Hor. Epp. 1. 19. 7 : cp. id. 2. 1. 50

> *Ennius et sapiens et fortis et alter Homerus.*

7. Curios for *Curiatios*: the form does not occur elsewhere. For *Horatia* cp. note on 3. 2. 11.   As Postgate points out, *Horatia pila* may refer either to the column in the Forum on which the spoils of the conquered *Curiatii* were hung, or to the arms themselves (Burn's Rome, p. 104).   But it is possible that there is also an allu-sion to the *pilum*, the characteristic weapon of the Roman legions.

The MSS. read **cecinit**, doubtless from the neighbourhood of *Ennius*, and not understanding the coherence of the passage.   But the sense requires **cecini**. The allusion to Ennius is slight; it occurs only in the pentameter; and to take up six lines with details of what Ennius wrote as a reason why Propertius should sing something different, has neither sense nor propriety. Propertius had tremblingly touched the mighty fount with his lips : he dreamed that he essayed, in consequence, to follow the example of Ennius, when (l. 13) he was stopped by Phoebus.

8. The allusion, without doubt, is to the triumphal return of L. Aemilius Paullus from his great victory over Perseus, the king of Macedon, B. C. 167. Livy describes his magnificent progress up the Tiber, 45. 35 *Paullus ipse post dies paucos regia nave ingentis magnitudinis quam sexdecim versus remorum agebant, ornata Macedonicis spoliis, non insignium tantum armorum, sed etiam regiorum textilium, adverso Tiberi ad urbem est subvectus, completis ripis obviam effusa multitudine.*

Those editors who read *cecinit* hold themselves compelled to pass by this unmistakeable allusion because Ennius died two years before the event occurred, and refer to the comparatively obscure defeat of Demetrius of Pharos by L. Aem. Paullus the father in B. C. 219. But even so, it is scarcely necessary to suppose that Propertius would have been so accurate in his chronology or his quotations.

9. **Victrices moras**, in allusion to the famous waiting policy of the Dictator Q. Fabius Maximus throughout the latter part of the year 217 B. C. : the words of Ennius were

Unus homo nobis cunctando restituit rem,

closely imitated by Virg. Aen. 6. 847.

10. **versos**, used exactly in the scriptural sense of 'turning' the heart: so 2. 28. 32

Et deus et durus vertitur ipse dies.

The reference is still to Fabius who, on the very day of being appointed Dictator, *edocuisset patres plus negligentia caerimoniarum auspiciorumque quam temeritate atque inscitia peccatum a C. Flaminio consule esse* Liv. 22. 9. See the extraordinary number of *pia vota* conceived, caps. 9 and 10, and the still more marvellous list of prodigies which had occurred previously, cap. 1.

12. **fuisse**. The infinitive is here used, dependent on *cecini*, after a succession of substantives with participles or adjectives : *tropaea vecta, versos deos, Lares fugantes*. So sup. 1. 26 *pulsas arces . . . fluminaque cominus esse.*

Jupiter is identified with his temple. The allusion of course is to the cackling of the sacred geese when the Gauls were besieging the Capitol.

13. Castalia. Immediately behind the town of Delphi rises Mount Parnassus, called δικόρυφον or δίλοφος (*biceps* Ov. Met. 1. 316, 2. 221, etc.) by the ancients. This name was due not to the shape of the summit—invisible from Delphi itself—but to two sharp peaks, separated by a deep cleft, which crown a tremendous precipice which overhangs the town. Down this precipice offenders against the god were hurled; and from its base issues the clear water of the Castalian spring, dear to Apollo

> *Qui rore puro Castaliae lavit*
> *Crines solutos*

Hor. Od. 3. 4. 61.

Modern travellers have drunk the waters of Castalia with varying result : Dr. Spen was seized with a fit of poetic ecstasy; Dr. Chandler with a shivering-fit and a stomach-ache. Castalia was in Phocis : but Propertius' dream was on Helicon in Boeotia. Postgate remarks on the fanciful topography of the Roman poets, and quotes Statius Silv. 2. 7. 4, who speaks of the Corinthian as one who

> *Pendentis bibit ungulae liquorem,*

in allusion to the fount Hippocrene. But this mistake, as we have already seen, arose from the identification of *Hippocrene* with *Peirene* which was between Corinth and the Lechaeum. See Pers. Prol. 4.

14. It would thus seem that the modern photographer has classical authority for his favourite background of a tree-trunk or a grotto.

15. demens, used especially of those who make vain pretensions, as of Salmoneus, Virg. Aen. 6. 590

> *Demens, qui nimbos et non imitabile fulmen*
> *Aere et cornipedum pulsu simularet equorum.*

18. Mollia. See note on 3. 1. 19.

19, 20. I. e. your poetry should be of a light kind, to occupy the leisure moments of a maiden in her lover's absence. *Scamnum* is 'a bed-step,' the natural place on which to put a book from the *lectus*.

21. N. has *perscripto sevecta*, others *praescriptos*. *Sevecta* occurs nowhere else: Postgate renders it ' deviate,' ' swerve aside.' Prof. Palmer in his edition has *devecta*; but he tells me he has now withdrawn that conjecture. The sense seems to require a question deprecating undue ambition, which *devecta* would not imply: and the change to *praescriptos evecta* is infinitesimal. For *evehor* with an accusative cp. Tac. Ann. 12. 36 *Unde fama eius evecta insulas et proximas provincias pervagata per Italiam quoque celebrabatur.* Similarly *egredi*, *exire*, etc. take the accusative.

T

21. gyros. The metaphor is from the laps of the race-course, to which *evecta* is strictly applicable. So *orbem* 3. 1. 39.

22. I. e. 'you must not swamp your bark by over-freighting it.' The comparison of a poet's craft to a ship is common : cp. inf. 3. 9. 4

> *Non sunt apta meae grandia vela rati,*

and ib. l. 35

> *Non ego velifera tumidum mare findo carina.*

24. turba, 'confusion,' 'trouble.' *Turba* and *turbare* are constantly used by Plautus in the sense of to 'work confusion,' 'make mischief,' as of the mystifications of Tranio in the Mostellaria. *Turbo* and *turbidus* are also frequently used of storms or foul weather : cp. Attius ap. Non. 524. 26

> *Non vides quam turbam quosve fluctus concites ?*

26. Palmer, following N., reads *quo*.

nova semita. Cp. *intacta via* 3. 1. 18.

27. He describes one of the artificial grottoes spoken of above 3. 2. 12.

28. tympana, 'tambourines :' the special instrument of Cybele and of Bacchanalian worship.

29. Ergo Musarum. So the MSS. Hertz. explains *ergo* as having its original meaning = ἔργῳ, 'in very fact.' He quotes Hor. Sat. 2. 6. 70, where *ergo* cannot mean 'therefore,' but rather 'so then,' or else 'after that.' The latter meaning is not appropriate : if *ergo* be retained it can only mean 'and so,' 'well,' 'to proceed,' 'and then ' (= Gk. δή), implying that the appearance of the cave naturally led up to the idea that it was a haunt of the Muses, adorned with their emblems. Hertz. suggests *organa* as an alternative ; Haupt *orgia*, while Müller conjectures *orgia mustarum (mystarum ?)*. Then the sing. *imago* is out of place ; and it seems strange to have images of the Muses when they were there themselves. The connection between Bacchus and the Muses is constant. Cp. 2. 30. 37–8.

> *Hic ubi me prima statuent in parte choreae,*
> *Et medius docta cuspide Bacchus erit.*

In 4. 6. 75–6 we have the connection in a grosser form :

> *Ingenium potis irritet Musa poetis,*
> *Bacche, soles Phoebo fertilis esse tuo,*

reminding us of the dictum of Cratinus as given by Hor. Ep. 1. 19. 2

> *Nulla placere diu nec vivere carmina possunt*
> *Quae scribuntur aquae potoribus,*

whilst in the next words Horace illustrates *Pan Tegeaee* by ranking poets with Fauns and Satyrs :

ut male sanos
Adscripsit Liber Satyris Faunisque poetas.

31. mea turba, 'dear to me.' Doves were sacred to Venus ; and in the grotto was a spring in which doves were dipping their red beaks. The idea was probably a common one for representation on wall or floor. In the museum of the Capitol there is a lovely piece of mosaic representing this subject known by the name of ' The Doves of Pliny,' so called because Pliny thus describes a work of the mosaic worker Sosus : *Mirabilis ibi columba bibens et aquam umbra capitis infuscans. Apricantur aliae scabentes sese in canthari labro.*

32. Gorgoneo lacu. Another far-fetched allusion to Hippocrene.

punica, used here of the colour, as in Hor. Epod. 9. 27, for the more common *puniceus. Poenus, Poenicus, Punicus, puniceus* are all alike derived from φοῖνιξ, the famous purple-dye having been discovered first by the Phoenicians.

33. Diversae has properly reference to motion, 'turned apart,' as *diversi abeunt.* Here it means ' each in her several place.' *Diverse,* read by N., would have the same meaning. Let the young student beware of translating *diversus* by ' divers.'

rura here is unmeaning, and it is obvious how the error arose. In the line before, N. reads *nostra* for *rostra* : Hamb. apparently has *nostra* in the margin. It would seem that the first letter of the word, probably also that of *rura* just below it, had dropped out : the *r* was then inserted by mistake before *ura* instead of, or as well as, before *ostra. Iura* involves a very slight change and gives a good sense. Each of the Muses had her own province.

34. dona, in the sense of **munera,** implying their several functions and capacities.

exercere, the strict meaning of which is to ' keep at work,' is here almost exactly = our ' exercise.'

35. hederas. The ivy, as sacred to Bacchus, was the plant of poetic inspiration, and hence busts of poets were crowned with ivy : Hor. Od. 1. 1. 29

Doctarum hederae praemia frontium.

Prop. specially connects the ivy with lighter themes : 4. 1. 61

Ennius hirsuta cingat sua dicta corona:
Mi folia ex hedera porrige, Bacche, tua.

T 2

35. nervis, the strings of the lyre, as in Hor. Od. 3. 11. 4

> *Tuque testudo resonare septem*
> *Callida nervis.*

36. Aptat, 'sets to the lyre:' the regular word for setting words to music, Hor. Od. 2. 12. 1, 4

> *Nolis longa ferae bella Numantiae*
> *Aptari citharae modis.*

The particular Muses are not to be identified.

rosam, because chaplets, especially of roses, were brought on after the *cena*, when mirth and music came on. Hence *sub rosa*, 'under the rose,' of a thing told under the confidence of hospitality.

38. a facie, 'a false etymology. Καλλιόπεια is from ὄψ (a voice), not ὤψ (a face)' Postgate.

39. Contentus. A somewhat amusing condescension. He was to put up with a seat in the car of Venus, drawn by swans.

40. ducet ad arma. Cp. 2. 1. 18

> *Ut possem heroas ducere ad arma manus,*

where *ducere* is used in the same sense as here.

nec fortis equi sonus. 'No neighing charger.'

41. Nil tibi sit, 'let it be naught in thine eyes,' 'deem it not to be thy business.' Postgate points out that the more usual phrase is *nil ad te sit*, 'let it be no concern of thine': Prop. not unfrequently using the Dat. for *ad* with the Acc. Cp. Lucr. 3. 830, *Nil igitur mors est ad nos.*

classica and **praeconia** are both properly adjectives, but both are used as substantives also. *Classica* is no doubt used simply for 'naval' as in 2. 1. 28. *Praeconia* are proclamations or praises: cp. Ov. Her. 17. 207

> *Non ita contemno volucris praeconia Famae.*

42. Flare, undoubtedly right for the *flere* of the MSS. The word is used no doubt in reference to the meaning of *classicum*, 'a trumpet,' or 'trumpet-signal.' Cp. Mart. 11. 3. 8

> *Quantaque Pieria praelia flare tuba.*

43. Mariano signo, a loose ablative of circumstance, not differing much from the ablative absolute: 'under the banner of Marius.'

44. In allusion to the two great victories of Marius over the northern hordes; (1) over the Teutones and Ambrones at *Aquae Sextiae* (Aix) near Marseilles in B.C. 102: (2) over the *Cimbri* at *Campi Raudii* near Vercellae in Lombardy in B.C. 101.

Stent, of the armies drawn up and ready for battle. Note that *Nil tibi sit*, l. 41, is the predicate of the clauses *quibus in campis* *stent . . . refringat . . . vectet.* The meaning must be ' let all these events be nothing, i. e. of no consequence, in thine eyes.'

refringat. Cp. Hor. Od. 3. 3. 28.

45. Some word equivalent to ' how,' ' in what fashion,' has to be gathered from *quibus in campis* to connect *vectet* with what goes before. The allusion is apparently to the defeat of Ariovistus by Caesar in B. C. 58. Ariovistus had entered Gaul to assist the Aedui against the Sequani at the head of various German tribes, among whom were the *Suevi,* a vague name assigned by Caesar to the tribes occupying the East bank of the Rhine. Caesar's victory was gained at a spot fifty miles from the Rhine: the defeated fled across the river, some swimming, some in small boats, among whom was Ariovistus. Clearly Propertius had but dim ideas as to the site.

perfusus, as if the surface of the water ran with blood.

47. coronatos, of revellers who have just left a feast.

48. ebria, the epithet is transferred from the revellers to the traces of their escapade. See above note on 3. 1. 8.

49. excantare, whence our 'excantation,' used here in its literal sense. Cp. Merchant of Venice 2. 5, where the Jew in vain warns Jessica :

> *Hear you me, Jessica:*
> *Lock up my doors ; and when you hear the drum*
> *And the vile squeaking of the wry-necked fife,*
> *Clamber not thou up to the casements then,*
> *Nor thrust your head into the public street*
> *To gaze on Christian fools with varnished faces,*
> *But stop my house's ears, I mean my casements.*

50. austeros viros, 'severe husbands,' or possibly 'curmudgeon fathers,' such as Shylock himself. In the former case, *puellas* would be 'young wives.' **ferire,** 'to cheat,' 'gull.'

52. ora rigavit, a proof that *parva ora,* l. 5, refers to the lips. Postgate quotes Ov. Am. 3. 9. 23, where the lips of poets are said to be watered by Homer as by a perennial fount. Our own 'Augustan' poets are fond of introducing the inspiring springs of the Muses : cp. Pope, Essay on Criticism,

> *A little learning is a dangerous thing ;*
> *Drink deep, or taste not the Pierian spring.*

And the same Propertian vein is to be discerned in the pride and care which Pope lavished on his grotto at Twickenham.

III. 4.

THIS poem is written in anticipation of the great expedition of Augustus into the East, when he was to bring Parthia and India, the Tigris and the Euphrates, under the sway of the Latian Jupiter, and wipe out the disgrace of Carrhae. Though the poet speaks of the Indian Ocean (l. 3) and of the furthest East, it is to be noted that he says nothing of Arabia : it might therefore be inferred that this poem was written after the failure of the Arabian expedition, B. C. 24. But see Introduction. Virgil is still more comprehensive in his anticipations of the successes of the arms of Augustus, Aen. 7. 604

> *Sive Getis inferre manu lacrimabile bellum,*
> *Hyrcanisve Arabisve parant, seu tendere ad Indos,*
> *Auroramque sequi, Parthosque reposcere signa.*

1. **Deus Caesar.** In no passage of the Augustan poets is the divine title so openly conferred on Augustus as in this.

Virgil and Horace generally cloak the flattery under poetical forms, or pave the way for it under skilfully prepared approaches. Thus Virg. E. 1. 6, 7

> *O Meliboee, deus nobis haec otia fecit :*
> *Namque erit ille mihi semper deus,*

a mode of statement that would scarcely shock a modern ear. Horace shows still more consummate art in the celebrated Second Ode of Book I, in which he formally proclaims his political faith. Reversing the order of Propertius, he descends from the divine to the human ; searching for one to whom Jupiter may assign the task of wiping out from Rome the stain of fratricidal guilt, he passes in review all the gods who care for Rome : he descends gently from Apollo the purifier to Venus and Mars, the mother and the father of the Roman race : then he passes on to Mercury, go-between between men and gods, who as *mutata iuvenem figura* may consent to abide on earth : then by carefully chosen human words—*triumphos, pater, princeps, Medos*—gradually paves the way for his identification, but only in the very last word, with Caesar himself :

> *Hic magnos potius triumphos,*
> *Hic ames dici Pater atque Princeps,*
> *Neu Medos sinas equitare inultos,*
> *Te duce, Caesar.*

Augustus never permitted himself to be worshipped as god in Rome ; in Spain and Asia he suffered temples and images to be put up to him, but even then only in conjunction with the worship of Rome, Suet. Oct. 52.

Caligula was the first Emperor who set up his own image in Rome, between those of the Dioscuri; and Domitian desired to be addressed as *Dominus et Deus*. How prone the Romans had become to such servile flattery appears from Tac. Ann. 4. 38, where the historian puts a noble speech into the mouth of Tiberius when refusing to allow divine honours to be paid to himself and his mother in further Spain. This refusal, adds Tacitus, *alii modestiam, multi, quia diffideret, quidam ut degeneris animi interpretabantur.*

Prof. Palmer suggests that *meus* may be the true reading for *Deus*, and compares *mei ducis* elsewhere. But in such a position would not *meus* be an impertinence?

ad goes with *arma*, 'an expedition to.'

2. gemmiferi maris, the Persian Gulf—the whole of which was embraced by the ancients under the name Red Sea—or Indian Ocean. The Romans, like the poet Gray—

> *Full many a gem of purest ray serene,*
> *The dark unfathomed caves of Ocean bear—*

imagined that all gems were Ocean products, and especially from the Red Sea. Cp. Prop. 1. 14. 12

> *Et legitur rubris gemma sub aequoribus.*

So Mart. 5. 37. 4

> *Cui nec lapillos praeferas Erythraeos;*

and Tib. 2. 2. 15

> *Nec tibi gemmarum quidquid felicibus Indis*
> *Nascitur, Eoi qua maris unda rubet.*

3. viri, 'gallants.' He addresses the army of invasion.

4. sub tua iura, 'under thy sway,' the word *triumphos* naturally bringing back the mind from the army to its chief. Distinguish between *ius dicere*, 'to administer justice,' 'to pronounce judgment,' the province of a judge, and *iura dare*, 'to impose laws,' the work of a legislator or conqueror. Thus Virgil, of Acestes in his new Sicilian kingdom, Aen. 5. 758

> *Indicitque forum et patribus dat iura vocatis.*

5. Sera sed ... veniet, 'Though late, will come all the same,' exactly parallel to Virg. E. 1. 28

> *Libertas quae sera tamen respexit inertem.*

See too Prop. 3. 6. 32

> *Poena erit ante meos sera, sed ampla, pedes.*

veniet, i.e. the East (included under *ultima terra* l. 3), or perhaps more specially Parthia, will come in under the dominion of

Rome as a province. Thus *veniet* is stronger than *fiet*, as if the East came voluntarily to place herself under Roman protection. The same idea is implied in *fluent*.

5. **virgis,** in allusion to the fasces. It may be a dative of possession, or possibly an ablative of description.

6. **Partha** for *Parthica:* see note on 3. 2. 11.

7. **prorae** is the vocative : so *equi* in the next line.

expertae bello, in allusion to Augustus' naval victories : first, that gained over Sextus Pompeius by Agrippa in Sicily B.C. 36, and, more notably, the battle of Actium in B.C. 31.

date lintea, 'spread your sails.' *Dare* is frequently thus used with an accusative in such a way that the phrase is equivalent to an intransitive verb. Thus Lucr. 2. 1143 says that one day the walls of the world

Expugnata dabunt labem putrisque ruinas,

which simply means, 'will fall in crumbling ruins.' So *dat sonitum,* properly 'causes a sound,' is equivalent to ' resounds.' See Munro on Lucr. l. c. In other passages *dare* with a predicative adjective is equivalent to a transitive verb: as Virg. Aen. 9. 323

Haec ego vasta dabo.

8. **ducite munus.** It is quite out of place to refer these words to the *Equites equo publico* or the *Equitum recognitio,* a ceremony long disused with a view to actual warfare, and only partially restored for mere form's sake (Suet. Oct. 38) by Augustus. The phrase is a confused expression ; *ducere* is appropriate to horses, ' lead forth,' or ' draw ;' *munus,* ' function,' would imply some such word as 'perform' before it. As it stands, therefore, the phrase will cover any work to be done by horses : *armigeri* confines it to the cavalry.

9. **piate,** 'avenge.' *Piare* is a transitive verb, used in the widest possible sense to denote any act of religious duty in reference to the thing or person which stands as its object. Of a god, 'to appease' or 'worship,' as Hor. Ep. 2. 1. 143 *Silvanum lacte piabant ;* of an altar, Prop. 3. 10. 19 *ubi ture piaveris aras,* 'hast duly honoured ;' of a bad omen, 'to avert its evil consequences,' Virg. Aen. 2. 184; of a crime, 'to expiate it,' 'wipe it out,' ib. 140. Here the idea is ' to avenge :' ' wipe out the impiety of leaving the Crassi and their slaughter unavenged.'

11. **lumina.** Rarely used, as here, of a fire.

12. **illa,** correctly, of a distant, uncertain day : elsewhere, as we have seen, Propertius uses *hic* in the same sense.

13. **oneratos axes,** the reading of the MSS., is perhaps better

than the conjecture of Muretus (adopted by Palmer), *onerato axe*. The car of Caesar laden with spoils would be the central and most important spectacle of the triumph : to make the poet relegate that idea to a subordinate clause, and make it his chief wish to see the horses shying at the plaudits of the mob, seems less natural. The omission of the copula presents no difficulty.

15. nixus has been objected to, and *vinctos, nexos* proposed : Bae. suggests *exuvias* on the ground that *spectare* needs an object. No criticism could be less sound : *spectare* is used technically and repeatedly for ' being a spectator ' at games. See passage quoted in critical notes, and especially the well-known line Ov. A. A. 1. 99 (wrongly given as 5. 99 in critical notes)

Spectatum veniunt, veniunt spectentur ut ipsae.
So *Spectantem specta* A. A. 3. 513.

16. Incipiam, more than simply 'to begin :' it implies to ' take in hand,' of some actual undertaking or operation.

et titulis . . . legam, a parenthesis ; *tela* and *arcus* in l. 17, and the infinitive *sedere* in l. 18, being governed by *spectare*.

Not only the names of conquered cities, but representations of them, as well as of striking incidents of the campaign, were carried along as part of a triumph. Cp. modern trade-processions.

17. ' The breeched soldier ' is of course the Parthian ; as early as the time of Croesus we hear that the Persians were distinguished by wearing breeches (Hdt. 1. 71), and Aristagoras adduces the fact to Cleomenes, king of Sparta, as a proof that they could be of no good in war (id. 5. 49). The Celts also were known to the Romans as wearers of breeches ; hence further Gaul was sometimes called Braccata, Juv. 8. 234. Caecina affected the Gallic dress, wearing a tartan plaid as well as breeches, *bracas barbarum tegmen indutus* Tac. Hist. 2. 20. It is an interesting and instructive circumstance that the ancient Southron was shocked because the Celt wore trousers, while the modern Southron affects to be no less shocked because he dispenses with them. The latter probably forgets that the kilt was a Roman military dress, worn by the Caesars : see the famous statue of Augustus in the Braccio Nuovo, referred to above in note to 2. 10. 13, p. 234.

18. subter goes along with *arma*. It would seem that in the triumphal procession captives were made to sit under stacks or trophies of arms taken from themselves. Thus Ov. Ep. Pont. 3. 4. 104 in describing a triumph

Stentque super vinctos trunca tropaea viros.

sedere depends upon *spectare* l. 15 ; in sense it is

almost equivalent to a present participle. Exactly parallel is 3. 6. 11–14

> *Nec speculum strato vidisti Lygdame lecto?*
> *Ornabat niveas nullaque gemma manus?*
> *Ac maestam teneris vestem pendere lacertis?*
> *Scriniaque ad lecti clausa iacere pedes?*

See below l. 20 *cernis. Ingredior ferre* 3. 1. 3, and *ibat videre* 1. 1. 12, are quite different; there the infinitive is equivalent to an accusative of motion towards.

19. tuam prolem, Augustus.

sit in aevum, 'live for ever!'

20. caput. See note pp. 220, 221.

21. haec, for *illa*, after the manner of Propertius.

Sacra Via. The most imposing point in the triumphal procession was when it descended from the Velia along the *Via Sacra* to the forum, with the Capitol full in front. At the far end of the forum, before the ascent of the Capitol begun, the captives were taken off into the *Tullianum* to meet their doom. Thus Horace, selecting the proudest moment of the triumph, Epod. 7. 7

> *Intactus aut Britannus ut descenderet*
> *Sacra catenatus via.*

22. mi. N. has *me. Mi* is both better in itself, and contrasts better with *illis* l. 22.

posse sounds weak and hesitating; but it is strictly in Propertius' manner. See Postgate, Introduction.

III. 5.

THIS poem is written in close connection with the last. Instead of offering to share in the perils of the war—as Horace before Actium in Epod. 1. 1—the poet explains why he must stand aside. He has no thirst for riches; conquered and conqueror alike will pass empty-handed into Acheron. Love and Song are his delight: when old age takes these away, he will scan the Laws of Nature, and peer into the secrets that lie beyond the grave.

2–4. 'I have indeed my battles; but they are battles with my love, and they are not waged for gold or luxury.' The only difficulty is in *tamen*, which answers solely to *stant praelia*, and takes no note of the mitigating influence of *cum domina mea*: 'I have indeed my wars of love; but I have no care for gold.' Paley quite wrongly explains *stant* as *durant, non facile dirimuntur:* 'I am compelled to wage war, yet not from avarice, but from differences with Cynthia.'

2. stant, of battles, means ' are set,' ' are ranged,' implying instant conflict. See above, 3. 3. 44

> *Mariano praelia signo Stent:*

not dissimilar is *stant littore puppes* Virg. Aen. 6. 902, ' are ranged,' ' drawn up.'

3. inviso auro has much the same meaning as Virgil's *auri sacra fames* Aen. 7. 57, implying not so much ' hated,' as ' worthy of being hated,' ' hateful.' The Augustan writers, especially Cicero, are fond of using the past participle passive in place of the adjective in *-bilis.* So Virg. Aen. 5. 591, of the labyrinth,

> *Falleret indeprensus et irremeabilis error.*

4. gemma divite. The allusion here is to drinking-cups and flagons hollowed out of a single precious stone. Such extravagances were known even in Cicero's time. Antiochus, a Syrian prince, lays out his plate before Verres: *Erat etiam vas vinarium, ex una gemma pergrandi, trulla excavata, manubrio aureo* Cic. Verr. 2. 4. 27. In addition there were *pocula gemmis distincta clarissimis,* i. e. cups with jewels set in them. Both kinds are probably alluded to in Juv. 5. 37–9

> *Ipse capaces*
> *Heliadum crustas et inaequales beryllo*
> *Virro tenet phialas,*

the former being cups made of a single piece of amber.

5. Cp. Hor. Epod. 1. 27, where he declares he will follow Maecenas to the war,

> *Non ut iuvencis illigata pluribus*
> *Aratra nitantur mea.*

6. miser, so the MSS. N. also has *aere* for *aera*, evidently mistaking the construction. But Palmer is probably right in reading *misera*, to agree with *Corinthe.* The *a* at the end of *misera* would easily get dropped before the *a* of *aera*; and the sentiment of *miser*, explained by Pinder to mean ' Nor mean enough to get money through thy fall,' is indeed by no means a Roman sentiment, or one possible in an Augustan writer. Even Juvenal, who magnificently denounces rapacity in the provinces, nowhere rises to the idea that the governor is morally degraded by spoiling the provincials; his highest sentiment is *miserere inopum sociorum* 8. 89. If *miser* be read, the meaning probably is, ' Nor have I, poor wretch! the luck to get a Corinth to sack.'

paro is used specially in the sense ' to provide,' whether for oneself or for others. Hence in the former case it frequently means to 'buy,' as Hor. Sat. 2. 3. 129

> *Servosve tuos quos aere parasti;*

in the latter, 'to bring in as income,' as Juv. 1. 106

> *Sed quinque tabernae*
> *Quadringenta parant.*

The allusion is to the wholesale spoliation of Corinth by L. Mummius B.C. 146, especially of its art treasures. For *aera*, statues, etc., in bronze, cp. Hor. Ep. 1. 6. 17

> *Aeraque et artes Suspice.*

7. fingenti, of the potter's art.

prima terra, the primordial clay (Horace's *principi limo* Od. 1. 16. 13) out of which Prometheus fashioned man. See Pausanias 10. 4. 3.

infelix, 'ill-starred in the potter's hand,' not with reference to the fate of Prometheus, but implying that he had made 'a bad job' of it.

8. parum caute, a pun on the name *Prometheus.*

pectoris, like *cor*, in the sense of our 'head' or 'brain,' not 'heart;' see above note on p. 220. *Pectoris* is a genitive of description after *opus.*

9. disponens implies the apportionment of the various parts of the body, each to its proper place.

in arte, of the product of his art.

10. I. e. 'the path along which the mind has to travel ought to have been made a straight path.' The words 'right' and 'rectitude' imply a straight line, which furnished to the ancients their figure for moral excellence: cp. the famous figure of the Pythagorean Y (written ᛉ), Pers. 3. 56. To a Roman engineer the first essential for a high road was that it should be straight; witness the remains of Roman roads in this country.

11. Nunc, 'as it is,' 'as matters now are.'

maris after *tantum,* 'over all these seas.'

14. The MS. reading *ad infernas rates* is inadmissible on ground of sense. The only 'conveyance' of souls was across the Stygian water; there is no meaning in the plural *rates;* and, as Pinder says, since l. 13 brings the soul to the bank, l. 14 must carry it across.

at is frequently written as *ad;* but is not good in sense, as there is not sufficient contrast between ll. 13 and 14. I would now adopt Palmer's conjecture *in inferna rate* as almost demonstrably correct. First, *rate* was turned into *rates*, because ll. 13, 15, 16 all end with *s; inferna* was changed to *infernas*, either because *rates* had been changed first, or because *s* follows at the beginning of *stulte; in* was dropped out, as Paley suggests, because it recurs in *inferna;* and lastly, when the omission was discovered, *ad*, as the most likely preposition, was inserted.

Nudus. Cp. Job 1. 21 *Naked came I out of my mother's womb, and naked shall I return thither.* So 1 Tim. 6. 7.

15. miscebitur. *Misceo* here, as usual, means an indiscriminate mingling, without regard to kind or quantity, in opposition to *tempero*, which means 'to mingle in due proportion.' Cp. *Haec ita mixta fuerunt ut temperata nullo fuerint modo* Cic. Rep. 2. 23. 42.

16. Consule. Jugurtha was captured in the year succeeding Marius' first consulship, in B.C. 106; but Marius entered the city in triumph upon the second day of his second consulship, Jan. 2, B.C. 104.

17. The Croesus of Lydia is contrasted with Irus, the greedy beggar of the Odyssey (18. 5, etc.), to represent the extremes of wealth and poverty.

18. A corrupt line, which no one has succeeded in emending or interpreting satisfactorily. The MSS. read *parta*, which is senseless, or *parca*. Bae. conjectures *carpta*, retaining *apta* before *die*. Lach. conjectures *parcae*, comparing Virg. Aen. 12. 150 *Parcarumque dies*, of a natural death; but the singular in this sense is unexampled. Other conjectures are *tarda* and (equally good) *propera*. N. has *apta* before *die*; Hertz. and Lach. read *acta*, comparing 3. 7. 30, which is scarcely in point. When H. is reduced to interpreting *parca dies* as 'a day which spares the life, i. e. puts off death, as long as possible,' and Paley as 'a day, or time, of poverty,' it is useless to consult commentators further. If we read, as in the text, *acta quae venit apta die*, we at least have sense: 'That death is best which comes at its own fit time, when one's day is done.'

21. Me iuvat reminds us of the refrain Hor. Od. 1. 1. 3 sqq. *Sunt quos . . . iuvat*, etc.

coluisse and *implicuisse* l. 20, alongside of *vincire* l. 21, show that no distinction can be drawn between the present and perfect infinitive. Pers. is fond of the same usage; cp. 2. 66

Haec baccam conchae rasisse, et stringere venas.

vincire. The phrase is borrowed from the idea of chaplets: see next line.

22. caput habere in rosa. 'To have one's head crowned with roses,' i. e. 'to carouse.' So Cic. has *in rosa potare* Fin. 2. 20. 65; Sen. *in rosa iacere* Ep. 36. 9.

25. For the whole of the following passage cp. Virg. Geo. 2. 475-486.

26. hanc mundi domum, 'this fabric of the world.' *Domus* means essentially a building, or structure of some kind. As pointed out above on p. 210, students are constantly led astray in translating *domus* by the analogy of our 'home.' Cp. Virg. Aen. 10. 1 *domus Olympi,* Geo. 1. 371

> *Eurique Zephyrique domus,*

and Prop. 2. 16. 50

> *Fulminaque aetheria desiluisse domo.*

So Shelley's *blue dome of air.*

27. deficit, as the contrast with *exoriens* seems to show, of the setting moon, not of an eclipse. Gellius however has *deficiente luna* of the waning moon, as opposed to *crescente;* and that may well be the meaning here. Lucan has *cornu coacto* of the full moon, when the filling in of the orb makes the extremities of the crescent appear to meet, Phars. 1. 532. For *coactis* cf. Ov. Tr. 4. 4. 35 *clavi mensura coacta est.* Note how indifferently Prop. uses the indicative and subjunctive mood throughout this passage.

29. superant, in its literal meaning, 'get up upon the sea,' 'rise.' So exactly Virg. Aen. 11. 514

> *iugo superans adventat ad urbem,*

'mounting by the ridge thus reaches the city.'

31. 'Whether *a* day is coming which,' etc. Lucretius affirms of the universe that

> *Una dies dabit exitio, multosque per annos*
> *Sustentata ruet moles et machina mundi.*

Several editors read *si* for *sit.*

32. Pinder points out that the ancients believed that the rainbow sucked up water from the earth and gave it back in rain.

33. The *Perrhaebi* occupied the northern part of Thessaly.

34. 'And the sun's orb mourned with his horses draped in black,' a grandiloquent phrase for an eclipse.

35. serus versare, 'slow in turning.'

Bootes, 'the Ploughman,' called also Arcturus or Arctophylax, 'the Bear-ward.' The former name was applied to it because it seems to represent the Ploughman or Waggoner who drives the whole team round. Hence *serus versare.*

36. An admirable description of the Pleiades. The stars which form the group (*chorus*) are so thickly set (*spisso*) that they appear to run together (*coit*).

37. Cp. Job 38. 11 *Hitherto shalt thou come, but no further,* *and here shall thy proud waves be stayed;* and Psalm 104. 9 *Thou hast set a bound that they may not pass over, that they turn not again to cover the earth.*

exeat, with an accusative, as in Ov. Met. 10. 52 *donec Avernas Exierit valles.*

38. eat, of the progress of the year; just as in 3. 1. 8, of the march of his verse.

39. sint iura deum, either 'whether the gods dispense justice,' or rather 'have jurisdiction, hold sway.' See above on 3. 4. 4.

40. Note the rare use of *si* in an Indirect question. *Expectare si, conari si,* etc. are conditional.

41. Alcmaeon slew his mother Eriphyle by his father Amphiaraus' injunctions: he went mad and was haunted by the Furies. Phineus, the blind soothsayer, was punished for savage cruelty to his sons; his food was always carried off or fouled by the Harpies.

I. e. whether the tales about Ixion, etc. are true.

44. pauca, to be taken as the predicate, 'are all too few.' Prof. Palmer would now read *pressa* for *pauca.* He thinks *pauca* arose from the transcriber's eye catching *auc* in *faucibus* in l. 43 after he had begun to write *pressa*, and compares Ov. Met. 1. 458 *tot iugera ventre prementem.*

45. An ficta fabula, 'or naught but tales and fancies.' See 2. 34. 53-4. Cp. *Fabulae manes* Hor. Od. 1. 4. 16.

47. Exitus vitae. So Nepos, Eum. 13, for 'the latter end, closing days, of life.'

III. 7.

A YOUNG friend of the poet, called Paetus, had been drowned in the course of a voyage to Egypt, whither he was bound on some trading venture. Assuming therefore that lust for gold was the cause of his friend's end, Propertius describes with much pathos the circumstances of his death, and moralises upon the avarice of man and the rash daring which it inspires. It is one of the most beautiful of his pieces, full of an exquisite tender pathos, and showing a high imaginative capacity, such as is rarely to be found in ancient poetry, for feeling and interpreting the wilder moods of nature. This poem would alone be enough to refute the common idea that Propertius was a mere love poet, whose one and only inspiration was found in Cynthia. On the contrary, it raises the presumption that Cynthia did as much to degrade or divert his muse as to create it, and fills one with regret that he did not devote his genius to nobler themes.

1. **Ergo,** used thus abruptly, implies surprise, almost remonstance, at a conclusion forced suddenly upon the speaker, and from which he feels there is no escape. Thus Hor. Od. 1. 24. 5

> *Ergo Quintilium perpetuus sopor*
> *Urget !*

Ovid. Trist. 3. 2. 1

> *Ergo erat in fatis Scythiam quoque visere nostris !*

In Hor. Sat. 2. 5. 101 it is an exclamation which bursts from the disappointed legacy-hunter on the reading of the will:

> *ergo nunc Dama sodalis*
> *Nusquam est ?*

Pecunia is here personified and treated as a Deity. The Romans worshipped, and erected temples to, a whole multitude of abstract qualities, such as Fides, Concordia, Honos, Victoria, Juventas, Fama, etc. Juvenal sarcastically observes that, as yet, Money is not so worshipped :

> *etsi, funesta Pecunia, templo*
> *Nondum habitas, nullas Nummorum ereximus aras,*
> *Ut colitur Pax atque Fides, Victoria, Virtus,*
> *Quaeque salutato crepitat Concordia nido.*

Most MSS. insert *es* after *vitae*, N. omits it.

2. The late H. A. J. Munro severely handled a translator of Gray's elegy for rendering ' the paths of glory' by *honoris iter,* declaring that the line

> *Ad tumuli fauces ducit honoris iter*

could have no meaning except ' The path of a public office leads to the gorge of a hillock.' We have seen above on 3. 1. 22 that *Honor* may be used in an abstract sense, like our Honour or Glory; the phrase *mortis iter* here is a warrant for *honoris iter. Immaturum* would certainly be condemned by an ordinary corrector of verses: the epithet properly belongs to *mortis,* not to *iter.* And it is almost hypercritical to say (with Postgate) that *adimus* is not appropriate to *iter. Adire mortem* or *periculum mortis* is as good Latin as *adire ad mortem :* ' to enter upon the path of death' is a perfectly natural expression, and *mortis iter* is analogous to *Phasidos viam* 1. 20. 18 and *caeli iter* 2. 1. 20.

3. This line is very modern in its tone, especially in applying an epithet like *crudelia* to *pabula.* Paley explains the word by ὠμά, i.e. ' causing so much bloodshed.' But the idea of bloodshed is foreign to the poem: note *curarum* in the next line.

4. **capite** is used with reference to the personality of *Pecunia. Caput* by itself, no doubt, and in a proper connection, may mean the

head-water or source of a stream, and *caput* can doubtless be used in such a sense, in a proper connection : but to address Money with 'The *seeds* of care take their *rise* from your *fountain-head*' would be a little too harsh even for Propertius.   Postgate supports this interpretation by *fontis caput* from 3. 19. 6 ; but the whole line reads
   Fluminaque ad fontis sint reditura caput,
which is a perfectly natural expression, involving no harshness or confusion.

   de capite tuo = *de te :* see above note on 2. 1. 36.

   5. tendentem in this phrase has the sense of 'stretching,' not of direction.   The phrase is equivalent to ' in full sail,' implying a prosperous course : ' all well.'

   Pharios portus, i. e. Alexandria.   See notes on Tib. 1. 3. 32, Prop. 2. 1. 30.

   6. insano.   Cp. Hor. Od. 3. 4. 30 *insanientis Bospori, insana Caprae sidera* id. 3. 7. 6, *insani Leonis* id. 1. 16. 15, and *insanis aquis* Ov. Her. 1. 6.

   terque quaterque.   A hyperbolical way of expressing the terrific nature of the storm : cp. Tib. 3. 3. 26
   O mihi felicem terque quaterque diem!
So *felices ter et amplius* Hor. Od. 1. 3. 17 and *bis terque mutatae dapis* Ep. 5. 33.   Possibly here successive waves are meant.

   7. excidit has no special reference to shipwreck.   The word simply means ' to fall out of :' as when Cicero says *verbum tibi non fortuito excidit* Phil. 10. 2, ' did not escape you ;' or of forgetfulness, *at mihi ista exciderant,* ' had escaped my memory,' Leg. 2. 18. 46. Here Paetus is said to have 'fallen out of' that which he lost or from which he disappeared, viz. his life.   So above 3. 2. 25 *nomen ab aevo Excidet*.   Still more curious is Ter. And. 2. 5. 12 *uxore excidit*, ' fell out of,' i. e. ' lost the chance of getting,' a wife.   (We say, in a different sense, a man *fell out with* his wife).   *Aevo* is the Abl.

   The juxtaposition of *nova* to *longinquis* doubles the force of the idea, each side of the relation being stated separately.   The fishes were distant to him (i. e. to his home) ; he was strange (*nova*) to the fishes. The principle is the same as that involved in such juxtapositions as Hor. Epod. 1. 21 *ut adsit . . . praesentibus*, Plaut. Most. 1. 1. 27
   Adsum praesens praesenti tibi,
Hor. Sat. 2. 6. 81
                                                    fertur
   Accepisse cavo veterem vetus hospes amicum ;
or more subtly, Od. 2. 4. 6, where *captivae* and *dominum* repeat the same idea,

Movit Aiacem Telamone natum
Forma captivae dominum Tecmessae.

8. natat. The verb *natare*, though applied to the natural swimming of men, fish, or other animals, is scarcely ever used of the natural floating of ships. It constantly denotes wreckage of some sort, as 4. 1. 116

Et natat exuviis Graecia pressa suis.

So *Ithacum lugere natantem* Juv. 10. 257 and Prop. 3. 12. 32

Totque hiemis noctes totque natasse dies,

in both of which passages the idea is that Ulysses was floundering about, with nothing but his swimming powers to trust to. Even of a ship in harbour the word denotes a wreck in Prop. 2. 25. 24

Cum saepe in portu fracta carina natet.

Metaphorically, the word is always used *in malam partem ;* as of inundations, of eyes swimming in death or drunkenness, of a wavering mind, Hor. Sat. 2. 7. 6, of an ill-fitting shoe Ov. A. A. 1. 516, where it is joined with *vagus,* a word of kindred meaning. To the Roman mind, whatever departed from the steady, the solid, the strong, the straight, was bad.

9. iusta debita, the offices due to the dead, especially that of sprinkling earth over the corpse, Hor. Od. 1. 28. 24.

terrae here is ' the body,' properly ' the remains when buried in 'earth,' as in 2. 13. 42

Non nihil ad verum conscia terra sapit.

The epithet *piae* is transferred to the remains, as all the offices to the dead have the character of *pietas.* Postgate's reference to *pientissimus* on an inscription is scarcely in point. To take *terrae* with Paley as a genitive is possible, but inelegant : besides, it is obviously to be supplied as the object to *humare* in the next line.

10. pote stands for *potis* feminine, agreeing with *mater. Potis* and *pote* are used of all genders, and with both numbers, indifferently. Cp. 2. 1. 46

Qua pote quisque, in ea conterat arte diem.

12. In illustration of this magnificent line—one of the finest in all ancient poetry—Postgate quotes an epigram from Glaucus (Gk. Anth. 7. 235), in which it is said, as here, of a drowned man, πᾶσα θάλασσα τάφος. These words, he suggests, may be an echo of the famous words of Pericles, Thuc. 2. 43, ἀνδρῶν γὰρ ἐπιφανῶν πᾶσα γῆ τάφος. But no two phrases, similar as they are in meaning, could be more utterly different in sentiment. Pericles meant ' Every land is a monument to our mighty dead.' Propertius means ' His mother has no spot to look to as holding the remains of her dear lost one but the wide blank sea.'   L. 12 conveys powerfully the idea of restless, homeless desolation.

13. Infelix, in reference to the result: 'disastrous,' 'causing misery.'

timor, 'dreaded by:' as we say, 'the terror of.'   The regular construction would be the dative of the complement, a construction which is used in Latin to avoid the awkwardness or untruthfulness of predicating an abstract quality of a concrete noun.

Orithyia, daughter of Erechtheus, was carried off by Boreas to Thrace, having unwarily strayed beyond the Ilissus.

14. spolia, with reference to *raptae*, l. 13.

16. I. e. the disaster was not deserved by the wickedness of those on board.   For ll. 13–16 compare Lycidas:

> *He ask'd the waves, and ask'd the felon winds,*
> *What hard mishap hath doom'd this gentle swain?*
> *And questioned every gust of rugged wings*
> *That blows from off each beaked promontory:*
> *They knew not of his story;*
> *And sage Hippotades their answer brings,*
> *That not a blast was from his dungeon strayed;*
> *The air was calm, and on the level brine*
> *Sleek Panope with all her sisters play'd.*
> *It was that fatal and perfidious bark,*
> *Built in the eclipse, and rigg'd with curses dark,*
> *That sunk so low that sacred head of thine.*

17. numeras would be more appropriate with *annos*. *Numerare pecus, tempus*, etc., quoted by Postgate, are less strange, as *pecus* and *tempus* consist essentially of parts which may be counted.

18. in ore tibi est. Cp. *in ore est omni populo* Ter. Ad. 1.2.13, *habere aliquid in ore* Cic. Att. 14. 22. 2, 'to be always talking of.'

non habet unda deos, most pathetic words: not implying that there were no gods of the sea, but that the waves which were engulfing him were pitiless.   Compare again Lycidas:

> *Where were ye, Nymphs, when the remorseless deep*
> *Clos'd o'er the head of your lov'd Lycidas?*
> *For neither were ye playing on the steep,*
> *Where your old Bards, the famous Druids, lie,*
> *Nor on the shaggy top of Mona high,*
> *Nor yet where Deva spreads her wizard stream:*
> *Ay me! I fondly dream!*
> *Had ye been there—for what could that have done?*

19-20. The ship had been moored for the night to a rocky shore, or a rocky bottom; the attaching cable had chafed (*detrito*) and parted (*cadunt*). *Nocturnis procellis* gives the general condition of affairs: it may have been the reason for their mooring, as well as the cause of the disaster. Unable to beat out against the wind, they would moor off a lee-shore, as their only chance; but the wind and sea were too much for the ship, her moorings parted or dragged, and she was lost. The *vinculo* and *fune*, after the manner of Propertius, refer to the same thing.

19. ad saxa may go either with *ligata vincula*, 'the cable secured to rocks,' or with *detrito*, in which case *ligata* will agree with *saxa*, the rocks being said to be bound instead of the ship, 'the moored rocks,' standing for 'the rocks to which she was moored.' The latter interpretation involves a confusion, not unnatural, between the *saxa* to which the ship was moored and those against which she was dashed: both formed part of the same rocky shore. Or again, translating *ligata* in the same sense, we may take *ad saxa* with *cadunt* and the general sense of 'striking' involved in l. 20: 'The cable chafed, her moorings parted, and she was dashed against the rocks.'

21-24. This passage is notable for Mr. R. Ellis' striking emendation of *Mimantis* for *minantis* in l. 22, and for the original interpretation which he has founded on it, and developed in his Prof. Dissert., Univ. Coll., London, 1872, now unfortunately out of print. Mr. Postgate has adopted his reading and interpretation.

21. curas. For *cura*, applied to love, see above note on 2. 12. 4. Here it is probably 'the beloved object,' as Ov. Am. 3. 9. 32

> *Altera cura recens, altera primus amor.*

For the plural in this sense cp. the use of *deliciae, amores, ignes*, to denote a single person, as in Cic. Phil. 6. 5 *sed redeo ad amores deliciasque nostras L. Antonium.* So in Hor. Od. 3. 7. 11 *ignibus* stands for 'Gyges:' *tuis Dicens ignibus uri.*

22. Whatever the true reading of this difficult line may be, there can be no doubt as to the general meaning of the couplet. 'Another shore besides this one testifies to the loss of a dearly-beloved youth.' I have ventured upon a reading which is very slightly removed from that of the MSS., and which appears to me to fit in better with the general tone of the passage than any which has been proposed. The passage is one of intense feeling. It rises in an ascending climax of grief and piteousness from l. 5, where Paetus' fate is first stated, down to l. 28: in a tone of agony the poet fills in every circumstance that can add to the feeling of horror and desolation at such a death. In the midst of this pathetic description come ll. 21, 22, in which Propertius compares the fate of Paetus to that of Argynnus, a youth beloved by Agamemnon, who also met his death by drowning. The ancient passages in which the legend is mentioned are quoted by Mr. Ellis, viz. Plut. Gyrilli 7, Athen. 13. 8, Clemens Alex. Protrept. 11. 20, Sylburg., and Steph. Byz. *Argynnus*. They all connect Argyn· nus with the mainland of Greece; in two the Cephissus is named spe· cially as the river in which he was drowned; in another the Boeotian lake Copais is named in connection with the incident. As the Cephis- sus is out of the question here, Mr. Ellis supposes that Propertius followed some other legend, which connected the drowning of Argynnus with some point on the coast of Asia Minor. Out of several names which might be connected with *Argynnus*, he selects the promontory *Argennum*, exactly opposite to the island of Chios, and conjectures *Mimantis* for *minantis*, showing that in MSS. *Mimas* has frequently been corrupted into *minas*, *minax*, and similar forms. Mount *Mimas* is one of the three mountainous projections into which the peninsula between Teos (S.) and Clazomenae (N.) spreads itself out. Mr. Ellis points out that Agamemnon was specially honoured near Clazomenae (Paus. 7. 5. 6); and there were probably Agamemnon legends all along the Ionian coast. Assuming therefore that 'the waters of Mimas' might be used to denote a point on the shore near to the promontory of Argennum, he proposes to read either

(*a*) *Quae notat Argynni poena, Mimantis aquae*,

making *aquae* in apposition to *litora*, and translating 'Shores sig- nalised by the punishment of Argynnus, the waters of Mimas which drowned him :' or else

(*b*) *Qua notat Argynni poena Mimantis aquas.*

He prefers the former reading, as involving a slighter change, and as being more recondite. The authority of Mr. Ellis will doubt- less commend this reading to future editors : but I venture, with much diffidence, to think that there are strong reasons against it. For (1) there is no legend that Argynnus was *punished* for anything. (2) The 'waters of Mimas' is a somewhat strange expression to denote a point on the shore near Mount Mimas. (3) Strictly speaking, the promon- tory *Argennum* was not on any part of Mount Mimas at all. It was on a spur of Mount Corycus, forming the Western spur of the three- pronged peninsula, while Mimas was the Northern. The passage quoted by R. Ellis from Strabo gives Mimas its true position, be- tween Erythrae and Hypocremnus. No great weight perhaps need be attached to this point, for *Mimas* was apparently the best-known name of the three, and Propertius may have had in his mind the words of Odys. 3. 172

ἣ ὑπένερθε Χίοιο, παρ' ἠνεμόεντα Μίμαντα.

(4) There is nothing in the words, of themselves, to show that Propertius meant here to identify the spot where the shipwreck took place. The Carpathian Sea is mentioned in l. 12, and no doubt the shipwreck took place in that sea. Now the Carpathian Sea lay round the island of Carpathus, between Crete and Rhodes; and though the Carpathian Sea was on the way to Egypt, Mount Mimas was quite away from that course, nearly 150 miles to the north of it. Mr. Ellis gives various quotations as to the Carpathian Sea, but none of them prove that the Carpathian Sea extended up the Ionian coast.

(5) The natural meaning of the words is, ' There is a shore too that testifies of Agamemnon's grief, where Argynnus was drowned.' The point of the illustration is not the place where the drowning took place, but the fact that a loved youth was drowned on some shore as Paetus was drowned. I take therefore the *natat* of F², and read *Argynnus* for *Argynni*. *Qua natat* is as near the reading of NO as *quae notat*, and less likely to be substituted for it than *vice versa*. *Natat* will be used in the sense illustrated in the note on l. 8, of the drowned body, tossed about by the waves, ' floundering,' and so almost equivalent to ' drowned;' the present tense will be partly used in place of the perfect (as referring to *Argynnus*) after the manner of Propertius (see note on 4. 4. 54), partly to convey the sense that Paetus is still at the mercy of the waves. To *Argynnus* the word *poena* is applied in much the same sense as in 2. 20. 31

> *Atque inter Tityi volucres mea poena vagatur,*

where *poena mea* means ' my doomed spirit.' Here, as applied to Argynnus, it will mean 'the doom,' almost 'the thing punished,' ' the victim,' of the threatening water.

Lastly, the words **sunt litora** may be used to indicate a spot known, but not further named. The translation will then be, ' There is a shore which tells of Agamemnon's grief, where floats Argynnus, victim of the angry waters.' Thus the attention is never turned away from the piteous case of Paetus: every word in l. 22 applies literally to him. The word *poena*, removed from *Argynni*, no longer suggests an offence on his part, but suggests parenthetically the innocence of Paetus, falling a victim to the cruel angry waters. *Minacis* would be more usual perhaps in this sense, but the participle is in the manner of Propertius. Pinder's interpretation, '*Argynni poena aquae* = Argynnus punitus ab aqua,' is extremely harsh.

23, 24. These lines I believe to be interpolated. They seem to be a dull prosy commentary by some wiseacre who imagined that the combination of ' Agamemnon,' ' shore,' and 'sea,' must necessarily refer to the much-harped-on detention at Aulis. Fond as

Propertius is of mythological allusions, he introduces them always appropriately, so as to heighten, not to interrupt, the feeling of a passage; this couplet, if genuine, would be almost a solitary instance in Propertius of lines dragged in inappropriately, for the mere purpose of parading learning, and that in a passage of strong feeling where the blemish is all the more apparent. To enter into geographical details, to drag in Iphigenia, and the Greek fleet, and Aulis, painfully interrupts the feeling of the passage, which is concentrated on Paetus and the mode of his death. And the legend knows of no connection between any youth and the delay of the Greek fleet. Further, as Mr. Postgate points out, it is clear that these lines refer to the usual version of the tradition, according to which Argynnus was drowned in the Cephissus. To connect the delay at Aulis with a drowning near Mount Mimas is more than awkward—it is absurd. Mr. Ellis himself doubts the genuineness of these lines, and while offering the following paraphrase, acknowledges that the connection is awkwardly indicated: 'Paetus was wrecked on the coast, which retains the name of the lost Argynnus, that youth whom Agamemnon vainly sought to discover, and kept the fleet at Aulis waiting in the hope of doing so—a delay which caused the death of Iphigenia.' Can any one believe Propertius capable of such an irrelevant and pedantic train of thought in the middle of such a poem as this?

25. Reddite, a vague address to the powers, whoever they are, who control the fate of Paetus' body. Possibly Aquilo and Neptune (ll. 13, 15) are included. *Reddo* (see note on 2. 1. 71) implies not restoration, but a giving of what is due, natural, or expected. All kinds of duty therefore are appropriate to the word: here the notion is that a body is due to the earth, as much as that it is the duty of friends to bury it. Professor Jebb suggests to me that the words *Reddite,* etc. give the key to the whole passage, and that the word *litora* l. 21, with the allusion to the legend of Argynnus, is introduced to add point to the prayer of l. 25, that Paetus' body may at least be buried. 'There is a shore near—the shore where Argynnus was drowned,—O waft the body of Paetus to that shore!'

posita est. So N.: much more pointed than H.'s *positaque.* As Jacob puts it, ' *Praedam habetis : corpus reddite.*'

26. sponte tua, i. e. as we, his friends, are helpless.

vilis, as though he were addressing the *nauta* of l. 27, not the sand itself. So Hor. Od. 1. 28. 23.

27. transibit, as in 2. 7. 9, = *praeteribit.*

28. timor, as in l. 13, for *timori.*

29. Intense feeling is shown by the abrupt way in which the poet addresses one after another the persons or things which have contributed to the death of Paetus, without taking time to realise what they are. Cp. l. 25; here the builders of ships are apostrophised.

N. has *curvae*, mistaking *rates* for a vocative. *Curvate* is the clever but unnecessary conjecture of Mr. Peskett and Mr. G. T. Lendrum. It is much more forcible to identify the *curvas rates* with the *causas leti.* The following line is the commentary.

30. acta, 'of impelling ships. Propertius means that those who go to sea are rowers in Death's vessel.' Postgate. This surely is to introduce unnecessarily a foreign idea. The words merely imply that those who make ships make occasions for death: a death like that of Paetus is brought on, caused, by human hands; **acta,** apparently in the widest sense, after the analogy of *agere vitam, agere otia, agere opus* (3. 5. 8), etc. The harshness of the phrase is mitigated by the fact that the death was a violent one—'brought on,' almost 'inflicted,' by the hand of man.

31. fuerat. Looking back to the time when this new channel for death had been devised.

fatis, of a natural death, like *Fortunae vias* in the next line. *Fortunae miseras vias* is generally taken, as by Pinder, 'Chance ways that lead to misery.' But in fact *fortunae vias* is exactly = *mortis iter; miseras* is an 'epitheton ornans.' 'The hapless ways of Fortune' is equivalent to 'the many sad forms or modes of death.' See notes on *mortis iter* sup. l. 2, and *animi via* 3. 5. 10.

33. For **teneat, tenuere,** cp. 2. 10. 14. Propertius was probably not conscious that he was using the word in slightly different senses. He uses common words like *tenere, agere, via,* with great width of meaning.

34. sua terra. Pinder translates, 'Earth, man's proper element,' as though the language was that of a hen seeing her duckling brood take to the water. *Sua terra* is obviously to be explained by *Penates,* l. 33, of his native country. Postgate quotes Ov. Am. 2. 11. 30, which is exactly in point.

35. paras. See note on 3. 5. 6. The word is here used of ship-building, = *facis, aedificas.*

36. Consenuit, the aoristic perfect, to denote frequency or habit. Postgate well quotes Cat. 4. 25 *nunc recondita Senet quiete.*

fallit ... fidem, 'breaks its word,' the opposite of *fidem servare* or *praestare.* The idea is the same as that in 2. 25. 24

Cum saepe in portu fracta carina natet.

37. insidians. So N. Many edd. have adopted *insidias* on slender authority, a reading weaker in itself. For the idea of *substravit* cp. Shelley :

> *I see the deep's untrampled floor.*

38. succedat, impersonally : ' that it go well with thee.'

Caphāreus or **Caphēreus,** the S. E. promontory of Euboea, on which the Greek fleet was wrecked coming home from Troy, allured by false beacons. Cp. Virg. Aen. 11. 260.

39. triumphales, in the very moment of their triumph.

40. tracta, another instance (like *teneat, acta,* etc., above) of a vague incomplete idea being used in place of a definite one. The verb *traho* suggests ruin and disaster ; it is used of the shipwreck without any special reference to currents or other possible causes for the mishap.

41. Paullatim, well explained by Postgate of the 'gradual piecemeal loss ' of his companions. by Ulysses. But the word goes rather with the whole sense of the line than with *iacturam* specially. Translate, ' one by one.'

42. N. has **soli** : **soliti** is due to Lipsius, and should be read.

43. Quod si verteret can only mean ' Were he now turning ; ' the imperfect is used rhetorically instead of the pluperfect, for the sake of vividness. Propertius throws himself back to the time of the shipwreck, when the action of *verteret* and *viveret* might actually have been going on. *Duxisset* is necessarily the pluperfect, as it refers to the choice made when Paetus determined on the voyage. The peculiarity is that the tense of *verteret* is determined by *viveret* instead of by *duxisset.* Had *verteret* been actually (as it is virtually) in the apodosis, there would have been no difficulty. ' If Paetus had paid attention to my words, he would now be ploughing his father's lands and be living in presence of his own Penates.' In 1. 17. 19–24 Propertius distinguishes accurately between the imperfect and the pluperfect :

> *Illic si qua meum sepelissent fata dolorem,*
> *Ultimus et posito staret amore lapis,*
> *Illa meo caros donasset funere crines,*
> *Molliter et tenera poneret ossa rosa :*
> *Illa meum extremo clamasset pulvere nomen,*
> *Ut mihi non ullo pondere terra foret.*

Here *sepelissent, donasset, clamasset* refer to acts done once for all, and past irrevocably ; *staret* and *poneret* to continuing states or acts, which might have been going on at the moment when the words were spoken. See note on the passage.

contentus is to be taken with *verteret,* and to some extent replaces the pluperfect : 'Had he been content to be turning.' If *patrio bove* be read, *contentus* must be taken ἀπὸ κοινοῦ both with *bove* and with *verteret.*

45. dulcis, ' an accepted, welcome guest ;' the meaning being transferred from the qualities which win favour to the favour with which they are regarded.

46. Pauper at, like *Sera sed* 3. 4. 5, 'Though poor, yet.'

flare potest. So Jacob, for the MS. reading *flere potest*, which has neither sense nor grammar in its favour. There has been no question of weeping or trouble, but only of life safe, in contrast to life lost. From l. 29 the poet has been harping on one theme, the dangers of the sea, the safety of the land. *Terra parum* l. 31 ; *sua terra* l. 34 ; *Ventorum est* l. 35 ; *insidians pontum* l. 37 ; *in mare*, etc. l. 42 ; *contentus verteret* l. 43 ; *Penates* l. 45 ; all carry out the same idea, and prepare us for ' Poor, but on dry land, where no storm can blow.' *Stridorem procellae*, l. 47, catches up the same theme. Postgate justly says that the rendering ' where blowing has no power' is very harsh : I would add, quite unnatural. But when he adds that ' where nothing can blow' is not true, he adopts a standard of truth so strict that it would condemn one-half of the body of existing poetry, and almost all metaphorical or exaggerated expressions. He proposes *sat est* for *potest*, and interprets 'He was poor, it was true, but he was on *terra firma, where freedom from misfortune (nil flere ?) is enough food for contentment.*' Do the words italicised contain more truth than the statement that land, as contrasted with the sea, is ' a place where no wind can blow ?' And the very next line tells us that on shore Paetus had not to hear *stridorem procellae*. Palmer ingeniously suggests *Pauper : at in terra nil ubi flere potest ?* ' Poor, I grant you : but where on earth is it possible to find no cause for complaint ?' This is harsh : and in this context *terra* could only mean 'dry land.' Hous. approves Baerens' conj. *at in terra nil nisi fleret opes*, 'poor, I grant, but on dry land his poverty would have been his only grief.'

47. Non tulit... audire, ' did not endure to hear,' i. e. ' had not the pain of hearing,' 'had not to hear.' Postgate, to be consistent, has to translate 'Could not endure to hear,' as though Paetus always dreaded storms. But if so, why did he go to sea ? Further, this interpretation requires *hic* to be taken as the pronoun, which seems not so good.

hic is emphatic, ' while he was here at home.' The lines 47–50 contrast the comfort of home with the terrors and labours of the deep ; and the point is, not that Paetus was nervous about storms, but that he was not conscious either of the comforts he was enjoying, or of the hardships he was about to face.

49. Thyio. So Hertz.: the MSS. have *Chio*. θύα or θυία was the Greek name of the citrus tree (*Thuia articulata*), to which the Romans attached extraordinary value for purposes of furniture. Persius speaks of luxurious couches being made of this wood, 1. 53.

thalamo is probably the bed made of *citrus* wood, though it might be taken of the chamber itself, furnished or panelled with that wood.

Oricia terebintho seems either to have suggested, or to have been copied from, Virg. Aen. 10. 136, of ivory set in a frame,

> *Inclusum buxo aut Oricia terebintho.*

The *terebinthus* is our turpentine tree. Pliny describes the wood as pliant, durable, *et nigri splendoris*. H. N. 13. 12, and says cups were turned out of it. He includes both the *citrus* and the *terebinthus* among the woods suitable for veneering purposes, the others being box, palm, holly, ilex and elder-root (16. 84).

Oricia, from *Oricum* or *Oricus*, in Illyria, the port of embarkation for Brundusium. See 1. 8. 20, where Postgate says it was 'famous for box and turpentine wood.' What is the authority for this statement? Pliny says that the tree grew to a great size in Syria, but that there was a small shrubby variety which grew on Mount Ida in the Troad, and in Macedonia, 13. 12, while in 16. 30 he says that, like the cedar and larch, it loves the mountains. In all probability the *terebinth* was called *Orycian*, merely because *Orycus* was the port of shipping, just as all Eastern wares were called *Syrian*, as *Sherry* derives its name from *Xeres*, and *Hamburg Sherry* from the port of Hamburg.

50. Effultum or **Est fultum**, an undoubted correction for *Et fultum*. It is hard to choose between the two: but *effultus* is twice used by Virgil.

versicolore pluma is difficult. We can scarcely doubt that cushions, *cervicalia*, are alluded to, as by Martial 12. 17. 8

> *Dormit et in pluma purpureoque toro.*

But if the cushions are only stuffed with feathers, why *versicolore?* Becker, Gallus p. 288–9, makes out that the *plumarii* exercised an art of embroidery with feathers, making 'feather tapestry.' This may be so: but Mart. 14. 146 applies the terms *cervical* and *pluma* to the same object, and *pluma versicolor* might well stand for 'a parti-coloured feather-cushion,' *pluma* denoting the contents, *versicolor* the ornamentation of the case. *Versicolor*, as Postgate points out, properly means 'changing colour,' like our word 'shot' as applied to silk.

51. Propertius now paints the painful details of the death. The human nails, which are continuous with, and a modification of, the scarf skin, will drop off with the scarf skin after two or three days' immersion in water, especially if the temperature be warm. Postgate says Propertius knew this, and imagined the same thing might happen during life from the mere force of the waves. Paley supposes the meaning to be that Paetus 'could not swim effectively because his hands were hurt.' It seems simpler to suppose that what Propertius meant was that the nails were torn off by the violent dashing of the body by the waves against the rocky bottom. *Vivos* is better than *vivo*, which is weak, and was probably suggested by *huic.* See Hor. Sat. 1. 10. 71 *vivos et roderet ungues.*

52. miser invisam express the horror of the moment; **traxit,** the long deep draught. **Miser hiatus** = *miser hiante ore.*

53. improba, one of the most difficult of Latin words to translate. As *probus* is constantly joined with *pudicus,* of a slave, to denote well-regulated, respectful conduct, so *improbus* almost always implies some form of *excess,* in a culpable direction, with its correlative, in a human subject, of effrontery. Thus *improbus anser* Virg. Geo. 1. 119, is 'the greedy goose;' *labor improbus* id. 1. 146, is 'excessive,' 'unceasing labour,' 'that knows no rest;' *improbus iste Dares* Virg. Aen. 5. 397, 'you braggart;' *improba ventris rabies* id. 2. 357, 'ravening hunger' (Mackail translates 'mad malice of hunger,' quite wrong); *Improbe Amor* id. 4. 412, of the reckless audacity of Love (Mackail 'injurious,' wrong again); *ingenti fruor improboque somno,* 'unconscionable,' Mart. 12. 18. 13; *negat improbus* Hor. Epp. 1. 7. 63, 'the impudent scoundrel.' The word may often be well rendered by 'bold.' Here the idea is that night adds a new horror to the situation, as if it were not terrible enough already. 'Cruel,' perhaps brings this meaning out better than 'pitiless' (Post.).

54. ut occideret ... colere, 'came together to,' 'combined for,' the loss of Paetus.

55. Flens, in the extremity of his fear. The ancients thought it natural to weep in moments of danger. An Italian boatman caught in a squall will resort to tears and the saints for safety, instead of paying out the sheet. Cp. *siccis oculis* Hor. Od. 1. 3. 18. See Prop. 2. 27. 7, with Postgate's note.

56. niger, in reference to *nox improba* l. 53.

clauderet ora, lit. 'shut his mouth,' to use our own colloquial expression.

57-64. This last dying speech affords a striking example of the artificiality of ancient poetry. and especially of that of the Alexandrine school. To a modern ear such a speech, in the mouth of a drowning man, choked with salt water, would be absurd: but it must be remembered that speeches were an essential part of the stock in trade of an ancient writer, whether of history or poetry. Such speeches are not intended to represent what any actual person ever said, or was supposed to have said; they merely sum up, in a pictorial way, the view of the situation taken by the author, or that which he supposes to have been taken by a bystander.

57. The gods of the Aegean are the winds: Horace calls *Notus* the *arbiter Hadriae* Od. 1. 3. 15 and *Auster* the *Dux inquieti turbidus Hadriae* 3. 3. 5; but that is not the same as calling them gods. Nor does Virg. Aen. 1. 52 sqq. assign to Aeolus any dominion over the sea, but only over the winds and storms.

58. degravat, 'weighs down,' 'sinks.'

59. miseros primae lanuginis annos = *me miserum in p. l. aetate.* So *nostram vitam* for *me* 3. 11. 1. Postgate refers to the imitation in Ov. Her. 15. 85.

60. longas manus, of the delicate tapering hands of a boy. A long hand was admired, Prop. 2. 2. 5.

61. alcyonum scopulis, i.e. 'rocks haunted by halcyons,' and consequently wild and rugged.

62. fuscina (*furca?*) a three- (or four-) pronged spear (τρίαινα), used by fishermen for spearing fish, and given as an attribute to Neptune. It was used as a weapon by the gladiator called *retiarius*, who first endeavoured to entangle his adversary with his net, and then attacked him with the *fuscina.* Cp. Juv. 2. 143 and Hom. Od. 5. 292.

63. evehat. So the MSS.: 'throw me ashore at;' not very satisfactory. *Advehat* has been proposed. But Postgate quotes Ov. Her. 18. 197, where Leander, before crossing the Hellespont, says

Optabo tamen ut partes expellar in illas.

Eveho is frequently used of passengers by sea, as Liv. 37. 15 *placuit tamen Regillum classe tota evehi ad portum Ephesi.*

64. de me, to be taken closely with *hoc*: 'this remnant of me,' 'these remains of mine,' 'will be enough, if only,' etc.

With the idea of this line compare Lycidas:

Ay me! whilst thee the shores, and sounding seas
Wash far away, where'er thy bones are hurl'd,
Whether beyond the stormy Hebrides,
Where thou perhaps under the whelming tide

Visit'st the bottom of the monstrous world;

. . . .

Look homeward, Angel, now, and melt with ruth,
And, O ye dolphins, waft the hapless youth.

65. torta vertigine fluctus form one idea, *torta vertigine* describing the character of the *fluctus*.

Subtrahit, 'sucked him down.'

69. Closely imitated by Ov. E. P. 2. 6. 14

Brachia da lasso potius prendenda natanti,
Nec pigeat mento supposuisse manum.

decuit subponere. The present infinitive is correctly used in Latin with the perfect of such verbs as *decuit, oportuit*, etc., where we say ' you ought to have,' ' you should have,' etc.

70. gravare, ' weigh down,' ' prove too much for.'

71. mea vela. *Mea* is emphatic: 'thou wilt never see *me* setting sail :' ' see sail of mine.' Postgate.

72. condar. There is no need to take this of his burial : the idea is simply that of uneventful, unventuresome seclusion, in contrast to the hardihood of Paetus.

iners has thus its proper meaning of 'inactive,' as in 1. 8. 10. Cp. Hor. Od. 4. 7. 12 *Bruma recurrit iners.* When *condere* refers to burial, the reference is always made clear by the context.

III. 11.

THIS truly magnificent poem presents to us the genius of Propertius at its best, and is constructed with the greatest artistic skill. It recalls to us Tennyson's ' Dream of Fair Women,' as it passes in rapid but majestic review the more famous women of antiquity : but the effect of the catalogue is strictly subordinated to the main end of the poem, which is to make the reader feel the immense issues which were at stake at the battle of Actium, to connect the victor with the great worthies of ancient Rome, and to proclaim that on that great day he had constituted himself the Liberator of his country, both on sea and land. The great shame of the whole campaign to the Roman mind was that it had been waged with a woman, and that a woman had been able to place the state in jeopardy ; the poets are never weary of expatiating on the infamy of seeing Romans enslaved to a shameless and luxurious Oriental queen, with her trains of eunuchs and her mosquito nets. To associate the highest kind of glory with victory over such an antagonist required no little skill : it was a scandal that such a foe should have been allowed even to

buckle on her armour, Prop. 4. 6. 22. Even Horace has not escaped
from the difficulty : were the Egyptian queen so corrupt, so effem-
inate and luxurious, where was the great glory of overcoming her?
Antony's great ability could not be recognised : for the cue given
out both by Caesar and Augustus was that Romans had never
triumphed over Romans.   Propertius solves the difficulty in his own
way.   He exalts the victory of Augustus by exalting first the genius
of woman, and by pointing to the master-minds amongst women
who had showed great masculine powers, and exerted empire over
men. The character of Cleopatra is not spared ; she is painted in the
vilest colours; but there is the sense all through that she was a great
woman, that she had been strong enough to conceive direct hopes of
adding Rome to her domain, and that she had all but succeeded in
her ambition. He makes us feel that there was indeed cause for trembling at Rome during the time when, as Horace puts it Od. 1. 37. 6–8

> *Capitolio*
> *Regina dementes ruinas*
> *Funus et imperio parabat.*

All this is naturally introduced, as from the poet's own experiences :
he begins simply, in his usual strain, justifying his devotion to Cynthia : his enslavement to her (cp. l. 2 *addictum sub sua iura virum*
to Horace's *emancipatus feminae*) is typified and justified by the enslavement of men to Medea, to Omphale, to Semiramis, and the all-but
enslavement of the Roman world to Cleopatra.   The subject grows
naturally out of his own life and feeling: and the panegyric on
Augustus is thus introduced more naturally, and with far more power,
than in the more elaborate and official description of Actium in 4. 6.

1. versat. The frequentative form of the verb makes it appropriate for expressing violence and passion. Thus in Virg. Aen. 7.
336 Juno declares that Alecto the Fury has power *odiis versare
domos* ('to overturn,' Mackail, but it is rather equivalent to *turbare*).
Cp. Liv. 2. 45. 5 *nunc pudor nunc indignatio versare pectora;*
Prop. 3. 17. 12

> *Spesque timorque animum versat utroque toro.*

meam vitam. A Propertian periphrase for *me*.

2. addictum, 'made over.' *Addicere* is said of the judge who
formally makes over any thing or person to a claimant. *Addictus*
is thus specially used of a debtor handed over as bondsman to his
creditor. Horace has the same idea in a similar connection of Antonius, *Emancipatus feminae* Epod. 9. 12. So of himself as a free
lance in philosophy, Epp. 1. 1. 14

> *Nullius addictus iurare in verba magistri.*

3. Crimina ignavi capitis, 'a charge of cowardice.' *Capitis* is used as above, 2. 1. 36, where see note. The neighbourhood of *addictum* and *crimen* is intended doubtless to suggest also the technical meaning of the terms.

4. nequeam, the subjunctive, as constituting the *crimen*. The figure in this line is changed to that of an animal under the yoke.

5. Venturam . . . mortem is the MS. reading. Hertz. adopts *noctem* in the sense of 'storm,' quoting no authority. Palmer in his edition reads *iactura*, to correspond with *vulneribus*; but he now proposes *Venturum . . . motum*, and for *motum*, 'a storm,' compares Hor. Od. 3. 27. 22, and Prop. 3. 13. 21. See too Virg. Aen. 10. 99 *Murmura venturos nautis prodentia ventos.* The four lines are an expansion of the maxim *experientia docet :* 'the sailor, the soldier, learn by experience to expect danger: bold as were the words of my youth, I have a like experience to offer you.' The sentiment is similar to that of 2. 27. 11.

R. Ellis, Journal of Phil. vol. 15. p. 19, ingeniously suggests that Propertius had in view Pind. Nem. 7. 17

σοφοὶ δὲ μέλλοντα τριταῖον ἄνεμον

ἔμαθον, οὐδ' ὑπὸ κέρδει βάλον,

σοφοί corresponding to *navita*, 'the trained seaman.' But I cannot believe in his suggested reading *molem*, which he illustrates by Virg. Aen. 5. 789 *quam molem subito excierit*, of the storm got up at Juno's request.

7. Ista verba, i. e. 'those words which you cast up against me now.'

9. adamas (ἀδάμας), iron or steel: used figuratively for the hardest conceivable substance, Ov. A. A. 1. 659

lacrimis adamanta movebis.

The word is here used to heighten the sense of the passage, as though 'to break bulls to a yoke of adamant' implied a more complete subjugation.

10. Cp. Ovid, Her. 12. 95

Arva venenatis pro semine dentibus imples:

Nascitur, et gladios scutaque miles habet.

humo, a local ablative.

11. Custodis, in adjectival apposition to *serpentis*.

clausit hiatus, again like our colloquial 'shut his mouth.'

12. Aeson was Jason's father.

14. Penthesilea, queen of the Amazons, who dwelt round the Lacus Maeotis (sea of Azov), came to help the Trojans during the siege, and was slain by Achilles. Cp. Ov. Her. 21. 117

Non ego constiteram sumpta peltata securi,
  Qualis in Iliaco Penthesilea solo.

15. When Achilles lifted the helmet from her face, he was en-
amoured of her beauty.

cassida, archaic for the more usual form *cassis.* So Virg. Aen.
11. 775. The helmet 'bared' her face by being taken off. An
elliptical or 'condensed' (Pinder) expression, similar to *placidi* ·
straverunt aequora venti Virg. Aen. 5. 763 and similar phrases.
Cp. 3. 22. 22 and note.

16. Vicit victorem recalls Hor. Epp. 2. 1. 156
  Graecia capta ferum victorem cepit.

candida, for 'beautiful,' seems strange as an epithet of *forma;*
but see note on 2. 3. 24. The word is frequently applied to a person
as a whole, or to some part of the body, as *brachia* 2. 16. 24, *colla*
3. 17. 29, *pes, humeri, cervix,* etc., and Ov. Met. 1. 743 affords an
exact parallel to the phrase before us,

  De bove nil superest, formae nisi candor, in illa.

17. All the MSS. read **Ōmphălē** which involves a hiatus, and a
shortening of the last syllable. Virgil and other poets have this
license not unfrequently, as E. 8. 108, in the first thesis of a dactyl,

  Credimus? an quī amant ipsi sibi somnia fingunt?

But, as Palmer points out, it is very rare in the last syllable of a
dactyl (see Virg. E. 3. 79 *vălē vălī inquit,* and Aen. 3. 211 *Insulăe
Ionio*), and it is unknown to Propertius ; so he most ingeniously conjectures *Iardanis,* 'daughter of Jardanus,' a name by which Omphale
is designated by Ovid, Her. 9. 103. He points out that in no less than
ten instances Propertius designates female characters by their patronymics ; thus Helen is called *Tyndaris,* Penelope *Icariotis,* Niobe
Tantalis and so on. *Omphale* would thus be a natural gloss, imported into the text. Further he points out that the scribe who
copied *Omphale* into N. had a rage for lengthening syllables in
proper names, and probably intended *Omphăle* to be scanned *Omphāle.* The same hand has elsewhere *Antīlŏchi* for *Antĭlŏchi* 2. 13.
49, *Ărēthusa* for *Ărĕthusa* 4. 3. 1, while other MSS. have *Cāpănēi*
for *Căpănēī* 2. 34. 40. One MS. inserts *et* after *Omphale,* but the
word is out of place, an evident interpolation.

tantum goes with *ut* l. 19.

in tantum formae processit honorem, a very strained expression : ' reached such a pitch of beauty.' *Honor,* as in its technical political sense of 'a public office,' is here used to denote 'an
external mark, stage, or degree' of beauty.

18. Omphale was queen of Lydia; **Gygaeo lacu,** a huge

reservoir which never failed, mentioned as a marvel in connection with the monument of king Alyattes by Herod. 1. 93. To what the word *tincta* refers is not known.

19. Columnas, i. e. the Pillars of Hercules, supposed to have been set up by him at *Calpe* and *Abyla*.

20. tam dura, 'in that hard hand of his.'

The next figure in Propertius' gallery is Semiramis, the fabulous queen of Nineveh, daughter of a Syrian goddess, and wife of Ninus, whose favour she won by her skill in taking Bactra. After her husband's death she ruled long alone; conquered many nations, including Egypt; built Babylon, with its famous walls of brick ; erected in Nineveh a monument to her husband a mile high; and did many other marvellous things.

21. The terms *Persians, Medes*, and *Parthians*, are used indifferently by the Augustan writers. In Od. 2. 2 Horace speaks of the Parthians first as Persians, l. 22, and a few lines further on as Medes. Cp. Luc. 6. 446 *Babylon Persea.*

22. ut, consecutive : ' so as to rear,' = 'rearing.'

cocto, of the brick walls of Babylon. Cp. Ov. Met. 4. 58

> *ubi dicitur altam*
> *Coctilibus muris cinxisse Semiramis urbem.*

Paley and Pinder both suppose Propertius' meaning to be that these great works, carried out by women, would never have been achieved by their husbands alone. There is no indication of any such comparison in the text. All that Propertius does is to indicate instances of female greatness.

23. in adversum missi, i. e. ' moving in opposite directions,' ' meeting face to face.'

24. N. and F. have **neo** ; others **ne.** If *ne* be read, it must be used in a consecutive sense, so that *ne = ut non.* Paley pronounces this ' an incorrect usage:' so also Pinder, while Palmer preserves the *nec* of N. and adopts *mitti*, the tempting conjecture of R. Y. Tyrrell for *missi* in l. 23. But all these editors have failed to see the true construction. *Semiramis* is the main subject of the whole passage, down to l. 26 : *statuit* in l. 21 being continued by *Duxit, condidit* l. 25, and *Iussit* l. 26. The whole three lines, 22-24, are subordinate to *statuit*, and *ne*, l. 24, is subordinate to *ut* l. 22. The whole passage reads literally thus : 'Semiramis built Babylon in such a way that she reared walls of brick, and that two chariots facing each other could not (i. e. needed not to) graze their sides in consequence of their axles touching.' *Ne* does not stand for *ut non*, but only for *non* after the preceding *ut* of consequence. Cp. Cic. Fin. 2. 8 *Ex* *quo efficitur non ut voluptas ne sit voluptas, sed ut voluptas non sit summum bonum.* Here no distinction can be drawn between *ut ne* and *ut non*, each signifying ' so that not.' Our passage is strictly analogous: *statuit urbem ut tolleret opus et ut currus ne possent stringere latus.* This use of *ne* as = *non* in consecutive propositions suggests that *ne* might similarly be used after *ut* in final propositions, in which case *ut ne* would mean ' in order that not ' and thus be = *ne* alone. This supposition at once explains the difficult passage, Hor. Sat. 2. 1. 37, in vain tortured by commentators :

> *Missus ad hoc pulsis, vetus est ut fama, Sabellis,*
> *Quo ne per vacuum Romano incurreret hostis.*

Ne here simply stands for the negative after *ut* final, and *quo ne* is = *ne*, ' in order that not.' The whole difficulty is thus removed ; and Palmer's ingenious but unnatural explanation, connecting *quo* with *vacuum*, ' unguarded of whom,' rendered unnecessary. Bentley quotes the Digest 21. 1. 17. 5 in illustration of *quo ne: si celandi causa, quo ne ad dominum reverteretur, fugisset.* But the authority is late, and the interpretation doubtful : Schütz punctuates *si celandi causa quo, ne ad dominum reverteretur, fugisset.* More to the point is Cic. Fam. 7. 2 *praefinisti quo ne pluris emerem.* Palmer says of this passage, ' It is obvious that *quo* is governed by *pluris*.' True : but *quo* contains either a final or consecutive meaning = *ut eo*, and therefore *ne* is used, not *non*. So exactly in Liv. 34. 6 quoted by Roby: *cautum erat quo ne plus auri et argenti facti, quo ne plus signati auri et aeris, domi haberemus.* Here *quo* is doubtless governed by *plus* ; but *quo ne plus* is the exact equivalent of *ut eo ne plus* or *ut ne plus eo*, and exactly illustrates the point insisted on. Another illustration is Hor. Sat. 1. 1. 40

> *Nil obstet tibi dum ne sit te ditior alter,*

where *ne* does not mean ' lest,' ' in order that not,' but is simply used for *non* after *dum* in the sense of ' provided that,' to which meaning, as indicating purpose, *non* would not be appropriate. The rule might perhaps be formulated in this way : ' After *ut*, signifying consequence, *ne may* be used ; after *ut*, or any similar conjunction, denoting purpose, *ne must* be used, in place of *non*.' Bohn (trans. p. 90 note) quotes three cases of *ne* for *ut non* in consecutive clauses, but none of these are consecutive clauses. They are *substantival* clauses only. The *nec* of N. however, combined with Prof. Tyrrell's *mitti* for *missi*, gives an excellent, if somewhat refined, meaning : ' Could meet on the top, *and yet* not touch.' See Hous., J. of Phil. xxi. p. 191.

    stringere, ' to graze ': its proper meaning is ' to grasp tightly,'

e. g. *stringere ferrum*, usually wrongly translated 'to draw.' *Stricto gladio* is 'sword in hand.' How it came to signify 'just to touch and no more' is not clear: perhaps from the idea of pressing or touching without penetrating. Thus Virg. Aen. 5. 163

> *Litus ama, et laevas stringat sine palmula cautes;*

and in Ov. Am. 3. 2. 12, of chariots just grazing the *meta*,

> *Nunc stringam metas interiore rota.*

ab, not exactly redundant: it states the causation in a more emphatic way, or denotes the effect as immediate. *Excidet ab aevo*, 3. 2. 25, quoted by Palmer, is different; *putris ab aestu*, 4. 3. 39, is 'in consequence of the heat.' It is hard however to give *ab* any special meaning in 2. 27. 11

> *Solus amans novit quando periturus, et a qua*
> *Morte.*

25. In allusion, apparently, to the great dykes attributed to Semiramis by Herod. 1. 184, by which he says the Euphrates, which formerly inundated the whole plain, was kept within its banks. *Duxit* is here used for the making of a new channel, and so 'leading off' or 'diverting' the wate s: cp. *aquaeductus.* Propertius' idea seems to be that she introduced the water into the city.

26. surgere. Propertius evidently makes a confusion between the taking of *Bactra*, which Semiramis accomplished, and the founding of her capital. *Bactra*, the capital of Bactriana, was known to the Romans as forming the most distant part of the Parthian empire: hence they use the name vaguely as synonymous with the extreme East. So Hor. Od. 3. 29. 28, Virg. Geo. 2. 138, Aen. 8. 688. In all three passages the city *Bactra* is used instead of *Bactriana*, evidently in ignorance. To a Roman mind the Euphrates would at once suggest the Parthians. There is thus no need to change *surgere*, with Burmann and Lachmann, into *subdere*.

27. Rapere in ius is a common expression: **in crimine** will mean therefore 'in advancing my impeachment.'

nam, as frequently, gives the reason not for a statement made, but the reason why the writer makes (or, as here, omits to make) a statement. 'I pass on from Semiramis—for what need to instance heroes and gods when we have the example of Jupiter himself?— and tell of our latest and greatest scandal.' See Hertzberg's references, especially Stat. Silv. 2. 1. 210

> obeunt noctesque diesque
> *Astraque, nec solidis prodest sua machina terris;*
> *Nam populos, mortale genus, plebisque caducae*
> *Quis fleat interitus?*

31. coniugis is read by N. and should probably be adopted. 'The price asked of her abandoned husband,' 'the price he had to pay.' If **coniugii** be read, it must bear the same meaning, as = *coniugis*. The *coniugium* was not foul to *her*: the disgrace was not in her making such a demand, but in his being ready to entertain it. The idea is exactly the same as that of Florus 4. 11 *Haec mulier Egyptia ab ebrio imperatore pretium libidinum Romanum imperium petiit.* The genitive is a subjective genitive: 'the price to be paid *by* the husband.' H. quotes Juv. 12. 62 *tempora prospera vectoris*, 'the weather *of*, i. e enjoyed *by*, the passenger.'

It is worth noting that the Romans laid no blame on Caesar for his notorious connection with Cleopatra, which nearly cost him his life and reputation in the Alexandrine war. This no doubt was partly because he *was* Caesar; but mainly because he did not allow her to be a disturbing element in his political career. What the Augustan poets brand as unpardonable in Antony was that he suffered himself to be estranged from Rome by Egyptian ties, and attempted to bring the power of the East to bear upon Rome in war.

32. addictos. See above on l. 2.

33. dolis aptissima tellus. The Romans, like most nations, believed all foreigners to be more treacherous and untruthful than themselves. They regarded the Greeks as a nation of liars and flatterers: *perfidia plusquam Punica* was a proverb with them. The Greeks shared their estimate of the Egyptians: Pinder quotes Aesch. Frag. 299

δεινοὶ πλέκειν τοι μηχανὰς Αἰγύπτιοι.

'Perfide Albion' affords another example: with us, again, it is a matter of faith that French, Germans, Italians, Americans—all nations in short with whom we come in contact—are less honest and veracious than ourselves.

34. totiens, referring to the various scenes of violence and treachery that had been enacted on Egyptian territory—the murder of Pompey, the famous siege of Alexandria when Caesar was in such eminent peril, and lastly, the scandalous excesses of Antony and Cleopatra.

35. arena, the Egyptian shore on which Pompey was struck down on landing by his old centurion Septimius, by order of the Egyptian king's advisers, on the 29th Sept. B. C. 48.

tres triumphos, i. e. Pompey's three great triumphs: (1) for his Numidian victories, B. C. 81 ; (2) for his successes in Spain over Sertorius, B. C. 71 ; (3) for his conquest of Mithridates, B. C. 61.

36. hanc, more Propertiano, for *illam*.

notam, apparently that inflicted by the train of Egyptian disasters.

37. Issent . . . tibi funera, a strange phrase : we have seen how fond Propertius is of applying *ire, via,* etc., in various meanings. 'Better hadst thou died.' The idea seems to be *res issent tibi melius si mortuus esses.*

Phlegra was an ancient name given to *Pallene,* the most westerly of the three peninsulas which form the extremity of Chalcidice, in which the battle of Zeus with the giants took place. The term is here used in the loosest way to denote the battle of Pharsalus, fought in Thessaly.

38. si daturus eras is here = *si dedisses.*

socero, because Pompey had married Julia, Caesar's daughter, in B. C. 59 : she unfortunately died B. C. 54.

39. Canopus, mentioned with loathing by Juv. 1. 26, 15. 46, etc., as a sink of iniquity.

40. ' That single stain burnt into or upon the blood of Philip.' The emphasis is on *una,* which has the force of *unica.* ' Cleopatra stands alone or pre-eminent in her character as a stain and scandal to the house of Philip.' Prop. would not have admitted that she was a blot on the fair name of Rome : nor does the idea suit the passage.

41. Anubis, an Egyptian god, with a man's form and the head of a dog. Similarly in Virg. Aen. 8. 698 Cleopatra has Anubis fighting for her at Actium against Neptune, Venus and Minerva.

42. Note the force and indignation of this line. In a somewhat different spirit Juvenal indignantly exclaims 3. 62

    Jam pridem Syrus in Tiberim defluxit Orontes.

43. The *sistrum* or rattle was the characteristic implement of the worship of the Egyptian goddess *Isis ;* it was also used by the Egyptians in war in place of the *tuba.* Thus Virgil, in his grand description of the battle of Actium, represents Cleopatra as brandishing a *sistrum,* Aen. 8. 696

    Regina in mediis patrio vocat agmina sistro.

44. Baris : a peculiar flat boat much used in Egypt. The word is used several times by Aesch. of Eastern boats.

Liburna, the small swift vessels, used by the Illyrian pirates, which formed the strength of Augustus' fleet at Actium, and are contrasted by Hor. with the huge galleys of Antony, Epod. 1. 1

    Ibis Liburnis inter alta navium,

      Amice, propugnacula.

45. conopia, ' mosquito-nets.' The still hardy Romans looked upon the use of this now indispensable protection as a disgraceful mark of luxury ; for a similar reason, the first wearers of parasols in this country, not a century ago, were mobbed in the streets. No less indignant is Horace, Epod. 9. 16

> *Interque signa turpe militaria*
> *Sol aspicit conopium.*

Hence our 'canopy.' κώνωψ is 'a gnat.'

46. Iura dare, 'to appoint laws,' 'to legislate,' 'rule.' The statement of this line appears to have been literally true: for Dion 50. 5 says that Cleopatra actually τῶν Ῥωμαίων ἄρχειν ἐλπίσαι, τὴν τε εὐχὴν τὴν μεγίστην ὁπότε τι ὀμνύοι ποιεῖσθαι, τὸ ἐν τῷ Καπιτωλίῳ δικάσαι. Doubtless Horace refers to this Od. 1. 37. 6.

> *dum Capitolio*
> *Regina dementes ruinas*
> *Funus et imperio parabat.*

et statuas inter et arma Mari. Hertz. gravely insists that *statuas* must not be connected with *Mari*, because there were no statues of men in the Capitol (except those of the kings and of Brutus) before the time of Caesar. But his history is as much at fault as his Latin. It would be impossible to separate *statuas* from *Mari*: and, as a matter of fact, the reference is to the notorious and daring exploit of Caesar during his curule aedileship B.C. 65. Sulla had passed a law forbidding Marius' bust to be displayed, or any monument to be put up in his honour. Caesar had already dared (B.C. 68) to violate this law by having the image of Marius paraded at the funeral of his widow Julia, Caesar's aunt. He now outraged senatorial Rome, and delighted the mob, by causing the statues of Marius, with the trophies representing his Jugurthine and Cimbric triumphs, to be replaced secretly by night in the Capitol, Suet. Jul. 11; Vell. 2. 43; Val. Max. 6. 9. 4.

Palmer conjectures **dares**, with a point of exclamation at the end of the line. In this case *ausa*, l. 41, is a participle, not the verb, and the whole passage, 39–46, reads as one sentence. But a long passage of this kind, reserving its one principal verb for eight lines, is scarcely after the manner of Propertius.

48. simili, i. e. 'with a name like itself,' in allusion to the name *Superbus*.

49. si ... fuit. Cp. *si versat ... et trahit* sup. ll. 1, 2, *si daturus eras* l. 38. Propertius is fond of *si* with the indicative. In these cases *si* loses almost all its hypothetical force. If on the one hand Propertius 'prefers the potential to the actual' (Postgate, Introduction, p. xl), so on the other he is equally fond of substituting the actual and the present for the hypothetical and the remote. Translate, 'If, after all, the rule of a woman had to be endured.'

50. Augusto is the dative, going with *precare diem*. But the conjunction of the name with *salva* is intended to indicate that Augustus was the saviour.

51. timidi. The Nile shrinks now in terror before Augustus, in contrast to the threats which it uttered before his victory, l. 42.

vaga, as already noted, is used frequently in a bad sense. It may refer here to the many mouths of the Nile, or to its inundations, when it spreads over country not its own. *Vagus* has frequently the sense of irregular action, beyond a thing's proper sphere. Thus it is used of a mast unstepped (Cat.), of a foot in too big a shoe (Hor.), of the Tiber beyond his banks, Hor. Od. 1. 2. 18.

53. Brachiā spectavit. Prop. thus tolerates a short final syllable before words beginning with *sc, sp, st, sq.* So *benĕ sponde-bant* 4. 1. 41 ; *consuluitquĕ striges* 4. 5. 17. For the plural *colubris* cp. *geminos angues* in Virg. Aen. 8. 697.

spectavit, read by Per., seems here to be the true reading. **Spectavi** cannot be satisfactorily explained. It could only refer to seeing in imagination, or to some representation of Cleopatra. Possibly, as Pinder suggests, that carried in Augustus' triumph.

54. soporis iter, like *mortis iter* 3. 7. 2 and *fortunae auximus vias* id. 32.

trahere is difficult. It seems to mean 'saw her limbs dragging along the secret path of death.' In that case *trahere iter* would be like *rapere, vorare, viam,* etc., but denoting *slow* and painful progress.

55. hoc ... tanto ... cive, ablative absolute, or ablative of circumstance. 'So long as thou possessedst so great a citizen as he.'

cive. Augustus specially studied to be *civilis* in his behaviour, and his *civile ingenium* was especially contrasted with the reserve and hauteur of Tiberius.

56. et ... lingua, 'nor yet that tongue,' i. e. her own. Horace speaks of Cleopatra's excesses Od. 1. 37. 14

Mentemque lymphatam Mareotico.

57. toto. N. has *toto* here, and is probably right. There is strong evidence that Propertius used the archaic declension of *unus, totus, nullus,* etc. *Nullae curae* occurs 1. 20. 35 in the dative, and *uno* in 2. 1. 47. It is to be noted that we often find analogies for Propertius' archaic usages in Plautus, who was, as Professor Palmer reminds me, Propertius' fellow-countryman.

58. timuit territa, pleonastic.

Marte, 'in war.'

59. Here follows a list of famous Roman exploits, introduced for the purpose of declaring that they are all thrown into the shade by Augustus' victory at Actium.

classes. Referring, apparently, to the incredible exertions by which Scipio had a fleet of sixty vessels built and equipped in forty-five days from the time of the felling of the timber.

60. Pompeia, used as an adjective for *Pompeiana.*

Bospore, i. e. the country adjoining the Cimmerian Bosporus (straits of Kertsch) which Pompey assigned to Pharnaces after the conquest of Mithridates.

61. monimenta, in allusion to the spot called *Lacus Curtius* in the forum, which marked the heroic sacrifice of M. Curtius, Liv. 7. 6. 5.

Syphax. A Numidian prince, taken by Masinissa in B.C. 203, and conveyed by Laelius to Rome to adorn Scipio's triumph.

62. An expressive line. Pyrrhus came over to Italy in the height of his reputation, being esteemed the greatest warrior of his time; in spite of his brilliant successes at Heraclea (B.C. 280), at Asculum (279), and in Sicily (278–276), he was utterly defeated, and his fortunes shipwrecked, at Beneventum (275).

64. Palmer unnecessarily adopts Scaliger's conjecture *Decius admisso* for the MS. reading *At Decius misso. Mittere* is frequently used where speed and strength are implied: cp. *mittere vocem, currum, hastam, fulmina, se ab saxo,* etc. The allusion of course is to the self-devotion of P. Decius Mus in the great battle against the Latins, B.C. 340. Cocles, apparently, gave his name to the street running up from the bridge which he 'kept so well.'

68. The mingled flattery and blasphemy of this line could scarce be matched.

69. At the southern extremity of the island of Leucas was a famous precipitous promontory called *Leucas, Leucatas,* or *Leucate.* On the summit of the cliff stood the temple of the Leucadian Apollo. There was also a temple of *Apollo Actiacus* or *Actius* at Actium, in Acarnania, at the southern entrance of the Ambracian gulf. Augustus beautified this temple, and instituted games here, in honour of his victory. Propertius apparently confounds the two places: for the Apollo at the southern end of Leucadia could not have been a witness of a battle fought some miles to the north of the northern extremity of the island.

70. Lit. 'so much of the work of war has one day made away with.' The idea seems to be that all previous exploits of war are destroyed, blotted out, because they will not be deemed worthy of being remembered in comparison with Caesar's great victory. Pinder supposes *operis belli* to refer only to the war against Antony: 'so much has the day of Actium done for deciding the whole war.' But

this interpretation weakens the point of the passage, which consists
in the depreciation of all Rome's worthies in comparison to Augustus.

71. **portus** again shows that Actium is meant.

III. 18.

THIS poem is an elegy upon the early death of M. Claudius Marcellus in B. C. 23, rendered so famous by the touching lines of Virgil,
Aen. 6. 861–887, and by the splendid generosity with which Octavia
is said to have rewarded them. In no passage is the delicate and
refined pathos of Virgil more nobly exhibited than in this, as he
brings before us the bearing and the promise of the youthful Marcellus,
the untold loss to Rome from his untimely death, the universal
mourning of the people. The premature death of Marcellus, in his
twentieth year, was the first of the series of family losses which fell
so thickly on Augustus, and which cut off one by one all the hopes
which he had formed as to the succession. Marcellus was own
nephew to Augustus, being the son of his sister Octavia and of the
zealous Pompeian C. Claudius Marcellus, who had done so much
during his consulship in B. C. 50 to hurry on the rupture between
Pompey and Caesar. As early as B. C. 29 Augustus brought the
young Marcellus into public notice; in B. C. 25 he seemed formally
to mark him out as his heir by at once adopting him as his son, and
giving to him his own daughter Julia in marriage, in addition to
other honours. In B. C. 24 he was elected curule aedile; in B. C. 23
he had performed the duties of that office with great magnificence when he was struck down by a fatal disease, of which he died
after a short illness at Baiae, under the care of Augustus' favourite
physician, Antonius Musa, who had vainly applied the same hot-
water treatment which he had found so successful before in the case
of Augustus himself. The nature of the illness was unknown: and
as ' Rumour is ever dark when dealing with the deaths of princes,'
we are not surprised to find that there were suspicions of foul play.
The series of catastrophes which cut off all Augustus' natural heirs
built up the fortunes of Livia's family: it was but natural, therefore,
that she should be believed to have plotted the deaths by which the
ambition of her life was gratified (Dion Cass. 53. 33). That the
suspicion attached equally to every case, without regard to evidence,
together with the fact that she retained the love and confidence of
Augustus to the last, is the best proof that the suspicion was in all
cases alike unfounded.

1. **alludit,** the conjecture of Lambinus for *ludit* of the MSS.,

must be taken with *stagna* l. 2, as in Cat. 64. 66, where of Ariadne's clothes, etc.,

> *Omnia quae toto delapsa e corpore passim*
> *Ipsius ante pedes fluctus salis alludebant.*

Elsewhere the word is used intransitively, or with a cognate accusative, as in Virg. Aen. 7. 117 *Nec plura alludens.* *Ludere,* with the accusative, is only used in the sense ' to mock,' ' to befool.'

Clausus ab umbroso : i. e. 'the sea shut out now from shady Avernus (by the new breakwater) plays upon the smoking pools of Baiae.' Postgate supports this interpretation by *insula ea sinum ab alto claudit* Liv. 30. 24. 9, where the island is said quite naturally to ' shut off ' a bay from the open sea. So Virg. Aen. 1. 160

> *insula portum*
> *Efficit obiectu laterum, quibus omnis ab alto*
> *Frangitur inque sinus scindit sese unda reductos.*

Here the water itself *frangitur ab alto*, which seems to mean ' is broken as it rolls in from the sea.' The *Julian Harbour* was the great work of Agrippa, constructed in B. C. 37 with a view to carrying on the naval war with Sextus Pompeius, whose fleet had its head-quarters opposite in Sicily. The dark and mysterious Lacus Avernus—the haunt of the Cumaean Sibyl—was separated by a mile of land from the *Lucrinus Lacus*—famous for oysters—and this again was partly protected from the outer sea by a narrow reef of rock called *via Herculis*, because laid down by Hercules to spare himself the trouble of going round the bay. Agrippa dug a canal between the two lakes, and strengthened the *via Herculis* into an efficient breakwater, leaving a passage for ships to enter.

pontus is the outer sea, which now *alludit*, i. e. washes up through the continuous channel to the quiet waters of the lake within. Virg. Geo. 2. 161, thus alludes to this great work :

> *An memorem portus, Lucrinoque addita claustra,*
> *Atque indignatum magnis stridoribus aequor,*
> *Iulia qua ponto longe sonat unda refuso,*
> *Tyrrhenusque fretis immittitur aestus Avernis?*

Pinder explains the MS. reading *ludit* ' of the quiet sportive motion of waters protected from winds.' But the sea was not calm because shut out from Avernus.

2. To make **stagna**, etc. in apposition to *pontus* is harsh in the extreme, and unmeaning. Baiae was situated quite outside the Julian harbour, and at some distance from it, on the western shore of the *Baianus Sinus*. It is clear, however, that *fumida stagna* refers to the Lucrine lake. The whole region is volcanic : and *fumida* refers

to the mephitic vapours and odours which in ancient as in modern times sprang up at various points from the shores of both lakes, and spread themselves over their waters. Hence the tradition embodied in the name Avernus (ἄορνος) that birds could not live in the heavy air above the lake. Propertius apparently confuses the sulphurous vapours exhaling from the shores of the two lakes with the warm springs of Baiae itself. Cp. Ov. A. A. 1. 255

> *Quid referam Baias, praetextaque litora velis,*
> *Et quae de calido sulfure fumat aquam?*

3. Misenus, the trumpeter or pilot (boatswain?) of Aeneas, whose fate is described by Virg. Aen. 6. 162-164, and who gave his name to the promontory south of Baiae which bounds the Bay of Naples to the north, and is still called *Punta di Miseno.*

4. sonat, i. e. with the beating of the waves. Some less well explain it of the sound of horses' hoofs. But the *Via Herculis* was no more an actual road than the Giant's Causeway. That Causeway *sonat* grandly, as all who have visited it know; but it is not with the hoofs of horses.

5. mortales urbes must stand for ' the cities of mortals :' the idea is more fully expressed by *urbes mortalesque turbas* Hor. Od. 3. 4. 46, 47.

quaereret, 'was looking out for,' or 'searching through,' with a view either to conquest or to putting wrong right. Hence **dextra,** ' by his conquering arm,' or, as Postgate puts it, ' in his conquering progress.'

6. Thebano deo, because Hercules was both born and worshipped at Thebes. His worship was often conjoined with that of Bacchus—hence the use of *cymbala*—and he was specially regarded as the patron of hot springs. As such he was worshipped both at Tibur and at Baiae : hence the force of *deus hostis* l. 8.

7. At nunc. These words mark the apodosis to the protasis of the first six lines, in a somewhat irregular and abrupt way. *At* conveys a sense of indignation, which is further heightened by the sentence being thrown into the form of a vehement interrogation. ' This spot so peaceful, so favoured, lies now under a heinous charge : what unfriendly god has taken possession of its waters ?'

magno cum crimine. *Cum* carries the idea of being involved or implicated in, mixed up with, the charge brought.

8. constitit hostis. Note the emphatic position. ' Has taken up his position as an enemy.'

9. pressus = *oppressus,* 'laid low,' 'borne down.' *Premere* is used vaguely to express every degree of evil or misfortune, from the greatest to the slightest, by which a person can be lowered or brought down. Thus it may mean mere mental depreciation, as in Virg. Aen. 11. 402 *contra premere arma Latini*, or, as here, the most overwhelming of misfortunes. Cf. Ov. Ep. ex Pont. 1. 7. 11

Nos premet aut bello tellus aut frigore caelum,

and Virg. Aen. 9. 330 *Tres iuxta famulos . . . premit*, where *premit* means 'slays.'

Baiae, in spite of its waters, was deemed an unhealthy place, as appears from Cic. Epp. Div. 9. 12 *Gratulor Baiis nostris, siquidem, ut scribis, salubres repentae factae sunt, nisi forte . . . dum tu ades sunt oblitae sui. Quod quidem si ita est, minime miror caelum et terras vim suam, si tibi conveniat, dimittere.* Malaria to this day pervades the district. **His** perhaps refers to the various adverse circumstances indicated; the mephitic vapours, the unhealthiness of Baiae, the presence of some hostile god in its waters. Palmer takes it differently: 'Hic (sc. undis) pressus in Stygias undas vultum demisit.'

vultum demisit in undas. The common interpretation that Marcellus was drowned in Avernus or the Bay of Baiae, is uncalled for. *Vultum demittere* is a euphemistic term for dying, suggested by the mention of Styx: 'sank, or was lowered, to the Stygian waters.' Such phrases as *demittere Orco* Aen. 2. 398, Hor. Od. 1. 28. 11, *d. neci* id. 2. 85, etc., are quite common, and *vultum* gives merely a more personal and poetical touch to the same idea. The idea of drowning may perhaps have been suggested by the beautiful words in Lycidas, which exactly illustrate *vultum demisit in undas*,

It was that fatal and perfidious bark
Built in the eclipse, and rigged with curses dark,
That sunk so low that sacred head of thine!

10. spiritus ille. There is obviously here a double meaning: the classical sense of *spiritus*, 'inspiring breath,' and so 'spirit,' is mingled with the idea suggested by the waters of Avernus, that the soul of Marcellus floats like a thin vapour on the water. Thus the passage gives a kind of anticipation of the later use of the word to signify a ghost. Postgate well compares the idea of 'The Lake of the Dismal Swamp.'

11. optima. The word *optimus*, on inscriptions and elsewhere, of a father or mother or wife, etc., is a stock term of praise, not denoting any special qualities, but merely a recognition that the natural duties of the relationship have been well and duly discharged. Thus Hor. Sat. 1. 4. 105 *pater optimus*, 'my worthy father.' Hor. S. 2. 1. 12 *pater optime*, 'Good Sir.' So in the vulgar phrase

' How is your good lady?'   Of Octavia, as Postgate observes, the
word could have been used in its highest sense.   The nobility of her
character is one of the redeeming features of her age.   Used as a
political puppet to further her brother's interests, she endured
patiently all the insults of Antony, and showed a true woman's devotion in taking charge of his children by Fulvia and Cleopatra, and
bringing them up as tenderly as if they had been her own.   She was
truly what Plut. Ant. 31 calls her, χρῆμα θαυμαστὸν γυναικός.

12. amplexum esse, i. e. 'What availed the fact that he had
been admitted to the very hearth of Caesar?' alluding to his adoption
by Caesar, which by Roman law admitted him to every right of an
actual son.   The term *focos* conveys perhaps more closely than any
other Latin word the ideas suggested by our ' home.'

13. Marcellus, as curule aedile, had celebrated the games with
great magnificence, and both his mother and Augustus himself had
helped him in every way to make the display as imposing as possible,
Dion 53. 28. 31, Plin. N. H. 19. 1.   The *vela* are the huge awnings
which were spread across the open spaces of theatres and amphi-
theatres to screen the seats from the sun.   On the outside walls of the
Coliseum there are still to be seen the sockets, carved out of solid
stone, into which the poles that supported the awning were fitted.
Lucretius illustrates the origin of thunder from the flapping of the
awning in a wind.   •

modo is to be taken generally with the whole line.   'The awning which late we saw fluttering,' etc.

14. omnia gesta, not ' all the things that were done by,' but
'the fact that all things *were* done by.' 'the universal agency or help-
fulness of.'   Nothing could be more tame than the former rendering.
Postgate supports it by 1. 6. 23

> *Et tibi non umquam nostros puer ille labores*
> *Afferat, et lacrimis omnia nota meis.*

But the sense there requires the same rendering as here.   ' May Love
never bring you pangs like mine, or a life all known to my tears,' i.e.
'a life like mine, every part of which has been bedewed by tears.'

per maternas...gesta manus is well illustrated by Suet. Oct.
29, who tells how Augustus executed great works in the name of
the members of his family.   Of this kind were the Theatre of Marcellus and the Portico of Octavia, whose remains are so picturesquely
interlaced with the Roman buildings of to-day.

15. steterat. Postgate explains this as an instantaneous pluperfect : 'Time suddenly stopped for Marcellus in his twentieth
year.   I cannot find any exact parallel.'   Surely the meaning is not

that his life was *cut short* in his twentieth year, but the more
pathetic one that he had just *reached* his twentieth year, and had
a whole life of hope before him, at the moment of his death.   Postgate's references scarcely bear out his meaning : 'to stand motionless,'
not 'to come to an end,' is the meaning of *stare* in *stent aere venti* Prop.
3. 10. 5, *stabant adolescentes* Liv.   The meaning is rather analogous to
that of 'standing firm,' of a solid work, as *ut praeter spem stare muros
viderunt* Liv. 38. 5 ; or of a completed work, as Ov. Met. 11. 205

> *Aedificant muros, pacto pro moenibus auro:*
> *Stabat opus ;*

or of an enduring work, as in the common phrase *stante republica ;*
or of a successful work, as Hor. Epp. 2. 1. 176

> *Securus cadat an recto stet fabula talo.*

So below, line 30, *stetit* is only a stronger word for *fuit*.   Postgate
quotes Prop. 2. 8. 10

> *Et Thebae steterunt, altaque Troia fuit,*

but there the meaning seems to be : 'Thebes *has* stood, Troy
has been,' i. e. '*stands* no more, *is* no more.'   The phrase *magno
stare pretio*, etc., 'to stand one in,' ' to cost,' seems to carry the same
meaning : see below, l. 30, and Virg. Aen. 10. 494

> *haud illi stabunt Aeneia parvo*
> *Hospitia,*

or Ov. Fast. 2. 810

> *Heu quanto regnis nox stetit una tuis!*

The event accomplished, the article secured, 'stand firm,' 'are
maintained,' at a certain cost, i.e. 'cost so much.' Here the twentieth
year of Marcellus ' had stood its ground,' ' had taken up its position
as an accomplished fact,' 'had been completed.' Thus the pluperfect
has its full natural force.

16. Tot bona, all his personal qualities, as well as all the external advantages of his position.

tam parvo orbe, i. e. in so short a life.

clausit ' included,' ' comprised,' shutting them off as it were
from the longer term of life which might have been his.

dies, time in the abstract, as Hor. Od. 4. 13. 16.

17. I nunc.   A sudden passionate apostrophe to one who is
supposed to read a different lesson from the facts.   So Juv. 10. 166,
after a contemptuous tirade on Hannibal's career,

> *I demens, et saevas curre per Alpes*
> *Ut pueris placeas et declamatio fias!*

i.e. ' Go forth then, if you still admire Hannibal, and,' etc.   So Hor.
Epp. 1. 16. 17, and Ov. Her. 9. 105.

tecum, i. e. 'in your own mind and heart.'

18. in plausum, with sense of motion: 'rising to cheer,' Postgate.

iuvent, 'be thy delight,' as in Hor. Od. 1. 1. 4.

19. Attalicas. See note on 2. 13. 22.

supera, 'outvie,' 'outdo.'

20. Gemmea, in allusion to the costly and extravagant novelties of decoration in which the exhibitors of games vied with one another in their efforts to obtain popularity. We hear of the scene of a theatre being overlaid with silver, ivory, or gold ; of the *arena* being strewn with vermilion ; of the cord of the *podium* being twined with gold, or covered with amber ornaments, etc.

ista, contemptuous. There is no authority or excuse for reading *usta*.

21. This line is very unsatisfactory as it stands in the MSS., **Sed tamen hoc.** *Tamen* seems clearly to be wrong : it is weak in itself, and gives a quite unnecessary emphasis to *sed*. *Hoc* appears in all the MSS. before *omnes* : if the more easy *huc* was written by Propertius, it is inexplicable how the more difficult reading *hoc* came to be substituted for it. On this ground Palmer suggests to me that *tamen* was introduced in consequence of *Sed*, and that the true reading is *Sed manet hoc omnes*. He quotes *Hoc quoque te manet*, Hor. Epp. 1. 20. 17 (to which may be added the remarkable parallel Hor. Od. 1. 28. 15 *sed omnes una manet nox*), and especially the following passage from the Epicedion Drusi, a poem modelled on Propertius :

> *Fata manent omnes ; omnes expectat avarus*
> *Portitor ; et turbae vix satis una ratis.*
> *Tendimus huc omnes: metam properamus ad unam!*
> *Omnia sub leges mors vocat atra suas*

This passage seems to be a distinct echo of the passage before us. Propertius probably wrote *manet ;* and *tamen*, which contains exactly the same letters, got accidentally substituted for it. But *Sed* is as much out of place as *tamen*, for the poet has already declared that all wealth, etc., will come to naught, in the emphatic words *ignibus ista dabis*. What is needed in l. 21 is not a contrast, but an amplification of that theme : 'all will go to the flames : but nevertheless all ends in death,' is a manifestly absurd connection. If we read *Hoc tamen, hoc omnes* all is clear. The repetition of *Hoc ... hoc ... huc* in one line was too much for the scribe : the corruption *tamen* naturally suggested that of *Hoc* into *Sed*. The repetition *Hoc ... hoc ... huc* is quite in the manner of Propertius. Cp. 4. 4. 37

> *Ille equus, ille meos in castra reponet amores ;*

1. 8. 25

> *licet Autaricis considat in oris*
> *Et licet Hylleis ;*

and again 1. 8. 37

> *Quamvis magna daret, quamvis maiora daturus :*

and 2. 31. 15

> *Deinde inter matrem deus ipse interque sororem.*

If we keep *sed* we may explain it as either (1) in reference to *omnes :* 'why speak of the rich ? Death awaits *all*, rich and poor alike ;' or (2) as a repetition and enforcement of the idea contained in *ignibus* or *dabis :* 'you may have all wealth, *but* all will go to the flames, *but* all alike end in death.' *Hoc* has been changed to *huc* in consequence of the *huc* later in the line, otherwise a verb of rest (*agimus* or *facimus*) would have to be supplied with *hoc*, a verb of motion with *huc*, the awkwardness of which was intolerable. The repetition of *sed*, l. 22, is another argument against *sed* in l. 21.

primus et ultimus ordo : i. e. 'highest and lowest '; perhaps in allusion to the fourteen front rows reserved for equites by the law of Otho.

22. mala, a strong word, expressing abhorrence. *Male sit* is a regular form of curse, and we may almost translate here ' accursed.'

24. publica. There is no distinction of rank or classes among Charon's passengers : the *primus et ultimus ordo*, the 'classes' and the 'masses,' all huddle together.

25. Ille. He passes from Marcellus and the person whom he has been addressing, ll. 17–24, to the representative of man in general. Perhaps *ille* may bear the sense of ' your famous captain ' (Pinder).

ferro refers probably to the coat of mail, greaves, etc. ; **aere** to the helmet.

26. protrahit, i. e. drags him out of his protecting armour, as though he had secured himself in a fortress.

caput, by the series of steps illustrated on 2. 1. 36, comes to mean as here ' the body ' rather than ' the life ' (Postgate), which is too abstract an idea for this passage.

With these lines cp. Dunbar, Lament for the Makkaris :

> He takes the champion in the stour,
> The captain closèd in the tour,
> The lady in bower full of beauty ;
> Timor mortis conturbat me.

Shirley also says,

> There is no armour against Fate.

Y

Nor can we help recalling the story in the Arabian Nights of the king who vainly shut up his son in a tower of brass to save him from his predicted fate.

27. Nirea: alluding to Hom: Il. 2. 673

Νιρεὺς ὃς κάλλιστος ἀνὴρ ὑπὸ Ἴλιον ἦλθεν.

Cp. Ov. E. P. 4. 13. 15

Tam mala Thersiten prohibebat forma latere,
Quam pulchra Nireus conspiciendus erat.

29. hic luctus, i. e. distress arising from this same Death, i.e. Death itself.

30. Atridae, the dative, not the genitive. See the passages quoted above, l. 15.

alter amor, his second love. His wife, Clytemnestra, was his first.

31. If the MS. reading *traicis* is right, then Bae. is probably right in supposing that some lines have dropped out here. Paley's conjecture *traicit,* adopted by Palmer, gives good sense, though the emphasis of the line makes it hard to believe that *tibi* and *nauta* refer to different persons. *Traicit* will bear its transitive meaning, 'who causes to pass over' or 'ferries across.'

32. animae corpus inane tuae may be either ' the body empty of thy spirit,' as Ov. Met. 2. 611

Corpus inane animae frigus letale secuta est,

or, 'the empty body of thy spirit,' i. e. 'consisting of thy spirit,' as though body and spirit were confused into one idea.

Palmer reads *hac,* to correspond with *qua* l. 33 : 'by this same road by which.'

33. qua ... qua. So the MSS. But *quo* seems supported by *huc* (l. 32), and would give a better sense, explained by *in astra* l. 34.

Siculae victor, the celebrated M. Claudius Marcellus, who conducted the great siege of Syracuse, B.C. 212. Archimedes conducted the defence, and was slain upon its capture.

Postgate observes that here, as in 4. 7. 57, Propertius supposes there were two boats. This is somewhat inconsistent with *publica cymba* l. 24, and is not absolutely necessary, as we may imagine Charon landing part of his freight at one point, part at another.

34. ab humana via. These words are difficult. They seem to support the reading *hac* l. 32 and the MS. reading *tuae.* 'May Charon carry thy spirit along that path by which Claudius and Caesar rose to the stars from the path of men.' For Prop.'s vague use of *via,* see 1. 2. 12, 2. 25. 46. Postgate well translates 'the ways' or ' haunts of men': probably Propertius was scarcely conscious that he was using the word in a double sense.

cessit in astra. Cp. Hor. Od. 4. 2. 23 of Pindar

> *vires animumque moresque*
> *Aureos educit in astra, nigroque*
> *Invidet Orco.*

III. 22.

THIS poem may be read in conjunction with 1. 6. They are both addressed to the poet's friend, Tullus, who, at the time of the writing of that poem, was setting out for Asia in the suite of an uncle, and had apparently asked Propertius to accompany him. The poet declined the invitation, declaring that he had no taste for war, and that he would rather stay at home to enjoy Cynthia's love than see all the sights of the East.   The uncle is generally supposed to have been L. Volcatius Tullus, who was consul along with Augustus in B. C. 33, and was son of the L. Volcatius Tullus, consul B.C. 66, best known as furnishing a date to Horace's wine-jar, Od. 3. 8. 12

> *Amphorae fumum bibere institutae*
> *Consule Tullo.*

Volcatius was setting out for his provincial command in Asia when 1. 6 was written, and the poet had the opportunity of joining his suite as Tibullus joined that of Messala, and Catullus that of Memmius.   How much Propertius lost by the refusal may be measured by what we have gained from the charm and interest thrown into the lives and writings of his fellow-poets by their travels in the East.   In the present poem, Propertius complains that his friend has stayed away too long, and assures him that whatever marvels there may be in the East, there is, after all, no country like Italy, which contains within herself all the charms and wonders of all other countries.   Closely parallel are Hor. Od. 1. 7 and the well-known praises of Italy in Virg. Geo 2. 136-176.   As to the date of this poem, we find from l. 1 that Tullus has for many years (*multos annos*) had Cyzicus as his headquarters.   When did he go out? Volcatius was consul in B. C. 33, and, according to the rule established by the Senate in B. C. 52, no consul or praetor could enter upon his provincial command until five years had elapsed from his tenure of office in the city.   If this rule was observed, we may suppose that Volcatius did not go to Asia until B. C. 27.   That would fix the date of 1. 6 : and this piece must have been written some years (*multos annos*) afterwards.

1. Cyzicus, in the Propontis, or Sea of Marmora, was originally an island. Strabo speaks of its being connected with the mainland by two bridges: and Plin. N. H. 5. 40. 2 says it was joined to the mainland by Alexander. At the present day, the connection is formed by a low narrow sandy isthmus about a mile long.

2. fluit Isthmos, therefore, probably refers to the unsubstantial character of the connection : 'where floats our Isthmus.' Pinder suggests that *fluit* may stand for *praefluit*, the Isthmus being said 'to flow with the waters' that pass it. So in Virg. Aen. 9. 105 the banks of the Styx are described as *torrentes pice*. It is possible that Prop. uses *Isthmus* for the channel dividing the island or peninsula from the shore, in which case *fluit* would be quite regular. See below 22. 28.

3. A much-vexed line. The MSS. read *Dindymus* and *iuventa* (*inventa* N.), whilst *Cybele* is variously written. Vossius conjectures *invenca*, which is supported on the ground that a cow frequently appears on the coins of Cyzicus. From the similarities existing between Cybele, Isis, Io (who gave her name to the adjoining Bosphorus), it is supposed that Cybele may have been worshipped at Cyzicus under the form of a cow. There was a Mount Dindymon, or Dindyma, at Cyzicus (Strabo 12. 8. 11) of the same name as the more famous mountain near Pessinus, the chief seat of Cybele's worship in Phrygia, from which she derived the name *Dindymene* Hor. Od. 1. 16. 5. If we read *Dindymus*, the mountain itself will be intended ; the construction must be either *qua Dindymus est*, or else *placuit* must be supplied from l. 1. Either construction is harsh ; whence Palmer reads *Dindymis*, a similar epithet to Horace's *Dindymene*. *Dindymis*, however, might also stand for the town, as we learn from Plin. N. H. 5. 40. 2, who says that Cyzicus was also called *Dindymis, cuius a vêrtice mons Dindymus.* He further adopts what he terms the *palmaris emendatio* ot Haupt, *sacra fabricata e vite Cybele*, on the strength of two passages, Apoll. Rhod. 1. 1117 and Strabo 12. 8. 11. Strabo speaks of a temple of Cybele on Mount Dindymon above Cyzicus, founded by the Argonauts ; and Apollonius describes how Argus made a statue of the goddess out of an old vine-stock, and set it upon a hill.

If **Cybelae** be read, it must be the dative, in honour of the goddess.

4. The tradition that Proserpine was carried off by Pluto at or near Cyzicus is only known from this passage, and supported by a single line quoted by Hertz. from the Latin Anthology.

qua. So the MSS.; but with that reading the interposition ot l. 3 between the *qua* of l. 2 and that of l. 4 is very harsh. It is to be noted that N. reads *quae* in l. 2, where it is clearly out of place : hence probably the mistake.

via. Cp. 3. 18. 34 and note.

5. si. The whole passage down to l. 17 forms the protasis : ' If you care for the sights of travel, and it is that taste which keeps you away from your friends, know that in all things Italy surpasses all other countries.' Some have supposed from the somewhat wild concatenation of persons and places brought together in the following lines, that Propertius referred to statues or other representations to be seen at Cyzicus. But this idea spoils the sense. The mixture of mythology and geography, without regard to the relative position of the places, is quite after the manner of Propertius, and we need not expect to find him mentioning persons or places in guide-book order.

Helles. Helle, the daughter of Athamas, gave her name to the *Hellespont* into which she fell.

6. movere. *Moveo* and *commoveo* are the special words used to denote strong feeling of any kind, both in prose and poetry. *Animo commoveor*, etc., is a frequent phrase in Cicero.

7, 8. I. e. ' whether you go to see Mount Atlas and the islands called the Gorgades.' Pliny mentions these islands as five days' sail to the west of Mount Atlas, and opposite the point *Hesperion*, the western promontory of Africa. Here the Gorgons lived : Hanno, adds Pliny, carried off two of their hides (*cutes*) to Carthage.

Phorcidos, i. e. of Medusa, daughter of Phorcus.

9. Geryonis, genitive of *Geryon* or *Geryones*, is probably the true reading, preserved as *Girionis* in N. : the common reading, *Geryonae*, would be the genitive of Geryones, as *Pelidae* of *Pelides*, *geometrae* of *geometres*, etc.

signa are no doubt the signs of the struggle supposed to be preserved on the spot. Of similar nature was the hoof-print left by the horses of the Dioscuri on the shores of Lake Regillus, and the mark left by St. Peter's head in the wall of the Mamertine prison. The palace of Antaeus, the scene of his conflict with Hercules, and the gardens of the Hesperides, were placed at *Lixus*, a colony planted by Claudius in Tingitana or Tangiers, Plin. 5. 1 ; while the island of Erytheia, on which Geryon fed the cattle carried off by Hercules, was identified with the island (now Isle de Leon), or islands, on which the Phoenicians placed their famous colony of Gades, regarded by Greeks and Romans alike as the westernmost limit of the world. Hence Hor. Od. 2. 6. 1

Septimi Gades aditure mecum, etc.

10. Note the unusual and rough elision of *que* at the end of the first penthemimer of the pentameter verse.

11. From the extreme west he passes to the extreme east of the Roman world, the banks of the Phasis in Colchis.

propellas, which should apply to the vessel, is here used by a Propertian inversion of the water through which the oars sweep, possibly with the idea that the water is itself put in motion by the stroke.

remige. The oarsman is regarded as a mere instrument: hence the preposition is omitted. This use of the ablative is near akin to the ablative absolute. See Munro quoted by Mayor on Juv. 1. 13.

12. Peliacae trabis iter, i.e. the whole voyage performed by the Argo, here called the 'Peliac ship,' because Jason, the rightful heir, was despatched from Iolcus to fetch the golden fleece by his uncle Pelias.

13. rudis may either mean the ship 'which was late an unshapen trunk,' like Cat. 4. 10

> *Ubi ille post phaselus antea fuit*
> *Comata silva;*

or 'inexperienced,' as going on her first voyage; so Propertius says of himself 3. 21. 17

> *Ergo ego nunc rudis Hadriaci vehar aequoris hospes.*

This seems supported by l. 14. Or it may denote the rough unshapen character of this first essay in ship-building. Cp. *rudis Argus* 2. 26. 39, if *rudis*, not *ratis*, be read.

natat. The same use of present for perfect that has been noticed elsewhere in Propertius: see 2. 7. 2, 3. 7. 22, 4. 1. 77, 121, and 4. 2. 3, etc.

Argos . . . columba. A similar use of the ablative to *remige* l. 12. The seer Phineus advised the Argonauts to let loose a dove before venturing through the Symplegades; the dove flew through with the loss only of the tip of her tail. Following this example, they sailed at full speed between the rocks, and escaped with a slight injury to the stern, Apoll. Rhod. 2. 562. Cp. 2. 26. 39

> *Et qui movistis duo litora, cum ratis Argo*
> *Dux erat ignoto missa columba mari.*

15. A corrupt line. N. reads *Et si qua origae*. Vossius conjectures *Ortygii*, which Lachmann changed into *Ortygiae*, referring in either case to an old name *Ortygia* given to Ephesus, probably from ὄρτυξ, because the coast abounded in quails. Scaliger has *Et si quadrigae*, understanding by *quadriga* the four cities of Ephesus, Smyrna, Colophon, and Miletus. Swans abound in the Cayster, Claud. Ep. 2. 12: hence *oloriferi* in Italian editions, and *cygnaei*.

Palmer's conjecture *Etsi quoi rigui* is commended by the ingenuity of his explanation : ' the *ui* of *rigui* was dropped before the
ui of *visenda*, and the scribe built up the remaining *rig* into *origae*.'
But what did the scribe take *origae* to mean?　Further, to bring in
travellers in general (*si quoi*) is scarcely in harmony with the spirit
of the passage which is addressed to Tullus alone (*tu . . . tuque
tuo . . . ipse legas*).

16. One editor imagines the *Rhesus* in the Troad to be intended;
another the *Ganges!*　But the seven-mouthed river can be none
other than the Nile; cp. Cat. 11. 7

　　　*Sive quae septemgeminus colorat
　　　　　Aequora Nilus,*

and Ov. Met. 15. 753

　　　Perque papyriferi septemflua flumina Nili.

Temperare means to ' mix in due proportion,' hence ' to moderate.' Propertius here means that the force or volume of the water is
lessened by being divided into seven channels : he expresses this by
saying ' the water moderates its seven channels.'　Cp. Virg. Geo.
1. 110, of water *scatebrisque arentia temperat arva*, i. e. ' moderates
the dryness of the fields.'　Closely parallel is *temperat ira manus*
l. 22.　There is no ' mixing ' in the case, as Hertz. supposes : *Nilus
denuo semper per vias suas effunditur, novasque aquas prioribus
addit, et has suis miscet.*

17. ' Will yield to the Roman land,' i. e. ' to the marvels of the
Roman land.'　So Juv. 3. 74 *sermo Promptus et Isaeo torrentior*, where
' more rushing than Isaeus ' = 'than the eloquence of Isaeus.'

18. Imitated by Ov. A. A. 1. 56.

19. As Pinder observes, the best commentary on these lines is
Virg. Aen. 6. 854

　　　Parcere devictis et debellare superbos.

But it is clear from ll. 27-38 that the words *commoda noxae* refer to
more than Roman mercy.　Propertius had the passage in Geo. 2
closely in view : the genial temperate climate, free from extremes,
the absence of noxious beasts, fierce animals, serpents, monsters, and
monstrous crimes, are all referred to in declaring Italy to be not
commoda noxae.

22. Stamus.　See note on 3. 18. 15.

temperat.　Just as in l. 16, the river itself, which supplies the
force of water, is said to moderate its courses, so here the rage which
nerves the arm is said to moderate it when it declines to put forth
its full strength.

23. Tiburne, adjective, ' belonging to Tibur,' through which

town is the most beautiful part of the Anio's course, with its celebrated cascade.

24. trames is properly 'a side-path,' 'a cross-road': hence
possibly 'untrodden ways.' Sellar (Augustan Poets, p. 273 n.) thinks
the word may = ὅρος, 'a hill-side.' So 3. 13. 44

Et si forte meo tramite quaeris avem.

Marcius humor. See note on 3. 2. 12. The lakes of Alba
and Nemi are still among the most exquisite scenes in the neighbourhood of Rome, and are combined in a single excursion. That of
Alba fills the deep basin of an extinct volcano, and finds issue
through the artificial *emissarium*—first built during the war with
Veii—some 400 feet below the lowest point of its encircling
banks. The lake of Nemi, bosomed deep in trees, and less formid-
able in appearance, also fills an ancient crater, and is drained
similarly by a tunnel into the *Valle Ariccia*, through which the
water passes into the sea near the ancient Ardea. The Alban waters,
on the other hand, drain into a stream which falls into the Tiber a
few miles below Rome. There is no connection between the waters
of the two lakes, but Propertius might well speak of 'the allied waters
of Nemi,' from the nearness and similar character of the two basins.
But Hous. reads *foliis Nemorensis abundans*, J. of Phil. xxi. p. 176.

26. In allusion to the well *Iuturna* in the Forum, near the
temple of Vesta, at which Castor and Pollux watered their horses
after their hot ride from Regillus.

27. cerastae, serpents with horns or feelers projecting from the
head. Pliny asserts they buried themselves in the sand and attracted
birds by the motion of their horns: a fable rejected by Cuvier, who
admits otherwise the correctness of Pliny's description 8. 35. 1.

29. pro matre, 'to atone for her mother's crime.' Cassiopeia,
the mother of Andromeda, had boasted that her daughter's beauty
eclipsed that of the Nereids. In revenge, the Nereids induced
Poseidon to send the sea-monster to ravage the land: the oracle of
Ammon advised that Andromeda should be given up to him. Hence
she was chained to a rock, and delivered by Perseus.

30. I. e. 'In Italy thou hast no unnatural banquets, like those
of Thyestes, to shudder at.'

31. When Meleager was an infant, the fates had prophesied that
he would die as soon as a log then burning on the hearth should be
burnt out. His mother, Althaea, hid it away: but enraged at
Meleager's slaying her brothers, she took it out and kindled it,
and Meleager died.

arserunt in caput, 'blazed to the destruction of.'

33. I.e. ' Here there are no frantic Bacchanalian orgies.' Pentheus, king of Thebes, being opposed to the worship of Dionysus, was hunted as a wild beast by his mother Agave, and two Maenads, and torn in pieces. Pentheus had climbed into a tree for the purpose of spying out their secrets.

34. I. e. ' Here no Iphigenia was ever sacrificed.'

35. Io was turned by the jealous Juno into a cow.

cornua curvare, ' to cause crumpled horns to grow.' This phrase supports the conjecture of *curvate* in 3. 7. 29.

36. bove, i. e. ' the form of a cow.'

37. Sinis of Corinth ' made trees into gibbets,' by fastening his victims to the tops of two pine-trees bent together, and then letting them spring apart.

37, 38. The accusatives of this couplet are governed by some verbal idea to be supplied from the previous passage.

38. saxa, supposed to be the Scironian rocks, on the coast of Megaris, where there was only a narrow path left between the rocks and the sea. But as *in sua fata* refers again to Sinis, who was hoist on his own petard by Theseus, *saxa* may refer to his abode.

40. honos, the career of public office.

41. ad eloquium, i. e. on whom to exercise your eloquence.

42. aptus. Here used for ' suitable,' ' proper.' This use confirms the reading *apta* 3. 5. 18, where there is the same confusion as here in the MSS. between *apta* and *acta*. We see from this line that Tullus was not yet married.

IV. 3.

THIS piece is in the style of the Heroides of Ovid. It is an imaginary letter written by a young wife from Rome to her husband, who has been absent for four years on a campaign with Augustus in the East. The names Arethusa and Lycotas are poetical and fictitious: but it has been supposed that they are intended to designate Propertius' friend Postumus and his wife Aelia Galla. For this there is no further evidence than that afforded by the charming poem 3. 12, in which Propertius writes a somewhat similar letter to his friend Postumus, upbraiding him for being able to stay away so long from his wife Galla, while warring in the East, and assuring him of her matchless constancy. The conditions are similar, and it is very possible that the circumstances of Postumus and Galla may have suggested the idea of this piece: but Bentley has pointed out that when Roman writers used feigned names to denote real persons they chose names of the same number of syllables, and of the same metrical quantity, as the originals. Thus Catullus writes of Clōdĭă as *Lēsbĭă*, Horace of Tĕrēntĭă as *Lĭcўmnĭă*. The poem before us is full of fine feeling and of delicate natural touches, which separate it *toto caelo* from the laboured sweetness and faultless artificiality of Ovid's Heroides. Hertz. puts the date of the composition at B.C. 20. As to whether Ovid copied Propertius in this style of poetry see note on l. 3.

2. Cum ... absis is subordinate to *si potes*. 'If, in spite of your absence,' etc. For the position of the *cum* clause cp. Nepos, Milt. 6. 3.

si potes. The indicative implies that the sentence is hypothetical in form only. There is no doubt about the *potes:* what she expresses is astonishment at the fact.

3. tamen is not easy to explain. It may refer to the supposed completeness of the *mandata:* 'This is my message: yet if it seem wanting in any part, know that it is my tears that are the cause.' But it is better to refer it to the doubt of his love implied in l. 2. ' Thou hast scarce the right to call thyself mine : *and yet* these lines are all blotted with my tears.' Cp. Ov. Her. 3. 3

> *Quascunque adspicies, lacrimae fecere lituras;*

and id. 11. 1

> *Si qua tamen caecis errabunt scripta lituris:*
> *Oblitus a dominae caede libellus erit.*

These passages are remarkable: it is scarcely possible to avoid the conclusion that either Ovid copied Propertius, or Propertius Ovid. Note the correspondence between *Si qua tamen*, and *Si qua tamen ;* *tibi lecturo* and *quascunque adspicies ; oblita* and *oblitus ; litura* and *lituras ; e lacrimis meis* and *lacrimae fecere.* Further, in the next lines of Ovid's epistle Canace speaks of her approaching death :

> *Dextra tenet calamum ; strictum tenet altera ferrum,*

while Prop. 1. 6 has *dextrae iam morientis*, words out of keeping with the rest of the poem, in which the young lady makes no reference to death or suicide. From Ov. A. A. 3. 346 it would seem that Ovid could not have been the imitator, as he claims originality in this kind of poetry :

> *Ignotum hoc aliis ille novavit opus.*

As Ovid was born in B.C. 43, and as the Heroides were probably the earliest of his works, it is quite possible that Propertius may have been acquainted with them when he wrote this poem.

5. fallet, ' baffle,' ' puzzle.'

tractu, ' the track,' or ' course,' lit. ' the space over which a thing is drawn,' ' the trail.' So Lucr. 2. 206

> *Nonne vides longos flammarum ducere tractus,*

of long streaks or trails of flame. So Luc. 10. 256 has *longo mitescere tractu* of the long course of the Nile.

7. modo, 'lately.'

iteratos . . . per ortus, = 'for many and many a day past.' The *ortus* are the risings of the sun.

iteratos means repeated, not for a second time only, but over and over again, so that it = *multos*. Palmer quotes Ov. Fast. 6. 199 for *Phoebusque iteraverit ortus:* but the first part of that line *Mane ubi bis fuerit* shows that a second repetition only is meant. In 4. 1. 82 *signa iterata rotae* are the signs of the zodiac, 'scanned again and again' by astrologers; and in Stat. Silv. 1. 2. 84 *iterata vulnera* are wounds 'repeated again and again.' Schultze supposes Lycotas to be compared to a star 'rising day after day' over Bactra.

8. Neuricus. The reading is uncertain: the text is a conjecture of Jacob, adopted by most editors, for the *hericus* of the best MSS. The Neuri were a Sarmatian tribe mentioned by Val. Flac. 6. 122 *et raptor agrorum Neurus*, and by other authors, while the Sarmatians were specially noted for their heavy mail-clad horsemen. See Tac. Hist. 1. 79, where the cavalry of another Sarmatian tribe, the Roxolani, are described. They were so heavily armed that once fallen, like the knights in the Middle Ages, they could not rise. Between B. C. 30 and 20 operations had been undertaken against the Daci and other tribes beyond the Danube, to which Horace often refers, and which would make an allusion to any Sarmatian tribe— as to the Getae in l. 9—quite natural. The conjecture *Sericus* is not improbable. The *Seres*, of whom the Romans knew little or nothing, are spoken of in three places by Horace as an extreme Eastern tribe within reach of the power of Rome, Od. 1. 12. 56, 3. 29. 27, 4. 15. 23; and it is remarkable that in the parallel poem to Postumus, Propertius speaks of the Median (i. e. Parthian) arrows and the mailed horsemen in one breath, 3. 12. 11

Neve tua Medae laetentur caede sagittae,
Ferreus aurato neu cataphractus equo.

10. decolor. There can be little doubt that *decolor* is the right reading, rather than the *discolor* of the MSS. The prepositions *di* and *de* are perpetually interchanged in MSS. Munro, Journal of Phil. vol. 6. p. 62, points out that *discolor* is read for *decolor* by an equal number of MSS. in each of the six places in Ovid where *decolor* occurs. Ovid uses the word specially of India and the Indians: and Seneca also has *India decolor*, Hippolytus 345. Munro holds, without sufficient reason, that *Eoa aqua* cannot mean 'on the Eastern wave or waters,' as an ablative of place. He shows that

Pliny and Mela had vague ideas of an *eous oceanus* or *eoum mare*, which they held to bound India on the East, and proposes *Eoae aquae*, translating ' And the Indian of the Eastern wave burnt to a discoloured hue.' But if the Indian could be described as ' of the Eastern wave,' he might equally well be said to live or be ' on the Eastern wave,' and to most persons the latter will seem the more natural expression. *Indus* is no doubt, as the whole passage shows, ' the Indian,' not ' the river Indus.' As applied to the river Indus, *discolor* would give a good sense, as it is a fact that the colour of its waters presents a strong contrast to that of the blue sea at its mouth. If *discolor* be applied to the Indian, it can only mean ' of a colour different from us,' or ' from the rest of mankind.' Cp. Virg. Aen. 6. 204

> *Discolor unde auri per ramos aura refulsit,*

where *discolor* means ' of a colour different from that of the objects around it.'

Eoa . . . aqua, on the above view, must be an ablative of place, ' on the shores of the Eastern waters.' Cp. 1. 14. 1

> *Tu licet abiectus Tiberina molliter unda;*

and 2. 13. 55 (if we follow the MSS.)

> *Illic formosum iacuisse paludibus.*

A simpler interpretation, however, of this passage may be suggested. The reference may simply be to sun-burning by the sea : ' The Indian burnt to a discoloured hue by the Eastern wave?' The Romans only knew of the Indian coast; they knew of the sea that washed it as being ever under a broiling tropical sun, and may well have attributed to this cause, at least in part, the swarthy complexion of the Indians. Cp. especially 3. 13. 16, where Easterns are described as *Quos Aurora suis rubra colorat aquis.*

11. marita, here used as a participle = ' thy wedded troth,' as in 4. 11. 33 *facibus maritis;* in Ov. Her. 4. 134 *fratre marita soror*, and perhaps in Hor. Od. 3. 5. 6

> *Milesne Crassi coniuge barbara*
> *Turpis maritus vixit?*

et pactae. Paley much improves the point of this line by reading *et sic pactae mihi noctes*, etc. ' Was it on *these* terms that I gave myself up to thee?'

12. rudis, ' all inexperienced,' ' a novice.'

victa, nominative feminine singular.

The ordinary phrase for ' yielding ' is *dare manus*, as 4. 11. 88.

13. deductae, of the marriage procession which escorted the bride to her new home. An exactly similar procession may be seen in some Scottish villages to this day—as in Leadhills in Lanarkshire

—where the whole marriage party after the ceremony accompanies the bride to her new home in a procession headed by a fiddler.

14. Nothing was more ill-omened than that the proceedings of a marriage should in any way come in contact with the paraphernalia of a death or a funeral. See Ov. Met. 6. 429: among the ill omens of Procne's marriage,

Eumenides tenuere faces de funere raptas.

During the Feralia no marriage took place, Ov. Fast. 2. 559

lumina nigra, not merely 'dim,' but 'dark' and 'funest' in their boding, because of their having been lighted from the overturned remains of a funeral pyre. There is perhaps an allusion to the fact that the marriage torch was made of the wood of the white thorn.

15. On reaching the door of his own house, the bridegroom presented the bride with fire and water, as symbols of the necessaries of life. Arethusa declares that the water was not fetched from a pure spring, but from some Avernian pool connected with the lower world.

16. The god Hymen or Hymenaeus, invoked throughout the procession in the marriage song, was supposed to be present throughout the proceedings.

17. portis. This word implies city gates, not the gates of a temple. At the city gates there were chapels or shrines to the *Lares Viales*, under whose protection travellers were placed. Similarly there were *Lares Permarini*, to whom prayers were addressed for those venturing on sea-voyages. See note on Tib. 1. 1. 20.

pendent apparently refers to tablets hung up with a record of the vow. See note on 2. 28. 43.

vota are not 'votive offerings,' as Paley supposes, which were not hung up until after the prayers made had been granted, but only the promise of such offerings accompanying the prayer.

18. Arethusa is represented as occupying herself at home with weaving her husband's military cloak, with the simplicity of an early Roman matron. So Lucretia, Ov. Fast. 2. 743, sits and works among her maidens:

Mittenda est domino, nunc nunc properate, puellae,
Quamprimum nostra facta lacerna manu.

19. vallum, the accusative of *vallus*, 'a stake;' *vallum* is a palisade.

20. per, 'by means of.' The preposition is rare in this sense, except with persons: such adverbial phrases as *per iocum, per otium, per viam*, etc., are common, but not parallel.

21, 22. An ancient fable is here alluded to, similar to our proverb of making ropes of sand, and represented in a picture by

Polygnotus. A man called Ocnus is employed in twisting a rope; as fast as he makes it, it is devoured by a she-ass standing at his side. Pausanias says it is emblematic of a hard-working husband afflicted with an extravagant wife.

obliquo apparently refers to the man standing sideways as regards the ass, so that he does not see what she does.

23, 24. The questions in *urit, atterit* are made direct for sake of vividness.

23. urit, 'chafes:' so Hor. Epp. 1. 10. 43 of a shoe,

Si pede maior erit, subvertet, si minor, uret.

27. tenuasse. Lycotas is said 'to have made his face thin,' instead of 'to have become thin in the face.' Exactly similar is 3. 22. 16, where the Nile is said 'to moderate his seven channels,' instead of 'to be moderated by having his waters divided into seven channels.'

28. iste, 'that paleness of thine.'

29. At marks the transition from the consideration of his state to hers.

induxit, 'has ushered in.'

31. pallia are the bed coverlets, which in her restless nights she keeps tossing on to the ground.

sidere, used like *sedere* in Ov. Am. 1. 2. 2

Esse quid hoc dicam quod tam mihi dura videntur
Strata, neque in lecto pallia nostra sedent?

32. Lucis auctores, i.e. the cock. So Ov. Met. 11. 597

Non vigil ales ibi cristati cantibus oris
Evocat Auroram.

33. Cp. Tibull. 1. 3. 85–88.

34. radios, 'the shuttles,' into which the woollen yarn was distributed in proper lengths (*secta*) for weaving. The MSS. read *gladios*, which Hertz. is half disposed to adopt as the true reading, with the same meaning as *radios*, on the strength of a line quoted from Ennius by Nonius,

Deducunt habiles gladios filo gracilento.

But the meaning of *gladios* in that passage is by no means clear.

suos, because each colour of wool would have its own shuttle.

35–40. She whiles away her evenings partly in work, partly in endeavouring to follow her husband's movements on the map, and in getting up particulars about the climate, etc., of the country he is in. Cp. Ov. Her. 1. 31 sqq. quoted above.

For the sense of the whole cp. Sir R. Aytoun:

Meantime my part shall be to mourn,
To tell the hours till thou return,

> *My eyes shall be but eyes to weep,*
> *And neither eyes to see nor sleep.*

38. docti ... positura dei is the disposition of the world *made by* a wise Creator. Cp. Virg. Aen. 12. 94

> *validam vi corripit hastam,*
> *Actoris Aurunci spolium,*

of the spoil *taken from* Actor.

39. lenta, as Paley remarks, is used of ' adhesive ' substances, such as honey, pitch, wax, etc., while *putris* is ' loose,' ' friable,' of a light soil, Virg. Geo. 2. 204, opposed to a clay soil which *lentescit habendo*.

ab, ' in consequence of.'

42. peierat, ' falsely declares.'

43. Hippolyte, Queen of the Amazons. Cp. 3. 14. 13

> *Qualis Amazonidum nudatis bellica mammis.*

44. barbara. Note the emphatic position of this word, in contrast to *Romanis* in the next line. As Pinder puts it, ' Happy in the freedom of her wild state.'

45. See the very interesting debate in the Senate, recorded by Tacitus, Ann. 3. 33, 34, as to whether governors of provinces should be allowed to take their wives with them.

47. Pater. If the reading *Africus* in the next line be correct, the title *Pater* must be applied to the wind in the same way that it is constantly applied to rivers. The only parallel given is Claud. Rapt. Pros. 2. 73, where *Zephyrus* is addressed as *Pater O gratissime veris*. If for *Africus* we read some word other than the name of a wind, *Pater* will stand for Jupiter, as in Hor. Od. 3. 10. 7

> *Audis ... et positas ut glaciet nives*
> *Puro numine Iuppiter.*

48. The MSS. have *Africus:* but *Africus* was *par excellence* the warm steamy wind of the Mediterranean, the South-west, the Greek λίψ, the sirocco of modern times, the last wind in the world to be associated with frost. Hence the various conjectures given in the critical notes. But elsewhere *Auster* is called *frigidus* Prop. 2. 26. 36, and Virg. Geo. 4. 261 ; *turbidus* Hor. Od. 3. 3. 5 ; and Tib. 1. 1. 47 has

> *Aut gelidas hibernus aquas cum fuderit Auster.*

Africus itself is often associated with storms : *Africis procellis* Hor. Od. 3. 29. 57 ; *praecipitem A.* id. 1. 3. 12 ; *protervus A.* id. Epod. 16. 22. Either then Propertius uses *Africus* vaguely of a wind that brings rough, coarse weather ; or else implies that in Scythia, whose cold the Romans greatly exaggerated, even *Africus* congeals everything with frost. None of the conjectures proposed are satisfactory. R. Ellis makes the tempting conjecture *Arcticus*, (Journ. of Phil. vol. 15. p. 19), but no authority but that of Hyginus is quoted for the word. Palmer is inclined to propose *adstrictam*, quoting Ov. Trist. 2. 196

Et maris adstricto quae coit unda gelu.

As the names of the winds are constantly recurring in Latin poetry, it may be worth while to give a wind-chart, showing the Latin names for the winds with their Greek equivalents:

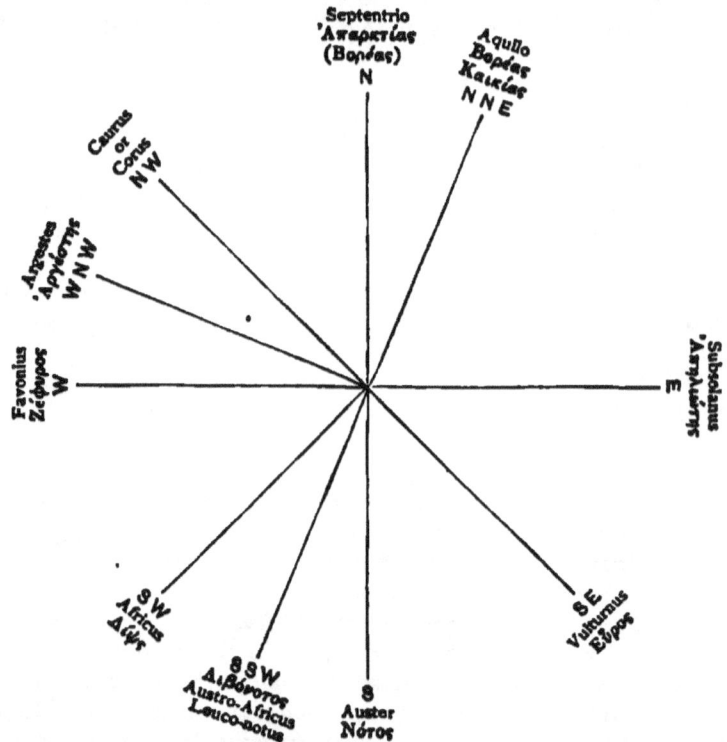

It is to be noted, however, that the names of the winds are often loosely used, and that each often trespasses upon the confines of its neighbour. This is especially true of *Notus*, who ranges over the whole S.W. quarter, from South to West: Boreas is more rigidly a North wind, but travels some distance to the East. Mr. Gladstone, Homeric Studies, vol. 3. p. 274, has pointed out that the Homeric winds usually hunt in couples, Boreas and Zephyrus being frequently associated as one couple, Eurus and Notus as another: in one place only (Il. 21. 334) are Notus and Zephyrus conjoined. Thus these four winds are not regarded as being at right angles to each other: Boreas is nearer to Zephyrus, Notus is nearer to Eurus.

49. aperto in coniuge, 'in the case of an acknowledged husband.' For *in,* attached in this sense to a verb of loving, cp. Hor. Od. 1. 17. 19 *laborantes in uno;* id. Epod. 11. 4 *in pueris aut in puellis urere;* and Prop. 1. 14. 7

     Perditus in quadam tardis pallescere curis
       Incipis.

50. Pinder points out the alliteration of this line.

51. tibi cannot be right here : there is no point in '*thy* purple' if the line be punctuated naturally as in the text, and to read with Pinder, Bae., etc. *nam mihi quo? tibi,* etc. is harsh as well as pointless. Palmer prefers *ter,* and suggests *quo . . . quo* as a possibility.

52. meas is clearly right. Bae. follows most MSS. in reading *tuas,* which can only be interpreted 'these hands which in very truth are thine'—an intolerable ambiguity, and not supported by such phrases as *Blanditias meas, oscula mea* ('kisses, etc., meant for me '), quoted from Tib. 1. 9. 77, etc. Coaxings and kissings are transferable, hands are not.

aquosa. The Romans accounted for the coldness and clearness of crystal by imagining that it contained water frozen into ice. Thus Claud. Epig. 11

     Dum chrystalla puer contingere lubrica gaudet,
       Et gelidum tenero pollice versat onus ;
     Vidit perspicuo deprensas marmore lymphas,
       Dura quibus solis parcere novit hiems ;
     Et siccum relegens labris sitientibus orbem
       Irrita quaesitis oscula figit aquis.

53. surda, transferred from the active meaning ' not hearing ' to the passive 'not heard,' noiseless. So *caecus* of a thing not seen ; as Lucr. 1. 271 of the winds,

     Sunt igitur venti nimirum corpora caeca.

Cp. Prop. 4. 5. 58

     Istius tibi sit surda sine arte lyra.

raris Kalendis, i. e. ' but seldom—on the first of the month,' ' no oftener than once a month.' *Raris* is a general epithet of *Kalendis,* not a determining epithet. Cp. *funus extremum* 1. 17. 23 and note. The *Lares* were usually worshipped on the Nones and Ides as well, Cato. R. R. 133.

adsueta : this was the regular duty of the *una puella,* the single maid-servant to whom her establishment was reduced. Prof.

Palmer would now read *ad sueta,* ' for their wonted rites,' and compares Appul.

> *Se ad sectae sueta conferunt.*

54. clausos, i. e. in the Lararium.

56. tui partem, ' claims thy place,' lit. ' thy function or office,' *partem* being used for the more usual *partes.*

57. verbenis. The *verbena* was a plant much used in sacred rites of all kinds, and especially in the ratifying of treaties, as we learn from Servius on Virg. Aen. 12. 120, Liv. 1. 24, 30. 43 and elsewhere. It is usually identified with our *vervain,* but it was used in a wider sense to denote the leaves or branches of any sacred tree or bush. Thus Servius, quoted above, says *Verbena proprie est herba sacra, ros marinus, ut multi volunt, id est λι-βανωτὶς, sumpta de loco sacro Capitolii qua coronabantur Fetiales et Pater Patruus foedera facturi vel bella indicturi. Abusive tamen verbenas iam vocamus omnes frondes sacratas, ut est laurus, oliva, vel myrtus. Terentius* (And. 4. 3. 11) ' *ex ara hinc sume verbenas*' *nam myrtum fuisse Menander testatur, de quo Terentius transtulit.*

58. herba Sabina, a kind of juniper, known as savin, used before incense was known, Ov. Fast. 1. 343

> *Ara dabat fumos herbis contenta Sabinis,*

or as an offering by the poor, Culex 403

> *Herba turis opes priscis imitata Sabina.*

60. Just as a tea-leaf swimming on the top of a cup of tea is called ' a stranger,' so a sputter in the wick of a lamp or candle was held by the Romans to herald an arrival, and had to be acknowledged by a libation. Thus Ov. Her. 19. 151

> *Sternuit et lumen, posito nam scribimus illo :*
> *Sternuit, et nobis prospera signa dedit.*
> *Ecce ! merum nutrix faustos instillat in ignes ;*
> *Crasque erimus plures, inquit, et ipsa bibit.*

We call a fungus-like excrescence on the wick of a candle ' a thief.' In the passage before us the wine is applied to the lamp.

61, 62. The ' fatted calf' would be slain on the wanderer's return : Hor. Epp. 1. 3. 36

> *Pascitur in vestrum reditum votiva iuvenca.*

62. Succincti, ' girt up for work,' hence used for ' active,' ' busy.' The opposite term, *male cinctus,* is used of an inactive luxurious person whose robe is loose ; hence ' profligate,' as in the celebrated warning of Sulla, who detected the ambition of Caesar under the foppery and profligacy of his youth : *ut male praecinctum puerum caverent* Suet. Caes. 45.

nova, because she had hitherto (l. 53) intermitted many of her religious duties.

63. tanti. The apodosis is left to be understood. 'Let not the glory of capturing Bactra be of so great value in your eyes as that for sake of that you should prolong your absence.' The full construction of *tanti* in such passages is seen in Juv. 3. 54 quoted above on 1. 8. 3.

64. odorato duci. 'Some perfumed chief.'

carbasa lina, as Palmer observes, is not more forcible than 'flaxen linen' would be. *Lina* seems a gloss: he suggests *picta*. It is possible, however, that *carbasa* may add a sense of fineness to the word *lina*: but in that case *lina* becomes tautological.

66. Another allusion to the Parthian and his well-known method of fighting; as in 3. 9. 54

> *Parthorum astutae tela remissa fugae.*

So Virg. Geo. 3. 31, Hor. Od. 1. 19. 12.

67, 68. tua . . . pura hasta, i. e. 'may a *hasta pura* be presented to thee, with which thou mayest follow in the triumph.' A *hasta pura* was a pointless spear, a reward of bravery to a young soldier. In Virg. Aen. 6. 760 the young Marcellus leans on such a spear.

67. sic, 'on this condition:' the condition is given in *conserva*, etc. For this construction see note on Tibullus 2. 5. 63.

70. lege, 'condition.'

71. Outside the *Porta Capena* stood a temple of Mars, in which returning warriors hung up and dedicated their arms. See Ov. Fast. 6. 192. Observe the dative *portae* after a verb of motion. The construction is somewhat softened by *votiva*.

IV. 4.

THIS poem, by many placed amongst the earliest (but see Introd.), is by no means the least beautiful, of the poems of Propertius. Hertz. is probably correct in supposing that, together with the first, second, ninth, and tenth of this book, it was intended to form part of a poetico-antiquarian book of 'Origines' after the model of the Αἴτια of Callimachus; and that, in all probability, these poems gave to Ovid the idea of his *Fasti*. There are obvious differences of style between these and the other poems of Propertius. Lachmann is of opinion that they were not published until after the poet's death.

1, 2. As in the first, second, and tenth pieces, Propertius begins abruptly with a short statement of his subject. The two lines before

us are exactly parallel to 10. 1, 2. For the legend of Tarpeia see
Liv. 1. 11, Ov. Fast. 1. 261 sqq. The account now generally accepted is
that there was originally a Latin settlement on the Palatine hill, a
Sabine (?) settlement on the Quirinal and Capitol, and that the infant
Rome was formed by the union of the two. Roman pride could not
admit that the Capitol was not originally Roman, and so represented
it as having been lost by treachery. See Tac. Ann. 12. 24.

2. **limina Iovis**, not the threshold of the temple of *Juppiter
Optimus Maximus*, but the approach to the Capitoline hill itself,
the whole of which was considered to have been the abode of the
god from the earliest times. Thus Virg. Aen. 8. 347, when Evander
conducts Aeneas,

  Hinc ad Tarpeiam sedem et Capitolia ducit,

Virgil adds,

  Iam tum religio pavidos terrebat agrestes
  Dira loci, iam tum silvam saxumque tremebant.

Evander goes on to explain that it is uncertain who the god is, but
that his Arcadians believe they have seen Jupiter himself. So *saxa
Iovis* l. 10.

antiqui . . . Iovis, as in 2. 30. 28

   antiqui dulcia furta Iovis.

3. **felix**, 'thick,' 'luxuriant.'

conditus no doubt ought to be read. **Consitus**, of a
natural wood, is unmeaning. *Conditus* means 'hidden,' 'retired,'
'withdrawn from view;' cp. such phrases as *nubes Condidit lunam*
Hor. Od. 2. 16. 3; *hostis in silvas armatum militem condidit* Curt.
8. 1. 4. Propertius means that the approach to the Capitol was
through a rocky thickly-wooded den or gorge, the rocks (*antro*)
being covered with ivy. All these points occur in Virgil's description: *silvestribus horrida dumis, silvam saxumque, nemus, fron-
doso vertice collem*. The details throughout are vague, confused,
and exaggerated, but it is vain to look for real topographical
accuracy in the poets, or indeed the historians, of Rome. The
Roman historians are notoriously inexact and vague in such
matters. Livy never helps us in his descriptions of ground, even as
to great battle-fields which he might easily have visited. And even
the careful Greek Polybius, who laboriously went over the scenes of
the campaigns which he narrates, never describes a locality with the
point and precision which are necessary for identification. The
Capitol has been so overlaid with buildings and ruins that it is impossible now to make out its original natural features: but there are
still two pieces of abrupt volcanic cliff—one of them at least sixty

feet in height—which lay claim to being the Tarpeian Rock. One is on the north side, overlooking the Campus Martius; the other is on the south-east side, facing the Palatine, in the garden of the modern German Hospital. The latter site suits history and the legend best, as the Sabine assault was made from the side of the Palatine and the Forum.

Through the den ran a little gurgling stream: in l. 7 and throughout the poem it is spoken of as *fons*, and treated indifferently as a stream and as a spring. Cp. *fonte, fontem* ll. 14, 15 with *amne* l. 24.

4. obstrepit . . . aquis. A curiously inverted expression. The natural construction of *obstrepo* is with the dative of the thing against which the subject chafes or sounds; but here the thing chafed against is the subject, and *aquis* is in the ablative: 'The trees echo or ring with the sound of the water.' Cp. Hor. Epod. 2. 27

    Fontesque lymphis obstrepunt manantibus,

'roar with their waters;' and Cic. Div. 5. 4. 1 *quae res fecit ut tibi litteris obstrepere non auderem*, where both constructions are used.

6. poturas ire, 'more usually *potum ire*,' Palmer.

7. fontem . . . praecingit, i. e. Tatius brought his lines close up to the *fons*, or pool, where the Roman garrison watered. Thus his palisade formed a kind of edge or·border to the *fons :* and when Tarpeia came down to draw water, the Sabines, bivouacking in the forum, were in full view.

8. coronat, as we speak of a ' ring-fence.'

9. Curetis, i. e. 'Sabine.' Propertius apparently alone uses this form. In Ov. Fast. 3. 94 the form *Curensis* is used, as by Varro and Pliny. *Cures, -ium* is the town.

11. dicuntur iura, ' law is administered.'

13. ' They had a mountain for their wall.'

ubi, etc., i. e. the *fons* was on the site where afterwards the *curia Hostilia* was built, the special meeting-place, first of the *curiae*, afterwards of the Senate. Close to the *curia Hostilia* was the famous *Carcer* or Mamertine prison, known anciently as *Tullianum*. Now the name *Tullianum* is derived from an old word *tullius*, signifying a spring, and in reality means ' Well-house.' There is a well still to be seen in the prison: it is therefore possible that the *fons* of Tarpeia is none other than the *tullius* of the prison, the sight of which wrung from Jugurtha his last words: 'O Romans, how cold your bath is!' See Burn's Rome, p. 81, etc.

14. This line is apparently a general description of the spring, without special allusion to the Sabines or Romans. The spring was apparently outside the lines of both armies: *Aquam forte ea tum* *sacris extra moenia petitum ierat* Liv. 1. 11. But Propertius makes no use of this point.

15. fontem libavit, i. e. 'drew water for the service of the goddess.' Besides meaning 'to pour,' especially of religious libations, *libo* means 'to taste,' 'to touch lightly,' and so 'to take' or 'select,' as Cic. de Inv. 2. 2 *Ex variis ingeniis excellentissima quaeque libavimus.*

at has no adversative force: it merely adds a new point to the picture.

16. Cp. Ov. Fast. 3. 14, of Rhea Silvia,

Ponitur e summa fictilis urna coma.

17, 18. The sudden contrast between the picture of the pure vestal, with her earthen pitcher, going about her simple duties, and the thought of the shameful act which she was about to commit, wrings from the poet the indignant outburst of this couplet.

17. satis una mors, i. e. no amount of deaths could expiate such a treachery. Cp. Hor. Od. 3. 27. 37. Lachmann's conjecture *urna,* adopted by Hertz., and called by him *palmaris,* is absolutely contemptible.

18. fallere, 'to prove false to.' As we have seen, the verb *fallo* is used in the vaguest sense, to denote any act or form of concealment, deceit, or treachery.

20. I adopt Palmer's conj. **frena** with great confidence. *Arma* came from *armis,* in l. 21, which would be a repetition if *arma* were read. The changes from *a* to *f,* and from *m* to *en* are of the slightest, and the picture of the horseman is incomplete without it.

Picta need occasion no difficulty to those who remember the lines:

Blue was the charger's broidered rein,

Blue ribbons decked his arching mane ;

The knightly housing's ample fold

Was velvet blue, and trapped with gold. Marmion, 1. 6.

22. inter, i. e. 'from between.'

oblitas manus, like *oblito pectore* Cat. 64. 208, and *oblito amore* 1. 19. 6.

23. immeritae, i. e. omens ' of which the moon was guiltless.'

causata est, 'alleged as an excuse for going to the spring.' Cp. Tib. 1. 3. 17.

26. Romula for *Romulea.* Cp. 3. 3. 7, 11. 52.

27. primo fumo, 'the first smoke of the evening,' when the fire was lighted for supper.

29. residens, 'sitting,' or 'sinking down,' with a notion of languor and dejection, after her ascent from the *fons.*

30. non patienda. The poet glances at her future punishment.

31. Paley says the speech of Tarpeia cannot extend to l. 66, because *flevit* is inappropriate to the passage from l. 48. But it is clear the whole is spoken by Tarpeia. She begins ll. 31–46 by a soliloquy: she then, ll. 47–66, goes on as if she were addressing Tatius, and discloses to him her plan.

34. Dum . . . conspicer, 'Provided only I may gaze on.'

35. montibus addita Roma. *Addita* is used here in a pregnant sense, to give the idea that Rome was something far greater than the site on which she stood. So in a bad sense, 'inflicted upon,' *Teucris addita Iuno* Virg. Aen. 6. 90 and Luc. ap. Macr. 5. 6. 4

> *Si mihi non praetor siet additus atque agitet me.*

Paley feebly explains 'the buildings add to the height of the *montes*.'

36. valeat, 'Farewell to.' She here meditates merely running away: the idea of earning her right to be Tatius' wife by treachery has not yet suggested itself.

pudenda, not in its usual sense, 'whom I ought to be ashamed of' (Pal.), but 'before whom I ought to feel shame.'

37, 38. Her mind reverts to the dazzling apparition of Tatius on his horse: a confirmation of *frena* in l. 20.

37. meos amores is generally held to refer to Tarpeia herself, ' my loving self,' just as in 2. 13. 22 *mors mea = ego mortuus*, and in 3. 5. 4 *nostra sitis = ego sitiens.* But Palmer is doubtless right in supposing it refers to Tatius: 'my love,' ' my darling.' So in 2. 28. 39, of Cynthia

> *Una ratis fati nostros portabit amores.*

Tarpeia is recalling in a hopeless dreamy way the vision of Tatius on horseback; she envies the horse his privilege of carrying his rider back to the camp; and then recounts with a half-approval instances of maidens who have been urged to bold wicked deeds by the urgency of their passion. To contemplate elopement would be out of place.

38. dextras. So the MSS. But why not *dextra?*

39, 40. Like Virgil, E. 6. 74, and Ovid, Fast. 4. 500, Propertius confounds Scylla the daughter of Nisus, king of Megara, with the sea-monster of Homer and later tradition, who lived on the Italian side of the Straits of Messina. The former betrayed 'her father and her country to Minos, king of Crete, by cutting off a certain purple lock of her father's hair. See Aesch. Cho. 615, Pausan. Att. 1. 19. 5 ' (Paley). Thus Prop. 3. 19. 21

> *Teque 'o Minoa venumdata, Scylla, figura,*
> *Tondens purpurea regna paterna coma.*

41. Prodita . . . fraterni cornua monstri, lit. ' The betrayed horns of the fraternal monster' by a strange inversion, = ' The be-trayal of her brother, the horned monster,' i. e. the Minotaur.

42. lecto stamine, 'by picking,' or 'taking up, the thread.' Cp. Ov. Her. 10. 104

Fila per adductas saepe relecta manus.

44. Improba virgineo. Note the strong juxtaposition of epithets. So in the Odes of Horace, *tenues grandia* 1. 6. 9; *insolentem serva* 2. 4. 2; *perfida credulum* 3. 7. 13, etc.

45. The Palladium was kept in the temple of Vesta, Ov. Trist. 3. 1. 29.

45, 46. Perhaps the weakest couplet in Propertius. The conceit is truly Ovidian : at once mawkish and exaggerated. Paley calls it 'a truly poetical idea.'

47. cessabitur. So Palmer; but he now prefers *potabitur.* The *pugnabitur* of the MSS. is entirely inconsistent with what follows, ll. 73-80, and especially ll. 79, 83. The account is modelled on the famous attempt of the Gauls under Brennus : the essence of the plan was that the Romans were to be off their guard, and the attack a stealthy one.

48. Note *capĕ* before a word beginning with *sp :* so 3. 11. 53, 4. 1. 41, and before *st* in 4. 5. 17.

49, 50. quippe ... aquas gives the reason why the *via* is *perfida.* It is always wet : but the water flows in a silent, and there-fore treacherous channel (*limes*).

52. Bae.'s correction **Hanc** is more forcible than *Haec.* All that mere words and prayers can do to help Tatius, she has already done : she wishes she had a more potent mode of helping him with her tongue. If we read *haec* we may translate, ' Then would my tongue too, like Medea's, have brought help to a handsome lover.'

53. toga picta, an embroidered robe worn by generals in a triumph, also by the statue of Juppiter Capitolinus.

sine matris honore, a negative, and therefore gentle, mode of describing the dishonour of Rhea Silvia, like *nec proba Pasiphae* 2. 28. 52.

54. Nutrit. Propertius is fond of this idiom, by which the present is used for the perfect of a past and completed act. So 4. 1. 77

Me creat Archytae soboles:

and in the same poem, ll. 127, 128, 131, 132, 133, the present and perfect are used alternately of the same events. See note on 4. 11. 39.

55. Sic, if correct, must mean ' on this condition,' viz. the condi-tion stated as a result in l. 56. The question of l. 55 is equivalent to a conditional proposition : cp. 'Is any merry? let him sing psalms.'

57. si minus shows that the preceding couplet has stated one of the two alternatives. The punctuation of the text makes the clause *ne sint* dependent upon *me rape*, etc. Others have a colon after Sabinae : 'let it not be said that.'

59, 60. In allusion to the legend of the Sabine wives rushing in between their husbands and their fathers, and so putting an end to the battle, Liv. 1. 11, Ov. Fast. 3. 217.

60. medium perhaps combines the idea of a treaty between the two parties, with that of bringing them to terms on the spot.

palla, the outer shawl or robe thrown over the female *stola*. It is here used for a wedding-garment.

62. vest. arm., 'the battle you must fight.' **torus,** 'marriage.'

64. V² reads *lassa* for *lapsa:* this gives point to *Ipsaque.*

65. de te. Pal. quotes Mart. 7. 54. 1

Semper mane mihi de me tua somnia narras.

67. permisit brachia happily expresses the *abandon* with which she surrendered herself to sleep.

68. furiis is used in a mixed sense ; partly for the Furies, avengers of the wrong done to Vesta in letting out the sacred fire, who in sleep are to goad her on to fresh sin ; partly, as *novis* shows, for the mad pangs of love, inflamed to new fury in her dreams.

accubuisse, 'that she has laid down beside.'

69. tutela, 'protectress,' as in Hor. Ep. 1. 1. 103.

70. condit in ossa faces. So Venus sends Cupid to Dido, Virg. Aen. 1. 660

Ut   .   .   .   .   .   .   furentem
Incendat reginam atque ossibus implicet ignem;
and in 4. 101
Ardet amans Dido, traxitque per ossa furorem.

71. ruit, of the mad fury of her movements ; not that she yet goes forth to meet Tatius, as she does later, l. 81.

72. Strymonis, 'some Thracian damsel,' from the river Strymon. The comparison is probably to a Thracian Maenad in her frenzy. Some refer it to an Amazon (Amazons are connected with the Thermodon Aen. 11. 659), but that would suggest quite a different idea.

sinu, the fold of the dress, torn off in frenzy.

73. Parilia. See Tib. 1. 1. 35 and note, also 2. 7. 88–9, and Ov. Fast. 4. 781 sqq.

74. primus coepit, redundant: as when we say 'then first began.'

76. madeo, *madidus,* often used in reference to wine, here of the richer dishes and dainties of the feast-day, which to meet the Italian taste would be well soused in oil. Tib. 2. 5. 85 specially mentions that on the Palilia the *pastor* is *madidus Baccho.*

76. divitiis. Cp. *gaza agresti,* Virg. Aen. 5. 40.

77. raros. The heaps of straw were placed at intervals.

81. suum, 'her own time,' and therefore 'favourable:' as in *vere suo* 'Virg. G. 4. 22 of swarming bees, *ventis iturus non suis* Hor. Epod. 9. 30, of Antonius after Actium.

82. Pacta. Propertius makes no mention of the bracelets which figure as the price of Tarpeia's treachery in the common tradition (*pepigisse eam quod in sinistris manibus haberent* Liv. 1. 11), as being inconsistent with his more romantic version of the story. *Pacta* is a kind of cognate accusative after *ligat:* 'she makes the bargain fast.'

83. ascensu dubius, from its natural difficulty, and on this occasion, in addition, *festo remissus.*

84. vocales occupat, i.e. Tatius. He strikes them down before they can give tongue.

85. Omnia praebebant somnos : a fine expression. 'Everything afforded sleeping to their gaze,' 'every spot presented sleepers ;' or, as Mr. Palmer well translates, 'wherever they looked there was a sleeping form.' *Omnia* is geographical, so to speak : a common use, far more graphic than Paley's, 'the holiday, the good cheer, the wine, etc., caused slumber.' Bae.'s *carpebant* is contemptible.

86. Decrevit, 'resolved ;' in l. 79 it is 'ordered.'

tuis, he suddenly apostrophises Tarpeia.

87. portae fidem, i.e. 'the gate committed to her charge.' But it might mean 'their confidence in the gate,' like *fiducia valli,* Virg. Aen. 9. 142. So Ov. Am. 3. 1. 50

Liminis adstricti sollicitare fidem.

88. ipsa, in withering scorn at the shameless request. Others read *ipse,* which is sufficiently disposed of by Paley's explanation, 'She leaves it to Tatius to name the day' (!)—a matter which all ages have regarded as specially within the province of the lady. The monstrosity consists in the demand for the marriage itself coming from her side, not the mere detail as to the time.

90, 91. There is something unexplained in these lines, as no pretext is suggested for the throwing of the shields on to Tarpeia. Can l. 90 mean 'Yes—thou shalt marry me—and here is the royal couch on to which thou shalt climb !' as though the shields were thrown down in cruel irony to form a nuptial couch ? .

91. armis, here = 'shields.' So Virg. Aen. 10. 841, *seque in sua colligit arma.*

92. The commentary of the poet. **virgo,** because she had broken her vows as a vestal ; **erat,** in reference to the time when the pact was made. Observe the ancient *dos* was given by the husband.

94. This line seems to be addressed to Tarpeius, who was *vigil* or guardian of the gate. He received the honour of having the hill called after him as a reward of his *iniusta sors,* i. e. in finding the gate betrayed, in spite of his own loyalty, by his daughter.

.

IV. 6.

THIS poem is a paean over the great victory of Augustus at Actium, like the ninth Epode of Horace. It has not, however, the merit of having been written at the time ; it was not composed till B. C. 16, on the occasion of the third celebration, under Agrippa, of the *ludi quinquennales* on the Palatine, games instituted by a decree of the Comitia in B. C. 28 in perpetual commemoration of the victory. They are not to be confounded with the similar games, also *quinquennales,* instituted on the spot itself by Augustus immediately after the victory.

1. Once more the poet assumes the character of a priest about to perform a sacrifice. The first ten lines contain the exordium worked out with more than usual elaboration. The description of the battle itself takes the form of a solemn hymn in honour of the Palatine Apollo, to whom the victory was due ; and the piece ends with an invitation to sacrificial revelry, as in Horace's Epode. The exordium and the hymn that follows are connected in exactly the same way as in Hor. Od. 3. 1 : see note on Prop. 3. 1.

3. Cera, though not wholly satisfactory, is better than any other reading proposed : though in sense, Paley's *hedra,* if possible, would do well enough. All through the exordium Propertius mingles the poetic with the sacrificial terms ; and in l. 3 *certet,* followed by *corymbis,* requires that its subject should relate to song. Thus *ara* (Haupt) will not do ; *serta* may be right, as it contrasts best with *corymbis,* and Propertius uses the feminine form, 2. 33. 37. *Cera* must mean the waxen tablet on which the song was written.

4. Cyrenaeas, referring to Callimachus ; **aquas,** to the holy water with which the hands were washed before the sacrifice (χέρνιψ).

honores, of a thing offered, as *laticum libavit honorem* Virg. Aen. 1. 736. See notes on 3. 1. 22; 3. 11. 17.

6. laneus orbis, the wreath or festoon of wool, such as we often see carved on Roman altars.

7, 8. The mingling of sacrificial with poetic terms, which characterises the whole exordium, is here almost grotesque. Lit. 'Let the pipe pour forth the libation of a song on the fresh-reared altar from a Phrygian jar.'

8. Mygdoniis, in allusion to the Phrygian pipe. To hunt up an obscure Phrygian town mentioned by Strabo, and write *Cadis* with a capital (so Scal., Baehrens, etc.) is absurd.

9. alio sint aere, i. e. 'Away with!' i. e. 'let them exist, if they exist at all, in another clime.'

noxae, all harmful, ill-omened things, whether of sight, sound or deed.

10. novum, probably of the poet's originality as an elegiac poet: 3. 3. 26. It might also refer to his first appearance in the character of a priest.

mollit. 'A soft carpet of bay-leaves is strewn upon the ground for the poet-priest to tread on as he leads the procession to the altar; cp. Ov. Met. 4. 742 *Mollit humum foliis.*' Postgate. The laurel or bay was peculiarly appropriate for Apollo.

11. Palatini Apollinis, see 2. 31. The temple was built in consequence of the Actian victory.

13. ducuntur, the usual metaphor from spinning.

14. vaces. Postgate rightly explains 'give me your leisure:' 'deign to listen,' Pinder. Palmer explains it as an apology to Jupiter for leaving him out.

fugiens expresses Virgil's *inque sinus scindit sese unda reductos* Aen. 1. 161, and expresses the great depth of the Ambracian gulf, which extended twenty-five miles east from its entrance at Actium. This gulf is described successively in the passage before us as *sinus, pelagus, monimenta* and *via.*

15. Athamana, for 'Epirote.' A good instance of the loose way in which the poets used geographical terms. The *Athamanes* lived away altogether from the sea, on the upper waters of the Achelous.

16. condit is surely more than 'receives' (Postgate, but see his excellent note); it implies the peace and calm into which the bay lulls the noisy waters of the outer sea. It is especially used of burial: and like *compono*, in the same sense, conveys the idea of rest. Cp. *inhumatos condere manes* Luc. 9. 151, which recalls our phrase 'to lay a ghost.'

18. Lit. 'a passage presenting no difficulties to the vows of sailors,' i. e. 'into which (harbour) there is a safe and easy channel.' The promontory of Actium (Ἄκτιον, from ἀκτή, 'a shore') was a long sharp point projecting from the south or Acarnanian shore ; between this point and the promontory which comes to meet it from the shore of Epirus on the north, the channel at one point is no more than 700 yards in width. On a height close to the promontory of Actium stood an ancient temple of *Apollo Actius* or *Actiacus*. Near this spot was the camp of Antony ; his fleet lay in the spacious bay within (now the Bay of *Prevesa*), and he was strong enough to occupy the strait itself, on either side of which he had thrown up redoubts. Augustus was encamped on the north or Epirote shore, on the spot where he afterwards founded the town of Nicopolis in honour of his victory: his fleet lay at Comarus, a point of the coast of Epirus outside the channel. He was unable to force the entrance: and the great battle was brought on outside the straight, when Antony, dispirited by failures and desertions, had made up his mind to escape with his fleet to the East.

19. **mundi manus**: for Antony, Virg. Aen. 8. 686

> *Victor ab Aurorae populis et litore rubro,*
> *Aegyptum, viresque Orientis, et ultima secum*
> *Bactra vehit.*

See Postgate's note on *mundus*.

moles Pinea. Antony had collected at Actium some 500 vessels, mostly of vast size—some rowed by ten banks of oars—protected with huge frames or bulwarks of timber, and carrying heavy engines for the discharge of missiles, etc.:

> *Pelago credas innare revulsas*
> *Cycladas, aut montes concurrere montibus altos :*
> *Tanta mole viri turritis turribus instant.*

Virg. Aen. 8. 691. With these monstrous hulks the poets are ever comparing the light Liburnian galleys which composed the fleet of Augustus. For the phrase *stetit aequore moles* cp. Campbell,

> *Like Leviathans afloat stood our bulwarks on the brine.*

21. **damnata**, 'condemned and made over to,' as in Hor. Od. 3. 3. 23

> *Mihi*
> *Castaeque damnatum Minervae.*

22. We have here exactly the same doubt as to the case of

manu which has been raised in the similar passage, 2. 1. 66. It is very probable that *manu* is the dative, and that the scribe has changed *femineae* to *feminea* from ignorance of the contracted form in *u*. See note on that passage. N. reads *apta*, the adoption of which makes the dative necessary, and it must be confessed that *apta* gives a better meaning than *acta*. There was nothing specially shameful in the manner in which Cleopatra hurled her spear, or in the fact that she hurled it at all, when once arrayed in arms against Rome: what was shameful and humiliating to the Roman feeling was that a woman should appear in arms against Rome, and herself take part in the campaign. It was the fact that she bore arms, that she commanded Romans in a war against Rome, that was intolerable: Hor. Epod. 9. 11–14

> *Romanus, eheu! posteri negabitis,*
> *Emancipatus feminae,*
> *Fert vallum et arma miles, et spadonibus*
> *Servire rugosis potest!*

If *femineae manu* be adopted here, we must adopt the dative *Tantaleae manu* in 2. 1. 66 also. See Hous., J. of Phil. xxi. p. 193.

23. Hinc, corresponding to *altera* l. 21. Virgil draws exactly the same contrast with *hinc ... hinc* Aen. 8. 678, 685.

Augusta; so *Augustus* l. 29, and Aen. 8. 678, though the title was not assumed till B.C. 27.

25. The fleet of Augustus advanced in crescent-shape, its two wings extending so as to enclose and cramp the huge ships of Antony.

27. In Virgil, Apollo Actius draws his bow from above, and at once strikes terror into the enemy.

linquens, used exactly as our present participle, 'leaving.' For the Propertian use of the present participle cp. *simulantem* 4. 11. 39, and note also *fugiens* above, l. 15.

stantem, 'fixed,' as Delos had been a floating island until bound down with chains by Zeus, Virg. Aen. 3. 76.

se vindice, a very rare use of the ablative absolute in place of the nominative, as it refers to the subject of the sentence. The justification is in *stantem*, which has practically the force of a verb with *Delos* for its subject. Cp. *se iudice* Juv. 13. 2.

28. tulit, 'had to endure.'

una, a certain correction: *unda* gives no sense.

29. nova, 'strange,' 'never seen before'; perhaps 'heavenly': cp. Virg. Aen. 9. 10.

30. 'Blazed out in a triple wave of light, so as to resemble a torch held slantwise.'

ter simply indicates there were several waves or curls in the flame; *ter* is a mystic, and therefore poetic, number. Virgil identifies this *fax* with the *Iulium sidus*.

31. attulerat, i. e. 'appeared with :' Postgate well compares Cic. Phil. 8. 8. 23.

in colla solutos, 'flowing in disorder on to his neck.'

32. inerme, i.e. he had come as the god of battle, as 'lord of the unerring bow,' and soon to be

> *All radiant from his triumph in the fight :*

not as a *citharoedus*

> *In his delicate form—a dream of Love—*

or as

> *The God of life and poesy and light.*

> Childe Harold.

33. 'But (he appeared) with such a look as that with which,' etc.: i. e. *quali—vultu* has a double construction: it is both an ablative of quality attached to Apollo as he appeared at Actium, and an ablative of the instrument in connection with *adspexit*. The allusion of course is to the description of Apollo when he smote the Greeks with pestilence in his wrath against Agamemnon for refusing the suit of Chryses, Iliad 1. 48 seqq.

> βῆ δὲ κατ' Οὐλύμποιο καρήνων χωόμενος κῆρ,
> τόξ' ὤμοισιν ἔχων ἀμφηρεφέα τε φαρέτρην·
> ἔκλαγξαν δ' ἄρ' ὀϊστοὶ ἐπ' ὤμων χωομένοιο,
> αὐτοῦ κινηθέντος· ὁ δ' ἤϊε νυκτὶ ἐοικώς.

34. egessit. *Egerere* properly 'to carry forth,' used here as equivalent to *efferre*, as in Pers. 5. 69

> *ecce aliud cras*

> *Egerit hos annos,*

'carries forth to burial.' The expression, however, is confused by making *castra* the object instead of the bodies, whilst *rogis* does not suggest of itself the funeral procession. It is not necessary to suppose that *egerere* means 'to empty,' either here, or in Stat. Theb. 1. 37 *egestas alternis mortibus urbes*. The literal translation is intelligible enough : 'carried forth (to burial), i. e. consumed, the Greek camp by the greedy funeral pyres.' So in the passage from Statius, 'whole cities taken out to burial by.'

35. solvit, of the muscles relaxed in death. As Postgate says (see his note on passage), *per orbes* goes equally with *solvit* and *serpentem*, which is here the participle. It means 'coil by coil,' just as *explicuit per membra virum* quoted by Postgate from Luc. 4. 629 means 'limb by limb.' *Per* gives the idea of successive stages.

36. ferae. I have adopted Palmer's conjecture. *Lyrae* must surely be wrong. The expression is very harsh, and un-Propertian in itself, and if it were possible to strain *lyrae* so as to make it equivalent to *Musae*, the answer is that there was no tradition of the Muses having been alarmed by the Python. *Imbelles lyrae* has crept in because of *inerme lyrae* of l. 32, and *fere* might easily drop out after the *vere* of *timuere.* As Apollo himself was the chief lyrist, the poet would scarcely have represented the lyre especially as quailing before the Python. This objection is not removed by supposing *lyrae = Musae.* Still we must not forget Hor. Od. 1. 6. 10

Imbellisque lyrae Musa potens vetat.

37. mundi, emphatic, as in I. 19. At Actium the fate of the whole civilised world was to be decided; just as Rome, in the person of Augustus, was to be suffered to reach *Quicunque mundo terminus obstitit,* Hor. Od. 3. 3. 53. **Ab Alba,** 'descended from': cp. *Pastor ab Amphryso,* Virg. Georg. 3. 2.

39. iam terra tua est, not strictly true. Augustus had as yet nowhere defeated Antony by land : and had Antony not followed the ill-starred advice of Cleopatra to decide the event on the sea, he had a splendid army of 100,000 trained legionaries to bring into the field, besides countless auxiliaries. Antony is generally represented as having staked his last chance at Actium ; but it would be no less true to say the same of Augustus : and had Antony won, his courtly poets might well have represented Apollo as saying to him before the battle, *iam terra tua est.*

42. 'Caesar's ship is freighted with a nation's prayers. A very modern expression.' Postgate.

44. non bene, i. e. the omen was a disastrous one, after all. All Rome and her career has been founded on a delusion.

45. Latinos, an almost certain correction for *Latinis,* which is due to *remis. Fluctus* needs an epithet : the scandal was that a *royal* fleet should venture into *Latin* waters ; and that too when Augustus was *princeps.* (Apollo commits an anachronism here, as Augustus was not made *princeps senatus* till B.C. 28.) *Et nimium remis* is not 'And so' (Postgate) : nothing yet has been said to disparage Antony's fleet. The words refer to what precedes from l. 39, *Vince mari: iam terra tua est,* etc. The land is already yours : you must save your country now by victory at sea. 'Ay, and their confidence in their ships is over-great' comes in quite naturally, followed by indignation that they should have been permitted to approach at all.

49. Guyet's conjecture *Centauros* is surely right. To take *minantis* as an accusative after *vehunt*, agreeing with some substantive understood ('forms threatening with (?) Centaurs' rocks,' Postgate, or 'figures threatening to hurl giant stones,' Pinder), seems awkward. With *Centauros* all is plain : 'and as to their prows carrying Centaurs which hurl stones.' The expression is confused, referring both to the Centaurs, which were often put as figure-heads (cp. Virg. Aen. 10. 195), and to the huge catapults for hurling stones, with which Dion. 50. 33 tells us Antony's ships were fitted. Propertius may have thought the two were combined.

50. Tigna, referring to the timber frames put round some of the vessels, either to protect them from being rammed, or to assist in boarding the enemy. These timbers would be found to offer no resistance (*cava*), and the engines to be mere painted bogeys.

pictos metus : cp. *as idly as a painted ship Upon a painted ocean.*

51, 52. Cp. Byron: *'Tis the cause makes all, Degrades or hallows valour in its fall.*

51. in, 'in the case of.' See 2. 10. 21 and 4. 3. 49.

53. committe, 'set them on,' as though Augustus were the controller of both forces. So *victores committe*, Venus Mart. 8. 43. 3 and *licet Aeneam Rutulumque ferocem Committas*, 'pit against each other,' Juv. 1. 162.

temporis auctor, because Apollo has suggested the moment for joining battle. It must be confessed that Apollo's speech is somewhat trite and prosy, as though written to order.

55. pondus, 'its contents' or 'freight.'

57. fide, for 'Phoebus was true to his word and true to the cause which he protected.' Postgate.

58. Sceptra fracta vehuntur, a powerful metaphor: the ensigns of Antony and Cleopatra's royal power drift shattered and helpless upon the waters.

59. Idalio, in allusion to Caesar's descent from *Venus*, to whom Mount Idalium in Cyprus was sacred. **astro,** the comet or meteor into which Caesar's soul was popularly believed to have passed, Suet. Jul. 88. Possibly the planet *Venus* may be indicated.

60. A very dull and egotistical remark to escape from the deified Julius on such an occasion. His style had not improved.

iste fides, i. e. 'this exploit of yours (*ista*) proves you to be of my own true blood.'

62. libera signa, 'the standards of freedom,' Postgate; but his examples do not appear to me to justify the translation. Our English 'of' is misleading: 'the path of truth,' 'the anvil of truth,' etc., are not analogous. The natural translation is 'the standards now free,' referring to the Roman force on Antony's side, which before the battle was enslaved to an Egyptian queen. Horace expresses the same thing in the words quoted above, Epod. 9. 12

Emancipatus feminae.

63. Illa, sc. Cleopatra: Pal. remarks how carefully the Roman poets abstained from mentioning the hated Egyptian queen by her name.

male, i. e. from the Roman point of view. See note on Tib. 1. 10. 51.

64. Hoc unum, in apposition to the sentence which follows *non moritura*, etc. Whether this be an Accusative or Nominative is doubtful. Greek analogy would favour the Accusative: but in this passage the Nominative seems the natural case, as in Virg. Aen. 6. 223

> *pars ingenti subiere feretro,*
> *Triste ministerium ;*

where the verb in apposition has a transitive meaning, the accusative seems suggested, as in Aen. 9. 53, 8. 487, etc. But see Conington.

65. Di melius, taken with the words that follow, is better taken as a statement, than in its usual meaning of a wish. 'The gods ordered better after all: for what (i. e. how trumpery) a triumph would it have been to see a woman borne along,' etc. The wish *Di melius !* would only be appropriate in the mouth of some one speaking before Cleopatra's fate was known, in which case *ductus est* would be required for *ductus erat*. Hertz. well quotes Seneca, Epist. 98. 5, who bids us solace ourselves under disappointments by saying *Di melius*, i. e. 'The gods, after all, have ordered it for the best.'

67, 68. quod eius ... rates, an extravagant and tasteless idea.

70. ad, 'with a view to joining.'

exuit, 'puts off,' 'lays down.'

71. Candida, in allusion to the cleaned or whitened garments worn on feast-days: Hor. Sat. 2. 2. 61.

72. Blanditiae rosae, 'the caresses, the allurements, of the rose,' i. e. 'caressing roses:' for the expression see Postgate, Introduction. The genitive is epexegetic.

74. spica Cilissa, i. e. saffron oil or saffron plant: used also for burning on altars, Ov. Fast. 1. 36

> *Et sonet accensis spica Cilissa focis.*

75. Scaliger's conjecture *irritat*, adopted by Paley, merely repeats a commonplace: *irritet* conveys an invitation and its excuse.

76. fertilis, 'productive,' 'suggestive.' For the sentiment cp. Hor. Ep. 1. 5. 19, 1. 19. 1–8.

77. paludosos, 'inhabiting a marshy country:' the *Sicambri* or *Sugambri* occupied the land on the east bank of the Rhine at the mouth of the Lippe. In B. C. 16 they invaded *Belgica*, and inflicted a disastrous defeat on M. Lollius, in consequence of which Augustus went himself to Gaul and spent two years in settling the country.

78. Meroe was practically co-extensive with the modern Soudan: in B.C. 22 its queen Candace had invaded Egypt, and had been repelled by the Roman governor Petronius. Thus early did Egypt look to foreign intervention—as to that of Britain at the present day— to protect her from the assaults of the hardy Arabs of the Upper Nile. *Cepheus* was a mythical king of Aethiopia, father of Andromeda.

79. confessum, 'humbled,' 'owning himself beaten' (Palmer), as in Virg. Aen. 7. 433 *dicto parere fatetur* expresses 'consent on compulsion' (Conington), and so 'submitting himself,' 'acknowledging his inferiority.' Hertz. quotes Ov. Met. 5. 215

> *Confessasque manus obliquaque brachia tendens*
> *Vincis, ait, Perseu.*

82. pueros, his grandchildren Gaius and Lucius Caesar, sons of his daughter Julia and Agrippa, and adopted by himself.

83. nigras, probably of the dark alluvial soil : if so, Propertius is thinking of Babylonia and the lower Euphrates.

si quid sapis. Cp. 2. 13. 42.

85. ducam, 'prolong :' so Virg. Geo. 3. 379 *Hic noctem ludo ducunt*, and Tib. 1. 9. 61.

86. The Plur. *vina* may mean 'cups of wine': cp. *ignes* 'torches,' *frumenta* 'fields of corn,' *fumi* 'wreaths of smoke.'

IV. 11.

THIS magnificent poem—'the masterpiece of the poet's genius,' as Paley terms it—is in the form of an elegy upon Cornelia, a noble Roman matron, pronounced by herself. Cornelia was connected, both by birth and marriage with the highest Roman families. Her father was P. Cornelius Scipio, described by Suetonius as of consular rank (Oct. 62: he was probably a *consul suffectus*); her mother was Scribonia, whom Augustus married for political reasons as her third husband in B. C. 40, and divorced in the year following, on the very day when she had borne him his only daughter Julia. She had a brother, Publius, who was consul in B.C. 16; and she was married to Paullus Aemilius Lepidus, a nephew of the Triumvir.

This Lepidus was *consul suffectus* B.C. 34, and censor in B.C. 22, in which capacity he completed the famous Basilica Aemilia, of which a portion, built of brick, still survives as the front wall of the Church of S. Adriano in the Forum. Cornelia left two sons and a daughter. The elder son, Lucius, married his first cousin Julia, grand-daughter of Augustus, and was consul in A. D. 1; the younger, Marcus, was consul in A. D. 6 with L. Arruntius, was employed in important commands by Augustus, and was named by him, shortly before his death, as one of the three possible aspirants to the empire : *M. Lepidum dixerat capacem sed aspernantem, Gallum Asinium avidum et minorem, L. Arruntium non indignum, et, si casus daretur, ausurum* Tac. Ann. 1. 13.

Of the daughter Lepida nothing certain is known. Cornelia herself died in the year B. C. 16, the year of her brother's consulship, as we learn from l. 66.

The form of the poem is peculiar. Cornelia is supposed to utter it after her death ; hence she addresses alternately her husband as to her past life, and the judges of the lower world as to her future.

Mr. H. A. J. Munro disputes the claim of this poem to be held not only the noblest elegy of Propertius, but 'the queen of all elegies,' as it is held by some to be, and denies that it represents by any means the poet's very highest inspiration. I should be inclined to differ from him. There is a noble stateliness, an unconscious grandeur of self-assertion, a true Roman strength in the way in which Cornelia describes herself, her life, and her family, which enable us to form a picture of the Roman matron such as can be gained from no other source—except perhaps by contemplating the statues of the Vatican —and which recall the words used by Aristotle of the μεγαλό-ψυχος, who 'thinks himself worthy of great things, being worthy.' And the simple pathos and delicacy of the conclusion are unexcelled in literature.

1. urgere, of any human emotion, implies force and insistance : used similarly of the importuning of grief, Hor. Od. 2. 9. 9
　　　　Tu semper urges flebilibus modis
　　　　Mysten ademptum.
In *urgere sepulcrum*, as so often in ancient poetry (and especially throughout this poem), the simple physical idea is confused with, and held to represent, the spiritual idea which it suggests.

2. ad, 'in response to.'

3. funera, the dead or the spirit of the dead. *Funus* is the dead body in 1. 17. 8

Haeccine parva meum funus arena teget?

Cp. *ossa* in the same sense l. 20.

infernas leges, implying the stern jurisdiction under which the world below is governed. *Leges* is equivalent to the world or region subject to the jurisdiction.

4. Non exorato = *inexorabili*. So *indeprensus error* Virg. Aen. 5. 591. The past participle has frequently the force of the adjective in -*bilis*, especially in Cicero.

stant, of the solidity and unbending strength of the entrance and the portals which guard it. See note on 3. 18. 15.

adamante. So Virg. Aen. 6. 552. Cp. Theoc. 2. 34 καὶ τὸν ἐν ῞Αδᾳ κινῆσαι κ' ἀδάμαντα.

5. fuscae denotes the absence of light, and hence of colour, which characterises the lower world. So Quint. 11. 3. 15 opposes *vox fusca*, 'a husky voice,' to *vox candida*.

5, 6. audiat ... surda. The converse of what Horace finely says of Orcus 2. 18. 40

Vocatus atque non vocatus audit.

6. Nempe sums up briefly and pointedly the whole situation: 'why,' 'say or do what you will, the result will be.' So Ov. Am. 2. 6. 20

Infelix avium gloria, nempe iaces.

The tears of Paulus are supposed to find their way into the lower world. All acts done to or in connection with the dead are concieved, not only as known, but as actually done, in the world below.

7. aera. The obol placed as passage-money in the mouth of the dead. A good instance of the idea remarked on above l. 1.

8. A good example of the confusion between the real and the imaginary already noticed : 'The lurid gateway locks up the grassy pyres.' The meaning is, 'The dark door is shut upon the occupant of the grassy grave.' There is no need to change *herbosos* into *umbrosos*. The pyre was built with turf, or upon it: no word would more truly and simply characterise the surroundings of the grave. Pinder's explanation that *herbosos* strengthens the notion of the grave as a *closed* place seems fanciful. But see Hous., l. c., p. 179.

9. Sic, i. e. 'Upon this principle,' 'With a full knowledge of this law.'

10. The body, while burning, is represented as being gradually taken down to the world below.

caput, as we have seen, stands for the whole body or personality, with a notion of tenderness and affection. Cp. the Homeric φίλη or ἠθείη κεφαλή (= *carum caput*), whilst ὦ κακαὶ κεφαλαί Hdt. 3. 29, μιαρὰ κεφαλή Ar. Ach. 285, etc. correspond to the use of *caput* in imprecations.

11. currus avorum. A triumphal car placed in the *vesti-bulum*, the open space in front of the door of a Roman mansion. Statues were placed there, especially equestrian: but the grandest thing of all was to have a triumphal chariot. In Juv. 7. 125-128 an Aemilius is mentioned who has both an equestrian statue and a triumphal car as well:

> *huius enim stat currus aeneus, alti*
> *Quadriiuges in vestibulis, atque ipse feroci*
> *Bellatore sedens.*

Postgate describes *currus* as a 'typical' singular, and compares 2. 14. 24

> *Haec spolia, haec reges, haec mihi currus erunt.*

12. pignora, probably her children, children being constantly spoken of as 'pledges' of affection. But the word may include also all the external marks of her character and position.

13. habuit, 'experienced,' 'found:' this sense also of *habeo* seems to be connected with that of 'to use,' 'to deal with.' Cp. 1. 1. 8.

If **habui** be read, **Cornelia** is emphatic.

15. noctes refers to the physical darkness below, as we see by the addition of *paludes* and *unda*: they may all be called *damnatae* as belonging to the region of the condemned. 'Nights of con-demnation' would more closely represent the meaning than 'nights of the condemned' (Postgate).

lenta, like *flumine languido*, attributed to the Cocytus, Hor. Od. 2. 14. 17.

16. implicat, equivalent to the *alligat* of Virg. Geo. 4. 480.

18. Pater is probably Pluto, so-called as supreme in the world below. Postgate suggests it may mean Cornelia's father, as women were sometimes handed over to be tried by their family. But **hic** corresponds to *huc* l. 17: to read **hinc**, 'in consequence of my innocence,' is unnecessary and far-fetched.

Det . . . mollia iura, 'May he judge me mercifully.' The phrase is used loosely: *dare iura* properly means to 'lay down laws,' 'prescribe a constitution,' etc.

19. si quis Aeacus, somewhat contemptuously, 'Some Aeacus or other,' Aeacus being a subordinate judge to Rhadamanthus. She desires Pluto himself to take her case out of the courts, and deal gently with her: if not, she is prepared to face Aeacus, and meet her doom.

19, 20. posita urna . . . sortita pila. As Postgate points out, the urn might be either (1) that from which the jury was drawn; or (2) the voting urn; or (3) the urn by which the order of the cases was decided. But there is no call to decide this point : 'the urn,' whatever its use, was a recognised accompaniment and emblem of judicial proceedings, and the poets, in using the phrase, did not concern themselves to consider to what special use it was to be put. The placing of the urn on the table—the drawing of the lot—are signs that there is to be a regularly-constituted trial, followed by a verdict and a sentence. This is all that Virgil means, Aen. 6. 430-432, by *nec . . . sine sorte, sine iudice* and *quaesitor Minos urnam movet.* The commentators refine overmuch : see Conington and Hor. Od. 3. 1. 16, etc.

20. vindicet in, 'pronounce sentence,' or ' inflict punishment upon,' in accordance, as Postgate observes, with the original meaning of the word *vim dicere.* Thus impersonally, Caes. B. G. 3. 16 *in quos eo gravius Caesar vindicandum statuit.*

sortita, either transitively ' by a ball which assigns me my destiny,' as in Hor. Od. 3. 1. 15 *necessitas sortitur insignes et imos :* or passively as in Prop. 4. 7. 55, *sedes turpem sortita per amnem.* If transitive, the meaning may be ' when the ballot has chosen a jury ' ; or ' when ballot has given me my turn to be tried.' In Aen. 6. 431 Minos presides as *iudex quaestionis,* just as Aeacus does here.

21. Assideant introduces the idea of assessors, often appointed to assist a *iudex* in the conduct of a case. The assessors are Minos and Rhadamanthus, sons of Zeus, and therefore brothers of Aeacus.

Minoida sellam, a certain correction for *Minoia sella* of the MSS. *Minois* is used for Ariadne 2. 24. 27. The objection to Palmer's conjecture, *Assideant, fratrem iuxta Minoia sella et,* is that the Eumenides could not be spoken of as *assessors :* they are avengers, waiting in court to execute the sentence so soon as pronounced. *Assideant* is applied non-technically to the Furies, by a kind of zeugma. Plessis reads *iuxta Minoa : sed astet.*

22. intento . . . foro expresses the silence and strained attention of the court.

23. mole, 'thy burdensome task.'

24. Tantaleo should probably be read, from a form *Tantaleus,* corresponding to a possible Greek form Ταντάλεως. *Fallax Tantaleus liquor* is weak : Palmer adopts *corripere ore,* supporting it by 2. 17. 6

Ut liquor arenti fallat ab ore sitim.

But *ab ore* there is emphatic and essential to the point of the line.

25. petat, ' make for,' ' attack.'

improbus. Postgate says : ' "Unconscionable" about hits the general meaning of the word.' Is this note an explanation ? Is it not an ἀνάμνησις of a translation once given of *improbus anser,* 'the unconscionable goose?' 'Unconscionable' is a word used in a humorous bantering way, of a thing to which we apply moral condemnation, but at the same time indicate we do not do so seriously. Thus 'unconscionable' exactly hits off the meaning of Martial, when he says of his country habits

Ingenti fruor improboque somno.

It is quite out of place here where the epithet is seriously applied. See note on *improbus* 1. 1. 6.

26. Cerberus' chain is to hang loose : no bar is to be drawn in the gate which he is guarding.

27. loquor. The MS. reading is more impressive and stately than *loquar.* Cornelia here begins a speech which lasts to the end of the poem.

poena sororum. Objective genitive: the punishment inflicted upon the sisters, i. e. the Danaids.

29, 30. There is a slight anacoluthon in the sense. 'If ancestors ever brought fame to any, the realms of Africa tell of mine.'

30. Cornelia mixes up together in one phrase the two great titles to glory of the Scipio family. Two of them gained the title *Africanus* for their victories over Carthage ; the younger, Scipio Africanus Minor, was also called *Numantinus* from his capture of Numantia, B. C. 133, Ov. Fast. 1. 596

Ille Numantina traxit ab urbe notam.

Nostra . . . signa. So Bae. *Nostra* seems needed by the sense. Scaliger's *Afra* is unmeaning. Palmer's former suggestion *Aera . . . nostra* is good : *aera* might mean 'spoils of armour' as well as 'family coins.' See Hous., J. of Phil. xxii. p. 108.

loquuntur, 'tell of.'

31. She passes to her mother's family, the *Libones.* It was a plebeian family : we hear of a L. Scribonius Libo, tribune of the plebs B. C. 16. Scribonia was sister to L. Scribonius Libo, who followed the fortunes of Pompey throughout the civil war, and commanded the Pompeian fleet off Brundusium before Pharsalia. His daughter was married to Sextus Pompey : and in B.C. 40 he was an important enough personage for Augustus to think it worth while to conciliate him by marrying his sister Scribonia, though much older than himself.

exaequat is used transitively, but without the usual dative after it. The expression is curious. 'The other side of my family (*altera turba*) makes my maternal ancestors, the Libones, equal,' viz. 'to the Scipiones' ; i. e. 'my maternal ancestors are not inferior to them.' An obvious exaggeration. Palmer suggests as an alternative,

Altera materni se exaequat turba Libones,

in which case *turba* would be idiomatic in apposition with a plural noun.

32. domus utraque, 'both sides of the house.'

titulis, in the same sense as in Hor. Od. 4. 14. 4

Per titulos memoresque fastos.

33. praetexta. The name given to the toga of childhood, whether of boys or girls, because it had an edge of purple or scarlet running round it.' This maidens laid aside at marriage for the *stola.*

34. The **vitta** was simply a band worn round the head by freeborn maidens and matrons to keep in the hair. It is thought from this passage and Virg. Aen. 2. 168, etc. that the maiden's *vitta* differed in shape from the matron's : but perhaps nothing more is meant than that a new *vitta* was put on at marriage. The line 4. 3. 15 shows that importance was attached to the ceremony of putting it on,

Nec recta capillis Vitta data est.

acceptas, 'caught up.'

35. sic either includes all the circumstances of her death, to part with you ' thus untimely,' or else it refers specially to *Iungor* : ' I became thy wife, Paulus, destined so to die,' i. e. as his wife, neither divorced nor a widow.

36. If we read **hoc** with the MSS., Cornelia must imagine herself standing before her tomb. It was a special distinction for a woman to be *univira.* Cp. Orelli's Inscr. No. 4530

HIC SITA EST ARRIA · M. F. MAXIMILLA · VNIVIRIA QVE VIXIT ·

IN CONNVBIO MARCO · AVRELIO AVGG. LIB.

Prof. Palmer suggests that *hoc* might be the neuter nominative going with *legar,* i. e. ' This will be read of me.'

37–42. She calls to witness her ancestors—the Africani and L. Aemilius Paullus—that she has maintained the purity of the house umblemished.

38. Captives had their hair shaved : and the editors are probably right in supposing that Propertius had in his eye a trophy erected to the Scipios with an inscription above, and at the foot a shaved captive representing the conquered Africa—like the eight statues of Dacian captives built into the architraves of the Arch of Constantine. The word **tonsa** however has the further meaning of ' fleeced,' ' stripped bare,' as in Plaut. Bacch. 2. 3. 8 *Hunc tondebo auro usque ad cutem.* There is a similar play on the word in

Prop. 3. 19. 22, where Scylla, who caused her father's death and ruin (as Delilah Samson's) by cutting off a lock of hair, is described as

Tondens purpurea regna paterna coma.

39. Persen. The name of Perses naturally suggests that of his conqueror, and is used here for it. These two lines have been much canvassed. They contain a reference to L. Aemilius Paullus Macedonicus (father of Scipio Africanus Minor), the conqueror of Perses. By an inversion characteristic of Propertius, he makes Cornelia appeal first to Perses himself (l. 39), whose name suggests naturally that of Paullus; then in l. 40, addressing Perses, he specifically describes his conqueror. 'I appeal to Perses too, him that boasted all the bravery of his ancestor Achilles; and him too who broke down thy house, Perses, for all thy boasts in thine ancestor Achilles.' The repetition of Achilles is strongly ironical: Perses and other members of the Macedonian house were for ever boasting of their descent from him, *aeternus carmine Achilles* Sil. Ital. 14. 95. Another explanation is to make *Persen* governed by *fregit*: 'him who broke Perses, and thy house Perses,' but this is harsh, and gives less excuse for the *tuas.* I cannot follow Mr. Postgate. Because Silius Italicus has the word *stimulos* in one passage (14. 93) in connection with Pyrrhus' boasting in his ancestor Achilles, and *stimulabat* in another (3. 609) quite unconnected with Achilles; because in a third (15. 292) *proavo tumebat Achille* is said of Philip; and in a fourth (3. 246) *vano corda tumore* is applied to a man proud of being Hannibal's nephew: for these reasons he thinks Silius Italicus had this passage of Propertius before him, and that *tumidas* (or cognate word) and *stimulantem* were read in the copy which he followed. In these passages the words *stimulos tumore,* etc. occur in a perfectly natural way, and Silius had no need to be guided to their use. But Postgate is entirely right in rejecting the rash changes proposed by H. A. J. Munro, Journal of Philology, 6. pp. 53-62, and in condemning his sweeping dictum that 'the Latin language peremptorily forbids that *simulantem* can mean "who formerly affected."' The use of the present participle is merely an extension of the use of the present for the past tense noticed on 3. 7. 22. Cp. Virg. Aen. 9. 266 *quem dat Sidonia Dido. Simulantem* gives an abiding characteristic of the man, almost equivalent to *simulatorem,* 'the pretender to.' Cp. also *tondens* 3. 19. 22, *fugiens* 4. 6. 15, and the present *nutrit* 4. 4. 54. A still closer parallel is Tac. Ann. 1-13 (quoted above), where Augustus describes M. Lepidus as being *capacem sed aspernantem.*

· **Achilli** is as good a form as *Achillis*, and is best supported here by the MSS.

40. proavo . . . Achille. The taunting repetition of these words is similar to Horace's *libertino patre natum* Sat. 1. 6. 6, etc., a taunt against himself which he repeats several times, half in pride, half in irritation.

The late Mr. Munro's great reputation makes it worth while to state shortly his view of this whole passage. Rejecting the MS. reading of l. 40 on every ground of grammar, sense, and metre, he believes that a whole distich has fallen out, l. 38 beginning with *Et* or *Et qui*, and that for *Achille*, l. 40, we are to look for some other *proavus* of Perses, to enhance still more the glory of his conqueror Aemilius Paulus. Suggesting first that this *proavus* may be Alexander, he proposes either *Atossa* or *Amastri*, two famous Persian queens, who would stand for the royal house of Persia : but finally he believes Alexander's paternal descent from Hercules to be alluded to, and Hercules himself to be described by reference to his last and greatest achievement, his breaking into Hades, dragging away Cerberus, and restoring Theseus to the light. Thus by a process of reasoning truly marvellous, and by a display of wholly irrelevant learning, he has persuaded himself that Propertius wrote the passage thus :

> *Testor maiorum cineres tibi Roma verendos,*
> *Sub quorum titulis, Africa, tonsa iaces,*
> *Et qui contuderunt animos pugnacis Hiberi*
> *Hannibalemque armis Antiochumque suis,*
> *Et Persen proavi simulantem pectus Achilli,*
> *Quique tuas proavus fregit, Averne, domos*
> *Me neque censurae legem mollisse,* etc.

This is indeed *rescribere, non emendare, Propertium* with a vengeance. Plessis reads *feras* for *tuas*.

41. Referring to her husband's censorship. He had no need, on her account, to relax the severity of his office.

42. mea emphatic ; ' by no stain of mine.'

43. damnum, for the more usual *damno*. See note on 2. 10. 6 *audacia certe Laus erit.*

45. aetas, well explained by Postgate, ' I throughout my life.' So 1. 6. 21

> *Nam tua non aetas umquam cessavit amori,*

i. e. ' You have never yet, in all your life, been in love.' Cp. 2. 5. 27.

46. Cp. Ov. Her. 21. 172

> *Et face pro thalami fax mihi mortis erit.*

47. An amplification of the proverb *Noblesse oblige.* Cp. Eur.

Alc. 602 τὸ γὰρ εὐγενὲς ἐκφέρεται πρὸς αἰδῶ. The idea is not quite that of Spenser, F. Q. 6. 3. 1, that

> *The gentle minde by gentle deeds is knowne,*

and again

> *But evermore contrary hath been tryde,*
> *That gentle bloud will gentle manners breed;*

but rather that those of noble blood feel compelled, by their very position, and out of an imperious regard for the honour and character of their house, to maintain a high standard of conduct. The words, of themselves, would apply literally to the modern law of heredity.

49. See above on l. 19. The urn here contains the decision of the *iudices.* Each juror was said *ferre tabellam,* to deposit his voting-tablet in the urn, ‘ to record his vote.’ Hence the urn itself is said *ferre tabellas,* because its contents pronounce or record the verdict.

50. assessu meo, ‘ by association with me.’ Possibly with a reference to friends sitting beside an accused person at his trial : or it may refer to the shades below, none of whom, however virtuous—not even Claudia or Aemilia—need shrink from contact with her.

51. The story of the matron Claudia, who proved her virtue by pulling off from a shoal on the Tiber the stranded vessel containing the image of Cybele, is told by Liv. 29. 14, Ov. Fast. 4. 305–328.

52. turritae, because Cybele’s head was surmounted by a crown embattled in the shape of a fortress.

rara, ‘incomparable.’ A favourite word with Propertius.

53. See Dion. Hal. 2. 67. The Vestal Aemilia having suffered the holy flame to go out, rekindled it, after prayer, by throwing on the ashes a fragment of her garment. Plessis reads *iam distinctos* for *commissos.*

cui, to be taken with *exhibuit.*

reposceret, ‘ demanded as a right,’ because it was the duty of the Vestals to keep the fire alive.

55. dulce caput, ‘ dear heart.’ See above on l. 10.

56. Hertz. quotes the common character given to wives on inscriptions :

> *De qua vir nil doluit nisi mortem.*

57. laudor lacrimis. Postgate well compares Consol. Liv. 209

> *Et voce et lacrimis laudasti, Caesar, alumnum;*

and l. 465.

59, 60. dignam vixisse . . . increpat, either ‘complains that she, who was worthy, etc., is no more,’ or ‘ passionately declares that she has lived worthy of.’ In the latter interpretation *dignam* has more force. Cp. 3. 10. 10

Increpet absumptum nec sua mater Ityn.

60. ire, scarcely, 'fall:' rather 'go forth,' 'have their course,' 'flow,' as in 3. 1. 8

Exacto pumice versus eat,

where see note

ire deo. So Consol. Liv. 209

lacrimas elicuique deo.

61. vestis, supposed to refer to a robe of honour presented to matrons who had borne three children: Dion. Cass. 55. 2. The phrase *stolatae feminae* on inscriptions has been held to refer to this distinction.

62. Nec mea ... rapina, 'I was not snatched.'

63. Her two sons: the elder, consul A.D. 1, was called *L. Aemilius Paullus;* the younger was called *M. Aemilius Lepidus,* and was consul A. D. 6. The elder brother, apparently, took the cognomen of his distinguished grandfather, *L. Aemilius Lepidus.*

65. Her brother, P. Cornelius Scipio, was consul B. C. 16, and had therefore presumably filled two curule offices previously, the curule aedileship and the praetorship. *Tempore* means 'betimes.' or 'just at the right moment.' (Cp. the similar use of *loco.*) Having seen her brother occupy two curule offices, and finally elected to the consulship, she was 'felix opportunitate mortis.' *Tempore* might also mean 'too soon'; or again simply 'just at that time,' 'at the very moment' (=*eo ipso tempore*), i. e. when he had been elected consul, and before he had actually held the office.

Paley explains the line as 'a brief or rather a confused way of expressing *qui cum consul factus esset, eo tempore rapta est soror eius,* or *cuius consulatus tempore rapta est soror;*' or else with Hertzberg would make *tempore* an ablative of the instrument. Munro, Journ. of Phil. vol. 6. p. 62, declares the former view meaningless, the latter out of place, and proposes

Consule quo, festo tempore rapta soror.

Postgate reads *laeto*, which has the same meaning. But the idea of either word is out of place here: she is narrating bare facts in this passage, in a tone of pride, not of grief, and the pathetic reference to her dying in a time of joy is uncalled for. Another solution is more probable. I would suggest that *quo* is used here, by a kind of confusion, in a double construction, to be taken *both* with *consule* and with *tempore:* 'At which time, just as he had been made consul, his sister was carried off,' or 'Who having been made consul just at that time, his sister was carried off.' Horace is extremely fond of placing words in positions where they are meant to be taken in a double, or even threefold, construction, as in Od. 3. 8. 20

> *Medus infestus sibi luctuosis*
> *Dissidet armis,*

where the force of the line is intensified by the fact that *sibi* may be taken, and is intended to be taken, with all the three words—*infestus, luctuosis, Dissidet*.

67. Appears to imply that her daughter was born in the year of her father's censorship. On what ground does Postgate translate *specimen* as 'a mirror'? It rather means a sample, by which a thing may be seen or known: so Plaut. Most. 1. 2. 51 of an illustration,

> *Tum specimen cernitur quo eveniat aedificatio.*

69. serie, i. e. by carrying on the line unbroken.

fulcite. Each son was a 'prop' to the house: see Postgate's illustrations.

70. The MS. readings *uncturis* or *nupturis*, and *malis*, are clearly out of place: but I cannot see that Postgate's *facta* is an improvement. *Mea fata* is quite a Propertian expression, used widely to denote her lot and position as a whole, including not only her death (=*me mortuam*, Schultze), but her life, her family, and all the circumstances of honour which she has just enumerated. 'I set forth in Charon's bark without regret, knowing that my own (i. e. children or family) will add yet more to my many titles to distinction.' It is surely inappropriate for a Roman matron to boast of her many *deeds*: but not of the many elements of honour with which fate had surrounded her. For *augere facta* in this sense Postgate compares Tib. 1. 7. 55

> *quae facta parentis Augeat:*

but the *facta*, in that passage, are the exploits of a Messala. Another interpretation, however, may be suggested. *Tot* may be taken with *meis*: she is addressing her children, and has just exhorted them to continue the race, *Et serie fulcite genus*. She may well add, 'I die willingly, leaving so many children behind me who will add fresh lustre to my name and life.' Nor would it be impossible for *fata* here to mean 'death,' as elsewhere: 'my children will add fresh glory to my death,' i. e. 'to me after I am dead and gone,' 'to me even after death.'

71. extrema, 'the highest, crowning reward.'

72. emeritum rogum, 'the pyre of one who has served her (or his) time.' The highest honour a woman can attain is that, having lived her full time, she should receive praise at her death. But perhaps it is simpler to interpret *emeritum* as 'well-won.'

ubi, referring to *Haec* l. 71. The more usual construction would be *ut* with the subjunctive = 'namely that.' *Haec . . . ubi* = 'In these cases, namely where.'

74. Hertz. well compares Cic. Verr. 2.1.44 *Cur hunc dolorem cineri eius atque ossibus inussisti?* The confusion of metaphor is natural, but glaring; *inusta* must refer to branding, as *adusta* in 3.11.40

Una Philippeo sanguine adusta nota,

the idea being suggested by *cineri*. 'To brand upon ashes' would be absurd: but the absurdity is relieved by the ancient idea that the ashes of the dead still live and feel, as in 2.13.42

Non nihil ad verum conscia terra sapit.

To suppose that *spirat* refers to the quivering flame (' = ζῆ,' Postgate) seems farfetched, and introduces the new incongruity of the flame being itself branded or burnt in.

72–102. An exquisite passage; full of simple feeling, true to human nature, and breathing a tenderness and delicacy worthy of the noblest type of womanhood.

75. maternis vicibus, 'the part of a mother:' the plural, as in Quint. Inst. proem. 4 *quando divisae professionum vices essent.*

80. oscula falle. *Fallere aliquid*, as we have seen above 4.4.20, means 'to exhibit deceit or treachery about something;' so here, 'give a feigned character to thy kisses,' *siccis genis*, 'by (presenting) dry cheeks:' 'let thy dry cheek disguise the character of thy kisses,' i.e. he was not to show, by the passionate nature of his kiss, that there was more in it than a mere father's affection for his children. A touch absolutely true to nature. Who has not seen, in a similar case, the tears for a lost love pouring themselves out upon the children? The words doubtless might mean 'Be false to, or cheat, their kisses by dry eyes (or cheeks),' i.e. do not let them see that you have been weeping, but meet their caresses by a show of indifference.

81. The nights, as though they were persons, are worn out by Paullus' lamentations: cp. Virg. Aen. 8.94 and Val. Flac. Aug. 5. 602 *Marte diem noctemque fatiget.* Still more strongly Sil. Ital. 12. 496 *curas fatigat.*

82. in faciem credita, 'which you deem to assume my form,' 'wrought by your fancy into my form.'

84. He is not to speak on continuously, but to wait after each *verbum* for an answer.

85. Seu corresponds to *seu* l. 91. She now turns to her children, and prepares them for a double alternative: their father marrying again, or remaining as he is.

tamen marks the contrast between the devotion to her contemplated in the preceding lines and the possibility of a second marriage.

adversum, because the *lectus genialis* was placed in the atrium facing the door. The door is here said to change the bed, either because it saw the change, or because the beds, old and new, had to pass through it. Propertius allows himself great latitude in his choice of a subject for a sentence.

86. **cauta**, implying rather the quality needed, than that necessarily exhibited, by a stepmother.

87. 'Speak well of and put up with.' Either one of these two by no means necessarily implies the other.

90. **Vertet in offensas suas**, 'will turn or interpret them into (i. e. as intended for) an attack upon herself,' or perhaps better, 'as implying hatred of her.'

92. **tanti**, i.e. as to abstain from re-marriage.

93. **sentire**, they are to put themselves in their father's place, and actually to feel, as he feels, all that coming age brings with it. **iam nunc**, as usual, anticipatory of the future: 'begin at once to.'

94. **ad**, 'to meet:' **nec vacet ulla via**, 'let no path be untrod,' or 'unguarded,' or, as we might say, 'let no stone be unturned.' Prof. Palmer would translate, ' Let no road be open for him to arrive at the troubles of a bachelor.'

95. There is perhaps more here than the idea of Ov. Met. 7. 168

Deme meis annis, et demptos adde parenti,

that the years of life taken from her might be added to make theirs longer. Rather she prays that her young children may have the tact and steadiness of a greater age given them, that they may be a comfort to their father. 'May the age that I have lost be added to you: so may offspring of mine bring joy to Paullus' old age,' i. e. because of the comfort they would be to him. That they should *survive* their father was only natural, and needed no special prayer.

97, 98. ' I die happy: I never lost a child : not one of you is absent from my funeral.'

99. **Causa perorata est**. Almost a technical form for the ending of a speech.

100. **humus**, apparently 'the underworld,' and especially the judges before whom she has been pleading. Propertius is fond of using such words as *humus, cinis, rogus*, etc., to denote any of the consequences of, or conditions subsequent to, death.

101, 102. I. e. some have been raised to heaven by their virtues : she will be satisfied if she be deemed worthy of an honourable burial.

THE PLEA OF CORNELIA.

(PROPERTIUS: *El.*, iv. 11.)

CEASE, Paullus, cease! thy fruitless tears withhold;
Unto no prayer will Hell's dark gates unfold!
From Death's dim bourne none cometh forth again;
Grief beats th' impenetrable bars in vain.
Tho' Dis should hearken, in his gloomy hall,
The deaf shores drink whatever tear-drops fall.
Prayers may to heaven and heavenly gods aspire,
But, when hell's ferryman hath ta'en his hire,
The dark gate seals the legacy of fire.
That truth sad trumpets pealed, when kindling flame
Dropped through the bier the ashes of my frame—
Mine—Scipio's child and Paullus' consort hailed,
Mother of noble children—what availed?
Found I, for all my fame, the Fates less stern?
Light dust am I, a handful in an urn!

Ye nights of hell! ye fens and marshes gray,
And snakelike streams that wind about my way!
Untimely have I come, yet guiltless all—
Lord of the Dead, soft let thy sentence fall!
If Aeacus, if judgment here there be,
Let urn and scroll speak justice' doom on me;
Judge sit by judge—let Minos' throne be nigh,
And the stern court, and Furies' company.

B b

Rest, Sisyphus! forego thy stone and hill;
Ixion, let thy whizzing wheel be still!
The cheating wave let Tantalus recall;
Let Cerberus no passing ghost appal;
Hell's bolt be silent, and its chain let fall!

Lo, mine own cause I plead! If false my plea,
Hard weigh the Danaids' urn of doom on me!
If trophied spoils bring heritage of fame,
Speak, Spain and Afric, of my grandsires' name!
Well matched with them may stand my mother's line,
And Scipio's stock with Libo's race combine.
Then, when I passed from maiden unto bride,
And wedlock's snood my virgin tresses tied,
Till death should part, to Paullus' side I came—
Wife to one only be my funeral fame!
Dead sires! whose threshold carven busts adorn
And conquered Afric's figure, slavelike shorn—
Bear witness from your ashes to your home—
Those ashes, worthy of thy worship, Rome!
Bear witness, Perses!—all thy breast on fire
To match Achilles' self, thy godlike sire—
Thou too, whose valour shattered from its base
That home of Perses' and Achilles' race—
That ne'er, for sin of mine, was law made tame,
Nor blushed our household for Cornelia's shame.
Thro' me no stain on our renown could come—
Me, crown and model of our glorious home!
I walked unswerving, held a stainless fame,
From wedding torch to funeral, the same.
For Nature wrought for me a law within—
Thou shalt not shun the judgment, but the sin.
What urn soever shall my doom decide,
No woman e'er shall blush to seek my side:
Not thou, O Claudia, who with spotless hand

Didst hale the ling'ring galley from the strand,
Cybelle's bark—thou matron of renown,
Servant of Her who wears the turret-crown!
Not she who erst, when anger'd Vesta came,
From stainless robe relit th' entrusted flame.
Thou too, dear heart, Scribonia, mother mine!
Ne'er have I grieved thee. If thy soul repine,
Say this—no more—*Too short a date was thine.*
Tears, true as thine, the weeping city gave,
And Caesar sighed detraction from my grave.
The mother of my Julia was thine,
He said; *thy life was worthy of my line—*
Farewell! and tears fell from his eyes divine.
Mine too it was, the honoured stole to gain;
Nor from a barren wedlock was I ta'en.
Ah sons, my twofold solace after death—
Propped on your bosoms I resigned my breath!
Brother, twice throned in power! the self-same day
Saw thee made consul and me rapt away.
Child, pride of Paullus' censorship begun,
Live thou like me, love one and only one.
Loyal to one, keep thou thy bed unstained,
And by thine offspring be our line maintained!
My race shall glorify my name—and now
Loosed be the death-boat—I am lief to go!
Of woman's fame, this is the highest crown,
When praised, and freed, and dead, we hold Renown.

Guard, Paullus, guard the pledges of our love—
My very dust that ingrained wish can move!
Father thou art, and mother must thou be,
Unto those little ones bereft of me.
Weep they? give twofold kisses, thine and mine,
Solace their hearts, and both our loves combine;
And if thou needst must weep, go, weep apart—

Let not our children, folded to thine heart,
Between thy kisses feel thy tear-drops start.
Enough, for love, be nightlong thoughts of me,
And phantom forms that murmur *I am she.*
Or, if thou speakest to mine effigy,
Speak soft, and pause, and dream of a reply.

Yet—if a presence new our halls behold,
And a new bride my wonted place shall hold—
My children, speak her fair, who pleased your sire,
And let your gentleness disarm her ire ;
Nor speak in praise of me—your loyal part
Will turn to gall and wormwood in her heart.

But, if your father hold my worth so high,
That lifelong love can people vacancy,
And solitude seem only love gone by,
Tend ye his loneliness, his thoughts engage,
And bar the avenues of pain to age.
I died before my time—add my lost years
Unto your youth, be to his heart compeers ;
So shall he face, content, life's slow decline,
Glad in my children's love, as once in mine.

Lo, all is well ! I ne'er wore garb of woe
For child or husband : I was first to go.
Lo, I have said ! Rise, ye who weep ; I stand
In high desert, worthy the Spirit Land.
Worth hath stormed heaven ere now ; this, this I claim
To rise, in death, upon the waves of Fame.

                                        E. D. A. M.

INDEX TO THE NOTES.

THE END.

13/9/99

Clarendon Press Series

OF

School Classics.

I. LATIN CLASSICS.

AUTHOR.	WORK.	EDITOR.	PRICE.
Caesar	Gallic War, Books I, II	Moberly	2s.
,,	,, Books I–III	,,	2s.
,,	,, Books III–V	,,	2s. 6d.
,,	,, Books VI–VIII	,,	3s. 6d.
,,	Civil War	,,	3s. 6d
Catullus	Carmina Selecta (text only)	Ellis	3s. 6d.
Cicero	Selections, 3 Parts	Walford	each 1s. 6d.
,,	Selected Letters	Prichard & Bernard	3s.
,,	Select Letters (text only)	Watson	4s.
,,	De Amicitia	Stock.	3s.
,,	De Senectute	Huxley	2s.
,,	Pro Cluentio	Ramsay	3s. 6d.
,,	Pro Marcello	Fausset	2s. 6d.
,,	Pro Milone	Poynton	2s. 6d.
,,	Pro Roscio	Stock	3s. 6d.
,,	Select Orations	King	2s. 6d.
,,	In Q. Caec. Div. and In Verrem I.	,,	1s. 6d.
,,	Philippic Orations, I–III, V, VII,	,,	3s. 6d.
,,	Catilinarian Orations	Upcott	2s. 6d.
Horace	Odes, Carm. Saec., Epodes	Wickham	6s.
,,	Odes, Book I	,,	2s.
,,	Selected Odes	,,	2s.
,,	The Complete Works (Miniature Text)		3s. 6d. and 5s.
Juvenal	XIII Satires	Pearson & Strong	9s.
Livy	Selections, 3 Parts	Lee-Warner	each 1s. 6d.
,,	Books V–VII	Cluer & Matheson	5s.
,,	Book V	,, ,,	2s. 6d.

I. LATIN CLASSICS.

AUTHOR.	WORK.	EDITOR.	PRICE.
Livy	Book VII	Cluer & Matheson	2s.
,,	Books XXI–XXIII	Tatham	5s.
,,	Book XXI	,,	2s. 6d.
,,	Book XXII	,,	2s. 6d.
Nepos	Lives	Browning & Inge	3s.
,,	Selected Lives: Miltiades, Themistocles, Pausanias	Allen	1s. 6d.
Ovid	Selections	Ramsay	5s. 6d.
,,	Tristia, Book I	Owen	3s. 6d.
,,	,, Book III	,,	2s.
Plautus	Captivi	Lindsay	2s. 6d.
,,	Trinummus	Freeman & Sloman	3s.
Pliny	Selected Letters	Prichard & Bernard	3s.
Quintilian	Book X	Peterson	3s. 6d.
Sallust	Bellum Cat. & Jugurth.	Capes	4s. 6d.
Tacitus	Annals I–IV	Furneaux	5s.
,,	Annals (text only)	,,	6s.
,,	Annals I	,,	2s.
Terence	Adelphi	Sloman	3s.
,,	Andria	Freeman & Sloman	3s.
,,	Phormio	Sloman	3s.
Tibullus and Propertius	Selections	Ramsay	6s.
Virgil	With an Introduction and Notes, 2 Vols.	Papillon & Haigh	Cloth, 6s. each, stiff covers, 3s. 6d. ,,
,,	(Miniature Text, including Minor Poems)	,, ,,	3s. 6d. and 5s.
,,	Aeneid I	Jerram	1s. 6d
,,	,, IX	Haigh	1s. 6d.; in Two Parts, 2s.
,,	Aeneid I–XII (in Four Parts)	Papillon & Haigh	stiff covers, 2s. each.
,,	Bucolics	Jerram	2s. 6d.
,,	Bucolics and Georgics	Papillon & Haigh	stiff covers, 2s. 6d.
,,	Georgics, I, II	Jerram	2s. 6d.
,,	,, III, IV	,,	2s. 6d.

II. GREEK CLASSICS.

AUTHOR.	WORK.	EDITOR.	PRICE.
Aeschylus	Agamemnon	Sidgwick	3s.
,,	Choephoroi	,,	3s.
,,	Eumenides	,,	3s.
,,	Prometheus Bound	Prickard	2s.
Aristophanes	Acharnians	Merry	3s.
,,	Birds	,,	3s. 6d.
,,	Clouds	,,	3s.
,,	Frogs	,,	3s.
,,	Knights	,,	3s.
,,	Wasps	,,	3s. 6d.
Cebes	Tabula	Jerram	2s. 6d.

*** *Also, Abridged School Edition,* 1s. 6d.

AUTHOR.	WORK.	EDITOR.	PRICE.
Demosthenes	Orations against Philip, I, Phil. I, Olyn. I–III	Abbott & Matheson	3s.
,,	II, De Pace, Phil. II, III, De Chers.	,, ,,	4s. 6d.
,,	Philippics only	,, ,,	2s. 6d.
,,	De Corona	,, ,,	3s. 6d.
Euripides	Alcestis	Jerram	2s. 6d.
,,	Bacchae	Cruickshank	3s. 6d.
,,	Cyclops	Long	2s. 6d.
,,	Hecuba	Russell	2s. 6d.
,,	Helena	Jerram	3s.
,,	Heracleidae	,,	3s.
,,	Ion	,,	3s.
,,	Iphigenia in Tauris	,,	3s.
,,	Medea	Heberden	2s.
Herodotus	Selections	Merry	2s. 6d.
,,	Books V and VI	Abbott	10s. 6d.
,,	Book IX	,,	3s.
Homer	Iliad I–XII	Monro	6s.
,,	,, I	,,	1s. 6d.
,,	,, III (for beginners)	Tatham	1s. 6d.
,,	,, XIII–XXIV	Monro	6s.
,,	Odyssey I–XII	Merry	5s.
,,	,, I and II	,,	each 1s. 6d.
,,	,, VI and VII	,,	1s. 6d.

II. GREEK CLASSICS.

Author.	Work.	Editor.	Price.
Homer . . .	Odyssey VII–XII . .	Merry	3s.
,, . . .	,, XIII–XXIV .	,, ...	5s.
,, . . .	,, XIII–XVIII .	,, ...	3s.
Lucian . . .	Vera Historia . . .	Jerram	1s. 6d.
Lysias . . .	Epitaphios	Snell	2s.
Plato . . .	Apology	Stock	2s. 6d.
,, . . .	Crito	,, ...	2s.
,, . . .	Meno	,, ...	2s. 6d.
,, . . .	Selections	Purves	5s.
Plutarch . .	Lives of the Gracchi .	Underhill	4s. 6d.
Sophocles . .	(Complete)	Campbell & Abbott	10s. 6d.
,, . . .	Ajax	,, ,,	2s.
,, . . .	Antigone	,, ,,	2s.
,, . . .	Electra	,, ,,	2s.
,, . . .	Oedipus Coloneus . .	,, ,,	2s.
,, . . .	Oedipus Tyrannus . .	,, ,,	2s.
,, . . .	Philoctetes	,, ,,	2s.
,, . . .	Trachiniae	,, ,,	2s.
Theocritus .	Idylls, &c.	Kynaston	4s. 6d.
Thucydides .	Book I	Forbes	8s. 6d.
Xenophon .	Easy Selections . . .	Phillpotts & Jerram	3s. 6d.
,, . . .	Selections*	Phillpotts	3s. 6d.
,, . . .	Anabasis I	Marshall	2s. 6d.
,, . . .	,, II	Jerram	2s.
,, . . .	,, III	Marshall	2s. 6d.
,, . . .	,, IV	,, ...	2s.
,, . . .	,, III, IV . .	,, ...	3s.
,, . . .	,, Vocabulary .	,, ...	1s. 6d.
,, . . .	Cyropaedia I	Bigg	2s.
,, . . .	Cyropaedia IV, V . .	,, ...	2s. 6d.
,, . . .	Hellenica I, II . . .	Underhill	3s.
,, . . .	Memorabilia	Marshall	4s. 6d.

. A Key to Sections 1–3, for Teachers only, price 2s. 6d. net.

www.ingramcontent.com/pod-product-compliance
Lightning Source LLC
Chambersburg PA
CBHW031051110726
47900CB00003B/888